P9-DMX-806

NOTRE DAME REVIEW

The First Ten Years

Notre Dame review

The First Ten Years

Edited with an Introduction by
John Matthias
and
William O'Rourke

~

University of Notre Dame Press
Notre Dame, Indiana

Notre Dame, Indiana 46556
www.undpress.nd.edu

Manufactured in the United States of America

Library of Congress Cataloging-in-Publication Data

Notre Dame review : the first ten years / edited with an introduction by
John Matthias and William O'Rourke.
p. cm.
Includes index.
ISBN-13: 978-0-268-03512-9 (pbk. : alk. paper)
ISBN-10: 0-268-03512-1 (pbk. : alk. paper)
1. American literature—20th century—Periodicals. 2. American literature—21st century—Periodicals. 3. American literature—Indiana—Periodicals.
I. Matthias, John, 1941– II. O'Rourke, William. III. University of Notre Dame. Creative Writing Program.
PS536.2.N687 2008
810 .8'0005—dc22

2008046017

This book is printed on recycled paper.

Contents

PROSE

Editors' Introduction

i.

Sometimes editors of literary magazines feel a little like Arthur Miller's Willy Loman, "out there in the blue riding on a smile and a shoe-shine." *Notre Dame Review* was founded by a group of creative writing faculty at the University of Notre Dame who, without the shoe-shines but maybe the smile that was almost in our case a prayer, established the journal on the initiative of Valerie Sayers, the first editor, with a computer self-publishing program in a coffin-sized office deep in the basement of the library. The first, pilot, issue appeared in 1995 and the second in 1996. From that point, *NDR* became biannual. All issues since the second have had an umbrella-like theme—"Dangerous Times," "Work," "Signs and Surfaces," "Body and Soul"—and have been committed to a wide open eclecticism that welcomes work from writers and artists of many different aesthetic persuasions. At the same time the journal was founded, the writing program also established, in memory of two fine faculty writers, the Ernest Sandeen and Richard Sullivan poetry and fiction book awards. The history of *NDR* and the history of these contests interweave. All of the winners of the two book awards, along with a great many who competed in the contests, have appeared in the journal and appear in this book.

Even the first issue of *NDR* indicates the direction the magazine would take. It includes work both by the famous and the unknown—two Nobel Prize winners, but also two poets publishing their first poems—along with fiction by Michael Collins, one of the first and most successful Notre Dame MFA graduates, and long poems by John Peck and Michael Anania, poets who would become regular contributors. When Michael Anania retired a year ago from the University of Illinois, Chicago, *Bluesky Review* published a festschrift for him in which Vainis Aleksa remembers Anania beginning a graduate poetry workshop by reading a terrific poem about Donatello's statue of young David. "We got riled up, outdoing each other with interpretations of the poem's rich resonance. 'Who's it by, Michael?' It was by one of the sophomores in his undergraduate class. We were hushed. Michael said, 'Poetry is not always a matter of experience, vocation, or sometimes even will. It can happen at any point of a writer's life, even in the beginning, and even only once.'" The editors of *NDR* have always assumed this to be the case; and that a story, like a poem, might also only happen once. You want to be there when it does. You never know; therefore, you must always be open as an editor. Moreover, it's wise to listen to good advice. From the beginning, *NDR* has had the help of our editorial assistants from among the MFA students, and from the group of advisory editors listed on our masthead. Many people, aside from the co-editors of this book and of all issues since number 6, have discovered and brought forward work that has been published in the journal.

When *NDR* began, America was watching the atrocities of the Third Balkan War on their television screens—the siege of Sarajevo, the slaughter at Srebrenica. Then came 9/11; then the Iraq War. This was all, of course, reflected in the manuscripts we received. Of the dozens, perhaps hundreds, of poems we received about 9/11, we published just one—the poem you'll find in this book written in imitation of Auden's "September 1, 1939." Somehow, of everything we read, only the formal rigor of that poem, along with its restraint, seemed right. Other occasions lead to different forms of response. And with the joys and pains of simply leading one's life, trying to think, trying to keep the imagination alive when it is numbed so badly by brutalities of history—who is to predict, much less prescribe, the forms that the best writing might take emerging from someone's daily struggle with words? In fact, it takes various and contradictory forms. There are a good many journals with a polemical, even a hysterical, agenda; but *NDR* is not one of them. One distrusts a reader of Pound who cannot admire Auden, a reader of Elizabeth Bishop who will not open a book by Susan Howe. Nor, in a decade's published work, are the contributions of poets who came of age at any one period—the 60s, the 70s, the 80s—exclusive spokespersons for our times. *NDR* and this anthology publish side by side a 90-year-old master and an undergraduate of twenty. There are poets here who could be called late modernist—Peck, Fisher, Kinsella—postmodernist—Latta, Strickland, Muldoon, Prufer—and traditionally formalist, even anti-modernist—Balbo, Thiel, Skloot, Gibb. Our contemporaries are all the people, whatever their age, who are alive in the world with us. Our fellow writers are those who work beside us, whether in the next room or on the next continent, whether in the form of sonnets and quatrains or with computer models and chance operations and graphics.

The poetry editor of this volume has decided to print just one poem, excerpt, or short sequence by each poet appearing. The order is alphabetical, rather than chronological by age or by the issue from which work was chosen. This makes for a fine serendipity. From A to Z, Agee to Zweig, "June grasses" to "tatters and wings," the poems range from very short to very long, very cryptic to very clear, very comforting to very frightening. The magazine has especially tried to be open to the longer poem, but limitations of the present format, along with the number of poets included, allows only James McMichael's "From the Homeplace" to represent this aspect of our editorial enthusiasms. We notice that, among the selections, there is not a lot of first person hyper-subjectivity or narrow manifestations of identity poetics; when the self appears, it seems to be fully conditioned by history, and conscious of that.

History, in turn, is often seen as a force field that the imagination can enter and engage, setting off sparks that can ignite unforeseen energies and urgencies. We are proud that a number of our former students are in the book; people we know well. And we are haunted by contributors who sent a single poem out of nowhere, disappeared, and cannot even be found in order to obtain permission for inclusion.

In the short time since we first published their work, seven poets have died: Denise Levertov, Czeslaw Milosz, Robert Creeley, Ken Smith, Edwin Bronk, John Engels, and Göran Printz-Påhlson. We think especially of them as the volume nears publication. In Chris Agee's opening poem, "Dark Hay," the harvest has left bales and stooks resembling Greek lambdas and windrows recalling, first, the stone spirals of the ancient burial chambers at New Grange in County Meath, Ireland or the Bogomil memorials near Stalac in Bosnia-Herzegovina, and then, as day darkens, outlines of Mayan temples in the stubble "in the late light breaking / Low from floes and plateaux." The poet is reminded by his imagery "that art is dark / For all its shining genesis," and goes on to evoke the stelae on the road to Stolac and the razed mosques nearby. But as the bales and stooks reminded him of stone memorials and ruins, so the stones remind him of hay again—for this is, in spite of all its consciousness of ancient and contemporary loss, a harvest poem, and it concludes with human work. The alphabetical order of authors' names—and also that lambda, symbol of wavelength in light wave systems—puts this poem up front as an almost perfect opening, part dolmen and part doorway. The rest of the poems in this anthology might be seen as variations on the themes it introduces.

J. M.

ii.

When you start a literary magazine near the end of the century (much less a millennium) it is almost impossible not to take stock of what sort of literary world you are joining. In our age of celebrity, our winner-take-all culture, no one pays much attention to the old notion of "generation," not to be understood in the sense of writers of similar age, one's immediate contemporaries, but the definition that takes into account the biographical links between writers, regardless of age, their mutual influences, the interplay of their work. Literary magazines showcase this connection, either consciously or unconsciously. When one hears the remark, "They publish their friends," it is often derogatory. But when the editors are writers, their friends frequently are writers, too. And what lies underneath that word "friends" is the deeply held conviction that some writers have been unfairly neglected, many too good to be adequately appreciated by large audiences, and those who occupy territory outside the most dreaded literary criteria: fashionability. Neglect is the most common form of censorship in our culture. The history of literary magazines is rife with such connections and convictions. Life always overlaps art; one might be short and the other long, but each happens simultaneously.

It is instructive to look into the early volumes of *The Best American Short Stories* series, which began in 1915. In the long history of American short story, it was first the commercial form. Jack London and Hemingway and Fitzgerald used short story writing as a cash cow. The magazines that published their work were highly profitable. And the list of their names and addresses in the back of an old *BASS* volume took one page; in the 2006 volume the list takes fifteen pages. The one page list was filled with the iconic slick magazines of the heyday of the print era, *Colliers, Look, The Saturday Evening Post.* Currently, the periodicals listed are, in the main, subsidized university-based literary magazines, paying not much at all. When an art goes from a high paying one to a low paying one it becomes, paradoxically, loftier in the literary pantheon. The short story is now the reigning art form; the novel, unlike in the days of Fitzgerald and Hemingway, is no longer the esteemed art object and ultimate goal, but functions as the commercial form.

It is impossible to separate the history of late twentieth century American short stories from the history of graduate creative writing programs. But not in the way they are often linked, derisively, for producing the so-called competent, but uninspired "workshop story." Both the journals and programs grew from the same root, the Baby-Boom era swelling of higher education's population. You educate more people, you get more writers—thankfully. The growth period of creative writing programs was the 1970s and the '80s. Notre Dame's program began in 1990. Our *NDR* does represent an aesthetic, a combination of specific tastes, that adds to the mix of literary magazines that exist. It is home to a number of writers of short fiction who are not found elsewhere and open to a variety of styles that often do not find partnership in other publications.

Editors announce their own deeply held positions by means of selection. The fiction that has appeared in the pages of *NDR* tells its own tale: what we like, what we think is important, what we think is necessary. *NDR*'s fiction has come from writers both accomplished and beginning. We favor writers whose own love of language is evident in their prose. Michael Collins's short story, "A Christmas Story," which is reprinted here, announced the arrival of a powerful new voice in contemporary writing. Five years later, in 2000, his novel, *The Keepers of Truth,* was short-listed for the Booker Prize. We value socially engaged fiction, regardless of its stylistic provenance. It can be the fact-based stories of Russell Working ("Inmates"), or the collage-based, Debra DiBlasi ("Oops. Sorry.").

Many of the young writers we published have been graduates of our creative writing program. They appear after graduation and, usually, after they have published a story or two in other venues. Tony D'Souza's story, "Taggers" (reprinted herein) appeared a couple of years after he graduated and we published ("Africa Unchained") what became the first chapter of his novel, *Whiteman,* which won the Sue Kaufman prize for the best first novel of 2006. But we also pluck emerging writers' stories from the so-called slush pile. "Love Beneath the Napalm," by James D. Redwood, was one such story (reprinted here); upon reading its first sentence, it was clear that this was fiction of the highest quality. We also publish writers whose careers have been long and honorable, R. D. Skillings, Arturo Vivante, Ira Sadoff, Richard Elman, as well as writers who are often thought of as writers' writers, such as David Matlin, Jaimy Gordon. Though we forbade the creative work of Notre Dame's faculty from appearing in the pages of *NDR* (though not critical writing in the back of the book), we did publish a story by Seamus Deane, as he was stepping into retirement. We are aware of where we are published (the Midwest) and who subsidizes us (the University of Notre Dame.) We take pride in both our location and our home and we look out for authors who represent both the region and the institution's mission. It is the *Notre Dame* Review.

Our growth and exposure, both of the program and the *Review,* has been rapid. Beginning with issue 5 (Winter 1998) we changed our initial cover design when Steve Tomasula became part of the English Department faculty and the *Review*'s Senior Editor. Steve has been responsible for the striking covers that continue to enhance the contents of the *Review.* Valerie Sayers stepped down from the editor's chair after issue 6 (Summer 1998); Kathleen Canavan came on as Executive Editor with issue 17 (Winter 2004), giving the production of the magazine professional continuity.

This anthology displays some of the poetry and fiction (and one piece of non-fiction) that has appeared in our first twenty issues, a ten-year span.

We have left out selections from the extensive amount of criticism we have run; we are committed to continue to bring such writing to the audience of the *Review.* More criticism has been devoted to poetry; it is a curious, but uncontestable, circumstance that poets are more willing to write at length about contemporary poetry than fiction writers are willing to write about contemporary fiction.

We have published over 1,000 writers, American and international during our first ten years. Our inaugural issue had 22 contributors; one recent issue, 51. The Sandeen/Sullivan prize volumes now number seven each. The creative writing program has over 150 graduates. Writing from the *NDR* has appeared in *The Best American Short Stories* and *The Best American Poetry* volumes, as well as the Pushcart Prize series, and has been reprinted in *Harper's* magazine, and elsewhere.

This collection does not claim at all to be a "Best of . . ." volume. It is meant to be representative. We have divided it in the simplest way, into prose and poetry, placing the writers alphabetically. Such a project—choosing some contributors, not others—is not an entirely happy experience. Both editors have had to leave out some favorites. At the end of this volume is a list of all the writers who have appeared in the first twenty issues.

Here, in one place, is a distillation of ten years of the work of many. Like any literary enterprise in these perilous times, our efforts are, and have been, a labor of love.

W. O.

POETRY

~

Chris Agee

DARK HAY

June grasses had burgeoned to monumental hay: slabs and beds
Printed in eights by the baler's sledge following its green coil
Of concentric windows like stone spirals at New Grange or Radmilja

To a last comma near the midpoint of the O
Where those eight dolmens stand at Giant's Ring. Then stacked
Into stooks "like lambdas" they darkened

To outlines of Mayan temples gathering shadow
In the late light breaking
Low from floes and plateaux, dark quadrilaterals

On the lit immaculate nap of shaven stubble
That reminded me that art is dark
For all its shining genesis. Seeing in stone

The image of hay, I saw too the vision polarized to God's glyph
Vanishing midpoint into nothing
(Swan-necked, double-helix, bull's eyes) on stelae swimming

In grass at the limestone necropolis on the road to Stolac
That passes the dumps of its razed mosques. Then, pausing to smoke,
Two men stood waiting to upend the last bales of an evening's work.

Sandra Alcosser

THE BLUE VEIN

To be human is of the earth, crumbling

~

Is humus. Is humility. Bleeding

~

We fall down. A dog licks our blood. Sometimes

~

We eat songbirds because we are hungry

~

A poet might refuse to speak after

~

Shelling. Another sings until they starve

~

Him, not because he plots against the state

~

Because he makes his own song. For the way

~

She loved his music, and the way he loved

~

The blue vein that rivered from her eyebrow

~

To her brain, the widower on the pier

~

Lifts his cello. Wrist becomes lips, tongue

~

Casals played Bach each morning to sanctify

~

The house, santify the mind. We are all

~

Ephemerals. Our blood so close to the

~

Blood of a tree. The cello too is pine

~

A body with ribs, belly. Below the

~

Winter bud each genus grows its own face

~

Vedran Smailovic walks Sarajevo

~

With a cello. He wears a tuxedo

~

Skeleton of the body is the music's

~

Shape. *I don't think about bombs, about*

~

Snipers. We have to remind ourselves we

~

Are human. *I go to the ruined place.*

Dick Allen

E-MAIL TO THE YEAR 2999

The last three digits of your year turned upside down
as if some car had flipped, the odometer
impaled on a cop's flashlight beam,
are the Devil's own numbers. But you know this,
just as we did a thousand years ago,
on the edge of the Great Eve. Like you,
we dangled our feet in centuries to come,
cast fishing lines a far ways into the mist,
wiggled our toes. *Revolution. Revolution.* There's always
some revolution—ours the computer one,
which made you what you are: machine-human, human-machine,
your revolution God knows what. Here,
leaves fall like airplanes, blue cake frosting
echoes our sky;
we live on pills and wild rice,
reciting our words:
accelerate, megahertz, microwave,
cellular, morph, RAM, gigabit, glitch,
save us, save us. We drown in choices,
we revel in sorrows. The last thousand years
have spiraled into a single computer chip
as the Internet widens. . . . If you wish to understand us,
imagine a lightening strike,
a car rolling over and over in the rain,
and the Devil among us,
nothing but a cursor on his screen,
yet typing away, because our world still matters.

Michael Anania

TURNINGS

for Enzo Agostino (1937–2003)
"e ca trovamu 'a luci d'a' memoria"

I.

Evening is liquid here,
  shadows welling into each shape,
    each valley, cut and crevice,

the sky, still bright, its lapis
  sun-streaked, the sea—both seas—
    darkening past Homer. "So soon

as the spirit has left the light,"
  rectangular slips of gold,
    embossed, their Greek, somewhat

Italic, found at Thurii
  and Piercastello-Laquari,
    suspended now behind glass

in the castello at Vibo Valentia,
  charms hammered, as though of fire
    and light, the sun offered back

to the dark flood, "so soon . . .
  on the right side of *Ennoia,*"
    a spring, in thought, that is,

lifting itself up out of
  memory. Though the reading
    is somewhat doubtful, folds

in the gold leaf obliterating
letters, parts of letters, words,
the sense is clear, prayer

and safe passage, "pure," it says,
"from pure to Purity, I come,"
gold out of earth and fire, speech,

spirit in light returning,
suppliant in her "blessed
company," funeral offerings,

of course, but folded and carried
by Greeks at the Calabrian edge of Greece,
the half-day journey from sea-froth

to sea-froth, following one river
upstream, the other down,
from Temesa and Hipponium

to Schilletion and Petelia,
merchants and colonists, death
touched each evening, rising

sounds and stirrings, the Sila's
mountains, caves and streams
—*Aquavona, Riventinu*—

rough passages that saddle
deep into shadow, chestnut
burs murmuring over leaf-mold;

in Calabria, *stasira, stanotti,*
Eleusis—"the enfolding
darkness"—is still underfoot.

II.

Or "beautiful, this evening's
evening," the sea running white
from Punto Stilo south past Locri,

a sparrow hawk wheeling above
    pebblestone, refuge, pinfeathers
        catch the mountain light, the west still

streaming eastward, out of reach.
    "I am," the gold leaf says, "like you,
        a child of earth and heaven."

Upland, from the tourist littered beach,
    Gioiosa—*Gejusa*—the sun plays
        its last, small strains, like mandolin

music, starlight and sound enshadowed
    there, your spirit drowsing, cradled
        at its home, in speech and light.

III.

A spindle-full of flax, its light,
    votive, drawn out and spun,
        bent fingers lifting bright strands,

like filaments from the still air,
    again and again, the olive wood
        bobbin bobbing above her feet.

Her song is whispers, names circling
    names, each one said into her hands,
        the thread, like a rosary

without pause or end, "Enzo,"
    and each other Enzo, Angelo,
        Michele, Dominic, Bruno,

Raffaele, so many passing
    from light into darkness and curled
        into the black folds of her skirt.

Jan Lee Ande

THE GHOST OF A FLEA

(Tempera on Mahogany with Gold Leaf, c. 1819)

The painting turned dull, cracked and darkened
over time, though a gold comet drags its blue tail.
Here and there—the stars are shimmering.

His vision, a speckled Flea, stunned William Blake.
Its massive body strides along on muscled legs.
The head (eyes bulging) sits on a knobby spine.

Eager tongue fluttering, the spirit divulges:
souls of bloodthirsty men inhabit these insects
—locked inside rigid bodies of bugs.

Robert Hooke engraved the form, one hundred
and fifty years before. Yet his flea was any flea
(a tiny leaping pest with long legs and no wings).

Blake's insect, a gothic fiend of a Flea. A ghoul.
Should the Flea swell to the size of a horse—
nearly all the people of London would perish.

Its tapered fingers hold the bowl of blood.
The Flea tilts forward, its long tongue lapping.
Imagine as William Blake tells John Varley

to reach him his things and step to one side!—
the astrologer in a daze. The grotesque figure
of a Flea, even now—warning this starry region.

Robert Archambeau

VICTORY OVER THE SUN

Here come the Futurists.
One wears a spoon in his buttonhole.

One signs an unknown hieroglyph.
One sings vowels, another consonants.

Here come the Futurists. It is 1913.
Kruchenykh, Matiushin, Goncharova,

Burliuk who leads his giant brother,
"I—Burliuk" on both their brows.

Here come the Futurists. Come, Kazimir Malevich,
saying "let the familiar recede,

let all by which we've lived
be lost to sight."

They come. Let all by which they've lived
be lost to sight—

let Moscow, drunk, serf-shouldered,
(a stunted mongrel, a cold and coal-blacked thief)

be lost. The massing of troops,
the Czar who calls a madman to heal his bleeding son,

the hunger,
the boy who beats his brother in a tailor's grimy shop—

let these recede, be lost to sight.
Here come the Futurists. It is 1913.

A flash, a clash of metal, projectors flash again:
They have begun.

They sing of victory over all we know,
a roar against the daily sun.

Then it is 1914, 1940, it is Moscow, Leningrad,
the Gulag, Buchenwald, it is the exile's empty room,

a daughter, grieving.
Here come the Futurists, long gone into the dark

with their victory over the sun.

Renée Ashley

SOME OTHER WOMAN SPEAKS TO ELPENOR AFTER HIS FALL FROM CIRCE'S ROOF

Youngest, least done with your days, you feel
stone-heavy past the windows of those rungs,
such a slender ladder as your life—all

that falling and the knot of your neck undone.
In the swinish yard, the remnants of long drink
wasted and the body of a boy who had a taste

for the stars; the men were off again, their own
descent joyless before them. The pale dust settled
and you, too, were gone. And all because some woman

loved a man! I say I dream you again, raise you up,
say that gravity with its perfect eyesight does not
see you, that your own weight is nothing, that you

do not struggle like a boy falling, but remain
passive in the air with your stars. No contrivance
is beyond love. You must listen: we can make

a comely magic now—in this dream you are falling
but timeless. Trust me: do not look down, not once.
Don't think of gods or of fate with its nasty

smile; don't think of men: they leave you. Don't imagine
the meaningless heft of your body dropping like rain
or the wide, insatiable hips of the earth rising to meet you.

Jennifer Atkinson

CONTURBATIO, COGITATIO, INTERROGATIO, HUMILITATIO, MERITATIO: GHAZAL ON THE FIVE PETALS OF THE SALT SPRAY ROSE

Overturned on the tide, eyes pecked out, mouth and gills exposed in a
clownish grin,
On the waves, the skate's flesh wings flutter.

Dog whelk, periwinkle, shark's eye shells—worldly repose in a whorled
paraphrase:
Zero, zero, zero. Zero from the lowest body whorl on up the columella
spindle of the spire.

Renounce your silence. Say *succumb* and I will lie down, your left hand
under my head.
Say *relinquish* and I will cede you the city. Hurry, my love. Day is near.

Under the sway of the sovereign moon and the rain, unwilled, under
water, the rugged beach rose
Blooms among the languid seaweed white, its fruit ripe, votive, sour.

How could I forget the pale green glamor of fireflies, my baby's shriek
of pain,
The gaze of a stranger, the color of honey, hunger, desire, fear, the taste
of salt on your shoulder?

Ned Balbo

AFTER HITCHCOCK

1. Descent and Aftermath

A long fall toward the grave, then toward the roof
Below the bell-tower, freefall into flight
That ends on impact—yours. Or hers. Or both.
And afterward, bowed strings filling the air,
Black disk spinning in place, you sit and stare
Expressionless: cramped room, and one old friend
Who won't let go, however far you fall,
No words to tell her if you're spinning still
In blackness or in light. How long she waits
We don't know, but no one should wait that long,
And when she turns, each slow step down the hall
Seems endless, like the space that swallows her,
Bottomless corridor . . . *Pointless to stay,*
She knows by now. *This patient needs his rest.*

2. Madeleine's Afterlife

Those weeks after the bell-tower—safe, alone,
A rented room, the green light of the sign
Hotel Empire left burning every night—
I felt, at last, I'd freed myself from her,
Suits pushed back in the closet, jewels set down
And shut away. Once only, hands half-healed
(Sharp twine and paper cuts) I left the store,
Just one more working girl "wandering" home
(That loaded word) on foot, and thought, *How good*
It would be now to slip into her life
A few more hours: to drive, sealed off from noise,
Crude pickups, and the rest, gliding down streets
Silent and dizzying . . . How good to fall,
Weightless, toward water, knowing that you saw. . . .

3. Melanie's Ascent as Metaphor

Their explanations always seem absurd:
Thick men (except for Ingrid) filling suits
That look inflammable, who drone on, glazed
Eyes fixed on some far point beyond the storm
Of their own rhetoric. We turn away
When Hitchcock asks and answers once again
What's madness? through the words of one who *knows,*
Some tensed psychiatrist . . . And yet, transfixed,
We watch as Melanie, flashlight in hand,
Begins her slow ascent late in a film
Where madness goes unmentioned, as she stops
Before the door she fears, then steps inside,
Glance frozen upward: shattered roof, blue sky—
Exploding from the bed, a thousand wings.

Mary Jo Bang

TO DANCE THE TARANTELLA

There will always be those who wear a felt hat
pulled over their face, a Fra Diav'olo
hiding in the mountains of Calabria, frater in exile,

renegade from the imagined hag, False-faith.
Which Edgar doesn't have a fiend? A Frateretto
who whispers that Nero lives as a trout in Lake George.

The jackhammer's *ratta-tat* reenacts
the tarantella, music once thought too frenzied
for the wearied ears of tourists.

But love in any language means
she invited the disturbance into the house;
locked all the doors, the windows, and stayed awake

for the better part of a century. Where can a person learn
Take me, will you? and the other catchy phrases
one never finds in guidebooks. To dance,

to dance the tarantella. To speak
a language of tongue rolls and lip twists. What sweeter?
Sweet rose. Sweet oleander. Sweet olive tree.

Wherever you are, I am: a jewel in the crown,
a bright cyclopic eye, bound to outstare. To feel the rush
of air, the soft breathe-out, brief as last night's sleep.

In the afterdance, everyone admits
that what they've fallen in love with is mayhem.
Oh you, yes, *you*. There's only you and I here.

Take off your felt hat, I beg you.

Tina Barr

THE PURPOSE OF JEWELRY

for Martha Osvat

1

I stared at the tapers of headscarves,
the long-sleeves of their blouses,
the white lengths that hid their waists and hips.
Eyes followed over me, my skin, my hair's color
The subway car was filled only with women.
I wondered about them, about their circumcisions.

In the silver shops, drinking maya madenaya
or mint tea, I sifted piles of silver dowry, heavy Yemeni
bangles sandcast with beaded patterns, three-inch
Turkomen cuffs set with bees of carnelian,
Nubian bracelets soldered with cut-outs and nuggets.

2

I looked into a big bowl piled with Bedouin
beads shaped like bird cages, oblongs, disks,
balls incised with arabesques, inlaid with glass,
filthy with tarnish. I thought I'd catch a cold
from inhaling dust, my fingertips grey with it.

From the ceiling hung dozens of khul-khaal,
thick hollow cuffs women wear on each ankle.
On the floor by Mahmoud's feet in a basin,
a stew of silver, earrings whose filigree spells *Allah,*
bent Bedouin hoops, lozenge-shaped cylinders
holding Koranic passages. Chains dripped from these
hegabs, swinging gilgilla, small hollow balls.

Siwa brides, clinking gilgilla, dressed their heads
in chains long as their hair. From huge yokes
around their throats, sun disks the size of small plates
hung over their chests. Rays of embroidery fanned
from the bodices, radiated through draped black caftans,
waves of triangles, hourglasses, stars in palm leaf,
yellow and orange. Girls arched over in the dark;
their families hung the stained sheets out.
Brides were given necklaces of carnelian beads
with five silver hands of Fatima, prongs clipped
for each child born to the wearer. A husband
gave a special bracelet if he beat her.

3

The woman on the train tied her black headscarf
so the beaded green edging framed her face;
heavy ends dripped over her ear. She kept
readjusting one other sheer scarf, so it tapered
down the back of her black overdress. She kept
smiling, tilting her head so her hoops
glinted, patting her temples while she fussed,
adjusting her scarves. Her coppery, soft hand,
covered with rings, touched her husband's
white turban. They leaned towards each other,
her face sixty maybe, her kohl smudged.
Near Sohag they got off. Plump, shuffling in flipflops,
she shifted her body inside two dresses;
on the station platform, she held her husband's hand.

4

On a Coptic tombstone, in relief, a stair.
The steps lead up or down.
The sun's rays lower, burning in leaves, water
a yellow fire. Each little girl was told to throw
the skin of her clitoris into the Nile.

Mike Barrett

ANGLES, ANGELS, ENGELS, AND EAGLES

Two lines in this conversation:
the first (what words say)
like 15 lb test that slants
upward from an earthworm squirming
on a pond's bottom;
the second (what words mean)
the line's thin shadow
across the sandy bed,
given its shallowness
and position of sun overhead.
That is, if we ignore the vertex
at the rod's smallest eye,
ignore that the line ends wound
round the spindle,
and then imagine it and pond
stretching infinitely.

After such talk
we mostly remember
what should have been said:
a fence that crosses
two widening boundaries
or point on horizon
that draws parallel lines
together. A light marvelously
bright, invariably distant,
Madonna's sidelong glance
from Gabriel's gilded script.
Too often in love I've mistaken
indifference for adoration,
punctuated memory with, "See?"
Heart like a cherub in flight
on a stone arch, plump with faith
that stuffs the belly,
Buddha ripe beneath his tree, fat,

begging the question. This belief
works through machinations
that render simple facts numinous,
"like the German custom to write
history as if it had fallen
from the skies." A way
to produce surplus value
out of space that's mainly glutted
with shadow. Heavy. Resolved
in neither friends, editors,
or lovers. Each rolls away
as if following the shape
of the earth into the unknown.
Guessing where keeps one sharp-eyed,
not for freedom or revolution,
but details of chance, opportunities.
Ending, then, grounded,
while thrashing in sleep,
I wake in too many rays of sunlight
and wait to take on wings.

Christian Barter

THE LOST WORLD OF THE AEGEAN

On the cover of *The Lost World of the Aegean,*
in a pile of reading on my kitchen table,
a painting portrays two Minoan women
in finely wrought jewelry feeding a monkey
between the pillars of a stone bathhouse.
Nearing the end of another relationship,
I'm at the point where
I don't want anything to die anymore—
the women, the monkey, the civilization,
even the creator of the Marlboro Man,
whose obituary photo in *Time*
is lying next to the book, a man
who lured millions to an early,
miserable death. His childish grin is lit up
in '62, sucking air and cracking jokes
just thirty-five years before being snuffed out,
oblivious to the whole idea of misery,
as I am on the refrigerator door
at twenty-two, waving to the crowds
of the future from my new pickup,
pulling out of the driveway,
going back to Portland where I will meet
a woman I do not love who will, a year later,
have a son I will never see.
And why shouldn't he be happy?
Jack Kennedy is beaming far from Dallas,
escorting his beautiful wife
down perfect marble steps
in The Greatest Country on Earth,
and new machines are going to
save us all from having to work,
perhaps, someday, from having to die.
Even the dry historian breaks down
and refers to Crete as "a lost and golden land,"
though the rest of the story is like the others:
an awakening, a series of disasters,
a pile of tablets not yet deciphered.

Wendy Battin

AND THE TWO GIVE BIRTH TO THE MYRIAD OF THINGS

—said Lao-tse, sage of waterfalls, who

knew how the courtly heart keeps trying the world.
Heart wants only the good: dreams like a glass

harmonica, ringing light's measures. Love like art
if art could grow from seed, unfolding the code

inside it. But what the mind has sundered
cannot stay long uncluttered. Innocent heart, I

think, good heart, it wants, wants just now good
hands to coax my shoulders loose. What are we

birthing, when one thing leads to another,
two swimming the body's heat together?

If you want to know how the Way makes
a world, desire. But if you want to know the Way,

want nothing. A tall order, either way, worse
in the wanting not to want, as if desire can only

redshift like the galaxies who fly from us, who never
knew us. The distant water insists on falling inward,

to earth, to hell with all the stars retreating around us. O
Lao-tse, o Hubble, o love. It all comes down

to the ocean in time, singing more deeply
the farther it travels. Its bass line thrums

the floorboards, the walls, such slow decay I can't
feel the dust on my skin until he is sleeping.

Nicky Beer

TO RADIUS AND ULNA

The two bones that form the framework of the forearm.

I sing of arms . . .
From their names alone,
they could have been another pair
of Virgil's jilted:
two slightly horsey,
big-boned sisters
lovesick over the same sailor
who had his hometown
stenciled on one tanned shoulder
in four indigo letters.
Would he have taken them
separately, hoisting
himself over one white
window sill, then the next,
or did he make it a game,
passing back and forth
between the two of them
at one time in the dark—
restless ship
in a heaving strait—
daring himself to guess
whose leg, whose arm?
What happened next, though,
is certain. The morning
they both found him gone
and the harbor emptied
of burnished masts,
they went down
to the shore.
Ulna, the elder, the homelier,
pulling her shawl over
her head until only the broad,

jutting nose she despised,
that *crow's beak*, was visible.
The younger leaning slightly
on one hip, the tip
of her slipper placed firmly
on the hem
of the other's dress,
as if she were
a plain, slow sea-bird
caught by the tail . . .
Time and the beach
slowly stuccoed
the pair in a white
mosaic: crabs emptied
and ossified at their feet,
the gulls dropped
guano and feathers,
the sea grass bleached
and wound into their hair.
Each dusk, the sun drowned
a doubled creep of shade
in the tide.

It's nothing
new for anyone to want
this, to be turned
to salt after a night
with someone who seemed
to have it pouring
from his mouth
in marshy lungfuls,
leaching from his fingers
that turned their tongues to paper.
Because we cannot first become
the bull, the swan, the lightning itself
for our loves, we prove
our devotion afterwards
by slowly becoming
unrecognizable.
But these two—they never became

beautiful, no matter what
we may want for them.
Think of how they must have
marveled at their own
stillness,
admired the chaos
that crafts
every quiet thing:
that thin, pale fan
dragged in by the waves
was once the rage of a fish.
This wind-diminished dune
was a mile of sea-roil.
These rocks were fire,
were women
who found,
beneath their tenderness,
an absolute,
an unadorned
yearning for the weight
of a familiar body,
a mute, stolid
lovesong of bones:
to hold.

Caroline Bergvall

MORE PETS

a more – cat
a more – dog dog
a more – horse
a more – rat
a more – canary
a more – snake
a more – hair
a more – rabbit
a more – turtle

a more – turtle cat
a more – turtle – more – cat dog
a more – dog – more – cat horse
a more – dog – less – horse – less – cat rat
a less – hair – less – horse – more – rat canary
a more – canary – less – turtle – more – rat snake
a more – canary – not – goldfish – less – snake – not – cat hair
a not – dog – more – hair – less – snake rabbit
a dog – not – more – hair – not – turtle turtle

a not – turtle – plus – rat catchat
a plus – dog – plus – rat – pas – chat dog
a more – hair – pas – chat – moins – chien horse
a more – chat – plus – horse – moins – chien – more – rabbit rat
a rat – not – plus – horse – more – hair – moins – canary canary
a rat – not – mon – canary – more – not – rabbit snake
a less – dair – mon – canary – pas – dair – dog – not – snake hair
a plus – rabbit – plus – dair – monte – lapin – not – snake rabbit
a plus – dair – rabbitnot – more – less – turtle turtle

a rabbitnot – catnot chatchat
a catnot – ni – more – ni – dogless dog
a ni – morecat – horsecheval – ni – dogless horse
a lessplus – notrat – monlapin – dogless – horsecheval not
a plusnot – notnot – notrat – goldfish – cancan canary
a notplus – snakenot – moinsplus – cancan snake
a snakenot – notair – lesscanned doghair
a nonnot – notair – plus – rab rabbit
a no – tair – plus – rab – more – turtle trtl

Richard Blanco

OCTOBER CROSSWORDS

for C. S. B.

The last week of October I watch you consumed
by the challenge of your puzzles in my apartment.
Twelve Across: adj. conflicted, diverted from attention
at the dining table, the low lamplight halloed over
you and the pen casting shadows against the grain,
filling in left-n-right rows and up-n-down columns.
Nine Down: unaffected by disturbance |s|e|r|e|n|e|
evenings on the chaise, writing against your lap,
lifting your eyes from the page every few minutes,
to gaze through the window into the courtyard
blooms sunned by moonlight, and pluck a word.
Six Across: a gem, but also a game (nine letters)
sprawled on my bed, your torso bearing down
on your elbows eventually buckling into sleep,
a still-life arrangement of defaced reading glasses,
the dictionary parted open to a field of *m* words,
a tabled glass of flat seltzer, the cat perpendicular
at your feet and my face parallel to your back.

And you never notice me searching for words,
trying to tempt you with my Spanish, the lines
across my palms, the palms down my streets,
cafe-con-leche mornings, *caribe-blue* twilight,
a seven letter *te quiero* to convince you to stay,
a *Ten Down* |g|u|a|r|a|n|t|e|e| that it'll all work:
the good job you'll find, the car you'll save for,
the two bedroom where we'll live with the bay
serenading bridges and doubling the city lights.
Four Across |c|l|e|a|v|e| *to cling but also to split*
you collect your toothbrush and patchouli oil,
your scarlet dashiki hung over the bedroom door,
your Yoga books, stacks of finished crosswords
and you return the closet space |v|a|n|i|s|h|

Eavan Boland

THE HARBOUR

The harbour was made by art and force.
And called Kingstown and afterwards Dun Laoghaire.
And holds the sea behind its barrier
less than five miles from my house.

Lord be with us say the makers of a nation.
Lord look down say the builders of a harbour.
They came and cut a shape out of ocean
and left stone to close around their labour.

City of shadows and of the gradual
capitulations to the last invader
this is the final one: signed in water
and witnessed in granite and ugly bronze and gun metal.

Officers and their wives promenaded
on this spot once and saw with their own eyes
the opulent horizon and obedient skies
which nine tenths of the law provided.

And frigates with thirty-six guns cruising
the outer edges of influence could idle
and enter here and catch the tide of
empire and arrogance and the Irish sea rising

and rising through a century of storms
and cormorants and moonlight the whole length of this coast
while an ocean forgot an empire and the armed
ships under it changed. To slime weed and cold salt and rust:

A seagull with blue and white and grey feathers
swoops down and rolls and finishes
its flight overhead and vanishes—
its colours stolen where the twilight gathers.

William Bronk

SUBJECT MATTER

Science is metaphor. So is truth.
It seems for all time. Others repeat
its experiments. Within its terms, it
is usable. How should we, inside
and of its metaphor, question it?

THE IMMORTALS

We think it's important what we do: it will last
and a story's expected of us. With a great world
wondrous outside us, our interest instead is to leave
on the shelf as we go out, a biography
we hope an insightful mirror will have written down.

THE MUTE DEAF OF THE WORLD

The stories we tell and are told and may believe
are what we call in music melody,
intently listened for where none is sung
except we sing ourselves. And all they sing
or all the stories tell is how we long
for song and story in the mute deaf of the world.

Richard Burns

FROM *THE MANAGER*

50

Hello. Hello. Are you there. Is that really you. What is the good of the traffic

The rushing to urgent meetings. The mortgages and bank loans. The research and the investments. The trees blossoming and fruiting. The in-tray and the out.

The percentages and bids. The train journeys to and from work. The car journeys to and from home. The gossip liaisons secrets. Mowing the growing grass.

The records signatures messages. The wavelengths and vibrations. The losses longings regrets. The weekends the flights the dreams. The bookings the tickets the seats.

The screens bars curtains panes. Le Quattro Stagioni. The borrowing the burrowing the prayers. The actual and imagined couplings. The new and the old machines.

When death will swallow us all. And we shall all go down. And our thoughts rot or burn with our bodies. And suffering never end. What is the good of the

Sorry. Sorry. Really, I thought you. Somebody else. Terribly sorry to have bothered. Wrong number. Sorry indeed.

Sharon Chmielarz

JEPHTHAH AND HIS DAUGHTER

> *If thou shalt without fail deliver the children of Ammon into my hands then shall it be that whatsoever cometh forth of the doors of my house to meet me when I return . . . shall surely be the Lord's and I will offer it up for a burnt offering.*
>
> —Jephthah to the Lord, Judges 11:30

Whatsoever cometh forth: Behind the vow,
the family history—his father's passion
for a harlot. And the offspring, Jephthah.
His half-brothers' disgust turning when
convenient into back-slapping praise.—
What do they want, his brothers, traveling
after all these years to Mizpeh, to his house,
offering oiled condolences on his wife's death,
eyeing his daughter. He sends her to her room,
keeping her from them as he would from
any ruffian. His gut curdles as it used to
at Father's table. "What do you want?"
They want war, against the Ammonites.
They want victory, from the Arnon to the Jabbok.
They want every city smitten, every Ammonite
on the run or slaughtered. They want to make him
Captain, over them, over all of Gilead.

Whatsoever cometh forth: Behind the vow,
a thought for the offering—a goat would do,
found at his doorstep, or a servant, yawning,
stumbling into morning, or a warrior
at the gate, too wounded to make it home.
Power opens as clause to sentence.
But the girl is the first out the door, dancing
to timbrel, tambourine. Next come the old,
faithful servants, a circle of ululation like locusts.
Then his voice, the Captain's, cracking,
Oh daughter, you've been a very great
trouble.— He lifts his arms, rends his robe.
She is hardly able to breathe as he wails,
in the stench of battlefield, *I've opened*
my mouth to the Lord and I can't go back.

Whatsoever cometh forth: Two months,
to bewail her virginity, to dance with friends
in mountains, to surrender as whatsoever,
an offering so shattering, each word
dries on his lips as the beloved's blood.

Kevin Clark

EIGHT HOURS IN THE NIXON ERA

The parabola of the suitcase as it flew
   from the Watergate balcony mimicked
my inner life the year the low voice
   on the phone said, FBI, do you know
a Bob Grant? My mother, a Republican

County Supervisor, was at church.
   It was a complex era. Did we laugh
too easily? Was I to tell the agent
   that Bob was a friend who'd palmed
a credit card for a wild DC ride

as Sam Irvin and the good guys were
   moving in for the kill? Bob, whose jet south
would pass DC-bound Air Force One
   that midnight, November 18th, 1973,
just after Nixon claimed he was no crook.

Bob had invited me for the gig, but
   I knew better—and I didn't know better
often. Bob seduced Ralph and Jenny,
   both staying the month in Jersey with me
and my publicity-conscious mother,

the same Ralph and Jenny who were on
   the verge of dissolution, ever since
I'd been falling for Jenny and she for me,
   though of course Ralph was my best friend,
and Jenny and I hated ourselves, hippie

clichés sloughing into a closet or basement.
   Even now I try to laugh it off. I told
Agent Kaplaw I'd never heard of Bob
   Grant. Boozy Bob, with whom I'd smoked
weed for six years in college while his muddy

Utah speakers alternately shook from
   Zeppelin sex riffs and Streisand show tunes,
who we later discovered longed himself
   to sleep with Ralph, *that* Bob had only
minutes earlier answered the suite phone,

hung up, looked at Ralph and Jenny with
   the gravity of a guy on bad acid, all
of them wordlessly putting into effect
   Escape Plan A, Ralph heading to the car
while Jenny and Bob packed the one suitcase

with the contraband of a good DC shopping
   blitz, compliments of a Mr. Robert Kitchen,
address at this point unknown, owner
   of a missing gold MasterCard. I hung up.
My mother pulled in the drive. The phone

didn't ring. It continued not to ring.
   As Ralph pulled to the curb and Bob and
Jenny descended down the elevator,
   exited, then stuffed the goods back
in the split suitcase and jumped into

the Cutlass, also rented courtesy of
   Mr. Kitchen, and headed for Dulles,
my mother and I chatted about Mass
   and Father Mulroney's somnambulant
sermon, though she didn't care to knock

the priest because she still harbored
   hope that my rejection of the family faith
was a temporary moral seizure and didn't
   want to sour the wine while I lapsed.
She went upstairs for her afternoon nap.

The phone rang. Agent Kaplaw assured me
   he would slap a warrant on my ass
for aiding and abetting and haul me down
   to DC if I didn't talk. I gave up Bob,
then hung up. Do we laugh too easily?

My mother's hero the President
   was a traitor—nothing else
she could call it. He'd lost her faith.
   And how could she win
her election next year? Car doors slammed

in front of the house. I met Ralph and Jenny
   outside. One look at me and they knew
trouble had trailed them. We called Bob
   at home in Gainesville. He would
turn himself in, as he'd promised. We

told my mother that rich Bob wasn't
   so rich as he'd made out, that he'd urged
Ralph and Jenny to DC for a weekend
   on him, that the weekend was stolen,
that the FBI had traced the billed calls

to *her* house. So practiced, we lied
   to soften the story, but
she had a Republican fit anyway.
   Soon enough Ralph left for California,
Jenny and I took a house, taught GED

in Jersey, Bob called the president
   of MasterCard and worked off
the three grand. No jail time. It's still
   a complex era, how the comic
can shroud regret. Jenny and I hit the road

for California, then broke up six years later
   when she became a Rolfer,
a Gestalt therapist, went in for enema
   and past lives therapies—
separately, I think. Bob is gay in Florida,

Ralph slept with another friend's lover,
   and now he's married to her.
I'm married, too, happy and faithful
   for two decades. In the adrenaline rush
of time, Ralph and I have remained

best of friends. We try to navigate
    all the old stories. When
our families vacation together, suitcases
    bloat, rarely fly.
I sometimes think of Nixon, how he failed us all.

Robert Crawford

ALFORD

Blearily rummaging the internet,
Aged thirty eight, not knowing where I was,
I found a site designed as an old harled manse,

Sash windows opening on many Scotlands.
Through one surf broke on the West Sands, St Andrews,
And through another Glasgow mobbed George Square.

Templeton carpets fluttered up and clucked:
Crevecouers, La Fleches, azeels, minorcas,
Cochins, Langshans, Scots dumpies, Cornish game.

The hallstand's canny, digitized gamp
Pointed to fading pixels; when I touched them
I felt *The Poultry-Keeper's Vade-Mecum,*

Though in the next room, where a bren-gun spat,
Its title changed into *King's Regulations;*
Tanks manoeuvred round the hearth and range,

Smashing duck eggs, throwing up clouds of flour.
Fleeing the earth-floored kitchen, an ironing table
Hirpled like girderwork from bombed Cologne

Into the study where my Aunt Jean studied
How not to be a skivvy all her life,
While my dead uncle revved his BSA,

Wiping used, oily hands on Flanders lace.
Ministers primed themselves in Jesus's Greek.
Bankers shot pheasants. Girls sang. My father

Walked me through presses with a map of Paris,
Though all the names he used were Cattens, Leochil,
Tibberchindy, Alford, Don, Midmill.

I understood. 'Virtual reality?'
I asked him. In reply he looked so blank
His loved face was a fresh roll of papyrus

Waiting to be made a sacred text,
Hands empty as the screen where he projected
Slides of our holidays at Arisaig,

His body fresh cotton sheets in the best bedroom
Of his boyhood home before he was a boy.
Waiting here, he waits to meet my mother,

For a first date at St Martin in the Fields.
Here, his father, Robert, catches light
On his own deathbed, pipe and *Press and Journal*

Combusting in a way none can control.
Manse rooms huddle, fill with shetland ponies,
London tubes. There is no here. Here goes.

En te oikia tou Patros mou monai pollai eisin:
In my Father's house are many mansions:
If it were not so, I would have told you.

Robert Creeley

FROM *HISTOIRE DE FLORIDA*

In pajamas still
late morning sun's at my back
again through the window,
figuring mind still, figuring place
I am in, which is me,
solipsistic, a loop yet moving, moving,
with these insistent proposals
of who, where, when,
what's out there, what's in,
what's the so-called art of anything,
hat, house, hand, head, heart, and so on,
quickly banal. Always reflections.
No light on the water, no clouds lifting, bird's flap taking off—
Put the food in mouth, feel throat swallowing,
warmth is enough.

Emotions recollected in tranquility . . .
which is what?
Feelings now are not quiet, daughter's threatened
kidneys, sister's metal knee replacement, son's
vulnerable neighborhood friendships, Penelope's social
suitors, whom I envy, envy.
Age. Age.
Locked in my mind,
my body, toes broken, skin
wrinkling up, look to the ceiling
where, through portals of skylight,
two rectangular glass boxes in the stained wood,
the yellow light comes, an outside is evident.
There is no irony, no patience.

There is nothing to wait for
that isn't here, and it will happen.
Happiness is thus lucky.
Not I but the wind that blows through me.
~

Another day. Drove to beach,
parked the car on the edge of the road
and walked up on the wooden ramp provided,
then stopped just before the steps down to the sand
and looked out at the long edge of the surf, the sun glitter,
the backdrop of various condominiums and cottages,
the usual collective of people, cars, dogs and birds.
It was sweet to see company,
and I was included.

Yet Crusoe—
Whose mind was that, Defoe's?
Like Kafka's *Amerika,* or Tom Jones come to London.
Or Rousseau, or Odysseus—
One practices survival
much as we did when kids and would head for the woods
with whatever we could pilfer or elders gave us,
doughnuts, cookies, bread—
Even in one's own terror,
one is proud of a securing skill.

But what so turned things
to pain, and if Mandelstam's poem is found scratched
on cell wall in the gulag
by anonymous hand,
and that's all of either we know—

Why isn't that instance of the same
side of world Robinson Crusoe comes to,
footprint on sand a terror,
person finally discovered an adversary
he calls "Friday,"
who then he learns "to be good"—

But I wouldn't, I can't
now know or resolve
when it all became so singular,
when first that other door closed,
and the beach and the sunlight faded,
surf's sounds grew faint, and one's thoughts took over,
bringing one home.

Ray DiPalma

PHARAOH'S HOUSE

Rubbing his hands with anticipation, he found the motion invigorating. The weather got worse. He sagged in his chair. Pencils rolled off the table. The music had been interrupted. He recognized certain words. But he waited for an explanation. This, he began to think, was a mistake. He intended to have a plan. Cómo está usted? Comó está usted? There had once been a parrot and a gardener. The Navajo rug resembled his signature. There were monkeys in the windows. These were paintings not windows. Moonlight spilled on the rug. At his side was an old key-wound timepiece that bubbled its tlick tlock tlick tlock from the bottom of a soapstone urn filled years ago with sea water. He shivered constantly. His chin was tucked into his collar. He tried once more to smile.

He remembered the cliffs. They went unmentioned. He wished he had taken more snapshots. No letters had been answered for three years. Rome—his white suits. Another argument. Three kings and two queens. Three aces and two jacks. All red cards. It wasn't possible. That's what he expected. Unambitious, he had underlined the books. Anxious for a change, he shaved his head. Instinct was indistinguishable from fairy tale. Painted stones for markers. He divided them further. Divination. The license number of the black car and the driver who wore the shirt with palm trees, matters that were now distantly related. Frayed rope around the mirror. He did a little dance. The radio was on. There was an answer for everything.

Slowly and distinctly. Fortunately. Certainly. He patted his left arm. Then his head. Competently. Not like everyone else. The story followed them. Apologies for having questions. Questions on behalf of apologies. They stood in place of answers. They blocked the way. They were a world unto themselves. They went along with the unformed plan and had no further questions. They shaved with their boots on. Struck over the head they died standing up. There was a room full of flowers. It was down the hall. He tipped his hat. Stiffly erect. He had a small bottle of linseed oil in his pocket. First soak the wood. Then wait. Illuminated by lightning. It had passed through the earth and come out in Shanghai. This was its return. An abduction.

He was painting the floor. Third in the litany. It could have been first. The shutters rattled. Now he waited with a newspaper in his lap. In three days the floor was dry. He had experienced similar moments in Russia, Turkey, and Japan. He had his feet then. Now he spent hours adjusting his glasses. The paper mentioned espionage, court intrigue, diplomats, and Zeppelins. He waited for the clock to strike. He had a desire to calculate. There was a compass in the pantry. Knowing that was enough. Could it estimate the time? Approximate the day of the week. These were standards beyond any imagined capacity. A tool for a tool. An aggregate measure from a perfect machine. Reaching from here to the pantry and back again. Just once. Anytime.

I know I do he said to his foot. Yes and no he said to his hand. This year he was waiting for the birds. It seemed like eight or ten years ago. But it wasn't. It was just as long as before. Before there was a this year. He had a sharp eye on the soapstone urn. It was a stunt. Guided by an exhausted finger. First bread. Then water. Then bread. Then water. The way of it. All the diamond-bright eddies in that crater of seawater. The come and go emptying the past. Semitones in languid descent. Spoken from the chair. The compliments of a rectangle. Furnished in the overlay. That is the waiting. Ankle-deep he wondered where his foot had gone. I know. I know I do he said to his hand. Yes. Yes and no, he said to his foot. Instructor of the spasm. The spiral was devious. Without pity.

He slid his arms around his knees. The paint had been dry for days. The remainder was a puzzling detachment. Posture meant nothing. It was just a changing of the guard. A way to wait for the attached. Attaching. Where not when was the question. Faintly but at all hours. Northbound. To magnify what might be found. Set it apart. Northbound. By the Pole Star. Its cunning formal power. Not distant, merely evasive. Difficult to call with a shrug. Cold light piercing the white taffeta and cigarette smoke. Starlight from the north. Northbound. Is that the gone back of it? Bound by common interests. Twirling out of a stud of light. Scratched out of the glare. Immediately recognized. Pressed for an answer.

Something provokes sometime. A way to operate. The stoop-shouldered pilgrim's become petulant. Where are you going? What are you that you would get there? Another excuse? Delivered to the obliged. Given the brush-off. That's how he got there from here. And that's how he got here from there. Steadied. Tapping out a few intimate inches. Unspoiled guest of the mirror. Streamlining the exit. Falling into the ocean. For a coastline or a road. The unfinished business. Built around the wall. The contrary divided into another intriguing remark. Gratified anonymity. Chalked on the door. Reaching with his stick. A pilgrim no more. But having been. He wears the lion's scar.

He said he was finished talking. And to further emphasize the point he said he was finished talking. The modulations of the voice. The fretted vowels. The discordant syllables. Walking and talking. Upper lip curled back. Vaguely flattered by the echo. That disappointing circuit. Squinting critically at the shape of the mouth going after its words. The nostrils involved. No apologies. In those days he could hear the turtle. To illuminate the situation. Put a seed on the tongue. Watch it grow. He hurried a short-tempered explanation into the darkness. Wordless gestures lifted out of the throat. Hands that decide. Convinced. He didn't care to begin. Even if important things would be lost. No attention. None. Making a place where he could find the inaudible answer.

Intimate as dust. Sealed and sequestered. He scruples to accept the speculations of a ghost. Both are full of trust. One in what he observes. The other in what he believes he absolves. He who is known as he makes a they with his unconscious impressions. A common sum of uncommon situations. Down to the stranger standing on the other side of the door. Making a living. An inexact one. The profits of surveillance and a loss of certainty. Uncertainty well attained. Bright sun and a muster of countenance. Its expansions. Excursions. Through the audible shadows. Melting in a mist of logical events. Being asked what. Or why. The Pythagorean letter. Deciphering the overheard calculations. Sheets of breath over all the witnesses. Concessions's gazette.

Parthians, and Medes, and Elamites. Modulators of the molehill. They fill the air with rumors of their cruelties. He says he sees their lips move. The marks of loot in the dust. The blue glow under a red cloud. It works the window. A small airplane makes the soft grey shadow towards which he stretches his fingers. Another polished tryst. Brass flashing in the pink crystal. Lids narrow. The woods are empty. Wet chalk underfoot. The sureness of the shingle. Rampant corners wedged with damp folios. Blank pages and the genial paradox. The fumes of Saint Nemo. He is among the mixed characters soothed by recollection. A proposal restored to oblivion. This is the loop. N'est-ce pas? A durable tender-conscienced grudge. A further message from the daughters of Odin.

The room came with a view. Enormous quiet folded in a leaf. He was home to the fading answer. The intimate spectacle of reply. It would apprehend the confusion of the place. Where the matter-of-fact ripens. A certain amount of imagined pain merging with pilgrimage. An idiosyncratic partnership between ambiguous ephemera and the appointed pursuit. A segment of thought preparatory to a silent judgement. Penetrating the imperfect choice. Dexterous and arbitrary. The direction of the hinge. To presume a step lower. One. More one less. Okay in both directions at once. The hallelujah scramble. Glue and the axe. Hammer and scalpel. Reading the notes for the legend. The puzzle of twilight filling the space left by disabused affections.

Now and then a further page. Incidence corrects the hoax. The Latin for it. And the Greek. Confetti to replace the constellations. The old man who wore pale yellow gloves. Apparitions and footprints. Night and day. The shimmy just before inertia. The spectator confounded. He was a very private person adjusted to the map. A noun at rest among the assessing verbs. Taken as it closes down. Not even a throb. A bargain thrown into the mix. An appropriate expanse. It has taken only what it needs to go from here to there. And from there to over there and over there. Scouring the careless fantasies. Turning away. He couldn't bring himself to add anything further. There are standards. Even behind the arras.

He is a corrosion of episode. Juxtaposed with distraction at the limits of premise. As the world turns he follows the equator and paces the room. The narrow road to the deep north flanked by vernacular indignities. No time for indignation. Only the next word. From a prospect of weeds a drunken dwarf offers his attentions. Cramp with his answer for everything. He's the only one to have repeated the reproach. Forward into the oblivion of surreptitious promptings. Rags of music stitched to the paper coat. A band of turnip greens instead of laurel. Circumscribed by rhythms and fractured patterns. Then repeated for any sparks they might give off. Salty aftermaths. The fathom count droned across the mist. Premature. Losing momentum. Useless.

He was the agent of unpromised possibilities. Convincing the prediction of risk. Tokens and portents. Nothing palpable. That's all he recalls. The all in recall. The giddy compromise. At the end of the shout. And outside. Just a place to shed some skin. Blank mortality. Good company. Their snarling music. Their one more once. Never again. This he could handle. Make another body count. Put some purchase on the soporific. A leg up. A hand over. A triumph of indiscretion and intuitive melancholy. The last warm-blooded success beating a hard retreat trimmed with words. Prolific. Well-known. Non-committal. Cruel. Prey to the glare. The remains of his ardor are a tiny trickle of sweat. The trace that stifles the allegory.

Knuckling his eyes. For the zones of light and color. He copes. To startle himself. And make the shadows jump. Secrets of survival. Lingering in the crevice and twitch. Making measure of the right reply. A finger stuck anywhere in a book. Six lines down. Heeding the last five words before the sentence turns a corner. Platinum threads on the tongue. He tunes the echo. An answer. Like birdsong. The miscalculated circle in a circle. An answer nonetheless. Cut within the cut. Smooth line following the ragged edge. Scratches and burls. Ink thrown at the collation. Passages from Phanodemus, Philochorus, Istrus. And the historians Hecataeus, Ephorus, Theopompus, Anaximines, Marsyas, Craterus. He rolls his hands and points at the window.

James Doyle

THE AMPHITHEATER

All of Babylon crowds
into the stone seats. Alexander's
generals file across the stage as the chorus.

The play is the Red Sea.
The actor who portrays Alexander
the Great slits his veins to show how it is done.

Different flags ring the theater.
One for each member of the audience.
The banners stretch to the Gulf of Persia.

Everyone wins and loses.
The pile of bodies keeps growing.
The chorus is trying to construct a history for the audience.

But no one wants
the show to end. The future
is booed out of existence. If Alexander is dying,

that is his tragedy.
If he had lived, for example,
would the Hanging Gardens of Babylon still be one

of the Seven Wonders?
But there is the tragic tale
of a blind king and incestuous gods to get through.

And Nero is waiting
a few centuries down the line. The actor
who plays him is even now reciting poetry in the wings.

Kevin Ducey

WEIL

Simone, near-sighted
soldier of the Spanish

war—distracted
(the whisper of an inner

ear) foot hesitating
above the campfire's

cookpot (set in your
path deliberately by

Stalinists) no doubt in
that moment of insight

the heavens opened and I
hear the sharp groan of

Henry Miller—bored with
all the whores of

Luxembourg. He dreams—
transports of

conversation with that girl
who took him for

several days—free. The
erotic love of

God looking not
taking one step toward

the friend, but flying
upward. Sit and taste

Love, the meat served
the requited guest.

John Engels

THE ORDERS

In this house
everything is where it ought to be.
The mirrors reflect
a perfect order. We cannot say

the same for what goes on
outside the doors and windows,
wilderness of up and-
down, slantwise, crosswise,

to-and-from—earth-
eating roots gone
every which way purposeless,
rain, great jumbles of snow,

a cardinal dropping from the cedar
into the spreadings of white alyssum—
all the processional put up against
the serenities of alignment

for which we've worked: stillness
of knives, spoons, forks
in their drawers,
the calm reaches of carpets,

flat clasp of wallpapers,
and the forceless diagonals
of banisters, even
the unbreathing, unsaying

stillness of the bouquets
of orange calendulas
in their shaggy symmetries arranged
to the precise centers

of tables. And here we are
standing here, looking on, trembling
with something more we knew,

for which we can invent no theory.

Beth Ann Fennelly

WINDOWS OF PRAGUE

Store Window: Restitution

A waitress suddenly owns
a department store, as property seized
by Nazis in the war is returned
to the descendants of the owners
of the loss. What has she to sell?
A wedding dress and auto parts.
In the window the bride's bouquet
is a wrench. Fixed in time, the Skoda
can spirit her away to church.

Castle Window: Defenestration

1419: Protestant noblemen charge
the Banquet hall, seize the King,
full bodied as his claret, and hurl him
out the window. This glitch in Hapsburg
succession is the Defenestration
of Prague. After history, the story
continues: moating the castle were peels
and carcasses fit for a King and chamber
pot refuse which pillowed his fall.
In three day's time he crawled out,
floated the Vltava downstream,
found an alias, became apprenticed
to blow glass. His windows were so clear,
it was said, that they fetched one hundred
crowns; as he made them in the field,
kingfishers died to fly to him. Bloody
feathers stuck in glass: the only proof.

Sky Window: Armageddon

The square's astrological glass dome:
a man discovers a thirteenth sign,
overlooked stars that are burning
to be recognized. All history is out
of line, fate's lacking. In the cracked,
unnatural sky, bears and lions
hurl against their cages, Orion pierces
the wine bag of heaven, and Pisces
thrashes his tail against the dome,
but the astrologer, unable to right
the fishbowl, drowns in his own dream.

Annie Finch

A LETTER FOR EMILY DICKINSON

When I cut words you may never have said
into fresh patterns, pierced in place with pins,
ready to hold them down with my own thread,
they change and twist sometimes, their color spins
loose, and your spider generosity
lends them from language that will never be
free of you after all. My sampler reads,
"called back." It says, "she scribbled out these screeds."
It calls, "she left this trace, and now we start"—
in stitched directions that follow the leads
I take from you, as you take me apart.

You wrote some of your lines while baking bread,
propping a sheet of paper by the bins
of salt and flour, so if your kneading led
to words, you'd tether them as if in thin
black loops on paper. When they sang to be free,
you captured those quick birds relentlessly
and kept a slow, sure mercy in your deeds,
leaving them room to peck and hunt their seeds
in the white cages your vast iron art
had made by moving books, and lives, and creeds.
I take from you as you take me apart.

James Finnegan

DIRIGIBLE DAYS

Its great shadow passed over us,
over our houses and town,
at times blocking out the very sun.
Our necks ached at night
from looking up at this
gas-filled leviathan of the air.
Sometimes you would shudder
when it came up suddenly from behind,
floating there, ominously, right overhead,
as though looking down, watching.
Some people claimed
they could see faces peering
out of the little round windows
that dotted its belly. Children
would run after it, trying to
stay in its shadow. "Ovoid"
was a word commonly used
in those days, and mothers
would hold up their infants
when it came into view. The steeples
of the town, needle-sharp, could never
bring it down, though at night,
being gray almost to black,
it may well have come down to earth,
at rest beyond the western hills.
 Then one day it was not there,
the sky immaculate, cloudless blue in all directions,
no shadow moved through the backyards and avenues.
There were many theories to explain
its disappearance, and the advent
of its return was often predicted.
But it was gone, gone for good or for ill,
and now the only ones who ever talk about it
are the old people, and the young,
hearing these stories, nod politely.

Roy Fisher

AND ON THAT NOTE: JAZZ ELEGIES

Wellstood, for forty-odd years,
guessed what there was to do next
and did it. Tipped
the history of the art half over
and went in where it suited;
and understanding that music's
more about movement than structure
proceeded to lurch, stamp,
splash, caper, grumble, sprint,
bump and trudge—mostly
on the piano—then sat down
in his hotel room before dinner
and, too soon, stopped.

Strange channels for new noises. That steely-eyed
old man, dapper,
sugar-coated in famous vanity
and endless glad-handing,
carried always somewhere about him
what he'd come upon early, a monstrous,
husky, thoroughly dangerous saxophone sound
never before heard on earth,
and on a bandstand if you put your foot
behind him hard enough,
out it would still come honking
with no manners at all.

Three piano-players
taking turns on the portable
stool. The first
tucks it close in
and perches like a hamster, as he must.
Second, I slide it back
to make good room to slouch
as I permit myself. Finally,
gaunt and purposeful, he drags it
to the extreme: Glenn Gould
plays Crazy Horse in crimson suede
pointed boots; extensible arms
reaching for distant keys, spine curved,
navel in phobic flight from the piano. The music,
after a moment's meditation, comes streaking out
in elasticated pulses: wild, dramatic,
timeless East European Stride.

Taking care never to learn
the ways of the world till the moment
the alto would assume its insinuating angle and get
blown straight into life. Seeing a waiting audience, then
blinking awake mildly, leaning down to whisper
surprise news to the pianist: "Trouble is,
I just can't seem to remember the names of
any tunes at all. Serious problem there." Prolonged
pause, prolonged. Again, after some painful night:
"How can those people go on playing
for twenty or thirty years and never even
start to want to learn their instruments?"
Serious question there.

Ears up, neck solid,
punching pretty tunes off centre
through a stubby *cornett:* "The way I figure it,
the sound comes out
that much closer to my face, and
that's where I want it." Lovely old
American tunes, and talking: "I guess you people
must all be thinking I'm just another American
loudmouth!" Talking: "What key?
THIS key!" "What tempo?
It's a BALLAD, for Christ's sake!" On a sofa
at a party in his honour, persuaded
to toot gently and graciously for his supper,
looses off at full volume and quells
New York Town Hall, with nothing
in pursuit but my quite small piano.

Whistling in the dark,
wobbling a pallid flame down
to the bottom of the bottle:
owl-sounds, muffled
squawks. Nothing
better to do but whistle
when there's so much dark.

Note: This poem commemorates some musicians, now dead, I used to play with, or alongside: Bud Freeman, Archie Semple, Duncan Swift, Dick Wellstood, Bruce Turner, Wild Bill Davison.

John Gallaher

A GUIDEBOOK TO THE BEAUTIFUL PEOPLE

I love to cuddle up with the white sandy beaches, Sadie said, there
on the ladder. And I'm really good at quitting smoking, to boot.
She knew more than she was saying, we could tell.

I get a kick out of guava and windward island settings,
she replied. We're really very curious is all. Maybe Jenny Hoyden
can help? We're into weddings here, where we can all be dressed

as the other person. That would be something.
Especially since we enjoy talking to people, all kinds of people,
Sadie added. John was very attentive and I was watching

the boats. The circus school's another basic requirement,
Albie said. We called it *The Mini-skirt Episode*, complete
with flying trapeze, trampoline, and the locals. Jenny didn't know

what to do with it. I'm still a little jet-lagged, she told us.
She was built with weather in mind, we knew, looking
out on the patio where she was swimming with a philanthropist.

They were taking photos the way one might take a bath,
Albie said. I also love to talk, Sadie replied, so let's talk. The
whole thing is why I love coffee with high quality introductions

and end notes. And I love to tan and wear sunglasses as well.
Other highlights include scuba diving, horseback riding,
several mirrors, and little plaid skirts. Other school girls

weren't so lucky, and are subject to availability. They've
their common interests, so the concierge told us not to worry
too much. Enough's enough, we shouted, and wrestled them

to the floor. As the name implies, Lover's Leap didn't
let us down either. And that's a place where you could stick
your Thanksgiving or New Year. In fact, Sadie found Mexicans

and Italians as well as a night out dancing. And I really enjoy
showing off for hours, she said from the landing. Look at her
there, Albie called, waving his flashlight. We were lost

from the beginning, we knew. So we skipped the funeral
entirely and concentrated on the cake. It was short of us, but
life's shorter. And dotting the horizon, as the signs say.

Richard Garcia

THE PEACEABLE KINGDOM

I wish I could write a poem about Squanto—
Squanto at our house for Thanksgiving
back in the fifties when I was a child, and all
of the family was still alive, younger, and together.
In the poem I'd introduce Squanto to my father,
John Garcia, former chef for the Matson Lines.
Thanksgiving was the one day of the year
he would cook at home. He'd adjust his chef's hat
at a cocky angle, cinch his apron, and while sharpening
his knives, ban my mother and sisters from the kitchen.
Only men allowed, just me, my brothers and cousins
and in this poem, Squanto too; after all, hadn't they
both sailed the world's oceans? My father had seen things,
he always said, that a man should not see. What things
I wondered? The child prostitutes of Manila? The public
sexual dance called "Toro?" Beheadings in Sumatra
or the slow Chinese execution by dismemberment
called "The Torture of the One Hundred Pieces?"
Squanto had seen a lot too—kidnapped twice,
taken, like Pocahontas, to London, but unlike her
he made it back somehow. Later, tricked into boarding
a ship in the harbor, he was shanghaied to Spain,
escaped, and managed to come home from that too,
only to find his entire tribe had died from the plague.
In the poem, Squanto and my father get along,
after all, both men spoke English and Spanish.
Squanto would make the pumpkin pies.
Maybe, if he comes into the poem a couple of days
early, I can take him to school and he can be
in the Thanksgiving play we have to put on.
Take that, Miss Kapelhaus!—my third grade teacher
who thought I was a complete idiot. Who didn't
believe I could read. Who couldn't tell me and Juan
and Carlos apart. Maybe she'll think Squanto
is the fourth Mexican at Dudley Stone Elementary.

At dinner we'll put three long tables together.
My cousins will be swinging from the lamps, sliding
down the banisters, and bouncing off the couch.
"Just like the first Thanksgiving," Squanto will say,
"those Puritan kids were pretty wild too."
In this poem I want to write, Squanto tells stories
about the Puritans. How surprised they were
to be greeted by an Indian in the Queen's English.
Maybe he'll joke and tell us his first words to them
were "How" or "Kemo Sabe." Maybe he will tell us
he waved-in the Mayflower like a parking attendant
saying "Easy now, watch out for that rock." We'll laugh,
careful not to ask him about the second Thanksgiving.
That'll be something he does not want to talk about
in this poem—blood seeping into the snow, crows
dipping deep into the hole that a blunderbuss makes
in a man's back. No, in this poem we'll just talk about
that first Thanksgiving that began a future
that never was. We'll even have our picture taken,
all of us around the table, our dogs, my Cousin Bob
down on one knee, me reading this poem out loud
like a proclamation. I'll add a lion, a tiger, some oxen
and cows, and I'll put my baby niece and nephew
sitting in front—The Peaceable Kingdom. We'll praise
and be thankful that time doesn't exist in this poem.
After dessert my father and Squanto will sit, smoking
big Indian cigars, swapping tales—abductions,
imprisonment, bloody mayhem, escapes, and
thankfulness for safe returns from the high seas.

Robert Gibb

THE EMPTY LOOM

I

Hiking through the Lake District, you watched sheep
Graze among the evening hills like a dusky, curd-
Shaped cumulus. Looms weave such clouds as these.

II

In his *Il Libro dell'Arte,* Cennini wrote that women
Took up spinning after the loss of Paradise,
But surely he was also thinking of the roundness
To their rhythms in the soft Italian nights, the moon,
Pale bobbin, coming on . . .

III

I'm sure he would have loved the simple buoyancy
Of these heddles, the warping board, and the way
The wood looks like it might burn even under water.

Have loved the sight of you in evening light, seated
By the window, inching your patient fabric past the lip
Of the batten where the patterns gathered into cloth.

Reginald Gibbons

SPARROW

In the town streets
pieces of the perishing world
Pieces of the world coming into being

The peculiar angle at which a failing gutter descends
from a house-eave; a squirrel's surviving tattered nest of leaves
woven into a high bare crook of an elm tree
(the last one alive on this street);

the small bright green leafing out of that elm;
a man shaking coins in a dry Coke-cup and saying
Small change, brother? Small change?;
a woman
in scuffed white running shoes and a fine suit hurrying
down the street with a baggy briefcase that must have
papers and her purse and her good shoes inside it
Perhaps a small pistol

Gusts rattle the half-closed upstairs window in the old office building that's
going to be torn down

Skittering across the sidewalk, a scrap of paper with someone's handwriting
on it, in pencil
A message that will arrive

Things in themselves

A few minutes of seeing
An exalting

Or a few minutes of complete shelter
A protectedness, a brief rest from the changes

Sparrow moments

~

But this emblem I take from the world—
able, fussing, competing
at the feeder, waiting on a branch,
sudden in flight, looping and rushing, to another branch,
quick to fight over mating and quick at mating,
surviving winter on dry dead seed-heads of weeds
and around stables and garbage and park benches,
near farms and in deep woods,
brooding in summer-hidden nests—house sparrow,

song sparrow, fox sparrow, swamp sparrow,
field sparrow, lark sparrow, tree sparrow, sage sparrow,
white-throated sparrow of the falling whistled song
that I hear as a small reassurance—

Would my happiness be that the sparrow not be emblem—
that it be only in my mind as it is outside of my mind, itself,
that my mind not remove it from itself
into realms of forms and symbolic thinking?

My happiness, that is, my best being

Words like branches and leaves,
or words like the birds among
the branches and leaves?

They take wing all at once
The way they flee makes flight look like exuberance not fear
They veer away around a house-corner.

Albert Goldbarth

INTO BLOSSOM

Of course we still love the idea of books, but we have an ever harder time tooling down to engage them as they were written to be engaged. Which is to say slowly, linearly, with single-track focus. Ours is now a world of high-speed action and reaction, of necessarily distributed awareness, of layered simultaneous involvements.

—arranged from an essay by Sven Birkerts

The Rapture, or a kind of Rapture, is going to come
and lift us with its claws in our nape or our waist-fat
(this is why "rapture" and "raptor" are cousins); or it
will take us the way that Zeus did Leda or
God did (fill in any one of the calendar's swooning
heart-speared saints); or, more to my current
purposes, it will land and say "welcome aboard"
as understood (in one of a hundred different languages
preprogrammed according to retinal scan) by an ever-ready
installachip behind our eyes, and we will take our place inside
that cybergenetic condor-jet-amalgam sensurround-vehicle,
and it will whoosh us away to the land of multistreaming screens
with neuro-plug-in capability, it will fly us across
an everyday hill of oak and scattered stone, and abruptly
into the vectors of info-boom and synchro-loop, oh it will whoosh us

—most of us. As for me, I'm sitting here pleasurably
with my back against one of those oaks. I can feel
the pattern of its bark—like Persian lamb—moiré my back.
The sun is out. A fly is insistent. I'm reading a poem
of James Wright's, on a printed page: I'm doing
nothing else. He's patting a horse now. He's breaking,
he says, into blossom. I'm small and quiet and rapt.

Barry Goldensohn

THE DEATH OF SENECA

If only he had stanched the wound of his mouth
and not placed an abstract power above
real power, appealing to a part of Nero
Nero didn't have, and tried to heave
His Unrestrained away from overpowering lust,
and left the Empress to the smart advice of her page
to find a new love, now love
was utterly lost, and had not urged on her
the higher justice of fidelity,
allowing her to try to kill Poppea
(The Empress also was an Unrestrained),

he would not have encouraged Nero's rising taste
for intimate murder, the most theatrical kind,
who then could play Fate in the tragedy
and Victim tra-la, and Executioner,
written just for him by Seneca
who would not have had to open his veins in the bath.

Lorrie Goldensohn

SEMIOTICS

An eye like a body of black
water in which the soul's swan drifts,
I have no words to give back
what we take from her, those rich gifts

at her command even now—drunk
out of her skull in a cement
doorway, October chilling her, sunk
to her muttering anger, bent

low to scald me with her talk, talk—
heedless of damage. But the tongue
that burns others turns on itself, balks;

she straightens, tips back her silk sleeve,
flashing the scarred wrist where the strong
blade bid. The wound wants me to forgive.

Jeffrey Greene

THE EVENING'S THEME

Let's say it's toward the end of the evening in a small town
in New England, with early November breezes and friends,

where the dinner discussion turns to a theme. Let's say
this time it's heroes, appropriate for poets over wine and stew,

but the definitions get stickier as they always do, ranging
from small acts of human decency to mythic figures at the end

of their journeys, and only what lies between gets interesting,
those lucky lunacies that changed the world, Copernican

or Lutheran, the unveering will of Magellan, down through
gradient heroes that make a nation and keep it dangerous,

until we are down to our own fathers, who must bear the heroic
flaws of our expectations. Then the discussion finally goes

to the hypothetical and from there to hell, where we
could start over with weaknesses. So we shift to places

where we grew up, things like bridges in Pittsburgh
or parishes in Wales or Raminski's daughter whom I thought

so brave to touch my brother and me near a coal bin.
I think of our landlord Raminski, the day he caught fire

burning paint off our building and pouring fuel on a lit pilot.
My brother cut his clothes off while blistering his own hands.

I know that it qualifies only as an act of human decency,
though my brother was only a kid. Still he looked mythic

with a carbon steel knife my father bought for dimes
at the flea market and Raminski sitting in shock on the beaten

earth of the backyard. Not even my brother's gin or cocaine
changes my mind. Achilles is nothing without Hector.

Debora Greger

THE LOST HERODOTUS

Here men pass their lives
separate from the animals they eat.
They do not knead dough
with their feet or take up dung with their hands.

Every day they bathe
standing up, and put on garments bearing names
of the small gods
who made their clothes. These people like to eat

in the out-of-doors
but relieve themselves in the house in secret.
After they drink
from metal beakers decorated with words,

these are collected
by a cart that requires not a single ox,
for burial at a special site,
for these people are mound-builders.

They leave their houses
to find cattle and chickens slaughtered,
and not by slaves.
And yet their buildings have reached the sky.

Their Parthenon I have seen,
farther away than any map could imagine.
The priest I asked did not know
how long ago it was built, only that animals

were no longer sacrificed there.
Birds may be seen to couple in the sacred precinct,
so the gods must be pleased.
Yet do these people have no great poet?

Robert Hahn

ELEGIAC QUARREL: CONCLUSION

in memoriam, James Merrill

You're off the hook. No messages. No dizzy-
Ing virtuoso zooms through cloudy sky,
Refracting sea, no blue middle distance

Where you have gone, only a dark shining
In the mind where fronds of the bronze palm stir
Where the bird burdened with its splendour sings . . .

. . . was the way I ended my elegiac quarrel with you,
But such a star-struck swoon, a dying fall,
Is far too easy, if the argument matters at all.
It leaves the world gasping with disbelief, as if
It were just what we say, no more than a mirrored globe
spinning through the abyss—

let me start again
Less artfully. We never met.
When I sent you poems, your cards came winging back
With praise I must admit
I feasted on—
and morsels of news
Life fanzine blurbs downloaded for admirers—

Dear RH, I'm winding up (or my w/p is) the memoir
I began 20 months ago, and have begun
Teaching the w/p to write verse. Sinister how much easier
It makes things. All best—JM

And now the posthumous memoir arrives, sifting gold from chaff,
The friends who called you Jimmy, from the rabble
Who knew you only as Sandover's "semi-fictional JM."

I saw your star, from a great distance, as one to be followed,
If at all, with misgivings—
shouldn't one do something

That mattered more, some praxis
Whose turnings on the lathe turned out
Bright scented shavings, yes, but more—
a mace, a staff?

Or is it true, as someone claimed, "to live as a poet
Is the equivalent
of a political statement"?

It sounds hopeful. I have hedged my bets,
Judging myself to be no worse than a bureaucrat
Of the Song Dynasty, those provincial governors
Who tried to rule as wisely as they could
or at least
to prevent harm.

Admittedly, it is art
We remember them for, their scrolling landscapes
Rising into clouds, not their local reforms

But whose life *does* hold up, worked over
By goons who straddle their chairs, holding cardboard cups of coffee,
glowering at the suspect?

Life reverts from gold to lead
In your recital of psychoanalysis, those precious chats which surely are
The hash of the leisure classes, no buried treasure there,
and when a robber baron heir
whips up a poem called *Ginger Beef*?

Art evades life
And life marches on, mocking art:

A late 90's item, this just in,
A film German soldiers made of themselves, some "pretending"
To be Nazis while others "play Jews," who pretend to be beaten,
And one wears a Hitler mustache, in case you don't get it,

Not the great winnowing, but the great leveling
Where we star in our homegrown follies, and skinheads film their rites
to recruit for the Aryan Nation.

But when did our high priests ever matter
To those who lived outside the Lion Gate,
Living and dying indifferent to design
the decorous deer pacing in violet
around the wine cup?

You have done
What you could, I have work still ahead,
A churlish son left to manage affairs of the island
from which your spirit fled

One day in Tucson when della Robbia blue
Glazed the sky, as you entered the inner room
With "every last comfort," leaving your poems by the pool

High in the gated hills, where cars pause at the guardhouse
Before they ascend, to views
And market values more breath-taking at every turn

Above the city whose long streets roll
From half-baked foothill resorts
Through the molten center and out once more
To the raw edge of town and a technical school

Where semi-fictional Guthrie characters, Jesús and Maria,
Prepare for the service professions—better surely
Than welfare and armed robbery?—
A paycheck, a costume, a walk-on role in the café scene

and farther south, where the road runs on
into dust, the spines of the mountains rise
like Mont St. Victoire in Cezanne's sky

whose "inmost depths of clear dark blue"
you plumbed, whose oblivious spheres are tuned
to a different scale, since you've been gone,

Since our sky—deep sigh—heard the last of you.
It's the wrong question, but: what have we proved?

Has anything been changed, if I mix in
Those topics you air-brushed from the picture?

But who would have thought that shimmering words
Could save a life. That art could change a world.

Among the angels, shining, free from harm,
You are judged at last, and you are pardoned

For writing well. But where we live today,
No one has been pardoned. No one is saved.

Corrinne Clegg Hales

GIRL AT A BARBED WIRE FENCE

after Dorothea Lange

1.

The mother waits a few yards back, the heels
of her good shoes sinking into thick dust; her shadow
slices dark toward home. She is thinner than the girl,
angular, and a plain, flat apron covers what must be
her Sunday dress. One long hand shields her eyes
against the brightness ahead of her daughter.
The girl leans into the fence, holding
the strung wire tight between barbs
with both hands. Why has she stopped
at such flimsy restraint? Her cotton blouse
is open at the throat, and there is nothing at all
growing behind her. Her short hair lifts a little
in the breeze. She looks at the ground over the fence
but doesn't try to cross.

2.

Say it isn't 1939. Say it's ten years later and beyond
that fence a star is bursting over the west desert
spawning a salmon-colored cloud that will cover the sky and rain
fine white ash on the girl and her mother and the vacant
sagebrush world around them. Then would the girl look up?
Would she hold out a hand to catch the strange warm snow,
let the powdery stuff dust her hair, her face, her throat?
Maybe she'd turn and see her mother's skin paling
behind her. But this is a photograph, so the girl
will stand forever in 1939, afraid to move, afraid even to look
too far ahead, and the photographer is lost on the other side
of the wire in the bright desert sun. The mother,
almost a stick figure now, sees her daughter about to cross over,
but she doesn't call out—she watches, silent as salt.

Mark Halperin

THE ELEGANT LADIES OF TALLINN

The elegant ladies of Tallinn
paint their eyelids purple
and wear felt hats with broad brims.
They are slender and the little
bulbs at the ends of their thin
noses twitch when they speak Estonian:

Aitah and *uks*, or rarer,
Stranger words for *thank-you*
and *one*. The winter sun rises later
than they do and breaks through
the clouds to shadow their fair
skin with icy blue hints of ardor.

Centuries of sea air have mellowed
the narrow streets and cobbles
their high heels totter along, and the yellow,
blue and orange stucco walls
they pass in their long coats,
hats tipped. There, restorers, Poles,

in the fifteenth century houses
of the burghers of Tallinn using shoddy,
imported bricks, survey the crowds
milling below them from rickety
platforms and spy on the proud
ladies of Tallinn. But the ladies have pity

and avoid them like mud or shouting
children with ice-cream. It could seem
nineteen thirty-five again, but without
Hitler to the southwest or Stalin
to the east, as the ladies chat about
news, hoping tomorrow's will find them

under more middle European than Soviet
cloudy skies. They look higher
than where Tallinn's intricate weathervanes pivot—
to "Old Thomas," on the *Raekoda* spire
from the thirteenth century, to his verdict,
as their mothers did and their mothers, and before.

(In Spring 1990, Estonia was still part of the Soviet Union.)

Jerry Harp

A MAN WHO WAS AFRAID OF LANGUAGE

The houses, the trees, and the dust had become
Sentences having nothing to do with themselves.
He seldom left his apartment now, the only refuge

He could endure, the dank spaces
And dim lights, the phone and radio unplugged.
Even printed words went on shifting

And crossing while stray phrases, echoes of phrases
Took up the burden. He tried to think
Of the same thing again and again.

He closed the blinds, but the boys still came
With their taunts and jokes and vulgar songs.
Sunlight slanted into their eyes.

A woman in blue made ambiguous gestures.

Mary Kathleen Hawley

CARL'S NECK

for Cin, who reminded me

There I was in the shiny back seat
of a baby blue Chevy Nova SS
with jacked-up wheels and an evil throated muffler
crammed between Marlene, fourteen, who had almost gone
all the way with Davey Hokkanen but stopped him,
to her eternal regret, especially later when he died,
and Verna, sixteen, who left the baby at her mother's
so we could ride down Main Street in Carl's car
carelessly smoking, shrill with the mix
of tobacco and syrupy liquor, as Carl,
eighteen, Verna's husband, drove the Nova
slowly down the street, and talked in short bursts
to his best friend Henry in the front seat
and we waved at the cars cruising past the other way

while I studied Carl:
how his tanned shoulders spread wider
than the back of his bucket seat
how his crop of thick blond curls was met
by fine gold hairs dancing
upward along his neck

so I knew when school started again back home
I could say if anyone asked or if they didn't
I rode in a souped-up car down Main Street
I drank sloe gin in a trailer
I know a girl my age who's married
some wild boys like me
you think you know me but you don't

Seamus Heaney

THE WATCHMAN AT MYCENAE

The rest is silence. The ox is on my tongue.
—Aeschylus, *Agamemnon*

Some people wept, and not for sorrow—joy
That the king had armed and upped and sailed for Troy,
But inside me like struck sound in a gong
That killing-fest, the life-warp and world-wrong
It brought to pass still augured and endured.
I'd dream of blood in bright webs in a ford,
Of bodies raining down like tattered meat
On top of me asleep—and me the lookout
The queen's command had posted and forgotten,
The blind spot her farsightedness relied on.
And then the ox would lurch against the gong
And deaden it and I would feel my tongue
Like the dropped gangplank of a cattle truck,
Trampled and rattled, running piss and muck,
All swimmy-trembly as the lick of fire,
A victory beacon in an abattoir . . .
Next thing then I'd waken at a loss,
For all the world a sheepdog stretched in grass,
Exposed to what I knew, still honour-bound
To concentrate attention out beyond
The city and the border, on that line
Where the blaze would leap the hills when Troy had fallen.

My sentry work was fate, a home to go to,
An in-between-times that I had to row through
Year after year: when the mist would start
To lift off fields and inlets, when morning light
Would open like the grain of light being split,
Day in, day out I'd come alive again,
Silent and sunned as an esker on a plain,
Up on my elbows, gazing, biding time
In my outpost on the roof. . . . What was to come
Out of that ten years' wait that was the war
Flawed the black mirror of my frozen stare.
If a god of justice had reached down from heaven
For a strong beam to hang his scale-pans on
He would have found me tensed and ready-made.
I balanced between destiny and dread
And saw it coming, clouds bloodshot with the red
Of victory fires, the raw wound of that dawn
Igniting and erupting, bearing down
Like lava on a fleeing population. . . .
Up on my elbows, head back, shutting out
The agony of Clytemnestra's love-shout
That rose through the palace like the yell of troops
Hurled by King Agamemnon from ships.

Brian Henry

BROKEN TOOTH

forgotten in the precipice of snag,

bury yourself before forces
marshal new growth into wagons
married to twigs and stones,

try darkness on against the odds
of gain, and turn in your hole
for each promise made, and buried.

The adherence to rules as such
augurs well for you, fallen sparrow
burning on a wave. Unbuckle

yourself from your deeper truth,
consider the hypotenuse drawn
as Tomaz sweeps into the room

bursting with light and remorse
for the living god shipped home
undone by bliss.

He would have blessed your pain
with an ardor more often reserved
for sicker creatures,

would have pulled the hurt
stirring at the root, sent the throbbing
packing. Forget the wit that swells

with wine and cross yourself, unblessed one,
for the air says it's time to dress
for starker days. All else breaks

in the balance. All else hangs.

Roald Hoffmann

TSUNAMI

for Maria Matos

A soliton is
a singularity
of wave
motion, an edge
traveling just
that way. We saw
one, once
filmed moving heed-
lessly cross
a platinum surface.
Solitons pass
through
each
other
unperturbed.

You are a wave.
Not standing, nor
traveling, satisfying
no equation.
You are a wave
which will not be (Fourier)
analyzed.
You are a wave; in
your eyes I sink
willingly.

Not solitons,
we can't pass through
unaltered.

Janet Holmes

YELLOW PERIOD

—that winter driving sixty dull miles
to work every day, sixty anxious miles back,
falling out of love: the odometer rolling each new number
relentlessly up, a taunt:
now? Now?
and from the radio nothing but the war:
live, up-to-the-minute reports. On Main Street
a storefront festooned itself with yellow bows,
and a second followed suit, and a few houses
hung them from their doors like holiday wreaths.
Ribbons streamed out from car antennae. At five o'clock
in Minnesota's pearl twilight, they were beacons,
advertisements for unrequited love . . .
She viewed them from the streaked windshield
as if witnessing a doomed wedding:
the bride devoted and ignorant, the angry groom
smirking behind his champagne during the feast—

Quarter the lemons—
                                        not all the way through
but so they open out to you, as a bud
unfurls itself in stop-motion, as the mouths
of chicks clamor upwards from the nest: pour salt
into the cloven fruit, and layer them
in a wide-mouthed jar, letting
fresh juice seep into the interstices.
Take care that the jar closes tightly:
each day invert it, and wait—

after a mouth you will have
preserved lemons to eat,
but all that time you will have the jar
yellow in your kitchen, a bottle
of fractured suns
half the time on its head,
uncynical, brilliant—

What opposite? Could it be that yellow patch,
the side of a house, that makes one think the house is laughing?

In the adobe church, candles gutter before the *bulto*
of *Nuestra Señora de los Dolores,*
a supernatural strobe effect:
the pale buttery halo around the saint
slightly unreliable—
her face now in shadow,
not lit and upturned, the eyes immeasurably sad.

Caution lights lining the highway (forever?)
—at least to the vanishing point, sliding along a curve
starting up the mountain, flashing their amber badges
every second; it was like (every second)
waking up from a dream: she shouldn't be driving:
she could imagine shattering the rail,
sending the car over, regretting it,
clutching the plastic wheel:
seeing the glowing disks, the last things—
(Later, in town, sweating:
she had pulled herself up there hand over hand
by the yellow lines in the road . . .)

Winter light in the afternoon.
Gainsborough's sky here in Minnesota,
nominally blue, but with a yellow glaze in the west:
aged overpainting,
oily and glistening, giving the clouds portent—
giving portent, rather, to the billowing steam
rising grand from the taconite plant
and drifting, pompous, over the icy lake—

Taxi! Taxi!
Yeah, get me out of here, let's move it—

Alison Jarvis

THE SAME HOUR HAS COME INSIDE MY BODY

for my husband

Here in Venice there are houses newly ochered
and some, once green are gone
to celadon. White light at noon
dazzles off stone; latticed and fretted
like handkerchiefs, white houses float
in surrender over the canal.
Even the palazzos of Venetian red—
color of clay, color of old blood,
wave in light off water. Everything moves
and nothing
                                        really begins or ends
in Venice, where color is memory
of color: umber, siennas—burnt and raw, the earth
of other places. Always as we near
each arched stone bridge that enters
the canal, there is that moment before
we apprehend the memory of the bridge
on the body of water. How much
fullness depends on surrender
and disappearance. The gondolas—
their black lacquer slipping through
darkening waters—look like coffins
and they look like cradles.

I used to believe in the orderly
progression of time; the slow shift of tenses.
Now month after slipping month,
the future falls back on itself. Damage
to your body. Disorder
in regions of your brain where each day
more neurons shut down. Once you told me
you pictured them like lights clicking off
one by one, in some alien town
where everybody goes to sleep at night.

Only in Venice
do you sleep all night. All night it seems
I watch you and I hear
bells in the campaniles ring, each
sound suspended through darkness
until it begins again.

And here, behind pine green shutters
in the slatted afternoons—
light splitting into ribs against the dark—
we can make love again,
not as a diminished act, but containing,
like a photograph. Or like a mosaic,
the way the Byzantines created them,
using just enough mortar for a single day;
placing the astonishing shards of colored glass
at angles that would refract the light
a hundred ways.

Devin Johnston

LOS ANGELES

The Colorado River flows—
sans silt—through fluted taps
in Universal City. Saturn nears.

Beneath millennia and shale
a riot growth of giant fern
and brontosauri decompose—
but through the auspices
of wildcats, blaze
                                        in incandescent beads
along a sliding mirror: long extinct,
their ghosts reticulate the hills
and hulks of studios—an Oz
of local urgencies.

Beneath the moon, emotions are
but vectors, dragging
                                                distant objects near.
As daikon sputters on an open flame,
the owner of Pagoda Inn
cradles the phone against
his shoulder. Neither party speaks,
yet leagues of fiber-optic lines
exchange their silences.

Paul Kane

THE DESERT FATHER

> *Both virtues and vices make the mind blind:*
> *with the first it does not see vices,*
> *and with the second, virtues.*
>
> —Abba Evagrius

Both virtues and vices make the mind blind—
so Abba Evagrius the Monk writes
from his solitary cell in Egypt.

Evagrius, son of a priest, had come
all the way from Constantinople in
flight from a "circumstance which threatened

his chastity"—better to take orders than
give free rein to free will in Byzantium,
city of glittering mosaic icons.

So the Abba, wide-eyed from warfare with
demons, attunes his soul to desireless
passion in the dry heat of the desert,

where at night cold stars cluster together,
mid-way between this world and all others
where virtues and vices blind the mind.

Robert Kelly

THREADS 37.

What the eye falls on
feeds the soul, the curious
relationship or
appetite lodged between
or amidst the ever-arising
and the never
completed edifice you are,
she said, quoting
from the book whose flimsy
dead elm leaf
colored pages still
managed to bear
the dark of word
after so many
fingerings, looking,
looking o they wear
things out
with their inspections,
checking the window sash
every night to know
what's locked out and
who's trapped in,
o tender curtain
of you,
words as words are
boundaries, words as
things, though,
her sweet
cuneiform, are doors,
so meanings trap you
and the wolf runs free,
but look
without reading
the shape

that matter dances
your way,
it is the property
and necessity of love
to be so ignorant,
just the ferocious
quiet pressure in you,
she said, reaching
you think the thing
beyond the shape
written before you
you stare at,
it could also be a plain
stretching through Silesia
shabby under old snow
and no one waiting,
as rails go on converging
in the ashen distances
and the Allied bombers
curiously spare
the lines down which
the already dead are
wagoned to the actual
article of dying,
their throes the strange
letters on her page
and the reek of gas
till no one left on the earth
knows what it means,
smell of a word.

John Kinsella

PARTING THE SORROWS

I tell you it's a nice day
though it's overcast.
Rain threatens dismay
as the State taste-tests,
and humour can't be
taken seriously
in the dark. Don't trust
those who'd die for poetry,
or worship stones.
No doubt you've heard
of the "outing"-sweetener
touring the blood, tabs
kept on colour-change
and systems of exchange.
Take potlatch and slick
crests in a new gallery space,
dirt under nail
brigades, combination
re-composition, fascinating
short circuits. It's cool
about stems, and conquest
rots gums—teeth
just don't stay in
and giving up food
still leaves speech,
failing to be heard,
hard to get out in spite
of precedent, gaps.
So open the casket
and defile a textual gate,
but with smiles all round
and no aspersions
sweet or otherwise: those flush
readings of privilege,
smallest publication

saddle stitched
and heard faintly
on a crystal radio,
that 'ol sucker punch
called "Drafts": I know
not my name but see the map
I wander; those geo-turrets,
seismic canisters sounding
reservoirs in hill-spaces,
the where I come from
undivested and vanguards
stuck in Mallory
doing little "up front"
about it: must ache
in plausibles and conquest,
to be THE unfinancial self,
it's milky diodes
plashed about the bonds,
solder in the bedroom,
hymnals and greeting cards
piled neatly in the cabin,
come from limestone stills,
water lavishing through,
patterning under-chambers
and less correctly
mirror-images, the cave-door
shut and the lights
bringing it up to best effect.
Phosphor and candor, bith and elision
in paper-spreads about the garden:
balcony with weeds,
near genetic decoding
places, a society
not necessary for this:
self wastes and dangerous cups
and loyalties—I still have faith,
vocal shields hissing on hot rocks
aside, famous statements
read (or foretold) to accolytes,
meant to trip up

stakes and ownership:
wood for the trees,
stone circles just out
to sea, fish traps
covering failed ecologies,
hardware of light fade, prospect
of rain, things that don't fit,
that haven't been seen here, the I's of bees—scrapings
of added selves, perfect music,
wretches and cedars,
kidnap ploys on the Swan River,
locks opened on the Cam,
cut-outs shading Mr. Sharpy's
escapades in joint-houses
where ferries annotate
a collected Wordsworth,
paternities and protectorships—
for which sublime thanks—
the disciple doesn't have
a daughter's love, or a guest's respect—
pierced from flank to navel
of feverishly taking souls
to task—bonfires in small communities,
the sparks reaching new york,
and newsmen phoning direct—
the heat; I move in script,
but we'll have none of that
"Look, no hands" stuff
amongst the following,
spilling wine, dispersing
gifts of sweetish sleep: sorbitol,
reasonable suppositions,
red faces in brush-bindings,
a pierrot troupes ousted
from Midsummer Common
settling into the privacy
of Lever's Passage,
taking full quota
of a correction allowance—WE
allow more than 10 percent,

BWV numbers consistent,
the semibreve being
a whole note in America:
multiplicity, unity, synthesis:
beneath electric light
and looking for guest-hosts
under the arctic circle,
lyrical and joyous,
sticking to recollection images
and suspect silhouettes: here
we are, none of it,
the plants too green
and brandnames unfamiliar,
the meat in their faces
antiphonal

John Koethe

THE MAQUILADORAS

They oversimplify our lives,
These stories, stripping them of context and detail,
Recasting each one as a journey, moving from the country
To a factory on the border, from a rural home

To one that I'd imagined, to this place
That I inhabit, locked in the idea
Of a room, a home, a city street, the country
Where I live and I was nineteen once

And where I find myself a subject of two states,
Of two distinct domains: a private one
Of furniture and poetry, pottery and silent monologues
While shaving in a mirror, thinking through

A turn of phrase, the course of an emotion,
Tracing the trajectory of a thought
That takes me to the kingdom of a single mind
Where what I think and feel and say all seem the same.

We all live in the other one. On the news
Last night a woman in New Jersey
And a man in Pennsylvania read my mind. More dead
Filled up the screen as someone read their names

Instead of mine, which would have been the same.
More Walmarts in Chicago, on the sites
Of some abandoned factories, while the doors keep closing
On the maquiladoras in Tijuana and Juarez

Through which the money flows, and flows away. Who says
That life is change, and change is for the better?
It can look that way when looked at through the blinders
Of an individual life, one constantly embarking

On a journey of its own, of everyone's,
From adolescence through late middle age. Nineteen
Was nothing special and I wouldn't want it back,
Yet sometimes when I think about the years to come

I see almost as many as the ones since then.
I feel a vague and incoherent fear, a fear
Of waking from time's dream into an even stranger place,
As different from today as now is from nineteen,

Without a sense of where I am or where I'd been before—
Which is always here, in my imagination. When I ask myself
What home was really like the answer is sheer fiction,
As I picture to myself an endless summer

Sky above a Culver's or a Dairy Queen,
A school, the Hansen-Onion funeral home, the modest
Mansions on the quiet, shady streets
Of a small Wisconsin town time left unchanged.

Sandra Kohler

MAP

i.

Nothing ties us to the past
like the longing for what wasn't there.
We want to sit down to dinner
at the table where we ate disappointment,
anguish, petty misery. A new room
cannot do it, a new table, a new meal.
The heavy food, the sweetened milk
have to be found again, the rough bread.

ii.

How do you know which map
to pull out, from the stack
in that drawer where you've kept them
for decades, folded, refolded
until the oldest most often used
are split along the folds, wrinkling
away from wholeness like the skin
of your hands?
                                        And if you find the right
map, open it, spread its fine skein
of departures over the kitchen table,
how do you find that corner, the set
of roads leading to the small village,
the house in which you were
immured?
                                    The remembered curve of a road—
you recognize a red line's shape, follow it
through green fields of loss until you are on
the street you once skipped down, counting
cracks, past the fenced yard with the cruel
white dog, the neighbor houses each speaking

a different family, and you come to the house
you've lived in since you constructed
its story from your terror, your desire.

Your back aches when you walk through
the door. The muscles of your arms strain
at the boxes you pack and cart to the curb,
the backs of your thighs ache with lifting,
your knees stiffen, fingers grow raw
from too much water, acrid soap, the steel
wool you need to scrub the grease of years
from every surface. Excavating, the oldest
labour, how deep you must dig, what layers
of rot leavings scraps of clothing skin you
scrape away, buttons that terrified you
as a child; china, crystal, pottery, shells
skulls.

All this is not enough: does not sort
through the attic, tell what to keep, what
to trash; mend the leg of the best chair, reweave
the seat, refinish the scarred oak chest, chisel
out wax glutting brass candlesticks, polish
the silver bowl. Your head aches, your body
shivers. The ground beneath your feet buckles,
reforms, dissolving kaleidoscope, map.

iii.

Who will take charge, start
auctioning all that has been left to me,
inheritrice? The dead mother of a dead
child willed me what has not yet been
unpacked, assessed: an old name, a scene
I walked through yesterday, last year,
last decade. The world is plaited,
its strands fine as the hair my mother
braided every morning, pulling, hurting.
Memory itself is plaited: I am the child
whose mother insisted on braiding her hair
and forty years later, the mother, braiding
a recalcitrant child's hair, angry, irritated.
Within the clock's minutes, a world
opens, I enter, live it through again, anew—
both, plaited. I am a set of real points
on an imagined line.

iv.

There is a time to bury the dead,
there is a time to shake them off like rain
and walk away from all graveyards.
Mow the grass, shovel the snow, fold away
the maps. Enter the minutes cell by cell
until every one is used, not one
is left, wasted, slack, empty.

Susanne Kort

DISPENSATION

The trick is to pick them up &
fling them, at first crack

or when the handle flies off, instantly, into the trash because
they're insidious. If you falter, studying

their impairedness for some other use
(dear old friends, Mother's melismatic

legacies) you are vanquished:
they'll remain

in your equal-opportunity house
& continue to clutter up your life

in their new identities: the ironstone
formerly soup tureen, violaceous with stock

& laburnum, the repatriated platter
couchant, rent shards of vases re-blent

with panic & mucilage: useless mouth-to-mouth:
What's gone.
It's best to stream on

& toss what you can out the door
as soon as it gives in to gravity, random

acts of God; get it over with, pre-fester:
the thing is to never

consider. We are older now:
our shins & pubises are bare

or nearly there: we are no longer
obliged to be such good girls.

John Latta

THE LIMITS OF LANGUAGE

Days like today, the intermittent rain
Drumming its particular rain—
Carnival rhythms off the eaves, its dense patter

Of faulty vocables, its unspeakable overlaps of
Noise, *thrup-thrup, thrup-thrup,*
With a skirling addition, a high

Persistent keening, a *thrip-thrip,* randoming
The backbeat, overburdening
The interstices: these days language is no good for.

If we itch to make mention of the rain
And its hugger-mugger way of talking,
We need—in all our endless primal itchiness—

To offer ourselves without intention,
Without words,
To other transports elsewhere—*intermezzo,*

Tintoretto, harlequinade, minuet—
Any smeary coincidence the world can muster.
Somewhere someone says:

"We cannot talk in simultaneous bunches of names."
Exactly. Talking we atomize the world
To rearrange it, to string

Strings of whatever few particulars can be strung,
Forgetting, like any child
Content with bead-stringing, how

The necklace only calls attention to the whole
Cloth of the chemise, how
It is not the essential wearable itself.

So we stop talking
Just as the rain,
In a lengthy diminuendo, thins itself to a temporary halt.

Though we hardly notice it:
Our feet, unbeknownst to our feet, move
Now in easy reiteration,

Now in cumbersome jest, speaking
The gone rain's story, happy
Geniuses of the story of the gone rain.

Freud says somewhere that every *move* is a *gesture*, meaning
We carry something along with us,
Some extraordinary kind of freight

Filling up our little carts,
The freight of a cart of raindrops,
The freight of a caboose of *rainingness* itself,

All hodge-podge and overlay, freight
We dearly long to discharge . . .
And if I pull my earlobe in a distant quiet way,

Will the whole load of rainy expressiveness get dumped, or
Shunted down a spur track, one
Just there for the unloading? Not exactly.

The instrumentality of the tug becomes its own end—and here
I remain, an upright animal
Toying with an appendage, standing

Akimbo in a kind of becoming perplexity
Like a painter whose smock is dotted and re-
Dotted to a pleasing *drench*

By the spritzing accident of the unbecoming rain.
There's a story I am longing to tell about the limits of language,
An untellable story.

I knew a man who, weary
Of the linear, the discrete, the successive
Order of words, wrote

What he called *A Novel on the Head of a Pin.*
He read some of it to me one day, a soothing babble.
He claimed it was about "everything, everything simultaneously

All words, all letters in a rush, a swirl, a concentrate."
He showed me a copy. It looked like this: •
What I want to say is this:

This rain, letting up now, still
Capable of a squall, a blurry contingency overloading
The whole wet scene, this rain is more than language can bear.

Denise Levertov

THE CULT OF RELICS

My father's serviette ring,
silver incised with a design
of Scotch thistles, the central medallion
uninitialed, a blank oval.
                                        The two massive
German kitchen knives, pre-1914, not-stainless steel,
which my mother carefully scoured with Vim
after each use.
                        My daily use
of these and other such things
links me to hands long gone.

Medieval con-men disgust and amuse us;
we think we'd never have fallen
for such crude deceptions—unholy
animal bones, nails from any old barn,
splinters enough from the Cross to fill
a whole lumber-yard.
                                    But can we
with decency mock the gullible
for desiring these things?
                                        Who doesn't want
to hold what hands belov'd or venerated
were accustomed to hold?—You? I?
                                        Who wouldn't want
to put their lips to the true chalice?

Moira Linehan

GENEALOGY

in memory of Honora Buckley Linehan

July 19th, 1860,
the census for Easton, Massachusetts.
The fourth child of Daniel and Catherine Buckley,
Honora—my grandmother—appears
a month old. Add four boarders—John Haydan,
Dan Rierdon, Pat Connell, Ed Sweeney. All
born in Ireland. All in their twenties. *Labourers*
says the record. Honora's father, too.
On that same day in the dwelling next door—
three families, thirteen names, the youngest
John Linehan, new-born son of Margaret and James.

1870. The Buckleys still have four boarders,
though the names have changed and they're much younger.
There's more detail of their work: *works on hinges*
this census says of Honora's father.
Works on railroad, of three of the boarders
while the fourth one *farms.* Home for Honora,
where so many would come and go. Imagine
the stories of longing she heard, all
in a language with no word for *emigrate. Exile,*
the closest they have. Each night at dinner,
Honora coming through that swinging door,
carrying bowls of potatoes boiled with cabbage
out from the kitchen into those stories
about the land they'd left, the mothers.

1880. Now Honora's father *sells milk.*
Eleven boarders *work in the shovel shop,*
the stories, now multiplied three-fold.
Now the Linehans own the place next door.
James and his oldest, John, *work in the hinge shop.*
I know what I want next and there it is
in the state archives: July 7th, 1885—
Honora marries John, the boy next door,
which is where I wish this story could pause
so Honora could speak, say what home meant
when hers stood next door for the rest of her life
while inside she carried twenty-five years
of exile, the longing of who knows how many
for the ones they'd never see again.
After hearing those stories, what mother
would ever let go of her child? Or worse,
ever let her child get too close?

1910. *Number of children born this mother:*
10. Number of children living: 8. My father,
now a name on the census, my father
who grew up her youngest, though not her last.
She died the summer before I was born.
Yet no story ever starts fresh and clean.
Straight and clear the path through the archives
back to Honora. And back to those boarders,
the stories that exiled her, me, as she'd tell them
again and again in the ways she did,
and did not, hold my father. He held me.

William Logan

AFTER THE WAR

That was before the time I carried a gun.
The hearings ran on for weeks, and then months.
Through the rippled glass, my name
still wrote a gilt verse in ancient Coptic.

Checked suits were all the rage that year,
but I cannot recall one newspaper headline
or who won the batting title.
One winter morning a woman had broken

her heel in a sewer grating.
She stood on the sidewalk weeping,
and clutching her red leather handbag.
She looked like my mother, or how I imagined

Mother had looked, twenty years before,
when she had come alone to New York.
The dresses of course were different then.
When young she had lived in Philadelphia

in a house owned by gangsters.
Her father had been an oatmeal salesman,
and through the Depression they had never
lacked oatmeal or a Negro servant to stew it.

They were wary of Jews.
It might be true that they hated the Jews,
they gave no thought to such things.
As for the man who would be President,

in a country house in Cornwall, you could see
the bullet scar in a wall of the room
where he slept with his mistress, who was his driver
and a famous brunette.

We did not know about such things.
My mother was a brunette, in those days.
That was before we knew how many had died.
There were rumors—or rumors of rumors.

Had died in the camps, I mean.
I remember a smell from the basement carpet,
the mounds of homely horn-rims and gold watches,
the beautiful ropes of human hair

sorted into mute and various colors.
By then it was much too late.
Long after the trials and the sentences,
my mother became a blonde.

George Looney

FACED WITH A MOSQUE IN A FIELD OF WHEAT

The hint of moraines on the horizon
argues against certainty. Unlike the ruins
of a shoe factory where it's said ghosts
murmur and often cry, barefoot and sore,
glaciers are in it for the long haul. But
rust only sticks around to repeat rumors
of couples laying blankets over broken
cement, holding one another, moaning.
Not even sex can disguise the flatness
of a place topographical maps turn
gray and the sky is blurred to protect
its identity. Guilt takes too long

to be sure of, and the vague history of
loss is oral. Everything depends on
the sad, moving tongue and the safe lies
of memory. Maybe rust doesn't have
a voice. Maybe it's a ventriloquist,
its act all distortion, like a mosque gone
gray surrounded by wheat. In the fall,
fields on fire turning it to smoke,
the mosque blurs into a definition
of what the heart gives up to live in
the flesh, or a prayer faith can make things
come back. It's said glaciers will come down

from the north again and erase scars left
the last time. But that's just rumor.
Nothing's certain but the hacking of sufis
in the minarets, the smoke forced out of
their mute lungs a kind of confession.
It is the world that's burning they love.
The chants they cough through are elegies
for everything consumed. They don't know
the history of ice and faith and loss
this landscape is. What they want to believe
is the world's formed by rusty voices
singing among ruins. That any voice

drifting with the ash of the right crop
can save everything. That cars hurtling
down the state route are driven by dummies
they can throw their voices into and speak
of sex and the anonymous sky. Smoke
can't hold up a mosque, and ventriloquism
relies on blind faith in an illusion.
It's hard to believe, but fire has
a voice. And its long argument with rust
is a map of longing lovers here have lost
the legend to. Direction is a chant
touch pulls from the flesh, and the landscape

is a name murmured in some raw voice. Local
stories tell of feet pulled loose by hooks
that drag the filthy river for flesh.
They're said to flatten wheat in patterns
that might be topographical maps of
countries the heart's had too much wine in,
where ruins are stone and ice never reached.
The heart is a foreigner everywhere,
a drunk says faced with a mosque in a field
of wheat. From the minarets, sufis read
maps flattened out by wind or feet, the sky
a chant in the bitter language of rust

or fire thrown into the throats of lovers
moaning in the ruins of a factory.
Ash isn't all burning leaves. Glaciers are
breaking off and moving south like ghosts
of feet burned blue with cold. It's been said
when they get here history will buckle
under its guilt and religion will lose
its voice, gone hoarse denying the world.
For now, farmers burn their fields to clear off
what hands can't. Sufis translate the smoke,
and discover the voice of the heart
whispering love to the wheat and the ruins.

Sheryl Luna

SONATA ON ORIGINAL SIN

It was all gone: memory, time, trees.
The sea was imagined. Music
a fog, and although unwhole,
I'm quiet night. No red cauldron,
no lightening eye, no quick Jesus:

dance of mosquitoes, whirr of crickets,
the moon's fated face. The order of nature
streaks sky, rain falls to music, smoke
rises. Work, rest in the stab
of love. Hold yourself like a warm
blanket. The saving always slow. Your Guarded song
a space of self along borders.

Love is gone in work. Gone
in a pin-striped suit, the appearance
of slick shoes. Gone in the way we mouth
nothing to one another. Guarded back. Watch it. Watch it.
Stiff chin. False hair color. Hide it all.

Your body and eye. *Paint your eyes,*
my grandmother tells me.
Buy a girdle.
Are Death and beauty bought?

Speechless and slanted in the walk,
I jog now, feel my joints loosen
to the tune of suns.

Death and beauty bought in faces,
in handshakes, in flatteries and hurried steps
to buses in slick towns, where women
wear lip gloss and highlight hairs, the electric
pang of music running through veins.

You played trombone like a wounded animal.
I am remembering snow on your hair in the yard,
the trees too capped with it. And then you came
like a ceramic doll smiling, a music box, set
to play the same tune for years, until the break
that Fall.

Original sin fell from our lips. Now
I am cracked in red lipstick.
An old maid counting and loving stars
alone. Carpe diem! Old lantern, black and costly,
antique chevy. The rust of poverty like lost love,
empty fiberglass pools.

My face a butterfly rash. Lupus, then a lover lost.
Then came the ash. Oboe slowness—. The way
you walked your dog each night
over the ridge. Arroyo empty. Gutted.
Chain-linked razor-wire fence always mended
and tended. The weeds overgrown. The ache,
muscle sore to the bone. This is the way of borders.

A slow series of breaths rising, falling. The way things
thirst. Tree without green, window
with no curtain, dog left to die.

We have to know
how to play. Pour like water,
patter as rain.
Beethoven was deaf.

Be Light in the silence, light in the noise.
I hold my rosy cheeks, my butterfly shape.
In the mirror I more than peer.

Time is breath smoked away. We were young
and flowered. Once, we were silent
in a perfect trance of sleep.

Endless deep throated voices of rage
turned to snow one night. The voices of women nearby rose
lighthearted with the sparrows.
I mourn the way we were too afraid to kiss
beneath the oaks, the moon laughing,

the moon crying. Us at the center of the small
universe. We two stars lingered in the bodied voice
of time, rising from dirges and requiems
like dancing stars, or the chaos of a blood sonata.

Derek Mahon

RIVER RHYMES

(for Wm. Rossa Cole)

I

Crossing the stormy Irish Sea
Our 'Lycidas' gets drowned, I see—
But, lo! Young Milton skips in view
Twitching his merry mantle blue.

II

Beside the Tiber's icky mud
John Keats spat up a spot of blood:
Sighed he, 'I'd hoped to go to Greece
But now have fears that I may cease.'

III

Drifting drunkly up the Yellow
Went Li Po, the Chinese fellow;
Reaching down to grasp the moon,
He climbed too far and toppled in.

IV

Beside the Black Sea's icy mud
The poet Ovid proudly stood:
'Miserae mihi plura supersunt,' quoth he,
'Old sport, *quam tibi felici.'*

V

Above the waves in Galway Bay
John Synge would smoke his pipe all day;
And later, when the day was o'er,
Listen to people through the floor.

VI

Beside the soiled and sunken Thames
Tom Eliot would play his games,
Impersonating a London cop—
Until his wife told him to stop.

VII

Way out upon Dun Laoghaire pier
A light went on in Beckett's brain—
'I'll get this down when I'm in the clear
And nicely settled by the Seine.'

VIII

The Quaker Graveyard in Nantucket
Was where young Lowell said his piece:
'Will you stop killing sperm-whales, f— it,
And give us all a bit of peace!'

IX

By Bantry Bay, his fame secure,
Jim Farrell lies who, taking ship,
Wrote *Troubles, The Siege of Krishnapur*
And, best of all, *The Singapore Grip.*

X

Beside the Lagan's oily murk
Seamus Heaney oft would lurk;
Though the clear waters of Lough Neagh
Were more his tea-cup any day.

Gerard Malanga

ALBERT GRIMALDI IN AMHERST, CLASS OF '81

You'd never expect it. You'd be heading out Main Street
swaying maples bisected
mid-winter when Miss Emily Dickinson walked into town
and no one took notice, not knowing she even existed.
Did you know that? Perhaps she lived down the street
from where you spent time browsing shop windows
or taking a breather now and then
out on the Common. She may have looked a bit homely,
so it would be hard to recognize her from the one or two cameos.
Photography was in its infancy.
It's amazing she'd come out at all.
Perhaps you'd come across one of her poems
in your studies. Don't know, for sure.
The one beginning, you would never expect it.
Well, come to think of it
she'd written several others just like it
where not much happens,
except for the light waning and the rustle of leaves
and echoes of children in the neighbor's backyard.
There's even a color snap of you heading back to the dorm
where you stop to talk with a classmate
her arms hugging books
and birds are flocking southward against a grainy red sky.

James McMichael

FROM THE HOMEPLACE

Occurrences are
runnings-toward. From who knows what all
else time might have
sent there instead, a place is

run toward and reached and taken

up by a thing when a
thing takes place. What it
takes for a thing to happen is a place time lets it

pose or
be posed, arrested,
placed in a resting state
as clay and soured rushes are for
one first gabled end. Allotting things

constantly their whiles of
long or short standing, time is each stance's

circum-, its surround.
Circumstantial that the same one gabled end should
again take place as it had taken place one

instant before. As
wide as the first, as tall,
and though time brooks few repetitions,
a second gable

too time lets take place. Handedness

left and right affords in time a
front wall,

a back. Before on
top of it all time lets take place as well
a wheat-straw roof,
sod over coupled rafters must be laid
grass up.

Some of a house's sides are
biased, some upstanding. Because a

house has its sides,

so also does the air that meets them have its
clement and less clement sides.
To the sides a house is posed as are opposed as many
standing and inconstant

things as you please.
As distance is the room
away from an opposing, sided
instance or stance,
the out-of-doors

itself is sided by a house whose indoor ways makes
room outside. Going outside,
the out-of-doors is gone out

into.
From the standstill house out
in it
(and with room between) are

hayrick and byre, a road, the moss, discrete

potato-beds, their
grass-to-grass closed hinges.
Room is by the laws of growth at

play there outside for parts related
all as one in increase in the

one thing. Along a root
        Earthed over, earthed
            Over again,
        The rose end, heel end,
            Stolon, skin

outward through the loose mold
part by part take room.
Enlarged to *membrum*

virile now in size
and now to fist, they are

parts in relation. There are goods as

yield at the home place sometimes as at
other times
not. Time is
equable that way.
With no parts to it in itself, indifferent,

without relation, time offers
nothing to be carried back. Persons are
separate in time when they are living.
When certain maincrop tuberous parts go on being

missed at the hearth, back as

one again with time are persons now
outside it for good.
Against a bad

outside time,
relation

sometimes takes its sundry parts
inside.
To a first part entered in
relation with them there, inside,

the other parts are sometimes only
relatively other.
Seized as in every way
relative and to the first part's taste
are such late

outside parts as are now
stew and colcannon.

As back along the tongue
palatably are carried first one
bolus and more,

        The circle of the Same surrounds
            The circle of the stripped,
        Assimilable Other,
            Pharynx-housed, tipped
down through a tenser muscle to the gullet. Equal

each to what was wanted,
each timely part means that
apart from her
outside

are parts to be

made same, partaken, had as that one
thought is had in thinking present any
morsel she eats. Laid
hold of when she thinks
are parts that just before were

other for her,
anyone's,
apportioned out

between her and her fellows.
She thinks of everything that it is

passing in its little parts. When back at

once to those same parts are drift and
purport carried,
meaning grants the time to have
returned to her from not-yet habitable parts

just what it is she thinks of those parts as.
Until she has meant them
as that,

configurative parts are still futures,

they await being
thought about by her as having

each been fitted to its
suitable outward look.
All parts that show are in concord in their
standing over against her,

all are directed toward
what it is about them that she might mean.
As one who sees them, as one whose
self is drawn away to those
among them she sees,

no sooner is she
scattered there outside than she regains the more

that self immured in seeing them as such.

To meanings she takes part in with them, she
too belongs.
All parts that mean are
home to one still enough the same herself to be made
solute with them

inside what they mean.
Her domain
within them is the time they
take her to think.

Other for that time and
outside,
absolute,

are interrupting second parties.
High time that in his
proper person
one of them approach her now.
Others of her blood are there

around her,
inside. His having come could pass as a family call.

She can take it as that. So can he,

if beyond the frugal
greeting she tenders
she does not speak.

To address him
puts her at risk of what might follow
straightaway.
He would be sure to answer. It would be

colloquy then. Irrecoverably
past thereafter would this mute

present time be.
Among such parts as
give themselves to saying, each leaves a

now-no-more-than-recent part behind.
Another now arrives,
another. Nows
track that way, they multiply,
the gaps that let each new part differ from the last

they override.
At the same time it carries
on to its own undoing,
the present

keeps to itself. Resolute,

she presents the present
time and time again by keeping to hers.
Homesick for the Same, the One,
she gathers at the same time what she
watches for in him

and how it sits with her to see it. How
lavish of him that he is

there to see her. As long as she
thinks him that and goes on saying nothing,
she keeps everything at the
one same time. At the same time,

to think does not always

go without saying.
Articulations sometimes are come
out with,

they are aired,
my goodness, my

word what reach a party of the first part's
voice has for incarnate
third and second persons who can hear.
From its hollow up from
the open glottal cords,

the next column of

breath she issues still gives
nothing away.
Not so,

The column after. As it leaves,
The lappets that she draws around it
Make it tremble so positions of the
Tongue, teeth, lips and jaw can sound it

abroad. Cast

forward from her thus are parts with their
own times each.

One does not have to turn to listen.
Airborne at the middle ear,
molecular,
each damped and stronger sound prompts its allied

hair-cell to fire. No more than a
smear at first,
the spell each sound is there for has its

onset and rise,
its temperings whose
play across the membranes no one
other repeats.
Dispersed toward him with the rest from what he

sees of her face,
the silences themselves are telling.
Of moment, every
nasal, glide and spirant,

every stop.
Time for them

all there is, these many, her express
fugitive and dative phonemes.
He has made them out.

Robert McNamara

SEPTEMBER 11, 2001

Awakened from the news
in the neutral *New York Times*—
a president ambushed by words
and patriotic greed
turning its back on the world—
I stare at televised crimes
at first I can only believe
the virtual hair-raising art
of a clever Hollywood crew:
the murderous plane banks in,
the flaming towers fall.
I hold my ticket to fear
as the theater opens to war.

How reckless and precise
the conception and command,
the fanatical scale of their work—
the discipline to stand
at the kicked-in cabin door
with visionary eyes
of Eros turned to crime,
indifferent or worse to cries,
the familiar love and distress
of man, woman, child—
and when the tower's in sight
to use what the enemy taught:
the accomplished turn on a dime.

Our pundits of the right
credit their Righteous God's
wrath at tolerant sin;
of the left, a world oppressed
by our blind imperial might
taking its just revenge.
They're ready to take to the air
in the name of all that's Good,
imperfections to erase,
a world to re-engineer—
so the beautiful ideas wither,
and the individual voice
calling to stopped ears.

Wanting not to be shamed
as a useless man of words,
Plato undertook
to teach the good of the state
and the law's didactic work
to the tyrant asking to learn.
But Dionysios proved
a bondsman to appetite,
desiring that men be slaves
and his philosopher approve.
Plato, wised-up to power,
sailed home from Syracuse,
nothing to declare or excuse.

All I have is words,
the hope of thinking flesh
wanting a better mouth
for shaping them to prayer:
for a disposition of mind
steadying after a fall—
beautiful Ideas loved
only as they hold
a skeptical leash on the will;
each day's grief the food
the adversary gives,
reminding us that the Good
chides us when we call.

Christopher Merrill

WEST WINDOW

for W.S. Merwin

Green as the palm that fans the hill and hides
Flames at its base, the lizard slides or falls
From frond to flower, a raindrop disappearing
Into the ferns below. The island's mimics—
Mynas and mockingbirds—sing when the cardinal
Flies from the hutch to the mango and beyond.
The bamboo creaks. Doors open. No one's home.

The cardinal preening   in the palm transplanted
from Indonesia   is not the island's
sentry nor the sea's   ambassador
winds waves and wings   whirl at the sound of the last
door closing   in the leper colony
below the bluff   where the *brilliant water* is
wearing down the wreckage   from the war

The dying man was still drawing up plans, this time for a prison. Candles flickered, and outside his window songbirds fell like rain; choristers trapped them in the cisterns to roast them over a spit. A priest opened a book and recorded the statesman's final words: *Who are the enemies of France? The German princes? Their lands are burning. The Holy Roman Empire is a leper colony. Open the window on the West. We shall leave seeds and feathers everywhere.* The Master of Royal Fireworks was in the courtyard, tasting sauces for the songbirds. Courtesans poured wine for the choristers. *The blows from a sword are easily healed. Not so the blows of a tongue . . .* The priest scribbled in the margins: *Delirium has set in.* Fireworks rained down on the city, like songbirds. The cisterns were filled with burning oil. Soon the swollen empire would split in two. Lepers were at the door. But just before he closed his eyes the cardinal heard the poet's voice: *Where are the snows of yesteryear?* And that is why it is said he died peacefully in his sleep.

Peter Michelson

THIS A.M. IN BATTI HAS BEGUN

A dog, scrofulous and bony, lies
inert beside Lloyd's Road.
The raucous crows convene nearby.
Otherwise, the day dawns clear.
Muslim prayers broadcast the rising sun.
Brightly saried women, men
in dress shirts and sarongs
pad their stately sandaled gait.
Kerchiefed kids in Uniform
gaggle on toward school.
They file through the checkpoint on the bridge.
Neighborhood goats browse shoreline trash.
A dainty billy rears and mocks a charge,
remembering some atavistic call.
A bullock cart is overtaken by
a foursome perched upon the family bike.
The parish bell rings the faithful in.
Now the dog has twitched its ear and yawned,
cancelling its comment on mortality.
No matter to the shrilly rising crows.
They know whatever route they fly
this hounded landscape's likely to provide
some thing or one with blank and tasty eyes.

Czeslaw Milosz

WANDA

translated by the author and Robert Hass

Wanda Telakowska (1905–1985), once a popular figure in artistic Warsaw, a painter specializing in color woodcuts, was renowned for her conspicuous stature, her organizing skills, and her sense of humor. In the interwar period she created pattern designs for the textile industry based on folk craft, in particular the handwoven fabrics of Eastern Poland. Her idea of beauty in things for everyday use stemmed in part from native sources (the theories of the poet Norwid), and in part from folk art. She received some backing for her project in government circles. Also a cooperative—called *Lad,* or *Harmony*—working along those lines, was founded in Warsaw.

The *oeuvre* of Telakowska, the colored woodcuts and the theoretical essays prepared by her for print, was consumed by fire during the Warsaw Uprising of 1944. After the war she saw the possibility of organizing state enterprises to produce, for internal use and for export, products of high artistic quality modeled on native handicraft. She met with resistance, and the transition from prototypes to mass production proved impossible. A collection of individual objects, sent to New York, was much admired by the big trading firms, which, however, wanted quantity. Telakowska traveled to America in 1948, hoping to secure markets for the export of textiles. She succeeded in interesting prospective buyers, but no supply from Poland was forthcoming. I tried to help her. Unfortunately, her case—of a socially minded person eager to serve her country—was typical of Poland at that time.

~

And so, Wanda of a bygone Warsaw,
Let the living pretend they are not concerned
With death, which is too common, too ordinary.
But I don't understand how it is possible
To live and to know that the hour strikes,
And to wait quietly for one's turn.
Something needs to be done. Protest marches?
Wallowings, howlings, curses?
At least let there be a skeleton with a scythe,
Scissors of the Fates, or a star that plummets
When a soul departs. But there is nothing,
An obituary in two or three lines,
And then oblivion forever.

We did not become romantically involved.
Traveling, we would take two rooms.
Because sex is diabolic. I believed that then
And still maintain it. And whoever
Believes otherwise surrenders to the power
Of the Spirit of the Earth, who is not good.

We are allowed it, but only with our spouses.
And, besides, Wanda, you were not a temptation.
Huge, heavy, and not too pretty,
A good companion in coarse laughter at the table.
And beneath, another Wanda, timid and tenderhearted,
Mindful—though with shame—of her maidenhood.

In our sorrows we find solace in a project:
To make the State a helper of art.
Factories and mills were to create beauty
For everyday, as country looms once did.

The elegant wives of ministers listened.

(Oh, elegant wives of ministers!
Where are you? In what department of oblivion
Do you touch up your lips, snap your handbags?)

~

During the war I used to meet Wanda at the Iwaszkiewiczes in Stawiski. From her accounts of wartime adventures I remember those testifying to her presence of mind—for instance, when she found herself in the middle of a roundup at the edge of Mokotowski Field, by Polna Street. "They were taking everybody, they walked straight toward me. What could I do? At the last moment I squatted and lifted my skirt. The German gendarme felt, after all, awkward confronted with a woman pissing and passed by, pretending he did not see me." Or when she moved to the mountains after the Warsaw Uprising and lived in Zakopane with a peasant family. "They were banging on the door. I escaped to the yard. There was a shed with sheep. I had brought my fur-lined overcoat from Warsaw, so I turned it fur-side-up and got down on all fours among the sheep. The Germans took a look into the shed and went away."

~

To be a witness, try to remember.
It cannot be done. Nor am I doing it.
I only know it's gone, that city,
And on its ruins the illustrious Red Army.
Also Wanda, who tried to convince yokels
Who pick their noses behind their desks
That it's worthwhile, important, that the State should . . .

Dull and sluggish, without the gentry or the Jews,
They were doing something, not too much.
And all daring seemed to them lordly,
Too risky, fanciful.

While you, Wanda, were of those who were ready
To straighten the bent axis of the globe.
People, as usual, did not care.
And soon, old age. Perhaps, you kept in memory
That trip of ours to San Francisco,
Which we both had hope enough to undertake.
What use medals and crosses of merit?
You remained alone in your defeat,
Lonely, not needed, going blind.

To bear it. And human beings bear it.
And what can be said is always too late.

Simone Muench

THE *MELOS* OF MEDUSA

It's the jitters that gives them a hard-on!
—Hélène Cixous

I once was a beautiful woman;
now it's come down to tricks and stones,
the wick of my voice sputtering

curses in the Mediterranean breeze.
I once believed that voice
was sustenance: beauty and weight

of a pomegranate—its wine-colored chambers,
a thousand rooms to lose
yourself in. Now I know

no one was listening but the goats
as they ate their way through night's
detritus: an orgy where men sang

and drank while women, thin as mist,
whispered on the periphery. *Lovely*
mouths gagged with pollen.

Perseus, as you move your back
towards me, I want to lick
the delicate skin where armor

doesn't sheath the elegance
of your neck as you peruse
my reflection in your shield.

I want you to see *me,* to stop
pursuing my image. It wasn't my face
that turned those poor men to rock.

It was the burn of me—even
  my navel, a thimble of fire. My hair,
    a catastrophe of fiery curls, not coils

of water moccasins. But the myth remains
  the same: someone is saved; someone
    dies a terrible death.

We know the rules.
  My song that has gone so long
    unheard will taunt you in your sleep

even as you sweep your sword
  across my neck like a finger
    tracing its own silence.

Paul Muldoon

LONG FINISH

Ten years since we were married, since we stood
under a chuppah of pine-boughs
in the middle of a little pinewood
and exchanged our wedding-vows.
Save me, good thou,
a piece of marchpane, while I fill your glass with Simi
Chardonnay as high as decency allows,
and then some.

Bear with me now as I myself must bear
the scrutiny of a bottle of wine
that boasts of hints of plum and pear,
its muscadine
tempered by an oak backbone. I myself have designs
on the willow-boss
of your breast, on all your waist confines
between longing and loss.

The wonder is that we somehow have withstood
the soars and slumps in the Dow
of ten years of marriage and parenthood,
its summits and its sloughs—
that we've somehow
managed to withstand an almond-blossomy
five years of bitter rapture, five of blissful rows,
(and then some

if we count the one or two to spare
when we've been firmly on cloud nine).
Even now, as you turn away from me with your one bare
shoulder, the veer of your neckline,
I glimpse the all-but-cleared-up eczema-patch on your spine
and it brings to mind not the Schloss
that stands, transitory, tra la, Triestine,
between longing and loss

but a crude
hip-trench in a field, covered with pine-boughs,
in which two men in masks and hoods
who have themselves taken vows
wait for a farmer to break a bale for his cows
before opening fire with semi-
automatics, cutting him off slightly above the eyebrows,
and then some.

It brings to mind another, driving out to care
for six white-faced kine
finishing on heather and mountain-air,
another who'll shortly divine
the precise whereabouts of a landmine
on the road between Beragh and Sixmilecross,
who'll shortly know what it is to have breasted the line
between longing and loss.

Such forbearance in the face of vicissitude
also brings to mind the little 'there, theres' and 'now, nows'
of two sisters whose sleeves are imbued
with the constant douse and souse
of salt-water through their salt-house
in *Matsukaze* (or "Pining Wind"), by Zeami,
the salt-house through which the wind soughs and soughs,
and then some

of the wind's little 'now, nows' and 'there, theres'
seem to intertwine
with those of Pining Wind and Autumn Rain, who must forbear
the dolor of their lives of boiling down brine.
For the double meaning of 'pine'
is much the same in Japanese as English, coming across
both in the sense of 'tree' and the sense we assign
between 'longing' and 'loss'

as when the ghost of Yukihira, the poet-courtier who wooed
both sisters, appears as a ghostly pine, pining among pine-boughs.
Barely have Autumn Rain and Pining Wind renewed
their vows
than you turn back towards me and your blouse,
while it covers the all-but-cleared-up patch of eczema,
falls as low as decency allows,
and then some.

Princess of Accutane, let's no more try to refine
the pure drop from the dross
than distinguish, good thou, between mine and thine,
between longing and loss,
but rouse
ourselves each dawn, here on the shore at Suma,
with such force and fervor as spouses may yet espouse,
and then some.

Jude Nutter

GRAVE ROBBING WITH RILKE

You want to write about life
but you keep coming back to the body;
back to this untended, overgrown graveyard
where your small, family mausoleum
has been broken open and the bone
ware of your parents' tomb keeps passing
out of one world and into another.

Even if god is something
in which you will not believe, you need
to believe your dead should remain
in one piece forever, and yet your parents
will not stop trading their earthly possessions:

you've seen them taken—clamped
in the jaws of the badger and the fox; carried
by the raven's mussel-black devices
toward a purpose even you would call
heaven; and once, you found a darkness
of children, slick as stones in the rain,
waiting, as the one boy willing
to touch the dead for them all stepped forward
into the tomb and came back

with pieces of your parents in the basket
of his fingers. Any fall toward knowledge is won
through disobedience to the gods,
and as you watched him go—little hero,
his pockets full of trinkets belonging to you—
you thought about Rilke, who claimed his god
was a dark god—*a webbing,* he said,
made of a hundred roots that drink in silence:

a metaphor, yes, but every metaphor reveals
the ghost of a literal world; and what acts
of desecration he must have committed
in order to claim it. He had his burden, and not once

did you think of calling that young boy back.
You stand now in sunlight, on the splintered
threshold of your parents' grave, looking in:
and this, you tell yourself, *is how it must*
have been for them when they stood,
in silence, in that brightly lit hallway just outside
the doorway to my room, watching
the rungs of my small ribs rising and falling.

Jere Odell

FRUIT FLY

Larvae under fruit skin, adults rising, ripened with yeast.
Ghosting, sometimes visible—the breath in a bowl of pears.
Bodies of ambered juice, confections for wings, eyes of candy,
    pectin for feet.
Impersonal, but at one's lips—this morning, the last to leave
    the party.
Hangers on, oblivious inebriates, clouded spirits
rimming the shot glasses & walking the wine bottles.
Sweet lover and the dew.

Or else, the object of science: 2 mm, reproducing in multiples
    x times a week.
Variables, few; traits, enough; the find, that rare recessive
    white-eyed male.
The object of science, the go-between to our genes.
Regenerative but small, the triumph of Mendel's genetics.
The fame of Thomas Hunt Morgan, the Nobel winner
    scanning his data incarnate.
& how he found his sample: Domesticity!
Left fruit on the window sill & let it swell.

Drosophilia, changeling, double soul living in the liminal:
come to the kitchen, vinegar bird, pomace fly, it's more yours
    than mine.

Andrew Osborn

HOMING

Now and again, through the background soundtrack
of Andrei Tarkovsky's *Nostalghia,* a circular
saw blade rips like a question. I keep asking: *a lack*

of devotion, devotion to shortfall, to blur?
The unseen gnawing my options apart,
each diamond-sharpened *which-is-it?* Or was it

that sepia clottage of rained-on pulp
homed in on like a landscape remembered,
sawdust heaped in hillocks on the floor?

So, too, are we asked by Flaubert
to hear above the story line, behind
the dormered window of an upper-story flat,

the lathe of Monsieur Binet, turning and turning.

~

Listen: *le percepteur et son tour—*
theirs is the sound of surveillance-and-taxing-
in-one, a keening unison. His rounds

of the village made, the payments exacted,
dinner taken at six, he works
the treadle, letting the vortex tap him,

ushering something merciless to true us
with or against our grain. And against
the back of my brainpan (I was rereading

aloud from the passenger side as you drove us
to Texas) something centrifugal weighed:
the way in Bentham's radial prisons

the watchman's central tower compelled
the back-lit inmates to feel they were being
seen at all times, and how their faces,

how the whole front sides of them took
the seen-ness on as something worn.
Can we not be weaned? Can we not—

the girl long since brought home from the wet nurse,
spinning-wheel judging and judging—be reined
aside from this whining knowing?

~

Emerson, coming to terms, if not
in touch, with the death of his six-year-old son,
and the Fall of Man: *We must hold hard*

to this poverty, however scandalous,
and by more vigorous self-recoveries,
after the sallies of action, possess

our axis more firmly. I had not thought
the "I," like a well-greased flywheel, spun
as each of us braked and bleakened.

~

But when I feel the ceiling fans we run
all year down here or, after supper, pull
my napkin through its wooden ring, I think:

there is an axis we've held to, how happy
we often are now, and of that night you say
you woke, coughing up pulped pages of a book

whose unread ending you'd mistaken for arsenic.

Eric Pankey

DOES NOT SUNDER

Yesterday is grainy, thumb-smudged, more than little out of focus, as if a mirror of departures,
As if a spirit house open to the elements—mice in the walls, mud-daubers in the eaves.
It ain't nobody's fault but mine, the old song goes.
No, it ain't nobody's fault but mine.
The three horses are the same horse, a dream-horse, I explain, so, yes, you can kill a horse more than once.
The reader had imagined them as three separate horses, and was still puzzled by the *why* of the killing.

I live with a hunger that satiety does not sunder.
Filippo Lippi paints the Holy Trinity,
Knowledge, that is, of the Holy Trinity, as three arrows lodged in the heart of St. Augustine.
The incidence suggesting each arrow was shot from above, the aim of a deadeye dead-on.
Further on up the road, somebody's gonna hurt you like you hurt me. Further on up the road.
I found, years later, a whorl of burled hardwood where my arrow, let loose, had pierced the sapling.

"This struggle and hybrid desire," St. Teresa called it, "to have God and keep the world too."
If I was not understood—the gibberish I rattled, the voice in my head—I can't say I spoke in tongues.
I stepped out of my body of fire and into a world of fire.
Estranged. Ill at ease. Unpurged. Alone.
From a low ridge in the woods, when leaves were not yet full on, I would watch the drive-in movies—
Silent figures of mote-light, shimmering on the wind-rustled screen. I put words in their mouths

Not far from the fence was an apple tree, wind-bent, scrawny,
yet in Spring
a cricked crown of blossoms,
And by the time school started, a burden of crisp fruit, sweet to the tongue,
but a clench of tart as I chewed.
I waited at the fence for the mare to come, up over the hill and down, to rest
her neck on the barbed wire,
And take from my left hand an offered apple and from my right hand an
offered apple.
For my offering, the horse, in an ancient language of shivers and twitches,
instructed me in reticence.

Suzanne Paola

TENURE AT FORTY

November morning in Bellingham, 40
degrees: leafmeal crusted, & frost.
Each step cracks, a little bone.
My neighbors have put plasticene
on the windows for the cold.
I'm checking the thermostat
& the pilot light, getting the flues cleaned.
Thinking of nothing else. Thinking
of how I'm thinking of nothing else—
How the outer life has become
the inner, the skin the body.

I lean forward to adjust the curtain
shocked for once to be *here* & not *there*
to have walked through the six realms
& somehow without knowing it
have chosen
& a corpse lies, done
with her bardo journey

five foot six one hundred
pounds large-boned, each hand
wearing the precise imprint of a lit cigarette
as if glimpsing a future need for proof—

Cliffhanger
without ending, nights
I can't quite remember—
Dragged out of the Capitol Theatre in Passaic by the manager,
    OD'ed, my friends gone.
OD'ed again on methadone, bloody at the lips.
Unconscious in a basement. Awake
in a hospital room. Lyric girl, who leapt

from one image to the next.

Like species consciousness, this memory, like knowing
an earlier stage of evolution—
Neanderthal girl with rabbit fur coat.
The redlipped mammal girl, the reptile

all cold blood & lidless staring.

~

This, then, is narrative.
Ironbluish light
of midmorning. No sun. Nothing that could be called
illumination—
Just a change in tint from the tint of nighttime.
Mountains somewhere
perhaps, their veins against pale horizon.
Neighbors perhaps. Fogbanks
more visible than landscape, more fraught with line.
As if I chose to live where the gods do, veiled
from any overwhelming splendor.

We're each a piece of spirit, she said
on television, *we're in, like, a flesh suit.*

I pull on nude pantyhose to stand before the dean.
Tenure meaning *held.* He reads my file

where it ends with Service to the Community (Local)
where it begins, with a name

~

& the letter (we formally recommend be granted)
& my students half
asleep, the room dotted with paper cones of coffee.
Tomorrow & tomorrow & tomorrow. The Psyche
of Keats, Isabella
who planted basil in a pot with a human head, these stories

The book opens. The cover has bled
into the pages. The cover is the book.

& the story I see in the figure
their bored eyes give back to me—

Middle-aged. A powderblue suit. Pumps. Necklace
of impossible moments.

I can just see it, she said.

A woman who came back from death
& couldn't stop telling it, & forgot why.

Like gloves or something, it just comes off

Elise Partridge

GNOMIC VERSES FROM THE ANGLO-SAXON

adapted and selected

Kings shall rule kingdoms. Winter cold is keenest,
summer sun the most searing,
fall freest with her hand. Fate is almighty;
the old are wisest. Jewels must stand upright
in winking bezels, blades break on helmets,
hawks hunch on the glove, the huffing boar
wander the woods with the wretched wolf.
Salmon spawn in northernmost streams,
the king in his castle gives his cronies rings;
bears haunt the heath, the hastening water
floods the rolling fields of the downs.
Lovers meet in secret, monsters skulk
in the swamp, stars seed the sky.
The troop stands together, a glorious band.
Light lunges at dark, life parries death,
good clashes with evil, the old with the young,
army against army battles for the land;
all of us wait in the Lord's arms
for the decree he ordains, darkly, in secret.
Only God knows where our souls will go.

Tom Paulin

NAMANALAGH

Somewhere in the pine trees beyond the lough
two stones are being knocked together
—once twice three times—very dry—maybe
it's a chain gang working in the quarry?
there is no quarry though
and there never was a chain gang
only the little chunks of red granite on the long
looping bog road tell of famine relief
congested districts that human weather
that sticks like salt stains or burns in your hair
—no I realize all these are not
in fact the case—it's a chough
I can hear—its clatt-
ery cry that's like the real hard stuff
—poteen distilled on stony hills
where the black craychur
should be sounding its red beak its curved bill
against the screes
not hiding out on the soft bog by the lough

Deborah Pease

ALTERATION OF BEING

I.

Afterwards you are never the same, nothing
About you is the same, not a single vowel, not
A single footstep, nothing of what you were before
Remains and yet to all appearances
You retain a semblance of the self
Known as *you*, the mannerisms, vocal
Stresses, even the laughter you make
Such an effort to produce
To show you are not destroyed, to show consideration
For the discomfiture of those who knew you before
And do not want to know
What you've become, *however*
One night at dinner your eyes wander, stare,
Fill with tears, your hands tremble
While trying to cut a piece of lettuce, your words
Stick to the roof of your mouth like crumbs, the language
You hear around you is like a foreign tongue, and then
At breakfast you choke
On a blueberry muffin, silently at first
In a corner of the kitchen while others joke
(About baseball or the antics of the dogs)
By the sunny window seat,
Then less silently as you trail after them
Into the library, then violently
As you grab the edge of the bookshelf, terrible
Clots heave out of you, noises
Nobody here has heard before, anywhere, ever—
This is not within a normal frame
Of reference, you must be locked up
In a facility where screams
Are a professional matter, but even
After the screams are stifled
And you are discharged into the world the screams

Continue as you try to fit in *because*
You try so hard to fit in, you fall into clumsiness,
Stumble over simple everyday matters, your presence
Is a problem, you rush out of rooms on cheery pretexts
To go scream into a pillow or the bunched-up bathrobe
You bought him one Christmas, you cry
Until your hair is matted with goo
Until you become sick and must stop
Must go on living.

II.

"This happens to everyone"
Is the eventual
Exasperated unspoken response
To prolonged grief
(No open grave
To leap into, no
Black vestments to declare
A state of mourning)—
Only dignity offers solace, the dignity of those
So alone that nothing degrades them
(The silence of bones,
The sockets of eyes) so
In your internal exile you rejoin the world,
You see fields acquiring new green in the spring,
Magenta clumps of azaleas, dainty chartreuse leaves
Of Belgian elms, the stalwart intricacies of daffodils
April snow blown sideways, the hawk motionless
As a kite in the sky except for a slight
Adjustment of balance, the sudden
Sure projectile
Of its body down a mile-long hypotenuse,
Geometries of rapture, but
This beauty fails
To move you, even the afterglow of a sunset
(Spectacular, all would agree, flammable
Leviathans coasting
Through God's fantasy, reflections

On the obsidian surface of the pond), this
Abundance of beauty, observed,
Fails to move you, how
Can you be moved except by love? Only love
Animates beauty, only *human* love, only and forever
Love, the love that withdrew
From your life despite your desperate attempts
To keep it alive,
To protect it, shield it, comfort it, breathe
Your own life into it, into your love
For him, for his life,
For his love for you—you failed, you watched
Love's long slow regard
Until it could breathe no longer
Until all breath stopped.

John Peck

VIOLIN

With all pasts and futures harboring in this present
then all, happiness and unhappiness, is a choice
if only because I have agreed to build here. Yet even
the most daring choose happiness alone, and thinking
will never get me through this, and feeling loiters in it—
only Great Harbor floats all of it, fresh, waiting.
Following descriptions of the North Pyramid at Dashur,
the Red Pyramid stripped of its red sandstone facing,
then photographs from recent expedition reports,
I found no speculations about precisely why
this pivotal structure slopes at forty-three degrees,
a matter of moment, perhaps or perhaps not, yet
I saw sand shelving along the base of the west face,
a ripply ledge smoothing along remnant facing
and blending with it—the same as on Plum Island,
barrier beach for piping plover and pale-belled sand shrubs
dropping its steep bevel sucked at for miles by surf,
the rolling sound momently sinking away in it,
its high edge fronting dune grass nervy against sun.
No Joseph among us to build granaries, no Jonah
to ironize destruction, no Jacob to hammer choice.
One third through the mere sixty years which saw the great
pyramids rise, this one, with the lowest inclination
at forty-three degrees, *cautious* some say to forestall
shiftings which skewed the vitals of the Bent Pyramid
somewhat earlier and three quarters of a mile off,
was the first achieved prototype. A slope which has me sense
greater mass and area than it commands. A discovery
about proportion and it may be an application
of lore no one yet has been able to read from the record.
This time the architect lifted the burial chamber
higher inside the mass—the squared cone of sunlight—
and for the first time aligned the coffin east-west
with tomb temple and the sun's track. Its capstone
pyramidion was of the same red sandstone,
not the gilded white stone or granite of later practice.

The entire casing bulged slightly outward much like
the faint entasis on a Greek column, though not
meant for Greek good looks, but rather for what would stand.
Altering the slope's angle rise by rise with
cord and peg, masons jesting with the overseer:
this innovation in masonry was not imitated.
Senefru, who enjoyed people, calling his staff *Dear Friend,*
the only king known for doing so, presided over
erection of the Bent and the Red pyramids, as well as
two others at Meidum and Seila, the start on Egypt's
Manhattan Project, four solar fusion battery casings
for his charged body, at three locations. He was buried
in this one if its hurried completion is any evidence.
Osiris's theology by then nosed ahead of the astral one.
An east-west journey at night with the sun in that god's boat.
Setting out through river reeds, their silken forgivingness.
On one side, barrier dunes thrusting up into solar acetylene
which tracks with me along their apex, while on the other
vast drenchings sink into the low slope. Four fiberglass
fishing poles shoot lines off into surf, their necks
bent studiously, their shanks in tubes rammed into sand,
their armchair owner dozing under a blue towel.
Four nylon zings of tackle as if sounding unison.
They baked loaves for him in the reliefs. He himself ran
a race in the Heb-Sed ceremony, as did his fathers,
all in renewal of their powers, his predecessor loping
hugely across the slab which seals a shaft at Meidum.
Though no tides any longer moisten the stones, those tunnels
smell of the sea. The burial of full-scale ships
began under his son Khufu near the vast piles at Giza.
My ears ring with a cricket-like susurrus that comes from years
of holding taut line out into the oncoming rush.
A certain age renders further ambition supernumerary,
my buried boats need no more cult. For all the forces
at play in this wide theater, its spaciousness declares
a propertyless state. May I now take up
the violin that nearly came to me at age ten,
my maternal uncle's gift? brought ceremoniously
on a special visit, yet it went back with him, the fact of it
raising an outsize grief in my mother for herself, perhaps.
Rest in peace and the mystery, with the silent thing in its case.

Or may I pursue this engineering further? surrogate
for the womanly body of that fiddle gone downstream.
Yet they were building spirit reservoirs, surge tanks
for seam voltage, soul-welding solar granaries, and one architect
had been chief priest. The hand tracking shadow at Dashur
from rod to rod for the foundation's first course of stones
may have held a lamp for priests in the last chamber
as rare privilege—for their ordained invocations
tested by many sequencings, happiness on alert
through ordeals, the chances awful and the aim real.
I woke with the sand grains of his destiny alive
across my maroon blanket, mustard golden spores
thrown over him by the king, a gift of land to that
Dear Friend. Deir of the geometries. His eye through the pile,
its red slope, the Forty-Three: design stabilizes the *mana*
of earth lofted into fire's force and held there,
steadies the dangerous changes. Guards against them
even before the end, so that a fine instrument
recharged and tuned during the royal run but at last
taken away may morph to mastery in some other walk
by another sea. May turn—mangled god—mischance into the path.
For this I sing: Deir of the triangle with plumb line
portable and pendulous in his eye's mind intending
this for the powers, the king and people, the realms
interlocking, past calamities, through dynasties dangling
in the shaky cycles of order.

I took from his case the still shiny
stream-bottom varnish of the thing and chin-clasped it
per his instruction, and before setting it back in the inky
blue plush drew one long wavery whine
from the G string, pushing up slowly with the bow.
Delight broke from his face. The dark closure not yet
having come across hers, she parted her lips, eyebrows
arching expectantly. Labored, nursed, caressed, that sound
could go on past the end of its own curve, such was
its Pythagorean hint even in my raw hand,
animal miracle among the ratios.
Next morning it was gone. This then sing:
that were I to walk that sand's bandwidth between desert
and facing stone, I would tread neither the waste

nor the monument, but one string stretched like the dune's world
behind my barrier beach, scrub and wiry foliage
nestled minutely into pockets of the in-between
and giving ear steadfastly to immensity.
That close to forty-three degrees is where the G-string
lands a bow's tilt, as a pro will testify.
That even the smudge across her happiness, and the murderous
touch of *creatura,* and the inept weight of fate,
dissolve where the soul burns and melts, where tone
and overtone release each other, and if all stabilized things vanish
in the furnace, truing the line and lighting the chant
give love to the fire. An immense fragrance rose
from the violin case's dyed velvet, the sealed wood,
strings, rosin, fogged bakelite of the chin cup,
the untreated inner wood of the curved body,
the equine substance of the glue, the fluted pegs,
ivory nut to tauten the pale sheaf of horsetail,
and a man's sweat and breath, when he opened these to me.
I have not imagined myself long in the burial chamber,
neither as carver nor priest, and only for a brief spell as builder
scanning the ceiling slab for telltale cracks. A vast
aroma lifted from that case among the bright faces.

Paul Petrie

ADOLESCENCE

for Tom Madsen

Under the streetlight's gauzy eye
we paced—
now on the walk with the dandelion cracks,
now in the street,
now half upon the curb, half in the street,
conversing
(Hands absorbed in intellectual arcs)
of Gandhi, God, Dos Passos, Stendhal, Proust,
and Young Peoples,
                                        and Madelaine Allersby,
the girl we both adored,
                                                  and whom before that night
was through, you gave to me, and I gave back to you,
and both gave up.

Through the cherry-blossom dark
the hours slipped.
"What should the novel be?" we queried,
and solved the problem in endless tomes of words
that made Tom Wolfe short-winded.

Fame perched above
in a halo of light.

Applause
dropped from the stars.

At half-past four, I walked you home,
                                                                      and turning
round—
            you walked me halfway back.

The lamps looked down, counting the glowing miles.

Donald Platt

LATE ELEGY IN SPRING FOR LARRY LEVIS WITH CARAVAGGIO & HORSES

Another May, drum roll of hail on our back deck,
                Larry Levis
one year dead, Shostakovitch's

                First Violin Concerto
played over and over until I know the Nocturne's
                every grieving

slow vibrato, then sun too bright to bear,
                the magnolia in our front yard
lighting its votive candles, masses of wisteria twining

                up the pines, asphalt
steaming, the gardenia's obscene perfume. Yesterday
                I saw for the first time

Caravaggio's *David with the Head of Goliath,*
                visiting from Italy
"on extended loan." There is no black so lustrous

                as that in the upper
right-hand quadrant, which looks as if the oils
                are not yet dry.

Because Larry had lingered for hours in the Borghese before that painting
                while he wrote
the poem "Swirl & Vortex," I felt him stand behind

                my blind left shoulder, looking
with me at Caravaggio who looks back at us from Goliath's
                glazed eyes

in the severed head held up by David, who grips
                a fistful of his hair.
Larry, it's not Goliath, nor Caravaggio's self-portrait, nor your friend

Zamora blown to bits
by a Viet Cong land mine. It's your own ravaged face, etched
with fine laughter lines

and time's coarser crosshatchings, your thick eyebrows, the slackening jaw, the hair
you let grow long
in your last days so that a friend said you looked like

"a defeated Southern general."
Because in one of your poems a man finds solace
talking to a gray-white

horse, I take my children Eleanor and Lucy to feed
the foals oats.
All bays, they come when we call them over

and rub their worn velvet
muzzles against the splintery top rail and nose our pockets
for the kernels that they know

are there. My daughters are scared, and I must feed
the gigantic
jaws myself, offering each handful of grain

on my flat palm
with my thumb tucked in so it won't be ground down
by the blunt, oblivious

teeth. Larry, when I close my eyes to see what you see,
I hear only
low whickering, a breathing more emphatic

than mine, sudden
snort, hoof stamp. The foal nuzzles my palm, a woman's breast brushes
me again, she grows wet

against my fingers, the horse's rough tongue licking
long after the grain
is gone. I stretch out my hand to the live darkness all around us.

Göran Printz-Påhlson

AELIUS LAMIA

Tankas for Robert Hass

Autumn: Stapleford.
The fine badge of air between
the branches of trees:
a squirrel jumping from one
to the other one, bending,

reminded me at once
of other squirrels in the parks
of my own childhood
in the cold winters of war.
They were red, like foxes' tails,

not grey, American,
silver-speckled tenderfoots.
Memories are eggs,
spotted, in colours, numbers
as in poems by John Clare.

But this is their true
significance: transience
in the permanent;
when blown, enduring as shell:
The man Aelius Lamia

(*vide* Suetonius,
who loved idle gossip)
was put to death by
the Emperor Domitian
"on account of certain jests"

of which the one is self-ex-
planatory, but not
particularly
funny, the other—of his
silence when exhorted to sing:

heu taceo:—has
to this day never been
explained nor understood.
There is, as you know well,
comfort in silence, sadness.

James S. Proffitt

SOMEHOW EARLIER, FIELDS OF BRUSHY PAIN OUTSIDE AND FLAT, THOUGH PAINFUL

If there was someone earlier, now there is not.
Not inside, nor outside, nor anywhere else.
Like a plain it is wide and flat and empty.
Though there may be grain and brushy fencelines.
It is the solitude of no others ever which is painful.
Like a plain not inside nor out, the solitude.
Wide and flat and empty though there may be pain.
Now there is not, even if earlier, there was someone.
Now anywhere else, grain and brushy fencelines.
Like pain, though there may be painful solitude.
And someone else not here, nor anywhere else.
Brushy fencelines wide and flat, like pain.
Though someone earlier was not inside, nor out.
Wide and flat, even if earlier, painful grain.
Not outside, pain, nor wide—but inside and flat.

Kevin Prufer

TROMPE L'OEIL

The dead are as an echo resounding off a wall
on which someone has painted the shapes of stars.

My mittens unravel. The long strands
flutter against my coat sleeves. I put my fingers in my mouth
where they will be warm. In the air again, the weave stiffens,

shells over. Snow falls as stars or, cast in a deceiving light, as dying
embers. Shadows thrown by street lamps so each black footprint
appears larger than it ought to be, the low crying

of wind, an echo thereof, the evening slowing, stopping—
does the mind tick to a close like this?

In January of 1610, cast adrift by a mutinous crew, Henry Hudson
and his young son were never seen again, or

it is 1912 and Xavier Mertz slips into a crevice, legs twisted
behind him. He calls and calls, but the rope isn't long enough.
Please don't ask me to explain—It is 1820

and the British load their lifeboats
with candlesticks and china, lash them with ropes, and set out,
dragging them across the Canadian tundra.

It is any year at all. The landscapes thicken, crust over,
all the people clicking forward, their minds

---

slowly unticking. I have seen from below the domes of cathedrals
designed to convince us that they are not there

at all. Someone painted them a perfect bottle blue,
traced over them with the outlines of stars which, later,
he gilded—so even in the weakest candlelight

they shone as though they were real. I stood, head tilted,
and looked into an unmoving sky. I whispered my name,
and heard the echo come back to me.

Peter Robinson

A TRIBUTE

About a train journey over the border,
I'm finding it harder
and harder to put out of mind or explain
why, when I came from a cramped waiting room,
a young girl or, rather, young woman
had me rooted to the platform—
for it wasn't as if, after all, I knew
or had ever set eyes on her before.
Perhaps because her thick fall of red hair
threw me back off down the years
to a towpath where I'm racking my brains
for a word to say as minute by minute
our time's made a series of tortures
(her silence, mine) with me like
one of those hapless government spokesmen
who's no sooner opened his mouth
than he puts a foot in it . . .

which was when the journey began in earnest.
Through seeming-deserted country, our train
at its new speed limit racketed on
across yet more debatable terrain—
everywhere owned and abandoned
even by trespassing walkers, depressed
farmers, their eyes
watering at fumes from ministry fires
behind a horizon, crooked smoke plumes
meeting the cloud-base above livestock pyres
like a tribute to the gods of brand and
profit; through hill fields, healthy areas
where the rest of the flocks still safely graze,
we're sent down false tracks till with house roofs
on Lockerbie's outskirts, it slowed again
by heaps of heifers' blackened hooves
pointing at the skies.

Pattiann Rogers

THE LEXICOGRAPHER'S PRAYER

Write for me now the name
of the hanging willow branch in cold
rain, then the name of the willow branch
moving with summer wind. Give me
the word for summer wind as ruffling
killdeer feathers, the word for cold rain
off black umbrellas.

Not the name of the poplar, not the name
of the coral-yellow evening sky, but tell me
the name for the single thing that exists
as they are one, a seamless union.

And what is the pine woods snake called
when it is unwitnessed, imagined beneath
forest leaf and litter? What is the name
of the same snake when exposed to the sky,
observed, in the hand, remarked upon,
a different entity? Pronounce
the words slowly.

And what is this—ice enclosing fallen
cattail stalks, not two together, but one essence,
each constituting the other.

Moon and moon and moon all over the lake,
broken, misshapen, fluttering, one of them
penetrated momentarily by my toe . . . these are not
sky moons, not rock moons, but something else.
Wavering-water moons? Elusive liquid moons?
One toe moon? One moon-wet toe? Or, being
without substance, no *moons* at all?

Here are my definitions: 1. street lamp
with no magpie atop 2. street lamp
with three magpies atop. Spell
the word for each.

And say the single sound for this: autumn-
morning-crow-call in the heart. Altered,
altered, I'm certain; neither call nor heart
is the same alone.

Come now to my aid. My book
is frighteningly incomplete.

John Phillip Santos

DEEP FIELD

I.

We unscroll bolts of damask linen, measuring each incongruous hem
with an Osage arrow, a Hawawir sword, any ruins left lying around
the place.
With open palm and fiery heart, bring in our whisperer of suras
crescent halo, penumbrae of a thousand shimmering kites.
Let words rise like ether of gardenia, bringing love, forgetting and
adrenaline.

II.

Roll back the sky now. Roll it back on a scroll
stapled with cactus spines, tightened around the polestar
every swath dotted with squash flowers and pine tar
all our parole glistening in a wash of opal sea foam.
That's how far back we had to go to find the way
again, that's where we left all the counted stones
where blood that runs as clear as honeysuckle sap
mingled with our breath, night air, turning burgundy
forever. "It was a poignant century," said the old priest
"a century when we thought we were doing good,
when we were really doing very bad." The sky
remembers everything, each pulse of fire, flame tracks
of the first songs, the first contrition of the void
giving forth, inexhaustible, leavening the quiet.
When we hear the song again, it's an old radio show
scratchy as if it had traveled across time
in a meteor of smoky quartz. When we embrace
an open canyon yawns beneath us, languid cool air
swirling, twirling us westward into oldest night.

Hillel Schwartz

BENEDICTUS

Grundke, leagues and treelines south of the other
grinder of lenses, five years dead and ex-
communicate, conceives a pharmacon of words
in stoppered bottles: adverbs spooled and corked, lex-
icons of heartfelt nouns, soothing adjectives,
verbs of a broken silence, prose and con-
tractions, glass pediments of infinitives
and filaments of exclamation, long-
suffering subordinate conjunctions which
stand alphabetical for heartache and hearts-
ease along his cedar shelves. The poor, the rich,
the middling squint through thick beryl and quartz-
yellow panes to see each invisible echo
afloat in the soft catoptrics of after-
noon light. Spinoza, rubbing the lens, would show
men *lux,* the Let-there-be; Grundke, master-
craftsman in a town of gilt and wooden toys,
will sell them what must at last be said, some-
time soon, before a daughter leaves, a father dies,
a godmother goes deaf. The sensitive, the numb-
skull both long for the truly apposite.
What is that howling at night if not were-
men, werewomen who have ever on the tip
of their tongues what it was they should have said thir-
four- fif- -teen -ty years ago ago. They seethe
with animal stammer, howl loud blanks into wind-
riven Nuremberg clouds. So come ye, come ye.
Good words are still unspoken-for: wheat, warm, mind-
fulness, to calm, soon, yes, abracadabra,
as if, little one, fortunate, open sesame, aha!

Neil Shepard

SIENNA

After you climb the four hundred steps to Torre del Mangia
and peer down from the belltower onto the scallop-shaped
Il Campo where hundreds of tourists sprawl across the piazza
and hundreds more bend under green umbrellas to nibble biscotti
and sip caffe, and the air's suffused with golden aureoles,
you'll know why swallows double-loop the campanile and circle
the nearby duomo, circle all afternoon without coming
down through shafts of Tuscan sun like a knife
and intercession between light's source and its deliverance
to the brick streets below. You'll know why the Council of Nine,
a level-headed, merchant lot, launched their earthly plans:
commanded tones of raw and burnt sienna for their houses,
umber for the city walls, and quarried colored marble
from nearby hills for the various facades, flat bands
of pink and green that paralleled the world below.
And puzzle-pieced beneath the pilgrims' feet black and white
inlays of marble, Sibyls and Allegories that spoke simply
for the divine mystery. Magnificence, yes. But earthly works—
to praise Him and to weight men's passions for the sky with marble
edifices. Today, it's all brilliant and dead as Jesus in his tomb
despite the Gothic arches, the golden stars of apse and dome,
the soaring nave, the pulpit carved of porphyry, the striking
bronze of Saint John, the famous *Maesta* with Mary serenely
poised between saints and angels—no, I tell you, up here,
four hundred steps to the belltower is as close as you come
to the light those ancient ones beheld, and still you must shield
your eyes from the milling ones below, vendors of gelato and vino,
crowds videocamming the hundred diversions of the square's
halved-circle. Or else, go down to ground-level and pass through
the duomo's bronzed doors and down her arching corridors
and slip into the Libreria Piccolomini where the books
of Pope Pius rest behind glass, and inhale the quiet
that companions books everywhere, like a body and shadow,
a hand and its gesture, an incarnation and its insubstantiation,
and press your palms against the case that keeps you from those

illuminated words scrived by monks whose faith was timeless
and who therefore worked on a scale of time we no longer recognize.
And witness next the margins of the page, eccentric figures
half-man, half-horse riding with bow bent to the hunt,
or monkeys cavorting with virgins, and know the original
confusion of impulses, the first fires in the blood
that lit a light too high and too charged for reverence
or serenity. And know that even from these familiar
desires you are cut off. Then, when you are ready, turn
to the Three Graces in the room's center, that Roman 3rd century copy
of a copy, pining for the Hellenic original, the longing
for pastness so strong it comes through each delicate, straining line
of the Graces' arms and legs, even the stumps, the severed, lost, smashed
limbs that strove as far as they could for a prophecy, a fate,
that reached *backwards* to a shared origin. Then return
to the courtyard and stand among the hordes of schoolchildren
with their frazzled, diligent teachers, among the shepherded
tour-groups with their staff-wielding leaders, among the many
and the few in need of instruction, and witness the uncompleted
floor-plan of the duomo's second phase, a few grand arches,
a staircase leading skyward, a few bold walls, the plans
for grand expansion cut short by the Plague of 1348
that cut short half the lives of Siena—65,000 bodies struck
from their souls and piled high in the Il Campo, stinking
under the burnt siennese sun—
and cut short their commerce and their fleet and standing army,
and converted them to an annex of Visconti or Medici powers,
and thenceforth, to a beautiful but inconsequential
city on a hilltop, and thenceforward, to a walled museum
whose every medieval scrap and stone was ordained
to be left as is, so others might climb the four hundred steps
of the campanile and behold the swallows slicing through
these shafts of light that fall on the passions below
and illuminate all that grand architecture framed in time.

Reginald Shepherd

POLAROID

1

Propositions, presuppositions,
a small summer in my palm.
It hollowed out a heart
in me, backdrop of burned leaves
already burning's color. October
evening recovers summer, renders it
Oil Drum Fire with Bum huddled
at horizon, glittering past
complacency. These

2

early lighthouses had wood fires
or torches in the open, sometimes
sheltered by a roof. Tungsten lamps
fizz on at five to six, flaring like myth
in the making with borrowed
bits of shine. No getting around that
smooth skin, sealed envelope of poison.

3

Let empire, let rage: I said
to worms, you are my mother
and my sister (unearth my then),
we are death's firstborn
festival. The young men
saw me and hid, and the old men
smiled like ash: waited for me
as for rain, acid, for the most part
memory.

4

I cover the sea's voice with chalk
and circumstance, having only myself
to say, scattered smattering of singed
doll parts. They make their way
by means of breakings (schist
and marl): collapse into a clamor
of crows before appearances'
sake, and stand simple

5

in their wreckage. *Coal by-product*
ovens extract ammonia, tar, light oils
wasted as smoke when coal burns:

the mindless heat of substitution
tended and intended, burning
razed fields flat as photographs.

6

Pillar and halt, pillar
and stall, a sinking
water table leaves behind
its salt: the man I made of him.

Charles Simic

DE OCCULTA PHILOSOPHIA

Evening sunlight,
Your humble servant
Seeks initiation
Into your occult ways.

Out of the late summer sky,
Its deepening quiet,
You brought me a summons,
A small share in some large
And obscure knowledge.

Tell me something of your study
Of lengthening shadows,
The blazing windowpanes
Where the soul is turned into light—
Or don't just now.

You have the air of someone
Who prefers to dwell in solitude,
The one who enters, with gravity
Of mien and imposing severity,
A room suddenly rich in enigmas.

Oh supreme unknowable,
The seemingly inviolable reserve
Of your stratagems
Makes me quake at the thought
Of you finding me thus

Seated in a shadowy back room
At the edge of a village
Bloodied by the setting sun,
To tell me so much
To tell me absolutely nothing.

Floyd Skloot

NEAR THE END

My mother came to live beside the sea.
She hated the sound of surf, smell of brine,
gulls circling before the window where she
sat all day in a bright rage of sunshine.

Everyone was old. Everyone was slow.
They went to sleep too soon, rose too early,
were content to watch films and play bingo,
chat with staff and kowtow to the surly
young women at the front desk. Everyone
had someone living close enough to come
for visits twice a week. One woman's son
tried to move in though he was much too young.

There was something wrong with the moon and sun.
Her worst time was near the end of each day.
The moon rose, the sun set. She was alone
with darkness, chill, and fog over the bay.

Ken Smith

THE DONEGAL LIAR

Far from her nest the lapwing cries away:
My heart prays for him though my tongue do curse.
—Shakespeare, *A Comedy of Errors*

Magowan the poet, who might have been Irish,
of one sort or another *Mac an Ghabhann,*
making his way in another disputed borderland,
wearing another mask, north of the south, west of the rain.

A blew in, a run-in, sometimes adrift on a black sea
of sweet black stout, with his companions the captain
and the navigator, whose identities
may or may not ever be revealed.

A ragged country, the roads under fog,
small towns and their flags of allegiance:
Prod. Taig. *No Bigot Parade. No Pope. No RUC.*
No Agreement. Dungevin supports McGahey Road.

No visible border, the miles shift into kilometers,
the signs into script, everywhere stone, stone,
mountains and scree, and the lough suddenly,
a long bolt of blue in the sheer sunlight.

Within him he fancies there was always a Donegal man
butting out from Inishowen, head into the wind
that bears off the Atlantic from the edge of the known world,
northwest corner of the continent of Europe.

Where the neighbours don't like each other much,
here as elsewhere. Ah, the Donegal Liar.
What does he know? He's on the road,
looking for lost uncles, out finding his lost self.

A singer, a fumbling romantic, wanderer,
chickencraw. And in him always the other:
the settler, the stranger, the foreigner,
the blue eyed English. Thirty years it has taken.

Thirty years before that asking *who was that man*
who was my father, a man whose life was all
a bad mood, most of that a bad temper,
whose first glimpse of the light was here in Buncrana?

In the town there was a dream night after night
of the wind and a loud knocking at my door,
over and over, and someone calling my name
up the B&B stairs and the rain over the lough.

At this point nothing is certain, little known.
Whether our man comes back changed from a journey
or whether he learns nothing, thereafter sifting
memory's scraps, silence, the blue moody sky.

In Grant's pub they have on the IRA tapes,
just for our benefit: *Have you no homes to go to,*
have you no homes of your own? Oh the English,
they'd steal the crack of the plate and the plate.

I can't argue with you there boys but I'd love to.
Are you a spy? What's your cover?
How long have you been with the British Army?
This with your father and your mother is bollocks anyway.

800 years of this and the rain. The people
you're after are all drunk and have no money.
Our man concludes a pub is a bad place
to begin researching his ancestors. This pub.

What is he with a name like Smith and his granny a McGrory?
Is he a left footer or a right for the sake of Jesus,
Mary and Joseph, not to mention St. Bridie
and St. Patrick that we thought cast out all the bloody snakes?

Maybe he'll go live in Cool Bay north of Letterkenny
and make finishing the whole of his story. Maybe not.
He could believe all he's told: the rock somewhere there
where the priest's head cut by the redcoat's sword.

Bounced. Three times. To this day where it struck
the grass does not grow, the man swears it,
that and the other stone Wolf Tone was chained to
when he was taken, along the shore there, somewhere.

Somewhere hereabouts by the long lake of shadows,
where the submarines sulk, sunk deep
in radio silence, watching each other. And there's a tree there
cannot be cut down. Men that tried it had sudden bad luck.

All that's certain in my case: a few names, a few dates,
the old man's certificates: birth, marriage, death,
all there is of him. John Patrick. John Smith.
And what manner of a name might that be?

I thought if he was someone else who then might I be?
If he could change I could, I too could be anyone,
anyone at all under the stars. Magowan for instance,
a worker in metal, McGrory, McGroary, McGroy.

His silence was absolute, nothing again nothing,
maybe he knew nothing, shuddered in sleep
in a dream over and over of nuns like angry bees
in a hive he can't get out of, though whether in his sleep

or my own I don't know, never will now,
till he's kicked down the wooden stairs
to the door for the last time, and thereafter
the nothing at all he remembered.

Out on his own. Out on his ear at ten years
one month, from then a working man,
most of his days an itinerant unlettered landless labourer,
a spalpeen in the English north country counting pennies.

Asked, he'd blaze into anger, subside into long silence,
till we buried him, weary, still angry,
angry for ever under the great map of the stars.
Unfinished, as everything is. As this is.'

Mike Smith

POUND

But came to me then   a vision

which I carried, though it pleased
me not, this reef and wrack,
resting place riding as it seized,
sudden, upon my back.

But came to me then and stayed:
The poem as canvas, dried and rot,
a worn-out, faded sailor's cot.
Clearly I saw then   and was afraid.

My father-in-law, Dr. Arndt,
met you once, not long before your release
in 58, while you held forth, pell-mell,
on the front lawns of St. Elizabeth's.
(Murray, not Walter, the butcher
of my beloved *Faust*.) Murray,
English professor and Salvatorian priest,
before he left a decade later
with that great American exodus, that
bold act which led, among other things,
to his granddaughter, Virginia, being born.
Virginia Marguerite, named
for two of her grandmothers.
In the Italian way. Virginia Marguerite.

He told me this on our way home
from Parke County, Amish Country, your
country once (before you shipped, were shipped out),
where we'd gone shopping for a chair
and to look around, had passed
on the road, seconds before,
two authentic horse-drawn buggies
with Indiana plates.

(Behind us, the great
golden sun dipping down,
wine-red bubble
under the back window blade.)

My favorite image of you
is in Rapallo, captured
opposite a middle-aged Robert Lowell
then included in Mariani's
uneven biography. A couple
of bona-fide reprobates, and you're
thin, thin as a rail, dressed neat in blacks and whites
and silver beard, but seem, for once,
almost at home in the world.

(Bald farms,
                    and this roadside wreath.)

He was teaching Christ and Bible then
at Catholic. You were a field trip
for bored students and peers
who saw you, if they saw you
at all, as sworn shock-jock and traitor,
the one-time editor of Eliot, then
committed enemy of banks and Jews.

Ah, what you were in life, you're less
and less in death, but per
this enterprise, bedeviler,
what would you make? I confess
I don't know what to make.

So this.

But then to set oneself (to be beset),
braced against the endless,
unquestioning present
and its all-embracing style? With this,

besotted with word-shadows, then the numb
clutch of madness (re: crutch), little thought
given to the suffering few
I hold dear, proceeding bankrupt, unheeded

and unheeding, poem after poem,
the poems like ciphers decoded,
then forwarded on in code? Is it dross,
this madness? Is it new? Is it mine?

> (It's been thirteen years since I first
> read you, 13 years but I still
> haven't read them all. For that,
> I weep, and am glad.)

And how should this obsession end, how
should it best be ended? With such hurried
speech, peppered with tricks
and the usual suspect questions?

With this pre-pressed image, a time-stripped
and faded glimpse, the stretched corner
of some abandoned, untraveled world:

Up and well and shipped out, the crack(ed) mind
capped against swells and the chill wind,
ship's prow ahead, the mast behind?

> (But to have done this much
> instead of not doing . . .)

The pitch (past pitch) and the price:
The true returns are endless.

stress *truth* stress *loss* (i.e. *the* loss)
which means Time. Venerandam,

then the catch . . .

Stellasue at *Rattle* sends
her succinct blessings. She writes
these "epigraphs are wonderful," but comments
she felt she could serve me best
if I sent her some of my "own work."

(A man of no fortune and with a name to come . . .)

Rapallo, now there's somewhere
I'd like to sail to and see.

The poem is an anagram of Ezra Pound's "Canto I."

Lisa M. Steinman

POTATOES, CABBAGES, LEEKS, PLAGUE, WAR

a meditation on a line from Pascal about wretchedness

What *was* the man thinking? Why cabbages
and leeks? Like potatoes, rock solid.
You'd think a mathematician would play
by the numbers: simple, compound, or

imaginary. A child by the civic
monument yells, "Hey, wait. Look. Art," then
hops between the pavement squares, singing
"Step on a crack. Break . . ."

Diving danger in the concrete, he walks
on slight fractures, but counts on the familiar,
practicing a tactful forensics. His mother
diagnoses herself with obsessive-

compulsive disorder and incipient
Alzheimer's. A sad state when you cannot
re-call what you're compelled to repeat.
Cabbages, leeks, potatoes. Compounded

of dirt and sun, tough green sprouts shrug off
the soil. Then plants, flowers, hung improbably
with small green lantern-like globes. Between
the rows, in the path, a small stone appears:

no, a potato, no, two, three, five,
eight, no: bouquets of potatoes,
hand gathered by forays—brief as
the body's delicate hold—on earth.

Are potatoes part of hunger then?
Hunger, sharp as blue cheese on bread with wine
fiery red as the sun on the south coast
from which it comes. The coast smells of fish and brine

in the town where an ordinary young man
pumps gas. He leans in windows, ominous
and amiable, giving change and judging
women's legs. He'll go fishing tomorrow.

If he were asked he'd say he loves his job,
which changes day to day, talk and money
passing back and forth. There's no reason to think
satisfaction is less complicated than desire.

Here, look: there's two more people on the town
sidewalk. His once-blond gray hair is
slicked back; he struts a little. His name
would be something like Dutch. He calls her "Mother."

After the army, he found a job fixing
small appliances. Heavy-set, she's just had
her hair done. You can tell she is pleased
with her new, bright green synthetic stretch pants.

They are holding hands absent-mindedly,
long-time companions. They are not thinking
about their complex compact of hands,
solid as solace, meat and potatoes.

No plague. No war. And not so simple:
meat and potatoes, cabbages, leeks. Mothers
and children, all falling through the cracks
of light where you'd least expect it.

Stephanie Strickland

WAVESON.NETS 14–18

WaveSon.net 14

and 5, she mapped, who veers
as she flies, who carries the tilted earth
on her back. This is hallucinated hearing
in the service of art, of Arthur's table,

R2, Artemis,
and Ursa guarding the Pole.
Welcome, then, Presence, Reflection, Shadow,
Refraction, She Who Stands,

Gnova, Gnomon, Goose, Ouzel, Orca, Longdark,
Hardware, Software, Wetware, a Dolphin
leaping, responding
to the bare boy on her back.

For a crown is a cradle.
Wings are conical baskets of grain, baskets of fish
slung from her shoulders.

WaveSon.net 15

She will apportion, determine, sustain
and guard,
Our She, if she keeps her cards going,
if she makes her pack,

if she burns the string figure holes in their backs,
peepholes to heaven, to check
on heaven and to check
heaven. If she serves

her mother, the Goose who is flying
into the gap, who uses
a hook, the hooked jaw of a salmon,
to tat, to get

from one side
to the other, a bird's only task
beyond keeping track,

WaveSon.net 16

a hook which appears
in the fourth year, the year
of its spawning,
the Year of its Leaping, dying, not eating, falling

apart as it travels up, flails
to breed.
Feel her power in bird or stone, or in her eyes
or breasts, alone, or even in

her hieroglyphs.
There is a woman in a conical hat.
When we chain her waist
with dice and cards,

a punished witch. The Jack of Knaves
comes up at 128, the one
who stole

WaveSon.net 17

her tart. She will sit
on a bird
or a broom. Or an axle-tree.
Or a mill wheel grinding.

She keeps time
timely, and you know her: Green, Great Circle, Noon.
My computer tells me
2:32

PM and so salutes her. Not P,
of course. Of courses, M
the *Maîtresse* (VV
reversed, please imagine), M the standard without which—

M not mother, but an anchorage, Anchoress, arbitrary
necessary prime first,
Royally

WaveSon.net 18

observed,
at the Green-wi( )ch
meridian.
A bee lives 28 days, that vaginal cadence,

nose swollen in honey.
The tree rings itself with another ring each year
and in its hollow live the bears—a world
tree closes. Major

and Minor, they circle the hole,
dipping honey from the hollow
at the tilted top
of the northern world, Polaris, star at the very end

of the Little Bear's tale.
To know
there is a pole, a polar axis to the earth

Marcela Sulak

COMFORTS OF HOME

When I buy vegetables I prefer to be in my country rather than yours—
though in my country, they are not so juicy and fancifully shaped—
crescent moon carrots, radish hearts.

I prefer to find you in a place your vocabulary carves
a secret door through which I can enter or escape.
Where syntax is not a floodlight on my blinded tongue.

I prefer to be here, where I do not have to lie, to say I'm married and my man
is the jealous type. He's with the police, and my father is the ambassador.
Here I am not a bare field in need of a flag.

In my country I am just like all the others and it is you who are different.
In my country, you don't recognize me or know where I live.
I can stare back. And when I smile, it means whatever I want it to.

Brian Swann

ESCHATOLOGY

The small body discovers the body dies, but
If it were a blackbird it would come back
Year after year and not stay down.
It is aware the world has seams.

Later yearning in hard dark, she has
The hummingbird fly out of its epidermis
As a lover would to feel the leaving,
And from the peel another bird double back

Into a rainbow. It is lovely, the whole range.
Now it will be alright. The world will race
And glow again like rivers. Imagine: All it takes is,
"What shall I tell myself?" And you have

A photo of a place you've never been
That takes you there, rapt in calm and quiet,
Intense and aureate, part of an evolving
Conversation that includes chasms that close

When you look at them, like in a fairytale,
And open too, done and undone the same,
And what was sitting on your chest
To stop your breath is now a marvel

You can enter as if it were ordinary,
Somewhere in a future that does not punish
But continues in different weather,
Much the same as this.

Brian Teare

POEM BETWEEN LINE BREAKS

[Why?]

So that after, every kiss could become metaphor but a metaphor for what?

[The old one—his body
a house? His body of locked rooms
and his brother inside?]

Okay. Here is the door—

[hollow, cheap pine
rickety with holes and how will it hold, how
will it hold the telling—]

where the brother tests the knob

[(locked) and behind that,
the room
where the boy looks up from his story]

as if his point-of-view could mean something here.

I give you the house—

[pink siding, blue shag rug
in the basement bedrooms,
wood paneling, mildew
creeping through the grain—]

how pipes knock plaster loose in the ceiling.

I give you the brother,

[but not what leads him
to crouch here. Tell me, what moves you
most? Instinct? Gullet and hunger?
A door he knows he could break
if necessary?]

To make him more than his actions,

[would it matter to you?
Out of his fourth institution
in as many years,
he's stopped taking Lithium
because "it" isn't the "real" him.]

I doubt anyone—the family, the boy—is able to *see* him

[except as "really sick," a pain,
as in : Can we trust?
What to do with?*]*

Does that change things?

I want to know

[what makes him make me tell
this story, the one
where I can't lie]

no matter how improbable the outcome.

The boy being young, the brother drunk,

[you must understand that the first
kiss does not so much begin here
as that it merely grows in probability.]

The boy afraid—

[long fibrillation, air conducting
the shock—the sound of the lock
being picked—panic prolonging
the breakage . . .]

What happens next is easiest—

[his brother fucking him—]

afterward is more difficult.

There are many reasons for this.

[Their parents in the room
above, not hearing
it happen, not making it real.]

Does that change things?

And what of that, the not-hearing?

[Because before that no story,
no metaphor, a body
a body, his brother his
brother. And even being fucked
just that : plain
pain predicated on correct
grammar, syntax : subject
verb object.]

And what of blame?

Perhaps you say "A moment like this, it—*easy*—is not possible,"

[and I say "Yes, true : tell me who
and how." Say "I said easiest.
The boy never confused
until after—the long not-hearing
in which he will remember

a kiss came to be

a house made real forever—

his brother inside the room—

his body."]

Maria Terrone

REREADING THE HISTORY BOOK: CENTURIES XX AND XXI

The Dark Ages:
So many pages of childhood taken up
        by sleep.
    Some nights my eyes opened
        to gray light, a man and woman
                framed across the alleyway,
then replaced by a white wall
    until she returned, or he,
                to pass through the frame
alone. The satin slip she wore
        crisscrossing
    their room left an afterglow,
                a white X
stamped behind my eyes: do not
        read this text.

                Skip to

The Nuclear Age.
Page after page of warnings:
    Beware of chromosome X,
        aberrant.
Double X makes female,
            double-crossing Eve.
    A blue X marks the spot
where they blast your breast
                with that invisible
        skull and crossbones.
                You're sick,
so this may cure you;
        If x, then y:
    fossilized logic unearthed
from the Age of Reason.

Diane Thiel

CHANGELING

Bernhard had nothing but their names.
He'd come there on his own.
He asked and asked, but no one knew.
So many had come and gone.

The boy had followed others west
and walked much of the way.
In the leveled continent,
Dresden had been saved.

The city was filled with refugees
when the markers floated down,
cone-shaped like Christmas trees
lighting up the ground.

For this—the city had been saved,
the people suddenly knew.
They poured into their cellars. Someone
brought the boy below.

Beneath the ground, he couldn't see
the rain of fire fall,
but he could hear each bomb explode
and feel the buildings crumble.

The heat melted all it touched,
bodies before the stones,
carving out the Frauenkirche
down to her catacombs.

Between three raids that night and day,
survivors left their cellars
and faced the burning homes next door
caved in at their centers.

The streets were heavy with rock and ash
as another search began—
turning over coats to find them
holding skeletons.

Alone in the hollowed city, Father
wrote on the church in chalk:
Where are you, Paul and Hedel Thiel?
I live. Bernhard

Ryan G. Van Cleave

ORUS, THE FALLEN ANGEL: AFTER DALI'S *ATAVISTIC VESTIGES AFTER THE RAIN*

Even God has a hole through his heart, an impurity like the
interworked spirals
that are the flesh of sky, the interlacing of bright worn smooth by
years of overuse.

With his son by the hand, the man points at the dark brook before
them, the water
deep and fast-moving with the faces of their dead like memory-
photographs

that cannot be destroyed; symphonic the horizon, how the light
shines even when
we are gone, its elaborate copper craftsmanship appealing and
dangerous,

like an unknown religion full of Celtic rituals and engirdled with
blood sacrifices.
The city ghosting from sight like the sleep's feisty door is darker
now than before,

the fading light dancing slow like the floor of a funhouse that
suddenly gives way.
Skin of animals, the vowels of reddish brick dust—surely there is
only enough time

for one last messiah. Ice, fire, whimper and bang, in the
trumpeting sky of fire,
the tide gushes back in a glassy wash of fish, and the cosmos comes
together,

its final headline: tender, frightening, the blossom of life bristles
foolish, still red.

Anthony Walton

TRAFFIC

Because we had walked, anonymous
past the barkers and grifters
the bootleg
            and jewel merchants
            of Broadway

past street cafes on Bleecker
                                on Spring

through a street fair that closed down
La Guardia
            only to swim the crowded Sunday
            of Sixth Avenue

            an empty bench in Union Square
            looked like landfall

Matter through matter
matter through space
here we are proving the world is matter
in motion
            here we are
            floating, alive, holding

each other like driftwood
through the wreck of an afternoon

working at being simultaneous
in the entropy of Manhattan

                the misses, near-misses
and collisions:
buses, pedestrians, the subway
rumbling underground—atoms, photons, buildings

how you see it is a matter of scale
and perspective

while the light changes, then the weather, the seasons
and, soon enough, us

All this matter, all these small defeats of decay
accidents of fate and grace

All this matter and so many souls
so many souls to face
                                        as I sit here so still
                                        and in transit

That leaves you, here, so still and oddly
with me
                how odd it is
                to be here in this photon mist
                of sunlight
                twilight
                streetlight

Marlys West

BALLAD OF THE SUBCONTRACTOR

During his senior year, Frances won every blue ribbon
Debate. *Every debate, Frances?* "Yes,
Yes, I won them
All," he answered with no false modesty and no true
Modesty, either. Our Frances argued the death penalty fifty

Times that year. He was like a star quarterback but
Smaller, brighter. Odd to think of it,
Now that the workers who deserted are finally
Caught, I mean. We threw them in the lift, debated
Knocking them around
A bit. Their manifold arguments

Will accentuate those you already
Have. The cranes broke loose, they said. *Not likely.*
They lost our papers, hammers flew over the edge. Pneumatic
Drills advised them to do as they were told
In the old country. Frances liked to open each debate with

A rhetorical question. "Imagine, for a minute," he would say,
"That you are on death row." Closing his eyes, Frances
Shivered. It was his best
Debate; he won both sides over,
And over. He'd bend and sway; clasp his hands. I can't
Recall his ever giving me a cigarette for my smoking

Pleasure. The electricians who cursed us were finally
Sorry. During my junior year, Frances led
The team to a championship and carried a gold-plated
Trophy home. His role
Complimented mine. I won nothing back
In the day. Frances took everything and then

Some. Judges met to welcome
A new champion who
Understood the industrial and ritual uses of
Metal. The industrial uses of steel as building fabric, exoskeleton,
Are many, but the damage
Was done. Since then I've been altogether too
Busy, working overtime, really, to thank him, but events have born out my
Fears and
Predictions. *You break a strike, you pay for it*
In spades, in the blocked road. In spite

Of the many arguments
Offered by those in favor of unions, I have
No opinion. In one
Corner a pile of bricks, in another
A jacket of Copper. Spatial order, but also, chronological
In that the bricks came first and the
Copper went up last with wired bits of glass so
That the foam of the capitol illuminates

The sun-blocked day and night.
This is my part in the skyline
Renovation project, brought to
You by someone or other, *those mugs,* money
Swindlers, fat cats, pocket shimmers, someone, I would
Guess, like that windbag Frances.

Eric G. Wilson

THE PERATAE, THOSE WHO PASS THROUGH

In the middle of the second century, on certain clear nights
at the core of summer, between one and two in the morning,
when the heat for an instant returned to the absent sun, when
the stars reflected a curious light hiding behind the darkness,
the Peratae, those who pass through, abandoned the walls
of Alexandria and walked out into the desert.
Called by the Christians, Gnostics, ones who know,
these nocturnal pilgrims burned beyond their flickering
hearts for the boreal sky, for Draco the serpent around
the axis coiled, cool portal to the fullness above wounded
sons and caves that lacerate, blood and stone.
To the sidereal snake, aloof as snow, the insubstantial soul rose,
through the scales it slid, husking away flecks of flesh,
through the threshold, now free of petty godlings and star-guards,
now around the first tree again entwined, near
the beginning now and now close to the end—ouroboros,
serpent curved to perfect hoop, caducuceus, two torqued to one.
Down again descends the soul to the hot heart but the vessels
are for a time soothed to calm vision: sand turns luminous
flakes, crystal reticulations: ice in Egypt. The invisible wick of the world
freezes. Unheated light everywhere shines. There is nothing that is not seen.
All was dream until the sun once more scorched its furious morning
over the skin, softer than night, and the hard grains.

David Wojahn

POST-DYNASTIC

Not all the Greek and Roman-era mummies
    are as carelessly prepared, though a specimen
        from Oxyrhynchus is a case in point:

the frontal portrait is a young man with a beard,
    but CAT-scans show inside a female, arthritis-wracked,
        approximately seventy years old. Is this

how you'd begin: "theory—they were mummified
    together, wrapped on the same day"?
        Their portraits, switched through carelessness

when sewn against the unguent-smelling faces.
    Such is the decline. You would tell me even the good
        seems arbitrary: for example, the carefully

fashioned artificial leg of Pepi-Ankh,
    a priest or scribe of no great consequence,
        who'd lost his real one in life, or to jackals

as he snoozed unresurrected in
    the preparation tents. (The salting with the natron,
        after all, took thirty days.) "Consider

the surprise of Pepi-Ankh . . ." who arises
    unhobbled in the Western Lands, and as his sins
        are weighed on Thoth's great creaking scale,

he can stand at least on both feet. Is this
    how it would go? The decline
        of the embalmer's art by Ptolemaic times

is everywhere in evidence. The cedar oil,
    the clove-paste, cinammon and myrrh, canopic jars
        of hearts and livers swimming in palm wine:

all replaced by cotton batting. "The cats
and ibises, the linen-wrapped pet snakes . . ."
—For what is Paradise without electric

pricks of fur along a sandalled foot,
forked tongues to beat tatoos up jewelled arms?—
all excluded. And only surfaces

are dignified: more post-modern than post-
dynastic. And what beyond this?
The bandaging techniques, evolving

to bizarre complexity. In the most
elaborate style the bandages criss-cross
diagonally, forming up to a hundred squares,

gold coins sewn to the mummy's skin beneath,
so gilt can seem to pulse from every square,
giving the impression that the mummy is

entirely bedecked with gold, twelve or thirteen
bandage layers on some—resplendent,
though unscrupulous embalmers could

replace the coins with yellow stucco buttons.
Pocket money—who would know? The bereaved
are always easy to deceive. . . . Would this

have been the poem you'd planned to write? The notes
just starting in the final months' entries,
along with, everywhere, pain? Nothing

substantial yet: just spidery jittery swirl,
and March five underlining *"grave goods, unguent,*
entropy (?)." And *"Memory of the morgue in Boston Hospital,*

finding it by accident when visiting T. . . ."
And glued to March eight a postcard, caption
set down in purple ink: "alabaster

canopic jars for Princess Sit-Hathor. . . . "You seem
to be writing it fast. . . . "*The jars*
should have contained the princess's

internal organs, but instead are filled
with lumps of mud and cedar pitch, the work"
—the letters formed more slowly now—

"of irresponsible embalmers."
Then something scribbled out. Then, *"how to connect*
with T . . . ?" How the bereaved

deceive themselves. Boston when? And who
is T? What shape of the room, and the light
raining down on the flat ones being washed

with sponges by a man in rubber gloves,
and he places a sponge on a face as he coughs.
He's not even half-way down the line.

The tide of silver pallets and the thirty-six closed eyes.
White stubble on their scalps and shaven genitals,
they give him their commands. And is it now

he turns to see you? Tell me, is it now?

Baron Wormser

BERNARD BARUCH

When I was a boy, people were always talking about
Bernard Baruch the Wall

Street wizard who unofficially advised presidents,
made a fortune for himself and sat

On a park bench from whence he tossed his wisdom
upon the queasy tides of human events.

He was always in the newspapers
where his considered yet snappy quotes

About how to give everyone a share
in the pie called "America" made

First-rate, things-are-looking-up copy
and he was always being photographed

On that park bench, an urbane yet somehow bucolic
philosopher who was securely rich

And hence credible because a poor man couldn't
have known much—if he did he would

Have been a rich man. When the wizard died
there were various encomia,

Though not from my Uncle Sidney who, though he'd never
met the gentleman, pronounced Mr.

Baruch a self-important windbag whose notion
of civic virtue had more to do

With preserving the prerogatives of finance capitalism
than altruism.
Sidney was an intelligent

But embittered schoolteacher who wanted to become
a trial lawyer but owing to

The circumstances of the Great Depression
found himself spending his

Life appraising tenth graders' inchoate essays about
Machiavelli and Pericles.

When Sidney died there were no telegrams from
politicians, corporate titans,

Or financiers.
Sidney hated the glib tone of newspapers.
His scruples were incorrigible.

I wanted to ask him what it all mattered.
Bernard Baruch would never visit

His stuffy, overheated classroom. Instead I listened
and thought at times I heard inside Sidney's

Clockwork rants about who got noticed in this
money-hungry world and who didn't

And who read Herodotus and Plutarch
and who knew them only as names,

Something more frightfully prideful
than either wealth or hurt.

Charles Wright

HIGH COUNTRY CANTICLE

The shroud has no pockets, the northern Italians say.
Let go, live your life,
                                        the grave has no sunny corners—
Deadfall and windfall, the aphoristic undertow
Of high water, deep snow in the hills,
Everything's benediction, bright wingrush of grace.

Spring moves through the late May heat
                                                            as though someone were poling it.

WAKING UP AFTER THE STORM

It's midnight. The cloud-glacier breaks up,
Thunder-step echoes off to the east,
                                                            and flashes like hoof sparks.
Someone on horseback leaving my dream.

Senseless to wonder who it might be, and what he took.
Senseless to rummage around in the light-blind stars.
                                                                                    Already
The full moon is one eye too many.

NIGHT THOUGHTS UNDER A CHINA MOON

Out here, where the clouds pass without end,
One could walk in any direction till water cut the trail,
The Hunter Gracchus in his long body
                                                                approaching along the waves
Each time in his journey west of west.

MORNING OCCURRENCE AT XANADU

Swallows are flying grief-circles over their featherless young,
Night-dropped and dead on the wooden steps.
The aspen leaves have turned grey,
slapped by the hard, west wind.

Someone who knows how little he knows
Is like the man who comes to a clearing in the forest,
and sees the light spikes,
And suddenly senses how happy his life has been.

Martha Zweig

COUNTER-FABLE

Dear preposterous
grasshopper of opposite-
angled knees, glitch, insistent screed
of disproportionate bliss, I put my trust
in domestic economy once, eschewed
excess of appetite & disrepute, kicked the likes-of-
you con-over-career—

I recant. Field pillagers, who conspicuously
overrun the locale, welcome!—infest my circumspect
securities & exchange, day-in-day-out
pester askew the topiary hedges. Offertory: I
resign my estate. Do I quibble some? then shrilly
buzzknuckles-&-shins
dismember & remind me.

What hideous best bug
face any one of you puts on & tilts
to fool me, will. Fill
of folly I laid up long ago exhales: stale
meadowy breath exhuming out of the crib & dry
disintegrating bales, savory yet of the odd blossom,
grass sex, inimical thistle. Choked down

mostly what exhaustible bowl of dust I get, is why I
crave more, why scrape the floor, next attic
shelves, hurl spinning
hats into the shoe trees. Strum cheek-
by-my-jowl any green musician at all!—instigate in my crawl
spaces fiendish undoings, strip my stewardly
jacket & leggings for tatters & wings.

PROSE

~

Chimamanda Ngozi Adichie

RECAPTURED SPIRITS

I am not the image of Africa, not like those sun-blackened, AIDS-ravaged people flashed across the evening news on ABC or CBS once in a while. My students look surprised the first time they ask where I am from, why I have an accent, and I tell them Nigeria. Sometimes some of them ask, the ones who want to show off how cosmopolitan they are: Are you from Lagos, the capital? I say yes, but it is not the capital anymore, Abuja is. Then they ask, what's Lagos like? And I say Lagos is like New York City, only Lagos doesn't have as many skyscrapers and New York City doesn't have as many street beggars.

I don't say more, don't say that my comparison is superficial, don't explain that Lagos is a city unlike any other, a city of rubbish dumps and fierce dreams and exhaust fumes. I don't say either that although I was born and grew up in Lagos, I am not really from Lagos. My students will hardly understand, they are wide-eyed young people who protest causes they do not fully grasp, who accept all my comparisons, who have been in the tri-state area all their lives.

But Bibi is different. Bibi, with her dreadlocks snaking down to her neck, streaked with gray even though she just turned twenty-one. Maybe it's the gray—the wisdom—that first struck me when she walked into my class a week into term in a kente-print top asking if she could add the class. It was the last day for Add-Drop; I never signed Add-Drop forms on the last day. Her top was loose fitting and she was clutching hard cover books to her chest, yet I imagined the cone-shaped rise of her breasts when I said, Yes of course, and signed the Add-Drop form.

And now, it is she who asks the first questions, who comes by my office with an extra can of Pepsi to peek in and ask, You busy? She who asked me once what Lagos was really like.

And I told her that the beggars look like caterpillars with stumps for arms and legs, sliding on boards at busy intersections, weaving between closely packed cars. That markets spring up and run the lengths of streets, their make-shift shelves crammed with tinned milk and cigarettes and in the evenings, the traders light kerosene lamps and bathe the streets in topaz. That in shantytowns people have houses made of zinc or cardboard, next to open gutters clogged with the rubbish that the same people throw in them. That only miles away, sleek compounds are outlined by palm trees, their gardens burst with red Ixora clusters and their gates topped with spiky wire are so high you can only guess the color of the mansions behind.

Bibi nodded that day, as though she knew Lagos. And I knew that with any other student I would have said something else, like—Lagos is like a mix of the worst of North Bronx and the best of the snazzy suburbs near New Jersey.

I am drafting my questions for finals today but when Bibi peeks in and asks, You busy? I say no, quickly, too quickly. She has some questions about Achebe and Soyinka, she says, sitting down. My office is so cramped I can feel her legs next to mine, underneath the table. I imagine slowly pressing my legs to hers.

She runs her hand across the piece of sculpture on my desk, the smooth, oval face, the long neck. I've always wondered what this is, she says.

My grandmother's god, I say.

Bibi's eyes widen. Your grandmother's god? Really?

I open the windows, because the air conditioners in Hurley Hall blow hot air. It's a long, fractured story, and I don't know where to start.

I have the whole day, Bibi says.

My Nigerian grandmother had two gods, one visible and one not, and my British mother wanted me to know both. How's that for a start?

Bibi smiles teasingly, says it would make a great thesis.

My mother was concerned that I stumbled when I spoke Igbo. St. Mary's School didn't help; the Irish missionary nuns didn't teach any indigenous languages and the offense of Speaking in Vernacular earned you detention. Once at a PTA meeting, my mother asked that Igbo or Yoruba or even Hausa be included in the curriculum, like in the government schools. They gave her strange looks because few British citizens, even those married to Nigerians, wore Nigerian nationalism so brightly. Then they told her learning the vernacular in school would confuse students.

So to make sure I did not become insipid, I received a yearly dose of culture. It was my mother's idea. Each Christmas, when my parents took me on the six hour drive to Abagana, the village where my grandmother lived, the village where I *really* come from, I would sulk in the backseat and say no thank you to each offer of biscuits or *gala*. I wanted to spend Christmas in Lagos, to go to the parties our neighbors had, where they strung green electric lights in their hedges, where Father Christmas came and gave out presents in plastic bags—toy cars for boys, white dolls for girls, sometimes Superman and Wonderwoman underwear thrown in for good measure.

I knew we were almost at my grandmother's when we got off the expressway and drove on a dirt road so bumpy the Volvo grazed the sun-baked soil and screeched. Mango and *Ugba* trees bordered the wide compound as though hugging it, protecting it. They cast mysterious shadows across the compound, filled it with the pulpy smell of ripe mangos and the crackling sound of ripening *ugba* pods. You could still see the faint patterns of fingers used to mold the lumpy mud wall that encircled the compound.

My grandmother would stand in the front yard and make a loud hooting sound, something like, "Wuuuuu!" She hugged my mother first, then my father, and finally me, the longest and tightest. She smelled so strongly of cassava that I held my breath the first few minutes. An eager neighbor would wash the red soil off the Volvo and then my parents would go off to the Holiday Inn in Onitsha for the rest of the week. These are my mother's words—we need to go and recapture our spirits, dear, we can only do it alone—when I asked why I couldn't come with them. Her British accent made it seem so formal, as though there would be a printed program with elegant lettering for recapturing their spirits.

Wasn't your mother being British the reason you didn't learn Igbo at home? Bibi asks, as though to say—You're being too easy on your white mother.

Step outside the status quo, I write often on the margins of Bibi's critical papers, because they are too precise, too safe, too predictable. Once, I wanted to write, Let go of your inhibitions, but I didn't.

Bibi has the sculpture in her lap, caressing it as one would the head of a new-born child. Do I tell her how my mother took me to the shantytowns in Ajegunle to give out old clothes because she distrusted the bureaucracy of St Vincent De Paul? Do I tell Bibi how protective of my grandmother's gods—both of them—my mother was? How she argued with my father when he said it was wrong for his mother to go to church and still worship the wooden thing in the backyard? But I will be careful, or Bibi will label her paternalistic.

We spoke English at home because of my mother. My father didn't speak a lot of Igbo because he said he lost his train of thought when she kept saying, "Say that again more slowly." Although, he could have simply said it again more slowly and we could have spoken more Igbo at home. And we lived in Lagos too, our neighbors were Yoruba and Lebanese and Indian and Israeli. It was like mixing different tea bags. At the end you don't get any of the individual tastes, you don't even get tea. Still, my mother tried. I remember our neighbor pinching his nose shut to mimic her British rendition of Igbo. She wore wrappers often, too, although her behind, flat as a dinner plate, could not hold the wrappers up.

Bibi smiles and I know that she is satisfied—I have been loyal enough to my white mother without vindicating her completely.

Say something in Igbo, Bibi says.

Isi adikwa gi mma? Are you crazy?

Bibi laughs. Her tiny teeth are so widely spaced, she will never need to use toothpicks. I imagine the tip of my tongue trying to lodge in between those wide spaces, my saliva mixing with hers.

Igbo was what my grandmother could make sensible conversation in, and it was what her neighbor shouted, in lilting strings, from the house across the mud compound wall. It was what the worn black Bible—the Catholic version with the deuterocanonical books—in the living room was written in, although my grandmother could not read. Even the rusting metal gate of her compound spoke Igbo, the creaking, sing-song sound it made when it swung open was like an Igbo Gregorian chant. There was constantly the high-low sound of that creaking every Christmas, behind all the other noises—goats bleating, children whooping, chickens clucking, adults talking. Neighbors strolled in to gossip. Friends home for the holidays parked their city cars outside the gate and came in to *gba Kristmas* for my grandmother with noisy turkeys, legs tied together, or fat yams so fresh that clumps of soil still clung to them. Mama Nnukwu—big mother—everyone called my grandmother. Funny because she was a tiny woman, bent over like a withered stick, a black Mother Teresa. She referred to herself in the third person.

"Come and greet Mama Nnukwu," she would say, before clasping me in her thin arms, pressing me against her bare, flat breasts and the smell of cassava.

"Help Mama Nnukwu take this bag into the house," she would say before leading the way inside.

The house had been built in the early twenties right about the time when, according to my father, the first Irish missionaries built St. Paul's on Mission Road. It was refurbished often but it still felt crumbly. I did not touch the walls or lean too hard against the door because I was afraid they would dissolve. My grandfather looked down from the living room wall, in a wood-framed photo so grainy he looked like he had no nose. He wore a flowing caftan and white shoes that continued, curving upwards, long after his feet stopped. Mama Nnukwu boasted every Christmas that the first white priest in our parts, the first *fada,* had given them to him. It was only special people that the Irish priests had given shoes.

What did you do for the week? Bibi asks. What did you do with Mama Nnukwu? She does a pretty good job of pronouncing "nnukwu." She is learning Fanti from a Ghanaian hairdresser in Brooklyn; she wants to do the Peace Corps in Ghana. I wanted to go to South America until I registered for your class, she told me once, and I've fallen in love with African Literature. On sleepless, sweaty nights, I have taken to replaying her words and replacing "African Literature" with "you."

My week revolved around Mama Nnukwu's kitchen, a small building yards from the house, big enough to hold a table, four chairs, and a food store where bags of rice and beans, yams, cassava bundles, and bunches of plantains lolled. It was where the other little cousins and I ate, talked, laughed, and cried, seated on raffia mats spread on the floor because the chairs were for the grown-ups. It was close to the other small building in the yard, the compact-like-a-matchbox building with the pit latrine at the center. My first Christmas there, when I was eight, I started to cry at the sight of that pit latrine, at the fragile dynamics of squatting without seating over that stark hole. I imagined I would fall into a sea of brown feces dotted with fat white maggots. Mama Nnukwu said matter of factly that the hole was too small to swallow me, that even the new baby goat could not fall in. It had wandered in there the other day, by the way, she added.

The goats wandered a lot around the yard, they wandered in, too, while we cousins bathed, scrubbing with *ogbo* that my grandmother made from sun-dried coconut husks, scooping water from a metal bucket. We bathed near the vegetable garden, in the space enclosed with zinc left over from the last house refurbishing. Mama Nnukwu would shoo the goats away from the vines of *ugu* and beans that crept up those zinc walls, clucking, clapping her hands.

You all showered together? Bibi asks. She straightens her legs and I feel their heat, their smoothness, next to mine. I wonder if she can feel the hair on mine, if she can tell that I have never shaved my legs, that I dream of showering with her and watching her shave hers.

Bathing together and sharing the buckets saved water. And the older cousins could help scrub the younger ones, to make sure they got at their backs and between their legs. The year I saw the python, though, I was old enough to scrub myself. I was following a chicken as it dug around the herbs in Mama Nnukwu's spicy-smelling plot, scattering the sand. Next, it pecked at wrinkled cassava peels spread on an old mat to dry, it even pecked at the black balls of goat droppings scattered around. Then it entered the zinc-enclosed shower space.

The python was coiled in a corner, the corner where we placed the extra buckets of water while we bathed. Over and over on itself like a pile of car tires. I screamed. Snakes didn't hear, because it kept sitting there. I dashed out, back to the kitchen in the backyard. My grandmother was sitting beside a sooty pot over the firewood-fed fire, she was breaking *ugu* leaves into little bits and throwing them into the pot.

"Mama Nnukwu! There is a snake!" I had forgotten the Igbo word for snake and so I said *snake,* in English. Mama Nnukwu could say the Hail Mary and Lord's Prayer in English, she had to know what *snake* meant. She did not even drop the *ugu* leaves in panic. She simply said, "Come with me."

Her breasts hung down her chest like flat slippers. She tightened the wrapper on her waist before walking up to the python, hands clasped behind her, bent almost double now, as though approaching a superior.

"*Nna,* Father," she said. "Please leave. We are honored that you have come but the child is scared. Please leave. I know you do not want to scare children."

The python slowly uncoiled. I was sure it would lunge for Mama Nnukwu, for daring to talk to it. But it simply slithered away from us, towards the compound walls and out through the hole in the mud wall made for draining during the heavy floods.

"It is taboo to harm the pythons," Mama Nnukwu said. "Our ancestors dwell in their bodies."

"Did it understand you?"

"Of course," Mama Nnukwu said, a little impatiently. "The ancestors always understand."

That night, the python appeared as I tossed and turned on the mat. It hissed but instead of the spiked tongue I expected in a snake, bursts of fire flew from its mouth. It started to take the shape of an ancestor, a stooped, bald male—that was the image I had of an ancestor. I had seen the hands dotted with age spots, the skin wrinkled and tough like palm fronds, when I woke up, screaming.

"It is only a dream . . . only a dream . . ." Mama Nnukwu was saying, holding me up, pressing my face to her bare chest. I had not even heard her come in. She took me by the hand to the backyard to pee by the Mango tree and then we lay back on her mat. It was a hot night and she left the door open. The sound of the night crickets floated in. *Krii-krii-krii.*

"The python appeared to me," I said.

"It means the ancestors are protecting you."

"But how can our ancestor be in a snake? Snakes are bad, a snake made Eve eat the apple," I said in Igbo. I remembered the word for snake now. *Agwo.*

"Close your eyes and sleep."

Oh my God, Bibi says, widening her eyes so much that I can easily tell where her hazel contact lenses start. She is still caressing the sculpture, almost meditatively, and I imagine that it is one of my now-south-bound breasts, the nipple hardening to Bibi's touch.

Mama Nnukwu arranged an outing the next day, to get my mind off the python. She wanted me to see the masquerades as they paraded past the main road, on their way to town for the *Ipia Agba* festival. She had taken me last year, and had roughly pinched my lips against my teeth when I asked if she knew the men behind the masks and costumes. I could see mud-encrusted black trousers peeking out underneath the raffia skirts.

"Don't speak loudly," she had muttered, "they are not people! They are spirits come from the land of the dead!"

But Mama Nnukwu was expecting guests that afternoon and so Uche would take me. The other cousins would come too. Sister Uche, we little cousins were required to call her because calling her just Uche was disrespectful and she was in her late teens, not quite old enough to earn Aunty Uche. Sister Uche liked to pull at me. She would pull my dress and say, "Is this from overseas?" Or pull my lips and say, "Can't you say any Igbo word right?" That afternoon, she didn't pull at me because Mama Nnukwu was there. She said she knew a shortcut to the main road, and we started off. Milky cobwebs swung from the trees, the ground was undulating and rough; I had to look down to determine how high I would raise my leg for each successive step. Two little cousins stumbled.

"*Osiso!* Hurry up!" Sister Uche said often.

We walked and walked. Sister Uche was starting to look worried, I saw balls of sweat on her upper lip, above the glaring lipstick she had smudged on after we left Mama Nnukwu's compound. I wanted to cry because we were lost and then, horror of horrors, I suddenly needed to go. Bad. Right there and then.

"I have to ease myself," I said, in a small voice.

Sister Uche stopped. "Okay, go right there."

I shook my head. It was not urinating, I said, it was *nsi*.

Sister Uche wrinkled her nose as though she could already smell the *nsi*. Then she asked the other little cousins to wait and led me further into the interweaving of trees, with branches hanging down, straining to catch at my dress. She said I had to hurry up. I pulled up my dress, pulled down my underwear, and stooped. I was woozy, afraid I would topple over backward, afraid that some of it had touched my shoes, purple flats my mother had gotten at Harrod's last Easter. Sister Uche looked around and gestured to a tree. "Take one there. It is the smoothest."

"What?"

"Take one leaf and wipe."

"A leaf?"

Sister Uche had grown impatient. She plucked a leaf from a tree nearby and handed it to me. I took it, still squatting. I did not have a choice, I thought longingly of my mother's purses, of the scented tissue she always carried in them.

Bibi smiles shortly and then stops. It is so like her, I can look in her eyes and see them accusingly spell Bourgeoisie. No cliché of ideas or thoughts, I often tell my students when I give writing assignments. Yet once I told Bibi, Something may seem wrong at first until you try it and realize how right it is. It is the closest I have ever come to telling her how I feel. She'd stared at me blankly for a moment before pointing at her paper and asking something. I still wonder if she knew, if she was too afraid to show that she knew.

Uche had to be mistaken about the smoothness of the leaf because it had hidden ridges on it, spiky, wicked things that left me so sore and itchy. I hobbled through our thicket wanderings until we came to the main road. The masquerades that paraded past were menacing enough, wielding long whips, lifelike masks glowering, strange bells jangling from their ankles. But I was distracted, I was hopping from leg to leg, thinking of new muscles to contract to ease the itching, thinking how horrified my mother would be if she knew I had sneaked a hand into my underwear in public. I told Mama Nnukwu as soon as we got back and Sister Uche had gone off to give the little cousins a bath.

"Bend down," she said. She pulled my dress up and my underwear down in one swift movement. She examined, prodded, pried. It was the *elimonu* leaf, she declared. What was Uche thinking, you never used an *elimonu* leaf to wipe.

"At least your mind was not occupied by the python," she said, with a sly smile, before opening her tin of palm oil and pouring generously into her palm. She asked me to bend over again, pulled down the underwear I had hastily pulled up, and spread the palm oil on me. I felt the orange-red oil dripping on my pink St. Michael's underwear and felt the itching, the crazy, prickly itching, stop immediately.

Later that evening, Mama Nnukwu scolded Sister Uche in Igbo too rapid for me to follow. And the next morning, Sister Uche yanked my ear as she gave the little cousins a bath, harder than the usual pulls, so hard that my gold earring stopper fell off. I was on my knees, combing through the red soil for the miniature metal long after Sister Uche had taken the rest of the cousins into the house to shine their skin with Vaseline. I did not find my earring stopper and I fixed the plastic bit of an old pen behind my earring. I would not have told Mama Nnukwu about the earring stopper if she had not noticed.

"Where is the thing that holds your earring behind your ear?" she asked when I came out. She was feeding the goats, throwing cassava peels into the narrow thatch-enclosed pen where the goats had clustered.

"It fell when I was getting dressed."

"Tell Mama Nnukwu the truth."

She already knew. She knew things. "Sister Uche pulled my ear."

"Did your mother buy the earring from across the oceans? In the country of her birth?"

"Yes. When we went to England to see my other grandmother."

I sat on the edge of the mat, my legs stretched out on the red earth. The soil was different here, thicker. In Lagos, it was faded, as though the rich red had been leached away by the sweat of millions of people.

"Uche should not have pulled your ear. She cannot go across the oceans to get another earring," Mama Nnukwu said.

"Mummy said we will go to England next Easter. Maybe she will buy me another pair."

Mama Nnukwu grunted, and gently pushed a young black and white goat, just weaned from its mother, towards a cassava peel.

"Maybe you can come with us, Mama Nnukwu," I said, and when she said nothing and kept throwing the peels down, I asked, "When will you come with us to England?"

Mama Nnukwu looked up. "See that lizard over there? When it starts to grow fur."

I laughed. It was funnier because she did not laugh.

Later, she roasted thin tubers of yam on the dying fire beneath her pot and scraped the blackened skin off with a knife. We ate from a plate she placed between us on the mat, dipping the yam into a bowl of palm oil floating with red peppers. The yard was silent except for the shuffling of the goats as they wrestled for the brown cassava peels and I prayed that the gate would not swing open in that sing-song way to shatter our peace. After lunch, I trailed her as she went to the tiny thatch shrine tucked away behind the kitchen. It was so low that even she, stooped as she was, had to bend to get in. I crawled in behind her. I had never been in the shrine, Mama Nnukwu did not let anyone in with her, she always said, "Wait for me," when any of us grandchildren tried to follow her in.

I waited for her to say, "Wait for me,"—to ask me to leave, but she didn't.

Two statues stood on the mud ledge. The Blessed Virgin Mary, a miniature of the life-size marble that towered in the front yard of St. Mary's, crushed the head of a snake with bare white feet peeking out under an azure cape. Next to it stood a wooden, unadorned bust painted a wet, glistening black, like patent leather. It had narrow, feminine features. A long head shaped like a slightly curved cucumber.

Bibi holds up the sculpture, as though to check my descriptions against the actual object. Her eyes are dreamy, half-closed. So this is something real, she says, stressing real, as though she expects it to open its eyes. And for a moment I am amused, and I hold back my laughter. I wonder what

Bibi will say, now, if I suddenly stop and tell her that what I am really trying to say is that between the old and the new, there is—there can be—a balance, a middle ground. That sexuality, like religion and race, is a continuum. Will Bibi sneer? Laugh? Agree? Storm out of my office?

Mama Nnukwu was muttering something, face down, as I examined the bust. This was what my father called lifeless wood when he had the arguments with my mother. "She has a right to worship what she's comfortable with," my mother would say.

"How can you say that?" my father would say, starting to stammer. "It's easy for you to say, your English mother is safely Christian."

And then my mother would laugh without really opening her mouth and say, "But what about your grandfather and his father? They weren't safely Christian."

I wondered then what Mama Nnukwu would think if I told her about my parents' arguments. I had the sudden urge to tell her, but instead I asked, "Do you like my mother, Mama Nnukwu?"

Mama Nnukwu turned to look at me.

"I want to know if you dislike her," I said.

"Don't you know that if I dislike her, or something in her, I will have to dislike you, and that same thing in you?"

It was the kind of moment when you realize something, when something dawns on you, abruptly like a person throwing your comforter off you on a winter night when the heater is acting up, but you don't recognize it until many years later. We were silent for a while, while Mama Nnukwu continued to mutter inaudibly.

"In catechism class, Brother Gilbert said God is jealous. God would be jealous that you have that statue," I said.

"God did not tell Brother Gilbert that."

"What about the *fada* in church? Doesn't he say to throw away all the wooden gods?"

Mama Nnukwu grunted, carefully breaking up the piece of yam in her hand. She had saved it as we ate, the softest piece from the center of the tuber.

"When your grandfather became a Christian," she started after a long silence, "the *fada* asked him to throw his *chi* away. So he hacked down his shrine with a machete, and burned the thatch. But his *chi,* he took it into the woods, behind the farm, and built a new shrine there."

I stared at my grandmother's face, at the lines and furrows criss-crossing it. A grown-up never told a child about another grown-up not following instructions, surely Mama Nnukwu knew that. It meant encouraging the child to flout instructions, it meant encouraging dissent in the child.

"Why didn't grandfather throw the wooden god away like the *fada* asked him to?" I asked.

She did not answer. She threw the last piece of yam at the foot of the statue, muttered slow, indistinguishable words. Then she turned to the door, and asked that I be careful not to bump into the ledge. A rosary dangled from the edge of the ledge. Its black beads were as round and shiny as the droppings that carpeted the goat pen.

Bibi puts the sculpture back on the table, with both hands, letting her hands stay for a while on it even after it is on the table. Her contact lenses have darkened to bronze. Do you remember anything else from that Christmas? she asks. As if she knows it was my last dose of culture, that I still try to remember things, things like the smell of the goats. The particular way the goats smelled that Christmas. Maybe she does know, maybe we were meant to be, our souls paired long before birth, mine leaving soul-land some years before Bibi's. (I permit myself one incredulous thought a day.)

The next Christmas, the year of my first period and the year of the Pope's historic visit to Nigeria, I was packed when my parents told me I would not be going to my grandmother's. It was the first time I had actually wanted to go. Mama Nnukwu was sick, they said at the same time as though they had rehearsed it. Her legs. She refused to see a doctor, she was eating herbs, she could not walk. I wanted to see her, yet at the same time, I did not want to. She could no longer negotiate with a python, could no longer feed the goats or crawl in to talk to the Blessed Virgin and the gleaming bust at the same time.

"So you won't get to go recapture your spirits?" I asked my mother when we were alone. She shook her head and her stringy blond hair caught the dirt-studded Lagos sunlight that streamed through our kitchen window.

"I think we've done all the recapturing and capturing we need," she said and smiled in that brave, bittersweet way that hides tears but lets you know that it hides tears. She smiled a lot that way two weeks later, as we drove the six-hour distance for the funeral. People filled Mama Nnukwu's yard, like many Christmases fused together, so many people my father decided to dismantle the creaking little gate to make it easier for them to come in. The requiem mass was said in the yard because the village church was too small. It was during the service that I took the black bust and slipped it in my bag.

Oh, but you *totally* had to, Bibi says, a little dramatically. She has picked up the bust and has it pressed to her chest. I feel an absurd pride, that I have entertained her, that we have not discussed Literature. That, perhaps, after exams, I will tell her other fractions of this story, and other stories that will lead to us, end with us.

We should leave the room to discuss Achebe and Soyinka, I say.

Jarda Cervenka

THE STRANGE RESTORATION OF J.A. SPLINTER

Until the arrival of Jan Andrew Splinter, the most memorable events in the life of the village would have been the typhoon with its eye right overhead, and one earthquake that measured 7.8 on the Richter scale. His coming was as unexpected as the volcanic quake. He fell out of an old U.S. Army surplus jeep in front of the Chief's hut, stretched, then helped the diminutive driver to unload an enormous red duffel bag with "Eddie Bauer" on it. So Eddie, people thought (those few who got the courage to approach with a smile). The tall pale stranger smiled too, and then shook the left hand of old Manolo, whose right hand was saving his falling pants.

"Eddie! Señor Eddie," Manolo beamed, and people nodded.

"Buenas tardes, padre," Jan widened his grin, actually bowed, and then climbed the stairs to the Chief's veranda. At the top of the stairs he turned around, descended, and asked Manolo to keep an eye on his Eddie Bauer bag. You never know. When he climbed up the stairs again, the Chief (who had been watching between the planks of his hut) stood there with a serious face like a mask, in a red T-shirt that said, "Vegetarians Taste Better."

They proceeded to greet each other with some formality while more villagers arrived to form a welcoming crowd. People gesticulated; some raised eyebrows; some opened their eyes widely; some opened their mouths widely; some shook their heads from side to side, while others nodded. They all exuded the excitement of bashful insecurity. The American had arrived.

Splinter's elegant spiral of DNA, his genetic endowment, was solely responsible for his sinewy build, his sandy noncompliant hair and impressive height—the traits ran in the family on his mother's side. Ma towered over her husband by half a foot, like most Scandinavian females would tower over most non-Scandinavian males. She was Norwegian, and Jan's father was of Bohemian extraction. He'd changed his Slavic name by simply translating it to English. It was better that way, in northern Minnesota, he surmised. But Mother towered over her hubby in her intellect, too, and since Father was no rocket-fuel scientist but still a proud enough male, family relations suffered. This caused Jan to search for a college that was geographically farthest from his home town.

Jan enrolled in a medium-sized school in the northwestern corner of Washington and double-majored in agriculture and botany. It was a solid and respectable achievement, of which he was justly proud. Cool. So he'd left the school with good feelings, despite a couple of regrets: no love story, and no real friend. He was wise and observant enough to understand that if had he not found a true friend in college, he would have opportunities to find only acquaintances, in the future.

It was his nature that served him so well in studies, but not so well when around a bunch of pals passing a joint at a beer party. Too serious, they said about him; a stickler for details bordering on spasticity, keen on particulars, those printed in small type on a page, and in life, too. He looked for perfection where perfection was not the goal. And he knew it, and tried to change, and when he tried, it came out so phony that everything inside him screamed *bullshit,* and he ran to the study or the library, alone.

All that said, he had been accepted well enough, because he was a good man. Helpful, sincere he was, not a trace of a mean streak in him. A good kid, that Splinter boy. Peace Corps material? Sure thing.

Jan did see the past as a mirage of placid days filled with study, but did not suffer from lack of dreams. So he decided that before committing himself to a career in the corporate world of uncertainty, he would join the Peace Corps and spend a year or two in the Third World of uncertainty, saving that meager three grand a year, but doing more for mankind than if he were at Monsanto. Because agriculture is the most-demanded specialty in the Peace Corps, he was accepted on the first shy try, despite some doubts by the elders on the admission committee about his ability to adjust to cultures remote from ours. Privately, he was warned by an old hand, to avoid there any excesses "in venere et baccho." Yeah—already ancient Latins knew these dangers to homo ludens and homo explorans, the wise man said. Jan could get really screwed in the Third World, man, and even more in the Fourth World, by fooling around and not paying attention.

~ Those unblessed ones who've ever fallen in love with village beauties would recognize some of their common and some uncommon traits and attributes: her facial components were in symmetric harmony and balance. There were no flaring auricles, dominant nose, nor pronounced Oriental epicanthi, but one would notice that her lips were exceptionally full. Facing her, one would vividly imagine them nesting a kiss, entrapping it in their wet snare, and one would go on imagining and dreaming about it, regardless of the topic of conversation or the importance of the matters of the moment. Her hair was simply the hair of her people: a mane of straight, plentiful wires, charcoal black, with the gloss of a black panther emerging from a jungle stream. She was of slender build, but her rump and breasts, that duo of anatomic parts commonly desired by males, were clearly present and could be envisaged to be of unaccustomed cartilaginous firmness, their caramel-hued and caramel-sweet surfaces silky smooth. They were always concealed by a sarong-like wraparound, the heritage of fanatical missionaries, those masters at induction of shame and guilt.

Her hands were interesting in their deception: the long, gracefully slender fingers were upper class, high society, but the view from the palmar side revealed four horny calluses, each the size of a penny, each the badge of callus-making labor. Her feet were just regular, beaten-up rural tootsies that had never ventured to explode inside the darkness of a shoe. The big toes were spread widely apart, as in hominid apes, and Jan marveled at what he'd got into, looking at them. They would never fit into a shoe (pumps? ha!), with the exception of Eskimo kamiks or illigamaks.

Often he would catch a glimpse of her in the village hurrying around with a wide basket on her head, erect like an amanita mushroom on the go, or lumbering under a load of firewood, a beast of burden—till she looked up. Never a strain would show on her sweatless face, and never would the load affect her graceful gait. So he thought about her, evenings, and allowed her to enter his dreams, where she dispersed images from his past like a barracuda hitting a school of fat, content pinfish.

The first impression he could make of her at close range came a couple of months into his stay. He was working on his project, planting a thousand seedlings of mahogany up Kunde Hill. He had half-fulfilled his work-plan for the day, planting a perfect twelfth row with even spacing. The villagers had helped him to clear part of the jungle on the hill next to a creek that would provide water for the seedlings.

A flock of women lumbered down Kunde with their loads of firewood, and stopped to watch the American, while pretending to drink from the stream. Jan approached her with some trepidation and asked whether the water was good to drink. Just a request for information, no smiles, and some would say that their following verbal encounter lacked sophistication.

"Is good, Señor Eddie."

"I am Jan, not Eddie, you know."

"Ia'n Eddie!" She smiled so that his stomach constricted and his heart fluttered in dangerous fibrillations.

"Well . . ." he said. "And what is your name?"

"Carmencita my name."

"Carmencita is a very pretty name," he said, grateful that he could say "pretty" to her. They exchanged two, three simple sentences and Jan, aware of the close scrutiny of the other women, went back to his mahoganies, humming and smiling while hiding their roots into the rusty laterite sprinkled with his sweat in the 95% relative humidity and the 95°F heat. When he stretched, he cheered the violin-bird displaying its plumes on the ravenea musicalis palm and marveled at the resplendent iridescence of the morpho butterfly homing at his neck, seduced by the scent of his sweat. He smelled, with exaltation, the sweet vanilla perfume from a spray of blossoms of the brasavola orchid swaying in the breeze like a roost of white minimal roosters. He took it all in with all his senses, this botanical Eden.

She was gone. He was alone. So at the green wall of the jungle he hollered: "Ain't bad, kid!" He flicked a drop of sweat from the tip of his nose. "Not bad at all!"

~ Jan Andrew Splinter was getting used to everything that comes with the tropics: tedious food, often more like bait than a meal; rough climate, diarrhea and skin fungus, and, frequently, the overwhelming kindness of the natives. He rejoiced in discovering his fellow villagers, their patient resourcefulness, their ability to do much with what little was available. Lozio had glued together the twenty shards of glass from the cylinder of a shattered hurricane lamp. Roberto had fixed the tiny clasp on Jan's camera by multiple feather-gentle touches of a two-pound sheet-metal hammer on an iron nail. Jan marveled at the many uses of Superglue (Jan's present to them) when mixed with fine sand, and more. The villagers took to technical imports with ingenuity and relish, but the cultural inventions of the outer world they rejected in confusion and often with a resentment of mysterious origin. This had been demonstrated to Jan most dramatically in the Affair Carmencita.

After the rainy season ended, Jan decided to chance it. One afternoon he waited for her at the end of the beach where he knew she would go at low tide to collect crustaceans and anything else that moved on the exposed reef. The creatures of the tidal pools were an important source of nutrition, since all the fish had been dynamited out. The beach, a ribbon of subdued gun-gray, was narrow, despite the low tide. It was bordered by a belt of salt-loving vegetation that made a wall hiding the village. From the Bogota-emerald belt, the coconut palms shot up to the sky, then curved above the water in gracefully audacious arches and bends. The tidal current made the water murky along the shore—only at the deepest part of the lagoon, by the barrier of coral reef, did the water clear to green and blues reflecting the moods of the sky. He used to come here sometimes to watch the killdeers, the sandpipers in their hunt for sand-lice, the brown pelicans like archeopteryx skipping inches above the lagoon, and the magnificent frigate-birds, perfect birds high above it all. Sometimes he dreamt of home.

When she waded onto the shore, he asked her to come see him in his hut tonight. He would cook for her a delicacy of his own invention: freshwater prawns from the creek near his mahoganies, steamed in banana beer. He would have breadfruit baked in platano leaves; she would certainly like it. He smacked his lips and generated a smile he thought to be irresistibly seductive despite his cracked lower lip. She looked down at the ground, then walked away whispering something like a chant. Or a promise?

That evening Jan waited in a newly washed T-shirt (Minnesota Twins), went to urinate three times, repeatedly combed his unruly hair, and rechecked the breadfruit in the open-pit fire in his outdoor "kitchen." Then she appeared next to him, all of a sudden, an ethereal apparition of the kind that, when touched, would disappear. He shook her hand several times and was moved to see that she was wearing a necklace of white cowry shells that he had never seen on her before, and that she had painted her lips with a reddish dye. He was astounded by the difference this meager tool of diluvial cosmetics made.

He rushed the prawns onto a steamer of his own design, and soon they were eating in silence, sitting not on the floor but at his hand-hewn table, facing each other. She looked apprehensive and did not respond to his simplistic small talk. At one moment she looked as if on the verge of tears; he did not know why and was afraid to ask, not knowing why he was afraid. *But the shrimps were great, anyway, goddamn it,* he thought, being a kind of Pollyanna man, out of necessity.

She left him after eating the prawns and the last tiny crumb of breadfruit, saying "Buenas noches, Eddie, it was muy rico." She tried to smile and then touched his forearm with the tips of her piano-player digits and moved her fingers down his arm as lightly as a dermatologist would pet a puppy. *The hell,* he thought, because a lump in his throat prevented him from talking. *The hell,* he thought, because she disappeared.

The next day he looked for her in all the places and niches she might be found, but without success. By evening, he'd noticed that the neighbors seemed to avoid meeting his eyes. Even old Manolo, his cheerful friend, would alter the direction of his stroll, on seeing Jan in his path, and the widow Margarita "Mirabal" averted her peek faster than when meeting the gaze of a spitting cobra. Only the dogs looked him straight in the eye; some even wiggled their tails; to them he was known as "the one who does not kick." So after several days of nervous gloom on the Island of Zombies, and no explanation forthcoming, Jan decided to see the Chief and ask what was his disease, was it as contagious as ebola? As repulsive as lepro-matous leprosy?

The evening before the planned visit to the Big Man, two young men walked into Jan's hut without the customary calling out of a greeting from outside. They stood by the door motionless and did not seem to notice Jan's welcoming gesture offering them a seat. Jan knew one of them; he was the oldest of seven brothers of Carmencita. The other, in his late twenties perhaps, was certainly a stranger in the village. He wore a sneer of disgust on his face which might not actually have been disgust since it was a result of a scar pulling one corner of his mouth downwards. He wore a baseball cap with the visor backwards, common sandals of tiretreads, black jeans, and a faded flower-patterned shirt with the collar turned up. Carmencita's brother talked to this man in their native ngolong, while the stranger translated into fairly good English, not Spanish.

"Eddie, we came to tell you," the tough fellow started, without the customary polite hesitation. "Know Carmencita? . . . It is sad. You maybe disgraced her, maybe you did not." His grin remained unchanged; his eyes looked at Jan calmly, but there was no steel, no snake hypnosis in them. There might have been amusement in those coal beads. Jan's hands began to tremble, so he folded them on his chest, then unfolded them to motion the visitors to sit down, again. They did not pay attention.

The brother said a few words to his companion in ngolong, which he interpreted. "It has been decided here, in this village, that you shall marry her." Toughie paused and contorted his lips. It was a smile, no doubt. Again the brother talked.

"You must marry her before the new moon. Come tomorrow to talk to her father and grandfather! That's what her brother here said."

There was a long silence. Maybe all was said. Jan wiped sweat from his eyes and turned his head, watching a brown moth fluttering across the room, hitting the wall. *The moth was trapped,* he thought. His nose started to run.

Carmencita's brother raised his voice, in anger it seemed, talking now in ngolong full of wildness directly to Jan. He ended, then opened his mouth widely, revealing two rows of perfect brown teeth, and stuffed his fist in his mouth, extruding his eyeballs in a frightening, enraged grimace. Jan stepped backwards and almost fell tripping over the kitchen stool. The brother turned abruptly and marched away, leaving the stranger behind to translate. Jan tried to control his tremor.

"He said that if you try to leave, to escape, you know, before marrying, you'll be caught. That is certain. Then your balls, las bollas, amigo, will be cut off. Then your balls will be stuffed into your mouth, and you will suffocate. That is what will happen!" The stranger turned, shuffled to the door, but stopped and returned with a scowl resembling an acceptable smile on the left side of his lips, but a sneer, scar-side.

"You see, that will be my job! Ha, Eddie? So you don't worry about . . . suffocation. You die before that . . . suffocation, mi amigo." The man seemed to be in a pleasant disposition now. "You'll die of . . .," he could not come up with a word, bent his head down thinking, shaking his forearm up and down. "Yeah, yeah, Eddie. You'd die first of terror, yes . . . t e r r o r!"

So there was a joyous wedding in the village of the Peace Corps volunteer Jan Andrew Splinter and his Carmencita, lovely (and virginal to boot). The marriage rites happened two nights before the new moon and, to the day, on the anniversary of Jan's arrival with the Eddie Bauer duffelbag. During the wedding, the groom oscillated from a bout of depressive stupor lasting several minutes to an exaggerated exuberance (of equally short duration) when he would scream songs with the locals, his fist flying up high in rejection of threatening gloom, accompanied by a bellow of some college profanity. In a solitary, quiet moment when everybody lay plastered, he leaned back on a tree, looked at his bride surrounded by old women and by the envious eyes of the young ones, mumbled "unbelievable," and remembered reaching this place a year ago with the thought that he was entering Tropical Cultures 101. He howled quietly, being certain, now, that he was not in a classroom.

"My shitting days are over; my shitting days are over," he repeated, without much linguistic imagination. He did not know, exactly, how he felt—but it was not a pukka sahib satisfaction. For that, his stomach was too giddy and his throat too constricted. He cheered up a little when a disorganized squadron of flying foxes, fruit bats, passed above, crapping on the guests and squealing at Jan: "Go, Eddie, go!" he was sure. It was a blue-bright night, hopeful for them, too.

During the ceremony and the festivities, it was impressed on Jan that he had become one of them. Now, Eddie, you are one of us, some told him cheerfully, and a few told him gravely. Then the "tuba," the palm wine, cut him down too. When he recovered, he would walk his bride, hand in hand, to his hut, despite the rule that she should walk a few steps behind him.

"Fuck the rule," he told her with the sweetest smile he could muster at that late hour, stumbled a few times, and to himself mumbled "this is goddamned exciting," before he collapsed on the four-poster bed of his own construction, only to wake up at light with a tuba-headache to find his wife (wow! wife?) lying on the split bamboo floor next to his bed like a vagrant on a subway grid. He lay down next to her.

~ Carmencita had grown up in a village that lacked philosophers, scholars of high learning, and social scientists. So she, like everybody else, knew that there were only three things essential for life: intake of fluids, sex, and food. Without one of them, life and life's renewal would cease. With a scarcity of one of them, life would not be normal, and the soul and body would be diseased. This had been passed down through the generations and well proven by cruel experiments of Nature. That was what she knew.

She had, however, been instructed by her mother that coitus was for procreation. Jan, of course, was determined to become a tutor in sex solely for non-procreation and, on the way, maybe to learn a thing or two himself. Since the behavior of lovers must be so refined as to result in the greatest mutual joy and laughter known to man, it cannot be hurried—nor, gods forbidding, coerced. The first lesson. Fortunately, she lacked deleterious bashfulness, and soon it became obvious that in her genetic makeup she carried a gene encoding for natural gregariousness in matters of intimacy, and also for plain love of fun. And Jan was a good boy, too, so the gods decided to reward them with friendship and intense liking for each other, which they knew was rarer than love and therefore considered by some as more precious. Not long into their relationship, Jan and Carmencita graduated from speaking from their brains to speaking from their hearts. It was a new and astonishing experience for both of them.

Food was another matter to be explored. Carmencita smacked her generous lips over the "mashed potatoes" Jan made, not mashing potatoes but mashing pounded yams with hot goat's milk. She liked Jan's bread, made of flourized manioc with yeast from well-fermented palm wine, baked in the pit with hot stones. Of course, the freshwater prawns steamed over banana beer were the hands-down all-time favorite. While Carmencita's cooking was mostly directed toward replenishing calories, in time Jan learned from her the sophistication of simplicity. A hen cooked in coconut milk and hot peppers was on the top of the list.

~ Drinks, as we know them, were a problem. But there was this invention that the Peacenik was so proud of, and both of them enjoyed it with glee and hilarity after they got used to each other. Jan mixed several day-old portions of tuba-wine with a little sweet guanabana juice and a dash of coconut milk, and re-fermented it overnight. A quart of this bubbly would do very nicely, at night, after they'd bolted the door. Carmencita used to catch gigantic click-beetles that have two fluorescent spots on their thorax of such an intensity that they could light up their room in psychedelic patterns, and when they were seduced to land on her naked body, they illuminated her beauteous curves from angles that cannot be imagined, and when seen, would not be forgotten, ever.

About two weeks into their married existence, a seemingly insignificant episode marked the beginning of the period of their life that resembled an excursion of a tightrope walker on a windy night with violent gusts.

~ Canuto "Barbarito," the one with one milky opaque eye, ambled into Jan's hut just as the rain stopped. He was in a tense disposition, which could be judged from the deep color of his facial hemangioma—the large birthmark that changed in the intensity of its red according to Canuto's mood. Jan had always marveled at his habit of sitting in front of his hut with a clove of garlic in each nostril, watching the pelvic gyrations of the women pounding cassava with the total concentration of a scientist studying the behavior of an ant. Canuto was slightly "different."

"Presento, Eddie," he said. He would not accept the offered stool, but waited with a nervous smile, "el presento" in his outstretched hand. Carmencita busied herself, keeping her distance short enough to allow her to hear every word said. Canuto "Barbarito" unwrapped the banana leaf and showed them a foot-long pale sausage that looked like a subject from a dissecting room in a course on pathology. He explained to the stranger who knew so little about the ways of his people: a rare delicacy, to be savored slowly, this piece of dog's gut, the intestine of a dog who had been fed only boiled rice for a week, every day just sweet white rice, then killed and the gut washed on the outside and boiled shortly, to be eaten slowly, this delicacy.

Jan thanked, thanked, nodded slowly. Carmencita licked her lips in secret. On the way out, Canuto "Barbarito" stopped and, with both the good eye and the milky eye fixed on the floor, added "Señor Eddie, if it would be possible, I'd like to sit behind the driver of the airplane. I would like to watch him to steer the airplane."

"Which . . . airplane, Barbarito?"

"Oh, oh," sounded the old man, amused. He hacked, clearing his throat, percolating there the mucus generated by smoking since he was five years of age. But it could have been laughter. "Krch, chrch . . . when you take us with you to America. That plane, Señor Eddie. The airplane we will all fly with you!"

A few days after Canuto's visit (. . . *poor guy, losing his marbles in a bad way,* concluded Jan), Margartia "Mirabal," the widow, sauntered in. Jan liked this woman and was undeterred by her laugh, the laugh of a hyena, with her hindquarters low to match. "Mirabal," besides all the chores of a woman, had learned to cast the throw-net into the surf like a man, and better. And she could pee standing up, too. *Atta lady!* Jan thought.

The widow was followed by Maja Dog, her constant companion, the mutt with the face of a Tasmanian devil and the loving disposition of a boxer, who would never be eaten. The collapsible Maja Dog folded herself down onto the floor while Margartia "Mirabal" displayed a half-dozen eggs in a basket. She swore that they were about ready to hatch, in a day or two at most, so the fetuses would be just right when boiled. When eating them, just the tongue should recognize the heart, by taste the liver, and the brain through the crunchy skull. Oh, so good!

And by the way, she would like to take with her a couple of her best hens. So please, could Eddie reserve a place for the hens, on the American plane, so that she, the poor widow, could keep an eye on her "best hens." And of course, another matter, she could not leave her Maja Dog behind, alone in the deserted village. Please?

~ They would come bringing things, offering to repair the roof, the stairs—all sincere, kind people, believing every word Jan said, maybe, because Jan did not say many. Would he give a seat to Paeng, next to Juanita, since she is afraid of flying in the sky so high that one may see stars too close and, maybe, see the dangerous secrets of the moon. Jan could not sleep well any more. He spent more time in his nursery, made love only twice a week, and walked through the village fast, his gaze straight ahead. Now there was no reason for denying the obvious. Jan sent Carmencita on a mission to verify. Wide-eyed she confirmed that, yes, Eddie is one of us; he will take us all with him. How great will be the future of all the villagers, in America, while there is no future here, under Kunde Hill, after the villagers dynamited all the fish and the coral reef to smithereens. Oh, America!

In the Southern sky, the stars were very bright, strewn across the holes between the clouds as they rushed behind the hill from the west, predicting rain. The breeze danced with the tall coconuts but ignored the clump of rugged oil palms near Jan's shelter. By the ground, the air was still, and the hardened laterite clay returned back the heat it had received during the day with a wisp of earthy scent added. Jan evacuated the flying zone of night-biting mosquitoes on his porch and joined Carmencita inside.

Old Manolo eased himself in, shook hands with Jan several times, and nodded his head with a happy face. He was Jan's favorite story-teller, this elder who had welcomed him to a village a year ago. On the hand-hewn table Manolo put an object of Carmencita's admiration. "Wonderful! So, so tasty!" She sighed and sat in the corner. It was a pig's stomach filled with coagulated blood, chopped pig's snout, and a fistful of boiled rice and spices—mostly crushed leaves from the renako tree, the tree without bark. Manolo wondered how Jan would remember the seat assignments for all the villagers. He worried that his window-seat reservation might be forgotten. Jan and the visitor remained silent for a long time.

"Why do you want to go so much?" Jan asked, finally.

"Everything is so plentiful in America. Everything. Even things we can not imagine!"

"And how do you know that, Manolo?"

"G. I. Joe told me, in a bar in the capital after the war. He was tall like you, Eddie." Manolo smiled at his memory, since old people often smile, remembering the past, and rarely smile, foreseeing the future. "Unimaginable things, he told me, G. I. Joe." The soldier had told Manolo that, there, petrol flows underground everywhere, so that pumps cover the land like a strange forest, as far as one can see, and they pump day and night as if the iron forest sways in the wind. "G. I. Joe told me," Manolo remembered, "that they have so many mummies from Africa, they use them for stoking fires in the locomotives, their iron horses. Imagine that land!"

Jan tried to imagine that land—but failed. He shook hands with the visitor several times, knowing he could not disappoint Maolo, his surrogate uncle and almost a friend. He had to get to work.

In a dry place under the pandana-leaf roof, Jan kept three little treasures: one-year-old issues of *National Geographic, Geo,* and the magazine of Northwest Orient Airlines. He pulled out the airline publication. There it was: a Boeing 747-400 can take 418 passengers. A DC-10 will take 290. But the right capacity seemed to be the Boeing 757, with seating for 194 passengers, three seats on each side, and a range of 2875 miles at a cruising speed of 530 miles per hour at 30,000 feet. And Northwest Orient Airlines owned 48 of these beauties.

Jan reached behind one of the rafters, carefully (scorpions hide there). He kept a few small bags of native medicine there (all useless, he suspected by now) and, also, pieces of chalk to paint one's face for celebrations and the festival. With the chalk he drew the cabin of a Boeing 757 on the planks of the wall of his hut, as big as across all the wall, three seats on each side of the plane, all tourist class, with the aisle between the triplets of seats.

"Yeah, sure," Jan snickered, after reading in the magazine that ". . . our refurbished interiors, coupled with the outstanding technical expertise and genuine commitment to customer service of our people, will give you an exceptional experience." He shook his head. "Yeah, my people need an exceptional experience!" He said it to Carmencita, who had just walked in and gazed at the white outline of the aircraft and the names of Canuto, and Paeng next to Juanita, Manolo on the window seat, and others. She did not say a word, sat down next to Jan on the bed. They huddled together. Jan put his arm around her waist, his bare foot stepping lightly on her foot, both gestures as unknown in the village as was their destiny unknown to them. Would their fate be common to both, was the question they contemplated, without asking it aloud. They knew that once words escape the mouth, they cannot be called back.

~ Rodolfo was the oldest man in the village, and it was believed he would have had 105 grandchildren, if half of them would not have perished, as have all his wives and most of his friends. So, he lived in poverty greater than was common. He brought one egg, put it on the table, and slowly, carefully, sank down on the stool, his elephantine swollen legs spread apart. He looked at the seating plan on the wall, silently. He could not read, but still he could comprehend there were only a few places left unoccupied, by now. Jan thanked him for coming and for the egg.

"I like Americans, compadre Eddie." It was a proclamation of clear meaning from a mouth without teeth and with gums that had atrophied decades ago. His speech was slurred but understandable—his intentions, too.

"I know," Jan helped his visitor, smiling at this "presento," this gift of accolade and of praise the old man had brought. "And where have you known . . . Americans, don Rodolfo?"

~ "Right after the war ended, they arrived at a town near the capital. I was there shooting Japanese, too." Rodolfo's teary eyes wandered somewhere to the corner of the roof, acquiring a look of absentmindedness. He looked back in time, through the roof.

"They were so tall. We were babies, next to them. They liked us. They gave us tins of meat—but we did not know how to open them." Rodolfo turned his head from side to side. Jan offered the old man a banana, but he did not want to use his toothless gums in front of Jan.

"Once, they drove through the town on their trucks as big as houses, waving at us. The people were happy, amazed. We loved them much." A smile lit the ancient face, rearranging nicely the deep wrinkles and grooves. "They threw condoms at us. Ha . . . we chewed them because we thought they were Chicklets—chewing gum. We didn't know nothin'."

"A long time ago, don Rodolfo. You remember well."

"Many years. We learned much since then, we did. Later we knew how to put the rubbers on: they prevent disease, they do! But I remember how the American soldiers laughed, like our children. They leaned their heads back and showed their big white teeth."

"Why did they laugh? You did not say."

"Oh, when we told them we take the rubbers off when we are with the women. So much they laughed, we laughed with them."

Jan put the name Rodolfo on Seat C, 24th row, next to the aisle. He helped the visitor to get up. The viejo bowed and shuffled out, thanking him.

When Carmencita returned with firewood, Jan told her that the aisle seat would be good for the old-timer because of his bad legs. He could get in and out of the seat easier. But there was no window seat available anyway, none left at all, even if he wanted, but still. . . . She stopped Jan's stream of words; the logorrhea was painful to hear.

"What does it matter? Look at me! Look at me, Jan. What is it with you? You must know it is just a game the villagers play and Jan plays. Game, Jan!"

He paced from one wall to another, raised his arms and let them down again. "We will be landing in San Francisco. . . . There is a beautiful view: the bay, the bridge—beautiful. I would want Rodolfo to see it. He would be amazed. He loves Americans, you see!" Jan sat down, jumped up again, and paced across the room, raising his voice, raving now.

"It all got fucked up by the Chief. He has to have the whole of the first row, just for himself, all six goddamned seats for himself, he demands! The Chief, the Big Man. But they will teach him in the States, he'll see. But what can I do here? Nothing, nothing." Sweat dripped from his brows. Breathing hard, he turned to Carmencita, who watched her man first with incomprehension in her eyes, then with plain fear—fear of the unknown.

A sudden sadness seemed to calm Jan down. He sat on the stool, hanging his head down. "The bay, Golden Gate Bridge, windsurfers like . . . like splendid butterflies." He shook his head and let silence rule a while. Then he started whispering, but there was a melody to his raspy mutter:

"Be sure to wear . . . flowers . . . in your hair."

The tune was beautiful. The whispered melody became quieter, till it ceased. Jan looked up with eyes filled with tears. "I wanna go home." Like a baby. "Home!"

"It will be O. K., Jan, everything." She knelt in front of him, trying to look up at his face. "I'll make the soup you like, with bitter leaves, dried fish—and I have bamboo shoots, too." She straightened his hair and held it in place with her hand for quite a long time. When she started the fire in the fire-pit, tears fell on the embers and hissed. In a woman's life, there seem to be many tears. Mother had told her there are never enough tears to extinguish the fire completely, but, often, they douse the bright flame enough to leave it just smoldering.

Carmencita shed more tears in the coming weeks, because Jan became a different man from the one who had taken her to his hut, holding her hand, saying "fuck it" to the old customs, then holding her so gently.

When Uncle Yasis caught a big dorada behind the reef, she was invited, with Jan and most of the family on loan to him, for the feast. Jan praised the fish—wow, a thirty-pounder mahi-mahi bull, what a treat! Then he spoke less and less. While sitting down he gazed at one corner of the hut. All the people were happy, and Jan sat there staring into that corner, silent, in an aberrant way.

Later, one evening, he brought home dried fish and did not want to say where he'd got it. He stole a hoe and a shovel and hid them under his bed. He stopped watering his mahoganies and sat at home for hours watching the plane-plan, oblivious to the gecko lizard dashing up the aisle in pursuit of a honey-colored cucaracha on the pilot's seat. When he complained that, at night, secretly, somebody was sneaking into their hut and switching the seating assignments, Carmencita went to see her mother.

~ On March fifteenth, in Mangayas, north of the archipelago, the Muslim guerillas kidnapped Peace Corps volunteer Jim Presley from Prospect Park, Minnesota. His parents and younger sister, who had just arrived for a visit, were also taken. It appeared to be a well planned action, occurring at night, silently, no evidence of violence, no witnesses, no tracks. A written statement in both English and Spanish was left on the table, weighted down by a freshly cut monkey's head with a cigarette butt in its clenched teeth. The monkey still retained an expression of horror, and the statement was signed "Cobras for Freedom," the most ruthless faction of the independence movement, the true believers in Allah.

The wording of the note was not made public, but a brief summary delivered to the media after a two-day delay stated that unless the conditions of the kidnappers were met within a specified time (the time not announced in the press release), the lips of each and all of the hostages would be delivered to an undetermined location. If there was further delay in meeting the demands, the heads of the Americans would be delivered. Independencia Total o Muerte!

Intensive overnight communication between the American Embassy, the State Department, and the Peace Corps Headquarters in Washington, D.C., resulted in an unequivocal decision: the activities and presence of the Peace Corps organization in that country would cease without delay, and all volunteers would be recalled from their posts immediately. All, including the staff, would be transported to the United States by a plane chartered from a commercial airline. Local army and police personnel pledged total collaboration with the U.S. Embassy.

~ A covered army truck lumbered through the muddy path into the village where a naked boy, holding his little genitals in one hand, pulled his index finger out from his nostril and pointed with it to Jan's hut. The truck stopped there, and several soldiers with submachine guns spilled from the back. They were joined by one man in civilian clothes who slid down from the driver's cabin. In silence and without hesitation, they surrounded the hut as if on a well rehearsed mission.

Two military men and the civilian disappeared into Jan's cabin. It took just a short time till they re-emerged with Jan between them. One of the soldiers dragged the red Eddie Bauer duffel bag. They had to carry Jan up to the bed of the truck. He seemed to have no power to walk, much less to climb up. His face was expressionless. He tried to look back, tried to turn his head backwards.

People gathered. Mute, they huddled together as if against a cold wind. The truck departed in a hurry, and the people remained standing where they were, hesitant to move. There ruled a dead silence that even the birds seemed to heed. Only the palms rustled like dried bones. From Jan's hut a despairing wolf-like howl cut through that still air, then a muted wailing which made all the people hide in their shelters and only whisper.

After a torturous journey through the jungle, the truck came to a stop in a small town with a fishing harbor where a Navy launch awaited them. Jan was assisted down from the bed of the truck, stumbling, wide-eyed, unprotesting. He was allowed to go to the bathroom in the dinky harbor bar, "Titas de Ramona." A soldier just waved his hand and smiled at the pale catedratico.

The troopers were in a good mood. Somebody had had the presence of mind to bring a couple of sixpacks of Tsin Tao. Their task in this dangerous territory was almost completed. Marines from the gunboat were ready for the transfer of the American. They seemed eager to go. The powerful twin inboard diesels were started, the throttle checked.

"¡Singa!" a soldier exclaimed, running out of "Titas de Ramona," his tiny fist hitting his forehead above his bulging eyeballs. "Cono maricon!" Then another soldier of misfortune appeared: "Me cago en Dios! Hijo de puta!" Then "fuck it, singa, singa" in a dissonant chorus.

There was no American! Even the most inventive obscenities were not as much help as usual. Bedlam, pandemonium, panic and alarm ruled the local police, all to no avail. Jan A. Splinter had vanished, faded into the thin, hot air.

In the coming days, many sightings were rumored, many rumors were reported, many reports rumored. An announcement was made that a tall white man had been seen crossing Tuluan Bay on an outrigger, holding a trident—but another sighting on exactly the same day would have put him on the opposite side of the island, where a white man of enormous height had been seen coming down the Merunga volcano with a blowgun in his hand. The only officially corroborated report received by the authorities was of Carmencita Splinter. She had disappeared without a trace on the night of the half moon, together with the steamer for freshwater prawns and the shaving kit that Jan had forgotten in the hut. This last news, when it reached the Embassy of the United States of America, caused additional confusion, since there was no record of Splinter's marriage, not even an application for the appropriate marriage documents.

~ After years of keeping the case open, it was finally filed as "inactive." For the record it was stated that J. A. Splinter was missing permanently (?) and the search would be resumed if any new leads appeared, that Splinter's last recorded words were: "I need to take a crap. Badly." No further mention was made (and no last words recalled) of the native Carmencita.

~ In the village, everybody knew that Carmencita and Jan were far away, free and safe. Everybody was certain they would come back. Jan would complete his mission.

As time passed, first years then generations, things became even clearer and better understood. In each village hut there was an uncluttered bamboo stand on which a small supply of food was kept for the journey to America: dried copra, lychee fruit, water coconut perhaps. It would be replenished every week or so, and arranged nicely around two statuettes carved of soft balsa wood. One was the image of a woman with exaggerated buttocks and long hair painted black with a mixture of soot and coconut oil. The fetish of the man was much taller, with a bushy beard and waist-long hair painted with a mixture of chalk and oil in the hue of the rare orchid found only on the ancient sacred mahoganies that grew in perfect rows on Kunde Hill.

The coming of Eddie was indubitable. Old men, around the evening fire, would explain that Eddie would arrive on a tall white ship on the night when the moon was brightest and the ebb tide reached the palms. He would tower over the roofs, an ancient man with flowing white hair, and with him Carmencita, young and beautiful, in a sarong of pure silk, her almond eyes illuminating the night a thousand times brighter than fluorescing click-beetles. Eddie and Carmencita would give American presents to every woman, man, and child in a joyous festivity. And then Eddie would ask everybody if they were ready.

"Are you ready to fly with me?" he would ask in a big thunderous voice, his white hair like rays of moonlight, his big round eyes as blue as the sea behind the reef. "Are you ready to see the clouds underneath you, not above?" And he would laugh, because everybody would crouch down, terrified of the big, big voice. Then all of us would start to laugh with Eddie, too, and then would begin the time of great happiness and joy for all of us, happiness so excellent that we, now, cannot imagine it even in dreams.

~ So two new demi-gods were added to the multiculturally and politically correct (no doubt) gallery of deities and supernatural beings, between the ju-ju gods of the African forest and that soccer team of Hindu deities, among the bearded padres of Christians, Jews, and Mohammedans, as well as others from everywhere. For enlightening us in this matter, credit is due to famed anthropologists Mathias Spudich, Horse Przewalski, and Josh ("Bubele") Shapira who, in their collective study, demonstrated the expansion of the Eddie Bauer Cult into all coastal villages of the archipelago, and the rejection of the Cult in the more conservative and animistic interior. Also, they presented a learned discussion on the bizarre, but understandable popularity of this Cult of primitives in far-away Slovakia.

But it was Hanelore Wolavka, of the University of Wiena, in her painstakingly wissenschaftlich treatise ("Neure Erfahrungen, Untersuchungen, Beitrage and Bemerkungen über der fröliche Eddie Bauer Kult des Süd China See") who was able to isolate the defining characteristics of the fetishes of the Cult and thus elucidate the one most intriguing mystery of modern social anthropology. She postulated that the obvious youth and exaggerated buttocks of the female figure (steatopygia) characterized rapturous joy. The loss of pigment in the capital and facial hair of the male fetish (Eddie himself) represented wisdom and senility, and his hypertrophied penis, extending to the knees, represented favorable exuberance and hope (well, you know Hanelore). The widely stretched lips (a smile?) carved on all the fetishes in almost gruesome detail also suggested hopeful expectations—the defining attribute of the Eddie Bauer Cult.

Yanbing Chen

GENGHIS KHAN

I

"What's up?" Lee sounded as upbeat as ever at the other end of the line.

"Everything," I said. "Rent, tuition, phone bill, insurance, everything except my god-damned wage, still four twenty-five an hour."

"You still washing dishes at the school?"

"What else can I do?"

"Too bad," he said. There was a short silence, as if he were trying to think of a way to get me out of my lousy situation. "Do you have to work tonight?" he said after a while.

"No," I said. Tuesday was my only night off.

"Good. There's a new casino open in Joliet. You wan' go?"

"I don't have any money," I said.

"Fifty bucks's all you need. We don't play no big. You lose, you leave. But who knows, maybe we'll hit a jackpot and never have to work again."

"If you wanna go, go yourself."

"I can't. That piece'v junk of mine broke down last week. Think it as you do me a favor, OK?"

By the time we pulled into the huge parking lot outside The Empress Casino, it was already packed with Mercedes, BMWs, and Lincolns. But there were the other types as well: a rusty '78 Oldsmobile with its passenger's side window missing, an ancient beat-up Mustang, a shiny little Yugo. My car, of course, fitted more comfortably in their company.

Lee made his usual car talk as we cut through the parking lot.

"That's a good one." Lee patted the hood of a Continental convertible with the top down. "V-8 engine, turbo-charged, 120 miles an hour no problem."

"How about this?" I pointed at a red Renault parked next to it.

"Junk." He kicked its tire. "Don't ever buy a Renault in this country. They're all junks."

With all his knowledge, it was funny though, that Lee had bought one bad car after another. The problem, he explained, was not the lack of expertise, but that of money. "You can't buy a Rolls Royce for five hundred bucks."

The admission turned out to be fifteen dollars, something Lee claimed to be unheard of.

"Fifteen bucks just to get in?" Lee challenged the girl in the black and white uniform behind the counter, "In Las Vegas, they even gave me money to spend!"

"This ain't no Vegas, sir," the girl said, hands perched on the computer keyboard, eyes glued to the screen. "You decide if you want to go in or not. Next!"

That reduced my fortune-making fund by almost a third. With the quarter tokens barely filling the smallest cup, I headed straight to the slot machines. Lee said he was going to look around for a while, checking out the dealers at the Black Jack tables.

I wandered along the aisles, dropping a token here, a token there. Finally I settled down at a machine that spewed out twenty on my second try. All around, the only thing you heard was the sound of tokens spat out of the machines, clink, clank, clink, clank. . . . For a moment you would think everybody was winning. I read the instructions: 1 for blank, 2 for cherries, 5 for any 2 fruits . . . 80 for 3 bars . . . and three cherries, the Jackpot—$5623.75 . . . $5624.50 . . . $5625.25 . . . The figure in the electronic display kept increasing.

"Put in three at a time, then you can get it to pay at all three lines," a middle-aged man in overalls at the next machine said, a tip. But having only thirty-five dollars in the cup, I alternated—three times single, one double, three times single, one triple—hoping that would last me a little longer.

Lee and I met working at a restaurant in Chinatown two years ago. I was a busboy, and he a waiter. I had just come from China, and was enrolled at East-West as a Ph.D. candidate in philosophy. Though my tuition was prepaid with my application—a policy which I found out only later was rare in this country—the monthly rent of $250 for my sleeping room in a rundown apartment house on Sam Davis Avenue was making my money run out like rice in a leaking sack. I was, therefore, very grateful to the Cantonese owner of the restaurant when he hired me, asking for neither work permit nor experience. Three-thirty every afternoon, I rode a squeaking bike, which I had picked up for five bucks at a rummage sale, through the dozen blocks swarming with people of all nationalities to the restaurant lodged between a bakery and an oriental pharmacy on Wentworth, pondering all along the ontological differences between Spinoza and Confucius. Lee had been working there for several months. Originally from Hong Kong, he came to the States fifteen years ago. He spoke Cantonese, Hakka, but no Mandarin, so the two of us had to communicate through pidgin English, which he was very good at. Lee taught me how to set the table, how to fold napkins into flowers, how to carry six glasses in one hand and then put an ashtray on top; and later, how to wrap Moo Shu, how to serve champagne, and how to take the change back to the customer non-offensively when it was not enough for the tip. But the restaurant went out of business a few months later. Lee found another job across the street, while I, it being no longer possible to ride a bike in winter, moved to the dorm and settled down to washing dishes in the school cafeteria.

My first big hit was "three bars," 80, but it came on a single shot.

"See, I told you to put in three at a time. It would've been 240," the man in overalls said, shaking his head.

But I was happy enough with this windfall. Scooping the tokens into my cup, I looked around for Lee. He was nowhere in sight. Ignoring once again my neighbor's advice, I continued with my pattern.

When the bell burst into a blast at the other end of the floor, I had altogether three decent hits, one 50, another 80, and one 160—finally caught one with two tokens.

The bell kept on.

"What's that?" I asked the man in overalls, who had stopped feeding the machine and was looking towards the other end.

"Somebody's hit a jackpot," he said. I followed his eyes and saw a little red light above one of the machines flashing and spinning like the kind on top of an ambulance.

"Really?" I asked.

"Oh, yeah," he said. Slowly, the corners of his mouth lifted into a grin, as if he himself were only beginning to understand the meaning of his own announcement.

"How much you think it is?"

"Oh, those are the dollar machines. Must be quite a lot. I've been here all the time since this morning and haven't heard the bell ring till now. Go and check it out."

I went over.

"Fuck . . ." Lee was grumbling two machines away from the one that was making all the noise.

"That was mine," he said, pointing to the old Latino lady sitting in front of the winning machine like a stone corpse, staring at the three 7s centered on the middle line—red, blue, and white, perfect order—deaf and mute to the uniformed attendants around coaxing her to take a picture. "That was mine," Lee hissed. "I was playing that one when she came up and said she was playing that one since yesterday and had just stepped away to go to the bathroom. Fuck ye mother I gave it to her!" He dropped the last two tokens in his cup into the machine and pulled the lever—nothing. "Ai," he slapped his thigh and stood up, heading for the change counter.

I traded all my tokens for plastic chips at the counter and picked a five-dollar Black Jack table to try my luck. It didn't go too bad. At least I wasn't losing. By the time Lee came over, I even had a small pile of additional chips on the side. I had just won three times in a row.

"What are you doing playing so tiddy-bitty?" Lee yelled when he saw I left only two chips in the hole for the next hand after collecting my winnings. "Play big. Got to play big when you're strong."

There were only two more hands left before the time was up for this cruise. I was tempted.

"Are you sure?" I asked.

"Of course. That's the rule," he said, and nudged another five chips of mine over.

The dealer hit a Black Jack right on, and swept the table clean.

"Big, big." Lee poked at me as I hesitated about the last bet. "Last hand, I don't think she be that lucky again."

I slapped a whole pile in the hole. Ten chips, fifty dollars.

6 and 5. The face card of the dealer was 3.

"Double!" Lee poked at me again. "She be busted."

I pushed another pile over.

"Te-n-n-n!" Lee intoned as if performing some kind of a black magic as the dealer drew out my double card. It was an 8.

"Not bad, not bad," he said, "you win for sure."

The dealer's turn. Her bottom card was 2. Ace, 10, and . . . 4! That adds up to 20.

"Fuck." Both Lee and I slammed down on the table with our fists.

The cruise was over.

Back in my car, I asked Lee if he had lost all of his fifty dollars.

"Fifty!" He jumped, as if my question were a great insult. "You really believed me, did you? Ten times!"

I didn't ask anything more, but figured how many tables he had to wait on before he could earn that much back.

"How's work?" I asked when we stopped for breakfast at a Hardee's along the Interstate, "Still working at the Cantonese Chef?"

"I quit."

"When?"

"Two days ago. Had a fight with that son of a turtle."

"What happened?"

"Don't ask me about it." He blew at the coffee the way one would a mug of tea with the leaves floating on top. "That son of a turtle, the hell with him!" Across the aisle, a man in a flannel shirt with rolled-up sleeves sat alone at a table drinking coffee from a thermal cup; two tables down, a fat sleepy-eyed woman was blowing smoke rings over the remains of her breakfast.

"You want to work in the restaurant again?" Lee asked after a while, crumpling the sandwich wrapper into a ball and stuffing it in his empty cup. "We can go and look for a good place together."

That was not a bad idea. The spring semester was about to end, and both the cafeteria and the dorm would be closed, which meant I would have to look for another job as well as a place to live.

"How about we wait till I'm done with school?" I said.

"When's that?"

"In three weeks."

"Nah," he said, wiping off the stain his mug had made on the table. "Too late. If you want to go, we go now. When everybody's out of school, you won't even have soup left."

II

After checking out a dozen Golden Dragons, Imperial Palaces and China Houses all around Chicago, we found a place called Genghis Khan in Wheeling.

"What can I do for you?" A man in his fifties sitting behind the bar reading a Chinese newspaper looked up at us from behind a pair of black-rimmed glasses.

That was Wong, the owner of Genghis Khan. It turned out that one of his waiters was going back to Hong Kong to get married, and another was opening a restaurant of his own. He said he would try us out that night.

"No use fooling around with me, OK? I can tell by just watching you wait on a few tables."

Compared with that little Dim Sum place in Chinatown, Genghis Khan was a real restaurant, and five times busier, but Lee and I worked as a team, and didn't have too much trouble. By the time the last table was gone, we literally had money dropping out of our pockets.

"Not bad, uh?" Lee said as I counted my tips in the car. I didn't change them into large bills as Lee did. It felt good having a pocket full of money, even just for a little while.

If you are someone who did not have enough sleep, then the alarm clock must be your worst enemy. It always starts to beep at the best part of your dream, though in most cases the dream is gone the moment you open your eyes. But that makes you all the more angry because you've just been deprived of even the memory of pleasure, which might be the only consolation you have to last you through the day. But that's something you just have to put up with because things would be only worse when the clock goes on a strike and you wake up to find half the day already gone. My daily routine during the last three weeks of that semester started at five with a mug of strong tea. After ironing my shirt, vest and trousers for the night—first things first—I would start working on the two fifteen-page papers due before the end of the term. On Tuesdays and Thursdays I went to class at one, and then, at three, headed off to Chinatown to pick up Lee and go to work—we had worked out with the boss that as soon as I was done with school, both of us would come and work full-time. By the time I got back home it would be around midnight. A couple of times I woke up early in the morning and found I had dropped dead on the bed without even taking my clothes off.

The day I went to turn in my last paper at the department office, the secretary told me Dr. Freeland, chair of the department, wanted to see me.

"You must have heard about Professor Skretkowicz," Dr. Freeland said after I sat down.

"No," I said. Skretkowicz was my thesis director. "What happened?"

"Professor Skretkowicz died of a heart attack two days ago." Dr. Freeland paused, taking off his glasses. "I am very sorry."

"I'm sorry, too," I said, but had no glasses to take off.

"I understand you have worked closely with Professor Skretkowicz and am so sorry that the relationship between you two had to be terminated this way." He replaced his glasses. "As I understand, you've finished all your course work, but have not completed your thesis yet. Am I right?"

"That's right."

"And your thesis is a comparative study of the philosophies of Spinoza and Confucius?"

"Correct."

"You may well know that Professor Skretkowicz was the only expert in oriental philosophy in our department."

"Yes, I know. That's why Professor Skretkowicz became my thesis director."

"Now that he's gone . . . eh . . . passed away, I mean, we are really diminished in our ability to guide your present thesis. Do you think there is any possibility that you might choose a different topic at this stage?"

"Well, I'm afraid it would be quite difficult now, Dr. Freeland," I said.

"Oh I understand your situation perfectly. I was only making a suggestion. Of course there's always the possibility that we hire somebody from another school to read your thesis, but that . . ." he paused ". . . could be difficult sometimes."

"The alternative," he said after a while, "though I hate to say it, will be you to transfer to another school." He looked away at the books on the shelf for a moment. "But don't get me wrong, we don't really want to lose you."

I followed his eyes to the bookshelf, saw nothing in particular, and said nothing.

"Anyway, you don't have to make the decision now. Think about it, and let me know before classes start next semester. All right?"

So, I thought as I walked down the dim corridor, that was about the end of the friendship between Confucius and Spinoza.

~ Lee was right. Almost everyday the first two weeks after we started working full time at Genghis Khan, people called or just walked in, looking for jobs. We were lucky to have made the right move in time. We made good money, an average of seventy dollars per day, not including our wage. The wage was fourteen dollars a day, well below the $2.19/hour minimum for waiters if you divided it by ten, roughly the number of hours we worked every day. But nobody really bothered to argue as long as the tips were good.

To save money on rent and gas, Lee and I moved to the restaurant.

The move was easy. Except for a few books and some clothes, I left all my things in storage at school, and all of Lee's belongings were packed easily into an old footlocker, two traveling bags and a few fortune cookie boxes.

Our "dorm," as Wong referred to it, was the space between two steel file cabinets and an old sagging canopy bed in the second-floor office of Genghis Khan. We were not supposed to use the bed.

"My wife might need to take a nap there in the afternoon sometimes, and when she's in there, you keep out, OK?" That was the condition under which the key—there was only one—was handed over to us.

Most times, however, Lee and I made our beds in the dining room by pulling the chairs together. Twelve chairs, and it was a quite comfortable bed. On some rainy nights when it got too chilly we would light up the fireplace, a fake with gas tubes hidden between cement logs. But we had to watch out for Wong, who sometimes after his midnight Mahjong party would sneak back and check up on us.

Upstairs, next to another "dorm" shared by the amigos—Anastacio, the Pick-up/Deep-fry, and Jose, the Dishwasher—Chef Wu, or Wu Shifu as we called him, lived alone in a small room. Thirty-six years old and wearing a pair of gold-rimmed glasses, he looked more like an accountant than a cook. Ever since coming over from Hong Kong six years ago, he had been working for Wong, twelve hours a day, six days a week. His salary, which he revealed only reluctantly after our repeated probing, was $1600 a month. He had a house about twenty minutes' drive away, but since his wife had run away with a white man two years ago and he had sent his son to his sister's in New York, he lived most of the time at the restaurant. Once Lee and I rented a Kung Fu movie from a grocery store in Chinatown and we all watched it in Wu Shifu's room. Aside from the TV and the VCR, the only things that could be called superfluous in his room were a few posters of Hong Kong movie stars printed by a noodle factory, and a framed photo of his wife and son propped up on a nightstand. When Lee asked why he kept the photo of a woman who had dumped him, he said that it was the only good photo he had of his son.

Anastacio used to be a professional bullfighter—Matador, as he called it. Six and a half feet, thick shoulders and strong muscles with a dash of black moustache, he did look like a man of the arena. Only his stomach was getting a little pouchy. "All this Chinese food," he grinned, patting his belly. He was saving his money till he had enough to go back and open his own Chinese Restaurant.

III

The days got warmer. Business was booming. At the peak hour, Lee and I would each handle seven to eight tables. Anyone could wait on one or two tables, but to handle seven or eight all at once required a certain level of coordination. The key was timing. Soup, appetizer, entree, and dessert—an experienced waiter like Lee could take all the tables at once and space them out in good order. "The Pot Stickers take about fifteen minutes, would you like something to drink in the meantime? . . . How about some Chinese beer? Tsintao, you ever tried that? . . . Never? What a shame! You have to try it. Believe me, you wouldn't be disappointed. . . . The Mandarin Fish's the Special tonight. It takes a little longer, but you'll see it's worth the wait." Clear and efficient in the kitchen, pleasant and graceful in the dining room, a good waiter leads the customers by his smile, his joke, and his authority, and never loses his pace and composure; a mediocre waiter, on the other hand, gets ordered around, tipping wine glasses and spilling soup into customers' laps from time to time, barely catching up at either end. It was clear I belonged to the soup-spilling type. There was no doubt about that.

But good or mediocre, you work hard. On Friday or Saturday night, by the time Wong and his wife counted the bottles of beer left in the cooler, locked up the box where the air-conditioning switch was located, and left in their white Mercedes, everyone was exhausted. Wu Shifu went to bed immediately, Anastacio sprawled on the grass across the parking lot, while Lee and I sat at the table in the waiter's section, for a long time not wanting to move. Only Jose seemed to have endless energy. After taking a shower and putting on his new shirt and black silk pants, he would slip out the back door with a cowboy hat in hand. Normally he wouldn't be back until three or four in the morning. For him, the day had just begun.

After a while, you got to know all the regulars: Mrs. Rosenberg who lived in the nursing home around the corner and wanted her tea boiling hot, Mrs. Culvert who came twice a week with her thirty-year-old imbecile daughter who beat her plate with the chopsticks like a drum; on Wednesdays, Mr. Jones would drop in for lunch with a roll of newspaper when almost everyone else had left, ordering always Chicken Chop Suey with no MSG and leaving two quarters as a tip. And there was the high school basketball coach with his skinny girlfriend, the insurance salesman in tie and suit adding up his invoices while waiting for his food, and the four Japanese businessmen who came late every other Friday night and drank three rounds of Tsintao and two pots of Sake, running the bill up to more than a hundred, using always a calculator to determine the amount of the tip, fifteen percent, not a penny less, not a penny more.

The thrill of earning cash daily, however, quickly decayed into tedium. As a waiter, all you ever needed to say was only a variation of about ten sentences—"How are you doing today?" "Can I get you something to drink? . . . Are you ready to order? . . . Is everything all right? . . . Great! . . . Here's your change. . . . Thank you, Please come again. . . . Thank you! . . . You have a nice weekend! . . . Thank you! . . . Good night! . . . Good night!" Sometimes I thought about writing a guidebook for working in Chinese restaurants and selling it to all those in China who were eager to come to the States. *How to Survive in a Chinese Restaurant in America,* I would call it, and I could guarantee it would be sold out overnight.

Since coming to live at the restaurant, I had hardly read anything, let alone begun working on my thesis. Waiting on tables had numbed my senses. But my body was getting strong. My muscles no longer felt sore by the end of the day. As for the mind, there was no need. "Walking corpse," Lee once said jokingly, "that's what we are!" But sometimes in the afternoon after the sidejobs were done, or at night when all the customers had left, sitting in the dining room, staring at the Happy Buddha in the half darkness, I felt the conversation with Dr. Freeland at the end of the semester grow like an ominous seed, bloated and sprouting in the tepid summer rain.

Changing the topic of my thesis was almost out of the question—I was already more than halfway through my first draft. Besides, I didn't find any other topic that really interested me. Transferring to another school, on the other hand, could be costly, in terms of both time and money. The mere thought of the coming fall sent my head spinning.

"How long you still have to be in school?" Lee asked me one morning while we were still lying in our makeshift beds.

"I don't know," I said, looking at the stained foam blocks of the ceiling. "Looks like it's going to be longer than I expected."

"Then what? Can you get a better job?"

"With a M.A. in philosophy, probably not," I said, turning over.

"What use of study if you can't get a good job out of it?" Lee sat up.

A good question. What was the point of studying if you couldn't get a job with the degree? Lee was right.

"Is it too late for you to switch the subject?" he asked, meaning my major.

"I guess it is."

"Then start all over again. Stop your stupid comparison of Confucius and Snowpizza. Go to another school and do something real."

Want it or not, I smirked, it didn't seem likely Mr. Old Con was going to eat Snow Pizza anymore.

"You speak good English. Why don't you go to a Law School? You'll make good money."

Well, that was what everybody else was doing and what I had been resisting up till now.

"You're young and smart, there're many things you can do," he went on, but then sighed. "Not like me."

Lee dropped out of high school just before graduation the year he came to the States with his brother, and had never gone back to school since. For a while, we lay in the dim morning light and remained silent. A flock of birds hopped back and forth on the roof. Through the cracks, their chirping sounded distant but clear.

IV

On Sundays, when there was no lunch at Genghis Khan, Lee and I went out. I would go and pick up my mail at the school, and Lee would either go have a haircut or buy a pair of new shoes—shoes wear out fast if you work as a waiter—and then wait for me at Three Happiness in Chinatown with a copy of Shijie Ribao—the World Daily. After lunch, we took Lakeshore Drive to downtown. On a good day, the lake would be full of sailboats; if we were lucky we could a find a meter on Columbus Drive and take a stroll in Buckingham Square.

Instead of bringing me comfort, letters from old classmates in China always left me even more depressed. So-and-so got married, with a girl once I knew quite well; so-and-so got a job in a foreign venture in Shengzhen, and was making 4000 yuan a month, ten times of the wage of an ordinary clerk. Another sent a photo of himself leaning against a brand new Mercedes: he was soon to be promoted to cultural attaché somewhere in East Asia. "How are you doing, buddy?" they would ask. "Going to be professor soon?" Or, "Hey, got an American girlfriend?"

As I sat on a bench reading these letters in the brilliant sunlight, the pigeons walking as unhurried and dignified as the ladies and gentlemen on Michigan Avenue, an occasional gust of wind sending a spray of water from the fountain over our heads, and the colorful sails out on the lake shimmering like a huge, live jigsaw puzzle against the fairytale blue of the water and sky, I wondered how I would describe my current situation to them. My parents' letters were worse. While telling me not to work too hard, they never failed to remind me how much was still owed to friends and relatives who had generously lent me the $7500 dollars for my first year, a debt my parents would never be able to repay unless they robbed the Bank of China.

"What you do if you win a jackpot?" Lee asked suddenly one day as we lay on the greens on the east side of Columbus Drive eating cones of ice cream.

"Pay off my debt."

"And then?"

"And then . . ." I really had to think about that.

"If I win a jackpot, I'm going to buy an Alpha Romeo, a new one, just like that." He pointed at a little red convertible parked along the shoulder. "You don't see many of this kind here, but damn popular in Hong Kong."

"Romeo?" I asked, squinting my eyes to make out the lettering on the hood. The only Romeo I knew was the lover of Juliet.

"Ro-may-o," he corrected me. "Italian."

V

One Friday night in June, Wu Shifu burned his hand. In the usual chaos of eight o'clock on weekend nights, Jose bumped Wu as he was switching a wok full of boiling oil to another stove. The oil lapped and splashed all over Wu's hand and forearm. Everyone in the dining room heard the terrible scream. By the time Lee and I rushed back, Wu was sitting on the floor, tears in eyes, and sweat breaking out on his forehead. Anastacio rummaged through the first-aid box for a cold pack, but only came up with a wad of half-soiled gauze.

Wong came in, stared a few seconds, and took the wad of gauze from Anastacio. "Everybody get back to work," he said.

We moved to fiddle with our jobs, but no one had left the kitchen. Realizing the gauze was dirty, Wong threw it in the garbage and went out. A few minutes later, he came back with a fresh bandage patch. But on close inspection, his brows tightened. "Shall I call an ambulance?" I asked.

"No. I'll drive," Wong said.

Louis and Anastacio helped Wu to his feet. But at the door, Wong turned back.

"You drive him to the hospital," he said, handing me his car keys. "I have to cook."

The drive to the hospital, according to Wong, should take only ten minutes. It took me twice as long, however, with the confusion of all the one-way streets and intersections.

At the Emergency, the doctor was furious. "You should've called an ambulance right away," he fumed. "At least you should have used coldpacks. Don't you have any cold-packs at home?"

The phone rang. It was Wong.

"You didn't tell them that it happened in the restaurant, did you?" he asked in a low voice.

"Not yet," I said.

"Don't! Just say it happened at home, will you?"

"Why?" I was not clear what he was getting at.

"They charge much more if it's going to be paid by the employer. It wouldn't make no difference if I had insurance for him, but I don't, you understand? And also . . ." His voice was now even lower. "That kind of thing could get me into trouble."

I thought for a moment, and said, "All right." As long as he took care of the charges, it would make no difference to Wu.

"And you tell Wu, will you?"

"I'll tell him."

"Good," he said. Then as if as second thought, he asked, "Is he all right?"

"I don't know yet," I said.

There was a short silence. Then his voice switched back to normal. "Drive carefully, OK? Don't wreck my car."

What happened later proved I was stupid to let him off like that. Wong did pay the hospital bills, but he refused to pay Wu for the two weeks he stayed at home. With his own false account of the accident on record, Wu couldn't do anything. Wong visited him once at home with a basket of fruits. But that, like the hospital bill, came out of Wu's own payroll for that two weeks as well.

As the result of the accident, Wong stayed in the kitchen for two weeks. To be fair, he was a good cook. Though Wu cooked good standard American Chinese food, Wong knew the little tricks in spices and fire temperature to bring the subtleties out. To most American customers whose palates were corrupted by Egg Foo Young and Sweet and Sour Chicken, such subtleties made no difference; and even when they did notice the difference, they didn't appreciate it. Mrs. Rosenberg complained that her Mongolian Beef had a funny taste, and she would like it the old way. But for all of us gourmets condemned temporarily to waiting on tables, it was a rare chance to offer some flattery to Wong without losing principles completely.

Wong, on the other hand, seemed indifferent. "What do you know about Chinese food?" he snorted and put on an air of contempt. "When I first started to work in the restaurant, you were still kicking in your mother's belly." This, of course, did not really apply to Lee, for Lee was just a few years younger than Wong. But Lee laughed and said nothing.

Monday was Jose's day off. So everyone in the kitchen had to take turns washing dishes.

"Who made this pot of tea?" Wong suddenly asked as he was loading the dishwasher. "Who did this?" he asked again when no one answered, holding the tea pot with the lid open like some evidence of crime. We all looked at him, puzzled. All the teapots looked the same, how could anyone know who made that particular pot?

"What do you do when you make a pot of tea?" he quizzed me.

"You take it from the big tea pot." I said. What else could you do?

"And then?" he was still holding the pot, looking relentless.

"Take it out to the customer, I guess." I shrugged my shoulders.

"My God," Wong shook his head and dumped the rest of the tea in the sink. "You been working here how long? Two months? Two months and you don't know you always mix half pot of boiling water with what you take from the big pot?" He shook his head again, defeated. Then he turned to Lee. "He doesn't know, and you don't tell him, either. You want to ruin my business?"

"OK . . . OK." Lee took a clean pot from the lower shelf and demonstrated it to me.

"You mix in half boiling water next time."

"Why should you mix in that much water in tea?" I caught up with Lee later in the dining room.

"Well, in most restaurants they make the stuff in the big pot really strong in the morning, so you always mix in half water when you serve. But here," Lee took a quick glance around to make sure no one was within earshot. "It ain't quite strong to start with. To tell you the truth, I don't put that much water when I serve it either. That's why I didn't say anything to you."

"So you think it's all right?" I said.

"Yeah, you got any complaints?"

I tried to think. "Guess not."

"See?" said Lee.

In the rest of the three weeks, Wong found more abhorrences: Cashew nuts sprinkled on top of Kung Pao Chicken, Sizzling Rice left in the kitchen so long it no longer sizzled, too much ham in wonton soup, too little ice in coke. "Good Heavens, you're really going to ruin this business, are you?" Holding a half bowl of left-over rice rescued from Jose, the Dishwasher, he slumped in the only chair in the kitchen and looked at us in disbelief, as if he were going to cry.

What almost ruined the business, however, were not our abominable deeds. One Saturday night, a birthday party I served found a dead cockroach in their pot-sticker sauce. The party threatened to call the Health Department. Wong's face turned white when I came back to the kitchen to report the incident. With his greasy apron still on, he rushed out and caught the party just in time at the door. It took him a long fifteen minutes of explaining, smiling, begging, and bribing to finally get everyone back to the table—the only thing he didn't do was kneel on the floor and kowtow to them. The bribery worked—all the orders were cooked fresh again, by Wong personally, all drinks on the house, free birthday cake and dessert, plus, everyone at the party was issued a coupon for a free meal on next visit. Such unusual generosity from Wong surprised us all. But it seemed only a small price when we learned later that two Chinese restaurants around Chicago had been closed recently by the Health Department.

VI

One Sunday after Wu's accident, a girl walked in in the listless hours of the afternoon.

"Can you fix me a Bloody Mary?" she asked, picking out a stool in the bar and drawing a Virginia Slim from a pack in her black leather purse with her long thin fingers with polished pink fingernails.

I had just been dozing off in the bar with a Chinese magazine Lee brought back from Chinatown, and was almost startled to hear her voice. Officially, the restaurant did not open until five o'clock, but sometimes people drifted in to have an early drink. I scurried behind the counter, looking for the tall glass and the tray of garnishes, at the same time searching in my mind for the right recipe—Bloody Mary: half vodka, half Tomato Juice and a wedge of lime—that shouldn't be too hard. But it was not until I laid the glass down with a cocktail napkin on the counter did I remember the black pepper and bitters. I rushed to make the amends, but in a moment of nervousness knocked the ashtray off the counter.

"You're not the bartender, are you?" The girl laughed, puffing out a sequence of fuzzy smoke rings.

My face must have turned red, for she looked at me with an amused smile.

"No," I said, and turned to look for the ashtray, which was now hidden somewhere under the cabinet.

"I figured." She tilted the cigarette to hold the ash still and reached inside the counter for a dirty coke glass in the sink.

I found the object of my quest, now broken.

"You sell a lot of drinks here?" She glanced up and down the bar, as if measuring spaces for a new coke machine, or some extra pieces of furniture.

"On weekends, yes." I combed the few strands of hair dangling on my forehead with my fingers, trying to regain my composure.

"Good," she said, and this time swept her eyes over the rows of liqueur bottles behind me on the rack. She pulled out a five-dollar bill from her purse and made a gesture for me to keep the change.

She took a big sip of the Bloody Mary through the straw, and got off the stool. "By the way, my name's Jane," she said, extending her hand over the counter—I noticed she was not tall. "What's yours?"

"David," I said, and touched her fingers lightly—they were moist.

"Good name." She was again amused. "Well, I'll be seeing you, David boy," she said, and waved before she went out the door, her black purse dangling at the curve of her hip. The next time I saw Jane we had reversed positions at the bar, with her on the inside, fixing Bloody Marys and Wakiki Hulas for my table's order. She was the new bartender. Instead of the lime, she had stuck a stem of celery in the Bloody Mary, which somehow made it more exotic.

"What you say, David boy?" She lined my orders neatly in on the counter. "Beats yours, uh?"

As most Orientals looked younger than their age to Americans, most Americans, young people especially, looked older in my eyes. Jane, for example, was hardly older than I, but the way she carried herself sprayed a mist of worldliness and sophistication about her slender limbs, her sharp vulnerable body of a teenager, and her almost cherubic face coated thickly in blue eye shadow, black mascara and purple lipstick. David Boy, she called me, with a flirtatious wink.

Jane worked on weekends only. The rest of the time she said she was going to school to be a hairdresser. The style of her own hair changed weekly, this week the shape of a chicken nest, and the next a cascade of golden torrents, then one day she cut the extra length off, and had it all frizzled like a thousand tiny, black, rising serpents. Black? "Yes," she said, tilting her head as if to give it a better display, "the color, you know, is just as much part of the fashion as the style."

Lee did not like Jane. "Big mouth," he said. Once Jane made fun of him for saying Margarita as Margaret. "Margaret? There's no Margaret here. My name's Jane." But as a bartender, she was good, and efficient. The usual complaints of funny tastes in exotic drinks made by Mrs. Wong turned slowly to subtle nods with smiles. Even Wong was pleased; when Wu came to work again, he resumed his usual seat behind the bar with the daily newspaper, overseeing our commotion above the rim of his hornrimmed glasses. "If you all worked like her," he said once while both Lee and I were at the bar, "I'd have a few more years to live."

Early in June, Lee and I made the dining hall our permanent bedroom. At night, I had dreams. In most of them I went back to the old college days in Shanghai, the dorm with eight of us packed in a room, the windows that leaked the damp and bone-chilling wind in the winter, and the occasional fistfight in the crowded canteen over a bowl of lukewarm soup with cold fat floating on top—yet in the dreams, all those mundane routines we once hated and tried every way possible to escape seemed to have lost their sharp, unpleasant edges and appeared warm and fuzzy in a nostalgic blur as in an old movie. In others dreams, I was back in my small hometown outside Wenzhou, now a booming port of trade on the east coast of China. The streets were as crooked as ever, the people forever familiar and young. In our house, my father, a shoemaker in the old fashion, still bent over his low working table, putting lasts into the half-finished shoes or nailing a sole with tiny black nails, while my mother, an old woman already at the age of forty, moved in the background, cooking, sewing, fighting a hopeless battle against the dust that fell, forever falling, on everything in the household where our family lived. In one dream, my sister, who ran away at the age of seventeen with an antique dealer from Canton and only sent money and a note home on New Year's Eves with no return address, came back. Her face was still the same, even her clothes were the ones she wore the day she disappeared; the only thing different was her hair, instead of the long thick oily black braids, it was now short, and straight, every one standing on its end, gnarled and coiling. I stared and stared until, waking up in a cold sweat, I realized with an inexplicable horror that it was . . . it was like the hair of Jane.

VII

Across the street, two blocks down from Genghis Khan, squeezed in between a stationery store and a place that sold used sewing machines and vacuum cleaners, was a small reading room of the *Christian Science Monitor.* Sometimes in the languid summer afternoon when the dining room was empty and the air was turned way low by Wong when he and his wife left, I would sneak out over to this cramped, but cool, haven. One day, digging through the pile of university catalogs and bulletins Mr. Wunderlich, the custodian, brought in occasionally for local high schools seniors, my eye was caught by a brochure from the MBA program of Saint John's University: a two-year program in New York City, and the possibility of a full scholarship for someone competent in doing research in Chinese. The application was enclosed. I noted the other things I needed to send along and filled out the forms on the spot, using the pen I carried around in my pocket for taking orders, making quite a few smudges with the ink leaking all over from the heat. I borrowed a used big brown envelope from Mr. Wunderlich, put Genghis Khan as return address, and dropped it off on my way back to the restaurant.

Jane was already there behind the bar, smoke from her Virginia Slim coiling between her fingers. The air was turned back on high. "Where have you been, Philosopher?" she asked.

Philosopher, that was the new name she had for me after she found out I majored in philosophy. "Now maybe you can help me on this. What are philosophers?" she said, coming out from behind the bar and settling on one of the stools. "What do they do?"

"They think," I said.

"That's it? That's too easy, anybody can think," she said.

"Not everyone."

She took a drag on her cigarette, as if considering, then said, "Maybe you're right. But I mean, what do they do for living?"

"Waiting on tables."

"No, seriously." She flicked the ash off her cigarette. "I never figured that one out."

Well, Wittgenstein, I told her, scrubbed floors in a hospital, while Confucius begged a good part of his life.

"That's pathetic," she said. "They've got to do better."

I told her about Spinoza.

"Make lenses?" the dark shadows on her eyelids peeled back. "That's cool! I like that."

But most of the time, Jane kept an aloof distance. Except for poking fun at Lee and me, she kept to herself behind the bar, clipping photos of new hair fashions from *Elle* or *Le Monde,* touching up her makeup with the tiny mirror in her compact, filing her nails, or just smoking.

~ Lee didn't hit a jackpot, but his luck at gambling seemed to have taken a good turn. Since I had told him that I was not doing him any more favors giving him rides to the Casino, he sometimes took the tour bus there on his days off from Chinatown. Once he came back in the evening with snacks for everybody: moon cakes, sweet rice chicken, barbecue buns, and Phoenix Claws—he went with two hundred, he said, but walked away with four thousand. One night he told me secretly that if his luck stayed with him like this for two more weeks, he would be well provided for the rest of the year. I was not completely surprised, therefore, when, one Tuesday evening, a golden convertible sailed into the parking lot with Lee at the wheel. It was an Alpha Romeo.

Though an '88 model, the car looked almost new. Lee wouldn't tell how much he paid for it, but it was clear he thought it was a good deal. That night after work, Lee took me out for a ride. We went all the way to the lake shore. The night was cool. On one side, the silhouette of the Congress Hotel, the Prudential Building, and the Sears Tower loomed on the skyline; on the other, the beacons on Lake Michigan blinked in the unknowable distance of mist and darkness.

VIII

The response from Saint John's came quickly, with a personal letter from the department chair, who happened to be writing a book on Chinese economy and needed an assistant. My credentials looked impressive, he wrote, and he would let me know about the scholarship as soon as the fund he was applying for got approved.

"MBA! New York! Good for you!" Jane said. "So you're going to be a CEO, huh? But what about your philosophy?"

The hell with it, I said. I didn't want to scrub floors or beg on the street, and lenses were not ground by hand anymore.

On Saturdays Wong did not show up until the afternoon. That was his day for golfing. Mrs. Wong had no interest in golf, and never went with him.

In fact, she couldn't if she had wanted, for one of them had to be in the restaurant. When lunch was over, she rushed home to catch up on her sleep—their Mahjong party on Friday nights usually lasted till the morning—and came in most times just before five, hair ruffled and eyes bleary. Wong came in at least half an hour early. So did Jane.

Now that I had two tutors, I took my bartending lessons seriously. Weekends between lunch and dinner was time for my practice runs. But once Wong or Jane was back, the bar became their domain. Sometimes, they came in one right after another. One day, filling salt and pepper shakers in the smoking section, I heard them talking.

"That really was a nice shot," I heard Jane say.

"You should see me play last year. My back's been aching since the rains this spring."

There was a stiffness in Wong's body when he looked up and saw me through the lattice that separated the bar from the smoking section.

"You wiped the mirrors yet?" he asked after a short awkward silence.

"I'm going to," I said.

"Do the mirrors first," he said, impatiently. "And don't forget to clean the big tea pot and the soy sauce bottles!"

~ Some noise on the roof woke me up in the middle of the night. Though the restaurant had two floors, it was structured in a way that there was nothing above the dining room. At first I thought it was mice, or the rain. But no, it was something larger, a cat, or a squirrel. No, not even that. Someone was up there crawling on the roof. I sat up. Lee was awake too. We listened. The sound was moving toward the other end. Lee switched on his flashlight, and motioned for me to follow him. On bare feet, we groped our way up the two rickety flights of the narrow stairs. There was a skylight in the office that was supposed to be our dorm.

Slowly Lee opened the door. The roof creaked, and we could hear the tiles being crunched. Pulling me after him behind a steel file cabinet, Lee aimed the flashlight toward the skylight. A yellow, haggard face emerged on the other side of the windowpane.

"Open la ventana! Open la ventana!" The window rattled. "It's me, Jose. Let me in!"

Mumbling a curse, Lee climbed on a stool and opened the window to let him down.

"Fucking cold, man." Jose shivered. His shirt was torn, and the black silk of his pants gleamed in wetness. A few strands of hair clung to his forehead, the cowboy hat nowhere to be found.

"Hey, you have thirty bucks?" he asked, wiping his face.

"What you need money for at this hour?" Lee growled.

"I got to pay the taxi. Thirty bucks, I give you sixty next week."

Lee went downstairs to find his pants. "I don't want your no sixty bucks—go pay what you have to pay, but just don't ask me to open the window again at four o'clock in the morning," he said when he counted the money out to Jose.

Grinning, Jose took the money and went out through the back door in the kitchen. By the time he was back, Lee had found a half bottle of vodka and a shot-glass from the bar.

"Good stuff! Where you get this?" Jose was grinning again.

"Just shut up and drink." Lee put the glass down in front of him.

Jose took a small sip, made a face, and then emptied it out.

"What happened?" I asked.

"Oh, fuck!" He combed his hair back with his hand, and began to take off his shirt. Only then did I notice there was a big bruise under his left eye and his face was swollen. "Fucking shit." He pulled off his soaked pants and wiped his ass with the napkins. It took us quite a while to get the whole story out of him.

It had been a long night. As it was payday that night, he headed as usual for the Cicero strip joints in a friend's car with two other Mexicans who worked in another restaurant nearby. Two girls stopped them and asked for a ride. They let them in. As their hands fumbled beneath the girls' blouses and skirts, the girls went straight for their pockets. It was only after they had sat down in the club that they realized they were penniless. They got into a fight with the guards who tried to throw them out, the police were called and they had to run, each on his own way, in the pouring rain. He walked for more than an hour before he finally found a taxi. Then the door was locked—it was probably Wu who did it, not knowing anyone had been out.

Jose rubbed at the bruise in his face. In Lee's black baggy pants and my college sweater, he looked funny, like a collage of incongruous elements from some wildly different parts of the world.

"How old are you?" Lee asked, eyeing him up and down as if seeing him for the first time.

"Why? Seventeen." There was a baffled look in Jose's eyes.

"Why don't you be like Anastacio?" Lee sighed. "When you get my age, you be just like me. Or worse."

"I don't know if I want to live to your age." Jose laughed. "When I get thirty . . ." He formed his hand into the shape of a pistol and pointed it to his temple.

IX

Jane would be finished with her cosmetic school in August. I asked if she would open her parlor in the fall. "If things work out," she said with a veiled smile.

Two weeks after Lee got his Romeo, my Datsun died. The transmission had to be completely rebuilt. The lowest quote I got from a garage was six hundred dollars, plus any parts if necessary. Not knowing where I was headed after the summer, I called the junkyard. "How does twenty bucks sound?" The owner offered after I told him the year and model. Politely, I pointed out that he could easily take off one tire and sell it for that much. "Well, you gonna let me make some money, right? Or you want to keep it and sell the tires yourself, that's fine with me." I said he could do that more easily. "Yeah, that's why I'm here," he said. "Hey, listen, I got other things to do. I'll give you five more bucks if that's what you want. But that's the best I can do." I said I appreciated it and asked when he would come and pick it up. He said he would be right over.

One Saturday afternoon around three, Mrs. Wong called in. "Is he in the restaurant?" Her voice had already told half the story.

"Mr. Wong?" I said. "Isn't he at the golf course?"

"I am at the golf course," she yelled. "How about Jane, have you seen her?"

"Not either," I said. "Is Mr. Wong supposed to pick her up today?"

"You tell me!" The phone clicked.

Whatever happened between Wong, his wife and Jane that afternoon remained beyond our speculation. The three of them came in around five thirty, almost half an hour late. It was going to be a big night—with three large parties, the whole dining room was virtually booked out. Except for the fake smile he put on for the customers, Wong kept a sullen face the whole night, while his wife's face glowed with a strange mixture of rage, contempt and satisfaction. Only Jane seemed indifferent, though she didn't poke fun at me that night.

The last customers left around ten-thirty. I was counting my tips of the night in the bar when Mrs. Wong slapped a cash envelope in front of Jane on the counter. "Take the money and get out!"

Jane didn't pick it up. "You didn't hire me, did you?" Jane asked coldly.

Wong sat at the end of bar adding up checks. "Just go home," he said, without turning around.

"All right, I'll go." Jane slipped the envelope into her purse, and started to leave. "But don't think you can fire me like that."

"Go please, will you?" Wong said. "We talk tomorrow."

"Tomorrow?" Mrs. Wong snickered.

Jane didn't come to work the next day. But the letter from the director of the MBA program at Saint John's came finally. I opened it before I got back to the restaurant from the mailbox at the street corner. It confirmed my admission and scholarship—full tuition waiver plus a monthly stipend of one thousand dollars. I had already gone through it several times when I stepped in the door, but I kept reading it, over and over again. Wong was in the bar, talking on the phone.

Jose was behind the door in the kitchen, listening on the extension. He chuckled so loud that finally I couldn't help looking up from the letter. He thrust the phone to my ear.

It was Jane's voice. "Fuck you," I heard her say, and then a click.

X

For Lee, in the meantime, things couldn't have worked out better. One night he came back from his casino trip with a bottle of Mao Tai. Enough, he said, he would not go to the Empress anymore. He had all the money he needed. A friend of his from old times had a Chinese grocery in California, and had asked him to be a partner. He would work till the end of August and then go over there.

"Never have to wear this black-and-white skin again." He tugged at my waiter's shirt and vest.

Wu went out and bought some snacks and a pack of playing cards that night after work. We were going to play "Catching the Pig"—or Hearts, as Anastacio said it was. The Mao Tai was too strong for Jose—only one sip, and his face was twisted in a grimace, but Anastacio liked it, and sneaked an extra cup when the rest of us removed silverware, salt and pepper shakers from the table, arguing about the different rules of the game's Chinese and Western versions. Wong stayed a little late, doing inventory in the basement. "Don't steal any beer, OK? I got them all counted," he hollered as he shut down the air and walked out the front door.

For a few minutes, we listened, waiting for the sound of the engine to start and disappear. We heard nothing. Jose stole to the back door.

"Come! Quick!" he called from the kitchen.

Two men stood by Wong in the shadow of his Mercedes. It seemed they were in an argument. One of the men gave Wong a shove. Wong shoved back. Then one of them had Wong by the collar, and the other started to punch him in the face.

"Help," Wong cried.

Wu dialed the police. But no one went out.

The one who had Wong by the collar swung him around, and slammed him on the side of the car parked next to Wong's Mercedes. He kicked his knee up into Wong's stomach. "Hey, hey, don't touch my car." Lee pushed open the door and went out. It was his Romeo.

"Easy, easy . . ." The one who had punched Wong in the face came up, blocking Lee's way.

The other one now dropped Wong. "So, this is yours." He pulled out something from his belt, and mashed it down on the windshield. It cracked.

"Fuck your grandpa!" Lee yelled and leapt.

The next thing we knew, the guy who had blocked Lee was groaning on the ground, hands in his crotch, and Lee was banging the other's head on the garbage bin.

Wong scrambled to his feet.

"Fuck him! Fuck him!" Jose cheered.

Then we all heard the sound: a loud but muffled thump, the kind of sound a chunk of thawed meat made being slammed onto the chopping block. Lee slumped. Caught by the side of the garbage bin, his body slid to the ground.

Then the deafening blast as the men bolted out the parking lot on a motorcycle.

~ The two men were never found. Neither were the police able to locate Jane, who disappeared the same night of the incident. Lee died in the hospital the next morning. The shot ripped through his chest. The police waited for three weeks and finally had to have the body cremated. There was no funeral. Lee's car stayed in the parking lot for two more days, and then a tow truck came and dragged it away, along with Lee's other belongings—the footlocker, the traveler's bag, and the fortune-cookie boxes. They were notifying, said the young officer as he filled out the police form, a cousin of Lee they had found in LA.

That same night, I left Chicago, on a Greyhound heading for New York.

XI

It was three years before I returned to Chicago on my first business trip. The last day of my stay I found myself again in Wheeling. What used to be the Genghis Khan was now the Royal Garden. It was three in the afternoon, the cook was not back yet. The waiter on duty, a middle age man from Chaozhou, asked me if I wanted a drink. I told him I used to work here. "Genghis Khan, you mean?" He looked at me. He knew the story. So I asked him what happened after I left.

"The Immigration came soon after," he said, "and rounded up the amigos. Fake green cards, you know. The boss was fined and locked up a couple days, his second time."

"And then?" I asked.

"Oh, he sold the place after he came out. I've been here since this new one opened," he said, and fixed a napkin flower that had wilted.

We walked around the dining room and talked about what all waiters talk about—tips, side jobs, and boss. The decor had changed. Instead of the old red and golden, it was now white and green. "That old owner was really a son of a turtle, I heard. Was he?" he asked. He walked with me out to the parking lot. I thanked him and was just about to leave when my eyes fell on a car at the back of the lot.

"Whose car's that?" I asked and walked over.

"This one? That's mine." He followed me over. "I bought it when I first started working here. It was a real bargain. Three thousand. Police auction, you know. Looked almost new. Only the windshield was cracked. Don't know what happened. But that was OK. I got it replaced." He patted the new glass.

I headed back downtown. It was four o'clock. The traffic finally ground to a standstill on I-290. A black young man knocked on my window and waved a bouquet of roses wrapped in cellophane at me. I waved no, but he didn't go away. I said I had no need for it, but, separated by the glass, he couldn't hear me, and started to show me the different colors he had. I lowered the window to tell him "go away," but he had already picked out a stem and thrust it through the window. All right, I said, and slipped him a five-dollar bill. God bless you, he said, thanking me repeatedly before walking down to the next vehicle.

Instead of going back to the hotel, I went past Michigan Avenue and turned north on Lake Shore. A sweep of black clouds moved on the horizon. The yachts and schooners were coming in. The boaters gathered their clothes and lowered the colored sails. On the other side, the skyline was steeped in the last spilling of the setting sun. I took the exit off at a recreation area near Belmont.

The beach was empty. Only a few coke cans lodged between the rocks clattered in the wind. I stood for a few minutes. The gulls, squeaking, hovered low on the lake. I remembered the rose, and went back to fetch it from the car.

It was a large one, a few tattered petals on the outside, but the rest still fresh, dark and crimson, like someone's bloody fist, or heart. I planted it in the sand and left, wondering how long it would be before the dusk turned into the night, and how long before the wind and the rain would pluck out the rose and toss it to the dark rolling water.

Michael Collins

A CHRISTMAS STORY

Christmas didn't just come; it had to be planned or it would be a disaster. Feeney knew all about preparation. His mind was always on the future. He had a saying, "Today is the future." In February he purchased a cow which he had mated immediately so that she could give birth before Christmas. He planned to sell the calf in advance of leaving its mother's udder, delivering it to its new owners in the New Year. The sale of the calf would pay for Christmas. It was a simple plan that he had learned from his people down through the years. They had been farmers, living on the bartered flesh and produce of animals for their existence. Now there were only two weeks to Christmas.

The sound of the factory horn competed with the church bells. Feeney waited for his daughter at the end of the long drive, leaning against his bicycle, dressed in a soiled long black coat. He had his right trouser leg tucked into his sock to keep it from getting tangled in the chain. Entrenched in the past, Feeney would never take to cars. The bicycle accompanied him everywhere. Even when he walked without it, he had his right hand out, perceptibly pushing the phantom. There were still few people with cars, but everyone knew Feeney would never be a man to take to them. He was one of the last of a breed of bicycling men.

His daughter came down the long school drive with her friends. The bicycle wheeled out in front of the gate, Feeney by its side. "Maria," Feeney said, nodding his head. The front wheel moved slightly, allied with Feeney.

The girls crowded around her, wide-eyed, staring at Feeney.

Feeney stood at the gate, the bicycle poised, the eye of the lamp staring at them.

"Maria?" Feeney said again.

Maria moved from the cluster of girls and went over to him, her face flushed with embarrassment.

"It's the cow," Feeney said, dipping his head. "I need a hand with her."

Maria curled her black hair behind her ear nervously. "I have to come back for a Christmas exam in Maths this afternoon."

Feeney ran his tongue over his teeth. He had strong blue eyes. "I'll take care of that."

The girls stood about in their disquieting pubescence, with blotched faces, big feet and hands, the secret biology of their lives lost to an unseen metamorphosis beneath convent blue uniforms. "Can you believe it?" they whispered, ashamed for the poor girl.

Feeney ignored their stares. He heard the giggles and whispers. Feeney looked in disgust.

Maria got up on the crossbar. Feeney took a running start for effect, swinging his right leg over the seat, mounted the bicycle, and headed down toward the town. It was all in one glorious choreography, like in the cowboy films. The girls stood by and turned their heads, mortified at a fourteen year old on a crossbar.

The midday sun hung weak in a sky that threatened rain. A strong wind carried the churning clouds low over the ground as he raced against the first showers, the wings of his coat flapping. The handlebars turned onto the main street, the balanced weight of his daughter accounted for in the unconscious flex of his buttocks, the back wheel licking up a trail of dirt onto his back, the ingrained stigma of all bicycling men.

In the town the sun barely peeked over the narrow streets, cordoned off by black roofs and solid brick. The bicycle glided through the premature coldness, a mechanical shadow, sucked into cracks and then reemerging on the walls.

A melancholy smell of lard and cabbage water hung. An invisible order verging on oblivion existed in the narrow stone streets. Everything was falling apart, but it maintained a Protestant severity, the shopkeepers clinging to an incorruptible pride in being associated with the British Empire, getting the papers about the war. Feeney participated in the intangibles of the place, its history and its Orangemen, getting money from the work he had done out in the fields, work these people had no interest in, or cared for. He took nothing as insult, nor did he feel inferior, only different. It was part of life on a border town.

Feeney's shadow stopped. He dismounted. "Right then." He brushed his coat, shuffling his shoulders. "I'll have to get some stuff around the place. Go across to Leahy and see if he has time to stop down in a while. I'll be waiting for you over at Mrs. Sweeney's. Right?"

Maria left. Feeney watched after her, seeing the red mark from the crossbar on her legs. He puffed up his cheeks. The money would be there when the cow dropped the calf. A grim satisfaction cracked on his face. He'd get her a bicycle of her own for Christmas. Setting his own against the wall of a shop, he stepped down a polished step into murkiness. A bell jingled on coiled wire. A purring ginger cat unwrapped itself and moved off the counter. "Hello," Feeney said tentatively, knocking on the glass inset in a door that led to the domestic quarters. There was no sound. Feeney clicked his fingers impatiently but was glad of the wait. The dimness shrouded him. Things would be wild enough soon with the birth. He went over a list of things he would buy with the money.

The shop was run by a wizened old widow, as were most of the small shops, spinster sisters or doll-faced little men waiting to rise and serve, to pencil accounts into tattered notebooks. Feeney waited, looking at cans of beans standing beside small figurines. It was all part of a disjunctive commercial proposition sealed by the omniscient surveillance of holy statues. What could he say—not that commerce wasn't all based on faith in the long run. Here morality was helped along by slant-eyed saints with ossified beads like droplets of dry blood. The hoodwink of statues was all right by him. Somehow nothing was stolen. The shivering bell called nobody. The burden of existence rested on those without. Feeney waited dutifully, the honest Catholic that he was.

Behind the counter, an army of empty milk bottles huddled in the darkness. Things were set in jars or tin containers, tea, sugar, flour, sweets, blocks of butter, wooden boxes of honey combs, a teetering poverty pivoting soundlessly on oiled springs, weighed to the ounce, two ounces of tea, an egg and a rasher for one solitary meal.

A diminutive old woman emerged from a doorway that led down to a fireplace. The cat brushed her legs and disappeared. She held a cardigan around her shoulders, smelling of sleep. "What can I get you, Feeney?"

Feeney bought a loaf of bread and two bottles of milk in the shop. Maria came across the road. "She was asleep again," he said to Maria. He stuck the bottles into his front pocket, took the handlebars and headed down the street. "Any word from Leahy?"

Maria shook her head.

"He's not in, or he won't come?" Feeney asked, although he knew the answer, reading it in her reluctance. He did not look at her face.

"His wife says he got nothing for the last time he helped you."

Feeney looked furious. He wanted someone to share in his triumph. "We'll do without him."

"Are you going to sell the cow soon?" Maria said as they walked along.

"I'm going to pack the whole lot of them in, the shagging mother and calf," Feeney nodded, his fingers spread out like a starfish on the black bicycle seat. He turned, agitated, enumerating the grievances he had against the town. He was not prone to cataloguing retribution, but as he walked along he kept seeing different faces of Orangemen who had wronged him, all shopkeepers who could not be challenged. They held a monopoly on his life. The town, if he stayed long enough, had its awful, trenchant fatalism, forcing him to the grim acknowledgment that he was born an outsider, that the world of money was beyond him. Small plots of land were his haunt.

He lived amongst animals. Usually, when he got like this he carried bags of hay from one end of the town to the other, or rode his bicycle hard on the roads. Animal exertion was a form of therapy.

A strip of light cut his face. He looked up and shook himself. "What was I saying?"

Maria looked at him.

They walked briskly. The cow wasn't well. All Feeney needed was a complication and he could lose everything. The noon meal simmered from the backs of shops, mingling with the cold. His stomach turned digested toast and an egg from the early morning breakfast.

"Can we eat first?" Maria lingered outside a doorway. A family ate at a table.

"Whist a bit." Feeney breathed hard. His lungs ached from the long days. He was severely realistic to the point of pessimism. If he was lucky and took some pigs to market along with the calf and mother, he felt he could afford the bicycle and have enough left to get a new litter of pigs. He calculated figures in his head, carrying out addition and subtraction, losing numbers, beginning again and again. Surely, the dealers wouldn't be that hard on him, give him a few extra pounds for the sake of Christmas. He'd have more animals in due time, but all pigs from here on out. His lips moved as he went on. He wanted to get back to the old routine, to the things he knew about.

Throughout the years he bought all sorts of animals, pigs, hens, turkeys, preparing them for slaughter. There were some farmers who preferred not to kill their own livestock. Feeney obliged. He was good at these things. Everyone knew that Feeney had a way with animals that could only have come through a long period of intimacy with a farm. They were somewhat wary of a dispossessed man who took to slaughter so easily. Yet, Feeney had a fixity of expression, an earnest face propped up by a family. Everything about him said, "Whatever I have done in my past, I will do you no harm. Trust me with your slaughter."

For all his association with animals, Feeney resolved that his children would never follow in his footsteps. He never let the children near the animals up to this. He had his own relationship with animals which he kept to himself, an ambivalence which he did not understand, but felt. For whatever the reason, God had set him among animals, and he took his lot with solemn accord. He knew about heredity from breeding animals, the crude eugenics of dog handlers playing God. In his younger years he had fought the filth and degradation of a farm life, the constant attention to animal needs, the six in the morning milking, the turning of the hay; a convolution of birthing and slaughtering. The lure of cities, their careless escape, led him through Dublin and over to Liverpool. However, the money soon ran out. World War loomed. It was only after marriage, that milestone of realism, that he came back to what he had always been accustomed, animals. The return changed his entire life. The frivolity of his youth soured into a conscious asceticism where he indulged in neither drink nor smoke. Sex took on its obligatory procreation, a purge of frustration. He wasn't beyond a good laugh, but somehow marriage and children threw him into the slavish need to provide. The memory of his people sitting in their own houses, on their own land, with their own animals, lurked behind his every thought. He had not only disinherited himself, but had destined his children to be landless people.

Feeney took a side glance at his daughter. It was best that she be down here with him rather than his sons. They were to be city men. She had a sensitivity that would keep secrets to herself. Boys were blabbers, and God knows, if any of them fainted at the sight of a cow giving birth, what would they think of themselves? He nodded to himself, yes, she was at that age where she understood something about things that were never to be revealed. Feeney had a secret awe for women; they held the unfathomable within themselves. They had the ability to reinvent life into a fancy of romance, of hope, of love, despite hidden channels of blood and pain which were never discussed. He had never come to terms with any of it.

Feeney knew he was in a bad way now. His head was at him. He turned the key in a heavy padlock and pulled back the gate. He kept the stock in a rented bit of land out the back of an old widow's place off the main street. The big yard stabled horses and coaches before the time of trains and motor cars.

Maria moved slowly behind him, exploring the walled enclosure of beasts. She had never come in there before. The animals knew Feeney's smell and nosed around their pens, the pigs butting the wooden boards. "Go easy, boys." He let them sniff his hot hand. From the previous night's rounds of the hotels and guest houses, he had some potato peels and carrot scrapings left. "'Come over here, Maria. You're not scared?" Feeney maneuvered a small pig over to Maria. "'There now, let him sniff you." The wet snout sniffed her pale hand. Feeney kept pressure on her arm, holding it steady. "Dad."

"Take it easy." Feeney got a good laugh out of her, the sly coercion that could be applied to women, the steady pressure of a hand holding with sustained power, not overtly harsh, masculine. He thought back to the girls at the school. He took a bucket of peels and emptied it into the pen. "There you are." The pigs went frantic, burying their noses in the ground. Feeney grinned. He liked pigs best of all. His mood brightened. He reveled in the unabashed animal humour, the tight coiled tail. Seeding the ground, he made a clucking sound with his tongue, calling the chickens. His animals were quiet beasts who demanded nothing other than food and shelter and a hand to sniff. The enclosed space did not distress them. The claustrophobia made them more at ease. When he was young, his people used to let the pigs into the kitchen near the fire at night. Pig was one of the first words he had ever learned as a child. In later life, when he came to know more words, he looked back on the simplicity of those domestic animal names, three letter words, dog, pig, cow, hen, cat, as though they had been named before other things had names.

"Don't be scared of them," Feeney laughed, sensing his daughter's apprehension. "All they are is hungry." The affinity was lost to her, the disease of the landless, the dispossessed.

Maria sat still, watching her father move amid his animals. The place seemed like some wayward ark.

A big stone wall with tufts of grass growing between the cracks surrounded the yard. It harboured darkness, concealing an antiquated solitude. A caved in roof aimed splintered beams at the sky. The yard walls protected the animals from the whipping winds. Feeney went to great pains to keep the animals content and healthy. He didn't want a scene or have to forfeit the yard. The pigs had sonorous snorts that could only be heard if one stood outside the gate and earnestly listened, and the cluck of the chickens bothered nobody. He was set in that regard. As long as he cleaned up the manure and washed down the place with a hose, the smell was tolerable, and nobody complained. Every morning before work, he got up at six o'clock, swept the yard of its muck and waste, sprinkling sawdust in the pens.

With the pigs fed, Feeney went over to Maria. He put the bottles of milk down on the ground and took out the wrapped bread. "You'd better eat something. We'll have a long enough time here." He felt her hands. "You're freezing. Do you want to go up home and get a jumper?"

Maria shook her head.

Feeney blew into his hands. "So now you see everything. Is this the way you thought it would be?"

Maria shrugged her shoulders.

"This is what has kept us for the last few years."

"I'm cold," Maria whispered.

Feeney pointed around the yard. "You see how hard it is to survive in this world. I took you down here to see this so you can remember what I did for you when the time comes."

Maria sensed something was being asked of her and smiled obliquely.

"All right, I'll say no more." Feeney rose. He knew she was not at the point of understanding him yet. He still lived his solitary life. "Listen, stay put awhile until I see that everything is all right." He walked to the back of the yard to a shed.

The cow remained unseen. Feeney stuck his head into the hemisphere of blackness. The cow moved silently. He stepped over the runny manure, reaching with his hand to stroke the long bovine head. The huge eyes glistened, the head turned. The cold nose bristled against his hand, a line of mucus frothing when it breathed. Feeney led the cow up toward the light in a strained hobble. He wiped the mouth with the sleeve of his coat. "There now." The cow's eyes roamed in its head, the skin damp and hot. Feeney trembled. The cow looked bad by his estimation. Jesus, what would he do if it died on him? The cow was too big to slaughter all by himself in the yard. It would have to leave the yard alive. He wondered if he should take it up to the fields for the birth. If the cow dropped dead in the yard, he had no access to a cart to bring it out dead. He'd be done out of even selling the meat.

The cow seemed to sense Feeney's mood. It held Feeney hostage, keeping the calf inside itself.

"Come on, you whore," Feeney said, pulling the cow forward.

The cow resisted and almost fell over. Feeney had tied a rope between the forefoot and back foot like the knackers did to keep their horses from straying. The cow limped everywhere. Feeney finally set it in the open yard. Its monstrous form, encumbered by the smallness of the place, shifted nervously. The pigs eyed it and snorted belligerently.

Maria swallowed and pointed at the cow's leg. Feeney hunched over. The shin above the hoof of the foreleg was shaved in a deep wound. He pressed the leg gently, fingering his way up to the breast, feeling if the infection had spread. The cow pulled away from him nervously. "Christ." The wound glistened, pink and tender. Puss oozed out when he applied pressure around the edges of the wound. The cow lowed.

Maria flinched. "Dad!" she shrieked, curling away from the sight of the injured creature.

Feeney untied the frayed rope. He felt the horror in his daughter's presence. He stood up and slapped the cow's nose in a spasm of rage. His daughter was lost to him. She saw him as cruel. What the hell could he do? The cow had gone mad a few months ago and nearly destroyed the yard. He had to tie the legs to keep the cow from kicking out at the shed door. Feeney wanted to say this to his daughter, but all he said was, "You go over to Leahy and get him, do you hear me?" Feeney glared at the cow.

"But he said . . ." Maria pressed herself against the wall.

Feeney grabbed her by the arm and took her to the gate. "Tell him the cow is sick. Go on, tell him." Feeney went out the gate and over to a chemist's shop. He came back with antiseptic cream and dabbed the wound. The cow lowed plaintively. "Whist," Feeney whispered, his fingers working the wound. "There, you see, you've cost me another two bob." His rough fingers worked the wound. "You did this yourself, didn't you?"

Feeney stood up and wiped his face and then mixed a bag of animal grain in a bucket, adding water from the hose, stirring the mixture. His body sweated under the black coat as he worked away. He poured the contents into a long shallow trough. The cow lapped up the mixture, impervious to Feeney's mood. It had its hostage. The food was set before it.

At least it was eating. Feeney breathed easy. He checked the barrel side of the cow, feeling the pregnancy inside, putting his chiseled face against the warm hide. It was over-pregnant by his estimation. Christ, after all this time, he soon would be rid of the beast. He resisted the urge to hurt it. He'd never experienced such disaffection with an animal before, but cows were different than pigs. They had an almost luxurious swagger to them, and long feminine lashes, eyes that regarded him with suspicion. Except for their milk, Feeney would have no part of them. The redness of their meat indicted, red and runny, cooked so many ways, unlike the placating white of pork, served one way. After a Sunday dinner of steaming cow organs, families had to walk off the bloated decadence of hard-to-digest meat. Feeney took no part in such ways. He had his pigs served hard and over-cooked, ungarnished, the bristle of hair singed, the rubbery fat, call it cannibalism for all it was worth, he had spoken to and loved this meat, it had eaten from his hands, now he ate it with his hands. Yes, slaughter was a necessity, eating was a necessity. He left it at that, if not reveling in its baseness, then at least acknowledging the crudeness.

When Feeney finished feeding the cow, he sat down on a smoothed stone. He looked wearily at his animals. The yard, another dimension beyond the dim street, cobbled stone out of the eighteen hundreds, the loose mortar and the big stones cut awkwardly. He imagined hot horses rubbed down for the night, the warmth of their breath and flesh mixing with heat from the blacksmith's fire. Everything lay in ruins now. The widow who owned the place had migrated to an upper floor of the old house, confined to a bed set near a window to let whatever light there was fall on her wasting body. The town lived on the ghostly memory of old money, the military pensions of deceased Protestants of the Boer War who left all to their brittle-boned brides. Feeney heard the one widow was leaving five thousand pounds to a cat's home.

The pigs snorted and clamoured against the pens, getting Feeney's attention. The smell of the antiseptic cream made them uneasy. "Easy boys." Feeney felt there must have been something immoral or sinful about himself, the prodigal son who received no homecoming. For all these years he had never asked that question of himself as he had begun to over the time with the cow. Christ, he knew he shouldn't have bought it. It wasn't a time to gamble.

For all his association with animals and slaughter, Feeney had a reserved regard for them. A crescent scar on his cheek marked him for slaughter himself, the wounds of animals. He stared at the pigs finishing the scraps. He would never openly admit it, but part of his nerves was guilt at having to do the inevitable, coming down on a Friday evening when the town was at its wildest and opening a pig's throat into a bucket, holding the shaking body. He did it sober, because he did not want to cut himself and mess up the whole thing, but the real reason lay somewhere beyond practicality. When he slaughtered, it was always a wholesale slaughter, no survivors, each one led away by the scent of his hand to the dark corner of the shed, his thick thumb making the sign of the cross on the flat forehead. He didn't want any of them to live on in fear or remembrance of what had happened to the others. Animals had memories. With the money he made from slaughter, he bought a new stock, innocent of murder, just greedy to sniff his hand and eat his scraps. That was how he was able to keep the pigs so quiet, giving them a false sense of security, treating them more like pets than livestock. Feeney was good at deceiving animals.

The problem had been the cow, witness to his massacres, sentient to the flow of animal blood, speaking in a language of smell to the frightened pigs huddled in the pen away from a marauding bloody hand.

Feeney ate slowly, turning the food over with his tongue. The sun dissolved on the horizon. He put the milk to his lips and drank, the coldness of the day getting to him. His kidneys were at him. He got up and urinated against the wall. The light traced its own shadow of piss. Everything was beset with its own ghost.

Feeney sat down again. His scrotum turned in on itself, migrating up into his body. The cow mooed. Feeney got up and led it into the stable again.

Where the hell was Maria? Feeney walked back and forth in the yard. The cow dropped splats of manure in the shed. Feeney expected the cow to start dropping the calf right there. He'd come so long with the cow. It had been his own fault, greed and stubborn pride, to have put himself up to a thing like this. If he'd left well enough alone, everything would have continued as it was. He knew from the start that cows were temperamental beasts. They needed an amount of grass and hay which could not readily be supplied by his sole means of transportation, his bicycle. It had been a long year. He felt the ebb of sleep, the drifting in and out of consciousness that had become so much habit over the year. He wore himself out in the first weeks, trying to buy feed for the cow. But nothing would sustain its appetite. He finally set on taking it out after dark up to the hill and letting it eat on the green out back of the Gaelic pitches where knackers' work horses grazed. The only problem was that he had to stay with the animal. He couldn't trust the knackers who would have sold the cow if they had the chance. On clear or rainy nights, he led the cow off, taking up his residency on a tree stump. The cow didn't react well to the night feeding. It's temperament tended toward day feeding and a long night ruminating. It took Feeney all his time to break the instinct in the animal. He stopped short of getting down on his hands and knees and eating with the cow under the moonlight. He was well capable of that kind of earnest lunacy. He had a family to feed and another child on the way.

Maria came into the yard. The lights in the houses were on already. "Don't let the pigs out," Feeney shouted. Two pigs harassed Maria, trying to push through the gate. Feeney got up and slapped the pink skin, making the pigs squeal and trot back to their pens. "Well?" Feeney said.

Maria looked at the ground.

"I knew as much. . . . I'll remember him. Well you'll have to hold the light for me then. It's over there. Get it."

Feeney went to the cow again. Maria followed her father. Feeney felt the rotund stomach, letting his fingers work around the hind, lifting up the tail, feeling for the first signs of water. The cow pulled away and lumbered to the security of its dark quarters. Its back legs were already parted. Feeney grinned, feeling the reproach. She couldn't prevent nature from taking its course. He'd have the calf from her. He rubbed the silky mucus thread on his coat.

Feeney filled a bucket of water. "She's nearly there." He went out and secured the pigs, talking to them.

Maria peered at him through the slashes in the shed door. He was laughing and rubbing them. He came back and sat down in silence.

The evening died into a blustery night. Errant sound drifted into the yard, plates being scraped in the back yard. Tea time was over. The cow moved anxiously, lowing, coming forward in the stable, nudging Feeney. He stared at the animal.

"Maybe she's ready now," Maria whispered.

Feeney put a finger to his lips. "Shoo. Let her get comfortable first. They have their own way of preparing." Feeney's forehead wrinkled. "Have the light ready."

Maria had her hands around her shoulders.

The cow bellowed plaintively. Feeney rose. "That's it, you whore." He took the cold bucket of water. The cow faced the wall, its hind legs far apart, like a big woman in high heels, the hooves scraping the concrete floor, trying to keep balance. The tail hung to the side of its rump. The margin of wetness spread down to the thighs. Feeney put his hands under his hot armpits to warm them before touching the cow. It mooed softly in resignation, the tremour of its legs holding it up above the damp hay. Feeney stared with the obligatory sobriety of a vet. He had done this sort of thing before. The shed filled up with the hot animal breath and juices of birth, closing around him into its own womb.

"You stand over there," Feeney whispered. "Light the lamp." He took his coat off and rolled up his sleeves. He blew on his hands once more to make sure they were warm.

Maria shivered in the corner. She lit the lamp, putting it on the ground. She looked at the dark figure of her father leaning into the hind of the cow as though he were trying to climb into it. She closed her eyes.

Feeney eased his hand into the soft suctioning warmth of the passage. The cow's legs nearly buckled. He supported them with his shoulder, his face inches from the dark folds of flesh. "That's it." His wrist pivoted, his fingers crawling along the creature's inside. He felt the slime of the sack. He drew his hand out into the coldness, hot and glazed, dipping it into the bucket of water. A shock of coldness ran through him. A dribble of urine ran down his leg. "Get more water," he whispered to Maria.

Maria had her hands to her face. Feeney barely distinguished her. "Get me more water," he shouted. "Come on." She was sobbing. She went out and came back with more water.

The cow was almost squatting, the contraction of the tunnel pushing the calf along. "Leave it there." Feeney tried to touch her. Maria jumped back in terror.

"Jasus," Feeney muttered. He went around to the head, letting the cow touch his hand, the tongue instinctively licking the scent of her own insides. She shifted forward and moaned. Feeney stroked the stomach, appeased at last. The cow settled for a few long minutes, breathing hard, her hind opening slowly.

The calf dropped into a bed of straw, a sack of mucus. Feeney spooled the dark entrails. The cow turned and pushed him with its head. The calf lay inert, like a small child curled up. Feeney panicked and pushed the cow's head away. It began to moo, butting Feeney. He fell to the side, scrambling on his knees to the calf. The limbs were stiff. "Jasus, no!" He moved away to the corner, his hand to his mouth, his tongue hanging out of his head. The cow leaned over the calf, nudging it, trying to bring it to its feet. He stared at the pit of cow's hole, panting in spasms, then turned off the lamp.

A half an hour passed. His teeth chattered. Maria held his hand. The cow stood motionless over the dead calf, invisible. Feeney lit the lamp again. The cow's face was smeared with blood. "Go home," Feeney said.

Maria pressed his hand. "Will it be all right?"

Feeney pushed her gently. "Go on." Maria stood up and looked at the dead calf and then at the cow and back to her father. She stopped herself from crying.

Feeney took the bucket of water and washed the cows face. It gave itself up, dazed and exhausted. He cleaned off the hind legs. "Go on now, you see she's fine."

Maria waited in the yard amongst the pigs.

Feeney lifted the calf into his arms and took it out into the yard. The cow followed him. He had to stop and push the massive head back into the darkness. The cow acquiesced. In the yard, the pigs were sleeping, the chickens with their heads tucked into their breasts. The sky overhead was black with clouds, the universe unseen. He was glad. This was his secret.

Maria walked behind her father. "You're not angry with the cow, Dad, are you?"

Feeney put the calf absurdly over the crossbar, putting its torso in the middle with the legs hanging on either side. He extended the forefeet onto the handlebars so the legs wouldn't get caught in the spokes. It looked like the calf was steering. Feeney turned up towards the Gaelic pitches. Maria followed behind him. He stopped. "You go home now, love."

"Dad."

"What?"

She had turned toward home. "Don't hurt the cow."

Feeney swallowed and said nothing.

When Feeney finished disposing of the calf, he came back down to the yard. He locked the padlock again. His shirt was soaked with blood. His body trembled, blue with cold. The cow stood in the shed, waiting. In the yard, Feeney slapped the pigs and woke them. He threw stones to disturb the chickens. They flew around and then landed again. "I want you to see what happens to animals who cheat Feeney." The animals shuffled around, nosing the buckets for scraps. They were accustomed to order. The pigs tried to touch his hands. Feeney opened the shed and led the cow into the yard. He questioned the cow, an absurd trial. He led pigs to an imaginary witness stand. He took hold of their hooves and shook them. The pigs grunted amiably, corroborating stories. Feeney got the lamp and brought it to the cow's face and then to the hind legs and told his version of how it all happened. Some terrible things had gone on in the yard. Feeney talked about the incontrovertible evidence, calling the cow "a slut." It stood with its head down in the middle of the yard. Its hind dribbled mucus. "You have been sentenced to death."

Feeney held the butchering knife in his hand. He took it to the neck of the cow and cut cleanly across the throat. The cow fell over like a cardboard figure. Its hooves tapped the concrete as though it was waiting impatiently to die. Its mouth opened and closed mutely.

"Now there, justice has been served, gentlemen of the jury." The pigs grunted around him. He let them smell his hand, the teeming sweat on the hair of his hand. He led the pigs into their pens, then left, locking the gate behind him, leaving the cow in the yard. He pushed his bicycle alongside him. He had done what had to be done. It was officially over. Now he looked forward. From the knackers he felt he would get enough for the new bicycle. He was adding figures in his head. There was always next year. The pigs were a sure bet. "Gentlemen of the Jury," he said in his most Protestant voice, then burst out laughing. The pigs had learned something out of this. There was a contract in life, between all creatures, between men and women, between religions, between countries, between him and the town of Protestants that had to be maintained, a life living on Borders. Himself and his pigs would continue through this time of struggle, in the love and births and deaths, in the slaughtering and the eating. "No," Feeney said to himself, "this wasn't a bad night at all." It wasn't a thing to ruin a Christmas.

Tony D'Souza

TAGGERS

Dean Mickelson, a kid I wasn't supposed to hang out with, called me up on a Sunday afternoon a week before school let out for the summer. My folks were at church with my little sister, and I was lying on the couch watching pro-wrestling on TV. I didn't go to church anymore because I didn't believe in that crapola. My dad said, "Rot in hell if you want, I don't care," about it, but my mom said it was only a phase I was going through and that I'd be back in the front pew singing my lungs out in a little while, just wait and see. My mom could annoy the heck out of me like that.

And it was her fault that I'd made my confirmation anyway. I wasn't going to do it, I told my dad all winter how it would be a lie if I went up there and said all that crap about God and the Apostles and Jesus and how I loved them, and he said, "Fine, Ted. Do what you need to do," all winter in his tight voice which meant he was trying to sound like he didn't care when he really did, and then my mother leaned in my doorway one night a week before the ceremony in her blue nightgown and looking tired and beautiful with her dark hair down around her shoulders and her slender hands on the doorframe like holding it up, like it was the pillar that supported our house, and she said, "Please make your confirmation, Teddy. For your daddy's and my sake. You'll embarrass us in front of the whole community if you don't."

So I'd gone up there to the bishop in an itchy suit my dad had bought me that week at the Men's and Boy's store where we bought all our clothes with the tie knotted too tightly around my throat as though he hadn't wanted me to be able to breathe, and the bishop had asked me what he'd asked thirty-five other kids in my grade, "Do you believe in blah blah blah and love blah blah blah your savior, Jesus Christ?" And I had said, "Yes," nicely while my aunt Tina, kneeling beside the altar for an angle, snapped Polaroids of me for the family album. Then the bishop wiped holy oil on my forehead, and that had been that, and we went to Red Lobster for all-you-can-eat Alaskan King Crab legs that night because it was my choice, and we stuffed ourselves. I had to loosen my belt a notch at the end of it the way my dad did. I guess it wasn't that big of a deal.

Dean Mickelson said over the phone, "Whatcha doing, Ted?"

"Watching Hulk Hogan kick the Iron Sheik's ass," I said, watching the wrestlers on TV.

"The Iron Sheik?" Dean said. "I hate that dirty sand-nigger."

"Me too," I said.

"We bombed the shit out of those camel jockeys, didn't we, Ted? We bombed Quaddafi's baby daughter."

"We fucked them up, that's for sure."

"We've got a great president, don't we, Ted?"

"My dad says he's the champ. He ain't afraid of the commies or anybody. My dad says we can be proud to be Americans."

"I'm proud to be American for sure," Dean said.

"We're the best nation on earth," I said. Then Hogan pile-drived the Sheik into the mat, and the sweat splashed off them like glitter through the light of the flashing cameras, and the Sheik's turban flipped off. "Hey, Dizz," I said, "did you know that the Sheik's bald under his towel?"

Dean said, "Hogan pulled the Sheik's towel off his head?"

"You bet," I said. "Hogan's slamming him all over the place. Hogan's wiping the place up with him. Ain't you watching, Dizz?"

"Naw. I'm listening to some music in my room. Want to come over and hang out with me?"

"What are you listening to?"

"I dunno," Dean said, "Dylan."

"What album?"

"*Desire.*"

"Is that the one with the getting stoned song on it?"

"Naw. I don't know which one that one's on."

"That's a killer song anyway," I said. "Hey, Dizz, got any doob over there by the way?"

"A little," Dean said. "Why? You want to come over and smoke up with me?"

"Sure," I said, switching the TV off with the remote.

~ I tied on my red and black striped Vans and skateboarded over there. It was six blocks down along the elm shaded streets of Park Ridge, my town, and Dean lived with his foster father on Touhy, the busy street I hadn't been allowed to cross when I'd been a kid. One time walking home from kindergarten, I'd been screwing around doing something, something like throwing mudballs with my pal back then, Danny Durkin, at his neighbor's house, and by the time I got to the corner, the crossing lady had gone home. So I had sat on the sidewalk and cried because I couldn't cross the street. After a long time of that, a police lady came and stopped traffic for me.

At Dean's place, in the driveway, I ollied off my board, caught it under my arm, and went around back and rang the bell. Dean's foster dad had a lot of flowers in his garden, and there were robins splashing around in the birdbath across the yard, and white blossoms all over the apple tree like snow. Then Dean was standing behind the screen door with a bottle of Coke in his hand, his blond hair down all over his shoulders, his gold stud in his ear, and his eyes were red and droopy like he'd only just woken up, and good old Dean was stoned already. He always made me think of a hillbilly with his hair long like that.

"Jesus, Dizz," I said. "When'd all these bloomers come up?"

"The last week or so," Dean shrugged, "I dunno. But ain't it beautiful back here, Ted?"

"It's probably the best garden in town."

"My dad works pretty hard on it," Dean said, smiling as he looked out at all those colors—reds and oranges and yellows, greens and blues and violets—bright as candy, like the colors of the rainbow, and then his eyes trailed over onto me, and he laughed like he was happy, like he was surprised and happy to see me. "Hey Jones-ey. Come on in," he said. "My dad ain't home."

We went up to his room above the garage. Dean's was the coolest bedroom I'd ever seen because his foster dad just let him have a mattress on the floor without any frame, and there were Zeppelin and Hendrix and Dead posters on the walls, and he was the only kid I knew who had his own computer. We sat on the mattress and looked up at the pages of the *Sports Illustrated* swimsuit issue he'd taped to his ceiling while we smoked a bowl of bud.

"Your foster dad's pretty cool," I told him, looking up through the smoke of the bowl at the long-legged models in their bikinis. They were all on some beach somewhere, and Elle MacPherson and that black chick whose name I didn't know were splashing through the surf like ponies, their long hair whipping behind them like tails. I looked at the smooth curves of their jugs beneath the wet cloth of their bikinis, at the bumps of their nipples through it, and then I had to look out Dean's window so I wouldn't pop the wood. There was a plane trail in the blue sky there, a long white line.

"I like it a whole lot over here," Dean said. "Lots better than over at Mercy."

"What the heck's Mercy?"

"This dump these bitch nuns run."

"Bitches, huh?"

"Yeah."

"They whack you around much over there?"

"I dunno. Not much. But they were always screaming about some shit. The littlest shit, you know. Like muddy shoes. I like Park Ridge."

"Were there chicks living over there, too?"

"Yeah, dude," Dean said and grinned, puffing a plume of smoke out toward the window. He tapped the bowl with his lighter to loosen up the bud. The bowl was nothing special at all, just a straight steel pipe, and you could see your reflection when you'd hit it. Dean said, "There was this Mexican chick named Carmella over there. She let me suck her tits."

"She did?" I said.

"Oh yeah. It was no big deal. We went into this closet where they kept the brooms, and she was about to put her hands in my pants, when this bitch nun opened the door. Then I got sent down to Flosmoor, and then I came up here. I didn't know what they did to Carmella."

"I got to kiss Debbie Lawler a couple of times when we played Spin-the-Bottle at Jeff Paulson's Christmas party," I said. "But now she's going steady with Eddie McGannon."

"Isn't she that girl you gave a rose to on Valentine's Day?"

"Yeah," I said and blushed. I glanced at Dean out of the corner of my eye to see if he was laughing at me about it, but he wasn't, he was sucking on the pipe with his eyes closed. "That turned out to be pretty stupid," I said under my breath.

Dean puffed out a plume. His eyes were nearly shut now, his lashes coming together like little black feathers over the slits of his eyes. He said, "Did you stick your tongue in her mouth at least?"

"Naw," I said and laughed. He passed me the bowl and I hit it.

"Next time, put your tongue in her mouth. Girls like it. It's French kissing."

I breathed out a long plume to the window. "I know," I said as the smoke wisped out the window screen, bending left with the breeze.

"Did you ever do it before?"

"No."

"How do you know about it if you've never done it before?"

"Oh, you know. Eddie told us about it."

"Is he on the basketball team, too?"

"He's our best player."

"Call him over to shoot the rock with us sometime. The three of us can break in the new hoop my dad got for me."

"He wouldn't want to come," I said. "We're not really friends."

"He's a dickhead, huh?"

"Yeah," I said.

"Forget it," Dean said. "We don't need dickheads like that."

We cashed the bowl, and Dean hid it under his mattress again. Then we just chilled for a while with our hands folded on our stomachs, looking at the posters on the walls. There wasn't any music playing, but that was all right. I felt too lazy to music right then. I said, "You a Cubs fan, Dizz, or what?"

"Of course I am. You don't switch teams just because you move around."

I said, "I'm always going to be a Cubs fan."

"Me too," Dean said.

"I used to go down all the time with my dad when I was a kid," I told him.

"Hey, Ted," Dean said, "why don't you ask your dad if we can all go down to a game together sometime. My dad can drive us."

"Are you crazy, Dizz? I don't want to go to a Cubs game with my old man. You and me can go. We'll just take the train. Hey, Dizz, got any smokes?"

"Naw," he said. "My brother always forgets to bring me some when he stops by."

"Is your bro pretty cool?" I said.

"I used to want to live with my brother," Dean said, "but they wouldn't let me. He got in trouble once."

"Doing what?"

"I dunno," Dean said. "Hey, Ted, how can I get some cigarettes?"

"It's easy," I told him. "There's a machine over at Perry's Pizza, and you can lift them pretty easily from Walgreens."

"When I lived with my aunt over by Elston and Foster last summer, everybody just sold them right to me. Nobody cared about anything over there. It was all Royals over there.

"I'd be a Royal," I said.

"You don't know anything about the Royals."

"I'd be a Freak, too."

"You don't know anything about Freaks and Royals is why you'd say you want to be one. Nobody in Park Ridge knows anything about it. They beat you in and then you can never get out. They get all their guys just to beat you in for an hour."

"I could take it," I said.

"They hit you fifty times as hard as they can in your chest bone with their rings on. They hit your legs with baseball bats."

"I could take it no problem," I said.

"No way," Dean said. "You'd be dead in a garbage can in the morning."

"You don't know anything about me, Dizz," I said.

"I know you're from Park Ridge, and Park Ridge's people don't know anything about the Royals or the Freaks or the Kings or anybody."

"It must be cool living over in the city," I said.

"I dunno," Dean said. "Park Ridge is pretty cool, too. I asked my dad if I could go to your school next year instead of Lincoln."

"Which dad? Your foster dad?"

"I asked Jim. My dad here."

"That'd be cool, I guess," I said. "What'd he say?"

"He said everybody's Catholic and it costs a lot of money."

"Ain't you Catholic?"

"No. I'm Lutheran or something. My brother told me what I was once. But I dunno."

"Well that could be cool," I said. "But let's cruise out of here now."

"Let's go by the pool, hey. I'll lend you a suit."

"The pool's closed on Sundays, Doof. Let's just cruise around. Let's just cruise uptown and see what's going on over there."

"Okay, sure," Dean said, and we got up to stretch our bones, and he got some air freshener out of the bathroom and sprayed it around his room.

~ We boarded across Touhy, down along past the Junior High where Dean went to school, and t-ball games were going on at the diamonds, and a little kid with his cap on backwards had a kite with long purple ribbons for tails way up in the sky, and it looked like some kind of bird hanging there, like some kind of purple jungle bird with long purple tail feathers rippling behind it, and people in shorts and sunglasses were looking up at it, just standing there staring at it with their arms crossed like waiting to see it fall down, and we skated uptown past the Unitarian church and its high, white steeple, past City Hall and its tall columns, to where the red-brick library was with its bell in the tower, and we slid down the staircase on the handrails, and we hopped up and down on our boards from the lip of the stone fountain where pennies were in the green water, glinting in the sun like old coins at the bottom of the sea. Then Mrs. Burdick, the old lady librarian, came out to chase us away.

"I'll tell your father, Mr. Jones," she said as she came out, wagging her finger, her glasses hanging down on her blouse by the chain around her neck. I'm warning you, young man. I'll telephone your father again. You're coming to no good."

I boarded a circle around her, laughing, and she gave up on me and pointed her finger at Dean who was standing there on his board as though he couldn't move. "And what's your name?" she said to him. "I'll call your parents too."

But Mrs. Burdick was like everybody, a harmless old bird who got worked up over nothing, so I hopped a few loud ollies, making as much noise as I could, making the wheels hit down on the cement like I was banging down a 2 x 4, and Mrs. Burdick said, "Stop it! Stop it! Stop it!" like I was going to make her have a heart attack, and then Dean and I boarded out of there. We passed the Youth Center beside the Lutheran church where they had pool tournaments on Friday and Saturday nights that nobody ever went to, and the florist, and the pancake house where the old people were always sitting in the windows and looking out and sipping their coffee with long faces, like they were in some kind of prison, like they knew they were supposed to be dead already, and when we got to Yankee Doodle Dawg, Dean pulled up and said, "Let's get a couple of Chicago Styles, hey Ted?"

"Sure," I said, "but I ain't got no money."

"Don't worry," Dean said, "I've got a little. My dad gives me an allowance."

We got a couple of dogs with everything on them from Mr. Frangella who owned the place, and a medium coke to share, and we ate the dogs at the counter in the window. We were just chewing, just looking at the cars pass by on the street and then line up when the light turned red down by the bank, when I said all of a sudden, "My dad says Jim's a fruit." Dean's forehead flushed. "Jim's not a fruit," he said.

"Well that's what my dad says," I said and shrugged.

"Does your dad even know my dad at all?"

"I don't know," I shrugged. "I guess not."

"Listen, Ted, I could bash your face in so you wouldn't even know what happened. I could fuck you up so people wouldn't even know who you were."

"What?" I said.

"Look—" Dean said, like he wasn't even in his head anymore, like he was about to take a step toward me, and then he stopped. He lifted up the Coke and sipped it through the straw.

"Hey-hey there, Teddy," Mr. Frangella said, setting his heavy hand on my shoulder. He was in his apron with his hair combed over his bald spot. "How's the dog? Staying out of trouble, pal? How's the old man? Want to make a little money today? I've got some flyers for you to pass around. The both of you. Hang on, guys. Let me go get them."

Mr. Frangella went back to get the flyers and Dean said to me like nothing had happened, like we were still friends, "Still hungry, Ted? I'd get you some fries or something if I had any more money."

"Naw, I'm cool," I said looking out the window.

"Sure?" Dean said. "We could go back to my house and I could get some money from there. My dad keeps a jar of change in the kitchen."

"Naw, I'm fine," I said.

"Want a sip of the Coke? You can just have the rest of it if you want."

"Naw, I'm cool. I'm fine," I said.

Mr. Frangella came back with a stack of yellow flyers in each hand. "Here you go, fellas. There's a hundred for you both. Just go around and stick them under windshield wipers. And here," he said, fishing his wallet out of his back pockets, "is two dollars for each of you."

Dean and I put the money in our pockets. "Thanks Mr. F," I said as we caught up our boards to get out of there. "We'll go over to the supermarket and get these out right away."

"Say hello to your mom and dad, Ted," Mr. Frangella said, wiping his hands on his apron. "Stay out of trouble, now. Come back and see us." Outside, I boarded around into the alley. I didn't care if Dean followed me or not, but he did. "Where are you going, Ted?" he said behind me.

I pulled up at the big dumpster out back, lifted the lid, and threw the flyers in there. I shifted around a piece of cardboard to hide them. "Just pitch them in here, if you want," I said to Dean who was watching me. "It's what I always do. I'm not wasting my whole afternoon on that old dago."

Dean lifted the lid and threw in his flyers. "I don't care either," he said.

I skated back around to the street, past the hot dog shop. I didn't care if Mr. Frangella saw me without the flyers or not. Dean just followed me, and I didn't care about that either. I skated around past the library and down Main Street where all the clothing shops were with him behind me like my shadow. I pretended he wasn't there.

"Hey, Ted," Dean said, calling loudly behind me like asking me to hold on. "What do you want to do now?"

I didn't say anything. I just skated along.

"Are you going home?" Dean called. "You're not going home now, are you?"

"No I'm not going home, Dean," I said. I pulled up at the hardware store, and caught up my board. "I'm going to get a can of spray paint and fuck around behind the movie theater. You can go home if you want. I don't care what you do."

"No, I'll hang out with you," Dean said.

"Give me your money. What color do you want?"

"I dunno," he said, looking over his shoulder at the street.

"You don't have to come with me," I said.

"No, I'll come."

"Then give me your money."

"I don't care," Dean said, giving me the money. "My dad gives me an allowance."

"You said that before, for Pete's sake. You don't have to say everything a hundred times, for Pete's sake."

"I don't care," Dean said.

"What color do you want?"

Dean looked along the street, at the cars driving along it, at the leafy trees in the planters, at the women along the sidewalk, looking in the windows, carrying packages they'd bought in the shops. "I dunno," he said. "Silver."

I went in the shop by myself, got two cans of silver paint, and went up to the counter where Mr. Lewis was leaning in his white shirt with his pens in his breast pocket, reading the newspaper. He looked through his glasses at the cans when I set them down. "What do you need those for, Ted?" he asked me.

"My dad sent me over," I said. "He's painting an old table."

"Painting a table silver, huh?"

"Yep," I said.

"Maybe I should give him a call and ask him why he'd want to do a ridiculous thing like that," Mr. Lewis said, lifting his eyebrow.

"Call him," I shrugged. "He's at his workbench in the garage right now, waiting for me to get home."

Mr. Lewis gave me a steady look, trying to figure me out, and then he said, "All right," and rang them up. "But tell your dad that next time he has to come over himself."

I carried out the brown paper bag with the cans in it, and Dean was sitting on his board under the window like he was tired. "Still coming?" I said, as I dropped down my board and skated away.

"Wait up, Ted. Hold up!" he called after me. "I'm coming! I'm right behind you."

~ The movie theater was across from the library, and I led us around it to the alley behind. Trash bags were out around the dumpsters, ready for pick-up in the morning, and the brick wall of the theater—and the back of the shops across the alley from it—rose up high around us, making the alley seem even narrower than it already was, and it was cool and dark back there. Cats lurked around by the dumpsters, too, their tails snaking around behind them.

"Somebody could come down here in a car and catch us," Dean said as we skated through the alley, our wheels and trucks rumbling over the concrete, the narrow walls echoing with the sound of it.

"Nobody ever comes around this place. See all these tags—" I said, pointing to all the names and signs and swears spray-painted on the walls, "—these are from me and my friends. Nobody ever gets caught back here. This whole place belongs to us." I pulled a can out of the paper bag, shook it so the bead rattled around inside, flipped off the cap to the alley with my thumb, and sprayed a long silver line along the theater wall as I coasted beside. "See?" I said to Dean, looking back at the line bobbing and dipping along the wall like the wavy top of the ocean. "What's there to worry about?"

"I dunno," Dean said. "Nothing."

"Haven't you ever tagged before?"

"Lots of times," he said.

"Where at?"

"I dunno," he said. "In the city."

"So let's see what kind of tagging they do in the city," I said, breaking like skidding on my board, tossing Dean the can. "Let's see your tag."

"I don't really have a tag," he said.

"I thought you said you tagged before. I thought you said you did it in the city. Just write your name or something. Just write your initials."

"I dunno, Ted. What if somebody comes—"

"Forget you, Dean," I said, and kicked off on my board like I was going to leave him there.

"Here," he called at me, and I circled back, and he wrote 'Dizz,' on the wall. It was nothing. It was just straight up and down letters, absolutely no style. Anybody could have done that. A little kid could have done that.

"That's it?" I said.

"I dunno—" Dean said, looking at it, squinting his eyes at it like trying to figure out what was so bad about it, "—I guess so, yeah."

"Come on," I said. "I'll show you how to really do it."

~ We hid our boards inside one of the dumpsters, on top of the garbage bags in there, and then I rolled the dumpster under the theater's fire escape, climbed on with the spray paint can in my pocket, jumped and caught the ladder's last rung. I chinned up, and pulled myself up there. Then Dean was up there, too. We ran up around the flights, and then we were on the black tar of the roof, high up, looking over Park Ridge. I could see the steeple of the Unitarian church poking out from the treetops like a slim white pyramid, and the treetops rolling off away from it like a hilly green carpet, like rolling grassy hills, and there were birds popping up and down from it in the distance like flecks of black paper, and the sun was bright over everything. Dean jogged across the roof ahead of me like an excited little kid, like drawn to what he saw, and before I could stop him, he was all the way over at the raised ledge, his hands on it, looking down at the library and the street. "It looks like a forest, Ted. It looks like we're lost in a forest," he called back at me over his shoulder.

"Get the hell away from there, dickhead," I shouted at him. "Somebody might see you. Come on. Come over here. Take a look at all this stuff I did."

Dean walked over to where I was standing in the middle of the roof, looking down at all the colors of the tags kids had painted up there over the years. A lot of it was faded, a lot of it was paint on paint, and showing it to him, I saw how it looked like a mess, like one huge messy mural, like every color of paint just splashed down however. "This one's mine," I said, touching the toe of my shoe to my tag in gold letters. It said, "Jonez," in slanting letters, in letters that slashed like knives, and it looked fast, too, like something on the side of a race car. Mostly, people had taggered their names, but they'd written all the swears there ever were, too, and "USA Rules," and "KKK," and somebody had painted a big white swastika in the middle, and "Die faggots," and there were all these hearts with initials in them.

"Did you write most of this stuff?" Dean said.

"Oh yeah," I said. "I hang out up here all the time."

"It's cool up here," Dean said, looking out around the trees as the breeze passed over us. "It's pretty up here."

"Come on, Dean," I said, crouching, shaking up my can. "Let's tag something." I sprayed, "Fuck you," in big, curving, cursive letters, like I was trying to be nice about it. Then I sprayed, 'D. L. is a bitch' and, 'E. M. sucks wad,' and then I could smell the paint in the air, and the silver of it speckled my fingers.

"What should I write?" Dean said, watching me.

"I don't care," I said. "Just something. Anything. It doesn't matter." I sprayed, 'Cubs rule.' Then I sprayed, 'I love Mary Jane.'

Dean crouched over to the side and started spraying something, but I wasn't paying attention to him. I sprayed a picture of this frog, with "Fuck Fuck Fuck," in a bubble coming out of his mouth, like how cartoons talk, like the frog was saying "Ribbit Ribbit Ribbit," except he was saying "Fuck," and I sprayed, 'T. J. + D. L.' in a heart, and I sprayed, 'D. L. + T. J. TLC 4-Ever,' in a heart. I wasn't bothering to style it at all. I was just spraying fast, like I had a lot to say. I sprayed, 'E. M. sucks cock.' I sprayed, 'Jonez Bonez.'

Dean said, "Here, Ted, look at this."

I walked over to where he was crouched and looked at what he'd done. It was this face, this square-headed face like Frankenstein with one eye winking and lines like snakes coming out of its head, and it had this huge ear to ear smile with big square teeth and all these gaps between the teeth. "What the hell's that supposed to be?" I said.

Dean looked up at me and grinned. "Can't you guess? Come on and try to guess," he said, smiling at me like I was suppose to know.

"Frankenstein," I said. "Frankenstein when he's stoned."

Dean laughed. "No, dude. Come on."

"I don't know," I said. "It's some fucked-up dude. It's Mr. Smiley-Teeth. I don't know. Who the heck is it?"

"It's me," Dean said. "It's supposed to be me."

"It doesn't look like you," I said.

"Sure it does," Dean said. "Don't you see my earrings in there? Don't you see—"

But his face closed up like a fist, his face turned dark like some cloud had covered the sun, and everything got quiet, and I turned my head to look where he was looking. A cop was walking over from the fire escape, his billy club hanging off his side, his gun in his holster, walking slow with his thumbs hooked in his belt like he wasn't in a hurry at all, like we were all down on the street and he was coming over to say hello.

"Lovely weather we're having, isn't it fellas?" the cop said to us when he came over, and he looked around at the sky, and took a deep breath like he felt pretty good. I remember the points of his hat against the sky. Then he looked down at us and smiled. "You stupid, stupid fucks," he said.

~ Dean didn't cry, not once, not even a little. Not even when Jim came into Sergeant Feldman's office in his tennis clothes, and put his hands on his shoulder, and said, "We're going to work this out." And I don't know what happened to Dean after that because I never saw him again, except that he didn't live in our town anymore.

Sergeant Feldman let me out of the cuffs as soon as Dean's foster dad signed some papers and left. "Why would you hang around with a kid like that for, Ted?" he asked me, sitting on the corner of his desk.

"Don't know," I said and shrugged, looking down at my fingers speckled with silver paint.

Sergeant Feldman shook his head. "Don't you know where kids like that end up? Come on, pal. You've got too much going on for you at home to be jerking around like this."

My father came in, in his Sunday suit, gave me a long look to let me know that I was dead, and shook the sergeant's hand. The sergeant said, "We caught him with that punk staying over with Jim Devorak."

"Devorak?" my dad said like trying to figure it out. Then he yanked me out of the chair by my collar, rattled me around, and shouted close to my face so I could feel his breath, "How could you embarrass me like this? Hey, Godammit? What the hell is the problem with you? You tell me. Don't I give you everything? Don't you have everything you want?"

"Take it easy, Will" the sergeant stood up and said.

These tears started falling out of my eyes, I couldn't help it, and my dad said, "See the big man now, officer? Ha-ha. Ted's just a little boy," and he cuffed my ear so hard, I stopped that.

I started up again in the car, not making any sound really, just letting the tears fall out as I watched my town and its homes and trees and happy people pass by in slow motion, like we'd never get home at all, and my dad said to himself as he gripped the wheel, "It's your mother's fault! It's your mother's fault! Her god damned bleeding heart just had to invite that urchin into our house."

He shouted at her about it when we got home, and I laid on my bed in the dark of my room with my hands behind my head, listening. My little sister came and stood in my doorway looking at me with her eyes wide because she was scared, looking as small and little in her dress as an elf, and I turned over and went to sleep. I knew nothing would happen to me. Nothing ever did.

~ Except they made me paint the roof of the theater. Not the whole thing, only the part where the graffiti was, and I had this black gloop in a white bucket that I had to get on my knees and spread around with a heavy, wooden handled brush. I went up there with the lady who owned the place, and she had on a tan suit, and tan heels, and she was very pretty with brown hair and brown eyes, and a pearl necklace, and pearl earrings, and a slim gold watch.

She looked like she belonged on TV, she was one of the ladies who did the news, and she kept her arms crossed the whole time, like she was mad at me, and stood well away from me, like she was afraid of me. I don't think she was from our town. She wanted to know which ones I'd painted.

"This one," I said, pointing out the 'Jonez' in gold, and "This one," I said, pointing out the 'Fuck you' in silver.

"And who did this one?" she wanted to know, stretching her leg out to tap Dean's face with the pointed toe of her shoe like she didn't want to get too near it, like it was a dirty puddle of water.

"The other kid," I said. "The kid who got me to do it."

"Is this some king of gang sign?" the lady asked me, toeing Dean's earring like it was a marble she could kick away. "I'd like to know the meaning of this."

"I don't know what it means," I told her. "I think it's just a silly face."

"No," the lady said, shaking her head, "this means something. I know this has some significance for you kids."

She looked at me like she expected some answer, and I shrugged, and she just looked at me a minute with her arms folded, looked me right in the eyes like trying to really see who I was, and then she said, "This roof hasn't been inspected for at least eleven years. Tell your friends that it's soft in places. Tell your friends that they could fall through at anytime." Then she left me alone up there.

I finished a couple hours later. The knees of my jeans were black with tar and ruined from my kneeling to work the brush, but it was time for a new pair anyway. I was tired because the day was hot and I laid on my back and looked at the sky.

School was out a week now, and I'd already forgotten what it was like to be cooped up in there all day. The whole summer before me—as endless and empty before me as the sky was deep and blue that day—and I was growing, I could just feel myself growing, my arms and legs stretching out, my muscles getting bigger, and I closed my eyes to feel myself grow. I imagined what it would be like to slam dunk a basketball over everybody to win a game. I imagined the cameras flashing as I arced through the air, I imagined the girls in the stands screaming my name.

Seamus Deane

D.

It was easy to go to Ireland with D.; I had not much to stay for in Paris. I trusted him. He had money. He would help with the baby. He liked me. I had no feeling that he would demand anything severe in the way of return, certainly nothing sexual, no kind of domination or squalor. He wanted something from me, of course he did, but he wasn't sure what it was and I believed I knew as well as he did. He wanted to appease my loneliness in place of his own, or as a version of his own, or as a prelude to learning how to deal with his own. That was my guess. He looked at me as though his own loneliness had suddenly become incarnate before him. O'Malley thought it was sexual, but O'Malley was always wrong—not by a lot, but by enough—in important matters.

Besides, there was the fear D. and I both shared and that O'Malley was at least tinged by—the fear of the young man in the café. He was looking across at D. and O'Malley and in the three-quarters profile it seemed to me that his eyes were stove into his head, as if they had been formed by someone turning a hot, burled stick into his pewterish flesh, the sort of texture and colour my father's flesh had when he was dying from pneumonia. Even as I thought this his gouged eyes turned suddenly on me and his face, the face, was that of a healthy young man, simmering with energy, yet still sexless, because it was the brilliant robotic imitation of a condition not of a person. How did I know so much then? Did I know it? Yes, I did, I did, I was so high-tuned, I could notice and recognise in one instant, as immediately as immediacy can be, anything that came into my ken. I knew it all but could do nothing with it. I needed someone like D. to bring it into a reality where it would slow down in that thicker air and become absorbed.

It began in that upstairs corridor, as one would expect. D. had a light installed; he had offered to make large-scale improvements, bring in a contractor, restore the whole house to something like its former self. But I was already more than beholden to him and wanted nothing else from him, just some time to myself and the child, some privacy, some rest from his increasingly sombre protectiveness behind which I could see his leaping love for me. I was grateful and was full of good feelings towards him, but I did not want to be surrounded all the time by his excessive civilities and assiduities, all the decencies in which he invested his increasingly intense longings. So he let me have it as it was, with minor improvements carried out by tradesmen, and some decorating. But I said I'd bring it into line myself, slowly, a bit here, a bit there, improving it maybe, preserving it as much as I could, making it comfortable. Sometimes I would see an elegant ginger and white cat ease itself over a drainpipe onto a sloping roof that lay beyond a bedroom window. It would go upward on the slates a few feet, then stop and lazily lick itself over one shoulder, then unripple slowly as it stalked sedately to the roof crown. It seemed so noble and brilliant a creature against the gray-black roof, the unmoving building, a mobile and indifferent occupant, not just of the house but of the whole vicinity, as natural to both as the two centuries that had passed since the house was built and the vicinity had reformed itself around the chunky new residence with its gardens and its noise and its vulnerable shimmies and reflection in the lake that it seemed to command.

Maybe it was because of that ginger and white cat, I decided I would redo that bedroom first, and was so readily taken by the decision that I had D. call for some window cleaners to come and do all the windows of the house of that side, inside and out, so that I could begin the renovation with the semilustrous light of the lake glimmering in that uneven old velvety glass or with the rising sunlight welling in it and turning its roundnesses into squares and rectangles that appeared like new windows themselves on floors and walls and made the whole house seem transparent instead of dark and fugitive.

So it was that on a morning, no more than a week after the window cleaners had come and a housepainter had painted the high ceiling a flat, solid white, when I was shifting rolled rugs, bundled curtains and the debris the painter had not yet removed into the hallway, that I looked up at a noise from the dark end, where the fallen staircase was, and the young man from Paris was standing there, hands in pockets, with a slashing red cravat at his throat and a pale grey linen shirt that seemed to billow slightly in a ruffle of wind that came from the open window behind me, standing and smiling towards rather than at me until I realized he was staring at little Carmel who was sitting on the floor holding her teddy bear and gazing very earnestly back at him. At once I straightened and practically jumped to stand between them, anger and terror lighting up in me, and, at that moment he was gone and only the wind in the baby's hair seemed real as I turned to lift her and hold her to me, softly, feeling that I was clasping a tiny cloud that moved out of my arms even as I held it and moved, moved so unknowingly and pitilessly away. Next time I saw him like that, he was standing on the water, about a hundred yards from the house. D. and O'Malley were with me, and D. was holding Carmel as we walked towards his car. It was the sound of birdwings that made me turn, as though a flight of moorhen were skidding in. But it was he, all in black but with a dab of redness at the throat and his arms outstretched, in mock greeting or embrace. Carmel pointed over D.'s shoulder and said, "Man. Man," but when D. and O'Malley turned obligingly to humour her he had gone again, as I knew he always would or would for as long as it suited him.

And he appeared like that maybe half a dozen times, three times in the corridor, once on the stairs leading to the front door, twice in the ruined garden, passing behind a shrubbery that had grown into a wall of twisted ivies and clematis, strangled rosebushes and ceanothus overpowered by weight and guile. Yet even in the midst of this some of the blossoms flared their blues and purples, and a lone yellow rose survived as though in midair, shaking itself gently to pieces. He passed behind these towards the muddied circle that had once been a lily pond.

It was his joke, I knew, his announcement that he was coming, that he meant harm, that he was subtle and unstoppable, that the child was in his sights, that . . . What was he not saying? I was ensnared in his evil, he was walking round me like a cat in heat, spraying the boundaries with his foul juices, and I was locked inside with the odours of the lakewind passing and thinning the foulness out though I still felt it eating, feasting even on my insides, lifting its moist face now and then smilingly. But I kept renovating the bedroom. And I vowed to renovate every room, one by one, until I had nothing left to renovate but the rotting end of the corridor, the broken stair, the ugly void into which the few remaining steps dangled by their chewed joints above the rat-streaked basement floor.

It was his part, no, not his part so much as it was a part of the house his kind belonged to, the pit that is in every house that cares to take the risk of opening it or is so sunk in apathy that it opens by itself with none to stop it. I would close it up here; but first, he had to be met and I feared and feared it night upon night before he actually came, as casual and as debonair as any visitor flying through and stopping to meet old friends he has taken the trouble to track down to their lair. He would speak openly of his pursuit but slanted his speech through the slats of convention so well that the declaration of war would have been inaudible to anyone else but D. and me, and was to us the louder and more terrifying because so modulated. Of the four of us, only O'Malley was deaf to his snarl; nevertheless, O'Malley disliked him, thought him a git, a sponger, a shady little shit. Had D. or I told him of the danger, O'Malley would have shot him, without a second's thought. But that would have done no good. We knew our only hope was that some other unfortunate or unfortunates would attract him more, that he would give us up for them; but once the appearances started, I knew that had not happened. D. would know when the creature actually arrived, but he saw none of the premonitory appearances and was at least spared that. Or so I believed. I said nothing to D. but knew he was sensing my fear and anxiety and felt his care for me widen and become more cumbrous, as though he were looking around the horizon to see who or what, and then looking in close to see if it might be this or that, the child, or a cold, or the weight of the house repair, or nostalgia for France, or a sense of isolation. He read his evidences so carefully and evaded acknowledging that all his guesses were looking the wrong way. For the time being, he would remain sympathetic and misled. But he would turn to me when I most needed him. I knew that. I wished I could have loved him. It was the least he deserved.

Corinne Demas

THE VILLAGE

Everything about the village has been transformed, except for the view. The deep valley below the village and the mountains across from it have held their own through the decades, while a string of new houses traverses the mountainside and telephone poles and television antennas have sprouted along with them. When Jane had been there, as a child, years before, the main road across the mountain range had been dirt and you needed a guide to help you find the rocky path that led to the village. Now the road across the mountains is paved and at the crossroads there are two signs. The larger town, nine kilometers away, has its name in Greek and English. Her father's village, fourteen kilometers away, has its name in Greek only.

Lewis follows the road straight into the village center where there is a marble fountain, empty of water, which Jane isn't sure she remembers from when she'd been there, or from a photograph her father had sent her of himself standing there with his cousin Panyotis. The entire male population of the village, it seems, has gathered here, around an old truck, to offer advice to the man who is working under its hood. They look up as the car pulls up and they watch Jane get out. She had been rehearsing what she'll say, but before she utters a word one of the men steps forward, and addresses her as if he knows who she is and directs her to Panyotis's house. If they are surprised by her arrival, they do not show it, except for a little boy, in high tops too large for him, who runs ahead to Panyotis's house to spread the news.

Jane had not written that she was coming. She wanted to come upon Panyotis without warning. Though she does not know why; does not know what it is she hopes or fears to discover.

She recognizes the house immediately, a stone house, two stories high, behind a concrete wall that is topped with stones the size of coconuts. It had been built by her father's grandfather.

Lewis, too large for the rented car, uncoils himself, and gets out beside her. He puts his arm around her and his thumb strokes her bare shoulder so gently it stirs the minute hairs, barely touches skin.

The little boy has aroused the occupants of the house and they come rushing out now, an old man and an old woman who is wiping her hands off on her apron—her father's cousin Panyotis and his wife, Irini. Jane has no choice but to allow them to hug her and kiss her and lead her up to the veranda of the house. They shake hands with Lewis and then hug him, too.

They refer to him as her husband, and Jane knows it is not that they have chosen to bestow this status upon him, but that her father had told them that she was married.

This makes her suddenly furious—that her father had willed her this lie, knowing that she would be stuck with it, at least while she was visiting the village. Her anger at him is fresh and vivid, an anger she hasn't felt towards him since he got ill eight months before and her sadness eclipsed everything else. Now it comes over her with a fierce familiarity and makes him seem in this instant alive and vigorous. Then, while Irini runs into the house for cool drinks, and she is left sitting there with Panyotis and Lewis, she cannot speak. Not because of the anger, but because of the grief that hits her, with remembering her father is dead.

As peculiar as his leaving had been his dying, and there was not much distinction between the two. They were both forms of absence, though one carried with it the possibility of return. Her father had watched her mother's dying. Strung out over two years with drugs and promises. Her pain went on so long you would expect her to become accustomed to it, except that pain is something you can never get accustomed to. When he became ill he knew that there was no real cure for him, only a prolonging. To circumvent that (though he never said so directly), he had gone off to this village he had visited only once before in his life, to die as his father had before him.

Her father disapproved of Lewis, but less than he disapproved of their non-marriage. He would not believe that Lewis had been asking her to marry him for two years and that it was she who had refused. He could not believe that she, his daughter, could live with a man, share a bed with a man, yet refuse to marry him. And when he fell ill he had not relented, but asked her to at least marry this man while he was still alive. But she had not done that. She could give him everything but not that.

"You mean you won't marry me, just to deny him?" Lewis had asked.

"No. It's that I won't marry you to please him."

"But what about you? What about please you and me?"

"I love you, Lewis," she'd said, "but I don't want to marry you—at least not now."

"You want me to just hang on forever?"

"No. I want you to hang on as long as you want to."

"So—forever, then," Lewis said.

~ The small garden in front of the house is ablaze with flowers, flowers whose colors are so bright they seem to outdo the heat of the afternoon, to penetrate into the shade of the veranda, where the air is still and somewhat cooler. Irini is beside herself that she has no cake to offer them and promises to bake one that very day for that evening. When Jane attempts to explain, in her minimal Greek, that they will not be staying the night, they are only just passing through (this was something she has agreed upon with Lewis ahead of time), Irini is horrified. She and Panyotis insist they would not only be hurt but deeply offended if she and Lewis did not stay in their house. They have already prepared the bed, they exclaim.

Prepared a bed? Jane wants to ask how had they known she was coming if she herself had not known, for sure. But no, they have expected her. And Panyotis himself takes her by the arm to show her the room which they have ready, the room next door to theirs, where their son, Theo, had lived when he had been a boy, and where her father—?

Panyotis answers her question before she asks it. No, her father had been given their room, the bigger bedroom in the front, and Panyotis and Irini had slept in Theo's room. The bed has a double set of pillows propped up against a mahogany headboard. They are giant, square pillows, stuffed tight in white cases that have been embroidered with white flowers, barely visible, white against white. At the foot of the bed is a folded cotton blanket that smells of cedar.

Panyotis opens the wardrobe beside the bed. His hand sets the empty wire hangers clinking against each other. He opens each of the four drawers on the side to show them that they are empty and awaiting their clothes. The drawers are neatly lined with newspaper. He takes Jane by the arm again, to show her the bedroom her father had occupied, and where, it is understood—though Panyotis cannot bring himself to say the word—he had died.

Jane draws Lewis aside. "What should we do?" she asks.

"Whatever you want," he says.

But there is nothing she wants except for it to be years before and her father to be taking her and her mother through the house, slapping the whitewashed walls and saying, "Rocks, Jane, that's all they had here. Rocks, so they built their houses out of rocks."

And it is not too surprising after all (though she is not sure she believes Panyotis) that he and Irini should give up their bedroom to her father. The house had belonged to her father and he had given it to Panyotis many years before. It was a small favor in return then, that he should be able to spend the last weeks of his life here.

Her mother had not been happy about her father signing over the house, but her father had done it anyway.

"Your grandchildren might want that property!" her mother had warned.

"In the mountains of Northern Greece?"

"It might be worth something some day."

"Fine. Then let Panyotis's grandchildren have it. My grandchildren will have enough, right here."

It was a sore subject between them—one of a half-dozen that recurred throughout their married life. Death didn't erase them—just made them seem, in contrast, rather absurd.

"It ended up costing my father a lot of money to transfer the property," Jane had explained to Lewis.

"Why's that?"

"Fees and lawyers—he needed one here in the U.S. and one in Greece. It took years. Endless red tape." She had laughed. When she was a child she'd thought there was actual tape and even now she cannot use the expression without picturing it. Now she pictures Greek officials wrapped up in red tape like kittens snarled in balls of string.

"Why was your father so eager to get rid of the house?"

"He said he didn't want the responsibility, the burden of being an absentee owner. But I think he always felt guilty about his privilege. His father had come to the United States, gotten rich. His relatives who had stayed in Greece remained poor. Panyotis never had my father's advantages. And there was something else, I think. My father really wanted to shed himself of his ethnicity."

"But he always seemed so proud to be Greek—at least that's what I noticed about him—"

"He was ambivalent. Look, he married someone Irish. He went by the nickname 'Skip.' He named me Jane. My mother would have preferred something Greek, but my father wanted 'Jane,' the quintessential American name, the little girl who walked out of his first grade reader."

"He took you back to Greece, though, showed you his father's village."

"But he wasn't like those Greek-Americans who run back to their homeland every summer they can afford it. No, Greece was just one country on our Grand Tour of Europe, a sort of cultural highlight. My grandfather's village was a stop along the way."

But it isn't on the way to anywhere. That is what's so remarkable about it—the only place Jane has ever been to that is totally remote, totally self-contained, surrounded by grey-brown mountains and not reaching out beyond.

"Come," says Irini, in Greek, touching her elbow now. "I will show you."

It isn't clear, at first, what she wants to show them. But when Jane sees the candles in Irini's fist she understands. Irini leads them all up the hillside. There is a small graveyard, in front of a small church, enclosed by a chin-high wall. All the graves are above the ground, as if the earth would not welcome them. They look like beds lined up in a mattress store. Some have little vases of flowers on them, set up like altars.

The marble of her father's grave is so raw and white it is hard to believe it has ever been anything natural, part of the earth. His name is chiseled into the stone in Greek—a spelling Jane has never seen before and barely connects to him at all. A photograph—absurdly modern—has been placed at the head behind a glass window.

Again, Irini is touching her elbow. She leads her into the chapel. The coolness is startling. Though they stepped up, rather than down, it feels as if they have descended deep underground. Irini lights some candles and sticks them into a sand-filled dish, like tapers in a miniature beach. She makes the sign of the cross several times, and then with a display of great tact, she tells Jane she will leave her alone, and she leads Panyotis away.

Jane watches the little candles fight the draft. The flames flicker, keep hold. She had forgotten Lewis's presence until she steps out again into the solid sunshine and the heat makes her dizzy. Lewis is there beside her.

"Oh, I hate them!" she cries.

She breaks away from the churchyard and runs—runs out along the dirt road away from the village, where the view is long and serene. Red wildflowers on slender stems, poppies perhaps, bob in a windy field.

But what does she hate them for? For the absurd white tomb they have built to trap her father in forever. Not just that. For having been the ones to see him through to death.

But it hadn't been they who had taken him off from her. It had been he, himself. Always in his life, he had been so sure he knew what was best for her. He had always wanted to control everything. Where she went to college, what she majored in, what job she got when she graduated, who her boyfriends were. Though he could not control the fact that he would die, he could control the way he died: he wasn't going to let his daughter suffer.

But in spite of his careful plan, he'd not been able to spare her suffering. Removing himself was not enough.

Lewis is waiting for Jane by the entrance to the churchyard. He folds his arms around her and she presses her face against his chest. A button on his shirt pushes into her cheek and she savors the awareness of it, the small round indentation, the not-quite pain.

By the time they get back to the house, Irini has managed to assemble a feast—spinakopita, lamb stew with okra, feta cheese, several loaves of bread, boiled potatoes, green beans. The refrigerator in the kitchen is as small as the toy one Jane remembers from her kindergarten, and the village has no shops where she could have bought anything. Jane wonders if all the neighbors have pitched in to help with this crisis. In spite of the plenitude, Irini is unstoppably apologetic.

"Tomorrow night then we roast for you lamb," says Panyotis. It's the first English he has spoken and it takes Jane by surprise. She had no idea he knew any English at all. She wonders if it was her father who taught it to him.

She looks desperately to Lewis.

Speaking slowly and carefully, Lewis explains that it is with the deepest regret that they can't stay that long. They would love nothing more than to be able to partake of such a generous thing, but they must leave in the morning. They have an airplane to catch back to Athens, and they'll just be able to get to it in time if they leave in the morning.

This isn't exactly true—and Jane marvels at Lewis' facility. He is someone who lies very rarely and only for good cause. She is immeasurably grateful for his rescue mission. The magic word for Panyotis is "airplane." "Aeroplano," Panyotis translates for Irini. The word has great power over her, too, and she succumbs to this airplane. Her horror at their early desertion has been replaced by reverent sadness.

After dinner Panyotis asks Jane to come with him into the bedroom. It looks as if there is something Irini has put Panyotis up to, and he seems ill at ease carrying out his mission. As she walks beside him, Jane realizes how much shorter he is than her father—he's just her height. Like her father's, his hair is barely beginning to turn grey, though he is two years older—seventy-five at least.

In the corner of the room—what Jane hadn't noticed before—are her father's suitcases, the same ones she had helped him pack to take to Greece. Panyotis hoists one up on the bed and explains that all her father's things have been packed away for her to take back with her. He goes to open the zipper and Jane can imagine the sound of it ripping along the three sides. She stays his hand.

"Please," she says, "I'd rather not—"

Panyotis looks at her, uncertain what she wants of him.

"Please," she says. She speaks slowly so he'll understand her English. "I'd like you to keep everything of his and give away to someone who might make use of it anything that you don't want."

Panyotis treats this as an act of extraordinary generosity, oblivious to the fact that the blackwatch plaid suitcases—which are the same ones they'd brought to Europe when she was a girl—are more than she can bear, and she can't even touch them, let alone encounter the contents.

She is eager to leave the room, to get back into the living room, to see Lewis's face, but Panyotis heads her off. He starts to explain something in

English, but he is so upset by what he is trying to tell her that his English deserts him and he pours it all out in Greek, forgetting, it seems, that she has trouble following what he is saying. They have no language in common which they both know well enough to convey anything complex with certainty—everything subtle runs the risk of being lost in the telling or the understanding.

What Panyotis wants her to know is that her father did not suffer when he died—he went to sleep just like a baby, is how he puts it. If he knows how drug-induced was that final slumber (her father's last letters had hinted at this part of his plan) he does not let on—nor does he succeed in conveying it to Jane. Jane is not sure if Panyotis has been planning on telling her about her father's death once they were alone, or if it is something that had just occurred to him to tell her about. She nods yes, yes, and backs to the doorway. At last Panyotis is finished. He is wiping his eyes, calling her father a saint.

It is time now for the afternoon siesta. Irini has not let Lewis carry in a single dish to the kitchen, but she has managed to clear the table on the veranda and put all the food away. She has also laid out towels on their bed, just as if they were in a hotel room.

"This is your room now," She tells Jane. "Next summer you both come and spend the whole summer here."

Jane smiles and nods. Irini asks several times if they have everything they need, and then she and Panyotis repair to their bedroom for a nap.

Jane and Lewis take turns washing up. In the tiny bathroom there is a hand-held shower mounted on the wall and a drain in the center of the tiled floor, as if the entire room turns itself into a shower stall. Jane takes off her skirt and blouse. She washed her face and arms and neck and lifts her feet, one at a time, to wash in the sink. When she gets back to the bedroom Lewis, in his undershorts, is stretched out on top of the top sheet. He is half-asleep. She lifts his legs and pulls the sheet out from under his body, and then covers him with it. She gets into bed beside him. From the room next door she can hear Panyotis and Irini, both snoring, out of rhythm. Lewis slides his arm under her and draws her close against him.

"When we get back to Athens," she whispers, "let's get married."

"Hmm?" Lewis asks.

"We'll go to the consulate," she says. "O.K.?"

"Um hmm," says Lewis. "Sure. Whatever you want."

When he is wide awake she will tell him what they agreed to. Now she watches him sink into sleep.

Of course it has to do with her father, putting him to rest. But mostly it has to do with Lewis, himself: the way, when they first arrived at the house, he put his arm around her and his thumb stroked her bare shoulder.

Debra Di Blasi

OOPS. SORRY

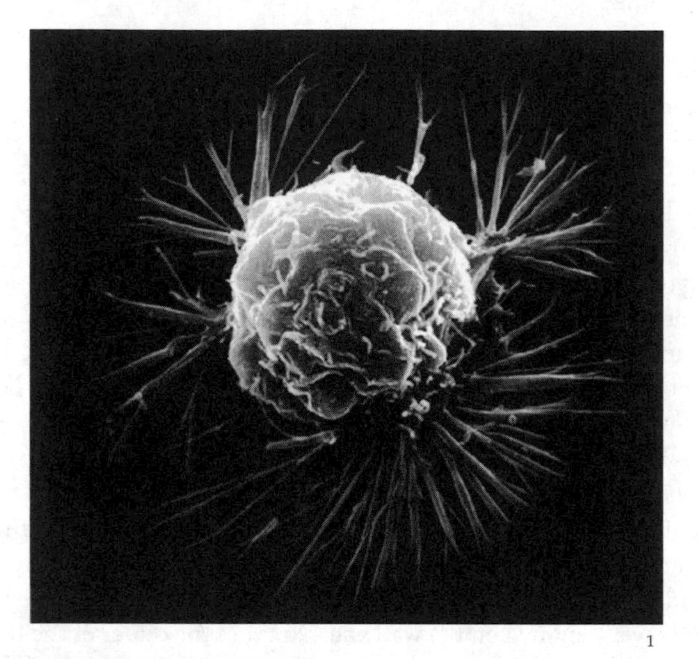

[1]

SPRING HAS SPRUNG

Jesus, what it must be like to die in the spring!

is what she thought. Just then her dying neighbor across the street looked up from the flower bed she was tending and smiled. Odd smile. Happy. No. More than happy. Calm. No. More than calm. Content? Yes, utterly. Utterly content. Smile.

I've never felt content in my life.

is what she thought. And

1. Magnification illustrating "breast cancer cells with intercellular boundaries on bead surface and aggregates of cells achieving 3-dimensional growth outward from bead." Credit: Dr. Jeanne Becker, University of South Florida. Source: Science @ NASA (http://science.nasa.gov/newhome).

Will you feel so content after you're dead?

is what she wanted to ask her neighbor. And rather suddenly, no, quite suddenly, as if a piano had just fallen out of a *757* en route to Prague and landed on her head . . . *that* suddenly, she loathed her dying neighbor. So that when she returned her dying neighbor's smile it was tight and oily. Disingenuous.

Cut your face in half, there's a phony smile on the bottom and genuine hate-filled eyes on the top.

You should be ashamed of yourself.

Should be
Should be
Should
Sh

You can never have too many beginnings!

Your neighbor across the street looks up from the flower bed she's tending, tending with great care, the tulips just now sprouting from the black dirt, the sedum returning green after a long brown winter playing dead. With great care, sweeping the dry oak leaves from around the new green shoots, picking out the litter of newspaper and Styrofoam and bits of cellophane blown in from god-knows-where. Carefully replenishing the mulch: cedar: scent: She raises a handful to her nose, inhales, closes her eyes, smiles. Looks up from the flowerbed, over her left shoulder to see you standing on your front porch staring at her in a yellow hat you know covers a bald head. Looks at you thinking how the yellow hat looks so cheerful against the periwinkle blue of her house she painted last fall, right after she learned the cancer had come back *en force,* was in her lymph nodes now, her liver, nothing they could do though they fed her chemicals anyway as if she were a Wandering Jew who just needed Miracle-Gro to get better.

She, your neighbor, has made it this far, into spring. Though she knows she will be dead when the chrysanthemums explode to yellow blooms, she plants them anyway. By seed. As if it's important she be there in their beginning: heat and oil and sweat of flesh the first world of seven worlds flowers must pass through to reach heaven: a place of light drifting across the plains of infinity.

You watch her brush her hands satisfied with efficacy, smiling wistfully at a future where chrysanthemums bloom in her absence, drop seeds, bloom again.

Boss: What's this word here?
You: Efficacy.
Boss: What the hell does that mean?
You: It means having the power to produce an effect. You wrote "I have my doubts about his efficiency with the client." Within the letter's context I think you meant efficacy.
Boss: Don't tell me what I meant. You're not paid to tell me what I mean, you're paid to do what I say, you're paid to type what I write, not to criticize my vocabulary. Is that understood?
You: I wasn't criticizing, I was just—
Boss: If I wrote efficiency then I damn well meant efficiency. Understood?
You: So do you want me to retype it?
Boss: No sense wasting time. Send it out the way it is.

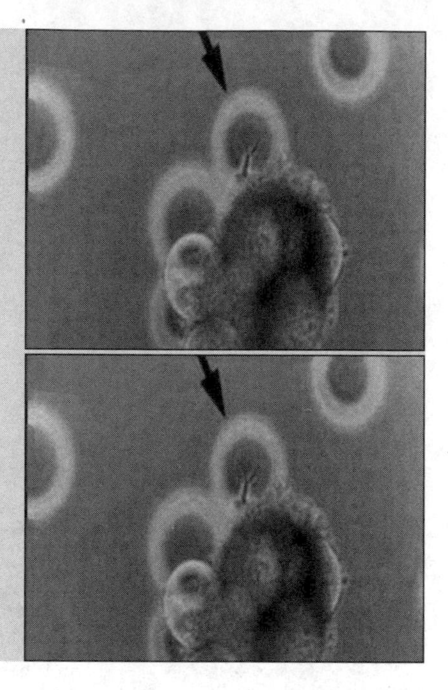

OF ALL THE THINGS THAT CAN KEEP YOU UP NIGHTS . . .

esprit d'escalier is the most persistent. Earlier in the day her BOSS whom she loathes scoops her heart out with a dull spoon. Now she tosses and turns in bed, attempting to alter the past:

Boss: If I wrote efficiency, then I damn well meant efficiency. Is that understood?
You: I was only trying to help.

Boss: If I wrote efficiency, then I damn well meant efficiency. Is that understood?
You: I was only trying to make you look good.

[2]

2. "Tumor cells aggregate on microcarrier beads (indicated by arrow)." Credit: Dr. Jeanne Becker, University of South Florida. Source: Science @ NASA (http://science.nasa.gov/newhome).

Boss: If I wrote efficiency, then I damn well meant efficiency. Is that understood?
You: I was only trying to make a silk purse out of a sow's ear.

Boss: If I wrote efficiency—
You: Wrote?!? Gimme a break, you can barely spell your name.

Boss: If I wrote efficiency, then I damn well meant efficiency. Is that understood?
You: Shut the fuck up, I quit.

Boss: If I wrote efficiency, then I damn well meant efficiency. Is that understood?
You: Why don't you go fuck yourself, you goddamn overpromoted addlepated ignoramus. Oh, and would you like a DICTIONARY to interpret that sentence, you fucking loser suckass butt-wipe cocksucker!

Finally her thoughts turn to homicide, or rather **ACTS OF GOD** perpetrated by She, Goddess of Justice, Queen of the Damned and Trodden and Nine-to-Fivers or -Eighters,[3] Omnipotent Potentatette, and she imagines HER BOSS WHOM SHE LOATHES strolling down the long hallway of the 21st floor when an earthquake with a magnitude of 9.9 on the Richter Scale rips the building apart, the floor opening up under BOSS's feet and BOSS plummeting into the magma-roiling pit of **HELL ON EARTH** where BOSS shall live out BOSS's eternity, missing the Second Coming entirely and regretting every shitty-BOSS-scourge BOSS cursed on employees, amen Amen *Amen* AMEN!

3. President _____ of the telecommunications company _____ sends a memo to all employees stating, among other dull but noxious edicts, that "although the work week is officiously [*sic?*] 40 hours per week, I expect all of us [read: 'you underfuckerlings'] to put in not less than 55 hours per week in order to boost productivity and consequencially [*sic*] declining stock prices in an incertain [*sic*] market."

The end is near?

It's always near. And nearer every day.

You're going to die.

Maybe not today, maybe not tomorrow but
sooner than you think because you think you'll
live forever, don't you.

You won't.

So what are you going to leave behind?
What are you going to take with you?
Hatred?
Deception?
Betrayal?
A life of lying, cheating, stealing?
A life of carelessness?

Wake up.
Clean up.
Time to die.

The leaflet guy is back. Or maybe it's a gal. Gal Friday. Out to save 700 souls on her 45-minute lunch break. 700 leaflets appearing like magic under 700 windshield wipers on 700 cars in the parking garage.

She can hear the chainsaws growling, tree trunks spitting sawdust, raw wood cracking, clatter of leaves twigs branches bark upon the underbrush vines ferns wildflowers moss. Somewhere on the once-a-forest floor a scarab beetle feels the rush of wind presaging death manifest in a falling pine and tries to flee its fate but the pine is big and the beetle's legs are small and there is only shadow shadow deeper than before the lumberjacks came before there is nothing.

Family SCARABAEIDAE, genera Dynastines. Best known for their immense size and the amazing horn-like structures that the males of many species possess. These structures are used mainly for defending feeding sites and during strength contests with other males over mates during the breeding season. Though the vast majority of these "rhinoceros beetles" are to be found deep within the great equatorial rain forests of the planet, there are a few species that live in more temperate latitudes such as NORTH AMERICA and Europe. . . . The larvae of dynastines primarily feed on the soft, decaying wood of dead trees. The larvae increase in size greatly as they progress. They often require many months to complete their growth, undergo METAMORPHOSIS within a protective cell, and then RE-ENTER THE WORLD as adult beetles.

—Source: www.naturalworlds.org

DOCTOR says, "I've got bad news."

Sh
Sh
Shadow shadow deeper falling.

"This is the route," he says, pointing to the line zigzagging across the CT-Scan.

IN WHICH YOU REACT TO THE LONG ROAD OF UNCERTAINTY AHEAD BY SCREAMING

I understand how you hate the world. Want to trip it as it saunters by smug knowing it's forever while you're just a flicker—sun caught in a speeding car's chrome. There. Then not there. The chrome not even warmed by your light.

Scream scream.

There's a place in your head like a windowless room where you scream to fill in the hole left by silence. Bury the fear in your screaming. Sure, let them shake their heads, those with their flesh not yet rotting; they'll know/rot soon enough. Know the ecstasy of a voice unleashed like the god of Moses.

O Eternal, what god is there like you, who is like you, so gloriously supreme, so awful, whom we praise for extraordinary deeds?

Eternal? You cannot believe in life beyond your death though you desire. And when you are dead, when your blood has been drained and your eyes sewn shut, and the nails of your hands blush black you will be only dead.

Absent from the world.
is what she thinks and picks an aphid from the leaf of the Wandering Jew and crushes it between her fingers.

A fate worse than hell.
is what she thinks.

At least in pain there's living.

"I don't believe in hell," she tells her BOSS, apropos of nothing. "Except the one here now," and she points the index finger of her right hand and maneuvers it around the office like a divining rod seeking water—and there is water everywhere: BOSS, Computer, Time Sheet (so much damn time wasted, wasted time recorded in the Book . . . no, the *Database* of Judgment), water even in the *Database* of Judgment), water even in the Wandering Jew with its aphids devouring—until her finger turns backward, curls backward, points backward at her breasts with their lumps, and she says,

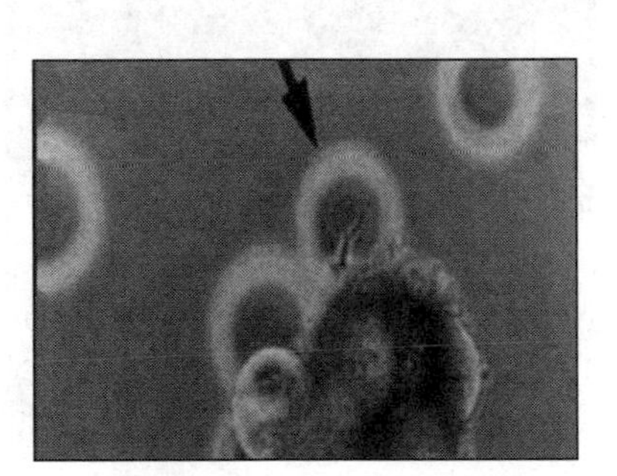

"Hell, metastasizing."

She cannot possibly remember them all, all the lumps blooming from coffee and push-up bras and homogenized hormone-laded milk and a gene whose sole purpose is to shiver awake when kissed by environmental toxins and rise and kiss awake another gene whose sole purpose is to grow lumps in breasts.

I cannot possibly remember them all but I remember my first—yes, remember like a first lover who takes me against my will, yet I harbor a secret desire for him nevertheless. My first at fourteen: big tender globe of fluid grown hard, tucked inside my armpit. I told no one because to acknowledge it was to make it real.

I told no one and it went away. Others replaced it, coming with their courting gifts of terror, going with their parting gifts of relief. And somewhere in between: God and all the scheming negotiating conniving bargaining that led me to believe prayer would save me, as long as the prayers were long enough, heartfelt enough, original enough, pretty enough, frequent enough, good enough for God.

I told no one. I prayed good.

This lump was different: pearl under the skin. Oysters of flesh on the sand of the bones. Bauble bead gem sunk in mud. Dig it out dig it out mining for gold those researchers with their white lab coats their stainless steel voices their eyes that never meet your eyes—*O do not see the human, the humanity, or you'll never make the cut*—and

Look at me goddamn it!

is what she thought. And

If I fire my doctor will the next one kill me out of vengeance?

is what she thought. And again

Pearl.

She once had a horse named Pearl. Shetland pony. Silvery-white and fat-bellied and interested only in eating, consuming—oats, carrots, corn, apples, clover, grass. One day Pearl consumed too much fescue and foundered:

hooves growing long so fast, blooming up and curling back like lilies into the silvery-white legs, the white bones, until she could not walk and the father hauled Pearl away and sold her for $20 to a slaughterhouse where she was shot and skinned and ground into dog food.

She is surprised by how much love she can still summon for a horse dead so many years but distinct in her mind in the shimmering green pastures lit with dew in the summer morning in the past that is unreachable, untouchable ghost, the ghost of Pearl.

The one time she tried to run away from home was on Pearl's back. Less than a mile down the dirt road Pearl spied sweet clover alongside the ditch and would not walk further. She dismounted and sat on the bank above the ditch and watched Pearl eat, waiting for Father and Mother to come looking for her. They never came. Eventually Pearl got full or thirsty or bored, and girl and pony headed home.

She can still smell horse sweat. Hear the long silvery-white tail swishing at flies. The comforting *crunch-crunch-crunch* of masticating teeth. See her reflection in a brown-black eye that seemed to always look beyond this world into another: long steady glimpse of perpetuity.

> *You lay your hand upon the hospital gown and pretend it's Pearl's winter coat beneath your fingers. You cry soundlessly thinking of the light in your pony's eyes doused. You would like Pearl back to run away for good. This time, not turn for home.*

WHEN YOU KNOW IT'S REAL

Fear is the worst of it. Makes you dizzy. Weak in the knees. Hair on the back of your neck bristles. Sometimes fear's so big it fills your whole life tight and you can't breathe and you think the cancer's in your lungs now fat lumps of consuming cells and you're suffocating so you call your MD who X-rays your chest and it at least is fine so your MD prescribes Xanax and you take one and then two and then three and go to sleep for twelve hours of dreamlessness and when you wake up you think it's dawn but it's dusk, so now there's just you and soon the looming dark and silence and somewhere behind a wall in the room of your mind fear still pounds its meaty fists against your heart that now beats fast and irregular and you think the cancer is in your heart now you're having a heart attack so you call 911 and the EMTs arrive and after a while your heart slows to 66 bpm but they take you to the ER anyway because you have cancer and the ER RNs hook you up to an EKG and take your BP and everything seems fine and you notice how safe you feel in the ER with the RNs and LPNs in their sea green scrubs and you realize that except for the cancer there's nothing wrong with you but fear and you ask to go home and they release you and the night is very crisp like you never felt before and you don't take a cab you walk home which is 12 miles and by the time you arrive at 5:37 AM the sun's coming up and you're covered with dew.

ART THERAPIST says, "Why don't you try using some color?"

It's my goddamn drawing.

is what you think.

It's my goddamn cancer.

is what you mumble. And you want to hit ART THERAPIST with your fists, hit everything, hit yourself until you bleed and the blood says you're still alive.

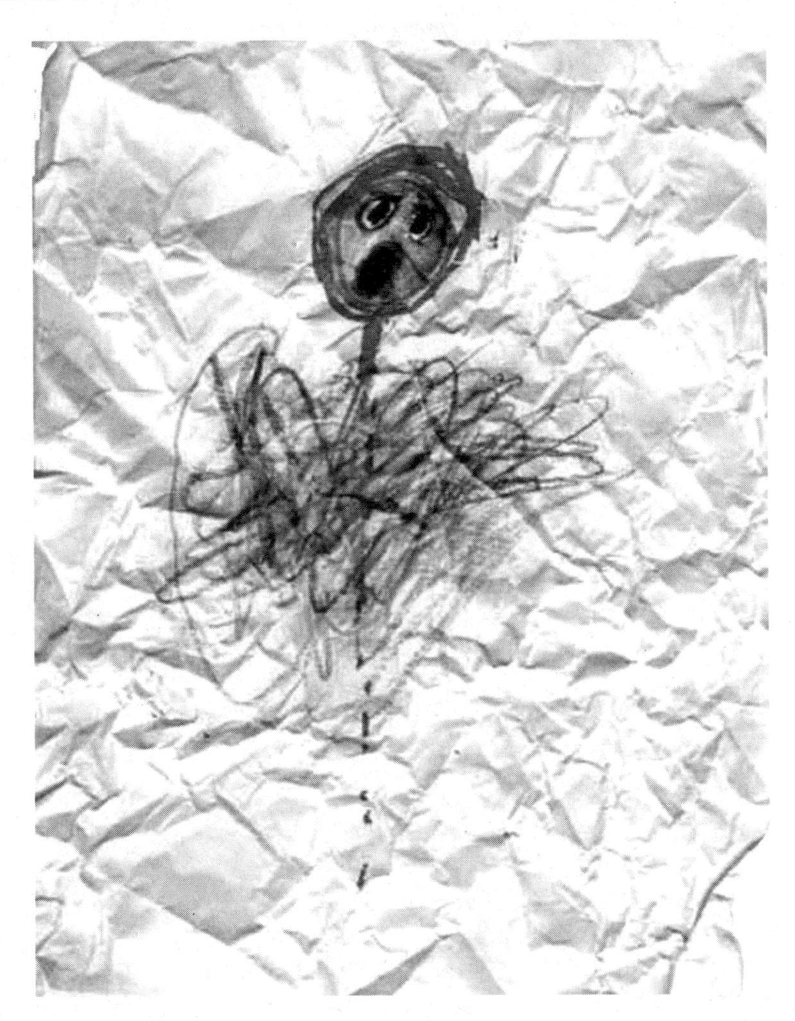

ART THERAPIST nods and says, "Much better!"

". . . new treatment that appears to have some positive results in some . . . combination of radiation and chemotherapy for six months . . . basically destroys your immune system with the cancer but . . . fatigue, nausea, skin discoloration, dryness, hair loss . . . best I can offer at this stage, so . . ."

CHEMOTHERAPY & RADIATION ALTERNATIVES

1. Breast Cancer Therapy Group
2. Art Therapy
3. Yoga
4. Transcendental Meditation
5. Focused Breathing Exercises
6. Stress Reduction Class
7. Tai Chi
8. Macrobiotic Diet
9. Green Tea
10. Chinese Herbs
11. Echinacea
12. Vitamin Therapy
13. Visualization
14. Acupuncture
15. Cranial-Sacrum Massage
16. Past-Life Regression
17. Smudging
18. Pray without Ceasing
19. Ozone Therapy
20. Colonic Cleansing
21. Crystals
22. Magnets

Suddenly it seems that everyone from your past is in your present and on TV. What they mean by your life passing before your eyes? Like the Czech BOYFRIEND-YOU-NEVER-LIKED of a FRIEND-YOU-NO-LONGER-LIKE who was arrested in Cuba for spying, the Czech, that is, Jirí Cêch. Which makes you laugh. And you feel momentarily healed.

30. Watch Comedies

And then, coincidentally (but you no longer believe in coincidence, your mind regressed to a primitive intuitive-laden state when women understood the net of the universe without having to take a course in physics) the FRIEND-YOU-NO-LONGER-LIKE is on the same TV news program, arrested for attempted murder somewhere in Prague and you stare at her as she's escorted by police, and you notice that her hair looks dull and unkempt, and she's wearing green which does not compliment her skin tone and it all makes you depressed and nostalgic for things you cannot name.

31. Don't Watch the News

Boss: I need you to be at the top of your game in your head even if you're not tops in your body. Understand?
You: . . .
Boss: Anyway. There are some typos in this proposal. I need you to fix them.
You: "Irregardless" is not a word.
Boss: Are we going to have this argument again?
You: And "profits are impacted by loose shipping timeframes" sounds like profits are constipated, as in impacted bowels. Whatever "loose timeframes" means.
Boss: . . .
You: It's "profits are affected by." Plain, simple, accurate English.
Boss: You need this job, don't you?
You: . . .
Boss: Well. Then. End of argument.

32. Kill My Boss!

God is not a vending machine.

You expect to put in a prayer and an answer will pop out.

Specifically, the answer you want.

Specifically, *what* you want *when* you want it.

God is not a fast-food joint, either.

Pray every day for other people in need. and you'll be okay.

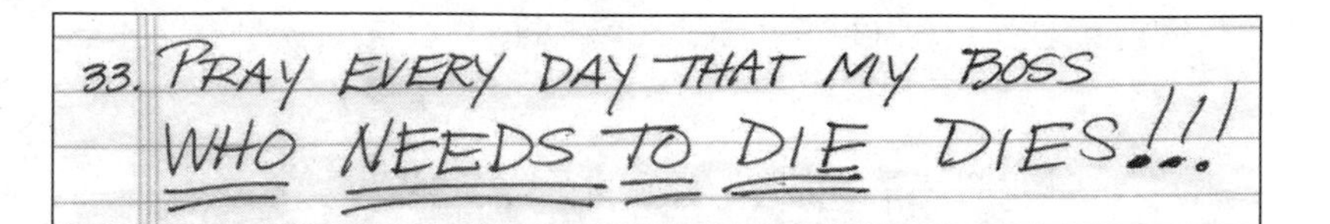

You say:	Are you the one who's been leaving this shit on everybody's windshield?
He says:	Not me. It's probably so-and-so down in accounting. She's a Catholic.

You say:	Are you the one who's been leaving this shit on everybody's windshield?
She says:	No, but I think whoever's doing it is probably evangelical.

You say:	Are you the one who's been leaving this shit on everybody's windshield?
She says:	What if I am?
You say:	Are you?
She says:	Maybe, maybe not.
You say:	Yes or no?
She says:	No, but what if I was?
You say:	I'd cram it down your fucking throat.
She says:	You're crazy.
You say:	I'm dying.

You put the leaflet in your 700 Club file folder with the other leaflets and close the drawer and fold your hands on your desk and stare at the Wandering Jew, searching for aphids, but there are none.

I don't want to die here.

is what you think. And

I don't want to die.

is what you think. And

I won't!

NOTICE

No one is allowed to use the word "death" in this house, nor any form of the word, e.g.,

- dead
- die
- dying
- deceased*
- deathly
- died
- deadly
- kill*
- cancer*
- fatal
- malignant
- passed
- etc.

*similar, if not from the root word

NEW SORTA BEST FRIEND says, "Hey, oh my god, you can't believe what I got!"

Cancer?

is what you think. But say

What?

"Two tickets to the *John Edward Crossing Over* show. Wanna go?"

34. Go to "John Edward Crossing Over" (www.johnedward.net)

TRANSCRIPT

"JOHN EDWARD CROSSING OVER"

TAPING DATE: OCTOBER 15

JOHN EDWARD: Okay, I'm in this area over here. Right here. [Points to center section.]

I've got a younger female, not a mother, not an aunt. A sister, like a sister, who's crossed over. She's on the same level as… [Indicates a horizontal line with his right hand.]

She's like a sister but I don't get that she's related. Like a friend maybe or…like a friend. Her name is Pam or Pamela or… I'm getting a P-M sound like… Pamela? Pam? … Does this sound familiar to any of you. [Looks at audience.]

I'm in this section right here. [Points to center section.]

There. Right there. [Indicates two women in top row of center section.]

Did you two come together?

[Women nod yes.]

JOHN: But you're not related.

FIRST WOMAN: No. We work together.

JOHN: So one of you knows a Pam or Pamela who's passed?

[Women look at each other and shake their heads no.]

JOHN: I'm pretty sure I'm with one of you. [Pause as he concentrates.] Okay, there's a yellow hat. A *very* yellow hat, bright yellow, like a… And she's…she had cancer in this area [indicates chest]. I don't know if it's breast cancer? But… [pause as he concentrates] I see a dark area in the chest and then in this area [indicates his waist] like the kidneys or liver or… [urgently] It's a very yellow hat, it's important, and there's no…there's no hair under it. She's bald. [frustrated] One of you knows this.

JOHN: Yellow flowers, too. Like those…what are those big fat yellow flowers called? Mums. I'm getting big yellow mums the same color as the yellow hat.

SECOND WOMAN: I didn't know her name.

JOHN: What?

SECOND WOMAN: She was my neighbor and she died of cancer, but I never knew her name, I'm ashamed to say it.

JOHN: So you understand the yellow hat?

SECOND WOMAN: Yes. She wore it at the end, after she'd lost all her hair.

JOHN: [relieved] Okay, whew! So I knew I was in the right area. And she's… Her name is Pamela, by the way. [laughter] Or Pam. She wants you to know that, and she's telling me it's okay that you…that you… [puzzled] Did you have bad… I don't know how else to say this… [pause] Okay, I'm just going to say it. You didn't know her, right?

SECOND WOMAN: No, we were neighbors but, no. We never spoke.

JOHN: But you were angry with her because she… because she had cancer?

SECOND WOMAN: [Nods. Starts to cry.] It wasn't… Not exactly the cancer, but… She seemed so happy at the end, I just…and I was… She painted her house bright blue, like a bluebird, and wore the yellow hat, and planted flowers in her garden right up until the day they hauled her…the ambulance came for the last time, and she was dying and so happy, so *content* and I was living and miserable.

JOHN: [gently] Okay. Well, there's a reason, then, why she's coming through to you today. She telling me… [puzzled] This is personal. This is a personal question, but do you have breast cancer, too?

SECOND WOMAN: [nods yes]

JOHN: Well, she's telling you to… I get this image of… You know those people who dive off those high, and I mean *really* high cliffs? Into the water? That's what I'm seeing, but not like a scary thing, like a—an adventure, a thrill. It's like she saying you need to just let go, you know, you need—

SECOND WOMAN: I understand.

JOHN: —to stop being afraid and find your own yellow hat.

SECOND WOMAN: [nods]

JOHN: Okay, she's pulling back. Just know that she saw this as her opportunity to come through and help you through your own difficult illness. Okay?

SECOND WOMAN: Okay. Thank you.

JOHN: Thank you.

The Egyptians believed in an afterlife. But it was a life without sunlight, a life of perpetual night.

35. Play Dead

Every night now the possum waddles out of the chrysanthemums growing wild across the street alongside the bright blue house for sale and empty except for furniture stained rank with the smell of a dying woman's last breaths and shits and pisses. The possum crosses the street, enters your yard, pauses a moment to stare at you sitting in the porch swing, trying to detect the predator's stink, the stink of the living, the gorgeous stink of life, and smelling nothing waddles forward, past your flower bed where only white stones grow, and slugs upon the stones, trailing their wet silver. And then moves on, the possum, ruler of night and six-legged insects.

But this time you rise from the swing just as the possum nears the bed of stones and you snap your fingers and clap your hands once and say, "Hey, fucker."

And the possum stiffens and falls over onto its side, still as a two-day corpse.

You go and squat over it, daring it to move. It doesn't. Barely breathes. Eyes open, staring, unblinking. You poke it with a finger, tentative at first, then hard. The muscles beneath the soft fur are rigid with pretend death. You snap your finger in front of the possum's eyes. It doesn't blink.

"Way to go," you say, and smile.

The next night and every night after that until the weather cools, you lay on your side in your yard, barely breathing, eyes open, unblinking, staring at nothing that will be here soon enough. Let the fear swell inside you like the gas bloat of afterdeath until it no longer hurts, until it is comfortable: All you know. All you want to be.

The possum waddles by as if you were a blade of grass.

After you're dead they will refer to you as "The late. . . ."

Late. As if for a party.

> *There will come a time when you are too weak to stand to walk to the bathroom and the bowels let go and the bladder empties and the bed is wet and you're lying in your own shit and a friend comes and says* It's all right it's okay *and bathes you and changes the sheets and strokes your*

bald head and kisses you good-night even though it's day and not good at all.

By now the house across the street is inhabited by someone else, a couple of young professionals who paint the clapboard a terrible brown.

They dug up the yellow chrysanthemums. Replaced them with rocks.

YOU ARE LATE FOR A PARTY

Someone has slipped another flier under your windshield wiper. You say, "Jesus!" Fold the flier into quarters and shove it into your purse. At the party you drink and dance. You grind your pelvis. You swing your hips. You shake and shimmy and imagine your breasts real: young buds not yet bloomed, cancer-free. You close your eyes and remember dancing alone in your bedroom when you were seven years old pretending to be a go-go girl a hullabaloo girl in your hullabaloo boots groovy chick in your love beads fringe vest fishnet stockings ID bracelet bandanna ankh.

You arrive. Late. Jirí Cêch is there. Just released from custody. Waving an autograph from Fidel Castro.

Jirí says, "You look hot tonight, woman," and flips that big Czech hand of his as if

The black ~~Whole~~ hole in the ~~Wide~~ World

were nothing more than gnats swarming/breeding.

You say that to all the girls, Jirí.

is what you say. And think

Oh, what the hell.

And Jirí grins. Winks. Slicks back his hair.

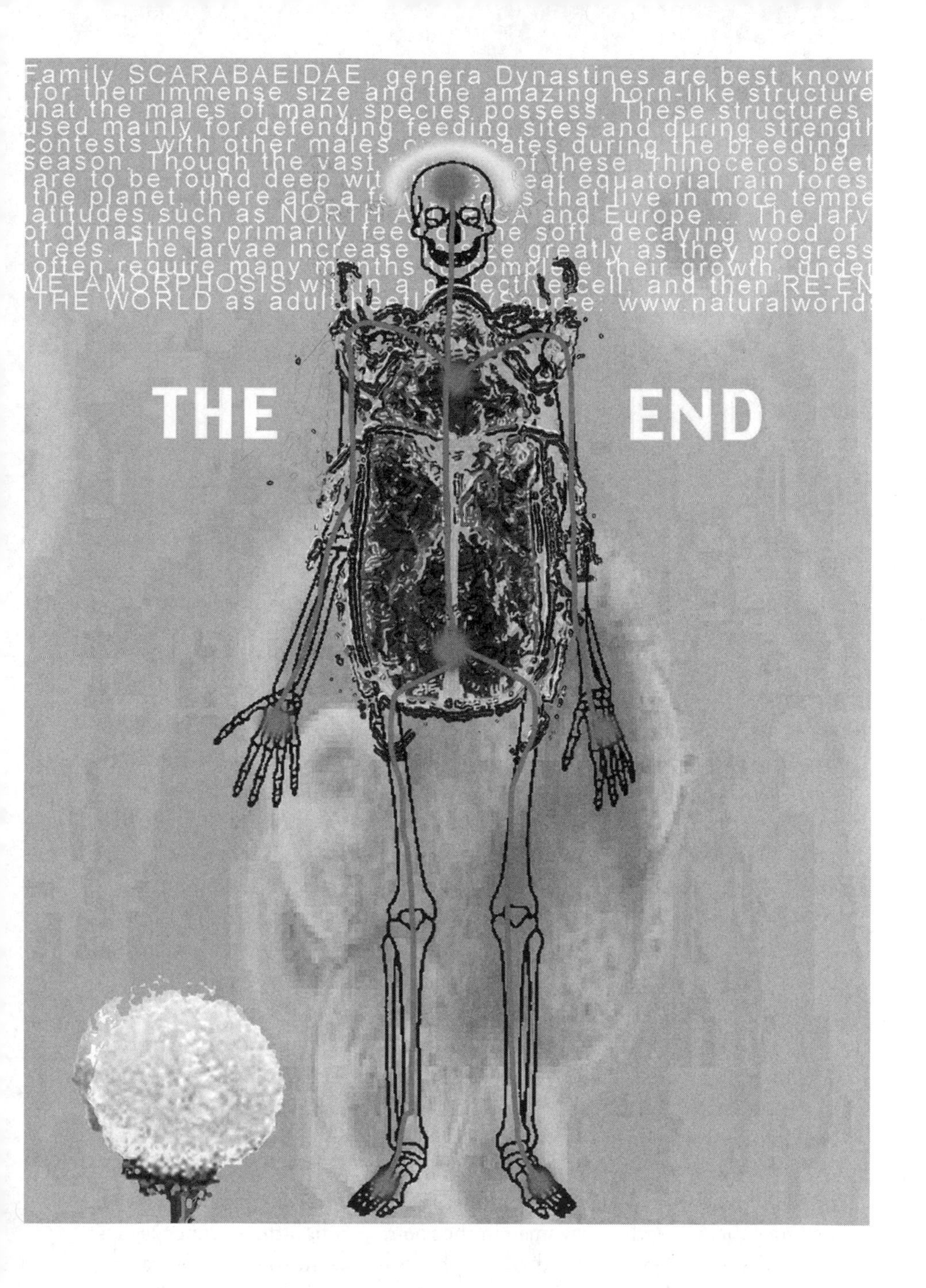
Family SCARABAEIDAE, genera Dynastines are best know
for their immense size and the amazing horn-like structure
hat the males of many species possess. These structures
used mainly for defending feeding sites and during strength
contests with other males mates during the breeding
season. Though the vast of these "rhinoceros beet
are to be found deep wit eat equatorial rain fores
the planet, there are a f s that live in more tempe
latitudes such as NORTH A CA and Europe.... The larv
of dynastines primarily fee e soft, decaying wood of
trees. The larvae increase ze greatly as they progress
often require many m nths omple e their growth, unde
METAMORPHOSIS wit n a p ective cell, and then RE-EN
THE WORLD as adul source: www.naturalworld
THE
END

Richard Elman

AS ALWAYS, "UNCLE BARNEY"

This is a very important right (the right to write badly) and to take it from us is no small thing.
—Isaac Babel, 1934

Sacred to the memory of Al Goldman, writer, friend.

I once had an "Uncle Barney." Barney Goldman. We weren't really blood relations, nor related by marriage. Barney was just a family friend of long-standing. He played handball and pinochle with my father at the Temple health club, and sometimes made love to my mother, and regularly came to dinner at our house with his wife, "Aunt Minna," and their spoiled rotten daughter, Masha, about three years older than I. Barney sold insurance and Minna taught public school. I was to call them "uncle" and "aunt" out of respect, I imagine, as well as affection. As I grew up, I sometime wondered what my mother called him in private, and what he called her.

My father always said Barney was "far too good-natured for his own good." He seemed to regard him as half simpleton, half sap and was more charitable toward his old friend than anybody else of his acquaintance. A big attractive galoot, Barney resembled a cartoon caricature of himself: he was fair, and open-faced, with a handsome mustache, and a commanding paunch on which he seemed to be buoyed through his various affairs in life like a finely crafted ormolu carriage in a royal procession.

He had a strong, clear basso voice and used to sing out expansively at weddings and funerals to earn a little extra money. In public, Mom seemed to have Minna's permission to fuss over Barney, along with Minna—as she could not with my brusque father—always straightening his ties, or picking lint off his jackets. "Barney Google," she called him, because I suppose he really did have "goo goo googley eyes" that were pale blue and always flirting gallantly with any woman in the room, through thick blonde lashes.

If my father ever noticed all this he didn't seem to care. He was too much in love with his own chances in life back then. Dad's temper tantrums toward me and Mom sometimes were catastrophic, though toward his friend,

Barney, he usually was placid, tolerant, amused. "Barney is a 'Bohemian' and a 'chaser'" was one of the first things I ever heard him say behind his back about their oldest friend. And the rejoinder from that other party was, "After all these years, it's harmless enough isn't it?"

Even Barney's wife, Minna, was always making allowances for him. My mom said Minna was just "very insecure." But she had reason to be. Minna was narrow, plain, dark as a squint, with straight hair, and lots of dandruff. A funky odor clung to Aunt Minna's dark school outfits; she never wore jewelry or did up her nails. She was rumored by Barney to be an excellent cook, but she didn't like to entertain at home because they lived in a small, dark apartment with Masha sleeping on a sofa bed in the living room.

Barney really wasn't much of a provider. He was always hard up for cash, and Aunt Minna and her daughter, according to the conversations I overheard between my parents, were simply not getting what they needed from Barney who really didn't enjoy selling insurance. Sometimes, irascibly, my parents felt compelled to subsidize the Goldmans. What they got in return was Minna's timid, "thank yous" and Barney's half-hearted expressions of good will, but no vows to reform their errant lives. Barney still preferred card playing to visiting clients, and he enjoyed afternoon jaunts along the Storm King Highway to the Bear Mountain Inn for a roll in the hay with some lady friend other than Minna or Mom. I wanted to think of Mom and Barney as lovers. I never really had any hard proof. After a while, I just took this for granted as I did a lot of adult behavior.

According to my father, Barney seemed incapable of that necessary day-to-day chicanery that bred success. He was "totally irresponsible." But, once, I overheard my mother talking to someone in a soft voice on the phone with such easy intimacy I knew she couldn't be speaking to Dad. I could not make out the gist, just that caressing tone of voice, and words like, "I could die."

Many other people also found Barney charming. He had a line of gab like most salesmen. Barney had briefly been a CP organizer, and he was now a solid ALP voter, and always sold his customers that Stalinoid line. Though no longer an active party member, he subscribed to "The Worker," and to cultural evenings at the City Center Theatre, and to fellow traveling "PM," and he loved to talk about current affairs: The Dneiper Dam, the Second Front, FDR, Vito Marcantonio and FEPC.

With his big deep voice and robust elocution, Barney could sound quite impressive. At a performance of OTHELLO, I can recall him confiding sotto voice to my parents, "A black man with a white woman has all the bigots in Venice going crazy with jealousy."

I also recall his version of the Hitler-Stalin pact which he continued to alibi many years after the U.S. entered the war as Russia's ally: it had been a deliberate ruse, Barney said, by a woman named Ivey Litvinoff, the wife of a high Russian official, to beguile the Germans while Russia prepared to defend the Sacred Homeland.

Barney's parlor pink attitudes were somewhat more problematical to Aunt Minna who had to fear the Livingston Street Board of Education; and they were probably embarrassing to Masha growing up, though she and I rarely talked at all. His family regarded Barney as potentially hazardous, unstable, though benign, this totally losing proposition. Barney was hardly making his "draw" from the insurance office, and, whenever something important around the house was needed, Minna had to borrow from her family or friends to make the purchase. Barney just never seemed to care about camp for Masha, or owning a TV, an air conditioner, or purchasing life insurance for himself, but he always had money to pay his health club bills, and for that weekend shack in Fire Island he occasionally shared with some other left wing insurance colleagues, members of the gang he called his "Rum Scoundrels."

"Life insurance is a capitalistic swindle," he confided to us once at dinner. "You pay and pay and pay and then you die. And who benefits? Your creditors. . . ."

"With the commission he earns from such a swindle," Minna pointed out, "it's no wonder I have to buy everything we need on time."

When they argued a lot at the dinner table about Barney's self-indulgence, my father and mother usually served as referees. As though this was a movie I saw only last weekend, I can still hear Minna overcoming her timidity to berate Uncle Barney for his behaviour at a sales meeting upstate the previous weekend at the Tamarack Lodge.

"Barney was being so firm for once in our life that business was business that I stayed home and wrote lesson plans and did the income taxes, and when I called him Sunday morning to ask if he'd be coming back in time for supper, as Masha and I were planning to see 'Gone With the Wind' again at the Patio, a woman answers his phone. I'm so embarrassed. Then she hands the phone to loverboy here, your friend, Irv, and he tells me I have it all wrong. The lady is a Vice President of his branch of the Utica Mutual in charge of annuities, which he's hoping to sell, if he can learn enough between now and Monday morning to write a business letter."

"I try never to miss a learning opportunity," Barney interjected, with a grin.

Even Minna thought that was amusing. And my father, when he was asked to intervene by her directly, acted as though he was more entertained than outraged by Uncle Barney's "impulsiveness." As an act of charity, he continued to buy all his policies through Barney, but he did get angry when he referred law clients so Barney could sell them, too, and, with great *panache,* his friend sometime talked them out of the "protection" they sought, and signed them up for a two week family holiday at the CP's Camp Beacon.

"What are you trying to do to me, fella?" Dad yelled into the phone on the little table in the hall in between our bedrooms. "Never in a million years will Abe Fogeller come out a Bolshevik. But I'm probably going to lose a client sure as I'm standing here."

"Suit yourself Irv," he later reported Barney saying while sniffling at his mustache. "If you don't trust my judgment don't make me such referrals."

"You do it for Minna and Masha," my mom always pointed out.

"Well little Mrs. Hoity Toity Minna can take care of herself very well thank you from now on," Dad said then, as though disturbed by any inference he could be less than magnanimous to his best friend.

"Barney and I were high school frat brothers when he first came to Newark from the Lower East Side," he reminded Mom. "He introduced me to you. We go way back. Can I help it if the guy has a screw loose?"

"I appreciate the sentiment," I heard my mom repeat, "but I told you it doesn't mean anything really," just as she always did when their talk was about Barney Goldman.

For a little while, after such episodes, Uncle Barney and Aunt Minna would not be invited to come around for visits quite so often. Then the friendship revived. My father must have felt some guilt for being so driven because he seemed to believe that Barney was a better person than he in some soulful, undefinable way, or else Mom might lecture him about keeping up old friendships. Mom once implied he needed Barney in his life to keep him from murdering me.

Ever since I had been old enough to talk back, Dad and I had been enemies. I was scared of his violent outbursts with his hands and feet, and he was convinced I was so totally loopy I would someday bring him shame. For some reason I never quite understood, my father thought of me as having affinities with "Uncle Barney" and he often called him over as a go-between when our relations became so bad they could get homicidal.

One Sunday, when I was fairly little, my mother went to Loehmann's on Bedford Avenue to buy a "formal" for an affair given by Dad's savings and loan association at the Waldorf Astoria; Dad was assigned to look after her only son. I pestered him so much with questions, I interrupted his perusal of the Sunday *Times'* real estate section and he threw me against the radiator head first, causing a big gash in my forehead. Uncle Barney was immediately summoned from a few blocks away to restore calm. He pressed a gauze pad wrapped around an ice cube to my head and eventually took me and my bleeding head to the Caledonia Hospital to get it stitched up.

"Just tell them it was an accident," my father said, as I bawled away, and Barney held me close and tried to soothe me.

"Don't worry Irv," he said, "they don't have to know everything you do. They just have to fix the boy's head."

"I feel awful about this," Dad said.

"YOU FEEL AWFUL?" I screamed at him.

"Easy does it, *boychick,*" said Barney. "Your father doesn't know his own strength. You feel awful and he feels awful, too. So sue him. He's a lawyer. What do you think you'll get?"

He signed off on all correspondence with "As always." He liked barber shop shaves and hot towel facials. I think I always liked "Uncle Barney" better than I liked my father in that I was never really afraid of him, but I also never thought we were at all alike. He'd gotten lost somewhere in his life where nobody could really rescue him anymore, and I was this outsider, this onlooker, who thought he knew certain things about this lost man so that comparisons to him weren't flattering. But, after one of my father's frequent atrocities to my head or hams, Barney was the perfect person to have on hand to diffuse our rages. After I interrupted a game of pinochle and got a slap in my face that loosened teeth, my father said, "Crybaby! If you want pity ask your Uncle Barney." Barney's ability to pity, like his loyalty to the family, was unquestionable.

As my father became more affluent and began to realize more of his dreams for himself and his family in the material world, his depredations against me happened less and less frequently. We also saw quite a bit less of "Uncle Barney" and "Aunt Minna." They were still called "best friends" and "like family." But now they were the sort of "Bohemian" friends my parents, as a couple, were all-too-glad to see infrequently. Every once in a while Barney's name would come up at dinner as an object lesson in why a simple heart and good intentions often brought one to the brink of outright disaster: He had asked to borrow money; he was out of work again; Masha was in trouble at school. . . .

I never heard happy stories anymore about Uncle Barney and Aunt Minna even when they did socialize, or take weekend trips with my parents, except from my mom, who always used to insist, "they're good eggs." Mom seemed to believe Barney was not as outraged by life as her stoical husband, and more fun to be with. When Minna got ovarian cancer and was in the hospital, Mom and Dad kept saying they must both go to visit her, and he never did. Then she died when I was about thirteen, and they both went to the funeral at Garlic Brothers, as Dad was their lawyer. It also turned out after the funeral that Aunt Minna had been a considerable squirrel, and she left bank accounts plus pension funds, and shares in IBM, and a whole lot of Utica Mutual insurance to Barney in trust for Masha's and his own upkeep.

Barney reinvested Minna's money shrewdly and he managed to live in modest comfort for the rest of his life. He quit selling insurance, dropped left wing politics, took up golf, bought and sold "collectibles," and did Sunday painting almost every day of the week, at first in the manner of Diego Rivera—huge, brightly mottled, peasantry Jewish faces surrounded by colorful sarapes, with hassids floating overheard as in a Chagall, and titles like, "Zippedy Doo Da Dearest Minna #4."

I was in first year high school then and doing very poorly. In every teacher's Delaney book I was considered a suspicious character, an outcast. I had an older girlfriend named Mona Anne Sequens, and she was two years ahead of me, a rightist *Irgun* Zionist, planning to immigrate to Israel with a gun. "Good riddance," said my mom.

My father was convinced the best I could ever hope for was to be "a sanitary engineer," his sarcastic way of saying "garbage man," on the Suez Canal. I rarely got to school, was in trouble with the Dean for telling him "Go fuck yourself," and was also thinking of immigrating to Zion through the leftwing *Hashomer Hatzair,* which was an embarrassment to my father, a *macha* in the United Jewish Appeal establishment.

Everybody recommended counseling for me, therapy. My father said in my case it would be a waste of money as I had a big mouth and just wouldn't listen. He wanted to send me off to a military school to improve my posture, but Mom reasoned with him to summon Barney from his new studio and residence in Valley Stream. The three of us could have lunch together at Lundy's in Sheepshead Bay, and Barney would help him to enlighten me about how I was fucking up my life.

I argued with my father that "Uncle Barney" was really his friend, and Mom's, and why would he care? And why should I listen? But Dad told me Barney really thought a lot of me. "He claims to think you have potential," Dad said. When I saw the gleam of menace covering over the dull hurt in those cold green eyes I relented, got dressed up in new chocolate brown slacks and a camel's hair sportcoat from Rogers Peet to have lunch one Saturday with my father and "Uncle Barney."

It had been some time since I'd actually seen Barney in person. He came dressed for sport, too, in a bright lemon yellow cashmere golf sweater, burnt sienna trousers, and a Greek sailor's cap. He'd acquired a neat brown tan, I noticed, and was wearing a toupee between his balding head and the dark blue cap that matched perfectly with the pepper and salt of his mustache and sideburns.

When we were seated my father ordered plates of oysters on the half shell for all of us, and then went off toward the Men's Room to make an important phone call, he said.

Then Barney reached across with his big paw and took my hand and asked me what was my favorite make of car.

"I can't even drive yet," I said.

"I own a new Austin Healey with a stick shift," he announced. "A *shtick* and a half . . ." He laughed silently. "So *boychickal*," he said, "I know lots of things are pretty lousy with you at school and in the home. So tell me is it like that in every way? How are the girls treating you?"

"They're all right," I said, flatly.

"You do like girls," he asked avidly, "don't you?"

"O, yes," I said. "But I'm still a kid and I'm not getting much really."

"Call me Barney," he smirked. "Forget the Uncle. At 14, I was a repeater pencil, as I still am . . . "

"You are?"

"More or less," said Barney. "The thing is be nice to them. Nice gets you nice, more than any other way from what you call the love angle."

"Thanks a lot," I said blushing.

To change the subject I complimented Barney on his ensemble.

"I should introduce you someday to my haberdasher," he said. "Really take you in hand and *handle* you, as it were . . ."

Then my father returned and he asked Barney when our oysters were being served to talk to me man-to-man.

Grimly, Barney nodded his head. "Your dad sure is worried about you."

"I need that like I needed a hole in my head," I said.

Dad bared his teeth.

"Even though you're growing up like a weed," Barney said, "it's important to listen to your parents and not waste your chances for a good education."

"That much I know," I said.

"It's really no joke," he said. "A boy like you could have real potential . . ."

"I want to make *aliyah*," I said. "Go on back to the Land."

"That's one way to get nookie, I suppose," Barney said, followed by that silent laugh again, so I knew he had me there, having had similar thoughts, and now they made me blush a second time.

My father seemed impatient with Barney's Socratic method. "I asked you to lunch," he said, "to give the boy some of your hard-earned wisdom about stepping off the deep end. You know how much trouble life can be."

Barney glanced about the large crowded room with its Moorish archways as if to take in the confidentiality of our circumstances. His pale eyes watered and he took a deep gulp of beer and swallowed. "If you don't ever do it when you're young and fit," he told me, expansively, "you'll never learn to swim like Lord Byron in Bosporus of Life. And only shmucks dog paddle," he added.

"That's not what I meant at all," my Dad said.

"He's not your stooge," I said.

"One or two days a week I still am," Barney said. "But on the whole that's neither here nor there! It's dog eat dog out in the world."

"The world should probably know better," I said.

"Birds of a feather," my father said, and looked off into space as another oyster slid down his throat.

When we finished lunch, Dad got the check and Barney and I walked out together into Sheepshead Bay's fragrant salty air.

"I guess I sounded pretty half-assed," he said.

"You did fine," I told him. "Thanks a lot."

"I did it for you and your mother," my father's best friend said. "But he's really not the worst. Just stay out of his way and he'll give you the shirt off his back."

"I really want him to leave me alone," I said.

"He can't do that," Barney said. "He's your Dad."

"So what?"

"What's going on, you two," Dad demanded when he came out through the revolving doors.

"Irv," Barney replied, "your boy here is teaching me all the facts of life."

I never did go to Israel back then. I never even saw very much of Barney again except from time to time when he would get in touch and invite himself for a visit and become part of my life and fade away again.

And the time we did see each other almost always involved a family crisis of some sort—mine, his, my parents', Masha's—so that there were periods when I thought of him almost exclusively in italics, or capital letters, moments set off from ordinary affairs of a young outcast from a family of comfortable strivers after the good life.

What little else I knew of Barney I learned from my parents, or Masha, if he was on speaking terms with either party, or from the times we bumped into each other at family affairs, though I fancied he was still my closest relation, almost a friend and comrade. Then, after many years of silence between my father and myself, when he was in a coma and my aunt begged me to come East to visit him before he died, there, waiting outside the Intensive Care Unit to which I'd been directed, was a meager replica of my "Uncle Barney," with a wispy white fringe of hair and a trembling lower lip, and wet rheumy eyes.

He seemed to recognize the grown man who had once been Irv Fishback's kid just as soon as I stepped off the elevator, for he called out my name.

I went over to Barney and we shook hands. "It's nice of you to be here at this time," I said. "Dad didn't really have that many old friends left. . . ."

Uncle Barney truly seemed glazed with shock that I was here for his old friend, Irv; he'd been visiting with a girlfriend who'd smashed up her pelvis in a car on the Southern State Parkway.

"There was a lot of internal damage," he said. "But she'll make it. How's your father? Ok?"

"He's dying," I said flatly.

"Poor Irv," he said. "I tried to see your mom before she passed away but he treated me like liver spots. Wouldn't let me enter her room. I didn't mean him any harm."

"Of course I remember," I said. "Don't you remember? I asked you to come. Dad could get crazy sometimes."

"He had his reasons," Barney said. He truly looked grim, more so than I was allowing myself to feel.

Looking me over again, he said, "You've filled out some. It's a good sign. You have a family?"

"I'm recently divorced for the second time," I said, "but I have a lovely daughter whom I see a lot of. . . ."

"It's probably better that way for all concerned," Barney said. "We're neither of us meant to be family men." His voice was very soft and vaguely quavering. "Is Dad still conscious?"

"I don't think so," I said.

"Could I," he asked, "come in with you? I'd really like to see him one last time.

I said I didn't think there was much to see, but sure; he could come into the Unit with me.

We entered this vast dimly-lit loft filled with cubicles and glass boxes connected by cables and asked a nurse to direct us to Irving Fishback.

Dad was stretched out between curtained walls on a cot, naked with tubes reaching out from his arms and legs. The air was very chilly; there was a bank of monitors above his head. He seemed to be trembling. From his left side a thick rubber drain drew fluids out of an open wound from surgery. His drawn handsome face was graven with pain, seemed blind to light.

But, suddenly, he sighed and his whole body shook, and then was silent again, breathing easily, though never once did he open his eyes to see us.

For all I was losing and never, in fact, had really ever had, I was fearful.

"It's terrible what happens to all of us," Barney said. "He loved you. I guess you know that."

"You were the best friend he ever had," I also lied.

"More like I was your mom's friend," Barney corrected me. "A lot of what I did I did for her."

"I think I always knew that," I said. "It doesn't matter now."

"I guess you were so smart you figured that out for yourself," he said. "But after a while I began to feel sorry for him anyway. He never really knew how to relax, but in a lot of ways he was a better man than I was. . . ."

"I think he probably felt the same way," I told Barney who turned away from me, quickly, and sobbed. I laid my arm across his frail shoulder.

"There's nothing really I can do for him," I said. "I thought at least we could say goodbye. But he doesn't even hear me."

"Try talking to him again," Barney said. "Make the effort!"

I came beside the bed and bent over low and mumbled, "Dad, I'm here."

"It's your son Ron, Ronald," I added. "I'm sorry we quarreled so much. I kept waiting for you to apologize to me for all the hurtful things you probably never meant to do but now it's too late so I'll do the apologies. I'm sorry, Dad, sorry we quarreled. Can you hear me?"

"LOUDER," Barney said.

I thought I saw Dad's eyes peek open a moment, but when I looked again they were closed, his breathing softening. He seemed even more remote from my words.

"TALK SOME MORE IN YOUR NORMAL TONE OF VOICE," Barney said, "and just keep on talking. He could come out of it. You'll see. You never know."

"Dad," I began again, "Dad, I'm here, your son, Ronald, I'm so sorry. Can you hear me? I'm standing here right next to you with Barney, Uncle Barney. . . ."

"Bastar . . . !" Dad's last utterance.

"I can't believe. And after all these years," Barney exclaimed.

"Father," I repeated. "Dad!"

"Have mercy kiddo," Barney said.

"Dad."

"Kiddo. . . ."

"Bo. . . ."

When I stopped and looked up, "Uncle" Barney Goldman was gone from the room like a bad smell. As though called elsewhere to his own accounting, he'd left without even saying goodbye.

I looked down at the figure in the bed. "Dad," I said, "Dad, I'm sorry. Barney's not here anymore but I still am. Can't you try to listen to me even now?"

I kept cajoling him to respond to me until the nurse told me there was no point in talking anymore.

~ I sometimes wonder if Uncle Barney could still be alive somewhere. He would have to be quite ancient, almost ninety. But, as Dad used to say grudgingly, "That palooka takes real good care of himself."

I was maybe ten or eleven years old when Uncle Barney took me out on the Pulaski Skyway to Bears Stadium in the Jersey Meadows to watch a minor league baseball playoff game between Newark and the Montreal Royals.

Jackie Robinson and Roy Campanella were Royals stars. This treat from Barney was on account that Masha was a girl and didn't like to watch baseball games all alone with him.

After the game we drove back to the City in his old grey Plymouth coupe. Barney let me sit in the rumble seat and scream and make faces at all the passing cars. The noise of traffic was sometimes ear-splitting, though upfront I heard snatches of his loud basso intoning, "My Bonny Lies Over the Ocean," to his daughter Masha, only he pronounced the name as "Barney."

"My *Barney* lies over the ocean
My *Barney* lies over the sea.
My *Barney* lies over the ocean
Bring back my *Barney* to me.
Bring back bring back
Bring back my Barney to me."

As we were late for the special dinner Mom was fixing at our house, he gunned the motor now and then.

I closed my eyes to keep out cinders. While Masha remained stony silent like an Easter Island statue beneath her babushka, Barney sang on:

"Bring back o bring back
Bring back my *Barney* to me to me
Bring back bring back
Bring back my *Barney* to me."

It was peacetime then, after many years of war. Inside the Holland Tunnel the car got stuck in traffic. Barney's lugubrious echoes bounded from the tile walls.

Exposed as I felt, I suddenly was fearful that all those tons of water and alluvial mud surrounding us might collapse their containing walls and we'd be engulfed beneath the river and perish. All seemed calm enough, the air stagnant with car fumes, and stifling, as Uncle Barney changed gears loudly, and dispelled my imaginary disasters with his stout vocalizing of another Rum Scoundrel tune:

"He don't own *term life.*
He don't own *whole life.*
And sucker buyers
are ripe and rotten,
but old man Barney
with all his blarney
he just keep rolling along!"

Ed Falco

PICK-UP LINE FOR POETS

Approach the one looking painfully bored. Take a seat nearby and say, "I want to go someplace dark." The response might be: "Like brindled fields at dusk? Where shadows gather before the sun's last breath?" (Remember, you're both poets.) Say, no. Say you want to go where crows unfurl black wings unseen; someplace away from cheering fans, the flag-waving hand-holding crowd; someplace where night sounds echo the tumult of your brute heart, where what you want rages in every word and you might touch and be touched in a place where the lies have burned away and you're left raw enough to feel.

Trust me, if you're really both poets, this line is foolproof. Try it, but be sure you've got the right other. With the wrong person, it's a disaster. But with the right one . . . Go ahead. Say, "Come here. I want to go someplace dark, dark."

THE BODY OF A WOMAN

What is it about some men and the body of a woman? For some men, a woman's body is like the deep sound whales make under water, a sweet urgent calling from another place, almost impossible to resist. Like Odysseus they must strap themselves to a mast and suffer to refuse the song of a woman's body.

What is it that makes his breath suddenly go shallow when a woman, undressed, bent at the waist, dries her dark hair with a green towel? Her breasts are small, nipples tucked in within enfolding skin. Why does he need to touch those breasts—with the palm of his hand, with his fingertips, with his mouth, the mouth most urgently?

It's not the animal urge to procreate. Not just that. Not for some men. For some men just to look is enough, just to see the body of a woman: the way the lower back dips along the spine, then rises to the parted flesh of the buttocks and falls again to that star of light where the legs meet the body, that small empty space, a diamond of nothing but desire.

This is not about love. This is not about a union of spirit that goes higher or deeper than the body. This is about the body itself, the body of a woman: the nape of the neck; the slope of a leg; the opening into her, the way flesh mounds there. Just to see it for some men is a reckless urge.

Does it have something to do with death or beauty? Is it only the instinct to survive?

In my dream the body of a woman was a luminous door, a glowing plane in a dark field, a passage, an entrance, a way into a hidden place I was meant to find.

What is it about the body of a woman? What is it about, the body?

ESSAY ON THE EVE OF WAR

October 2002

Her desire to touch while mouths bellow this and that about war, about killing. The need to, in this season of random shooting, of bomb and poison. She's sick of the posturing, of the attitudes of righteousness, after which so many wind up dead. And that's part of the desire to touch and be touched without the hand then closing like a fist and yanking her into the bloody feast, the civilized hall. Leave us out, but do come here because out there it's blood weather again. Come here and let's make a place where we know each other by what's in our hearts, where we worship and nurture with sheltering bodies, reaching through skin to the place where it's not just one person anymore but all the teeming others ageless, multitudinous, beautiful in various skins that in this place we know to be one body so that our touch touches everything that breathes and is alive. And then, maybe after that, we can go out together and tell stories of a different world, a place where we know the loved one in others and act accordingly, where swords in the hands of warriors are playthings, toys with which they gesture like bellicose children or harmless fools.

Amina Gautier

AFTERNOON TEA

A women's organization decided to adopt the girls in our school for the year, but we weren't supposed to feel lucky. We were selected, not for our scholasticism or high test marks, but because our school had the highest percentage of eighth grade girls dropping out to have babies. The organization selected us out of all the other junior highs in Brooklyn as the most need-worthy, designated us as the most at-risk. Ten women from the group would serve as volunteer mentors. Time spent with the women was supposed to raise our self-esteem. It would keep us from making negative decisions that could permanently alter and impact our lives. Translation: the program would keep us from having babies at an early age and living off of welfare.

Today was the registration and the welcome for the program and my mother feared we would lose face by showing up late. She rapped on the bathroom door to get me out of the shower. "What, do you think you're a fish? Make haste!"

Once I came out, I said, "I bet this is going to be really boring."

"It will be good for you," she said. "Just give it a try. You have nothing better to do on Saturday mornings."

This was true. Most Saturdays I stayed at home alone while my mother went out. She visited our extended family, making sure they were getting acclimated to life in the States, shopping for them and helping them barrel up goods they wanted to send back home to Jamaica. Because she was the first to come to the States, she was the veteran, the expert, the one who helped everyone else out, the one whom all our relatives came to live with first when they moved here.

She was taking a break from visiting to accompany me to the program today.

"I still don't see why I have to go to this," I said.

She tsked at me, grabbed my shoulder and pushed me towards my room. She ignored my question. "Hurry and dress."

Breakfast was on the table by the time I was fully dressed. "Bun and cheese," she said. "You don't have time for anything else."

I checked my watch. "It doesn't start for another half hour."

My mother sucked air through her teeth. "On time is too late. A half hour early is right on time."

"They'll probably feed us there," I said. "I can skip breakfast. That'll save time."

My mother shook her head. "You are only to nibble while you're there. You don't want to stuff yourself on their food and look like a glutton. When people are watching, you have to make a good impression."

"Who's watching?" I mumbled as I chewed.

My mother frowned at me. "They are."

At different times, depending upon who my mother was talking about, they could be anyone. *They* applied to all Americans, and sometimes specifically American blacks, and on rare occasions to the family my mother had left behind in Jamaica, proud and aristocratic, constantly watching from across the sea and waiting for her to fail and go back home.

I finished off my breakfast and got up from my chair.

"What are you doing?"

"You said to hurry—"

"You'll clean up after yourself first."

"I thought we were late."

"There's always time for that," she said, watching me carefully as I took my plate to the sink and wiped the table off with a dishcloth. "You have no servants in this house."

Thirteen years ago, my mother left St. Elizabeth with the seed of me inside of her, leaving behind a life of affluence for one of struggle. She had grown up a rich little girl in St. Elizabeth, Jamaica. She'd lived in a house with servants. There were women whose job it was to cook and serve dinner and these women were different from the ones who gathered the laundry and washed her unmentionables. Now my mother worked in a hospital five days a week, changing bedpans and dealing with other people's filth.

Twenty-two of us girls showed up at the school's library with our mothers. Ten black American women, all dressed impeccably in blue and red, waited for us. Three women met us at the door.

"Good morning."

"We're so glad you could make it."

"Please sign in at the table to your right."

They rushed to greet us, all speaking at once, then checked our names against their list to make sure we weren't crashers. Another group of three stood behind a long table loaded with red and blue gift bags. The last group of three poured cups of juice and lined them up on another table, next to plates piled high with cinnamon rolls and bagels. One woman stood apart from the others, watching and nodding as we entered and sat nervously.

"Why are they all dressed alike?" I whispered as my mother led the way to an empty table.

"They're a sorority," my mother said, pointing to the coat of arms on the colorful banner the women had strewn between two scarred bookshelves. Our library had been redone, transformed by these women and their presence. "Those are their colors."

"What about those?" Each woman wore a gold pin with indecipherable symbols above her left breast.

"They're Greek letters," she said, surprising me with her knowledge. My mother was a woman of many secrets. She knew many things, but only told me what she thought I needed to know at any given moment. When I was old enough to notice that other kids had fathers and I didn't and I asked her what my father was like, my mother gave the briefest of descriptions. "He was big like so," she said, stretching her hand over her head, describing a man anywhere between five four and seven feet tall. "And black like so," she said, pointing to the darkest object near at hand. No matter how many times I asked for more, her descriptions never went beyond this. I was never to know from her if he ever laughed, if he was stingy or carefree with his money, or even how they met. In describing my father as big and black, she told me all she thought I needed to know.

The one woman who stood apart, the leader, went around the room, pumping all of our hands vigorously. She introduced herself as Miss Diane. Then she introduced the other women. Each one came forth and said a little about what she did. The women were engineers, physicians, computer specialists, lawyers, and scientists. They gave us a history of their sorority, Zeta Alpha Delta. We all rose as they sang their sorority's hymn.

My mother took pains to tuck her skirt beneath her as she sat back down on the small chair. These women, dressed in their elegant color-coordinated suits and pins put our own mothers, dressed in their best, to shame. As Miss Diane explained the program to our mothers, thanking them for bringing us and saying that we would benefit from additional positive female role models at this crucial stage of our development, I listened and heard what sounded like a death knell to me. During these times together, we would focus on math, science, critical thinking and writing skills, but they would make sure to cover the niceties as well, teaching us etiquette, hygiene and grooming. We wouldn't have to pay for anything. We were to spend two Saturdays a month with them from ten until one for the remainder of the school year.

As Miss Diane talked, the other nine women circulated the tables, handing each girl a gift bag to thank us for coming. When I was handed mine, I looked at the other girls at the tables near me. Some of them I already knew, most I didn't. We were all wearing the same expression, a combination of fear, awe and distrust. Although they didn't say it out loud, the ladies' message was clear: they wanted to keep us from becoming the kind of women they would shudder to see. They wanted to save us from ourselves. The girl directly across the table from me caught my attention and whispered, "Who they supposed to be?" She was my age and American, with bad skin. We were classmates, but I couldn't recall her name. Besides the red eruptions of pustules on her brown cheeks and forehead, nothing about her looked crucial to me.

~ My mother pushed her way to the front of the room while other parents were gathering their coats and bags to leave. "I think this will be a wonderful program for my daughter," she said. "She wants to be a doctor. She comes from a long line of doctors. Her grandfather and her uncle both practiced medicine in Jamaica."

I hated the sight of blood and needles terrified me. I wanted to be a librarian, to live a quiet and orderly life. To walk among stacks of silent shelves, to know every book by its number and let no book go astray. I loved to read worn books, dog-eared by people who had loved them. I wondered why she was lying. I tried to stand apart from her, to disappear each time she gestured to me, saying, "This is my daughter, Dorothy. She's a good girl. Smart."

You could tell my mother was from the Caribbean. Even though her accent was almost completely gone, eroded away through the years, her foreignness appeared in phrases and on the ends of certain words, like my name. In school I was Dorothy, at home *Dorotee*. I absorbed my mother's sounds and phrases, but didn't repeat them. Her way of talking sounded more natural to me than the everyday language I heard outside of our home, but in her voice I heard an act of erasure, a code embedded in the words she couldn't rid of her special pronunciation. A warning I heard in those words not to repeat them. Her words told me Don't.

"Come," she said to me. I walked to her side, towering over her. I had to listen as she sang my praises. The women looked me over. I wondered if I looked crucial enough to them, if they saw themselves saving me from heated embraces with experienced boys, or if they could tell that I was always one of the last to be asked to dance at a house party. I was almost thirteen, but I might as well have been ten for all of my experience. I had never been kissed. Never attended a sleepover. Never done anything that did not have my mother's hand in it. Like my mother said, I was a good girl. I didn't see myself as being in a crucial stage, although I liked the way it sounded. *Crucial stage.* It was as if I were on the brink of something, standing with one toe at the edge of a cliff. At any moment I could plummet off the edge or be sharply pulled back in. Crucial. It meant I was one step away from my complete destruction. The slightest false move and I was done for. It gave my life an added sense of desperation that I liked immensely and didn't want these women to take from me. And if I were truly on the brink of something terrible, it was arrogant of them to think that they could save me.

"What was all that for?" I asked as we made our way out of the school and walked home.

"Just making sure they know who you are," my mother said. "Who you know is important. These women here can take you far."

I didn't say anything else as we walked home. My mother had already made up her mind, so there would be no getting out of the program. I watched her as she walked slightly ahead of me, swinging my gift bag in her right hand.

~ Leon was out emptying his garbage. He waved us over when he spotted us. We lived three blocks away from the school, on a street populated by other West Indians and Leon owned the Laundromat on our street. His Laundromat was more than a place to wash clothes. It was a place to buy phone cards and key chains, a place to ship goods. Twice a year, my mother bought two barrels and loaded them full of dry goods, taped them up and sent them to relatives I'd never met.

"Where the two of you been all dressed and thing?" he asked.

"Dorothy started a program today at the school. Can't have the mothers showing up raggedy and such, eh."

"That's right now. You have to represent and show them you mean business!" he said, slamming the lid of the dumpster down hard. "It's good to see young people with something to do to keep themselves occupied. Remember when we were that age? Our parents kept us busy. There was no lying around all day, watching TV and such. Leave you with too much time to yourself and you run around and get in trouble and all kind of mess."

"Not Dorothy. I have no worries on that account," my mother said.

"That's so," Leon said. "You doing a fine job with her."

My mother smiled modestly.

Leon was encouraged. "You sure look fine today," he said, giving her a wistful look as he grinned and showed off his gold-capped teeth.

I stood there for ten minutes while they discussed me like I was invisible, watching girls my age wheel their shopping carts full of dirty clothes past us and up the three steps to the Laundromat. Leon's infatuation was obvious although my mother pretended not to notice it. I wanted to warn him about my mother, to tell him that she preferred to be left alone. There were no men in our lives. My mother's father died during my infancy and her one brother had no desire to come over. This uncle of mine now had six children and my mother was always packing barrels full of Sweet'N Low to send to him. I had never seen my mother go out on a date, never seen her stop and smile or respond to any of the many men that expressed interest in her. Nice as he was, Leon was all wrong for her. Although he'd been living here for some time, he still seemed new.

~ On our first session, the Zeta Alpha Deltas showed us a video featuring "famous women of African descent." Then they gave us notebooks and asked us to write an essay about a woman of our choice who hadn't appeared in the video. When we were done, they had us read them aloud.

One by one, we each stood up and read essays about our mothers. Halfway through the eleventh essay, I could see the women's faces falling. They seemed bewildered and disappointed. Miss Diane looked as if she were going to cry.

When we were done, Miss Elaine put a hand on Miss Diane's shoulder. "I don't think they understood the assignment, soror."

Miss Diane took a deep breath and stood in front of us. She seemed to be making an effort to smile. Miss Linda motioned her to sit back down and she spoke to us instead.

"Well, girls, I commend you for your efforts," she said.

Miss Tracy chimed in, "To write such beautiful essays in so little time!"

Miss Anita added, "And it's certainly encouraging to know that you all love your mothers."

Miss Diane cut them off. "Yes, it was very good. But why don't we do this? Why don't you girls take the assignment home and work on it for our next meeting?"

We all groaned aloud at the thought of another essay, but Miss Diane was undaunted. She said, "This time, try to think of women outside of your immediate sphere. Try to think of dynamic women, women who were the first of their kind to ever do something, women who broke the race and gender barriers. Women who carved a space for themselves outside the realm that people have come to think of as a woman's role. Now do you understand?" she asked us.

We all nodded. I raised my hand.

Miss Diane called on me. "Yes, Dorothy?"

"My mother was the first woman in her family to leave Jamaica and come live in the U.S."

~ Although I came to hate them, my mother was pleased with my Saturday sessions. She wanted me to distinguish myself from the others in my class, to stand out. She wanted to write home about me, to finally be able to use me as an example for my relatives over the sea who all thought I was lazy and spoiled. I imagined that my young cousins hated me. Here I was going to school in whatever type of clothing I chose, watching music videos until it was time for dinner, and having the time of my life while they were forced into uniforms and still had to go to the kinds of schools where the teachers could hit you and your parents would thank them for it. Where girls who spoke to boys were fast and loose, where they didn't have time for television after school because they had chores. These were my mother's recollections of her youth growing up in St. Elizabeth and although two decades had passed since she'd been a girl in grade school, I imagined that much had not changed.

I hated the Saturdays, but there I was session after session. My grades weren't suffering, so I didn't see why I had to give up my Saturdays to learn how to sit, when to cross or uncross my legs, and play with knives and forks. But, like the other girls, I didn't have a choice. None of us wanted to be there. We took our frustration out by barely participating, by looking past and through the women so bent on saving us. Our mothers could make us go, but they couldn't make us like it. So we slumped in our chairs and answered in monosyllables. Of the women, we took no notice. We doodled while the Zeta Alpha Deltas talked. We smacked our gum. If we'd have liked each other, we would have passed notes. But we did not think of leaving or skipping out. We were all there because our mothers made us go. Because the Zeta Alpha Deltas took attendance and we couldn't cut. Because we didn't have anywhere else to be. The library surrounded us, our sounds echoed off its high ceilings. Normally, we felt crowded in there with several classes meeting at once. But with just us there, the room seemed to swallow us. We filled only two of the eight tables. We had journals to write in, but after the fiasco with the mother essays, no one ever checked them to see what we wrote.

~ I showed up late for one of the Saturday meetings. The girls were clustered around the tables in the library. Something was different. They weren't their usual sullen selves. No one seemed to be biding their time. Not one pair of eyes was watching the tedious movement of the minute hand on the clock at the front of the room. The girls were all whispering. A current of energy filled the room. After I hung my coat over my chair and sat down, I heard one of the girls say, "Wait until I tell my father. He'll probably go and buy a new suit."

"Who are you going to bring?" she asked me.

"To what?"

"To our tea," she said. She slid me an ivory colored envelope from a stack off the table. While the sorority women were setting a game up for us, I opened it and read the invitation. They were samples of the invitations the ladies were sending to our homes. The tea would commemorate the end of our year's program and we would all be awarded certificates for our participation. The ladies thought we would be excited about the chance to get dressed up and show off. They said the tea would give us a chance to show off our social polish.

"What's the big deal about tea anyway?" I didn't understand why we needed a special event just to sit around and drink tea. Tea was what my mother and I had each day after school when we sat in the kitchen together, before we did anything else, before we turned on the TV or prepared dinner. Tea was how we settled into the evening. It was our private cozy shared intimacy.

All the eyes at my table turned on me. Four girls started talking at once.

"Duh. It's not just tea," the girl to my left said.

One girl said that it was good practice for social functions we would attend in the future.

The girl to my right said that it would be like a miniature debutante ball, only without boys.

"Rich people go to things like this all the time," the girl with the bad skin said. I could tell that they were just repeating what they'd heard before I arrived, but their enthusiasm was genuine. The women had finally gotten to them. They'd found the one activity that would make the other girls come alive. Up until the mention of the tea, our Saturdays had been boring. Each time we came we were forced to play stupid games we hated. One of the sorority women made us play Jeopardy, only the questions she made up for us were all in math. Another time, we'd played Bingo. Every square on the board was a fact about their sorority. Sometimes, we didn't play any silly games. We would just gather around one table, knotting and pulling embroidery floss into friendship bracelets. In February, they quizzed us on famous black inventors and scientists. Most sessions ended with them awarding some prize to the winner. Once I won a sachet made of rose-scented potpourri that I kept in my underwear drawer long after the scent had faded.

Everyone seemed to be excited but me. Girls who were normally despondent, who didn't speak until called upon, were chattering away and making plans that included their fathers. Those that didn't have fathers were borrowing their uncles or grandfathers for the day. I was the only one in the group without someone to escort me as I made my debut. I could see it now. Each girl would make a grand entrance into the rented hall as the ladies called her name. She would leave her father momentarily as she went forward to accept her certificate; then she would return to him and take his arm as he led her to her seat. Each girl but me. I didn't even have an uncle or older brother I could get to stand in. I felt sick, imagining how freakish I would look that day, all dressed up with no escort. Instead of a father, I had only the barest description.

"What will our mothers do? Do they have a special role?" the girl with the bad skin asked.

Miss Diane smiled as if it pained her and said, "Your mothers will be there to support and encourage. That's an important enough role for them."

Another girl asked, "What if mine can't make it? She works weekends."

This time the leader's smile was genuine. "Then we'll just have to make do."

Fathers, or male figures, were required. Mothers were optional.

The girl with the bad skin looked at me, eyebrows raised. Neither of us were surprised. The Zeta Alpha Deltas had not been subtle in the least way about their desire to wean us from the women they didn't want us to become. They kept encouraging us to look beyond our immediate circle, to expand our definition of role model to include women who had made real contributions to the world at large. Women such as themselves.

"Are there any more questions?" Miss Diane asked.

The girl on my left raised her hand. "Yeah. Why do you all wear blue and red all of the time?"

Miss Diane flushed with pride. She was dressed in a blue pantsuit with a red silk scarf knotted at her throat. "That's a good question, but I can't tell you the answer."

"How come?" she asked.

"Because only Zeta Alpha Deltas know the answer. These colors are symbolic to our sorority. Perhaps, one day when you're older, you'll join our organization. *Then* you can learn what the colors are all about."

~ The official invitation arrived a week later. My mother was in the kitchen making fried fish and festival when I dropped the stack of mail on the table.

After she read the invitation, she got on the phone and called the mothers of some of my girlfriends. Nine of the original twenty-two girls had dropped the program and my mother now called their mothers to gloat. She didn't come right out and say that she had told them so. Instead, she predicted great things for me, of which this tea was only the first. The Zeta

Alpha Deltas would take me under their wings and give me a scholarship when it was time to go to college. Once I got to college, I would pledge their sorority and be connected to all the right people for the rest of my life. Doors would open for me left and right. All because I gave them a few of my Saturdays and was willing to drink tea.

When my mother got off the phone, she announced, "You'll need a dress."

"Leave me the money, and I'll go down to Pitkin Avenue and get one," I said. I'd been picking out my clothes for the last year because she was usually too busy to go with me.

She shook her head. "Not a dress from there. It has to be A&S or Macy's."

"Okay." I shrugged. "I'll go downtown then."

"I'm going to go with you," she said, surprising me.

~ We took the three train downtown on a Sunday afternoon. Once inside A&S, my mother passed by the juniors section and took me straight to the dresses in Misses.

She scrutinized rack upon rack of formal gowns. All the dresses were meant for evening wear and looked expensive and uncomfortable. My mother didn't let me select any dresses, nor did she ask my preference on my choice for style, color or length. She made her decisions silently, rubbing her thumb across one dress's material, only to frown and hang it back up. She pulled dresses off their racks and held them up against the side of my body—long dresses with satin tops and velvet skirts, sequined dresses with spaghetti straps, dresses that were concoctions of lace, dresses that came with gloves, dresses with the back exposed—dresses that all seemed way too formal for an afternoon tea.

"Here, try these on," she said, pushing me into the fitting room, after narrowing her choices down to three.

I came out in them one by one, with an ever-growing sinking feeling. Not only were the dresses way too formal for my event, but they were hard to get into and each dress cost between sixty and one hundred dollars.

"Well? What do you think?" my mother finally asked, once her choices were back on their hangers and lying across her arm. I didn't know how to tell her I thought she was making a mistake and that I needed a simpler dress.

"I don't know."

"Which do you like the best?"

None, I thought.

"What's wrong?"

"They all seem, well, kind of dressy," I said.

"Of course," my mother said.

"Just to drink tea?"

"It's much more than just tea, Dorothy," my mother said. "It's not like what we do at home."

"They cost a lot," I said.

"You get what you pay for and quality costs money," my mother said, choosing one for me when I still couldn't pick. The winner was a cream-colored dress with a satin bodice and lacy skirt that ended in long points. Once we got to the register and my mother paid, she said, "Anyway, you're worth it. This is your chance to make an impression on them."

For just such a chance my mother had been waiting, each year growing more and more frustrated and disappointed in me as I let golden opportunities to advance myself pass me by. I coveted no plum roles in school plays, won no medals at the annual field day competition in Betsy Head Park, and could not sing well enough to ever get a solo. I made good grades, but there were other students who made better ones. In short, I was adequate, and she had been despairing I would forever stay that way.

~ The rest of our Saturday meetings at the school were devoted to preparations for the tea. The Zeta Alpha Deltas were using the tea as a chance to teach us how to put on a social program, so we spent our three hours learning about hall rentals, going over seating charts, ordering flowers, debating band choices and menu selections. They wanted us involved in every aspect of the planning. The day of the tea, we were supposed to show up two hours early in our work clothes to set up the room. As the tea drew nearer, it was all the other girls could talk about and images of my own father haunted me.

Neither my mother nor I had yet to mention what I could do since I didn't have a father to escort me. When I finally reminded her, she said, "We have more than enough family. I'll find you a father. No worries."

I didn't want a substitute father. I wanted my own. Or at least enough information about him so that I could recreate him and pretend, but my mother lived in a private world of memories she did not share.

I know he must have been handsome for my mother to love him. Handsome and big with very black skin. This is as much as my mother has told me, but not as much as I know. I pieced together images of him from what I knew of her. She wouldn't have liked him at first. It wasn't her way. She must have met him and loved him against her will. She wanted to love a safe man, preferably an older one that didn't have many demands. She wanted to bear children, cook meals, keep house and be left in peace. She wanted something simpler than what she'd grown up with. She didn't want servants around her or a house that took more than two people to clean it. She wanted comfort, but not luxury. My father must not have been any of these things. She couldn't know that I often wondered about him. I didn't even know if he still lived in Jamaica. It seemed most likely that he never knew about me. My mother left her family's country home for America when she was two months pregnant with me. I never understood why she left him, but I guessed it was because he had the power to make her change her mind.

Still, she must have suspected that something like me could come about. Used to being protected and cosseted her whole life, she must have thought herself immune and panicked upon realizing her body was just as human as every other woman's. I used to fantasize that my father had been one of the servants in my grandparent's house. In my mind, I saw feverish and clandestine meetings between my mother and him in closets and bathrooms. It wasn't until I got older that I realized it would have been impossible for her to love him had she met him in her home. For the most part, my mother was a proper girl. Raised in a house with servants her whole life, she would have no more noticed one than she would the wallpaper, let alone run off with one or let one drive her out of her country. Unlike here in the States, where we were all lumped together regardless of status, there class made a world of difference. Kinsmen or not, in those days, he would have been beneath her.

~ My mother didn't say anything else about the tea. Whenever I asked her if she'd found someone, she told me not to worry.

The night before the tea, she came home from work excited. "I finally found a father for you!" she said.

"Who?" I asked between mouthfuls. I had microwaved the previous night's escovitch fish and started eating dinner without her.

"Leon!"

I almost choked. There was my mother, standing before me, telling me that she'd gotten the laundry man to pretend to be my father, looking at me like I should be happy. She said he would meet me there. I could see it now. The other girls would laugh me right out of our rented hall.

"Leon?" I asked. I had been secretly hoping that she wouldn't find anyone and I wouldn't have to go. I hated taking pictures and being looked at. "What happened to all of our family?"

Everyone was busy that day, she said, or else too young or too old to pass for my father.

"He's not even related to us," I said. "We don't even look alike."

"You don't resemble your father anyway, except for the height. You look most like me."

I wondered if Leon had a real suit, or if he would just throw a blazer over his outdated jeans. Years ago, it had been the style to have artwork spray-painted and graffitied on the front and back pants legs of jeans. The fad had come and gone but Leon still wore his. Every other day, he wore a pair of stone-washed blue jeans with Mickey Mouse or Donald Duck spray-painted onto the legs. He would embarrass me with his tight jeans and his gold teeth. "But people will see. Everybody will see us!"

"And so?" my mother said. "Leon's a hard-working man and he's always been good to us." Her focus on class had gradually eroded but I wasn't as accepting as my mother. Leon was nice enough, but I didn't want anyone to believe he was my father. Not Leon with his outdated jeans and his camel suede shoes and his loud patchwork shirts in multi-colors. He was everything I was trying not to be and I didn't want anyone to think we were related.

"But Mommy, he's so—"

She made a sucking sound with her teeth to silence me. "Hush. What's done is done. I already invited him and he said yes. I can't take it back now. Besides, it's only for the one day, Dorothy."

My mother waited silently for me to nod or do anything to show that I agreed, but I remained still. We had never had an argument before. I had never talked back, disobeyed or sassed her before. Neither of us knew what to do now.

By an unspoken agreement, we didn't yell. Instead, we retreated into separate corners of the kitchen, fighting with brooding silence. In the silence between us, my mother began to make our tea, lashing me with her careful, studied indifference. She had no words for me. My mother's anger hung in the air. In the clang of stainless steel against aluminum as she fitted the opened neck of the kettle to the faucet as if choking it. In the kettle she filled and banged down on the burner. In the three clicks it took before the gas came on. In the hiss of the tiny beads of water at the spout as they evaporated into the heat of the flames.

When the water was ready, I fought back with my own sounds. The accidental slam of the cabinet door after I'd pulled down my cup. The dull clanging of my silver spoon hitting the ceramic bottom of the cup as I stirred too hard. The spill of sugar into my cup as I made my tea just the way I liked it—too too sweet—and dared her to say something.

~ The day of the tea, I showered and dressed in street clothes, wrapping a scarf around my head to keep my hairstyle in place. I took my new dress and put it into a bag, along with my shoes and stockings and headed out the door.

I passed the Laundromat when I turned the corner. Leon was open early this Saturday. He was bent over in the doorway, sweeping dust from the welcome mat. On either side of him, by the door, there were barrels and barrels waiting to be sold and shipped. I wished, for the moment, that I could climb into one and hide, that someone would seal me up and send me far away, that the ceremony could go on without me.

I walked quickly by before he could see me and caught the three train at Saratoga. I didn't switch to the four at Utica like I should have. I didn't know exactly what I was doing, but I got off at Grand Army Plaza, a stop which wasn't mine. I don't remember doing it on purpose, but I found myself far from where I was supposed to be.

There was a small Caribbean store on the corner by the train station. I went in and ordered a beef patty and a cola champagne and took it to one of the three small tables in the back. It was early still yet and not many people were in the store. No one bothered me as I sat in the back and ate the flaky yellow patty and tried to make myself disappear.

Later, I would regret this act of rebellion. On college campuses, I would see sorority women like the ones who tried to mentor me. I would go to their step shows and social programs, watching them hungrily as they all dressed alike and wore the same colors and melded into each other, distinguished only by their hair styles. I would see them pass each other on campus and call out special greetings, see them cluster together on lines in the cafeteria, see them never being alone. And I would think of how I missed my chance to know their secret ways, how I had closed myself out. I would watch them as if through a window of thick glass and I would want to break through and get in. But for now, I was satisfied to thwart their attempts to mold me into someone else.

I never showed up for the tea.

I sat in my corner of the shop and I imagined the other girls in their finery, being led into the banquet hall on the arms of their tall and strong fathers or grandfathers and thought of how I had no one. I blamed my father, whom I had never met. I didn't blame him for leaving us because he hadn't known about me. I blamed him for loving my mother in the first place, for loving her so much and so hard that she felt compelled to flee him across an ocean. I blamed him for forcing us to be alone, for leaving my mother emotionally paralyzed, scared to meet another man because she might find that same intensity again, the kind that could take her away from herself and scared to meet another man because she might not. Had it not been for that,

I could have had another father. There were plenty of men willing enough. They flocked to my mother wherever we went. They watched her as she carried bags, knowing she would not allow them to help. I watched them eye her when we rode the subways and buses and whenever we went to visit relatives, there was always a new man, a friend of so and so's waiting hopefully to be introduced. But she would not entertain any man's company. And I was left with Leon.

I killed the hours in the back of that tiny shop. The woman at the counter didn't bother me. After I finished my patty I bought a bun and cheese and played with it. I wasn't ready to go home just yet, but eventually I would have to face her. I didn't know if my mother were still at the rented hall, out somewhere looking for me, or already home and waiting. I had no idea what would happen between us when I finally made it back. But on any other day, I knew how it would be when I got home.

After a day of family duties that it would never occur to her not to perform, my mother would go through the house and head for her bedroom. There she'd undress in front of the mirror, revealing herself slowly.

A tissue from a box of Kleenex would take away her outside smile, leaving her house lips in their place. She'd pick up the brush off her dresser and pull it through her hair, not one hundred times, but just enough to quell the itch in her scalp and to direct the thick, unbending hair into order. My mother would shrink in front of the mirror as her shoes came off. She wouldn't bother to get her slippers. The rest of the afternoon and evening would see her barefoot. Small curling toes with fading paint would guide her to the kitchen where she'd fill our kettle with water and light a flame under it. All this would be done without sound. She would have had enough in the street and in the living rooms of all the relatives she has visited. She would leave the kettle to its own devices and settle on the couch in the living room. There she'd sink into the couch as if dissolving, feeling at this moment that she could leave the world and never look back. Then my mother would think of me. First she would wonder what I was up to and hope I was minding myself. She would wonder if I were behaving well. Maybe, for one moment, she'd think of my father and wish she hadn't left him. Thinking of me, she'd laugh at herself for making our usual afternoon tea for two when I wasn't even there to drink it. She'd get up and walk to the kitchen to turn off the kettle. And that's where she'd be when I returned. When she heard me enter, she'd call out and ask me how my day went and I would tell her fine.

Justin Haynes

BUILDING RAIN

It was raining and the boy was missing. The rain had come swooping in, indifferent, wetting the world because it could. It was when the rain began that the wreck of a father missed the boy.

The last time that the father saw the boy was the day before, prior to the rain, when the boy was on the roof of the house in Belmont, Trinidad, dangling down and banging on the roof metal with the Coca-Cola yo-yo with the never-pop string, zip-pulling it back up to his hand between Walking the Dog, Rocking the Baby, and Going Around the World, the roof being the place where, over the past few weeks, the father had rocket-launched just one of many yo-yos. The father didn't see the boy go up or come down from the roof the day before, the boy staying up there and waiting out the cut-ass he knew the father had scheduled for him for breaking the you-know-what, waiting until the father was too tired and went inside to fall asleep on the couch in front of the broken you-know-what.

It was the day before the rains came, the same day that the boy went onto the roof that, in the living room, the father had first fallen out with the boy, the boy still Going Around the World even after the father kept asking the boy questions like why was he not inside with the sister and sick mother, and didn't he know better than to be playing with a damned yo-yo in front of the TV all day, and the boy instead kept going Around the World in front of the TV while it was on, trying to get the moves perfect, circling the Coca-Cola yo-yo with the never-pop string beside his body like he was developing gravity for his own planet.

To be fair, that day that the father rocket-launched the yo-yo up onto the roof, the father had been tired, too tired for the Brain Twister, the Forward Pass, or the Loop-the-Loop, him blacking out on his last job earlier that day at a one-story construction site that was still a steel skeleton and where the foreman paid him and asked him not to come back, the father landing on his side, and bruising all his ribs.

That day, the father had limped home to the mother who was shivering under the covers, and the girl who was looking after her, and the boy who was standing in front of the TV practicing the Man on the Flying Trapeze, and the Sleep Beauty, both of which he couldn't quite get yet, instead coming closer and closer to breaking the screen of the second hand black and white Panasonic that the brother-in-law had given to the family. It was after a failed Four Leaf Clover, when the boy succeeded instead in smashing the power knob on the television, reducing the picture to a dot, and the TV to a you-know-what, that the father had had it. The father had been trying to watch the minister on television when the boy knocked the set out of commission while trying to go Around the World, and it was here that the frustrated wreck of a father decided to send the boy to his room to think about what he had done instead of administering a serious cut-ass. It was later that day when the father went into the room to see if the boy was sorry about breaking the you-know-what that he saw the boy practicing at throwing a Tidal Wave and at ignoring the father. This was the end of something and the father snatched this yo-yo too—*where did the boy get all these yo-yos?*—and rocket-launched it onto the roof as part of the growing collection there, the father telling the boy, absolutely and positively, that he didn't want him playing with any yo-yos again.

During the father's rant, the boy was not listening to the father, instead throwing a fast spinner, sliding the second finger of his free hand along the string, while at the same time pulling back on the string so that the string moved over his finger until he was just a little bit away from the yo-yo, then flipping the yo-yo out and over his hand so that it made a loop inside his wrist, after which it returned to his hand, a perfect Tidal Wave, the boy finally and proudly, in a moment of divine inspiration, dropping the perfect Tidal Wave just in front the father's face, the father once upon a time knowing how to have fun and enjoy a good yo-yo trick, and maybe would be proud of this.

However, with the you-know-what broken and the boy not sorry, and the boy's glazed over eyes not even looking at the father, not even acknowledging him, the father finally snatched the yo-yo and with a scissors, cut the string of the Coca-Cola yo-yo with the never-pop string and rocket-launched it onto the roof where the boy was afraid of heights to get it or the other yo-yos. That, the wreck of a father said smugly to himself, would teach the boy some brought-upsy.

But now it rained and the boy was missing and he was not on the roof.

The father went back inside out of the rain and checked on the mother. She was shivering and sweating although the day was cool. He rearranged the blanket over her and smoothed it out. When the father had taken the mother to the hospital a few weeks earlier, the doctors said that there was nothing they could do. If it was any consolation, they said, it would not be long now. In a strange way, this *was* a consolation. For although the mother was suffering, the father could not afford the around the clock pain pills that the doctors had given her at the hospital which made the mother tell everyone that she loved them *all* very much. Now, in a quick act of contrition, the father thought about the boy in the rain and decided that he didn't want the boy getting sick on top of everything else.

The father sat himself at the kitchen table that was loose-tooth wobbly from termites, and bent the muscles in his jaw, debating whether to punish the boy. He told himself that if the boy were in the rain then he would *have* to cut his ass, this being the way to pound some serious sense into that head that was as useless as a broken you-know-what. The father looked outside at the rain that fell a bucket a drop, which collected on the streets like a debt. The rain had not come for weeks, but now that it was there it seemed as if it would not stop. That day the rain struck the house like nails driven into metal—reliable, construction-sounding rain. Building rain. The father hoped that the boy at least had the good sense to be at the brother-in-law's place. These days the boy had been spending more and more time at the brother-in-law's. Maybe if the boy were at the brother-in-law's and was out of the rain, the father told himself while his leg sewing machine-pumped, maybe he would not cut his ass.

~ When the boy showed up at the brother-in-law's, the brother-in-law didn't know what to say or do anymore, other than handing the boy a towel to dry himself, the boy running away from home and showing up at the brother-in-law's place at all hours of the day now becoming a habit, a habit made worse and intensified on a day like today with the rain pooling and ramajaying like it was.

The brother-in-law didn't want to tell the boy a story about his mother getting better, he having told the boy enough stories over time, stories to flood the world, the boy standing arrogant in his favorite brown-plaid shirt that the brother-in-law had taken the boy to get from the orphanage's family day that was held on the faith revival field during one of the hottest days the week before, the shirt being the only way that the boy would not be afraid at the mere sight of the orphanage on top of the hill which was across the street from the brother-in-law's rented room and the faith revival field.

The boy stood there in the brother-in-law's doorway wearing water over his shirt and over his face like so many tears, with the Coca-Cola yo-yo with the never-pop string that the brother-in-law had bought him—maybe the sixth yo-yo that the brother-in-law had bought him in the past few weeks due to the circumstances—*where did the boy lose the yo-yos?*—the never-pop string wrapped around the boy's middle finger like a bow on a surprise package.

The brother-in-law dried the boy off and pulled another yo-yo out of a drawer and taught the boy the Three Leaf Clover and the Dog Bite, yo-yos being what the brother-in-law and the boy's mother had played with while they were growing up, the brother-in-law telling the boy that he shouldn't run away from home in the rain like this—didn't he know that the Rain Man, with violent desires and tendencies, looked out for children by themselves in the rain, and took them away to the orphanage away from their parents *forever*—the same orphanage on top of the hill across the street?

The boy listened, and watched the brother-in-law's hands, the brother-in-law flipping the yo-yo without thinking while talking. The boy followed the brother-in-law's actions with his hands, saying that he wasn't scurred of no Rain Man, that he would put a silver tooth in his mouth to look like a bad-john to pay out the Rain Man before the Rain Man could get him, that he had something for the Rain Man, if he ever came to get him. The boy wiped at his nose and said that he had seen the Rain Man just that day and that he had escaped him, the Rain Man probably wanting to cut his ass like the time the boy was up on the roof.

The brother-in-law sighed and told the boy not to talk like that. The brother-in-law knelt before the boy and rubbed his shoulders one more time with the towel, and told him to sit on the couch, that he would make him something hot to drink, some cocoa or Milo to fight the Rain Man with, the boy nodding while still trying to work the new tricks on the yo-yo. But when the brother-in-law came back out to ask the boy if he wanted sugar or condensed milk in his Milo, the boy was gone, leaving behind a rain-soaked wet spot on the plastic couch and taking both Coca-Cola yo-yos with the never-pop strings in exchange.

~ The father looked under the mother's bed to make sure that the boy was not under there looking for the yo-yos with the never pop strings, under the bed being the place that the father at first hid the yo-yos because the boy was afraid to even go into the room to see his mother the way that she was, no longer his mother, unraveling from the inside out. But by then the boy was no longer afraid of slithering under the bed and slithering back out without even the mother noticing, him grabbing the yo-yos and thus causing the father to learn new places to lose the yo-yos, to commence rocket-launching them onto the roof. The boy was growing older, growing tougher. The father smoothed the mother's sheets again and went into the boy and girl's bedroom and then into the kitchen where the girl was making tea.

The girl told the father that the last time that she had seen the boy was when he was flat on his back wearing his favorite plaid-brown shirt, upside-down watching Ernie and Bert on the black and white Panasonic that the wife's brother had second-hand given to the family before it became the you-know-what. The father sat down at the table and drank the tea, looking at the rain that was falling as if the world was coming to an end, and remembering that the you-know-what was once a living breathing TV, reminded himself that he would cut the boy's ass for real now for having broken it, the father flexing his ass-cutting fingers.

The father stood up. The pain in his side cheered. He grimaced and sat back down. He told the girl that he was going to look for the boy and that the girl should check on the mother often. The girl nodded; she loved the boy even though the boy had learned a figure four leg lock from a wrestler on TV and had used it on the girl (along with a sunset flip), the move not forming an eight with their legs as the boy had hoped, but still causing her pain nonetheless. The girl still loved the boy in spite of all this. The girl was nine and sensible. The father stood up again and bared his teeth through the pain. Not having a raincoat he wore another shirt.

When the father stepped outside, he shielded his eyes from the rain and looked on the roof again for the boy. The father didn't understand how the boy had gotten up there the day before the rain, there being no trees near the roof.

That day before the rains came, when the father had seen the boy on the roof, the boy had sat at the edge of the roof while waiting out the cut-ass and lazily worked his foot under the sheets of galvanize on the roof with his toe, lifting the sheets enough so that the father finally had to borrow a ladder the next day to place some rocks on top of the galvanized sheets to hold down the roof that might blow away in the rains that were supposed to come any day.

When the father borrowed the ladder and climbed onto the roof, he wondered again how the boy was no longer afraid to climb onto the roof, how come he was no longer afraid of heights like the father had been all his life and still was, the father forgetting that fear to take a job in construction of all things, climbing beams to support his family.

Shaking his head, the father made off toward the brother-in-law's, deciding that the boy was probably there, the boy not liking to see the mother wasting away like she was, her body fraying from the inside out like overused string. The father opened the front gate and headed off to the brother-in-law's, the rain tagging after him like a starved animal, the idea of lightning following as well.

~ To get to the brother-in-law, the father cut through the faith revival field. The faith revival field was empty now and there were hidden rivulets and secret sinkholes everywhere from the water. Across the field separated by a road was St. Dominic's orphanage. In a corner of the field, under a shed, there were a few delinquent chickens with their heads burrowed into their chests. The chickens had lived in the field for such a long time that no one knew anymore who they belonged to. There was a goat under the shed too. The animals were never there when the field was being used for faith revival tent meetings.

The father had been to a couple of faith revival meetings, but being there embarrassed him. He had not been to church for a while, not since Easter three years before, church being a habit that the mother kept with the boy and the girl; the father had always been working. Now that the mother was ill, he felt ashamed that he had not gone more often. He'd wanted to start back but he'd felt that aside from the glances at church, his prayer would be hollow. Finally the mother suggested the faith revival tent meetings. She told him that the tent revival was where people went to be saved, and after that, maybe he would feel better about going to church. The father agreed that maybe this was so, but decided to first watch the minister on the second hand TV instead, the same minister who ran the faith revival tent meetings. The father said that watching the minister on TV first was like strengthening a broken bone after an accident, relearning to use muscles. The father liked watching the minister on TV.

Eventually the father went to a revival meeting, dragging the boy and the girl with him, the girl praying intently while there, and the boy too, even though he had one hand in his pocket as the father later found out, and was playing with the first yo-yo that the father would eventually rocket-launch onto the roof, the little boy so bad that day that he was even rude to the minister when he came to shake his hand, telling the minister in the sweated-out suit that *he smelled,* the father clouting the boy and the minister guffawing, saying that children will be.

At first, the father felt awkward talking to Jesus while the minister in the sweated-out shirt and sweaty face stood up front and shouted about everything from floods to the end of the world. The earnestness of the children with their heads bowed low made the father feel more ashamed. When he told the mother about this she replied that it was only instruction—meant as guidelines more than anything else—what was in the father's heart was what was important, and the father agreed and it was this that kept him going back, the minister on television serving as a cast on his broken soul. Having looked at the mother suffering under the sheets, the father decided that he would return that week; the tent revivals were held monthly and there was to be another one that Wednesday.

~ The father shivered as he walked through the field. He had his arms wrapped around himself when he tripped on a water-covered hole that one of the pylons for the tent had produced, falling onto a left-behind spike that pushed into his upper arm.

Bleeding and cursing, the father climbed the steps to the brother-in-law's room. These days the brother-in-law was taking a vacation from working at the oil fields in Icacos in the south of Trinidad. He said that he needed to get the smell of the oil out of his system for a while. The father nodded. He never could stand the smell of oil even though from what the brother-in-law told him, there was good money to be made from working with it.

The father knocked several times before the brother-in-law came to the door. When the brother-in-law opened the door, the father sneezed his way into the room and all over the brother-in-law. His bleeding arm had soaked right through the levels of clothes that he had worn, causing the brother-in-law to run into the back room and come back with the same towel that he had used on the boy and tell the father not to move as he sopped the blood up, turning the towel a bright pink. The brother-in-law shook his head at the blood and said that the father should go to the hospital, and the father shook his head—*no more hospitals!*—the brother-in-law nodding and saying in that case that he was going right away to buy some bandages to dress the wound, telling the father to keep pressure with the towel. The brother-in-law was gone before the father asked after the boy.

The father sat on a mustard-colored couch covered in plastic, looking around the room for signs of the boy. He saw that the boy was not there, but that there was whiskey on a cabinet near the front door in the shape of a ship's steering wheel, each spoke of the bottle carrying a little bit of grog. The father got out a glass and gave himself a shot of the whiskey, telling himself that that was all that he needed to dress *any* wound.

Walking to the window, the father looked down at the whiskey in the glass. He drank some and it burned through his chest. He looked down into the field and drank some more. Everything was gray between the drops. But the shadow that moved on the field was definitely the boy. He was filthy. In the rain. How did one stay filthy in the rain, the father asked himself.

The boy was covered with mud over his favorite plaid-brown shirt and was walking toward the brother-in-law's room with a yo-yo in his hand and with his head down, the boy running through the tricks that he couldn't quite get yet, maybe thinking of questions to ask the brother-in-law to get them right.

It was after a soggy Four-Leaf Clover that the boy looked up and saw the father in the window.

It was then that the boy stood in the rain and ran through the tricks for the father: Around the World while offering the middle finger, Walking the Dog while offering the middle finger, Rocking the Cradle while offering the middle finger, the boy getting all the tricks right this one time; the boy had been practicing. The boy was good.

The father poured himself another drink while watching the boy, his lantern jaw lit in anger. Finally the father shouted at the boy, telling him that he would get a cut-ass that he wouldn't *believe* when he walked through the doors, a cut-ass to end all cut-asses, one that would raise the dead, etc., etc., him playing with a damn yo-yo in the rain while his mother was home sick. The father yelled at the boy for him to wait, just wait and see if he didn't get a brand new cut-ass when he reached home, the father saying this as the boy turned and scrambled off, sliding through pools of water, leaving a rooster's tail of water behind him. The father was still yelling through the window when there was a knock on the door. Thinking it was the brother-in-law returned, the father found the faith revival minister instead, with an umbrella and his hat in his hand, wearing a too shiny suit.

The minister said that he was a friend of the brother-in-law's and often visited the brother-in-law to chat and talk about God and sometimes even to collect a donation for the continued existence of the faith revival ministry from the brother-in-law and could the father tell the brother-in-law that the minister was there? The father said that the brother-in-law had stepped out for a few minutes and would the minister like to come in? The minister thanked him and once inside asked the father if he did not want to join the congregation of the ministry that took place in the field just beyond the galvanized fence, and in so doing become one of the hundreds that were saved each fortnight? The father said that he was *already* a member and that he had been to the minister's last two sermons and even looked at the minister on TV before the TV became a you-know-what, and didn't the minister remember the father's rude rapscallion of a little boy? The minister, squinting at the father's face, admitted that *yes*, the father did look familiar. He told the father that, without meaning to offend him, that by the looks of things, that the father seemed as though he had been through many trials and whatnot and looked as if he needed Jesus' extra special love and devotion. The father nodded and the minister continued that, in that case, would the father like to make a donation to the ministry and have the minister pray directly to Jesus for him?

The father said no, thank you, that as far as he knew, that Jesus wasn't too interested in money while on earth, and too besides, wasn't there specifically a story in the Bible—a parable—that warned against money as being the root of all evil? The minister said, with his pointer finger pointing to heaven, that it wasn't money but the *love* of money that was indeed the source of mankind's problems. The father, holding the brother-in-law's door slack in his hands, and still upset over the boy, said that he had lots of problems, some of which could be solved with money, and some that couldn't, but him not having enough money anyway to justify any of the problems that he *was* having wasn't going to get him to tithe to no damn churchless church, saying that maybe he would hold a press conference with Jesus himself, and the minister should have a good day and try to stay dry.

The shrugging minister told the father to suit himself, but that he had a direct line to the savior, him being a minister and all, and could the father please tell the brother-in-law that he had stopped by? And with a tap of the hat on his head, the minister nodded to the father, popped open his umbrella and left, stepping away from the threshold just in time to avoid a door slamming into his Achilles tendon.

The father closed the door and poured himself a drink from one of the spokes of the wheel and rubbed his chin. When he sipped the whiskey, he felt it in his nose; his eyes burned. Outside, the rain continued. It had slowed down enough that on the brother-in-law's roof it sounded like applause.

As he was thinking about the rain, the father had an idea that maybe the minister could say a prayer with his wife, that the minister could go say a prayer with his wife for free, and that maybe the minister could get her in good for the long haul, the father thinking that even the most money-grubbing minister would do something that noble. With a final hammer-toss of liquor to the back of his throat, the father stepped back into the rain, pulling his already wet-through shirt on, pushing away the towel that bandaged his arm, trying to figure out which way the minister went.

It was when the father turned the corner of the faith revival field that he saw the boy squatting against a wall in his favorite plaid-brown orphanage-issued shirt looking tough with—a silver tooth in his mouth?—the little boy having wrapped some aluminum foil found God knows where, around his front tooth to look like a little bad-john, running through some trick with the yo-yo, the boy with his leg raised to rabbit-run upon seeing the father, but the father stretching out a hand and catching the boy by his collar and quick-swatting him twice on his behind before the boy broke loose, leaving the cheap material collar of his favorite plaid-brown shirt behind in the wrecked father's hand, in his blood-weakened arm, the father falling again on his already spike-gutted arm, falling and skinning his knee on top of everything else, the boy run-splashing through the water that had filled the gutter up to his ankles.

The father held the collar up to his mouth between the cup of his two hands and told the boy to run, to run like the rain, because if the father ever caught him then he would lose him up in the orphanage, that as sure as the rain was falling from the sky that he would lose him in there, that the time for cut-asses was *over.*

~ When the brother-in-law showed back up with the bandages, the wrecked father was swabbing his wrecked arm with the blood-soaked towel and told the brother-in-law about the minister from the faith revival field who came by, the father continuing about the boy before he was stopped, the brother-in-law stopping the father in mid-breath, telling the father that he had just been to the father's house, and that the mother had taken a turn for the worse, the brother-in-law saying that the father should come with him to hunt down the minister to administer the final rites, saying all this to the father's back as the father was already half-way down the steps and into the rain heading home.

When the father finally hobbled into his house, the minister was already there, hovering over the mother with the brother-in-law who had come in the minister's car. The father saw that the girl was there too, wiping her mother's brow with a damp rag, everyone quiet, even the rain had subsided.

It was while the father was holding the mother's hand, listening to the silence between the rain drops, that he heard the sound of the boy, the boy bang, bang, banging on the roof, the boy dangling down and zip-pulling his yo-yo so loudly that the father was not hearing the minister saying that maybe the father had better bring in the boy. It was only after a tug on the shoulder from the brother-in-law that the father nodded. Then the father followed the banging on the roof with his eyes to the front of the house where it was loudest, listening to the boy Walk the Dog in the rain, do the Tidal Wave in the rain, and do the Loop-the-Loop in the rain, the father starting to run when he heard the minister whisper to hurry, the father running and saying to the boy that all was forgiven—there would *be* no cut-ass—the father running out the front door with his eyes turned up to the sound of the yo-yo on the roof, not seeing the huge spider web that the boy had constructed from all the never-pop strings of the yo-yos that he had taken from the brother-in-law and that had been rocket-launched onto the roof, the spider web set up for the Rain Man in the dark suit who the boy saw go into the house with the brother-in-law but not leave, the same Rain Man that the boy had seen on the you-know-what and the same Rain Man who during the family day shook and beat a little boy similar to himself in a corner of the faith revival field when he thought no one was looking because the boy had stolen a piece of ice, the day being so hot. And instead of seeing the spider web, the father, looking up, yelling for the boy to come say goodbye to his mother, ran straight through the web of never-pop strings, some of which had unknowingly slithered around the boy's legs, the father still yelling for the boy as he ran through the spider web of never-pop strings that were tied at one end to the doorknob, and tied at the other end to the constellation of rocks that held down the rain-wetted, galvanized metal that sat there to keep out the rain from falling on all of their heads.

R.M. Kinder

SMALL COURTESIES

The Fan-T-Sci conference descended on the Delmar Hotel on a Friday afternoon in November. The Missouri sky was already shading toward its winter gray, moist, and low, but shimmering, as if a colder layer moved above. Inside the hotel, the employees, though all decent people, were tired and harried, and felt disconcerted by the nature of the guests. The clerks tried not to stare, but they covertly assessed the arriving group. The night supervisor called the manager, and moments later was instructed to provide extra security for the duration of this conference. Costs would escalate, but possibly food and drink sales would more than compensate. Hotel security contacted the police station and requested five of the city's finest for an off-duty job at good pay. Just in case.

Truly, this was no common conference. A new world mingled in the lobby, then dispersed in singles or small groups toward the stairs, elevator, or bar. One woman was dressed in silver sequins that clung to her torso and limbs as if they actually grew there. Only her face and her pale hands—the latter with silver nails at least three inches long—indicated that flesh lay beneath the sequins. She rippled when she moved, a most mesmerizing sight for everyone in the lobby. She noticed the attention and laughed. The sound brought chills to one clerk, and glances among them all. Another female wore flowing red chiffon—with nothing underneath but billowing body. Huge and rolling, she registered using her own pen, and the red ink name sworled violently. Most of the women were in black; most were buxom; all were on display. Male gazes could move from breasts that peeked, perked, to those that swung or hung pendant like sinking moons. The men seemed less colorful, but more ominous overall. Only a few were proportioned or attractive, and they highlighted their best features: A young man with the body of a dancer wore tight briefs, from which narrow silk bands led down his legs and over his upper body, creating the illusion of shirt and slacks; another wore form-fitting silver, no sequins, but with the sides missing, the front and back laced together. Most of the males, though, were misshapen, too tall, or too thin, obese, squat, or perhaps with skinny legs beneath a pear body, or narrow shoulders above a globe of rump. A cadaverish man in black leather had somehow shaped his long orange hair into spikes, so no one could stand near him. Beneath the jutting front spikes, his eyes appeared like black holes. His teeth were orange or had been painted so.

A gnomish man in green velvet looked up at the doorman and said in a low, soft voice, "We're not freaks. During the year we're just normal people with normal jobs. This is our holiday. Our chance to be different."

The doorman, who had a nice home in the suburbs and two children in college, didn't understand why this guy was explaining to him. He didn't know whether to feel threatened, because maybe the dwarf was flirting, or complimented, because he looked like a man one should explain to. "Well," he said, "we all need a vacation from time to time."

"We won't be causing any trouble or anything."

"Well, that's good. You might tell the manager that."

"We will. We're always good guests."

Behind the desk, a nightclerk mumbled, "We're in for something different this weekend," and read a few names to his coworker. "Dala Coflera, Zi Ki Lai, Larry Lech, Mylaika Rakon." He scrolled down the computer list. "Hey, a John Brown. Probably a spy." He was pleased with himself and had managed to pass from trepidation to anticipation. Usually he was bored at work. "Let it rain, let it pour," he said, sat on the high stool by the desk, and watched what was shaping up.

One of the night staff told the supervisor she needed to go home. Her babysitter had just called and her son was ill. "My God," she said to herself, hurrying across the filling parking lot, "it's like hell opened up." She was afraid of her own imagination and what such guests could induce in her. Even in the car, she felt unsafe, as if something horrible would pop up over the back seat and speak to her. When she got home, she asked the babysitter to stay for a while, but the girl couldn't. The woman and her son watched a comedy on television. The frantic, crazy humor made her tremble.

Meanwhile, on a one-way road from a small university miles away, a midwestern couple who had been dating only a month or so, and were already struggling for conversation or a tinge of passion, drove toward the conference. Their headlights turned the heavy mist into sparkle, but they couldn't see much beyond the light, just black shapes that must be a house, or barn, or closed country store.

"Where do people in this country go?" she said. "The houses are always dark even early in the evening, like people are already in bed. Sometimes it's like the world has died and I'm coasting alone."

"People save electricity. If you look close, there's probably a light toward the back of the house."

"I leave every light on when I'm home, and some when I'm not."

"I've noticed."

She didn't like that statement, and he knew it. Both understood the implication, that he found her wasteful with money. He was a saver, a healthy man who worked out daily, read much, and had a strong sex drive. She was older, thin, chainsmoked, loved fat and chocolate, read much, and also had a strong sex drive. Both were headstrong and lonely. She liked houses that were warm, that glowed at night like invitation to life, and she resented this bleak moist country of homegrown tightwads and tiny spirits. "I think," she said, "a house should look warm and inviting."

"Yours does, that's for sure. It's a nice effect." He meant that. Although he would never waste electricity in his own home, driving up to hers always made him feel the lights were for him especially. He thought perhaps she had a generous spirit and he hoped he did, too. "I'm always comfortable at your place," he said.

The moment was saved and they settled back into their new lovers' closeness. She was the one who had received notice of the conference. It was in her mailbox at work, with "FYI, Keith," signed at the bottom. Keith was a fellow professor from another department, who sometimes smoked outside with her, where they talked of writing and individuality. When she told him she might attend the conference, he said, "Good, but let me warn you that it's not traditional, not academic like you're accustomed to. These people are into science fiction and fantasy. I think you're pretty liberal and will enjoy yourself. I know you're bored with the normal routine here." That she was. But, being also wary of new things alone, she had invited along her friend, the thick-set man who had recently proven they were compatible in bed.

Now, she worried. "What if we don't like it? I'd hate to cost you time and money for a bad weekend."

"At the worst, we can stay in our room for two days." He took her hand and placed it on his thigh, then patted it. "You worry too much."

They felt very comfortable the rest of the drive, very much together and ready to risk a step into the unknown. One wing of the hotel had been reserved for the Fan-T-Sci guests, but other guests were certainly aware of them and grouped closer together when entering the dining room or bar. A few ventured into the special wing and read the legend of events posted in that registration room. It seemed bland enough, listing introduction, icebreaker, awards, dance; for Saturday, readings, mixers, games, stage play, special sessions. One brave brown-suited man managed to swipe a fuller program from a table near the bar, guarded by a green-dressed gnome.

"Just checking it out," the guest explained. "Looks interesting."

The gnome seemed saddened. "Those programs are for members only. You don't look like one."

"I may be by morning," the guest laughed, and waved the program as he walked away. It made for good reading with his wife: "Listen to this.

'Condom prizes, Fleur-de-lis room 8:00; Cross-dance by Leonard the Lion-hearted, 9:00. Saturday sessions: 10:00 Leather, Centurion Room; Metal, Skyline Room; Silk and Softer, Dahlia Room; Surprise, Charleston Ballroom.' God," the man said, "I'd like to go."

"They'd kill you for smirking."

"Probably." But he wondered if he could somehow dress to pass, just sneak in for one session. He wanted to see this other life.

The policemen, having conferred with the night supervisor, stationed themselves discreetly apart, covering elevators and exits. One had a full view of the rear parking lot, where lights were dimmer, especially in the heavily descending fog, and anyone dressed in black would be indiscernible. That policeman would occasionally have a smoke while he strolled the lot and sensed anything inappropriate. He was told by a green gnome, who startled him by appearing silently and suddenly at his side, that, "We're just ordinary people, you know. We assume a role this one weekend of the year. I'm an accountant myself. We're a courteous group, overall. We don't tolerate poor behavior." The policeman found that little guy somewhat sinister, maybe because of the fog, maybe because he had a slight lisp, maybe because he was too damned ingratiating. Sort of a protests-too-much guy.

Having become lost in the city streets, where signs were in ridiculous positions, and two-way streets became suddenly one-way only, without any indication of the direction of the one way—north, east, south, or west—the midwestern couple arrived later than they planned. Both were slightly embarrassed that she had used a green garbage bag for a dress-carrier. He felt a little more worldly than her, because he would never have carried such a contraption into a nice hotel. He would have left it in the car and brought it in later, draped over his arm. She held it up so the bottom of her pink dress wouldn't touch the carpet. It seemed to him like a flag of mediocrity, perhaps low-class. She, however, quickly decided that it was a sign of her true individuality, since the really wealthy, the really secure, broke all the damned rules. Only the middle class worried about correctness and they were the ones who made the world truly monotonous, because they were cowards. He signed them in, registering by two names but for one room, because, what-the-hey, they were what they were. Unmarried and together. Modern enough to be blunt about it. He steered her toward the elevator.

"We couldn't get in the reserved wing. It's all filled up. Might be best anyhow, to be separate from the main group since we're not really fantasy writers."

"I am. One of my published pieces is a fantasy."

"Okay. But we still can't get in that wing. The clerk said the introduction has already started. We can drop our things off and get right over there." He carried the suitcases and thought briefly about liberated women. She hadn't offered to carry her own suitcase.

A cop by the elevator said, "Good to see you folks. Thought there weren't any normal people left in the city." He had a goodhearted laugh that brought crinkles around blue eyes. He was too heavy for a policeman, but then, the woman thought, a good nature was a strong force. She sure liked that trait.

"I got a feeling," her lover said, "that we're not going to fit in."

"Why?"

"Didn't you hear the officer?"

"Maybe it's a young group."

"Maybe."

In their room he wanted to make love before they began the evening. The wide bed with the gold bedspread sank deliciously when he fell backward, and he wanted her to immediately be taken by the manliness he presented, lying on his back, hands behind his head, so his broad chest expanded even more. If she would just unfasten his belt, unzip his pants, without his having to say a word, she'd be the woman for him, but she was worrying aloud about whether to change clothing now or just get to the meeting. He reluctantly rose, and put his arms around her from behind, cupping her small breasts. "We could skip the first meeting," he whispered. "Why don't we shower together and then change? We can go for drinks afterwards and meet the crew."

"I want to see what's going on," she said. "We can make love later."

"Planning things ruins them."

"Spontaneity can ruin good plans."

So now neither could be truly happy with the evening. He had been postponed and devalued; she had been made selfish and staid. Both felt guilty and in risk of loneliness. Why didn't anything ever just work out right? They left dressed as they were, in search of the conference registration room.

And there, though all but one of the conferees had gone on to the introduction leaving one member to man the table, and though all the other tables bore the familiar paper cups, coffee urns, beer cans, and plastic glasses of conferences all over the world, the midwestern couple knew they were at the edge of a decision, because the one person left had orange spikes for hair, and eyes buried deep in shadows and sinking flesh. She strode up to the table and her lover, though hesitant, followed, feeling that he might be enlisting—which he had avoided during the last war. He didn't like confrontations of any kind.

"We want to register for the conference," she said.

"I don't think so," the orange-head said. "Are you already members?"

"No. Do we have to be?"

"If you've ever been to one of our conferences, you are. If not, you can sign up. But you don't look as if you're into sci-fi."

She couldn't bear being told what she could and could not do, and the chagrin brought her connection to mind. "Keith Parmenter suggested I come. I write fantasy." The dark holes seemed to shift to her partner.

"He's with me."

"I don't think either of you will be very comfortable."

"I want to register."

He allowed them to. He gave them blank lapel cards to fill out, and obviously read the names they wrote. "You better wear the cards all the time," he said, "so people will know you've paid to attend." Her lover was amazed anew at her fortitude. For a few moments he felt that he traveled in her wake, which he didn't particularly like. He did like the sway of her hips, and the curl of her hair, and that stride that was nothing less than bold. He held the door open for her to enter the gathering room.

Actually, there was no silence when they entered, though both felt as if there were. And both felt the prickle that comes from unseen eyes, though each, if turning, could have seen all the eyes. No one missed the couple's entrance. The speaker, laughing, had a brief lapse of sound, then launched off into the grand introduction of the guest entertainer, none other than Leonard the Lionhearted.

The couple had to sit up front, near where they had entered, because the room was full, full, full, to standing creatures in the back, and they had seats only because a small man dressed in green carried forward two folding chairs. "Welcome," he said, and the couple felt warm toward him for a human gesture and a familiar word. They sat.

Now the speaker was joining the audience, and music rolled out from behind them, fast and rumbling, a rock boogie, and people clapped and hooted and squealed. The couple didn't turn, because whatever was coming, was coming their way. A man gyrated past them into the space before the podium. He bumped, high-stepped, turned, wiggled that bottom, flipped his wrists, manly wrists, with strong hands. He was tall, muscular, with wild black hair falling mid shoulder, and with a black beard heavy enough for two hands to get lost. His long legs were hairy, too, so very male and strong, but the feet were encased in black stiletto heels that never faltered in intricate turns and quick, cute little twists. His tight buttocks were covered by black lace stretching to a bodice top, above which his chest hair curled ludicrously or sensuously. His red-painted lips synched the boogie words and he wooed the crowd with winks and kisses, all to a boogie beat. Keith Parmenter.

Leonard the Lionhearted. He stopped one moment in front of the couple, his hips and hands in rhythm, and capped each head with one of his hands for one beat, switched hands for another cap, then was bouncing off, swishing past, shaking that bodice top as though breasts might fall out. The couple now felt better. They had been touched and welcomed and were special guests, not outsiders. They were the anointed. When he danced back down the aisle, the couple applauded as loudly as anyone and even turned in their seats, surreptitiously skimming the crowd and meeting a few glances. Not all were cold.

They had to sit for another few minutes while awards were given to the conference planners. Black and orange condoms, blown slightly full, some with faces painted on the ends.

She wondered if she would be sickened by herself later, for having not walked out, for being pleased at the dancer's recognition. She hoped her lover didn't blame her for the coarseness of this meeting. He wasn't suited for this kind of thing. He was more conservative. A nice guy. Beside her, the lover thought by God he might not be happy, but he hadn't sunk this low. He was going back to the room and maybe back home. He had nothing in common with these crazy loons. Sick cries for attention. Losers all. Jesus. He didn't know what to make of her, sitting there so calm. But maybe she wasn't. Maybe they'd laugh and get the hell out of here together.

Keith, now dressed in a gold-mesh jumpsuit, was waiting for them by the door, and drew them aside. "I'm glad you came," he said. "I hope you're not shocked. I warned you."

"You did, but I didn't know what you meant. Now I do."

"And you're offended?"

"Maybe. I don't know. I've never seen anything like this. I tell you what, though, you were really good. I was fascinated. You can dance like crazy. I never knew that."

"I'd prefer no one at work know."

"I'm not going to say a word."

Keith glanced at her partner who shook his head. "Don't worry. This isn't the kind of thing I would talk about."

"You two," Keith said, "are a little noticeable. If you've got some more casual clothes, you'd feel less conspicuous."

"We both brought conference clothes," she said. "Will they kick us out?"

"Of course not. Just wear your name tags. And have fun." He patted her hand, while nodding at someone yards away, a lovely black girl whose body was painted the same array of colors as the chiffon scarves she wore, so that she looked like a wispy tropical bird or a blossom coming into being.

He hurried to her and the couple watched this perfect match impossible anywhere else in the world they knew.

They went back to their room and made love with the lamps out, but the drapes open, so the window was all moon-filtered gray. He poised himself above her as if he were a bird and would swoop into her forever. That's how they both felt when he entered her, like they rode a fierce warm wind together. Then they lay side by side, sweating, tired, and each still charged as if the night wouldn't let them rest.

"You want to go home?" she asked.

"Was thinking about it."

"I'd like to see the dance. Just for a little while. Then we could go if you want. Or we could get a good night's sleep and leave in the morning. Or maybe shop a while."

He thought it odd that she could think of shopping. What was shopping, anyhow? His head wouldn't clear enough to get hold of that thought, or any thought equally common.

Across town, the nightstaff woman let her babysitter go home, and she checked on her little boy who hadn't been sick at all, but who wasn't sleeping easily now, maybe from popcorn and cookies so late at night. Maybe from her own tension. Certainly, she herself wasn't feeling well. Her breath was ragged, which meant she needed to calm herself or she'd start hyperventilating and get panicky. She hated her damned nervous nature, having to guard against her own tendencies. But she'd had sense enough to take off work. She'd be vomiting by now if she had stayed there. Crazy people scared her to death.

The back-lot cop had an intuition about which one would be the troublemaker. It was that creepy green runt. He was too damned friendly. The other cops said he'd talked to each of them, gave each the same line about being normal people all year and just acting out fantasies during this conference. What kind of fantasies? Maybe there'd be a murder from someone thinking he was goddamn jack-the-ripper. Heaven knows the women were dressing like they longed to be victims of something.

The silver-sequin lady had to take six pills before she could attend the dance, and apply fresh makeup. She was a mass of pain and sometimes nausea. Beneath the silver, surgery scars crisscrossed her abdomen. Her breasts were foam and she loathed them. But she loved the reflection of Mylaika Rakon. She could swim there, in that vision, because visions never took treatments, felt terror, never lied, never died. She was her own mantra.

The midwestern lover refused to dress any differently for the dance, and besides, he couldn't if he wanted to. The change he brought was dressier than what he had on. Well, she asked, would he attend with her if she was wearing only a slip? Because that's what she was going to do. She had a black, long, half-slip, and if she wore it pulled up over her breasts, wore black stockings, let her hair down and put on gobs of makeup, she'd fit right in.

"What about shoes?"

She solved that. She pulled houseslippers from her suitcase and waved them at him. Silver slip-ons, with elastic pulling them tight. "Will you go with me dressed like this?"

"Why not? We're never going to see any of these people again."

Now each felt superior to the other and were separate as they walked down the hall to the elevator. When they emerged, he avoided the cop's eyes by lighting a cigarette, and falling a little behind her. He was with her when she entered the elevator to the other wing.

"Ashamed of me, I see," she said. "You don't need to accompany me."

"Somebody better. You're acting strange."

"I'm the same woman you came with."

"Maybe, but you're not attracting the same kind of man."

She thought that was astute, that he was caring for her in his way. "I do feel ridiculous," she said. "I mean, this is obviously a slip. Maybe I should change back."

"You've done it, let's go. Or let's go home."

"You're right. I made the choice. But if you get the least bit uncomfortable," she said, "we'll leave."

"I can take it as long as you can." He put his hand on the small of her back to guide her down the hall. "Whatever you do, don't stare. You don't know these people."

The small ballroom had a fountain in the center, with a low wall on which some guests sat. Others danced on the square tiled floor. The music was haunting and frantic, metallic, like wind through huge flutes. Colored globes hung like moons across the room. The couple sat on the fountain wall. Near them, a tiny, fragile blonde, who held a posture so rigid she looked like a statue, spoke with a brown-draped monk. He turned to assess the couple. Moments later both left, followed by the others, and the midwestern couple were alone by the fountain.

"I never felt so naked," she said. "I'm having chills."

"It's the water. Did you know you forgot your name tag?"

"My God, I did."

Across the dance floor, the statue and monk had stopped by Keith Parmenter. Now he crossed to the couple, smiling slightly. "So you found something to wear after all."

"Is it okay? I feel foolish."

"No. You're trying to fit in. That's good. Why don't you dance? Show everyone you want to mingle, not just watch."

"So people *are* noticing us."

"Yes, but that doesn't matter. Relax. Dance. Laugh. Get acquainted with the members."

They did dance, because they were certainly no worse at it than most of the others, better in fact, except for Keith and his lovely flower, for whom the dancers applauded. The couple envied that grace, though when they considered the source of the appreciation, were glad enough to be just competent dancers. He wished she had not worn the slip, because the excitement flushed her neck and chest with a funny bluish-red color that made her look older and more worn, and because with no waistline in the slip, and with her tiny breasts, she was a slat woman, not feminine at all. He wanted to desire her, even if it were just protective, but he felt she was asking for ugly attention and that made her ugly. She felt terribly alone in his arms, because he had a way of withdrawing that she could sense, even when he denied it, so he was like a force against her. It was wearying. She couldn't bear the weight of his discontent. Her own was heavy enough. Someone stopped them from dancing by touching each simultaneously. It was a small man, dressed in green velvet. His shoes were green, too, with curling tops.

"We have to ask you to leave," he said.

They were both taken aback, partly from his statement, but mostly from the lisp in which it came, childlike and soft, but from such an aging face.

"Why?"

"You obviously don't belong here, and you're making everyone uneasy."

"We're just dancing. Minding our own business," the lover said.

"And we paid our way. I'm a member now."

"You're not wearing a tag."

"I couldn't pin it to this outfit."

"Still, it would be better if you left. Everyone thinks so."

"You got it, buddy," from the lover. "This isn't my idea of a good evening anyhow."

"I paid and I'm staying."

Keith appeared again. "What's the matter here?" The green man bowed deeply, backed up while still bent, and spoke toward the floor. "I've asked the gentleman and lady to leave so the guests can be at ease." "They're friends of mine. It's okay. Leave it to me."

The little man backed up a few more feet and turned before he stood upright.

"That's Pietro, the Peacekeeper," Keith said. "He tries to make everyone at ease."

"Why did he bow to you?"

"He bows to anyone he respects. That's his only direct communication other than peaceful greetings."

"Well, he sure didn't make us feel any better," she said.

"I'm sorry it's not working out for you two. I didn't know when I invited you, that you'd bring a guest. I should have been more explicit."

"I, fellow," the lover blurted, "am perfectly willing to leave right now."

"You don't have to do that. But you might skip the dance, and come down for some of the games tomorrow. Though, if you haven't enjoyed yourselves thus far, I don't imagine you will tomorrow either."

"What are the games?"

"Depends on the room you choose. The titles are suggestive. You're both intelligent, and I imagine you can guess fairly accurately. I can't just stay with you, and I hope you understand. It might cause hostility and these are my friends. They buy my books, they feature me at conferences. I have a responsibility."

"Why did you invite me? Why me and no one else?"

"You seemed different from my other colleagues. Are you sorry?"

"No. I just want to fit in." She and they knew that wasn't true, but it couldn't be *unsaid,* and she couldn't be uninvited. Now he had demolished all of her worlds.

Her lover felt the other man, Keith the Creep, had somehow violated the woman he was with, and though she wasn't truly attractive, and wasn't as intelligent as he had first believed, she was with him and therefore in his charge. "We're leaving," he said. "You can count on that."

"And on your discretion, I hope."

"We'll see," the lover said, and felt he had retrieved a little pride.

In their room, she cried deeply, so that makeup ran her face into a dissolving mask. "I must have looked *so stupid,*" she said. "Damn. Goddamn. Like such a fool, showing up in a slip. I insulted them. That was it. I made light of their costumes by pretending a piece of underwear could make me one of them."

"Why do you care what they think? They're a bunch of sickos. Crazy people who can't lead normal lives, and you're crying because of them?"

"But if even they reject me, what in the hell am I?"

"You rejected them before you even entered."

"Then they're better than me. Can't you see that?"

"No. What I see is a college professor who's tearing herself to pieces over a crowd of jokers. You must want to dislike yourself. You have to really twist things to take the view you've got."

"You don't care about anybody but yourself. You never see what's going on. You even make love like you're watching your own body, or watching me watch it. You're as self-centered as any of them."

The possible accuracy of that stopped him cold. He had thought she appreciated his body. Now he wasn't certain of anything about her or him.

"Are we leaving?" he asked.

"Let's do."

She showered, dressed in a suit with padded shoulders, the one she had planned to wear to a conference session. The rest of her clothing, including the pink dress, she folded, wrapped in the garbage bag, and stuffed into her suitcase. When they checked out, her hair was still wet and her reflection was pretty ugly, as if her head were too small for her body. In her heels, she was taller than he.

"You want to carry your own suitcase," he said, though it wasn't a question.

"Glad to." She teetered toward the door and in a moment he swept up, grabbed the handle and carried the suitcase for her, angry but oddly grateful at the same time. In the back lot, the policeman recognized them as having arrived only a short time earlier, and felt he should investigate.

"You folks get driven out by the creep show?" he said, trying to be light, though he meant it.

"Yep," the lover said, stuffing the suitcases in the trunk. "We were actually asked to leave by a green runt."

"Bet I know who you mean. He's a troublemaker. We spotted him early on."

"We didn't know what kind of a conference it was," she said. "We made a mistake. They didn't do anything to us. We shouldn't have come."

"You shouldn't be driven away, though. If you don't want to go."

"Believe me," the trunk was slammed shut, "we want to go."

"That right, lady?"

"Yes."

They rode off into the fog together and they welcomed it. It seemed actually warm, and the vague, filtered lights along the highway seemed like suns that would guide them home and rise tomorrow on a new day. They held hands, and felt genuinely close, forever close. Even when they entered the backland leading to the small university town, even when the road was one-way, and absolutely dark, houses and stores closed down against the night, they felt good together.

"We're hitting it off really well, aren't we?" he said.

"Yes. Better than I thought we would."

"We had to team up tonight. That was an experience, wasn't it?"

"Yes. Scared me somehow."

"I'm glad I was with you. It wasn't pleasant, but you needed someone."

"I did. And I'm grateful."

He squeezed her hand. She held on and thought about the houses along the road, how people turned in early, snuggled against one another, maybe whispered in the dark. She sighed. "I guess life is easier if you're not alone."

"Maybe we won't ever have to be alone again."

They both thought that sounded right and good. They were suited to one another. If they hadn't attended the conference, maybe they would never have known.

In town, the nightstaff woman paced the hall. She had taken two tranquilizers and still her heart was buzzing. She could feel it, like someone had an electric charge going through her. She was going to die. She knew it just as she knew it wasn't true. This was a panic attack. Nothing more. She wouldn't die. She couldn't leave her boy alone to go to the hospital, and she couldn't very well drag the child there again. Poor thing, with a neurotic mother, a crazy mother. She should've stayed at work, faced it. Then, if she went crazy, her son wouldn't see, and she couldn've gone to the hospital and then come home sedated, and he'd not know the ugly, terrified woman who wanted him raised with none of her fears. Still, she had to wake him up and get him in the car with her and drive to the hospital, because now breathing was difficult and her heart was going to stop. She wanted it to. She wanted to die rather than to feel fear like this. Unshakable, horrible, rushing fear from absolutely nothing, nothing.

The back-lot cop called his buddies for support because something was brewing out here, something big. A spikehead had kicked the green dwarf to kingdom come and now had a knife out threatening the little twerp. The cop headed that way, where the two were moving shadows in the misty light, but he didn't run, because this was a strange crew and he wanted his backup.

He heard the spikehead repeating a grunted "Bow! Bow!" but heard nothing from the shifting, smaller form till he moved nearer, and then the sound was soft, a steady mumble. "No, never, never, never."

"Bow!"

"Police," the cop yelled. "Hey! Assholes! Police."

The tall spiked man kicked out, caught the short one in the face, and then ran right over the fallen man, the sole of his shoe pressing against the throat. The cop called "Stop," but he didn't really care if the guy stopped or not, and besides, his friends were now on the scene, one taking after the running man. He himself knelt beside the green velvet punk, checked his pulse, though obviously he was alive—he was turning his head back and forth as if still saying no, while he struggled for breath. The cop called an ambulance and wondered if he were capable of cutting a breath hole in the guy's throat. He'd seen it done, and it looked easy enough. The struggling ceased and he thought there goes one little loser, but he was wrong. The paramedics arrived, said the man was alive, carted him into the vehicle and sped away to a hospital.

The cops had a talk about the group of weirdoes, about never being able to identify orangehead if he washed out the paint, and wondering if he would or not. They ambled back to their stations, feeling pretty damned good about how well they did their job. It was even sort of fun as long as no one got hurt. Pity about the little creep. He didn't give in. Had some guts, at least. The back-lot cop was glad he'd been wrong about the guy.

Inside, the nightclerk thought this was the best evening he'd ever worked. Excitement every place he looked and no trouble to speak of. These people tipped, too, or so he'd heard. And one woman obviously was drawn to him. She didn't talk at all, or maybe she did, but it was through lips that didn't move. He wondered what making love to a statue woman would be like? It gave him quickened breath. Life was damned good most of the time.

At the hospital, the nightstaff woman turned on her table, sedated now, slightly guilty about her son sleeping in the visitors' lounge. Through pleasantly blurred vision, she saw a green twisted dwarf wheeled past her, insisting that he was not harmed and should be released immediately, please, immediately. The sight didn't bother her at all. Poor ugly creature. Her life at least was better than that.

The couple went to her house, where all the lights glowed welcome to whatever moved around on such a night. She unlocked the door and he carried in the luggage. He turned out all the downstairs lights and she didn't protest, because she knew what he was doing. He undressed her slowly and lovingly, like he enjoyed unwrapping this surprise for his body, and then she undressed him. They twined together standing, while the streetlight outside softened the dark enough so that they could recognize each other. Then they lay down together, still twined, knowing that this wasn't love, but it was the best they could make together and would have to do. It might be enough.

On Sunday, the sky had settled into stillness, lowering over the city and the rolling countryside the muted gray of a common midwestern winter. In the Delmar Hotel lobby, the Fan-T-Sci group said good-byes amidst the amused or frightened gazes of incoming guests. The silver-sequined lady was the first to leave. She was wearing a tiara with three diamonds sparkling a triangle just above her wide brow. It had been presented to her at the last session, in honor of her many publications of high fantasy. But she was no fool and recognized compassion behind the gift. Now, she gathered her waning strength, and with a haughty laugh, strode boldly toward the exit, so their memory would be of grace and happiness and determination. The doorman found himself bowing as she passed, though he never stooped to such servile behavior—it wasn't one of his duties—and wondered why he felt that small courtesy not only appropriate but most pleasant.

Marilyn Krysl

IRON SHARD

The cries of first birds with first light have passed. The day will be vast: Radika feels the rise of its approach. She sits on the bed, watching dawn come in millions of little pieces loosely sewn together, like breathing. Sun is a line of fire along the horizon. From where she sits she can see the gate, and along the cadjun fence the banana trees and oleanders, stately, ancestors gathered together in council. She knows also what lies beyond: more lanes, then the lagoon, its water a soft slapping. And beyond the lagoon the sea, that great, mothering water infinite as the goddess herself. The mesh of world surrounds her, its green and gold, its froth and foam, and perhaps it's this that holds her enough. Radika feels the iron shard in her palm. For the first time she finds the courage to contemplate the fact: their mother isn't coming back.

Though at first the idea was unthinkable, there came a time when the thought presented itself, almost shyly, a little waif of thought, at the edge of consciousness. It was only when Radika acknowledged its presence that this orphan grew to have a substantial body, a history. Now, the seventh day, she is ready to look into its eyes. Six days ago, when she woke and saw blood on her nightgown, she'd tried—for a moment—to pretend she hadn't. Though bleeding marked an important passage, there was a saying. *If you see it first, it's a flaw, but if your mother sees it first, it's a good thing.* She'd hurried to where her mother slept, touched her shoulder, told her. Her mother turned over. Like one of those hibiscus blossoms slowly unfurling, sleep opened around her and she sat up and drew Radika into her arms.

"In seven days we'll have your ceremony! Remember when we did it for Sivarani?" Her sister Sivarani of the black waterfall hair. At thirteen, she'd never cut it. It hung over her waist. She brushed it every morning and evening, as though each stroke down its strands was a prayer. Radika remembered Sivarani's excitement, how on each of the six days of seclusion friends and relatives came to offer congratulations. "You got to help serve sweets, remember? This time we'll let Maheswary help."

This blood, her mother had said, was not like the blood of bullets. It was good blood: a sign that from Radika's body could come a baby, out of almost nothing. Only women, she'd said, can do this.

That morning her mother had gone off to the market with her friend Praba. They'd made their purchases, and as they walked out beneath the arch, five Tiger guerillas had suddenly appeared and surrounded them. The

Army checkpoint was only a few hundred yards away, but you couldn't see the market entrance from the checkpoint. The Tigers liked to kidnap people right under the soldiers' noses. It made the Army look ineffectual. Quickly, in spite of Praba's protests, they'd taken Radika's mother away.

Praba had come to the house, carrying her mother's bag. Inside some tomatoes, a bottle of oil.

Each day Praba goes to the Tigers' jungle headquarters, and each day the sergeant promises to release Radika's mother. Yesterday he'd promised absolutely: her mother would be back for the ceremony. But what he said, Radika thinks, is not the truth. He is like this time, which is not a good time. Which is why Praba gave her the iron shard: to ward off evil. Her mother had given her the arica nutcracker to hold, but later Praba brought this iron splinter—a bit of a grenade? Or is it a sliver of metal from a mine? It would work, Praba insisted, because it had The Troubles in it. You used a piece of the evil against itself.

Radika sees the way the trees are there, rooted, leaves swaying above this rootedness, like women standing, intent on some task, humming to themselves. They are presences, meshed with live molecules of light, the living breathing threads of water, of air. She imagines Praba, her hair of mane, scolding the guerillas. Why question the good woman who collected money for their cause, a woman whose son and daughter themselves had become Tiger separatists? But the one in charge spit in the dirt at her feet. When Praba demanded her friend's release, the Tiger sergeant spoke bluntly. "Possibly your friend has kept some money for herself."

Radika imagines Praba, straight as the trunk of an oleander, her countenance fierce, shaking her great mane of hair. "Never in a thousand years."

Now the sun begins its gleaming climb. Morning arcs upward. The heat begins to swell, warming the sand. Later the light will be white hot, rising from sand in waves you can see. If she could see the lagoon, it would look like a mirror laid along the edge of the town. The leaves of the oleanders are tiny bells that tinkle when a breeze riffles them, the banana trees' leaves wide fans, fringed along the edges, the fringe murmuring.

The loose knit of breath extends, includes the gecko on the stone step, a dry leaf. The gecko is good at waiting, Radika thinks. And I am like him. These six days of seclusion have felt familiar, a reenactment of other waitings still going on. Waiting for her aunt, waiting for her brother Chilliyan, waiting for her father and for Sivarani. And now for her mother. You can't stop waiting until you know, and she doesn't know, not yet, for sure. Not knowing makes space for a small hope, pecking away at its shell like a baby bird chipping its way out.

Now Maheswary carries in the tray, sets it on the bed. Her small hands flutter around the bowls of rice, of dahl. "Is it enough?" Radika kisser her sister's cheek. When Maheswary was born, Radika had helped care for this baby as though she were one of its two rightful mothers. Their father had seemed to Radika merely an admiring presence, and Chilliyan and Sivarani were too old to be much interested. The baby smelled like flowers, and her softness resembled the softness of petals.

"You smell like jasmine," Radika says. She notices the fine hair on her sister's arms. Maheswary has never known a time without The Troubles. She's never been allowed to play outside after dark. Always there have been government soldiers on the streets and in the surrounding jungle Tiger guerillas, some of these fighters boys not much older than Radika. And yet Maheswary seems not to be afraid. Her exuberance resembles heat escaping from beneath the lid of a pot.

"I have to get your sari ready. Don't leave the room!"

She darts off. Radika sits in the blossom of morning. In her palm the iron shard is warm, as though just now burst off from its explosion. Their father had explained how The Troubles began, but Radika has forgotten his description. She remembers the story a school friend told her about two sisters in the capital, walking home. Suddenly there was a crowd, men and women shouting, shouts around the girls like stones flying through the air. One man kicked the eldest girl hard, and she fell. Then a woman grabbed the younger sister's hair and yanked her down.

So many shouts, each shout a stone.

Then the gleam of a machete, two machetes.

Afterward two heads lay on the pavement.

The story had entered Radika suddenly, as though one of those shouts had hit her. She and her friend were eight. They didn't know what to do with this story. That was why her friend had told her. Radika wanted to tell her mother. But it was not a good story. How could you ask about such a thing?

This land is the color of sand and dun cadjun, as heat from the sun is the color of lightning, and lagoon water a slice of silver, too bright to look at long. The washerman's doty is white, a way of warding off heat. He comes through the gate, as he comes for all the girls, to prepare the house and grounds, lays his stack of white cloths in the shade of the fence. Radika remembers when she felt safely surrounded by the fence, before three aunts and uncles moved across the strait to India. The fourth aunt, her father said, had been given, unfairly perhaps, almost all the beauty in the family. It was true: gazing at her was like drinking a glass of water when you were very thirsty. Radika's uncle, a doctor, had traveled to the capital for supplies and was arrested by the Army on suspicion of passing medicines to the guerillas. The aunt believed if she could get to the capital she could convince the government to release him. It happened that the family next door was taking their son there, to send him to London to study. Radika's aunt paid bribes to get a pass, then set off on a bus with these neighbors.

When they got down at one of the Army's checkpoints, the sentry had examined the aunt's pass, then taken her aside and waved the others through. He spoke in Sinhala. None of them could understand him. The couple and their son protested. They tried to find a soldier nearby who spoke Tamil. Then a jeep pulled up, and the sentry gestured toward the aunt with his rifle. She got in. He climbed in beside her, motioned the driver on.

Such a simple thing, driving away in a jeep. Radika imagined the jeep returning, bringing her aunt back. But her father, when he told them what had happened, did not say so. What he said was, "She was too beautiful."

~ If you could look directly at midmorning sun, would it resemble a god's shield, gleaming? The world keeps moving like a breath, in and out and in, over and over, there is no seam. If you listen, if you pay attention, you can rest there, rocking on this motion. But if there are gods, why shields? Is destruction a threat ever to a god? For six days Radika has not let go this iron shard, not even while she slept. Though iron is not a girl's material. Iron comes from deep inside the earth, taken out by men and forged by them—she has watched the smith at his fire—into objects sacred to men, which men use to hurt other men, and women and children. With which they themselves are hurt.

If iron keeps away the evil eye, you'd think fewer soldiers would die. But bullets and grenades don't protect soldiers. The government soldiers are supposed to protect people from Tigers—not just Sinhala people but Tamils too—but these soldiers are like an occupying force. If they need to move troops, they commandeer the local buses, and if they need space, they commandeer your house. They can't keep the Tigers from kidnapping Tamil businessmen, demanding ransom. And sometimes the Tigers show their videos at the school, enticing boys and some girls to join them. If the soldiers find out, this daring makes them furious. They carry out house to house searches, or arrest fishermen they suspect of aiding the Separatists. At checkpoints they riffle women's bags of rice, searching for weapons. They do these things in a language no one understands.

The Tigers speak Tamil. Anyone who can understand them. And they are fighting for Eelam for the Tamil people. Everyone wants Eelam, that heaven on earth. But Radika feels confused. Don't they have Eelam already? Aren't her parents, brothers and sisters, their relatives and friends Eelam? If the government soldiers went away, would that be Eelam? The Tigers wouldn't have to fight then. They too would stop being soldiers.

The way it is now the Tigers act like the government soldiers. They take a farmer's rice harvest, without explanation, and don't pay. Once Radika watched two Tigers steal the clothes a woman had hung out to dry. Or several may appear suddenly in your doorway and demand that you cook a meal for them. If they need gas, they siphon petrol from your tank. And both the Tigers and the government levy taxes. Both sides make people passing on the roads dig up mines. And both help themselves to girls. Just last week two girls left the high school as usual, and no one has seen them since.

And Chilliyan, her brother. When Radika was little, he used to swing her up against the sky, laughing. She remembers him grown, a smaller version of their father. Then three years ago he joined the guerrillas. They've received only two notes from him, cheery but vague. He did not say where he was or when he might come for a visit. When they finally get Eelam, will he come?

The washerman gets busy setting up the pantel that will shade the guests from the sun. Though it's early, Radika watches the gate. This is the gate through which their aunt walked away, the gate through which Chilliyan left them. And it was through this gate, one evening at dusk, that Tiger soldiers came into the compound. Their father had come from the telegraph office, then gone back out to bathe. He liked to shower with the hose at the same time that he watered the porrulaca in his garden. Radika and Maheswary sat at the table, doing schoolwork. It was their habit to sit there together, and when Maheswary asked, Radika would help her.

Their mother was setting rice to boil. She sent Sivarani to the market, under protest. Sivarani liked to be home when their father got there. Her love for him was like equatorial weather which one by one opened thousands of water lilies. She brooded around him, bringing him little attentions, and she liked to accompany him to the temple where, as *pusari,* in rites made puissant by repetition, he attended the goddess. You could see Sivarani's devotion to him. It was as though her gaze was unbroken illumination in which she held her father up before them.

But their mother needed oil and had sent Sivarani to get it. Radika's father came from his bath wrapped in a sarong, humming a little song Maheswary had taught him. He plucked a banana from the bunch, and, still humming, pulled back the peel and took a bite.

Radika saw the Tiger soldiers first. One by one they stepped from the haze of dusk through the gate, each with his rifle pointed toward the doorway.

"Father," she whispered. He turned. There were nine. It seemed to Radika that her father was strangely unafraid. He held the banana before him like a taper, by the light of which those assembled might examine each other.

All of them recognized Vadevilu, Chilliyan's friend. When Radika had been a child, Chilliyan and Vadevilu used to take her and Maheswary with them to the lagoon to skip stones and look for fish. Vadevilu had been welcome in their house, as Chilliyan had been at his. The boys had been sixteen when the Tigers had come to the school with videos. The videos showed boys advancing, rifles ready. One told how one cup of rice and one cup of water a day was enough, because it was for Eelam. The Tiger girl who'd lost both arms spoke defiantly. She'd rigged her rifle so she could pull the trigger with her teeth. She stood, flanked, a girl fighter on each side, the empty sleeves of her shirt riffling in the breeze.

Both families had begged the boys not to join, but Chilliyan and Vadevilu insisted. The evening of Chilliyan's departure, his mother wept. But her anxiousness had not persuaded him to change his mind. Afterward she'd offered to collect the Tiger's' tax from the people in her ward.

"Don't try to dissuade me," she'd said to Radika's father. "It will help keep him safe."

"Maybe," he said. "But suppose you can't get as much money as they want? Or suppose someone decides to tell the Army soldiers what you're doing."

The Tigers stood in a line beneath the trees. A current of air stirred the banana leaves so that their fringe rattled softly. Vadevilu stepped forward. "You have to come," he said, addressing Radika's father. "It's because you operate the telegraph. The leaders think you've passed secrets."

Radika's father also stepped forward, as though to meet Vadevilu. "What secrets?" he said. "Question me. Ask."

"You have to come."

"Vadevilu," her mother said. She stepped forward and stood beside her husband in dusklight. "You know I collect the money."

Vadevilu shook his head. "This isn't to do with you. The leader wants your husband."

"What will Chilliyan think?" she said. "Look at this man: this is Chilliyan's father. Think what you do."

"Don't make trouble," Vadevilu said. He spoke as though furious at the necessity of having to speak at all. Later their mother would say his commander might have sent him as a test of his loyalty. You heard such stories. It was a thing soldiers did to each other. "Your husband has to come. It's an order."

Their father's back straightened, and Radika thought he was going to refuse. The banana in his hand could be a reason. If a man was eating, you didn't take him away, not then. But he turned to their mother and handed her the banana as though in doing so he gave away his last possession.

When Sivarani came through the gate and across the sand, the banana lay on the table, one bite gone.

~ Perhaps the sun is not a god's shield, but the blazing countenance of the goddess. Isn't that why no one can look directly at it? See how she bares her shining throat! Bow down, open your mother, utter the white hot syllables of asking. Bring fruit, bring garlands. Make an offering. Bring something alive to feed the goddess, give it into her fiery teeth. But if her eyes are just, why doesn't she burn the bad ones, keep the innocent from burning? Shhh. She's not so simple. She is peace in the water, conflagration in the atom. She's the opening, the closing and everything between.

The washerman mounts the steps and walks through the rooms, chanting, sprinkling the floors with tumeric water, purifying the house. It's supposed to be women from your family who perform the bathing. At Sivarani's ceremony they came like a delegation, diplomats in saris, each carrying a water jar. The washerman filled each jar with sacred water. Each woman spread a white cloth over the jar's mouth. When it was time the women rose as one body, and as one body poured this water over Sivarani. It's the water that has the magic in it, lifts you by its lustrum into the realm of grown women.

But the aunts and their families have gone across the strait, and the grandmothers won't be here either. One grandmother died before The Troubles. The other grandmother went across the strait too, after Radika's father was taken, after Sivarani left home.

Before that she had visited them often. And Radika had especially liked this grandmother. She especially liked to help her wash Sivarani's hair. In the cool of early morning Sivarani would appear, holding out the soap, the towel, the comb. "Please, Grandmother. Will you help me?" Then they went out to the spigot near the oleanders. Beneath the low branches Sivarani bent forward, and Radika and her grandmother began.

Women's hair was valuable, like gold jewelry. You let it grow. Sivarani had let hers fall around her like a queen's gown. Her hair made her feel grown, and she'd acted, as a grown woman might, to find their father. She'd sent word to a girlfriend who'd joined the Tigers, and this friend had reported she knew the camp where they kept him. Sivarani had gone with this friend, leaving in the night while the family slept.

A month had passed, and another month. One day before the monsoon began they'd received a letter in Sivarani's handwriting. *I am a revolutionary now, like Chilliyan. I know how to make a land mine. We have to, to fight for Eelam. The Leader says there is no other way.*

The letter did not mention their father.

Their grandmother sat like a stone carving.

"Will Sivarani come back?" Radika asked. Her mother stood as though held by two strings pulling in opposite directions. "Maybe I shouldn't have collected money," she said. "It must have looked to Sivarani like I wanted to help them."

"She went after father," Radika said. Her mother did not speak. Mentioning their father was like the bad story. No one knew what to do with it. Radika remembers looking out into the compound, seeing the leaves of the banana trees swaying slightly. Looking at their green resembled a slacking, like wetness, water drunk down slowly, deliciously.

Their mother read the last part of the letter. *I have cut my hair,* Sivarani wrote. *All the girls do it, to show we're loyal.*

Radika had never seen a Tamil woman who'd cut her hair. It wasn't done. She could see the spigot where they'd knelt so many times. The Tigers were supposed to be good Tamils. Why had they done this to the girls? How could such a thing be Eelam? Their mother had pulled Radika and Maheswary against her belly. Her hair fell around them, an airy veil. Radika felt light come to her filtered through this dappled cool.

Their grandmother had wept, and Radika and Maheswary and their mother had come around her, so that the four of their bodies, grieving, formed a mount. That was how you did it, and then, after a while, the grief was almost gone. But this grandmother persisted in grieving. As the weeks passed, Radika cast about for means to distract her—prayers, little love gifts, hopeful pleading. She'd lied the way adults lie to comfort children. Sivarani would return when the war was over, Sivarani's hair would grow long again.

But grief was a stone around which the old woman shrank like a drying fruit. Finally she had gone across the strait where her younger son lived, away from The Troubles. She lived there a while. Then one night while the others slept, she let go of the thread of the world.

Father is dead, Radika thinks. Wasn't that why Sivarani hadn't written one word about him? And what but the certainty that Sivarani would never see her father again could have prompted her to pledge herself to the Leader, to cut her hair?

Sivarani won't come today because she doesn't know about Radika's ceremony. Their grandmother won't come either, nor will the aunts, uncles, cousins. Her mother had explained this on the first morning. Travel is too dangerous now, and everyone has less money.

~ The sun is neither gleaming shield nor goddess' countenance, but the mound of a woman's belly, that round, red heat where flesh comes to fruition. The mesh of flesh, the flesh of the world. Green, gold, silver leaves, heat, water, the gate of the body, the gate beneath the trees. They tell you you'll be happy with a husband, you will make your husband happy, and your strong body will make a good baby. What they don't tell you is the banana lying on the table, one bite gone. Or the lamentation of hair, slashed off, flung across the ground.

Now the washerman lays a white cloth across the ceremonial board: how bright, this slab of light where she will kneel. It occurs to her to wonder. Should she hold the iron shard through the ceremony?

"Look, Radika, red!" Maheswary says, dancing in with the sari, chirping. Red, the color of the hot cries of parrots. The color of women's heat. Radika tucks in one end of the sari, then twirls, turning into Maheswary's winding. "Look! They're coming!" Maheswary points. Their mother's friends, by twos and threes, begin to come through the gate, each with her jar. And here, across the sand, comes Praba. Maheswary's energy is a flock of tiny birds. "A red sari, Radika! And mother's gold necklace, all for you!"

Because Maheswary reaches up to fasten the clasp, Radika sees the lorry first. The driver, a girl of Sivarani's age, halts, keeps the motor running. Beside her a boy in uniform, with a rifle.

Another boy with a rifle leans out from the back.

Maheswary runs out of the room, flies across the sand to the gate. She and the girl speak. Then Maheswary hurries toward the back of the lorry. The banana trees and the oleanders suggest spaciousness, a grateful calm.

The boy at the back bends down.

Later Radika will remember one of the women had lifted her water jar onto her shoulder, as though ready to pour. She will also remember the sound that goes up from the women, the rush of air from a flock of birds beginning to rise, then falling back.

There in the dirt a rolled up blanket, a blanket with holes in it.

From the blanket's rolled edge a single foot protrudes.

The boy holds his rifle and looks down at Maheswary with the curious interest of someone engaged in a novel experiment who now observes the outcome.

How long, how many are those moments in which Maheswary looks back at him? Then she looks down. Their mother was a small woman with long feet that seemed to connect her securely to the earth. Radika remembers feeling safe walking beside her, observing how solidly those feet fit the sand. She sees Maheswary reach out, stroke this foot as though to soothe it.

A grating of gears, the lorry pulls away. It is all still there, the green, the gold, the light, the heat, the sand an esplanade all the way to the gate, and beyond the compound the lagoon and the sea, spilling benedictions of water into the world. It keeps moving in and out and in, all the tiny pieces loosely sewn together, liveness that never stops breathing. Perhaps it is this that gives Radika the courage to walk out onto the stone step. The gecko is gone. Heat rises from the sand in shimmering waves. The spaces between her and the gate has taken on the aspect of terrain difficult to negotiate. She passes the washerman where he squats, a dumb tool. The women have collapsed against each other like jars thrown down and cracked, one or two broken. Radika hears Maheswary's weeping, and beyond this, the barely audible ticking of the heat, the sound time makes, going on. It's the sound of waiting and not knowing, of knowing but not knowing who, of knowing who but not knowing when, of knowing when but not knowing how.

The truth is the sun is a burning star, and there are no favorites. Its heat illumines Tamil and Sinhalese, soldier and civilian, man and woman. The young and the old, the living and the dead. Did their mother keep some of the money she'd collect for the Tigers? She might have kept a little, anyone might have.

Enough to buy tomatoes, and some oil.

Radika sees Maheswary's gaze resting on her belly, as though she imagines it *was* Radika's belly she slid from, as though, if she could, she would climb back inside this motherly sister. It was men who had to deal with the blood of killing, and they used iron. But how can iron make anyone invincible? Iron splinters and breaks apart: here's a bit of it, in her hand.

Radika lets the iron shard fall onto the sand. There may have been a time when iron kept evil away, but that time is gone. The nature of iron has been changed by the violence with which men hurl it through the air. Now iron draws death toward you. Already a similar bit of iron may have sped toward Chilliyan and found him. Or toward Sivarani. There are many, many bits of iron flying through the air. It could have happened easily to both of them. Is the messenger even now hurrying toward them with the news?

Michael Martone

STILL LIFE OF SIDELINES WITH BOB

The Game Away from the Ball

Basketball coach Bob Knight of the Texas Tech University Red Raiders is riding the referee. It is the opening seconds of the home game with Oklahoma University, and the ref lucky enough to pull the assignment to patrol the bench-side corridor from Texas Tech's back court to Oklahoma's base line is weathering the sniping coming from Knight pacing parallel. After a few minutes of this criticism, the ref has developed a twitch. He is flinching, his head turning toward the Coach then shying away. Every call, no matter who is calling it, is being questioned, commented upon, underscored. The ref's attention is being divided. His reaction time dulled. Running up the court, he stalls sooner after crossing the timeline, adding a bit more distance from the glowering coach. He is being conditioned. He can't take his eyes off his own periphery now. And then, like that, Coach Knight lays off, slumps into his chair and assumes the position, his arms wrapped around his broad chest, his head down, brooding, Olympian, his dark eyes looking out from beneath his dark and darkening brows, intent on the game before him.

I have no idea what is going on in the game. I have been forcing myself to watch this drama on the sidelines, one of Coach Knight's calculated contributions to the flow and tenor of the remaining minutes of play. Roger Angell has pointed out that in baseball, the only game where the ball doesn't do the scoring, the spectator must widen the field of vision to the whole playing field. Basketball fans certainly know of the game away from the ball—the screens and constant cuts, the choreography of checks and switches, pick-ups and blocking-outs performed covertly while the player in possession dribbles into position or coils in anticipation of the perfect bounce pass to the now open man. In spite of sensing the complete action of the court, the fan's attention is more than likely by the bouncing ball riveted. Its trajectory through the air mesmerizes. That is why I have had to expend so much energy to ignore the attractive nuisance of that ball in its flight and the furious action swirling around it to focus on the now still center that is Coach Bob Knight.

In his thirty-five years of coaching college basketball, he has constantly shifted our attention to the game away from the ball. By that I don't mean simply the machinations of his players on the floor or even his psychological gamesmanship on the sidelines. It still matters that teams he coaches win, that the ball goes through his team's hoop more than the other team's. After thirty-five years in the presence of Bob Knight, however, the game away from the ball has expanded way beyond the game on the floor, in the arena, in the league, in the season. The game away from the ball has expanded to include institutions, state governments, whole peoples even. Our vision has shifted. We no longer keep our eye on the ball. Our eye is drawn to Knight.

Dazzleflage

Coach Knight, inert in his chair on the sidelines, wears a black pullover. Black is one half of Tech's colors. The other is scarlet, the shade of the collar of the golf shirt he has on beneath the black sweater.

There are a couple of things odd about this black. For one, it's not red, or more exactly, crimson, a color of Indiana University where Coach Knight coached famously for twenty-nine seasons. The scarlet at his throat today is a tease, sharing some of the same frequency of that other red, but it is eclipsed by that expanse of smothering black. This black, the black of his sweater, is matte, flat, a color drained of color, and it could stand for all that will not be spoken about the history of all his years in Indiana and his departure from the university where he was, until recently, so closely identified. The media guide I got along with my souvenir basketball scrupulously records his statistics of victory, the irresistible climb to eight hundred wins, the three national championships, the Olympic gold medal, the histories and careers of the scholar athletes he nurtured during those years. It also scrupulously deletes the acrimony of his firing from IU, the legacy of controversy, the public displays of anger, the accusations of bullying, the actual acts of violence. There is then this absence. The black is a hole at the core of the excitement about the commencement of this new winning tradition at Tech.

The color of the sweater itself is not what I want it to symbolize, its black does seem to absorb light, to flatten the figure who wears it. It is a kind of camouflage. It is a countershading that is goofing with my ability to read, in folds of cloth and the way light falls on fabric, the distance and depth of an object. The object I'm looking at, Coach Knight, is collapsing, collapsing in on himself. As I stare at him, from my perch on the mezzanine, he is beginning to, well, disappear.

It's funny I should be thinking of camouflage as this is the game where students, on their own initiative, have created a new T-shirt on sale for the first time in the arena's Double T shop. Rising behind the bench and Coach Knight, the stands emit the traditional broad swatches of black and scarlet clad boosters arrayed in bands of color into which the coach is beginning to blend. Here and there among the solid blocks of color are veins of these new camouflage shirts. The usual smattering of forest camo browns and greens, the woodland splotches and smears, have been replaced on these tees by shades of scarlet, white, pink, and black. The shirts' jumpy patterns disrupt the ironed-on message. "The General's Army" it says, invoking Coach Knight's nickname. As the game goes on, the camouflage pattern extends deeper into the crowd, marbling through the monochromatic black and red sections as more and more fans snap up the shirts and put them on.

There is another style of camouflage used in nature and war. Dazzle. Zebras, for instance, or referees for that matter, running in packs, are visually obvious to the predators that stalk them; they aren't blending into a background. But the high contrast of their striping creates another type of illusion, not blending, but that of an explosion right in front of our eyes, a scattering of the whole into many odd parts. For awhile there at IU, Coach Knight had a liking for loud plaids and patterns of crimson and cream, the harlequin design of dazzleflage warships so obviously there in the sights of the submarine but so hard to get a bead on.

Bob Knight has always hidden himself in plain sight. His world class temper could be either the real thing or a stunning act of diversion. The discipline he brings to bear on his players might be sadistic meanness or a calculated performance deployed to motivate and inspire. Or they could be both. They could be both real and a simulation of what is real. When he explodes, he could explode or simply seem to explode. It might depend on what we who are watching desire to see.

The Coach Knight I see on the bench is like a duplicate, a replica of the real Coach Knight. This Coach Knight, in the black sweater, is a quotation of the former red-sweatered Coach Knight. Getting down the sartorial look, the mane of silver hair, the beady stare, is relatively easy. It will be more difficult to duplicate the career at Indiana, its heights of success and its spectacular crashes. In a column introducing Coach Knight to Texas quoted in the media guide, Cynthia and Randy Farley liken him to one of Hemingway's heroes, but they neglect to connect both the coach and author to the danger of their powerful creations, the trap of self-parody. Playing one's larger-than-life self becomes a monumental task. Perhaps reconstituted in Texas, this Coach Knight's only remaining real disguise is a satire of a former self.

To advertise *A Season on the Brink,* ESPN's first made-for-television movie, the network features a reenactment of the moment during Indiana's game against Purdue in the '84–'85 season when Coach Knight launched a plastic bench chair onto the court while a Purdue player was shooting a technical foul shot. The verb is important. "Launched." "Threw." "Hurled." The coach in his new book, *Knight: A Coach's Life,* deploys "toss," transforming the verb into a noun to title the incident, "The Chair Toss," and says only that he "sent it scooting" while devoting a mere page or so to it all. He professes he is baffled by the notoriety and the longevity of the scene. Its power, however, is undeniable.

It may have been the impetus for John Feinstein, author of *A Season on the Brink,* the book from which ESPN's movie is adapted, to approach Coach Knight in the first place for access to cover the '85–'86 season. Feinstein views it as the nadir of a Knight decline bracketing the previous year with the pinnacle of the summer's Olympic victory in Los Angeles. Coach Knight, the student of history, discounts the chair toss in comparison to the other sideline antics of other coaches. "I consider my link to infamy," he writes, "a pretty tame one." The critical turning point that afternoon represents to him has to do with what he was wearing. He writes that it had been the first time, in a fit of frustration, he had not worn a coat and tie for a game. Had he, he says now, the jacket would have been out on the floor not the chair. Ever since then, however, he has worn those golf shirts and the sweaters.

Not only did ESPN feature the pas de deux with chair in the commercial, it was, in each commercial, repeated several times. There it goes again and again in a kind of action stutter cut like the multiple renditions of tables tipped in a music video's cliche of rage or a Wild Bunch ballet of blood where the same wounded cowboys fall over and over to the ground. The image of the chair sailing out over the floor is indelible, and the gesture does seem inexhaustible in its ability to deliver a kind of aesthetic delight to its witnesses. Let's see that again!

Why should the legs on the graphic images of the event surprise Coach Knight? For him it was only an act. It was staged. The coach admits as much in his memoir when arguing its trivial nature by pointing out that no one was hit.

"I made sure," he writes, "it didn't come close to anyone." It looks, to everyone but the coach, like a spontaneous authentic eruption of extreme emotion, a kind of inarticulate expression of feeling, but we are told that it was, in fact, under control, scripted even, choreographed. He would have us believe that what we are seeing is theater, but what we believe we are actually seeing is real life.

Coach Knight is toeing a line here as delicately as he toed the sideline when he threw the chair. He didn't actually go himself out onto the floor. That would have been a real transgression. In order for theater to work its Aristotelian magic, the audience must recognize that what they are seeing is within the context, the frame, of a theater. There, in the confines of art, we can exercise those emotions that if expressed outside of the theater in the real world would be truly dangerous. We watch in horror and pity as Oedipus blinds himself at the same time we know that the man before us acting as Oedipus has not really been blinded. Art is framed deviance. The artist doesn't simply create the picture but also creates the means for the audience to see it.

Bob Knight is, then, a kind of performance artist. And the various arenas, gyms, and field houses are the sites of the theater of Bob Knight. So often we can see the results of his art, the stunning residue of basketball genius performed within the painted lines that frame the varnished wood floors. But at other times we miss or he neglects to transmit the signal that he is performing. Often the frames he creates, if in fact he creates them, are less clear. There is a kind of slippage in the viewers' perception that results in the registering of real horror, not its simulated aesthetic twin.

Look, here is another piece of tape. Coach Knight throttling a player's neck. Here is another. A player head-butted by the coach on the bench during a timeout. And here is another. A scene before Assembly Hall in Bloomington, a student drawn up verbally and physically after exchanging a few words with the coach. In all these instances the frame Coach Knight asserts for these confrontations is that he was in the midst of a performance, a performance of instruction. What we are being asked to witness is a teacher, teaching. There's the frame. Can we see it that way? We are compelled to watch these moments over and over again to try to assess the shadowy context. This confusion itself is interesting. Is the actor out of control or is the actor acting out of control?

Not Oedipus as much as Hamlet here. Early in the play Hamlet tells us he will feign madness in order to attain his ends. Later Hamlet apologizes for his part in the deaths of Ophelia and her father. He reminds anyone who'll listen that he was mad.

There is drama on the basketball court, but it is drama you can see because of the frame of "game." The chair, a light plastic floating shell of a chair, tossed onto the court that day shattered the illusion that it was a game. It was no longer play or a play.

In the seats behind Coach Knight on the bench are four men who have paid $750 apiece to sit there. One of them holds up a hand-lettered sign occasionally. From where I sit, it is hard to read, but I see the words "Hoosiers" and "Knight." Hoosiers for Knight perhaps. They have come from Indiana not only for the game but for proximity to the man. They've attended a practice and the Texas Tech training table and later, after the game, will sit by me at the news conference. They bid for their places today some months ago at a fundraiser in Floyd's Knobs, Indiana, hosted by Coach Knight that, until recently, had raised money for Indiana University.

It is a weird coincidence that the United Spirit Arena in Lubbock is on Indiana Avenue, that it is made of bricks made in Indiana, that its inaugural game three years ago was won by a Bob Knight-coached Indiana team. The landscape of Lubbock itself is like a Bizarro Indiana. It is flatter than the flattest part of my home state. Its surrounding farms seem more farmy, the fields measured in sections not just acres. And the township grid, a signature of the quilted Indiana countryside, is even more pronounced here. Lubbock has out Indiana-ed Indiana.

Bob Knight, from Orrville, Ohio, spent twenty-nine years in Indiana, a state identified, if it has any identity at all, with the game of basketball. The ESPN movie features documentary interludes where real Hoosiers speak adoringly of their coach and their game. My mother reports from Fort Wayne that now the malls not only stock IU and Purdue licensed merchandise but Texas Tech stuff as well. Bob Knight's story has always been and continues to be a story also about Indiana.

Believe me, it is a burden being nice. When you inhabit The Heartland in this country, which this country also calls The Flyover, you begin to live this crazy contradiction. You believe, on the one hand, that you are the center of all that is good, true, and valuable. You are, you believe, the embodiment of American values and traditions, whatever they are. But simultaneously you know, in your heart of hearts, you are also in the middle of Nowheresville. So you keep up appearances. You're honest, optimistic, innocent, polite, respectful, and most of all, nice. Nice is us. We are nice to the nth degree. And yet it wears on you, keeping alive the flame of civility you believe is the flame of civilization.

In my favorite episode of *Law & Order,* a New York City woman who has murdered her sister to assume her identity is finally cornered by the DA. You took your sister's life, he accuses. And she answers, "My sister lived in Terre Haute, Indiana. She had no life."

Hoosiers, being nice, won't talk about this: Bob Knight is a monster. But he is our monster.

Because he won, because his program was clean, because his players graduated, because he played by the rules, especially because he played by the rules, because, finally, all of that was, well, nice, we allowed him to be something more. Because he was so very nice he could also become, for Hoosiers, the anti-Hoosier as well. He became for us, who constitutionally can't act out, our designated hitter, our surrogate rage against those stupid rules, our projection of the best suppressed Id on any forbidden planet. He is the thing in us all spoiling to be not nice.

You, who are Not Nice by nature, cannot begin to imagine how thrilling it is for the Nice to witness such public displays of emotion, any emotion, that Bob Knight could concoct. How the pent-up grudges, the slights, the nagging doubts, the inferiority, the martyrdom, the secret vanity, the righteousness even, and all those virtues that we must maintain and nurture, all of it gets bled off by the maniac in the bright red shirt. All heck, as we say, breaks loose.

I look at the four Hoosiers hovering behind Coach Knight. I wonder if the change of venue to this Bizarro Indiana will still work its empathetic catharsis. I can't imagine Texans plugging into this dynamic. Where is the understatement to foil the flamboyance? It's not quite the same. Bob Knight sits quietly on the Texas Tech bench. All around me Texans are going nuts as their team takes a commanding lead. But all the Hoosiers in the house wait on the Coach and on what he will do next.

David Matlin

IN OUT O

Wesley found a small apartment, painted the walls white, moved in stray furniture, tried to settle. The swing shift, 3:00 to 11:30, gave himself and everyone else on the fourth floor where they worked, fifteen-and-a-half hours. Eight on (with a half slice for lunch), fifteen-and-a-half off. And you might try a hundred ways to juggle it, twist it so it came out a square or a triangle, think of a Jacaranda spilling its purplest flowers for a flock of desert parrots and it always, no matter the intricacy of the dance, sounded like an autopsy with the number fifteen transformed into seconds, and each of those eight hours into segments and cross-segments of time the wizards of the American tropical jungles thought might be too heartless even for their Gods. The freight elevator was rickety. Anything over ten bodies and that thing seized into an intrigue of earthquake simulations. The fourth floor opened up onto a time clock with a wall of punch cards—simple, direct, merciless which produced a snicker in everyone who saw it. "Sumthin better sumthin worse, like a bad lover with an infection you couldn't take yer eye off of " one of the women workin the presses called it as she looked over Wesley, him freshly arrived, she and a couple of other girls havin a friendly smoke and doin a study. Lucille, Betsy, Janine. Two from Tennessee, one from Kentucky, daughters of hard scrabble farms and mines who "Come up either alone or with sumbuddy, any way a girl cood," Lucille from Tennessee told Wesley once on a coffee break.

Mon.	In	Out	O
Tues.			
Wed.			
Thurs.			
Fri.			

The names of the week abbreviated as if to spell out the complete noun might bring on a money spill beginning at the mystical crossroads where the phantom letters struggled in the renunciation of their appearances and if there was "O"vertime that information was written in by hand with the floor manager's initials "Travis P" who drove an impeccable show-room perfumed '58 Edsel, from Windsor to a neighborhood where Edsels or Fairlanes or Grand Prixs or LeBarons or GTO's or Impalas or Barracudas, Regal

Turbos, Futuras, Mustangs, Chargers, Cameros, Pintos, Chevelles and Cutlass Supremes; if they didn't have the proper reservation ended up lookin unwed and unled, sinners driven to final destination cause their owners forgot about the stop watch masters who come uninvited into the really impersonal night, unglue transmissions, engines inside six minutes, head for that garage in Conshohocken, Oshkosh, "Pahrump" in Nevada, and Arizona where at the end of all the darkest rides loaded with the smoothest contraband twentieth century steel had to offer, you end up in "Nothing" up a couple of valleys and mountain ranges from "Yarnell" and "Octave," a little off as it always is and far away as you can get. Wesley and me'd take the change we'd accumulated hoeing weeds or digging ditches under the eye of his father's Kiowa foreman and spend a Saturday afternoon in the "Grove Theatre" (because it was orange grove country) and watch juvenile delinquent Hot Rod films where we saw "Hot Rod Girl" and heard such phrases as "cool cats" "squares" "dig"—"Drag Strip Riot" where Fay Wray herself after being ravished by King Kong, ends up (along with a gestation period suitable to the primordial frenzy with her ardently doomed King of Kings) as the mother of a disturbed street racer—"Hot Rod Gang" where we heard Gene Vincent sing "Lovely Loretta" and "Baby Blue." There was also "The Choppers" which starred Marianne Gaba "Miss September" *Playboy* Magazine, 1959—"Dragstrip Girl"—we went to it for the beautiful Fay Spain and "TV" Tommy Ivo who hooked up four blown, injected Buicks onto one thin rail, pointed it a quarter mile down an asphalt tube in Pomona, a gravity visit to see what velocity and torque would do to the muscles of his pretty star-boy face.

No one we ever knew had an Edsel, so when, once in a while, Travis P offered to give Wesley a ride home Wesley'd ride shotgun and wonder about chopped channelled pin-striped customized Edsels, whether I'd want one—sent a picture to prove it existed, two-tone orange and white after my unit had poisoned a bunch of village wells.

After a tour of all the fourth floor processes; packing, punch pressing, assembling, inspecting, Wesley was taken to his "station." Five other people there; they were responsible for the final stages of assembly and inspection, a last tuning of the measuring gauges for oil tanks and containers that'd find their way to practically every oil field in the world "that had to do" as Travis P told Wesley, "with America's power." The five people held their faces tight as the floor manager stepped in among their tables and chairs tools and lunches to introduce "the new hire." Five Black faces and, this suddenly among them, one, extending his White Man's hand. And they paused for the moment to look it and him over. Wesley knew immediately it wasn't for the exact shade of his blue eyes. It was quick, unlike any measure he'd ever experienced. Though there were two wars, the spasm where I was that made that painting by Goya called "Saturn Eating His Son" seem like a nostalgia for innocence, and the one on the streets of America's towns and cities, those five faces were concentrating only on Wesley. What took no more than a second's glance; he didn't know anything else other than he'd find out. There was Darius ("Named after a King, and any King'll do, baby"), Marvin, Bob, JT, and George. JT about 6'7" or 8" (and Wesley estimated two hundred sixty pounds) stood up, extended a palm, a set of fingers that looked like small bananas. He squeezed Wesley's disappeared hand, not too hard, but enough to let anyone know it wasn't a seance and be sure as shit to keep yer eyes square, neither friendly or unfriendly. Darius was next. Wore a "Do Rag" to keep his "process" in place, sweet cologne, front teeth were split about an eighth inch, finger nails polished and trimmed and he had a little red portable radio one of his girl friends gave him "a surprise Easter present, and along with it some fine pussy, fit for a King, my Man" followed by a show of easy laughter, and an "Uh Huh, Muthufuckuh" for a touch of emphasis. It was obvious Travis P was getting nervous when he got around to Marvin, thin, light enough to almost "pass" but wouldn't ever consider it, eyed Wesley and rather than shake hands, pulled out a cigarette, lit up, doused his match, nodded down at Wesley's boot encased feet said, "Jack here, look like he know some horse shit." Bob, wore a red sweater turtle neck "dickey" under a long sleeved ironed blue shirt ("never gits dirty"), black slacks, Italian zipper boots, a gold left front incisor, pulled an apple from his lunch box, a business-ending knife from a pocket, began to cut the fruit into slices, handed one to Wesley, and then to the other four, didn't say a word ignored Travis P as if he were worse than a ghost, a humble fart slipped out with no chance for restitution and too sneaky for any secondary complications. George wore a felt hat he never took off, a couple of diamond pinkies, had a honey smooth baritone and used it to say "Wesley. Now that sounds like a lucky number."

Who's to say a Shawnee or Wea up from raiding Tennessee wouldn't along with scalps to be paraded for review of the British at Detroit bring Black slaves who'd escape into Canada and their offspring to attend the "quiet convention" in Chatham, Ontario May 1858 planning a provisional government with John Brown and a slave uprising against every plantation master. Michigan provided the secret region where a Black escapee drowned in one world reappeared in another; the St. Clair River wide too as the South Atlantic there though it seemed no more than a string in the usual Earthly comparison and by those properties of immigrant glacial waters forged shackles into invisible "Railroads":

1765/1840: Slave Population grew from 500,000 to 3,500,000. Each slave counted as 3/5 of a Person—They the great artisans of the South: carpenters, masons, blacksmiths, tanners, barbers, tailors—The Fugitive Slave Law passed 1850 to stop the disasters of "Immigration" along with collateral legislations: Capital offense to teach a Slave to read and write.

Virginia: The Slave Breeding State.
Shipped its product: 1830 to 1860: 220,000
no clod of cotton-worn dirt left unturned

Weight of rain
upon the genitals

Rupture of snake's breath
smeared from ear to ear

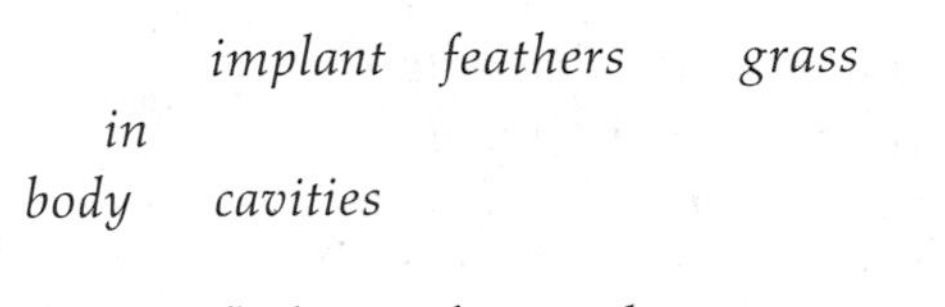

implant feathers grass
in
body cavities

flight of souls

incinerated by Magpies

Travis P left Wesley to his introductory shift and Wesley picked up a "gauge," examined the top-most red plastic cylinder-housing with its window of numbers indicating by the thousands or hundreds of thousands how many gallons a storage tank either held or didn't hold as a shrill whistle blew for five seconds (like an exotic form of epilepsy he'd later come to think). Marvin pronounced directly, "Break Little Jack. Nine minutes fifty seconds cause company policy subtract whistle time too." They pulled up a table, their lunches, took out some candy, some smokes, shuffled a deck of cards, laid down a short stack of ones, poured coffee.

"You kin watch," Darius commented. "If you got cash to lose, join up brother. Ain't the army here. And don't fret over them pieces of Company plastic. Soon enough you'll know, and then we git yer spare change." George held his hand out, palm up, and Darius touched the almost white skin there, with his fingertips to seal the gesture and the words. They gave Wesley half a "Snickers," dealt each other a hand of five card stud.

"Where you from, Wesley?" Bob asked sucking at his gold tooth.

March 6, 1863: Civil War Detroit Race Riot considered the only major "Midwest" conflict though there were similar epidemics in Buffalo, Boston, Brooklyn, Toledo, Cincinnati—One, William Faulkner ("col'd") accused of molesting two 9 yr. old girls:

> *Ellen Hoover ("col'd")*
> *Mary Brown ("Wh")*

The accused, forty one years, sentenced to life in prison for rape. The citizenry, driven to frenzy by the girls' testimony and the local newspapers attempted to lynch the prisoner. As the waves of the riot spread, the rioters, burning and pillaging Negro residences, began hunting women, children, old men focusing its hysteria on anyone it chanced to find. Frederick Douglass wrote in response to this episode and its implications for a return of Northern sympathies for slavery:

> *"The whole North will be but another*
> *Detroit where every white fiend may*
> *with impunity revel in unrestrained beastliness*
> *toward people of color; they may burn their*
> *houses, insult their wives and daughters,*
> *and kill indiscriminately."*

Summer: 1942: 35% of America's World War II weapons came from 185 plants in the immediate geography of Detroit. 55 of the major factories had not one single black worker, while skilled black workers by the thousands were either replaced or refused positions on the line in favor of recently arrived southern whites. Every factory in this crucial War Year was swept up into walk-out, sit-down strike, fixations of hate flooding outward from the line into the City. Gerald L. K. Smith called Negroes "universally syphilitic" their diseased sweat dripping onto the machinery shared with white workers.
The Packard Foundry: Three highly skilled black workers were upgraded according to their seniority and Federal Law as 25,000 white co-workers abandoned the line and a loud-speaker-aided voice bellowed that a victory of Hitler was preferable to spending a work day "next to a nigger."
"Life Magazine" August 1942 printed the headline:

DETROIT IS DYNAMITE
teetering on the two extremes:
either blowing up Hitler
or the "U.S."
Sunday June 30, 1943: Detroit ravaged by a race riot, one of the most fearful in American history.

Post-Riot fact finding committee blames violence on Negro demands "for racial equality which played an important part in exciting the Negro People . . ."
July 15, 1943: Attorney General Francis Biddle in his secret findings for President Roosevelt stated, "I believe that the riots in Detroit do not represent an isolated case but are typical of what may occur in other cities throughout the country. The situation in Los Angeles is extremely tense."
Biddle concluded that a possible limit be enforced on domestic "Negro migration" as a part of "post-war readjustments."

"Now from the Death that holds you walk
into growing life life that grows
grows to be seen

Walk

Begin

Begin To Be Seen

Where you are a Ghost
eat the wind that'll
make you sick there
The wind that'll starve you there"

"Around a little river called the Santa Ana," Wesley answered.
"Can a man go fishin?" JT asked.
"Depends" said Wesley.
"Depends. On what?" JT wanted to know.
"On you and yo pick pocket assed Mama" Darius interrupted shuffling the deck of cards like the original gaudy serpent causing everyone around that table to take a moment and nearly fall out of their chairs.

Marvin glanced at his watch said "Whistle up and sure enough it blow unsweet and loud as a shade in its Fourth Second After Death," as he gathered his hand and the couple of quick bills he'd won "To keep up with the Fords and Kennedys."

"Um huh," Darius shook his head, "Muthu here think he a preacher or a poet." "Discover what in those four seconds, my brother?" George pressed Marvin, but not too hard, letting the question go houseless.

"Baby, Baby," Darius clicked out the four syllables, "Why you bring up such things. Give Santa Ana Man over there the wrong impression about how far down the Tax Code seeps?"

These men. He understood they'd taken a pulse; his color, dress, voice, body movement, general carriage as if he were either a mug shot or a featherless nestling fallen before them. It was deliberate, an essential study. And it scared him a little. The remote contract coming forward as it did without insulation, contorted and contorting any identity it touched. We worked the potato harvests. The machinery churning spuds up, dewed soil stunk and crusted near to boiling at that unlocked afterpoint with snarled potatoes birthed out into the cruel blanknesses of the air, human hands pecking at it like flayed rooster heads; the mix of cut soil, sweat, tractor exhausts, bent bodies racing plow blades for their lives; a whole hundred acre field inside a day end up as Tom Green'd say, loading a last sack on to a sundown shrouded flatbed, "Tore as a broken grave." Our fathers had us do that as children, and later, at seventeen eighteen we hit the warehouses and fields ourselves, the money being what it was, though you'd gear yourself up for twenty hour days potato dust swelling your throat and gums; a hive or two from heat, the repugnant filthy noise of a harvest warehouse stirring up a desperate reckoning for the boys and their girlfriends we'd known, to escape, sign up for a war "Fuck and die or come back to this shit, you choose ese" the vocabulary rolled out slick as lacquer, animal, mineral, barrio time-slipped for revenge. End of the day we'd see'em, other exhausted laborers, black mostly with some white mixed in; a husband, wife fixed there too turning the piles of rotted throwaways they'd later boil for soup, a thin stew, mix it with runny pork, sleeping next to their thinned metal held with wire cars on the same ground they'd pick next morning, themselves and it shrunk mutually to a just before dying just after living hushed there, semi-blistered like everyone else sixth decade of the twentieth century in our California towns. It wasn't the work. Wesley knew he could do that. Knew after the death in life of his father and the collapse of the farm and the dreams of a farm, the Jew distant from the soil once more as if he covered himself with the landless past of Russia and Poland. The Farmer and Tom Green taught'im to be silent in hard labor, taught its finality and fragility, the study, gentleness, the murderous belittling breath of the hours and never, never to be broken by it (it was the reason we wanted him in Asia, next to us).

"You like Jazz, Santa Ana Man?" Darius asked, turning up his red radio.

> *Life of Black Detroit in the late nineteenth century was the subject of constant mockery by the City's newspapers which portrayed the daily struggles of its "col'd population" as if it, the City, was itself a Plantation "they passed day after day, eating and sleeping, working and playing, apparently as happy and as jolly as though they were back on the plantation itself " the "half dressed pickaninnies" at once mannikins of the grotesque and pitiful—horror visions of miscegenation, nightmare subvertors of white force lying beyond estimation or the "to reduce" as the initial verb risen in American colonial speech—the symptom and diagnosis a cosmology of the punitive: fantastic, impervious, throat cut as the mouth regions in the fangs of water stranded in its Vulture Form to draw existence in:*

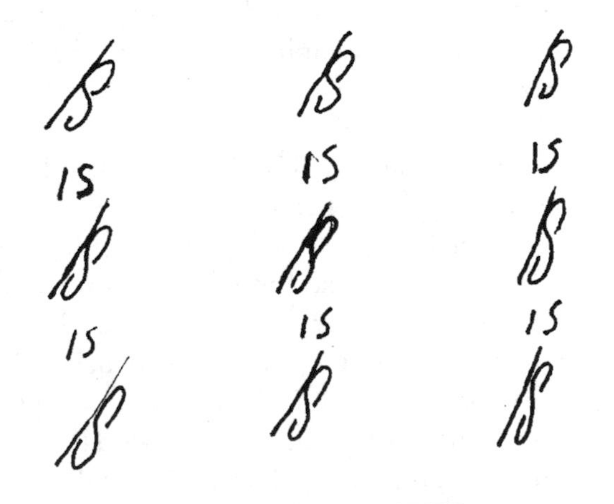

PLUS THE WAR VERB
DESIGNATING BIRTHLESSNESS
AT THE CORE OF APPEARANCES

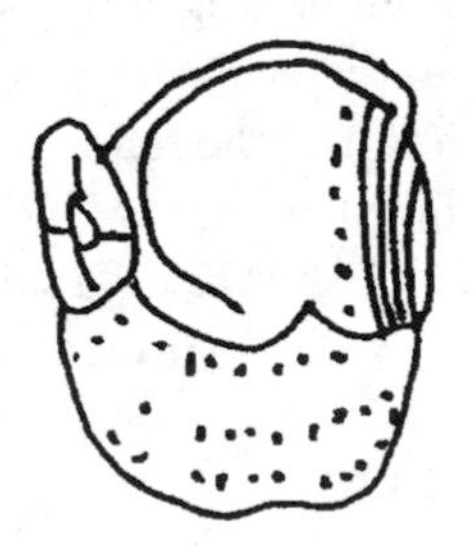

Wesley didn't say anything for a moment as each man looked, unmoved, a little ugly, as if the "new hire" and themselves because of it were a kind of corpse; Black hollowing White to a distant summer haze ("An evil inscription, come to stunt the whole wishing well" as George later would tell it not as apology, but living fact).

"Some. A little. I suppose," Wesley answered breaking the silence.

"Suppose what?" JT flexed out the words like he and the other mourners were about not to honor the dead and line the grave with the best unconsoling trinkets ten days after the Moon was born and touched the Earth with that water lily light o' hers knowing she was the only one ever who had six toes just enough distraction and deformation for everyone under her incandescence to want to sit on each other in the ways best suited to ardency, indecency, trembling, horsemanship, the laughter of heartless rabbits in far galaxies.

"My family had records so I listened. Just like I'm listening now to that bass in the background. I heard it before. Sounds like Paul Chambers. And yeah. I like Jazz."

It was "Miles Davis at Carnegie Hall" riding the radio waves to the fourth floor of this factory. We'd listened to the recording and tried to imagine from our palm and walnut lined Southern California side streets what New York or Chicago'd be like and sometimes we'd drive, Wesley and me, to the "It Club" in LA, hear Roland Kirk, the blind player, serve up notes and experiments that'd cut at us kids, cause questions to come up outta' nowhere; hear Sonny Rollins, Lee Morgan at the "Lighthouse" in Hermosa and then walk the beaches, discuss what we'd listened to and didn't understand a thing but that it seemed irresistible and held us like nothing else ever had almost like a hurt around a corner we couldn't see, one we wanted more than anything like the glow of some lake sliced into multiple shades of quarter moon light with sounds of our own voices gone aerodynamic as the other high strung bullets sunk and stirred and become instantly inaccessible to the beginnings of the night that brought us to this music. Then sneak back into the fields we worked, hear Tom Green cussing cause we hadn't showed at sunrise like we were supposed to and haul our asses to sundown and like Wesley'd said maybe it was that Kiowa after all who was trying to help us see it was us who could arrive late to a death zone.

"Is Paul Chambers," said Marvin who looked around at that moment at the others, and added "Uh Huh, Jack here might know some shit after all."

"Be shallow or deep, Marvin?" George asked.

"You and that funny assed nose a'yers git to go fewst George, if you wanna know."

They squared off long enough for Wesley to think over why exactly Travis P put him here, slapped a palms up "Brother" signal, each of them laughing, telling Darius to turn up his "Red Box" so everyone could go back to work. It was a picture he'd never expected. Poor Whites, mostly from the Ohio River Border States, and Blacks wound tight into the machinery that had to be shared. Some of the White women had the hands of their ancestresses, cracked and bled from overwork, corns erupted over knuckles, in some cases, as if those, the parts that told the silentest stories about where a woman goes to and gets from in her American Journey, were worn on their lips as tornadoes, deadening heat and cold, starvation, loved ones trampled by plough horses, whole countrysides during the seasons of brain fever so sick, no one able to bury the dead so up they crawled when the chance came to this factory or others with their memories of fathers or grandfathers, legs bowed a lifetime from stumbling over turned-up clod, either followed or not by husbands, sons; daughters, granddaughters sitting at a punch press waiting on the break whistle for a smoke. "A little lost nail" Janine called her, "two pack-a-day and more habit from bein' nervous. Musta' bin them Kaintucky Hills that did it," she'd laugh, offering her Black women coworkers a country girl wink. If this American Corner was a dead-end no one on those four floor'd whisper such forlornest sorrow over the Space and Depths of the country with all its possible footsteps and places to go. The loneliest Bride and Groom of the color codes in their ceremonies sat before each other here; displaced rural Whites and urban Blacks trapped in the details of sameness changelessly arranged for each generation. "Exact ones," Wesley wrote in his hundreds of letters, "we'd seen hacked by the mid-day sun working next to a Black man or woman, as if the Nation had suddenly deciphered itself." No one on any of those four floors forgot though what was waiting outside. Viola Liuzzo, the woman from Detroit had had her brains blown out on a drive-by suddenly abandoned Southern country road coming home after registering Black voters in Mississippi. Someone drove past her, fired point blank, kept going into the kind of murder as easily found in the Delta of the Mekong or the Yalobusha. And the Detroit Press in honor of its former traditions as to the properties of the Question tried to defame the murdered woman as drug addicted, educated, and sexually promiscuous.

"Men git the habit early," Lucille from Tennessee said about those who killed the civil rights worker one day. "Beat the women till they cin barely tell anymore whether a woman's alive, or alive enough to git beaten one more time cause he knows she'll find a lid for it. Couple bastards like that think no more of it than a lynchin 'cep they do'wanna in'dup in jayel and'd never figur on other women takin her place, scerd iver second as they might be. One woman, yeah maybe, cause she was alone. Beat a woman's OK, but be a woman killer. Even'n Soddy Daisy, where I'm from, no man'd be allowed to live the night."

Lucille was tall, 6', 6'1" "Black Irish" with "a quarter tinge Choctaw" in her "thirties sumwhars" liked "to go dancin, liked marijuana: put that on my gravestone too," and was respected by both her White and Black female co-workers for her wit, "fer the whiff of style she brang to it." The women who heard this comment on the murder of a courageous fellow woman cast a reluctant gaze on their Tennessee sister knowing their own morbid trials, and yet, though they reckoned, each of them, what had had to be abandoned personally in the face of this "vice" as it broke their worlds, they still had time to ask whether she considered herself "the Soddiest Daisy of Soddy Daisy" not to wrap any of it in disrespect, but to plumb the recesses of humor which might instantly radiate into necessity and extravagance for them to be as instantly undercut by glances at a watch, bitten fingernails, smears of mascara, a sudden shuffle through a purse to make sure everything (lipstick, powder, perfume, nail polish "in case a someone out there still likes to fondle female toes," capsules of amphetamine), were properly inventoried for an afterwork date. The edges of an almost resentful beauty still hovered over Lucille's jaw line and lips. Her face was cheekboned high with the strain and curvature of Southern Forest Indian and Runaway Slave blood. She was wiry, had long strong fingers, an ass Marvin said was "gonna haf 'ta wait before it got placed in a Museum" and a pair of washed out blue Irish eyes "that provoke" like Betsy (also from Tennessee) said, "late afternoon suspicions."

"Girl, whar'd yu say yu wuz from?"

"Ain gon' say, iver'gin."

"Name didin start with an 'S' did it?"

"Yeah. 'S' fer 'Stray Parrot' who beats her wings outside the windez a'pretty men on theeze Deetroit Jewly nights."

"Say agin, honey. Have a boy tatoo a feather on yer ass or mine, black, white, purple anytime."

"Wuz yew iver thar?"

"Whar's that?"

"Why that little town this side a' the Snow Bird Mountins."

"Yew mean the one has an actual Daisy pinned to her good uz pink 'ole White ass?"

"Why, Girl Bride, the very one."

The women could almost set themselves free with talk like this. Let the language go for a ride among themselves defining an utterable, communal preservation and an obstinacy against the rushes of hollowness which stole them: replaced the natural trust they might have had with the shrewd amusements that come with watching so much broken male traffic.

And they could break themselves as easily too.

If a new woman came, set an overhigh production pace, got the attentions of the efficiency experts forever waiting to rephrase those details affixed to seconds and minutes which meant wrists, forearms caught and mangled in presses—one arm for every 150,000 to 200,000 hours production time as the statistics proposed and those women knew intimately in the exact type of morbidity applicable to their "machine" and the rare but nonetheless occasional transformation of one of them into a partial or whole amputee; her beauty, at least the one that gave her negotiation, and even if it was a transparent dignity, it was, dignity—that beauty was "gutted"—if a new woman "went past rate" and forced the rest of them up that notch, increased the grotesque statistic they knew attended them, why then, in an adjacent alley the "girl" was kicked and bit, brought to know (because she needed the job "and there could be no other whereelses") the sisterly assault didn't have really a limit. It was the initial, the only warning.

Dear Wesley,

A war, or a something, came to the mid-continent countrysides around 900 A.D. The archaeologists who uncovered the skeletons were unable even in their trained language to insulate a personal shock over the Late Wood land mortuary mounds and what lay there on those bottom plains between the Mississippi and Appalachians for a thousand years—a taste for ghoulish violence no one ever, them or us, wants, but steams up and catches whoever's alive like they were a thing too under blood or whatever waiting to be dilated and dialed up and tainted and handed over—

Weapons of Preference: *Bow and Arrow*
Knife
Clubs insetted with flint spikes
(As if those forest stalkers up
and went club footed before their
own human flesh in what they got
to bear, their time helpless as ours
them and us hearing the same "Awful
Roaring" as Columbus while he was
still offshore?)

They were good at growing corn, the plant most like men and women who cultivated it. The cereal grass of the Ancient Americas wholly dependent on humans for survival as were humans dependent on it and because it liked sex, had similar appetites to its human progenitors, the thing least it play too hard and fast needed constant watching. Free genetic exchange between hybrids was allowed, even an occasional visit to bordering weedy grasses OK too long as it didn't interfere in seed quality and maintenance of healthy varieties. Every feature; firmness of cob whether hard or long, size of shank, shape of ear, width of cupule has something to do with replicas, reproduction, reincarnation, abandonment, hot mousepits, hand held hard penises and women's fingers, patient, inquisitive, alert, anticipant for corn, for other females, for men always slippery in their ass-worn ways and arriving like they'd only this morning crawled out of an accident, uneasy, cold, with those fine lines that go right to the rawest spot in a woman's eye.

Their mounds overlooked a landscape shimmering with what was immediately underfoot—contour of land and its forms, smell of the living, the dead, movement of humans, birds, animals, clouds, noises of life, path of blood in the body, wind risen above the knees, above the breast, no higher for the noon spread of air. The dead too are halfway, half waterlily. Flayed human face, shell of the Sun's Light that crawls now as a monster over night's claim upon day's swelling the petals—the halflily's terror over the incomplete amnesia inverting the realm of death. There are fields of flowers, perfumes for the predatory ruler of petals in or out of death's adherences. Dwarfs pluck them, pluck the petals. Their ears twitch in fury.

They occupied the same ridges and bluffs for at least three thousand years. One generation to another wanting to recognize the unrelaxed incarnations they'd carry in them about having lived, about having walked the same graciously dangerous, unyieldingly exact, miraculously detailed meadows, creeks, turns of soil and air so the dead might hear the patter of children's feet and who'll take up the arduous studies, know the stinging winds that'll rob a breath in or out of this life.

A large population of small villages planted, hunted, fished, built tombs, "crematories," cord-marked conoid clay vessels indicating the depth and shape of the women's minds who crafted the every-day object, brought it to a firm, mournfully simple luxuriance. The attractive complex of mounds and natural bluffs had to wait for 1940 in the twentieth century for road graders and bull dozers to transform the ancient "occupation zones" into modern highway fill—"treasure hounds" timber crews "collectors" wanting skeletons grooved axes projectile points fragments of a portable anything laid the rest to rest as if the whole outfit wuzza race a' stainless werewolves cum'ta lick it slick.

The revelations of these mounds and the discovery of the figures at Etowah both took place in 1962, the mysterious ocean and its creatures let loose now to imperceptibly crush us, draw us toward its secret smoothness we can't or won't be able to avoid even if we want to with its beauty so breathless, so exhausted, so poisonous as if it were a Venus-lit wall making us pliable, luring us to devotions, portals, raptures of destiny the previous generations knew they could not let well up, knew that no generation must ever inherit.

The killings of children appear to be prevalent by digging out their brains with flint-spiked clubs, bashing their faces in. Village life overcome by a continuous state of crushing evil enveloping even the youngest who were not spared beheadings and mutilations. We have no stories in these northern plains and forests that tell us the Lords of Death can be enraged and swindled into having to undergo their own darknesses. There were huge pyramids with plazas and cities but no one can say whether those landscapes were the sacred replicas of the earliest creations the Gods allowed to unfold.

Mandibles of gray wolves found among the skeletons; perhaps weir signs marking the days and nights of terror still untraversed by any story

Female skeletons with missing feet who walked into their trances one thing, and walked out another

It was found too that woodchucks in their generations had a taste for the skeletons, breaking and carrying away the bones to who could know, an anywhere, and remold the parts into some sort'a bastard faeries to weigh down and cause a drift to the living so that no one ever again in those lost decades'd know the difference from land and the primordial ocean on which it floats

Evidence of teeth gone; someone pulling them out of the fresh, the about-to-be fresh dead

Crushed femurs; who or what took their time to think out the applications

Hasty burials; skeletons with projectile points lying under or near indicating fatal soft tissue wounds

Skeletons without hands or feet; taken for trophies

Projectile points embedded in vertebra, pelvises; scattered around immediate excavated sites indicating episodes of random fury

No one spared

Some fishhooks in the graves that didn't match any of the other objects because they were so foreign, had the signature of deep sea marine expertise imported all the way from what's geographically Southern California—gang war trinkets from the Funeral Mountains, Rancho Mirage, an expedition come up the Mississippi to trade, had a Jivaro warrior along? Stayed a season. Two seasons? Enough anyway to fully absorb the whispers about the ways of ancient murder and who or what gets to be the fingerprints incalculable in their hard parasitic evasions

Traces of even earlier "prehistoric marauders" who came periodically through these landscapes of Pleistocene ravines, valleys, terraces, bluffs, limestone cliffs, as well as "emergency" shelters for hiding

The investigators think it was an "in-between" world worn out by the void of overpopulation, the need for land and the living things on it that couldn't be found unless one population decided to begin murdering another. Could'a been that, Wesley. Could'a been it was a one hundred year visit from the OtherWorld, the Death People breaking through, able this once, to reach across the rules of sentience which held them, held their appearances to disease, infection and its fear/shames, the swarms of rot conspiring to eat courage—their materializations allowing no further distance. Who's to say they didn't watch the ancient rules for billions of years, watching for the right thinness, the only one through all the galactic fractions of days and nights to arrive at the inconstant ZERO numbers can no longer affect as if the humans to come after are a boat of severed toes standing in the duplicate convulsions of the living?

The infection from Venus Light
has seared her cunt.

It is reported she was made of shells
and had normal eyes.

Sex was
particularly
beautiful with her

and brought forth the child

every one hundred thousand years

with the snake-headed foot

Throw the mind
back or forward
uselessly

sky's blue today

leave hole in smallest
utterance for lesions on the
pre-breath formations of our words

Thinning water for study
thinning water

and rocks

dry before it

trout listless

catch by hand

Dry lightning
Roar of Thunder

Leaf tip's curled

seared wind
to push
the nostrils wide
walk the meadow
find out if lightning eats humans

There are Kiowa and Sioux here too Wesley.
One of 'em said as we went into battle

"Where no man's word cut in stone
no liars"

What a Relief! Love, Lupe

Once the lesson sunk in a "new hire" girl, Black or White, took up "home." She and her machine and the clock dividing themselves into a seamless progression, the small and large as it dwelled in the shifts, the weeks, the gearage of years a woman'd sit under, the packs of smokes sucked down, tubes of lipstick popped up like some whiz-kid pecker to properly grease the expectant, righteous female anatomy; "maybelline" pencils in case a young lady of fortune needs to do the arithmetic about how much money a boyfriend borrowed, powder puffs, sanitary napkins, clandestine rubbers at the desperate bottom of a purse for that elusive hoodlum any girl hopes to see gliding by on a merry-go-round cheating at cards and waiting for his nomination "to become the honest mayor of a one-night stand" as one of the country girls from Tennessee arched up her eyes and said in range of Wesley's ears. A "Peach" fresh up from Georgia, soon as she got to know about the production cycle and its combinations—the floor bosses, the gloomy mosaic identitied snitch—the one no matter how hard the workers tried would never be teased into appearance—moon calendars, numerologies, permutations of that Fourth Floor Civilization—she began to sing. Not loud at first but the voice flexible, twangy with the soil of her Chattahoochee origins (Bob said it was like his older cousin "Effie's waffles; needed some sugar to get a grip, but after the first swallow, felt like ole friends."). It was one incomplete lyric from "High Noon" when Gary Cooper does his lonely impeccable ready-for-oblivion walk; Katy Jurado watching in the sexiest unconsoled anguish ever devised by any movie to humble eternity and its conjunction with everything inferior but this one mortal; Grace Kelly trembling in her distant science of virginity remove and this Georgia Peach when the noon time whistle blew though this "High Noon" was at 7:30 pm sang:

"Do not forsake me
Oh my Darling . . ."

as if she were Stephen Foster stumbled into the treasure vault of American melancholies spacious as the Heavens of Beulah as they mingle with the Starry Seas of Ruin. It kinda spooked the floor after a'while. She let the words ride the dolorous recesses of the syllables unraveling into sorrow, insomnia, alien murmurs of infuriated ancestors, or "the plain voice of a fine White woman" as George thought, who was checking over previous calculations about who'd she'd slept with and where, and whether this was another of those blunders that forced women to look at Paradise as a kind of enforced low-level gloom; didn't spare anybody, didn't necessarily either kill anyone of the millions of sisters out there getting through the successions of days impatient with the arcane innocence of male lovers who

The Song. It was passed down from an apparently "untameable aunt," was straight gorgeous as a girl, poor too as a fountain of piss, a country faun whose mother got rolls of undyed used cotton and managed to re-do those actual sacks into dresses, blouses, the pictures cut out of magazines used as templates to give the one daughter/child a sense of pride and singleness, a sense she was something other than "poor" even though after school she had to pick cotton and clean pig pens to help her father and mama on an eight acre piece of North Georgia mother stone.

War came along with a munitions factory, hired the women from miles around, "Wuz, over a bunch of them back country roads, not a man. Least not a man with a real scent, even the ones to go cold and mean; the way you have to be a woman at those times to please yerself so's ta know ya ain't deyad." They gave her the job of dipping the tips of 50 caliber machine gun tracers in red paint every twelve hour shift day. The job seemed to move from one war to another and after that bloodbath in Korea she watched the movie and decided those'd be the only words to be said at work, dippin' those bullets in a sea of preparatory blood and bein' the Seven Word Singer, slightly scaring anyone near her, humming, packing the tracers good n' tight for their "mured'up" destinations. Passed on the song and the movie as if they were her children, to the niece. Kept at those 50 caliber ingredients till one day, after twenty-some years, and "feelin' like the fumes could be crawlin with more than a couple ghosts" bought a trailer, a pick-up to haul it and herself, ("Because bad girls gotta save too") and lit out for "I don't know—Silver City; Wilcox down in Arizona sounds good. Wasn't Rex Allen from thar? One a'his brothers. If he got brothers. Never know who'll invite a girl for a quiet breakfast."

Darius, when he heard the lyrics start up decided he'd feel no bother and since it only happened once a night, five nights a week minus overtime, "What's the difference. Other women tore a part'a her away after she made grade. Thang may as well stop there." The Seven Words started a kind of work on Darius. "Done two tours. Don't need no one singin' in funny corners." He upped in '64. "Seen sim shit. Done sim shit." Second time, "Walked into the Ia Drang Valley. Felt like I'd been eaten by a scorpion. Still can feel that. Sittin here, tuning the Red Radio; piece of that scorpion hair'll rub up against me. Sweat start fillin' up my shoes." Wesley asked me about it. It was the kind of killing zone where the really heartless demons, the ones holding the indexes about unmanifested diseases of the blood at the end of this Creation, and in the Creation to come, went into a kind of reverence over what human beings do. And if you were in places like that you know you were only a tourist in your before "The Day" innocence, and after; an owl who can't get enough mice with those magnified eyes claimed by index varnished sunsets that started without any of us ever knowing, in this, or some other soon to be previous world. Darius, when she sang, rubbed his Red Radio (like Bob said, "Rub that thang, muthufukuh, and one night, it will turn into a ruby. Yes it will! And none a' us'll eveh, eveh hef ta' come back to this'yer hole"), hold on to the channel playing Lester Young, Art Tatum and his favorite, the guitarist sprung up from the same Detroit streets as himself, Kenny Burrell, "Play the electricity so sweet man, you wanna go shine the churchyard." "Done sim jail too, after I cum back." Darius reckoned it was for the change, "A lid'a Maryjane here and there to keep the ends from turnin to dog shit. Didn't have enough evidence to ripen up the real deal, but I did almost a year anyway. When the poleeze found out about my Silver Star they turned even nastier, sayin it was a miz-take given such medals to a common nigger while not a one'a them went anywheres further than their own assholes. Shackled me up once too, cause I wouldn't talk. Wouldn't say 'Jack.' Got to fill in the day somehow, and if you that kind of White Man the dazs muz really git long." Darius finished such soliloquies with a sharp, short laugh, one, that as JT summed it up, "Caused the windiest rivers to go straight." Darius became in-country expert with the formal handwork can only be compared to an overdose of chloroform and the inquisitions emerging from the flesh, the branches and summits of the refined exhaustions a knife, a fixed bayonet imposes on the fully encircled sleeper watching his aorta get pruned. "Poleeze lucky 'The D' wants to hear Lester Young," Bob said. "Folks in that jail never slightly curious how the blind Art Tatum helped separate Darius from his rage with the keys to a simple piano. Yes indeed, those blue suits gits to walk and talk like they still be alive." If Ray Charles came up Darius turned the radio loud for the girls, for Travis P, any traveling salesman, and "Wesley." "Want you to git to know the Raylettes," Darius said to the body surfer. "Take a dive into the sounds through them. No cure then, baby. Hear the Blind Man sing. Hear the Blind Man till the story," even though, as JT said "The D" took to leaving notes on the bodies he made in those Asian Jungles:

Peck you clean, muthufukah
  Till you pockets gleam.
  Peel them bills
  Till you ride the hills

"Wuz like a brand. Let'em know who'd been there. Who'd be back."

JT was Darius' cousin. "Fahthah's brahthah's son. Gits no closuh." Thought Darius "Went ovah a man; come back a stunned sparrow. Sumpin hapin ovah deh. 'D' ain't the only one dribble back like he been drained and ain't discussin his blood neither. Like he went and climbed a big ole' magnolia. Not de ones in Louisiana we wuz in, building them boy houses, hammerin, beggin uncles and aunts faw nails, extra boards. 'D' better now. But man, when he come back at the beginning, wuz like he climbed the branches a' death. Got up there fer a good look." JT upped but they sent him to Germany instead. Four years ridin a peculiar jeep up and down the border with the "Democratic Neighbor." "Vehicle was a pop-up murder machine, Jack. Uh huh. Danube valley's peaceful, quiet in spring with the rustle of them winds; eagles and thangs flyin. Sum Brahthah C.O.'s said birds up from Africa. Try git ovah that one, man! Africa! Since I was sorta like a bird handler muself I'd take muh glasses, watch them muthuhfukuhs fah awuhs. Baddest flyers I evah seen, and shrink from nawthin killuhs. Dive like dey wuz the devil's own impersonal bizness, watchin out fah the coin closest to the Night Man's balls. Like to fuck and fight elephants feh de scraps. Did that whenevah I got me the chance cause they wuz like Dolomite come straight out the egg with them words SUDDEN DEATH stamped middle o' they eyes. Yah dig it? Africa, man! Ain't dat sum sweet shit?"

JT'd look over, make sure Darius and his Red Radio were loud and clear in what he hoped at least was a temporary suspension. He'd put packing boxes together with their order sheets, set the destination stamps whether it was Arabia, Celestun, "Malang near the Java Trench. A geography lesson, plain and simple; if only the company give me sum ticket. Be gon. Yessuh, like sumone het the wrong button on the right toilet."

George said, "JT paid a price too. A taller one than Darius. It's quieter in'im, thas it, quieter, but trouble cum out the same barrel. That jeep JT rode in, or whatever the fuck it was; it was shrunk. It was like he say "Ground Zero on Wheels" no one be able to sniff out. Him and a driver. Thas it, baby. Jeep nothin but a portable missile silo ridin through those meadows, carryin midget warheads. 'Bout the size he say of a saxophone case. Ridin those four years. On leave in Spain, Paris next, Amsterdam and Crete. See a life he never thought possible. Then back to that trigger again. Waitin. Fine tune the last minute of the last day of the last second till them dreams cum to'im, whole clouds of fish gulpin for air; a world running outta luck sign. JT, he cum to it too. Like the Lord sent'im to the farthest snowstorms."

Cris Mazza

BREEDING

The bitch warned us every step of the way. Ten days after her season started, when she was in standing heat, probably ovulating—flagging her tail and flirting with Fanny—we brought her to the wolf. He indicated that she was ready, becoming erect immediately and testing her rump with his nose to see if she'd let him mount her. But the husky bitch whirled around with a shriek, ears flat, teeth bared and hair bristling.

"No," Fanny screamed, "he'll kill her if they fight." Oh yeah? The wolf just seemed bewildered for a moment and went to pee on a fence post.

So we had to muzzle the husky. That didn't stop her from growling and bristling, spinning around to face the wolf every time he approached her rear. We tied and held her, one on each side of her, Fanny's hand on her belly to keep her standing up, me holding her tail to the side. The wolf mounted, the husky growled and snarled and tried to twist away.

"Did he find the spot, is he in her?" I asked, trying to tip my head and see what was happening under the bitch's tail.

"No, I think he found my hand," Fanny laughed, pulling her hand away and releasing the dog. The wolf was left humping air, a stupid look on his face.

"What a pansy," I said. "I thought he had some pride." I was sweaty, dog hair sticking to me, scratch marks up and down my arms, my own hair getting in the way every time I bent my head to see what was going on. "Maybe I'll throw the two of them in the pound and go back to German shepherds." I swatted a fly with a towel which made the husky start barking. The wolf was lying down, panting. "Oh shut up," I snapped. "Jeez, I could kill the both of them."

But Fanny continued laughing. Why was she always laughing? Sort of a high-pitched breathless giggle, even while she talked, making everything she said sound shaky and too fast.

I sat watching the bitch lick under her leg. The wolf closed his eyes to slits like a stupefied animal in a zoo. Finally I said, "We're going to have to get an A-I kit."

"I thought you were giving up."

"I don't ever give up."

Silly girl with her silly mop of hair.

So we came back with the artificial insemination kit. It's a long floppy funnel made of rubber attached at the small end to a hard plastic test tube. Then there's a syringe, and a thin hard plastic tube that goes into the bitch. The wolf's owner made us sign a waiver saying we wouldn't sue if the wolf hurt us in any way. We muzzled him, but he just stood there, his back and butt jerking, while I made the collection, holding the rubber funnel over his penis, my fingers in a ring behind his knot. The little test tube filled with cloudy liquid. Then with the bitch on her back, her butt elevated on Fanny's lap, Fanny put the hard plastic tube into her dog while I kept the sperm warm between my hands. If anyone ever says this wasn't done kosher, I had read exactly what to do. I drew the sperm into the syringe, attached the syringe to the thin tube, and slowly shot the liquid into the bitch. After that we just had to hold her on her back for 20 minutes, the same amount of time the animals might normally be tied, allowing the sperm time to get to their destination. The wolf stood off to the side, his erection hanging eight inches out of him, unable to pull it in until the knot subsided. Fanny stared at him as she held her bitch on her lap. "I had no idea they were so big," she said, strangely. "And so . . . almost human shaped."

I wanted to laugh out loud but didn't. But I couldn't help it, later, when we let the bitch up and immediately there was a puddle of liquid on the ground.

"Oh, puppies!" Fanny said, pretending to pick up microscopic dogs and put them in the palm of her hand. "All our puppies spilled out!"

"They're also all over the front of your pants," I said. The whole crotch area of Fanny's pants, where she'd held the bitch, was damp.

Fanny looked down at herself, touching the wet denim. A minute later she was laughing again, when the husky was pawing at my leg, then rushing to the gate and staring out. Likely she smelled a cat, but Fanny said, "she wants an abortion."

We inseminated the bitch 3 more times, and, as if that was the way dogs were supposed to get pregnant, she started changing shape three weeks later. I told Fanny to keep her inside during the last few weeks, so she wouldn't hurt herself or the puppies charging around the yard, jumping at the fence and chasing airplanes that happened to be flying across.

When the time to whelp came, the husky told us once again that she had no intention of having puppies. The contractions started. We were ready with towels and rubber gloves and gauze and a heating pad, scissors and iodine and surgical soap. We shaved the bitch's underside, prepared the whelping box with blankets, charted her temperature.

The dog kept asking to go outside, then standing in the yard trying to poop, squeezing out a shard, then coming back inside. "She thinks the contractions are the same thing as having to shit," Fanny said. "She's afraid of making a mess inside."

The dog was standing at the bedroom door, sniffing through the crack, then turning to look at us over her shoulder.

"Do you think this dog is *afraid* of anything?" I said.

But afraid or not, the bitch put a halt to her contractions. "She's refusing to have the puppies!" Fanny laughed.

"It's been 45 minutes, they could be dying inside her, call the vet!" I had to shout, it's like she didn't take *anything* seriously.

So while Fanny held the dog on her lap, I drove, weaving in and out of traffic, bursting through red lights and stop signs, half hoping a police car would chase me so I could pull up at the animal hospital and scream "it's an emergency!" at someone who wouldn't *laugh.*

Then it was the dog screaming when the first pup came halfway out of her and stopped there, waiting for the next medically-induced contraction. The little blind thing also opened its mouth and screamed, but silently. We were sitting on a blanket on the floor at the animal hospital. After the first puppy, which the vet took and cleaned up in another room, the pups came too quickly in succession for the bitch to see what they were. By the time she ate the placenta and gnawed through the cord, another contraction was coming, so she never had a chance for that important initial bonding with each pup.

"God, she's more interested in eating the afterbirth than taking care of the pup," I moaned.

"She has her priorities," Fanny said, holding a puppy onto a nipple. We had to do the bitch's job and make sure each pup got its first meal, took its first shit, and could breathe without bubbling.

But, I have to admit, despite the laughing, Fanny seemed to sacrifice everything, at least for a few weeks, to ensure the survival of our eight half-wolves. Her sink was piled with dishes, dirty clothes thrown like pillows on the sofa and chair, her face pale but eye sockets dark and puffy, her house kept overly warm for people but just right for the pups, smelling damp and sour, the washing machine going twice a day to clean the towels and blankets that were quickly soiled by the puppies. Half the time when I arrived in the afternoon, Fanny's hair was matted and dirty, and I would have to tell her to go take a shower, but even then Fanny might simply throw herself across the foot of the bed for an hour first before she dragged herself into the bathroom.

So all the early problems were really *one* problem—it was all because of the one thing the husky bitch *didn't* have on her resume, the one thing I hadn't had the foresight to doubt, the one thing that couldn't be verified in play or behavior tests: the bitch had no maternal instinct. There were nine black puppies, still blind, each sleeping curled in the shape of a kidney bean, five males and four females. Yet, for probably the only time in her life, when the bitch looked at them, there was no spark in her eye, no eagerness, not even curiosity, just sort of a dull glance, when she was willing to look at them at all.

The *physical* problems caused by the bitch's disinterest were easy to solve—Fanny had to put the bitch into the whelping box every hour or two, round the clock, and make her stay there until all the pups had eaten. She had to smear each pup with butter to make the bitch lick and clean their little butts. But if pups and mother don't bond like they're supposed to, they won't look to her as their link to the world. If she doesn't interact with them, play with and discipline them, they'll not only have no pack experience, they won't learn behavior and attitude from her, they won't imitate, they might not gain her spirit and drive.

Before the breeding and during the pregnancy, I went to the library almost every other day, ordered books out of dog magazines, rented videos on wolf pack studies. But no one seemed to know how much of the instinct, personality, energy, boldness, or other traits of the spirit were genetically passed to offspring, and how much was learned. It shouldn't have even mattered: when you have a bitch with *everything* you want, physically and mentally, then if the genetic code doesn't carry the personality, the bitch will still be there as the center of the universe for the pups' first three months and they could learn the traits. For all I knew, the vigor of a bitch's tongue licking them would show the pups her intensity and keenness. But this bitch showed them nothing.

"She told us, from the start," Fanny laughed, despite looking haggard and not changing out of her sweat pants and T-shirt for two weeks because she was sleeping on the sofa, an alarm set to go off every 90 minutes so she could feed the pups. She dozed an hour or 45 minutes at a stretch, day and night, her hand hanging off the sofa and into the whelping box as a thermostat so she'd know if the heating pad was getting too hot or too cold. She was usually up in the afternoon, when I came for several hours to sit beside the pups with a journal so I could note everything they did. "We should've listened to her," Fanny said, her dark-circled eyes staring at the pups with half-lowered lids, "when she didn't want to come into season. She was telling us. She told us all along."

The bitch would bring me a ball or an old sock tied into knots and drop it into my lap, then stand braced and staring at the toy, waiting for it to move so she could pounce and kill it. "You crazy thing," I said, unable to stop my smile, "take care of your damn puppies, will you?"

Fanny bent over her bitch, reaching to pick up the toy. The dog, leaping to grab it back, smacked Fanny under the chin with the top of her head, snapping Fanny's mouth shut. I could hear Fanny's teeth clack together; her head flew back, her hands held her jaw, she made a noise like she'd been punched in the gut, a squeezed sound that seemed to come out her ears. For a second even the pups stopped making their mewing noise. Then Fanny moved like bad animation, from holding her face in both hands, eyes shut, to a hard fist raised over her head, glaring down at the dog, "Damn you to fucking hell!" And the husky bitch actually cowered, ears back, head down, shrinking body. "Oh my god." Fanny's legs folded, she collapsed beside her dog, holding her around the neck, burying her face in the husky's back. "I almost slugged her." She made a sound that wasn't laughing.

But the bitch, despite her neck being heavily yoked by Fanny's arms, was once again staring with ultimate concentration at the toy on the rug. *That's* the resiliency and determination I wanted in these offspring. They were two-and-a-half weeks old. The smallest male had his eyes half open, lifted his head and rested his chin on the back of the sleeping body beside him. A sure sign of dominance, and so early. I turned to point it out to Fanny, but she was flat on her back, limp like a deflated rubber life raft, unconscious on the sofa.

James D. Redwood

LOVE BENEATH THE NAPALM

Mr. Tu leaned forward on his haunches, and with the aid of a trowel, gently dug out a weed which had insinuated itself between two pansies and threatened to choke them. It was late afternoon. A sharp breeze broke from the Helderberg Mountains seven miles away. Winter was coming, and he greatly missed his native village of Long Dien, which would now be entering the long hot dry season. Mr. Tu did not look forward to the death of his flower garden and the eight long months of wait before he could bring it to life again. He shivered in his thin, second-hand flannel jacket, a gift from Mrs. Hai-li, the Chinese owner of the Golden Dragon Restaurant on the corner of Peach Street and Route 138 in downtown Schenectady. She paid Mr. Tu thirty dollars a week to tend the two square boxes which stood beside the stone dragons in front of the restaurant.

"Hello, Uncle," a voice said to his back, in Vietnamese. Mr. Tu arched his neck in surprise. It had been months since anyone had spoken to him, aside from Mrs. Hai-li, and more than a year since he'd heard his own language. He turned.

The girl gave a sharp little cry and stepped back. She placed her hand over her mouth and stared at him, her eyes wide. Mr. Tu's jaw crinkled as he flashed her the resigned little smile he gave everyone. If he had not been peering down at a nice bauhinia flower on the An Loc battlefield when the bomb hit, his eyes would have fried like eggs and he would never have seen the look his face always inflicted on strangers. But then he noticed how much the young lady standing over him resembled Le. She had the same lush black hair, the same doelike, almond-shaped eyes, the same playful smile of a kitten toying with a coil of hemp, now that she had recovered from her shock. Even the tilt of her shoulders was the same as she leaned forward again. Mr. Tu's heart pattered joyfully.

"Why, hello, Little Sister," he said, struggling to keep his voice from quavering. Mr. Tu then spotted the man beside her. He was American, and had looked away, of course.

"I like your flowers," she said. "Wait, Phil," she added in English, tugging her companion's sleeve. The American was big, blond, and handsome, though in Mr. Tu's opinion not as handsome as he himself had once been. Mr. Tu sensed the man's irritation at being stopped from the way his fist tightened around the restaurant door handle.

"Come on," the American growled. "I'm hungry. You can squawk with this guy later."

The girl blushed at her companion's comment and stepped back from Mr. Tu again. The implication that their tongue resembled the talk of chickens would have caused Mr. Tu to blush as well if the plastic surgeon who'd repaired his face after An Loc had left him any color to work with. This man reminded him unpleasantly of his induction training in 1971. The American advisers at the Thu Duc Military School had mocked his beautiful language, made fun of his eyes, his skin the color of Cham drums, his inconsequential stature. Their innuendos about the inadequate size of the Vietnamese male member filled him with humiliation and rage. Mr. Tu glanced at the beautiful girl again. Had she taken this blond ape because of the bulk of his penis?

"Hoa?" the ape said, nudging her arm. His voice whined with impatience, and Mr. Tu felt perversely tempted to goad him.

"So your name is Hoa," he said conversationally, leaning back on his haunches. He tapped his garden box with his trowel. "It's a name I like." He was tired of hearing only the Chinese word for flower.

The girl laughed like a wind chime tinkling nervously in a breeze, and the sound filled Mr. Tu with delight. Mrs. Hai-li carped at him constantly and gave him nothing but scowls.

"I can see that," Hoa said. Mr. Tu was impressed at how quickly she picked up on his implication. This girl was smart as well as pretty, just like Le. Mr. Tu sighed at the memory of his fiancée. He'd met her in 1970, shortly after his father died and he moved to Saigon. Le was studying at the Faculté des Lettres and living with an old aunt in Gia Dinh. Back then Mr. Tu was something to look at, and their courtship blossomed like his pansy patch in summer, until the day he was called up for duty.

Hoa crouched down beside him.

"Did you garden back . . . there?" she asked.

The word *there* coursed through Mr. Tu's veins like a spring flood rushing along the Mekong. He watched as she indolently ran her fingers through the dirt of one of the flower boxes and then carefully straightened out a pansy which had bent in the breeze from the Helderbergs. *A girl from the earth,* he thought with satisfaction, *a true Vietnamese.* Yet what was she doing with this American?

"Not after I went to Saigon," he replied. "The ground wasn't suitable, you see. And—"

He stopped talking. The girl had suddenly snapped her head back over her shoulder. The American was staring at the street. Mr. Tu was disconcerted at the interruption but looked on.

A red Thunderbird convertible with the top down chugged along the street toward them and screeched to a halt just beyond the Golden Dragon. Russet-colored maple leaves whipped up by the little car fluttered to the ground beside a clapboard house across the street. Two teenaged girls in the front seat, a blonde and a redhead, turned their heads and whistled at the handsome American. Hoa leaned toward Phil but then froze. The scowl which had overspread his face when she began to talk to Mr. Tu melted into a big smile. The redhead, who was slightly overweight and had a half-empty bottle of liquor in one hand, jutted her breasts forward in a gesture which Mr. Tu found both vulgar and inviting.

"Hey guys, wanna party?" she crooned, swaying in her seat.

She winked at Phil, who burst into a laugh.

"Later, girlie," he called, giving her a friendly wave. "Save it for dessert."

The redhead giggled, and the convertible took off. Mr. Tu's brow darkened as the woman beside him bit her lip and glanced down at her own tiny breasts. Suddenly she jabbed Mr. Tu's trowel into the potting soil and almost tore off one of the pansies. She threw the trowel down and looked away. Mr. Tu hastily leaned forward to fix the flower, but it flopped forlornly on its side, its neck broken. His heart yearned for the girl. He shared her humiliation as though it was another mark of their national disgrace, like the size of his penis.

The American leered at the Thunderbird as it disappeared up the street. The wind whipped through the man's hair like an autumn breeze through wheat. Mr. Tu sighed. Phil was just the kind of loon who would appeal to a superficial woman like the tramp in the convertible. Such swine never lifted their snouts out of the muck. Mr. Tu eyed Hoa longingly. How could the tow-headed lout *ever* understand this lovely girl who'd seen through his face to the very heart of him? Only the Vietnamese appreciated the pearl within the oyster. But still he was uneasy.

Phil glanced down, and his face tightened in a frown.

"Come on," he said coldly, tapping Hoa's shoulder. "That's enough. Let's eat."

Hoa barely looked at Mr. Tu now.

"Goodbye," she said, but her voice was distant. Mr. Tu gazed regretfully at her as she rose to her feet. He was hoping for another smile, just like Le's, and felt a pang of disappointment when instead she turned and edged close to Phil. Yet he knew she had to keep up appearances, and he took comfort from the fact that she held her body rigid beside the American. Mr. Tu thought of the many conquests of his youth, when women had dropped into his lap like persimmons from an overladen tree. Of course she was standoffish, reluctant to look at him! No woman likes to struggle with her affections.

But she was beginning to fall for him, Mr. Tu felt certain. He could tell that from the way she'd laughed at his little joke about her name. He had a sense of these things. They were both Vietnamese, after all, linked by bonds invisible to the Americans. Mr. Tu felt suddenly exhilarated. His soul had peeked through his blistered skin at her like a crocus through the snow. As he leaned back on his haunches again and watched them enter the restaurant, he realized he was in love.

~ "Let's row out to the middle of the pond," Le said, grabbing his arm.

It was March, 1972. Mr. Tu, twenty-three and crisp in his new lieutenant's uniform, removed his white kid gloves, folded them neatly in half, and slipped them into his pocket. He turned to her and smiled possessively, like all acknowledged lovers, and led her carefully along the dock which jutted into the crescent-shaped water lily pond on the grounds of the Botanical Gardens. It was the trysting place of lovers, but the disastrous Lam Son offensive of the year before had thinned the ranks of males, and solitary females could not take pleasure in a spot like this. Tu and Le had it all to themselves, briefly. He had to report to his unit the next day. A new North Vietnamese offensive was rumored.

When they reached the end of the dock, he unmoored a rowboat, got in, and assisted her to board. He seated her in the stern, sat down amidships, fixed the oars in the rowlocks, and shoved off.

"How I shall miss you!" Le cried, leaning towards him. Tears glittered in her eyes like sun-spotted diamonds glancing off the surface of the lily pond. Their marriage had finally been set for the following month. Le had waited patiently for two years with the old aunt in Gia Dinh for Mr. Tu to finish his training. Now they would have to wait some more.

A doleful-sounding vespers bell clanged in a nearby Buddhist monastery, and Mr. Tu felt a weight upon his heart as heavy as the iron from which it was cast. The bell seemed to toll their final moments together. The sweet scent of jasmine and rare orchids from the greenhouse on the far side of the island toward which they were heading only added to his sadness, and he pulled at the oars with long desolate strokes, like a mourner lugging a funeral barge.

"Don't think about it, my dearest," he said bravely, but Le burst into a torrent of tears. Mr. Tu quickly rowed beneath the Japanese bridge which crossed over to the island and stopped beneath one of its arches. Here she could indulge her sorrow in peace. He made the boat fast against the bank and seated himself beside her. He kissed her eyes, her lips, drank in the warmth of her body, the panting of her breath. She was beautiful, and he was happy and sad at the same time.

"My big strong soldier," she wailed. "How I shall worry about you!"

Mr. Tu nodded grimly and drew her close. In their two years together in Saigon other women had tempted him to kick over the traces, as was only natural with a man of his looks, but Le had managed to hold the reins tight and keep him on course. Never had they imagined she might lose him to the war.

"You will take care, won't you, darling?" she said, her voice choking.

"Of course," he responded, trying to sound cheerful. He hoped she would not notice his trembling, however. He thought of his father, who'd been caught in an airstrike while out tending his rice field on a foot-powered paddy pump. All they found of him afterward was a white powdery residue which looked like the chalk dust on the erasers at the Long Dien village school. Mr. Tu gripped the gunwales hard to stop his shaking. His unit was headed into the Iron Triangle, the jaws of the tiger. Le would have plenty to worry about, and so would he.

"Oh, my handsome one!" she exclaimed, collapsing on his shoulder and breaking down completely. Mr. Tu slumped in his seat. His carefree days were over. She fluttered against his chest like the last bird before winter . . .

~ The wind snapped off the Helderbergs again, and Mr. Tu shuddered and shook off the sad memory. He heard a noise and looked up. Mrs. Hai-li stood over him, staring down.

"What are you still doing here, blockhead?" she asked, her voice shrill. "Take yourself off."

She craned her neck and scanned the sidewalk for customers. Business had fallen off lately, and she blamed it on Mr. Tu's face. People lost their appetite when they saw him. The sidewalk was empty.

She turned back and frowned at him.

"Shove off now, that's enough for tonight," she said, waving him off the stoop with the back of her hand. "You'll frighten the whole neighborhood if you stay here after dark."

Mr. Tu rose reluctantly to his feet. He longingly eyed the restaurant door and thought of the girl Hoa seated somewhere behind it. Would he ever see her again?

"And don't forget that trowel," Mrs. Hai-li barked, pointing to the tool which was barely visible in the dim light. "If it rusts in the damp air, the replacement will come out of your pay."

Mr. Tu attempted to bite his lip. He leaned over and picked up the trowel, gazing fondly at his beloved pansies one last time as he did so. Their ugly little mugs reminded him of his own, and they comforted him in his distress as Mrs. Hai-li continued to berate him even while he trudged sadly away. Why had fate linked him to such a doltish shrew? Once he wouldn't have given her a second thought, but now he had to march to her tune, all because of An Loc. Truly his lot was a hard one.

When he stumbled into his darkened garret a few minutes later and switched on the light, the drabness of his lodgings further dampened his spirits. Rodents pattered behind the plaster, and the wind howled through a window gap covered with cheap masking tape. Boys who lived in the neighborhood had thrown a rock through the window soon after he moved in and then laughed at Mr. Tu's pink hairless skull when it peeped through the jagged hole. Mr. Tu shook his fist at them, but they just laughed harder and strolled away in a leisurely fashion to show they were not afraid of him. Afterward Mr. Tu kept his head covered with a New York Yankees baseball cap, but he still felt aggrieved. The boys were Vietnamese.

The wind whistled through the window crack again, causing Mr. Tu to shiver and fluttering the candle which stood inside a tiny spirit lamp on top of his bureau. He thought how nice it would be to have the girl from the restaurant to warm his bed, and then he stared at the photograph beside the spirit lamp. Le smiled alluringly at him from a painted Chinese background, a sprig of *mai* blossoms in her hand. He'd taken the photo himself, and at the time he was very proud of it. But after he parted from her that last day in Saigon, with the North Vietnamese inexorably closing in, Mr. Tu succumbed to the superstition that cameras took away a person's soul . . .

~ "This is my favorite part," he whispered, leaning over in the crowded movie theater and touching Le's sleeve. It was April 30, 1975. On the wide screen in front of them a tall Chinese warlord, girded for battle, strutted about his palace bedroom, gesticulating wildly at his wife, who stood scowling in the middle of the room, her fists tightened in a bunch. In the far corner the warlord's favorite concubine lay weeping.

"Yes, *thuong anh,*" Le said, nodding. She kept her eyes glued to the screen. "Just let me watch, will you?"

Mr. Tu thrilled with pleasure when she called him her beloved one, words he had not heard since that sad afternoon in the Botanical Gardens three years earlier. Given the way she'd greeted him that morning, he would not have expected it.

She'd shrunk behind the statue of the Virgin Mary in the deserted square outside the National Cathedral to protect herself from the unknown mutant who kept calling out her name and insisting he was her fiancé. Mr. Tu was hurt and chagrined until she remembered his voice. But Le too had changed. She was dressed in a pricy western mini-skirt, her hair curled in false ringlets, her mouth and cheeks painted red as a *Hat Boi* actress's. Still, he had recognized *her* immediately.

A rocket screeched by overhead, close to the theater, and Mr. Tu instinctively ducked. When it hit, his and Le's seats, as well as those of the other patrons who'd come there hoping to escape the war, shook in their sockets, and several people cried out in alarm. Le glanced at him anxiously, and Mr. Tu put his arm around her shoulder to comfort her. They clung to each other and watched the conclusion of "Endless Passion," quaking whenever another rocket hit.

~ Mr. Tu spotted Hoa from the far side of Liberty Street, late in the afternoon, near closing time. She was sitting in a chair by one of the tall library windows, reading something and basking in the rays of the declining sun. The gardener darted between some fast-moving cars and gained the other side of the street. He peeped in at her from several feet away, his heart pounding. With her head bowed over a magazine, her face at an angle, she reminded him of Le even more than she had the evening before. She was dressed in a leather mini-skirt that reached above the knees, and although from the tilt of her head he could not tell if she was wearing makeup, her hair was curled in exactly the same way as his fiancée's. Mr. Tu's heart beat faster as he scurried toward the entrance.

After the movie, Le had insisted on going back alone for some traditional clothes to make it easier for her to blend in with the hordes fleeing the capital. Mrs. Lanh, the madam, was fed up with men and would surely create a scene, she said. She would not be long.

He waited for her on the crowded dock which jutted into the Saigon River at Newport, where the big American ships used to land. Artillery shells pounded the city, and a pall of thick black smoke ringed the metropolis like a funeral wreath. Mr. Tu ran back and forth along the dock, glancing frantically about, mouthing out her name, trying to avoid the bodies trampled in the final rush to freedom and now lying crumpled beneath some crude woven mats. He started peeking to see if Le was among them, but stopped when the third body he came to had a face as mutilated as his own. A boat horn blasted behind him. People yelled at him to come on. Slowly, reluctantly, her name still on his lips, with tears struggling to form beneath the dead skin beside his eyelids, he turned away . . .

~ The librarian date-stamping books behind the checkout desk glared at him as though his face might set off the security alarm, but Mr. Tu glanced only briefly at her as he pushed back the door flap and strode intrepidly toward the stacks. Departing patrons whisked by him, some of them with books crooked under their arms, and paid him hardly any mind. Yet Mr. Tu started to tremble when he saw the row of sunlit windows up ahead and spotted her, poring over her magazine still. Hoa was seated all alone. His feet began to drag, and he froze in his tracks. The dust particles which danced in the air all along the bookshelf separating them seemed to Mr. Tu's distracted mind to be playing with her hair, which had lightened to a beautiful shade of auburn in the glow of the sun. He had difficulty breathing, and might have stayed there forever, just watching her, if a young man impatient for a book on the shelf beside him had not roughly ordered him aside. The man was rude, contemptuous, as though Mr. Tu's face gave him the right to be that way. Mr. Tu winced beneath his skin grafts and stepped uncertainly forward.

"Hello," he murmured, coming up to her. He was embarrassed when she didn't hear him. "Hello," he repeated, so loudly this time she jerked her head up from the page.

"Oh, hi," she said mechanically, and Mr. Tu's heart faltered. Didn't she remember who he was? No one could forget a face like his.

"So you come here also," she added, but her tone was flat, devoid of interest. She gazed at a bookshelf behind him. Mr. Tu knew he should leap at the opening which lay before him like a dropped handkerchief in the movies, but just at that moment his Adam's apple snarled up his windpipe and his courage flagged. The girl shrugged and lowered her eyes again. She flipped the magazine page, and Mr. Tu heard the paper snap as if she was angry at it.

He shifted awkwardly on his feet. Now that he was standing over her, he didn't have the slightest idea what to say. Hoa remained silent.

"May I join you?" he asked at last, indicating a chair across from her. She flicked her hand, impatiently it seemed, and Mr. Tu settled in and tried to make himself comfortable. But instead he became quite nervous as he stared at the beautiful bowed head and the tantalizing body opposite him, which had stiffened since he sat down. Occasionally, she glanced up at the bookshelf again, but not at him. Mr. Tu started to sweat, and the thought that she might smell him filled him with horror. His mouth went dry, and what finally emerged from his throat was little more than a croak.

"Aren't you glad to see me, Miss Hoa?"

She looked at him and smiled slightly, for the first time. Mr. Tu was encouraged.

"Oh, you remembered my name."

"How could I forget it?" he blurted out.

Her face immediately darkened, and Mr. Tu's hand jerked spasmodically on his chair arm. He was going too fast. She was trying to sort out her feelings for him, and he had to proceed cautiously.

"I work with flowers, remember," he added, trying to sound casual.

"Ah, yes. So you do." But she shrugged a second time.

Mr. Tu decided to hazard a smile, but stopped midway, afraid his defective face muscles might turn it into a sneer. For a moment he almost envied his father's fate. No one had been indifferent to the little pile of dust which was heaped up in the middle of the old man's rice field and which was virtually indistinguishable from the powdered fertilizer USAID had given him to increase his crop yield. It was the talk of Long Dien village for months.

The sound of raucous laughter suddenly came from behind the bookshelves, and Hoa popped her head up once more and frowned in its direction. The laughter was followed by giggling, then the hurried whisper of voices, one male, one female. Hoa looked across at Mr. Tu, visibly upset. He summoned up all his courage and flashed her the most engaging smile of which his blackened lips were capable. His smiles had cheered Le through many a troubled time. Hoa trembled slightly, and Mr. Tu felt emboldened. But his skin crinkled like a strip of tanning leather when he spoke again.

"Would you like to get a coffee somewhere?" he squeaked. He sank back down, embarrassed.

She twitched as though someone had yanked a rope around her neck.

"With *you?*" she said, her voice barely above a whisper.

She quickly shook her head, but Mr. Tu did not lose heart. He'd picked up the breathlessness of her reply, the rapid twittering of her fingers on the page. Women were programmed to demur, then to yield. He waited.

"I can't," she said, glancing anxiously at the bookshelves yet again.

Mr. Tu waved his hand as though her refusal was only to be expected. He tried to fix her with his eyes, those beautiful unscarred eyes which the gods had spared from the napalm at An Loc. Le had melted at the sight of them.

"Well," he said, attempting to keep his voice steady, "the Stockade Diner's just up the street."

She peered at him.

"But you're so . . . different," she said.

Mr. Tu's heart finally sank within him. He thought of Mrs. Hai-li, who never looked him straight on, as though his face might blind her like a solar eclipse.

"You think I'm ugly, don't you?" he said feebly, unable to look at *her* now. He felt as insignificant as a mound of dust.

The laughter resumed behind the bookshelves. Hoa's magazine abruptly snapped shut, and Mr. Tu lifted his head. The girl darted to her feet and moved away from him.

"You're *Vietnamese,*" she said, her voice filled with sudden scorn. Her eyes were glued to the bookracks. Mr. Tu's jaw dropped as far as it was capable.

"But . . . so are *you,*" he stammered, his face contorting itself into something resembling a look of confusion.

She glared down at him and shook her head vehemently.

"That was before," she said. "I want to forget all about that now, and you remind me of—"

A rustling came from the stacks, and Hoa paused in mid-sentence. Mr. Tu felt angry and hurt. He shot to his feet.

"Of *what?*" he said, his voice rising. He tried to grab her hand, but she drew away from him. "What do I remind you of?"

She didn't answer, for just at that moment Phil emerged from behind the bookshelf. Mr. Tu turned and spotted a wisp of red hair disappear in the direction of the checkout counter. Hoa flitted to the American's side. She scowled suspiciously at him and craned her neck in the direction of the exit. Phil grasped her roughly by the arm and twisted her around.

"Ow!" she yelped, trying to disengage herself. "You're hurting me!"

In spite of her curious remarks to him Mr. Tu stepped gallantly forward. Only her own people could help her in such a predicament.

"Be gentle with her, young man," he admonished, wagging a stern finger at the American.

Phil stared at him and then gaped at Hoa.

"What the fuck is this bird talking about?" he demanded. All of a sudden, Hoa wrenched free from him and turned on Mr. Tu.

"This is *our* business, so stay out of it!" she yelled. "And yes, you're right. You *are* ugly," she added savagely. "I would never go out with *you!*"

Mr. Tu was astounded. Never had Le treated him like this, nor any of the other ladies who had swooned over him in his youth. He drew himself up proudly in front of her.

"And I would never be seen with a whore like *you,* either," he snapped, tossing his head self-righteously and twisting his face into what he truly intended to be a sneer this time.

Hoa turned white and trembled all over. In a single bound she sprang to Mr. Tu, and with the swiftness of lightning she raised her hand and slapped him hard across the face. Mr. Tu's skin smarted as though it had been set on fire a second time. He felt dizzy, disoriented, and the tears which had been so many years in coming burst from his eyes at last. In his blindness the angry young woman with her fist still raised looked as though she stood at the edge of another world, beckoning for him to come back to her. Mr. Tu stretched his hand out and tried to call her name, but no sound emerged from his throat. He staggered against the chair he'd been sitting in and gingerly lowered himself into it. He bowed his head to calm his nerves. When he looked up again, a minute later, he was alone.

Mr. Tu's heart felt as thick and heavy as lead. His face burned fiercely still, and the pain, as it settled deep inside him, was much more intense than it had been the first time, when all he lost was a battle. A librarian began to switch off the lights in the stacks. She spotted Mr. Tu and started. Slowly he rose from his chair.

Ira Sadoff

AT THE MOVIES

Willie Houghton's father had provided the cash to celebrate the Reeses' thirtieth anniversary: all that was required of Willie was, sometime during their two-week vacation, to give his friend Umberto, owner of his father's favorite London restaurant, his best regards. But Elizabeth and Willie, who'd been saving for years to go to England, couldn't even negotiate that task with grace.

"He doesn't have that much money left. I don't want to owe my father anything," Willie said.

"He left you thirty years ago: how does one meal at a chic restaurant even the score?"

"He just wants to prove he was elegant and had good taste."

"So let him. Luxuriate in it. Take advantage, for once."

Elizabeth was strong-willed, and, after she made reservations, enlisting Peter and Ruth in her cause, Willie reluctantly agreed to go. Peter Reese taught at the Trinity School in Kensington, and since the Reeses rarely made it back to the States, they made an occasion of their last night in England, planning a first run movie and a big, expensive meal. Perdido's, complete with a resident violinist and a six foot long desert tray, was heavy on atmosphere, decorated with gold lame wallpaper, gold-plated chandeliers, palm front green rugs, chartreuse tablecloths and pink napkins with embroidered flowers. "Very subtle color scheme, " Peter said. "Very classy."

"Well, Willie's father was in show business," Elizabeth said.

"What's that supposed to mean?" Willie asked.

"We'll have none of that on our anniversary," Ruth said, wagging her finger at both of them. "Families are verboten. Especially Willie's family."

"That's right," Elizabeth laughed. "Don't get him started." She looked at Willie, turned down her lower lip and patted his hand. "Don't get sulky, baby. I know you keep thinking of your dad."

It was at Perdido's where every day Willie's father used to eat lunch with his former second wife, who'd become, in her third marriage, the Countess Berevka. After their meal, graphically and in great detail, Willie's father told him how he'd brought her back to his tiny room above the restaurant, licked the inside of her thighs and recited the poems of the Hungarian poet, Istvan Agh, a particular favorite of his, since no one else had ever heard of him. The Countess still claimed to love Willie's father, of course; but when he could no longer afford her, she was forced to leave him. She did generously continue to shower him with raincoats, Chopin recordings and expensive chocolates discarded by the exiled Count, and promised Willie's father that as soon as he got "back on his feet" she'd leave his Royal highness and they'd move back to the apartment above Perdido's, where they'd restore their resplendent life.

Willie looked at Elizabeth as she described her declining civil rights practice to their friends. Her firm had begun to take on foreclosures and divorces. "What can you do?" She shook her head. "It's the nineties." She was trying out a new hairstyle, one of those short, asymmetrical cuts, dying her hair a popular sienna shade no one had ever seen on a natural scalp. "It's dramatic," she'd claimed. "And I'm not going to lose clients to a pushy thirty-year old." But the years had taken their toll on her. The lines under her eyes, though pencil thin, were visible through her make-up and she'd lost enough weight so her face looked too tight, almost skeletal. And when pushed into a corner, she could use her tongue like a street-wise city kid, which she was not.

For an antipasto they ordered braised eggplant and peppers (the foccacio never arrived, but Willie was the only one who noticed), a salad of goat cheese and greens, rigatoni with capers, prosciutto and wild mushrooms, hand-made ravioli with pesto, a thin pizza of nicoise olives, fresh tomatoes, hot peppers and fontina. They splurged on a good Barolo and had one too many deserts: zabaliognies and chocolate cheese cakes.

"Fortunately," Peter said, loosening his belt, "Willie's father had an excellent palate!"

"Do you remember the Italian restaurant in Jersey?" Willie asked. "We were at some conference, completely lost, and we just drifted in by accident. There was a line half a block long, but Peter told the maitre'd he was a second cousin of the owner and they sat us right down."

"I have some Italian blood," Peter said, laughing. "It's possible."

"That was a great restaurant. God," Elizabeth said, "It's so boring without you. We need you. The goddamned country needs you."

"I'm happy not to be there," Peter said. The two couples shared a long political history: demonstrations, election campaigns, petitions and the like, and though they'd softened their rhetoric, they still believed in terms like "the oppressed" and "the oppressor." "The country's gone to shit. I couldn't turn on the television."

"But," Ruth said, smiling, "he can't keep from reading three newspapers a day either."

"I remember an eggplant parmesan to kill for," Willie said. "Of course we were all against killing."

"I'd like to say it was just the ball scores," Peter said. "But it *is* my country."

Elizabeth raised her glass, and, in a voice almost querulous, said, "You can have it, Peter. I bequeath it to you."

"Hon, we're still working hard," Willie said. But she kept on talking about how she hated television and how she hated the way the media folded up and died, how the left was so laughable now it was beneath parody. Willie managed to interject a story about how early in their marriage, the last time they were in London, Elizabeth and Willie had accidentally run into a May Day parade and joined it, thinking it was a labor strike. They waved flags and passed around flasks of vodka until they passed out on a tram.

After they'd finished off their second bottle of wine, Peter and Ruth chimed in, and soon they were exchanging stories about their respective courtships. Elizabeth said, "He was so attractive I couldn't keep my hands off him."

"Was? What do you mean *was?*"

"After twenty years of marriage, darling, I can keep my hands off almost anyone."

"Let's hope so," Willie said. She knew what he meant.

"My husband," Elizabeth said. "The Last Romantic. Every casual remark stings to the core. He makes Young Werther look like . . . who's that guy on TV with the smile plastered on his face?"

"Willard Scott? Chuck Wooley?" Ruth shook her head. "Did you guys settle on who's picking up the tab? If we're paying, I'm not ordering another round of expresso and biscoti."

Elizabeth stared at Willie and tilted her head. Willie wanted to say that it didn't seem to matter that it was his father's money, that he was the one who would have to deal with taking his gift, but the issue had apparently already been settled. "Well, love, you persuaded me," Willie said. "On one condition: you tell the waiter not to charge us for our missing foccacio. I hate hassling about money."

"I know you do," Elizabeth said, rolling her eyes. "Sometimes I think you'd be happy if you got an allowance and left *all* the bill paying to me."

"You bet. I also don't like to be cheated."

Elizabeth stared at Willie and snapped, "So the hands-off remark really stung, didn't it?"

"Since this bill's on my father," Willie said, "we can forget it, unload our pounds some other way."

"After this meal," Ruth said, holding her stomach, "we'll have a lot to unload."

They were sipping their expresso when Umberto arrived, making his rounds of the tables to be sure the paying customers were satisfied with their meals. Umberto wore a cream-colored silk shirt with the top three buttons opened: a Janus-like medallion and a cross hung from his hairless chest and was accompanied by a number of gold chains varying in width from wire thin to the thickness of a garter snake. He was slightly overweight, he had thick steely-gray hair and was sprightly in his step, so one was left with the impression of a boy inside a middle-aged man's body.

When Elizabeth pointed at Willie and said, "He's his father's son," Willie cringed. But Umberto's expression brightened, as if someone had turned up the volume on an old radio. "Ah, your father and I. How we used to confide in each other." So slight was his Italian accent that if you didn't listen for his syntax you'd have sworn he'd been born and bred in England. "My buddy," he said and brought his fist to his heart. "We used to share the mistresses, you know. And like you," he chuckled, surveying the empty plates on the table, "he had a taste for the finer things in life." Umberto must have seen making his customers laugh as part of his job. "It was a tragedy of course, how the Countess died, how she ascended before he had a chance to win her back. She used to come in here with her husband for dinner. She was very different with him. There was no, how do you say it, *joi de vivre* in her face. It was a job, being married to him." Then, turning away from the women, draping his arm over Willie's shoulder and bending toward him, he almost whispered, "She was some piece of ass."

Umberto picked up the tab without blinking, scribbled a note for Willie's father's edification about the good old days, then removed the thinnest chain from his neck, wrapped it in the napkin and handed it to Willie. "I know he's going through hard times. Let him know I haven't forgotten."

After Umberto left, Peter asked, "Could you read the inscription on his medallion?"

"Very elegant," Ruth said. They all laughed. "But you know what I don't understand? How did a man like your father,"—Ruth had three grown children of her own—"a womanizer, and—I don't know how else to say it—a shameless materialist, end up with someone like you for a son?"

Willie thought for a moment. "I've spent my whole life defending against being him." Elizabeth reached over and held his hand. Tightly. "Thank you," Willie said, with a tremor in his voice. "Thank you both."

"Don't thank me," Elizabeth said, trying to lighten the moment. "I only *work* here."

The theater was only three blocks from Perdido's. The Reeses walked ahead of the Houghtons, holding hands. It occurred to Willie to ask Elizabeth why she'd been so cranky in the restaurant. Something had gone wrong in between the time they'd left for London and the moment they sat down at the restaurant, or between the argument over who'd pay for the meal and Umberto's theatrical blessing, or between the good, solid, loving years of marriage and the unforgiving present. In between her childhood and their last night together, something had gone wrong. Willie knew, even then, whatever it was, he could not fix it. One thing was certain: three city blocks wouldn't have even given them time to begin to figure things out. He settled for, "Babes, are you OK?" and she nodded slightly, yes, and kept walking.

At the movies, Ruth and Peter sat between them: it just worked out that way. As they walked in, Willie remembered hearing some groans from behind them, vague murmuring, thinking, oddly, they must know we're Americans. The film was an Epic, in French, with sweeping landscapes and wonderful acting by Philip Noiret. But, all the while Willie kept thinking of a little town in Oregon, the story his wife had begun at the restaurant about how they'd met at a demonstration against the Vietnam War. There had been only twelve of them—it was early 1964—and they'd endured a lot of heckling and jostling from other students. They all looked so clean-cut, Willie recalled, in their white oxford shirts and khaki pants. His uniform was the obligatory blue work shirt and jeans. When a few of the fraternity boys surrounded him and when one of them began to push and curse him on the picket line, Elizabeth stepped in between them. "If you want to push somebody, big man, push me," she said. "Come on, Gonad brains: you're brave enough to push a woman."

The boy with the seventeen-inch neck and crew cut stared directly through her. "You don't look like a woman."

"Why don't you boys sign up?" she said. "You won't have to worry about such complicated distinctions."

Naturally they went for Willie. Two of them grabbed his arms and twisted them behind his back hard enough so he fell to his knees; then the third one punched Willie in the stomach until he collapsed. Then they walked away, snarling.

"Thank you," Willie said to Elizabeth as she stood over him and held his hand. "Next time you wise off I hope you'll wait till after I'm out of thug range."

"I'm sorry," she laughed, and Willie remembered the next twelve hours as if they'd lived them in slow motion. They walked all around town, ate jelly donuts heartily under the florescent lamps of Waldo's Diner, sat for hours at an all-night coffee house drinking cafe-au-lait, listening to Richard Farina's fractious guitar, interrogating each other about their majors, their families, their political commitments, naming all their past lovers and diagnosing what went wrong with each—if, Willie wondered, the word could still be used—relationship. The most touching story, and it was a story she'd never again repeat, occurred when she was sixteen, the night her own recently divorced father took Elizabeth's younger, prettier sister (that's what her mother used to say) out to dinner. Adrienne wore Elizabeth's prom dress, and her father pinned a carnation on the strapless organdy gown while Elizabeth silently watched. She waited by her bedroom window till almost one a.m. for him to drop Adrienne off. It was a scene that hurt Willie's heart even now to recall it, but he could never allude to the story again. She had to do a laundry, so they went to her apartment over the movie house and Willie watched her gather her pink underwear from under the bed and from the various chairs, looked at her poster reproductions of Goya's paintings, and he glanced at her shelf of books while she was in the bathroom, sighing in relief when he found Camus and Dostoevsky.

They watched her clothes tumble in the dryer as if watching the Academy Awards, and then, in the middle of the laundromat, somewhere near dawn, Willie remembered how she cried when she talked about her brother, who'd just enlisted in the Navy and was being sent to Vietnam in a week and how he refused to speak to her because she was so unpatriotic. They even read Ho Chi Minh's and Robert Bly's poetry aloud to each other on her bed. And Willie held her in his arms, not knowing what else to do, loving her even then, telling her how they would end the War.

"I thought I was going to be a poet," Willie told Peter and Ruth.

"Who didn't?" Elizabeth said. Willie remembered having told the story of their romance many times with great joy and gentle irony, but as Elizabeth told it this night, before the movies, he couldn't forgive the smugness of it, the banality of their being just two kids out of thousands who'd lived out, unselfconsciously, the script of their age.

By this time Willie had lost whatever slim hold he'd had on the movie's plot: now the actors were walking through debris in the aftermath of a great battle in World War I. A period piece, he thought, complete with bodies strewn over the Bordeaux hillsides, by the old grape vines. Though he knew his feelings bruised too easily, he couldn't stop thinking about how after he'd confessed the power his father still held over him, Elizabeth had said, "Don't thank me, I only work here." Had she picked up Umberto's saying that being married to the count had been work for the countess? Did she really think that attending to his feelings was that much work? He excused himself to go to the lobby, then did the most childish thing: in passing, he stepped on his wife's foot, wanting her to notice, to see how pained and confused he felt; she looked up briefly, shook her head and went back to the movie. Willie whispered to Peter, "I'm going to the bathroom."

And he did go to the bathroom, mostly to find a distracting, quiet place. In the lobby, for three bucks, he bought his first pack of cigarettes in years and smoked three of them consecutively, until he felt dizzy and a tart numbness on his tongue. Then he heard an elderly and high-pitched woman's voice, tinged with an accent, Hungarian or Viennese, with lots of lingering around the guttural consonants. "Whose fault do you suppose it is, this noise?"

Her voice was followed by the creaking sound of metal on wood, a wheel, and the uh-uh-uh of a stammering male voice. Then Willie saw them both: an older woman and old man in a wheelchair, his head tilted by some paralysis, his arms waving in the air like an out-of-synch conductor. And behind them, equipped with a flashlight, the sixteen-year-old usher was hanging his head, mumbling.

"But madam," the boy said, "he was creating a disturbance. All I can do is get the manager."

"Well get him then," she said. She wore a fox stole (the fox was curled around the breast of her obsolete navy blue pin-striped suit) the exact color of her dyed hair. She was heavy set, and though she must have been only five-six or seven, she looked much taller. Her face was intensely red and she looked around the lobby for anyone who might stand in her way. The old man in the wheelchair, however, was now moving on his own. He had a steel band around his forehead, similar to those doctors wear when they look into your eyes, but attached to this band was a pointer he could push by dropping his head down or turning it left or right. With these motions he could reach a lever that operated the motor in his wheelchair. He began to utter the most violent human moans as he worked the lever, as if someone were beating him, and his jaw fluttered from left to right and his tiny arms spun in circles. He had no legs. The wheelchair let out the low hum of a toy crane, but the noise was constant and, coupled with the young man's moans, factory-like.

Soon, except for them and Willie, the lobby was empty. When the woman looked over at Willie and sneered, he put out his cigarette. "If this happened in the States," she said, "the owner of this theater would lose his license." Willie shrugged. "This is his only entertainment. If he lets out a sound every fifteen minutes he's no worse than the couple talking in front of me. You know what they were saying? They said, 'I wish I had those boots.' Dead bodies everywhere, all of Europe is changed forever, and they admire the lieutenant's boots. Shame." She caught up to the old man, took a handkerchief out of her purse and wiped his chin. "How would you like to be him?" she asked. She asked Willie, because he was the only one left. "Where is the damn manager?" she said. "I could smash something."

But there was nothing to smash, and ten minutes later, after she stood at attention in a corner of the lobby, her face tilting toward the ceiling, her hands gripping the handles of the wheelchair so the old man wouldn't go too far afield, they walked toward the front door of the theater.

Willie looked at the old man, his atrophied body. What could he do for him that she wasn't already doing? He turned away as they passed, half-ashamed, half afraid they'd see whatever expression appeared on his face. No, indeed, Willie thought, he would not like to be like him.

At the end of the movie, when Elizabeth and the Reeses came out, Willie asked, "How was it? How did it end?"

"Badly, of course," Ruth said. "He decides to stay in the Army."

"The cinematography was amazing," Peter said.

"You missed a good movie," Elizabeth said, smirking.

Willie said nothing. But as they walked out into the London air he lagged behind his friends until he saw the usher and the manager, leaning against a wall, laughing and smoking. He went up to them and shook his fist. "It's disgraceful," he said. "How could you treat a human being like that? Answer me." He cornered them, sticking his finger in the manager's face. "How could you?"

A crowd had gathered around them. Willie heard that murmuring sound again. After a moment Elizabeth took his hand and silently dragged him away. Willie's friends stared at him. Finally, a few blocks later, Peter said, "Are you all right?"

"Mind your own business," Ruth said. They made it to their hotel silently but safely, and not before Willie made them backtrack, to take one last look at Perdido's, or, more accurately, at his father's second-story apartment. He tried to place him there, in the window which was closed, with the lights off, the night his countess did not come back. Did his father regret, for one moment, leaving him?

Willie and Elizabeth said good-bye to their friends in the lobby, knowing it would be a long time before they'd see them again, before they could make the evening up to them. Then Elizabeth and Willie got into bed and Willie prayed they would just, for one night, be quiet. Do we need to hear the accusations, the who did what to whom and when, how he or she could never please the other, how that time when he saw how she looked at that other man, or the time he said that horrible thing about her mother, or how he couldn't bear that staccato unforgiving voice of hers, or what gave him the right . . ., or whose fault it was they never had . . ., or any of the blanks that are filled in on a daily basis whenever two people promise their hearts to each other until the promise becomes a large and breathing thing, almost a person, standing between them, chiding them? No, and it is not necessary to say that when he closed his eyes he tried to remember all the kindnesses and care that had passed between them over the years, the gifts and the gasps of pleasure. No, Willie would have simply rather turned out the lights and listened to the dim street noise of London, the random sirens and voices, begging and refusing, arguing and whispering. But Elizabeth couldn't resist murmuring, almost under her breath, "You're such a professional victim."

After they fought, after they said everything that shouldn't have been said, they undressed in separate rooms. Willie's insides felt as if they had been rubbed with a scrubbing brush and he assumed the same could be said of Elizabeth. Neither could sleep; they rolled around from side to side, and finally ended up staring straight up at the ceiling without touching. Finally she took his hand and said, "Let's make up. We're both under a lot of pressure."

Willie turned his back to her and pulled up the covers. He couldn't help wanting her to apologize, to let him know she understood how painful it had been for him, that having his father back in his life had brought back a flood of feelings out of his control, and to acknowledge, to say at last, that no matter how disappointed she was in Willie, how disappointed they were in each other, how they'd wounded each other, wittingly and unwittingly, they could still be tender. When they woke up, they said nothing. They went back home and, for a while, tentatively, almost peacefully, they lived together. But nothing changed until, in a final flurry of mutual rage, Willie packed his bags.

Much later he wrote his father a note, thanking him, finally, for the wonderful meal, writing out a check giving him back his money. Willie tried to remember everything they ate and the nice things Umberto said about his father, wrote them down dutifully, then mailed the letter and the gift. Then he closed his eyes and remembered hating how, at the restaurant, his wife, his ex-wife, had called him, in that bristly voice of hers, "Darling." But he also remembered the scent of good garlic, the rich chocolate cake that stuck to the roof of his mouth, the oak of the Barolo, the laughter of his friends and the creaking sound of the bed over Perdido's, that ghostly joy accompanied by poetry.

Frances Sherwood

YOUR THIN GRANDMOTHER

Thanksgiving was when she asked me. We were in the kitchen, she on a stool by my counter, I rinsing dishes to put in the dishwasher and weary from making the pies—a pumpkin, a pecan, and a custard-coconut from a Bisquick recipe and doing the table á la *Family Circle*—corn cobs dressed as powwow Indians, their eyes bright red tacks, swatches of green felt wrapped around for miniature blankets, pilgrims from wooden spools found at the Goodwill.

"Like drive me to the Women's Clinic, like tomorrow?" Nina asked.

Nina and her family—Mark, and their two sons, Dali and Duchamp—had been responsible for the turkey. They planned to roast it in a hole in their backyard Hawaiian luau-style. I could have told them our Indiana ground was too frozen in November for a pit, but no, like 49ers intent on gold, the two boys took turns with a pickax, the pale carcass wrapped in tin foil patiently lying on the ground beside them. At the last minute, they had to throw the cold bird into the oven turned full blast, burning the skin to a crisp, leaving the inside bloody raw, delivering it, Happy Thanksgiving, with a bottle of blueberry schnapps. I ate it faithfully. My husband, John, and my daughters didn't.

"The Clinic?" Naturally, the men were in the den watching the game. Kids were somewhere and Francisco, Nina's tenant, had ambled over to join the guys with a hardy ho-ho. He had done the turkey thing, he said at his mother's, but was hungry for dessert, a night cap.

"I love you, Connie," Francisco cooed. "Like a Mother, and Nina . . . like a . . ." He wiggled his eyebrows provocatively, grabbing cookies like a bear fattening up for a long winter's nap.

"Are you escorting at the Clinic, Nina, is that why you want me to go with you?"

"Not exactly."

I had read in the *Telegram Gazette* that The Young Christians were having a marathon picketing at the clinic the day after Thanksgiving. Volunteers were needed to shepherd clients in from the parking lot.

"Counseling?"

"Nope. You're my friend, aren't you? Jesus Christ, Connie, it's post Roe versus Wade."

Barely post Roe versus Wade. We were in the early 90s. To Nina, history started in the late 60s, the heyday of the "Movement"—Berkeley, Ann

Arbor, Madison. The most I did during those exciting times was go to Catholic grammar school in my pleated skirt, participate in Spelling Bees. Now in Worcester, I helped out at the Rescue Mission, contributed conscientiously to the local PBS station in Massachusetts during pledge week. "Everything will be all right," we could hear one of her sons, Duchamp, singing from upstairs, but of course, Bob Marley was dead of cancer. Duchamp, wearing a spiked dog collar, a reggae tam, and one dripping earring looked like a grown boy nostalgic for dress-up games. Nina wore the other one of the pair of earrings, explaining that they were in son/mother matching outfits. My husband, John, was not amused. They're our next door neighbors, I had justified, be a sport.

"Is Mark using the car, Nina? Can't you use the bread truck?" It seemed that I wouldn't be able to get all the dishes in the dishwasher, would have to do it in two shifts.

"Mark is in a mood, and I won't be well enough." Nina was fiddling with her wire-framed glasses, rubbing the lens on her sweat shirt, holding them up to the light.

Mark was prone to depression through association, Nina genetically inclined. Every afternoon, after her bread route was over, she arrived on my doorstep to deliver the state of the union address, updating me on her battle with the Big D, no details withheld. Of course, there were times I was not in a great mood myself, but it never got to the dramatic extent Nina experienced. My daughters, Sophia and Theresa, teenage Curious Georges, using John's binoculars for bird watching, were able to keep tabs on additional doings and ditties next door since Nina and Mark did not bother with bourgeois amenities such as shades or curtains. Nina liked to say: My life is an open book, take no prisoners. My life was an open book, too, but not an exciting one. At six in the morning, if they were ambitious enough, my two girls could catch Nina and Mark hopping into their big, square bread trucks, twin, rusty red missiles. Side by side, barreling out to the bread warehouse, they picked up the loaves to deliver to supermarkets in the area before the first customer. Nina said she liked to work for her bread like a real person.

"Francisco will not be able to drive either."

Francisco, the tenant, had joined the men in the den.

"Since when has Cat-man-do not been well enough to drive? What am I missing here?"

"Shell-shock."

I thought perhaps Francisco's sleepy ways had something to do with marijuana. The one time I tried it, at Nina's insistence, I wanted to lie down in the middle of the day. Anyway, Nina and Mark let Francisco, a Conceptual Artist, live free of charge in exchange for fixing the basement up. Which he was slow at because his creative time was best spent constructing installations of Styrofoam named after great lovers, Palo and Francisca, Eloise and Abelard, Romeo and Juliet, a series to be submitted to the Whitney Biannual. Nina had to explain to me what an honor that would be, and how talented Francisco was, for I, not knowledgeable about art, mainly viewed him as a serious keeper of cats—twenty, not counting drop-ins for meals and mating—himself resembling his brood mare, Beany, with his droopy underbelly and a sleepy, stupid smile.

"Cats don't care," Francisco once informed me. "They even do it with their kids."

"I didn't know Francisco was interested in 'Woman's Right to Her Body.'" I could see something would have to be done with the turkey leftovers. I could chop them, fry them with onions and potatoes, make soup out of them, or throw them out the window.

"Hell, Connie, Francisco is the prime suspect." Nina gave me a satisfied little smirk.

I opened a cupboard, stared hard at my everyday china thinking of the years of meals, breakfast, lunch and dinner, eggs and sandwiches, casseroles, a steady march to the nearest graveyard. My husband was allergic to nuts, my daughter, Sophia, was lactose intolerant, and Theresa was on Atkins. I read about diets in magazines. Nina said it was a state of mind, said I had to think thin.

"Are you saying I'm too over the hill for birth control, Connie? Francisco is really cute in the buff, you know."

"Is that so?" I was not a very good judge of male beauty. But I admired Nina's energy. My husband and I had been married for over seventeen years.

"It will only take an hour max; you can get back in time for your soaps."

"Thanks." I have never watched a soap opera in my life except on Masterpiece Theater, and Nina knew it.

The roar of a touchdown emanating from the den, lapped into the kitchen. Nina pushed her glasses on the top of her head, gave me her nearsighted look. "Remember that Hemingway story, 'White Elephants,' when the guy is trying to convince the girl to do it, a little air in, out. No Biggie. Zip, zap."

"But, the guy in the Hemingway story didn't know what he was talking about, Nina, and the girl. . . . The *girl* in the story was scared."

"Be a pal, Connie."

"There must be somebody else you can ask, Nina."

"You're my best friend, right? Right?"

"I am your friend.

"So what's the problem? It's not like you are doing it yourself."

"It's just that . . ."

"You practice birth control, right."

"Yes."

"Do you tell your priest?"

"Of course not."

"Well then."

I looked closely at Nina, trying to see pregnancy softening her face, filling out her body, but she was as thin and girlish as ever, her sharp face cutting the air like scissors through paper. She still wore bangs, a high ponytail, but most of all, she was eager, forever the earnest graduate student she was once. Keeping her dissertation, she recounted to me, during those precomputer days, in the fridge against fire, in a safety deposit box against theft, and under the bed to slip out at a convenient moment to show off to admirers. Speaking of which she slept with everybody on her thesis committee, which is, she confided, what people did in those days.

"Even the women?" I had asked, thrilled. Nina's area of study at Berkeley was Early Childhood Development and I couldn't imagine a womenless Dissertation Committee.

"Thighs were in," Nina went on. "We looked like drum majorettes in our miniskirts. A bump, a bump, a bump, bump, bump."

Despite the fact that she was my senior by a good ten years, Nina *could* be imagined as a majorette in white boots with tassels on them or as a kid jump-roping red hot peppers till she fell from exhaustion, or as a Girl Scout honor bright, her beret slightly askew, a devilish glint in her eye. She put her coffee cup down on my butcher block kitchen table from Sonoma-Williams. Material things, she once told me, will possess you, and I knew she was right. She picked her furniture at St. Vincent De Paul, wore castoffs. All her possessions, which she said were merely temporary were recycled, and each item was rich in history, the rings on her table, the scuffs on her chairs, the spots on her mattress, her books from the library sale. My husband, John, did not share my admiration, said he didn't know how they could live that way. Even the washer and dryer in the basement, in Francisco's "apartment" amid the cat litter containers, were from the used appliance store.

"God will reward you for your good deed."

"Sure."

I didn't sleep a wink that night. Around two, I slipped out of bed, drove to the Holy Cross campus in my robe, went to their church because all other Catholic churches in town were locked. But Our Lady, overseeing her corner of candles in serene alabaster, cloaked in baby blue, although available, offered small comfort. A guard asked what I was doing there.

"Praying," I answered.

I was praying for the usual things, Nina and her family, and also, a kind of dispensation, if you will, for I would be aiding and abetting the enemy, going against policy, practice, all that I had been taught and a good deal of what I felt. My last prayer was that I wouldn't see Father Michael or anybody else from my church.

My luck, the next day, there were some familiar faces among The Young Christians. Out in force, they were wearing choir robes, some dragging heavy crosses and others carrying big pickle jars of diluted catsup, or maybe it was real blood. Nobody could get through, although standing in the horseshoe shaped parking lot, not knowing whom to serve and protect, was a team of Worcester's Finest. The "Woman's Right to her Body Coalition," in a half crouch position, arms linked, legs together so that nobody could charge in from the ranks of Young Christians to kill a doctor, surrounded the building and were chanting in unison:

"Hey, hey, what do you say? Coat-hangers make the day?"

As we approached, a Young Christian, a middle aged man, lunged at us. "Murderer, murderer," he spat.

"Racist, misogynist fascist," Nina taunted back.

The Woman's Body Coalition chorused: "Five, six, seven, eight, go home and masturbate."

Francisco looked like he wished he had thought of that earlier.

"Maybe we should go home."

"Shut up, Francisco," Nina said.

Francisco—Mr. Cool Cat, the ogre under the bridge, who goes there? Which is where it probably happened when Nina came down to do the laundry. Nina didn't fold anything or believe in ironing. I wish I could be less obsessive about wrinkles. Anyway, they must have "done it" amid the dunes of cat crap and shadowed by the piled cardboard boxes, the cat condos. If they hadn't used the basement, it could have been the bedroom while Mark was out drinking in his bread truck or sobering up in his "den," a bear's lair of baseball memorabilia. Mark was like a big bear himself, shaggy and handsome, and he could recite poetry, had studied the classics at Princeton, went to graduate school at Berkeley, same as Nina. In the summer he rested himself out back in the hole Dali and Duchamp had started to dig as a swimming pool—Mark and The Czarina, their pet beagle at incline on the sides of the pool in the shade of the lilac bushes which divided our yards. Our garden featured tulips in the spring, roses in the summer and lilies in the fall. My husband was a master gardener, wrote the Gardening column that ran in several papers. Summer now seemed a million miles away.

Nina and I prepared to make a break, but the picket line was too thick and the crosses the kids were dragging looked like what they were, instruments of torture. Strains of song from the other group "We are young and old together / we are gay and straight together," wafted sweetly over our heads.

"I wish they would stop singing," Francisco moaned.

"Shut up, Francisco," Nina said.

"If we break through the picket line and accidentally brush against somebody, would that count as assault?"

"Shut up, Francisco."

Then, finally, two of the Woman's Right protectors left the human barricade they had formed against the wall of the clinic, parted the line of pickets, saw us safely across to no man's land. "It will be over before we know it," Francisco consoled us all as we entered the drafty, darkened hallway.

"Shut up, Francisco."

Then we were in the "reception" area, which had the feel of a locker room for an under-funded girls' sport in a rinky-dink school, a hefty and rather mature team, by the looks of it, the game lost.

"You have to take a number," a large white woman told us. "Up there." She looked like a Michelin man in her down winter coat.

Facing the rows of folding metal chairs was an unattended desk with a little number rack. White plastic disks with the numbers in bold red hung like the deli counter at Martin's Supermarket. Nina was number 16. They were calling out 8. We settled in. Mark and Francisco were the only two men there and everybody looked at them with curiosity and approval.

"Are you sure you want to go through with this, Nina." My stomach suddenly was betraying me. "One more kid is all, you already have the room. I could be the babysitter. Once babies come, people love them, they can't help it."

"Be a pal and stop trying to convert me, okay?" She showed me her pointy teeth. "Okay?"

"Okay."

"I've run with the bulls, posed nude for art classes, I've told you that."

"You have." She was an exceptionally brave woman.

Another time she told me that she had decided as a kid when she read the Dorothy Parker line—"Men don't make passes at girls who wear glasses"—that *she* would make the passes. In the end, she did not get her PhD because Mark arrived on the scene. Together they made bricks for the Peace Corps in Barbados, followed by L. A., scriptwriting, then driving in four furiously rainy days and nights to New York for years of editing legal documents third shift. Mark, who actually had a PhD in American Culture, became an academic gypsy, teaching here, there, and everywhere. Dali and Duchamp were born in New Mexico and Montana respectively. Last December, during a huge blizzard, John and I were getting ready for bed, I sitting at my dressing table putting on hand-lotion and night cream, John plucking the grey out of his eyebrows in the bathroom, we heard a clanking and chugging in the driveway next door. A car dragging a muffler rolled in. A woman crawled out of the front, saw me looking out the window, waved as if she had just pulled into Shangri-La, she her own welcome wagon. I knew immediately that we would be friends. Soon, a grand piano arrived. That actually had belonged to Nina's father, who was a doctor. They cut the legs down so the kids could practice cross-legged on the floor, and my daughters also observed Dali putting a garter snake down his underpants.

"What's a little pain, Nina?"

"Shut up, Francisco."

The woman sitting in the row before us gave us another look.

"It hurts?" Nina squeaked out.

"Damn straight," the woman said.

Mark and Francisco slipped down in their seats. They were holding hands.

"Want a sip?" The woman handed Nina a thermos.

"What is it?"

"Vodka, honey. Take a shot."

"Will it help?"

"A candy bar will help."

"I'll go to the liquor store, buy some booze."

Nina gave Francisco a poke with her elbow, and he slumped back down with a sigh, began to stroke his face. I will not say Francisco has a beard because beard would be a euphemism. More like patches, tufts, sprouts of fur scattered haphazardly. Meanwhile, Mark had stuck his fingers in his ears as if he were watching a scary movie and not to hear the creepy music lessened the horror.

The woman gave me a once-over like I had done something to cause all this, then darted a glimpse at Mark and Francisco because now the two men were holding hands again and Mark was humming his favorite song, "Sunrise, Sunset" from *Fiddler on the Roof.*

"The thing is they will at least be giving me something for the pain," Nina said, "and if I mix that with alcohol, I might go into a coma."

"You wish." The woman turned back to her two children who were busy with their coloring books.

"I took a good shower this morning," Nina offered.

Compared to Nina I was obsessively neat. The last time I had seen Nina's upstairs bathtub it was full of clothes, books, ashtrays and newspapers, the curtains drawn, Nina's idea of cleaning house. My husband, John, won't set foot in Nina's house. Furthermore, he does not think that it is legal to have commercial vehicles parked in our residential neighborhood, and occasionally, threatens to call code enforcement on their bread trucks. Actually, he doesn't know that when the cops arrested Mark for disorderly conduct, he had hidden himself in the back of his truck, hunkered down among the metal bread racks shouting: "You won't take me alive." Nina wanted me to help her bail him out, and although I dreaded being one of the people who go to the police station, I went with her.

There were other times as well, one requiring a lengthy sojourn on the Psych. Ward of Mass. General and weeks of nightly AA meetings for him and AlaNon meetings for Nina, which she said was a dating service because everybody had everybody's phone number. Several men contacted Nina, she told me, which did not surprise me one bit. Mark had even been to a rehabilitation place. I envisioned it a kind of Betty Ford Clinic. Nina said it was more like a funny farm, the kind you'd read about in a Raymond Carver story with old guys out on the porch in rocking chairs crying in their 7-Up. Nina could make anyplace interesting just by her description.

At the moment Mark, sober, a green-grey cast to his face, was in clean jeans and a grey sweat shirt which said Holy Cross, just the outfit for an abortion clinic. Francisco was in his painting clothes, not the white clothes of a painter who paints houses, but bohemian black. Black chinos and a black turtle neck into which he was retracting his neck. Are you a cat or a turtle, I wanted to ask.

"Sure you don't want to go to my doctor for this, Nina?"

Nina always went to clinics, didn't believe in private medicine, but I thought, in this case, that she could compromise on her principles.

"Connie, you always believe in comfort," she accused.

She was right. I spoiled myself.

"Hey," the large woman said. "She's not supposed to be coming out the front entrance. They have a back exit." She pointed to a woman coming down the hallway holding on to the wall for dear life and walking as if she had ten sanitary pads wedged between her legs, which she probably did.

"I need a fucking cigarette," Mark muttered, putting his fingers in his ears again.

"Don't worry, folks, no way am I going to be hobbling out like that."

But Nina came out worse.

And the trip home seemed forever.

And I prayed that nobody was about with the binoculars when we pulled up in Mark and Nina's driveway.

"Upsy daisy," Mark said, lifting his wife out of the car, grabbing the pillows I had brought. Nina, all bird-bone and beak, was carried with ease up the stairs and he put her on the mattress in their bedroom.

"What happened?" Duchamp wanted to know.

"Mommy just had an abortion," Mark said.

Duchamp was wearing his spike bracelet, the one he had dipped in mashed potatoes and eaten from during Thanksgiving and he began hitting himself with it.

"Stop that this instant," his father said.

"If you need me," Francisco said. "I mean, if I can help, I'll be down in the dungeon."

"You've helped enough," I replied tartly.

"I guess, then, it's *au revoir* and *auf wiedersehen*, adios and *ciao*."

"What's wrong with Du?" Dali emerged from his room. Unlike Duchamp, Dali always wore a buttoned-up shirt, carried a kid's briefcase to school. A prodigy, he had built a giant Lego city in the basement, fixed the mother board of their secondhand computer himself. When of legal age, he was going to change his name to something like Newton, he told my daughters.

"I better see to the boys." Mark went down the stairs.

Then, quite suddenly it was quiet. Looking through Nina's window towards my own bedroom, instead of concentrating on Nina, I remembered that Sophia was conceived shortly after I met John. He said we were going to get married someday anyway. It just put up the date by about three or four years. We were married in his church, the Greek Orthodox, the whole service chanted. John told me that the first time he heard an organ in church he nearly jumped out of his skin. On Greek Easter when he was a kid, they all had to go outside the church, run around it six times.

"You were right after all, Connie. It wasn't like in that story by Hemingway, when the guy says, they just let a little air in. They take the air out, do it with a vacuum, The Hoover Maneuver."

"Mom, would you like to have some tea?" Dali poked his head around the door.

"Thanks, Dal, that would be great."

The poster above Nina's bed, mattress rather, was Che Guevara. At one time every campus bookstore in the country sold them. Poor fellow had asthma. How many Saturday mornings had I spent in the Emergency Room of St. Joseph's Hospital with Sophia's asthma attacks. Once, when I didn't think it was that bad, John had been the one to rush her to the hospital, save her life, something I'll never forgive myself for, and for which John will always be my hero. On my bedroom wall there are prints by Romare Bearden of women ironing, washing dishes, which I framed myself at the Ye Olde Framers Workshop. They reminded me of my mother.

"It *was* a vacuum cleaner," Nina looked better as she sat up and drank the tea Dali had brought her. "But it felt like fire going in. Like the flame thrower we saw in World War I on *Masterpiece Theater.* I thought I was going to die in the trenches."

"You didn't." I squeezed her hand.

"There you are up in the saddle staring at the holes in the asbestos. Somebody comes by, swoops away the bottle, but you see it, Connie, shreds, patches, a bucket of blood."

"I'm so sorry, Nina," was all I could think to say.

"It's not your fault, Connie."

"Shh," I stroked her arm. I wanted to say something, but I am not good with words, although at U Mass I started as a French major, had taken two years in high school, was supposed to spend my junior year in Paris. One day they changed the classroom of my French III class and it being the rule in the department only to speak *Francais,* I spent three days unsuccessfully trying to find the correct room. Finally, I went into the woods around the observatory, sat on a bench and had a good cry. John came along on his way to his Business Administration class. I don't know why, but I suddenly burst into tears right there when I was supposed to be strong for Nina.

"Not the waterworks, come on Connie." She laughed, coughed, winced in pain, had to put the mug of tea on the floor by the side of her mattress. I got some Kleenex out of my purse so she could blow her nose, went to the bathroom and looked, to no avail, for a washrag to wipe her face. When I came back into her bedroom, Dali and Duchamp had dragged in their sleeping bags and were setting up beside the mattress. The Czarina had ensconced herself in with Nina on the mattress, her head on a pillow. The dog began to snore, and under the covers, wiggle her tail, feet, give little yelps.

"Do dogs dream?" Duchamp asked.

"For sure," Nina answered.

"A nice warm house," I offered.

"Running away," Dali chimed in.

"Eating mud," Duchamp suggested, for he, too, ate mud, paper. My daughters had seen him.

"Getting petted," Mark, who had snuggled in on Nina's other side, added.

It was getting dark; I had to go home, see about dinner. Tiptoeing down the stairs, out of the house, I closed their door quietly, got in my car and drove into my own driveway. My story was to be that I had gone to the Mall to do Christmas shopping. That was what you are supposed to do the day after Thanksgiving. Now, I would have to smile mysteriously as if all the secrets in the world were hidden in the trunk of the car. Fortunately, John did not look up from the TV when I came in. They were doing a football score rundown.

"Sophia, Theresa," I called.

"They went to a flick, a Frenchy, *Entre Nous.*"

Both my girls, still in high school, already spoke better French than I ever did. Sophia was born in Bloomington, when John was finishing up his degree. Teresa came into being without premeditation, too, but at least, by then we were married. No Teresa, no Sophia? Unthinkable.

"What's for dinner, Constance?"

Not being able to face the turkey, I opened the cupboard and took out a can. I heated the chili in the microwave, grated some cheese over it, and put the whole concoction on toast, with a sliver of pickle on the side.

"*La piece de la resistance,*" I said setting the tray down in front of John in the den.

While he ate, I put the dirty dishes from breakfast into the dishwasher, cleaned the counters, sponged down the stove, played the phone messages back. My mother, who had spent Thanksgiving with my sister in L. A., was going to do all her Christmas shopping when she arrived to stay with us in Worcester. She had raised the two of us in Gary, Indiana alone, and now we couldn't spoil her enough. My reading group was meeting on Wednesday, a message said. The book was *Ya-Ya Sisterhood.* There was a meeting for Concerned Catholic Mothers.

"Milk," John roared.

When I brought it in, and leaned down to place the glass on the coffee table, he lifted my skirt up, gave me a little whack on the *derriere.*

"You still have a gorgeous ass, Constance."

I knew what was to follow.

"So how about it?"

"I'm not in the mood."

"Oh, so we have moods here too, do we. Suit yourself."

I went back to the kitchen, sat at the counter. A full moon illuminated the dead leaves which flooded Nina's swimming hole. I thought I saw the wisp of a little ghost, fragile as smoke, float up and out of Nina's bedroom window. Then, I saw a shadow which materialized into Francisco skirting the swimming hole and dodging the bare bones of the lilac bushes.

"Francisco." The last person in the whole world I wanted to see.

He plopped himself down on a stool, opened my cookie jar and took out a cookie in the shape of a pilgrim hat. Above us, I could hear the exercise bike in the bedroom going a mile a minute.

Francisco reached for his second cookie, a turkey.

"It could have been Mark's. *Anybody,* Connie," he said.

"I don't want to hear another word out of you, Francisco."

"Whatever. Nina is a big girl. Bigger than you think."

"She's not a giant is she?"

"I'm splitting to Seattle."

"Good for you, Francisco."

He ambled out with a handful of cookies, disappeared into the hedges. I set the dishwasher, went into the living room. In front of the house, the sidewalk tinged with frost gleamed with malice. I left the front lights on for the girls, dragged myself upstairs. Mark was already in bed. I put on my nightgown, the one with roses all across the front, the one I made myself, got in beside him, turned off my light. Across the room, I could see the family pictures stuck in the dresser mirror curlyqueing up at the edges. There were some from our trip to Greece, the four of us standing in front of the Parthenon. There was one photo of me and John, and for some reason, the lighting, something, our legs were faded off. Not a leg to stand on. I would have to destroy that picture, for I looked fat in it. Already I had weeded through the albums. I wanted to be remembered thin. Your thin grandmother.

"Have you always been faithful to me, John?" I said this out of the blue. The shells in the glass lamp by his side of the bed seemed to shift.

"I just want to know. It's okay . . ."

When he turned to me at that moment, I realized that his eyebrows, grown together at the bridge of his nose, were too grey to pluck, that his eyes held fear. Dear God, the terrain had been smooth a moment before, and I had planted land mines.

"You don't have to tell me," I said quickly, wanting to swallow back my dumb words.

"I *want* to tell you."

I braced myself.

"Connie." He took my head in his hands. "How could I be unfaithful to you, to the girls, to the family. I would see the Virgin Mary before me if I did anything to hurt you. I have too much self-respect."

I didn't know if the sudden sinking feeling was relief or utter dismay because for some reason I felt like crying. But I didn't; of course I didn't. I had cried at Nina's. That afternoon before Mark, the boys and The Czarina came upstairs to keep her company, she whispered, as if she had won the game after all. "I want to feel bad, but I don't. I'm a player, Connie, I'm still a player."

R. D. Skillings

ALL THEY WANTED

The Post Office steps is the most dangerous place in town. I just stand there until some disaster strikes, and then I go home and hide till the next time I'm seized with the need for mail. I could have it delivered, but then I'd never go out.

Just this morning I was sorting through my handful of nothing—junk mail and bills—wondering who might turn up if I waited just two seconds more, when I had it quite nakedly inflicted on me that whatever your state of mind at the moment—and mine never changes, thank God—there is also no such thing as past history in this town.

First comes Freida, still wearing long skirts, hair down to her waist. We smile, but what must she be thinking? Bayou and Grumm loved her, not me. She was mad for Brade, another fool of crazed ambition, who never loved anybody in his life, but who liked to treat me to grand dinners and fuck all night.

Next comes Alibi Arby Ruzo, sozzled as usual, Freida's first husband, whom she could never completely let go or get free of, who tried to console himself with me. We half-nod like we might have met once but can't quite remember where, then resume our absent faces. It's like being at the wheel of a ship in a bottle.

After that every person that came along—I'll spare you the list—reminded me of some side of The Crime of the Time, which nobody has the whole picture of, even after all these years, least of all the perpetrators.

These were people I was intimate with for a brief period leading up to the denouement—shall we call it?—then went on living in the same town with, but hardly ever came across, for years on end, except at the P.O. Maybe that's why the past remains so vivid, there's so little to bury it between then and now!

Of course everything else has completely changed. When I first came to town you could live on nearly nothing here. Surviving it was called. I had a lot of crummy jobs and I moved around a lot. There was a lot of drinking and drugs and a lot of sort of wild romance, not to mention how dingy it was, with people trying to commit suicide all over the place and murders in the dunes, ODs, rapes, mutilations and so on.

Too much happened all at once, even to register, much less digest. Bare feet were just being banned in the bars. Manny Zora was already a legend, and he didn't die until 1979. Hoffman was still alive. Nina Simone and Ella Fitzgerald had sung at the A-House not too long before. Only the Little Bar at the A-House was gay in those days. The Ace of Spades, where the Pied Piper is now, was lesbian, but discreet, very sedate. Women could dance together, but not men. There were still plenty of fish, and the Portuguese still had their swagger.

In New York it was the start of the Be-in and what I think of as anti-art. Down here I got arrested for cohabiting with the boy I came with. We had to lie that we were married to get a rental. The judge was an old walrus with a white mustache, last of the patricians. He got most indignant. "Perchance you think this is a brothel?" he says. "Begone by noon tomorrow."

Outside the court room—in those days it was right in Town Hall—one of the cops who was always trying to date me says, "Don't worry about it. Nobody takes him seriously."

My boyfriend split to Mendocino, I never heard from him again.

Vietnam was driving the country berserk. The people I fell in with refused to read the papers, or even hear about it. They'd come here to get away from all that. Music and marijuana were the only medium of truth. Words were rigid, evil, lies. Mind was the enemy. Love was all. I was a child quite wide-eyed, though I know you can hardly imagine that now. I wasn't pining to get married, but I certainly wanted a man of my own—not other women's men, all in a clot, which was what I got. I think it cured me like a thrombosis.

Anyway, at that time nothing in my life seemed to fit but my name. My flutist father loved birds and every night, just at dusk in the summer, he would play me the veery's call, like a falling spiral. It still haunts me. I grew up, as you see, to be cinnamon-colored like the bird—at least in hair and clothes—and like the bird I am—or rather used to be—too easily deceived by imitation distress.

Youth loves misery that doesn't know itself. By middle age invisibility and silence are more valid, more adroit. Anyhow my social virginity ended when I met Grumm's mother.

She was like a postcard of a lace doily. She looked sweet enough to eat, with her little girl's voice and her tinkling enunciation. We drank about ten crème de menthes together one Sunday at the Colonial Inn, and then somehow we took to sitting around in the wicker furniture there at all hours of the empty afternoons. It was so dim in the bar, so far from the windows across the dining room, that on certain hazy days the bay looked moonlit. We kept saying how beautiful everything was, but I wonder now, how much did it affect us? From her I learnt of avarice. I think she wanted a daughter. Eventually she tried to rule her son through me.

Grumm was a guru, and come to think of it I probably *did* first see him on the Post Office steps, just smiling his mustache up at the sun as if it were an old pal of his. He was into eastern wisdom, and he was always surrounded by pretty girls, but he was above sex. He was a marvelous wood-worker, a master craftsman, a designer and maker of furniture, but he didn't care about material things. He wanted to be a philosopher. When I disagreed with him he'd wind up saying things like, "Good God baby I'm not going to discuss this ridiculous matter with you any more, you're clearly befuddled."

It was Bayou's mind that fascinated him. They both did a year behind bars, but neither was ever quite sure how he got there. For a while afterwards they each kept trying to pry out of me what the other had said, and what Grumm's mother had said, and how exactly they came to get caught.

What Grumm really wanted was eminence, prestige. He was secretly impressed by wealth, background, culture. But he wanted it to be absolutely independent and unconventional. He was trying for a certain nonchalance, self-invention of a sort. By the end he wanted to disown the whole sham so much he moved out of town. At the time it was the thing in his life he was proudest of, maybe the first thing in his life he'd ever *been* proud of, it was who he really thought he was, or at least who he wanted to be, but he couldn't breathe a word, never a hint, till he let me in on the secret. That must have been the one thing in connection with the heist that Grumm ever did without asking Bayou first.

When they got out early on good behavior of course people asked embarrassing questions. Bayou made jokes about it in public. He seems to have enjoyed jail the way he enjoyed everything else. Ridicule that wilted Grumm only seemed to make Bayou more luminous—I think—because he had such a knack for people, for seeing who they were. And no prejudices. Not even preferences. He was the most truly democratic man I ever met, though one must admit that in his private polity he was definitely First Citizen.

Him I met at the old Sun Gallery. The first thing he said was, "How'd you like to go to Zanzibar with me?"

"Lead on," I said, straight to his bed. He was fantastically handsome and clever, and he looked like the quintessential beach bum with his ragged straw hat, seersucker cut-offs, no shave and those teeth. He had the kind of charisma that comes of seeing everything as possibility, as funny, even the grossest, grimmest things. He was a natural criminal with a taste for extravagance. He had a pedigree a mile long and all these diplomas from Princeton and the Sorbonne. He left his investment bank and his several families and did nothing but scheme. He was wry in a way and brilliant, neither brave nor afraid, and he never spoke a serious word, much less an honest one. He always smiled, and he made people laugh. From him I learned to listen, and forgive. He had a strange power over Grumm, not sexual. Grumm admired him because he was unmoved by any human being. Bayou would say things like, "Baby, you've got to stop hating me, it's no good for you."

He and another fellow quite larcenous planned to steal Columbian art, but the forgeries were getting so good he had to come back and study to tell the difference. Then he was going to smuggle cars to Peru. Then he tried to persuade me to go to Saigon with him. He'd pimp and we'd make a fortune. I thought that one a bit much. In court he claimed Grumm was the brains. The judge just laughed.

All the while I knew nothing. While they were thinking I suppose exclusively about *it*, I was thinking about *them*. I marvel to remember. I didn't even know they were friends, much less in cahoots, until I had slept with them both. Then I kept trying to choose, though neither minded. They were most complacent, Alphonse and Gaston.

Eventually the robbery got noticed. It took forever because the museum was closed all winter and the custodians were always stoned or lost in their own affairs—poetry or whatnot—but suddenly the word hit town like Mardi Gras. The local papers were full of it. That's all anyone talked about. Overnight the thieves were famous, heroes, giants. There was a lot of respect for their brilliance and professionalism. Rip Off Artists! People were impressed, completely admiring. No guns, no blood, no harm to anyone, considering whose loss it was. There were rumors that the whole swag had gone for a fortune to a ham baron's chateau in Bastogne. They were romantic figures, whoever they were. Gods! It was terribly heady stuff. But Grumm was still only Grumm to the world, and there was no one he could tell, which was definitely a downer.

That's how I became the art heist moll. Sometimes he would even deign to make love to me—but one night when we were just getting into bed he said, "Veery, you've got a good head on your shoulders. I need to take you into my confidence, I need you to check my perceptions."

It pleased me to think he meant some kind of exotic foreplay, but nothing followed but more talk. Little by little I began to wonder what he was saying, or not saying about the big brouhaha. I was lying there licking his shoulder, pinching his nipples and pushing my bush against his thigh. So I wasn't really paying attention until he fell asleep.

Bayou was the passionate one. It would take him suddenly, without any warning. One night we were on our way to a party, and he dragged me into the shrubbery, people going by on all sides. That sort of thing was so contrary to his cool nature, it almost had to be put on, but he seemed to enjoy it. He snorted like Poseidon. Another thing I learned from him: never wear underwear in the summer. Pardon my digression. I know you like this sort of thing. A bit more?

It never occurred to me that I was becoming an accomplice. For a while it was all quite exciting, quite flattering, too—which took the crassness off. Even at conception the theft itself was never merely a matter of money. It was ingenious how they foiled the security system. Then they waited for one of those deep February fogs when you can stand in the middle of Commercial Street and look both ways and never see anyone for days on end, plus of course it was about three o'clock in the morning. They got some small works by minor European masters. Real ones. More's the credit to them for that. The museum was full of forgeries. Already there was gossip. A whiff of scandal hung over the place. The owner was said to hold orgies there, though as a matter of fact I doubt that. Though at this remove why I should doubt anything is beyond me. There really was no limit to what people did in those days.

Here, finish that. We'll open another.

But the main thing, la pièce de la résistance, was a little Vlaminck. It was truly beautiful. Perfectly diffident, unobtrusive at first glance, but it was an extraordinary painting, sheer magic, and it saved my life one day—I'll tell you about that, when we get there. Enough to say now, it was just a narrow village street, cobbles, cracked walls on both sides, very somber, deft strokes, brickwork in the right corner, a sort of purplish, dark center leading away, some chimneypots, doorways and shutters, just pure genius, spontaneous joy, absolute truth, not at all nice, bleak as could be, but undeniable. It probably took half an hour to do. Of course one doesn't know it didn't take him twenty years, but it had that look of casual mastery, of something simply done in a wink. Like something done just because it *could* be done, like the point of a life well-lived.

Now spare me your long-suffering look! It was hardly the most precious painting they stole, but it was the only one they really cared about. The others they chose for dollar value—they got quite a few really, but all together they didn't fetch the price they should have got for the Vlaminck, if the world had eyes and paid fair. Which it doesn't. And the money they did get didn't last long, as money won't. They were broke by the time I met them.

Grumm's mother's name was Katherine, by the way. She liked art—who doesn't?—but she was not sentimental about the Vlaminck, especially once Bayou had found a new fence, someone eminently respectable, with good contacts, whose discretion could be counted on, someone absolutely beyond the law. It was getting to be quite a classy caper, and safe, with a whole fantastic future coming into view!

Bayou and Grumm doted on this painting. They were proud of it, not least of how they got it, and by the time I came on the scene it was the last one they had left, which made it all the dearer, a trophy, nostalgic, you might say.

They had created a world around it, down in Grumm's mother's basement, a little replica of a drawing room with gurgling, singing pipes overhead and all this stored junk and spiders and little sand ant-hills along cracks in the cement floor like a range of volcanos and the furnace chugging away with the Vlaminck on one grungy wall with a spotlight on it. They had installed a little antique table with lion's feet and two old oak chairs and they would have a drink and look at the painting, and talk about it. They acted like lords.

Katherine almost never came down. She was too nervous, but she still wanted her cut. When she would ask when the great transaction was due to take place, and what they expected to get, Bayou would discourse about how priceless a work of genius it was, how shameful it would be to part with such a treasure for mere money, or at least how foolish it would be to let it go before they had lived in its aura for some considerable time. He even suggested they might sneak it back into the Museum so everybody else could enjoy it, which made Katherine go quite icy. After all, he said, they could always steal it again. He was amusing himself no doubt, which was what he did best, but Grumm took him seriously, and fell in love with the painting. Or got infatuated with possession, or the high remove of secrecy itself.

Bayou was not one bit romantic, but he did love to dream up macabre scenes of French peasant life behind the doors in that painting, which he said looked like black tombstones. They were more like miniature cathedral windows at night, according to Katherine, who could match him whimsy for whimsy, if it came to that. "Not my rainbow at all," she said to his grisly imaginings. For some reason he was intrigued by animal squalor, and he had pigs and sheep living inside with the people.

Those were the great days of smuggling—not rum running like Manny Zora, but cannabis from Mexico and the Caribbean. Brade was going to make his fortune. He was the chef at the Colonial Inn, where Freida was hostess, poor thing. I resented her then, I don't envy her now. She could neither have him nor get away from him. And Arby drank there every night at the bar, his mournful eyes following her around, and she always found an errand or a chore for him.

Brade invested in a few voyages. He was going to buy the Inn. A boatload was worth a bundle. You'd see people suddenly driving Porsches. The F.B.I. was all over the place about that too. It was a bit creepy when you met somebody new. You had no idea who they might be. "Seduce him and find out what he's up to," Bayou said to me, when some stranger started mooching around for friends. That might be the only thing he ever told me to do that I didn't.

It wasn't all a bed of roses. I saw Mick Mulligan the day he got back from a year in a Jamaican jail. He was sitting on a bench looking out at the bay. I hardly recognized him. I said, "My God, where've *you* been?" He was always a very cocky guy, very big. He looked as frail as a boy. Or an old man. I never saw him like himself again.

Meanwhile, consorting with all these older men—there were several other affairs I won't mention—I consumed my youth. It went by without my even noticing. I was a frazzle. Everybody drank all the time. I don't mean they were drunk. There was just always an open bottle around, or they dropped into the Foc's'le for a quick shot—it souped them up, like race cars. Some of them at least. Not to mention hash and mescaline and mushrooms and acid. People would turn up in town with a suitcase of pharmaceuticals. It was going to be a new world. The millennium was about to dawn, never mind that things were going smash at the moment. Smash was what was going to save us.

I listened to a lot of talk. Men seemed to do nothing but talk. I didn't know what to take to heart. I was typing for Wilberforce at the time. He was writing a book named *The Autobiography of a Nobody,* which he planned to publish himself. I remember Bayou saying, "For the kidnapper the child is the great imponderable, but the just-finished manuscript of a millionaire—that's the ideal hostage. Let me know when it's done."

I was mad for Bayou. Maybe you can imagine. He was pure, in a way. He lived to scheme. He was completely charming, kindly, solicitous, and distant as a star.

I wonder now if that wasn't when he gave himself the idea of getting a fat ransom for the Vlaminck. They discussed it, but in the end he decided there was more hope with the insurance company than the museum, since the owner was a shyster himself. He drank champagne for breakfast every morning and always wore an ascot, a blue blazer, and a black beret. He was notorious for acquiring paintings from poor artists. He'd wait till the middle of winter, and then he'd say like everyone else he was a bit embarrassed for cash, but it would be good for their career to be in his collection, and he'd give them a show and a nice opening—well, he would put out some Soave and cheese—after which the painting went into storage until the artist got pricey, in other words dead, and he never had to pay them.

Grumm would have liked to play Robin Hood. That would have been a real feather in his cap. He talked about sharing some of the proceeds with the artists. They—not Katherine—spent hours trying to think up safe ways to funnel money to various of their favorite painters, but finally Bayou got bored with philanthropic fantasies and faced the obvious, that they'd never squeeze a cent out of the owner. This was a man, by the way, who preferred repute to real possession. He was not deterred by forgeries. I think he collaborated in his own deception. And who's to say what's real if you don't want to know?

Then Bayou got the idea that once they'd banked the ransom for the Vlaminck, they'd demand some fantastic sum for the return of the other paintings, which they'd threaten to burn one by one if the money wasn't forthcoming pronto. It was all preposterous, but I never asked myself where it would end. It was like I was not really there—in more ways than one—I was in all these beds though.

Grumm got to be a nervous wreck. Katherine could hardly contain her impatience. She had to contend with a lot of talk herself. All she wanted was just to live a little. Grumm would have been glad to have her gone and out of his hair. Bayou simply got more whimsical and pretended to shilly-shally. The reason—the occasion—for these wild, new schemes was that the great new fence in Boston had warned Bayou never to communicate with him; he'd call Bayou when the time came. But he never called.

So they had time on their hands, and nothing to do but sit around and dream up more and more impossible things to do with the money. Which made it necessary to imagine a bigger and bigger payoff. They lavished themselves as if it were millions, a few paltry thousand dollars apiece, nothing on today's scale. Also I think Bayou just liked juggling ideas. As soon as he said something, he'd unsay it, or refine it till only a geometer could have made all the angles fit. I think he loved impossible puzzles.

Katherine of course wanted him to stay home every moment, in case the fence called. She'd get excruciatingly jumpy while he and Grumm hung around her basement with the Vlaminck. So long as there was enough to drink and smoke they could muse all day about the good life—which according to them meant having perfect mobility and no ties to anyone or anything. Katherine's eyes would go around and around the walls as if she were trying to find her way out of a maze. She begged for one of us always to be in Bayou's apartment 24 hours a day. She offered to do a shift herself, but of course he wouldn't hear of that, and the simple fact is, he never liked to hurry. He had a languid streak, like a mental voluptuary. He was hatching more schemes, and I think he wanted to keep the Vlaminck to amuse him until he had a new jewel to sit on.

His phone did ring one time when I was there alone. Whoever it was hung up when I said hello. I wonder now if it was Bayou. He'd just stepped out for cigarettes.

If Grumm hadn't spilled the beans that night in bed I would never have been sitting around with them all that time, listening to them pontificate. Poor Grumm—what he wanted was to *be* somebody. Money was a side-issue for Bayou, too. He loved the adventure, the challenge of it.

Bayou said to Katherine, "Veery could make us give her a cut, too."

"Veery is not mercenary," Katherine said. "She has no part in this."

I don't think she thought she did either. She assumed some saintly judge would be too gallant to involve her. After all, she was just Grumm's mother, and he owed her homage. It was her way of restoring him to his class, her class. She felt he'd fallen to manual labor and low companions. She wanted him to dress better and shave off his beard. And squire her around and be polite. She cared more for appearance than substance. She wouldn't have denied it. Of course Grumm always talked in terms of spiritual levels, and claimed she couldn't understand. About that stuff she could be quite derisory in a sly way. She was not a stupid woman.

I suppose in the end Grumm was standing me against Bayou and Katherine both. Once he'd told me about the Vlaminck he never made love to me again. From then on it was all just talk. We spent a lot of time in bed too. He claimed he wanted my advice, but he always scoffed at anything I said. And there was no reason really even to open my mouth, if you'll pardon me. He just wanted a way to listen to himself. He was almost always high by then, he never came down any more if he could help it. He needed me to soothe his jitters, bolster his ego. He'd started screwing his little acolytes—against all his principles. It was pure escapism.

All the while Freida was driving him mad. She couldn't help herself. She had to exercise her charms. Bayou and Grumm might have locked horns over her if she'd given them the chance, but she never flirted with them except separately, so neither knew what she was up to. They figured her for a frigid tease.

She was just honing her skills, trying to make Brade jealous, but he cared not one jot. Every once in a while he would give her bottom a good, resounding slap, like a connoisseur. And she would blush over her shoulder, with eyelids lowered. It was embarrassing. Love is a ludicrous thing. I don't mean he wasn't nice to her. It was an appreciative whack, nothing affectionate. She used to present herself, she couldn't help it. He was nice to everybody. It made no sense to him to make enemies.

Me he treated to lavish dinners on his nights off. He liked the best—formality, waiters in white uniforms, the perfect bottle of wine, the finest liqueurs, and then a walk on the beach with a tremendous joint like an after-dinner cigar. He didn't like complications, which was why he liked me. For me he was a rest, pure luxury.

Brade was a would-be power-broker. He aimed to own the whole East End. He was seething with energy and ambition, hardly what you would call cool. Odd that Freida fell under his sway. Out of the kitchen he wore tweed jackets and looked like a doctor. She was the acme of hippie gypsy, all bangles and beads, black eyes and ethereal voice. She could almost float in those scarves and dark tresses. But he was absolutely impervious to anyone that didn't advance his fortunes. He was playing the market, according to him, like a violin. Down-payments was his mantra. He had a line on various ventures, and he did a little dealing in cocaine too. That was back before it came into vogue. Not my cup of tea, fortunately. In later years coke brought lots of my friends down, including Arby in due course, who in those days was always saying, *Seek what you will find.* It was like a shield against all follies. But all it was was an excuse. It meant absolutely nothing. What he found was Freida. Ten years before. And never another thing in his whole life. And Freida was all he was ever true to. Even today he keeps her lawn mowed, fixes her faucets, does odd jobs, no matter that she's on her third husband.

Everything else he betrayed or lost interest in. Many beginnings, no ends, or at least none of his own. He wore his shoulders up in a perpetual shrug. He was pure pathos to me, weak, or, as he would have said, strong in his weakness. I suppose I just wanted to comfort him. I couldn't stand to see Freida winding Bayou around her finger. It seemed out of sync with the universe. He was my god. I was already horribly tormented. But that was like an assault on my pride. By then at least I'd got my fill of Grumm. The faster he fell apart, the more sententious he was. There was a doomsday atmosphere around everything anyway. Live now, die soon. It's hard to imagine this is 1985, that whole world gone and forgotten, except for vestiges, like ourselves.

Ah, yes, the painting. Another little taste? So much talking dries the tongue. Katherine turned into a monster once she learned about the Vlaminck. Before that she was only Madame Crème de Menthe to me—that sticky green. I used to love it, it almost did me in, or something did. I suppose it was the mix.

She'd try to pump me about Grumm, give me bees for his bonnet about moving back to Cleveland. She said I'd love it there. This had started even *before* she learned about the heist.

Grumm was living with a lot of people out on Race Road, and couldn't hide the paintings there. Bayou wouldn't let them in his house. All but the Vlaminck went out of her basement in duffel bags one or two at a time to a fence in Providence without her ever noticing. But one day when Bayou and Grumm kept coming up for ice she went down to investigate and found them like acolytes at an altar. All that was lacking were some candles. She wound up feeling cheated not to have been cut in from day one. It was her basement after all. There was a loud, dumb song in those days, We want the WORLD, and we want it NOW.

Fortunately she could never figure out—and for a long time neither could I—where all the money from the first paintings went. Bayou had a catch-all phrase for plans gone wrong, "Gurgle-gurgle," which always made Grumm wince. I finally deduced that Bayou had talked Grumm into letting him try his luck in the futures market, and once they started losing, it just went down the drain. I'm glad Katherine never knew, she was already miffed enough that it was all gone, and never a penny spent on her.

She was relentless, she never let up on my sympathy, aging away in this sordid burg with her degenerating son. She wanted me to reform him and settle down en famille in some idyllic suburb—anywhere really, so long as it wasn't Provincetown—with her ensconced nearby, though what she at present most urgently needed and justly deserved after her recent life of privations was a sojourn in Paris, where she had once had the "summer of her life," as she called it, back in her salad days, before she got married and had Grumm.

Of course I would never have tried to influence Bayou—or even hint that the painting should be unloaded sooner rather than later. I could not have conceived of such presumption.

In this at least Grumm by now agreed with his mother, but he didn't talk to her about it. Or anything else. They were never in collusion. For this once they happened to be on the same side. He just wanted to get it over with and get the money. He had begun planning to open an ashram in the Green Mountains. A whole swindle of yurts. He certainly hadn't told her any of that.

I was experiencing memory loss, I mean blackouts, finding out days later what I'd said or done from someone else. Other people knew more about me than I did myself. They'd say, "Well, yes, Veery, you did, you actually did that, it was pretty impressive, it really was."

Crazy things were going on all around. There were continuous accidents of one kind or another. Fires especially. Contusions. Car wrecks, walking off of roofs. Everyone seemed to be wearing a cast or an eye patch. I was scared of myself, I was so volatile. I'd fly off the handle and give anyone, particularly strangers, a piece of my mind on whatever subject was being talked about, never mind whether I knew or cared one bit about it. I had all the answers to everything except my own questions. A little like you used to be, come to think. And now look at you!

Thank you. And to yours. That's all that matters now, isn't it? Life is simpler at least. Shorter. What's left of it. I have no regrets. I wouldn't want to do it again. Or I would do it differently. Who wouldn't?

Arby was cheering on the Viet Cong, ranting about The System. He wanted to see the country's face rubbed in its own filth. Up the Revolution! Down with everything! Destruction is creation!

Bayou laughed at me for being possessive and I slapped him. Then he laughed at me for calling Freida a slut.

Brade got flying one night. He talked about running the town some day, having henchmen on all the right boards. He wanted to put a boardwalk around the town like the Fontainbleau in Quebec and build a causeway with a pleasure palace on the end of it out in the middle of the bay, a huge casino with everything anyone could imagine. Kubla Khan. After which he'd be a billionaire, and ready to move on.

"Money is all that talks," he said. "You just have to know the language. And buy, buy, buy. Don't let anything stop you. Never. Not for one minute."

Grumm kept himself so high he almost disappeared. At that point I guess he'd braced himself to wait it out. He kept repeating, "All in the fullness of time," as if I were disputing him.

I was desolate. The worst was I didn't trust myself any more. I'd resolve to sleep alone, but after I'd got done my day with Wilberforce—there's another tale, believe me—I'd need a few drinks, and by the end of the night I'd be in somebody's bed, like as not listening to some dreadful sob story about how the guy had lost his wife by having a fling with somebody like me. Some interesting characters I met.

Eventually of course the fence called and the Vlaminck had to go. That was the very day I decided to visit Elena. She'd written recommendations for me. Her house was always a refuge where I could take stock and pull myself together. She was a very elegant person, genteel without being naive or foolish. She was fond of me, I know, and I would always go away with a good feeling. She was a real pick-me-up, an inspiration and a lively conversationalist, very wise, kind and calm. She was sixty-five-ish and still beautiful. She never wore makeup and she always dressed very nicely. Her husband left her some money.

Well, she was drunk. I'd never seen it before. I didn't want to see it. I didn't want a drink either, but she made me have one. She made me sit down and stay a while, just for form's sake. She was horribly slow and sloppy. I'd worn a beautiful pair of boots she'd given me, that I never could have afforded. I don't think she even noticed. After a bit she sat sideways and looked out the window. It was two o'clock in the afternoon. She was still in her slippers and dressing gown. Her wig was askew. I didn't even know she wore one. Her face was all pouched and red. Her eyes were watery. Her words were like moths on her tongue.

I was sick in my heart, sick in my soul. I could see her sinking into silence, losing her will to speak. It was absolutely appalling. The silences got longer and longer. I'd ask her a question. It was a great undertaking for her to answer. She said she'd stopped going out, she'd stopped reading, stopped going to the hospital—she did volunteer work in Hyannis—stopped everything actually but feeding her Schnauzer that she always carried under one arm when she left the house.

I tried to commiserate, but she wouldn't respond. It was like she was beyond despair, as if I wasn't even there. Nor her either. I was terrified. After a while she talked out the window at the water, just meandering, making chat about nothing, about how beautiful deers' eyes were, is what I remember. Apparently she'd been up in Maine, in a cabin with The Colonel, this English leech she was attached to somehow. I didn't like to think about that.

Anyhow, he hung a gutted doe from a tree outside and when she woke from a nap and saw it she threw up. The Colonel was quite irritated. She said, "We can't all be soldiers, I suppose."

That, "I suppose," was so like her. Only once did she turn her head and look at me straight on, and I had the strangest feeling that she pitied me. On my way out she said, "It's always nice to see you, Veery. I'm glad you're doing so well."

I couldn't help seeing what a mess the house was. It was like a vision of hell. She was usually impeccable. I wondered if The Colonel had moved in or something. I never understood what she was doing with him. I thought: Is this what's going to happen to me?

I was in a state of shock, my only prop in this town—in my whole life—knocked right out from under me.

All I wanted was to get blotto. Just forget everything. I went to the Bradford, and ordered a rusty nail. I haven't touched one of those things in years. I must have been looking for lockjaw.

Bayou saw me in the window. He came in and said, "Want to have a last look?"

"No," I said, "I don't."

"It's going tomorrow. Come on, we're having a Bon Voyage party."

He looked a little subdued. Of course I was bereaved too, but that painting seemed the least of my losses. I felt like I was becoming a multiple personality monster, trying to minister to so many men. But I never said no to Bayou. So I pounded down my nail and we walked over to Grumm's mother's in the rain. It was drenching weather, with a lot of wind. The trees were thrashing. And it just blew into my head that my life and the whole world I lived in was a worthless botch best blown sky high. I should have had a stick of dynamite.

Grumm was there. And Katherine. And a bottle of vodka. And the Vlaminck. We all stood around like it was an opening. Katherine put out some cashews. Still, it seemed as hushed as a wake. With this pile of packing materials in one corner, just waiting for the last rites to end. I had no reason to be there. I didn't belong. There or anywhere.

It's so hard to gauge the reactions of youth. I might just as well have been thankfully looking forward to a more normal life, such as skipping town, like them. But what happened—I can hardly explain this—I simply became mesmerized by the painting, like I was stoned in some new way. I walked away from the talk—there was a third and fourth chair now—and it caught me somehow. I stared at it for the longest time. I'd already looked at it plenty. I knew quite well what it looked like—I can see it now—but this was different, some sort of coalescence in the eye. Deafening too. It was a very powerful sensation, like leaving everything behind. I can still feel how stunned I felt, how exalted. I can remember in the abstract too what I took from it, and keep to this day—aside from the gratitude that comes of awe of the human—the sense that all things are malleable and one both. Is this mumbo jumbo? Where's Grumm when I need him?

We were sorry to see it go, all right, even Katherine. It became a solemn occasion, even while they slavered for the payoff. So, the long-awaited moment was a bit of a bummer, I never heard what the agreed-on price was. That's how much I cared, because suddenly they seemed like crazy strangers, and then I'd look at the painting and get separated all over again. It was like making my getaway.

From then on things went wrong. The next morning the fancy fence in Boston halved his offer, and by noon he'd withdrawn it entirely. Then there were endless wrangles in Katherine's living room about how to proceed—she'd developed quite decided opinions—and after that pretty much nobody went there except me. She would summon me, or they would send me to reconnoiter, and I would drink little sips of vodka in her living room and tell her I didn't know anything about anything and didn't really want to. I remember her looking at me quite cold-eyed, like a traitor.

Which was more or less warranted. I'd canceled the whole thing out of my mind. She never let slip anything I could take back to Grumm and Bayou. By this time I was nothing but an emissary or a spy. I was supposed to keep them all up on each other, I was a way to keep them all on the straight and narrow. I don't mean they thought any of them would sell the painting and abscond, only that someone might crack or say something careless somewhere.

It got more and more ominous. The rain never stopped. One of Grumm's little tricks came down with a baby of her own, but it had no effect on him. "She's an adult," he said. "I can't worry about the whole world. Abortions are easy."

They were now preoccupied with finding a new fence who would give them a price equal to their deserts. They refused to go back to the small-time thief in Providence whom they now considered to have fleeced them on the earlier paintings, and they demanded the Vlaminck compensate for that too.

Grumm said, "And for the wear and tear on the nerves."

"For our loss," Bayou said. "When the time comes. Right, Veery?"

I just nodded. I didn't say a word any more unless I had to.

The Vlaminck never got unwrapped. It stayed in its layers of plastic and blankets in a special wooden box Grumm had made for it, absolutely beautiful too. Even Grumm never went back any more. One day—or rather night—they packed up the basement. Bayou retrieved his table and chairs. The spotlight came down. I think they knew they'd never have it so good again. They were planning to rob another museum up-Cape—of course they didn't tell Katherine—but there was nothing there they really coveted, nothing that really took their fancy. Their ardor was gone. This was strictly business.

Things had gotten serious finally, and want of money owned them. And cabin fever. There was a lot of talk about palm trees and out-of-the-way, little beach towns in Puerto Rico where no one ever went, where life was simple and the people were nice. The minute they got rid of the painting they were all going to get out of town, they were going to scatter, even me, when June came. I wonder where I would have gone. People were always talking about leaving—it was practically an occupation—and some succeeded, generally on the lam or in a coffin, or so it seemed.

According to Bayou it would all have worked out if it weren't for Katherine. He says they agreed to hold off till the heat went down. Rumor was that some of the first paintings had turned up and certain dealers were being squeezed for information. He says Katherine disguised her voice as a man's and called the fence in Providence, whose phone was tapped.

Katherine claims Grumm played F.B.I. and called the museum to ask what company insured the painting. The curator said he didn't know, but he'd find out, if Grumm would call back the next day, and the cops covered the pay phones and caught him.

Grumm insists Bayou lost his address book at some stranger's party he wandered into when he was drunk. Someone took it to the police and they recognized some of the phone numbers and tapped his phone.

Of course the indictment got all snarled up. "Just don't lie," Bayou told me. Grumm said, "Deny everything." I was the ghost that never got called, never even got mentioned. In the end they didn't make much of a defense, didn't even try. Grumm was too flummoxed, Bayou too flippant, and all of them were too ornery. And unworldly. Katherine was half-right at least. She didn't get charged, but only because they both upheld her alibi that she knew absolutely nothing. The judge said, "Meet the son you raised."

And the Vlaminck? The Vlaminck went back to the museum, which moved out of town too. The owner felt unappreciated. You could say I was the one who got to keep it.

The other thing I've never forgotten—a second sort of saving grace—I went to see Elena again. It took me about a week to screw up my courage. By then I hadn't the courage *not* to go. I meant to try to befriend her, after all she'd done for me. I was really afraid of what I'd find. I went about noon, for fear she'd be plastered if I went any later.

She was fine. She acted as if nothing had happened—or wouldn't deign to give it the time of day. I was certainly too young to bring it up. She made me a nice lunch, and I went away very much reassured—I can't tell you how much it meant to me.

She's dead of course—out in the cemetery with her husband, whom I regret I never met—but I remember her quite clearly. She was like . . . what . . . a meadowlark? Freida would be a blackbird, I guess, Ruzo a sparrow, Brade a scarlet tanager, Bayou a grosbeak. Grumm a mourning dove, Katherine some sort of wren. You, I'd hesitate to say, maybe an ovenbird, once removed. Twice.

Can you read that? I know—to you we're all magpies, parrots, cuckoos, crows. I shouldn't make light. The time is gone. People grew into themselves, like cages, wherever they meant to go. We were the last of the troglodytes. After that it was all feminism and CR groups. People coming out left and right. And whoever you were or whatever you'd done, tell all! The worse the better! Mortification! The new glory! Not for me. I didn't want to gang up on men either. I just wanted one of my own, but that never happened for long, and finally I got over it. After which I went from fag hag to recluse, and now it's years since I could put up with a lot of talk in my house.

My cat's enough. He's sixteen. But he still limps out at night and sleeps all day and he still gets chewed up every time some female yowls. And then I have to pop the pus out of his boils. Otherwise they get infected. I can't be taking him to the vet all the time. Not on my salary, with my rent.

He's my lion tiger, he leaves a carcass on my back doorstep every dawn, bloody little chunks of fur, for which I have my special broom. I guess it keeps him going, and I'm used to it. What can you do? Even domesticated mammals can't be made to change. Of course I would never geld a cat. Nor fix a female either, nor have one for a pet, I must admit. I never wanted children, thank God. I don't envy anyone. Not anymore. I've got my window on the woods, and a good pair of hiking boots. That's all National Seashore out there. Audubon would love it.

Of course I never dreamt I'd end up here. I didn't know any place like this existed, even after I'd been here a while. I doubt I ever would have come if I had, much less have stayed. I wouldn't have dared. I wouldn't have known enough. Life's a risk, I guess. All surprise, good or bad.

Well, I don't know about you, but I'm going to bed. Coming? Pardon my humor. You know, we might have done once. So many years ago. We almost did, the night we met, remember? That would have been quite something! Can you imagine? We would have been too young. What use? I can't say I'm sorry. We never would have had this night. Still, I wonder why we didn't. Good luck, I guess. Shyness. Fear of incest. Pride.

Maura Stanton

THE RIDDLE

All of the people who'd been at the party where Jillian Kennedy had her heart attack attended the memorial service in her honor. Everyone was strongly affected. It was one thing to lose a colleague in her prime, but quite another to actually witness—or almost witness—her death.

Anders Peterson was more disturbed than most. Even a month later, he was having trouble sleeping. He'd lie in bed going over every detail of the party, an annual event held in the walled garden behind the alumni house that celebrated those in the department who were retiring or leaving for other jobs.

Everything began with a buzz of whispering from the group of people standing near him on the terrace. At first he didn't notice, for a loud plane was going over, and he was concentrating on not spilling his plastic cup of chardonnay as he tried to pinch a cracker from his plate of buffet goodies. He and his wife were hoping to get enough to eat so that they wouldn't have to make dinner at home that night, but stuffed mushrooms and chilled, tasteless shrimp and a few carrot sticks and crackers weren't going to do it, unless they could get back for seconds. And where was the dessert tray?

Then he began to notice what the people around him were saying.

"Does anyone know what's wrong?"

"She doesn't look good, does she?"

"This has happened before, hasn't it?"

Anders swallowed a bite of brie. "Who are you talking about?"

His wife pointed with a celery stick.

"Jillian. Look over there."

"Who's that with her?"

"Her boyfriend. He's a painter."

"Look, he's taking her pulse," somebody said. "Something's wrong."

"It must be her heart again."

"What do you mean, again?" Anders' wife asked the person who had spoken.

"Arrhythmia."

"Jillian's giving one of the speeches, isn't she?" somebody asked. "For Herb?"

Anders shaded his eyes against the setting sun. He'd first heard about Jillian's heart condition a couple of years ago and knew she was on medication.

Now he had a good view across the lawn. Some of the people sitting near her had gathered around her chair. The boyfriend, who had his hand on her forehead, was thin and swarthy, wearing tight black jeans and espadrilles. His grey hair was cropped short. Anders had never seen him before and was surprised. He'd noticed Jillian talking in the halls a lot with Herb Dorsey, the fiction writer, and speculated that they might be having an affair, even though Herb had two kids and Jillian was fifteen years older than him. Over the years Jillian had been involved with several men in the department, so it was the kind of thing Anders expected. Now he realized he'd been wrong.

Jillian kept shaking her head. He could see her lips moving, and her free hand went up, waving people away. She sat up straighter in the chair.

The crowd shifted. The speeches were about to begin, and people started gathering at different tables, moving lawn chairs around the grass or grabbing folding chairs from a stack on the terrace in order to be closer to the portable microphone. Those inside the alumni house wandered out to stand in clumps. Anders' view kept being blocked. He stepped to the side once, then had to move over once again. Luckily, he was taller than most men. He found a good place to stand, behind some retired professors. He noticed thick, greenish veins protruding from the temples of one of them, a former chairman who had terrorized him before he had tenure. So it was true, the fellow didn't have real blood in his veins. Brown spots, like fruit bruises, speckled the neck of another old professor standing in front of him. But the younger ones were changing into their future selves, too, skinny assistant professors promoted to pot bellies, to sagging chins or deep furrows between the eyes. He picked out Herb Dorsey standing with a beer at the back of the crowd with some of the newer, untenured professors who still dressed like graduate students, the women in long skirts with painted green toenails, the men in Hawaiian shirts. Herb was wearing baggy shorts and a Cubs T-shirt, and Anders hoped he didn't make a scene.

Anders spotted an empty folding chair next to his wife, but as soon as he claimed it he was forced to give it up politely to the large, melon-faced widow of a retired professor of Old English. Standing again, he had a good view of Jillian. She was still in the lawn chair, her legs loosely spread, her Birkenstocks kicked off. Her eyes were closed; her hands hung limp at her sides. The boyfriend was stroking her arm, still murmuring in her ear.

Twenty years ago, when they'd both been newly hired young professors, Anders and Jillian had been lovers for a short time. Jillian was the second creative writer ever hired on the faculty, and from the beginning her Irish accent, her loud laugh, her funny jokes, and the long black braid that hung down her back announced that she belonged to a completely different species than the rest of them. She had a love/hate relationship with Ireland,

and had a store of jokes about priests and nuns. Because he was lonely, unmarried, and a writer, too, though he also had a Ph.D. in Postmodern Studies from Cornell, he'd quickly fallen under her spell, and for two months they had spent every weekend together. After they made love, he'd go out to the kitchen and fix gin and tonics and a snack of peanut butter and crackers. When he came back, she'd be sitting up in bed, pillows propped behind her, the sheet pulled up to her waist, the long dark hair festooned over her bare shoulders and breasts. She told him stories about growing up in Ireland by the sea, how a yellow rain slicker, sticky with salt water, had been almost her second skin, and he began to fancy that in another life she might have been a mermaid. But when the sheets got gritty, and he joked that the crumbs were scales or sea salt from her tail, her anger surprised him. "I'm not a mermaid," she insisted, "anymore than I'm queen Maeve, Grace O'Malley or Caithleen Ni Houlihan. Why do you think I left Ireland? To get away from all that prettiness, all that repressive crap." Then she laughed and told him that if he really thought she was a mermaid, then he'd better be careful, mermaids were dangerous. And she kicked her real, human legs out of the sheets, and cut her toenails in front of him, letting them flicker to the floor so that he stepped on invisible sharp stingers on his way to the bathroom. But when she badgered him to go to Europe with her in the summer, he refused—he needed the money he'd get from summer teaching to pay off his student loans—and she really got annoyed. When she finally broke it off—she told him she was going to Sicily with a professor in the Italian department—he'd been stunned and deeply hurt. But he was also secretly relieved. How could an ordinary looking man with thin, reddish hair and large feet, even one who'd written a dissertation on the post-modern use of fairy tale motifs in *Lolita,* and had published a well-reviewed but quickly remaindered novel about Swedish immigrants, ever manage to keep up with an Irish mermaid like Jillian? He'd known from the beginning that it couldn't last. Depressed but resigned, he threw himself into the hard job of building the creative writing program. Three years later, at a committee meeting, he met Emily, a recently divorced Education professor with a flat, Midwestern accent and strong calves. Their honeymoon was a two week bicycle trip around the Upper Peninsula.

Gabe Puckett, the current chair of the department, a trim, bearded man in his early 50's who never looked anyone in the eye, blew into the microphone. As soon as the crowd quieted, he welcomed everyone, then reminded them of the letter he'd circulated recently about a retired faculty member who was failing rapidly and needed a kidney transplant. No one had volunteered yet, he said, but if anyone thought they could do it, they should contact the hospital. And now, he said, let's turn to more cheerful matters.

After a retiring medievalist in a blue suit and red bow tie had been honored with speeches, applause, and the gift of some gardening tools, it was time for Jillian to say some words about Herb Dorsey. Herb was leaving to take a job in the South. He hadn't been put up for tenure because he'd never gotten his novel accepted for publication, though everyone liked him, and wished him well. Apparently he didn't wish the department well, however. Anders had heard rumors about some bitter things he'd said.

Jillian got to her feet and walked barefoot to the front of the crowd, where she took the microphone from Gabe Puckett. He whispered something in her ear as another plane roared over, no doubt asking her if she was OK. She nodded. He touched her elbow and moved away. She lifted her chin, and when she pushed her long black hair, now salted with grey, out of her face, Anders saw that she had some kind of colorful tattoo on her shoulder. He leaned forward and squinted, but he couldn't make it out.

Jillian's eyes seemed especially penetrating as she looked at the crowd. She waited until another jet taking off from the airport, only a mile away, had soared into background noise. "Although they look like gorgeous flowers," she began, her voice as lovely and musical as ever, "sea anemone are treacherous creatures, covered with stinging cells."

She paused. People looked at one another. "What could you expect from a poet?" said their faces. "Jillian dramatizes everything, doesn't she?" Anders saw quick, nervous smiles all around him. He craned forward to catch a glimpse of Herb Dorsey, but all he saw was his back.

"Sea anemone prey on small fish. But clown fish—those are the bright yellow fish you've probably seen from glass bottom boats, or on PBS shows about underwater diving—have learned how to exploit sea anemone."

Again she paused. She took a deep breath, and wiped her glistening forehead.

"Is she all right?" someone murmured behind him.

"How do clown fish exploit the sea anemone, you're probably asking." Jillian's voice trembled, and Anders cracked the empty plastic cup in his hands. Why didn't somebody get her to sit down? She was clearly unwell.

"They do it," Jillian went on, after another deep breath, "by hiding from other predators among the tentacles of the sea anemone."

She paused again, lowering the microphone. Was it a dramatic pause, or was she going to faint? A ripple of unease passed through the crowd as people uncrossed their legs and leaned forward or stepped to the side for a better view.

"And how do they manage this wonderful feat?" she went on, her voice stronger at the same time that the hand holding the microphone was shaking. "They do it by secreting a special slime that stops the release of the stinging cells."

The crowd waited, hushed, expectant.

Jillian slowly turned her head, gazing at everyone, deliberately including everyone. "You all love riddles, right?" she continued. "So here's a riddle for you. What creature is covered with slimy camouflage like a clown fish but also enjoys stinging its prey like a sea anemone?"

A few people laughed. Others looked uneasily at their neighbors.

"Well," Jillian said. "Who can answer the riddle? I'm waiting."

It was so quiet that Anders could hear the bees at work in the honeysuckle bushes.

Then the wife of a retired faculty member whispered loudly. "Can anyone tell me what she's talking about? Is she reading a poem?"

"You're thinking this is just total bollocks, aren't you? All right then, think about it for a while. Now it's time to talk about one of the finest fiction writers in the country today, one of the best teachers and one of the truest of true friends. Herb," Jillian said, "I for one will miss you. I want to say—I want to say—" Jillian swayed. She dropped the hand holding the microphone, and her boyfriend rushed up and took her arm. The microphone fell to the grass with a screech of feedback.

Gabe Puckett stooped to pick up the microphone and waited. Jillian was led back to her chair, taking deep breaths. Several colleagues hovered around her, but across many turned heads Anders could see her waving people away, indicating that she was all right, that she just need to rest.

It was a relief when Gabe Puckett took over. He told a couple of jokes, made a thoughtful little speech for Herb that sounded convincingly warm, and when Herb came up to accept his farewell gift, an L. L. Bean briefcase to replace his notoriously shabby backpack, he was brief and gracious and said he'd made a lot of friends around here that he'd miss.

Anders debated going up to Herb to explain once again that the reason he'd voted against putting him up for tenure had nothing personal behind it. It had only to do with his knowledge that the college committee would have turned Herb down without that published novel, a humiliating experience both for Herb and for the department. He poured down another glass of wine, to give himself courage, but when he looked around Herb was gone.

Emily was ready to go, too. She'd dropped her plastic cup into the trash can, and had her purse tucked under her arm. They headed inside the alumni house, but when they looked down the hall to the front door, standing wide open, they saw Jillian lying on the floor. Several people were huddling over her.

"They've called 911," one of the non-tenure track instructors told them. He and his pregnant wife were standing back against the wall, nervously watching. "There's nothing any of us can do. We have to get home to our babysitter, but we can't just walk over her."

"There's a back gate," Anders said. "Follow us." And he and Emily stepped back out onto the lawn, where a few groups were still milling about, unaware of what was going on inside. He led the young couple to a gate in the high fence that opened into a parking lot.

"Thanks! I hope she'll be OK. People say this has happened before." The young couple hurried away to their car. Anders and Emily, who were parked in front, but further down the street, cut through a motel parking lot. When they reached the front of the motel, they heard the ambulance, and saw it pull up in front of the alumni house.

"I guess there's nothing we can do," Emily said, hesitating for a moment, watching the ambulance.

"We'd just be in the way." Anders hurried down the street. He didn't realize that he was almost running until Emily, in high heels, called out for him to stop.

~ No one had expected Jillian to die, not even the faculty who stayed with her until the ambulance arrived, and watched the paramedics at work. Gabe Puckett notified her family, and arrangements were made for a funeral in Ireland. A memorial service, organized by her students, was held in the campus chapel, and Anders, as the director of the creative writing program, was asked to speak. For three nights he'd been unable to sleep. He kept trying to answer Jillian's riddle. Was she talking about him? Did she mean him? Was he the slime-covered clown fish who enjoyed stinging his prey to death?

She'd been angry about Herb, he knew that. But there was no way that a man who'd been on the faculty for five years and had published only three short stories, even if one of them made it into *Best American Short Stories,* was going to get tenure without a book. The department would have turned him down for one thing, and if his friends had managed to muster enough support for a yes vote, the college committee would certainly have shot him down. Anders had explained this all to Jillian, going over the facts of the case time and again, but she wouldn't listen. "That's crap," she kept saying. "What's wrong with you, Anders? Are you suffering from a dose of piles or what?" She wanted him to support Herb all the way in spite of the odds. But it would only have made creative writing as a discipline look bad, as if it had no real standards. He'd been working for years to get the program accepted by supercilious theorists and suspicious deans, and passionate support for a doomed cause would have sent them back to square one.

One of Jillian's graduate students, a young woman with short, feathery hair who looked on the verge of tears, was standing outside the chapel, handing something to the arriving guests. Anders, a few steps in front of Emily, held out his hand. He opened his fist inside to find a little net sack full of dried purple flowers and leaves.

"What is this?" he whispered to Emily after they'd slid into a pew.

"Potpourri."

"What's it for?"

"Smell it."

Anders brought the little sack to his nose. It smelled sweet and old-fashioned, like the inside of his grandmother's velvet-lined silverware box. He remembered that as a boy he'd loved to open the hinged mahogany lid, and stroke the garlanded handles of the knives and forks and spoons that were only used on holidays. What had happened to that box? His grandmother had brought it from Sweden. It must have been sold at the estate sale after her death.

The chapel was crowded, and people were standing in the back. Folding chairs had been set up at the ends of the pews, and Anders saw Herb Dorsey, in a sport coat for a change, hunched in one near the front, twisting a piece of paper back and forth in his hands, his speech, no doubt.

"Who's in charge?" Emily whispered.

Anders shook his head. He glanced at his watch.

The crowd rustled. Gabe Puckett finally stepped up to the lectern. He welcomed everyone in a quiet voice, then made a few warm but general remarks about what a wonderful colleague Jillian had been. He read a message from Jillian's family in Ireland, then announced that a scholarship had been set up in her name, and that donations were welcome.

One by one Jillian's students stepped up to the microphone. A speckled redhead and a boy with spiky hair each read, or choked out, one of Jillian's poems; others sobbed as they told funny little stories about her zaniness and kindness. Somebody had accidentally spilled a whole container of pizza peppers into Jillian's lap at a restaurant one night, and felt horribly embarrassed. But Jillian laughed it off, and then to make the person feel better, threw a handful of peppers into her own hair so that they glittered like red sequins. She'd invited her class for a brunch one Sunday and made blueberry muffins, except she'd forgotten to put in the blueberries. She'd jumped into a pond to rescue what she thought was a drowning dog, except that the dog beat her to shore. And when one young woman wanted to get a tattoo, but was scared to go by herself, Jillian had gone along and gotten a tattoo of a starfish on her shoulder. By the time the soloist stood up to sing "Amazing Grace," everyone had tears in their eyes, including Anders. He now understood why he'd been given the potpourri. He kept squeezing the little ball in his palm.

Now it was the turn of her faculty colleagues. Anders got to his feet, his throat prickling, hoping he didn't break down. He really *was* going to miss Jillian as a colleague. She was way too emotional about some things, and her sex life had been a little on the sleazy side, but she was a supportive teacher and a prize-winning poet who would be difficult to replace.

Luckily, he wasn't going to give a speech. He'd chosen to simply read a poem from her first book called "Dancer with Bouquet." Nevertheless, when he got to the final lines "You stare / at the unknown audience, elegant as clipped / iris, unable either to dance / or run off stage," his voice cracked. He rushed back to his seat, his face flushed. Emily took his hand.

Two women professors who'd been on several committees with Jillian gave moving little speeches. Then Herb Dorsey stood up, his rumpled paper clenched in one hand, and Anders felt his buttocks tighten and he sat straighter on the hard pew.

"Jillian set us a riddle," Herb began, just as he soon as he'd smoothed the paper across the lectern top, and Anders felt a cramp in his gut. This was the moment he'd expected and feared. He only hoped he could endure it.

"She asked us if we knew what kind of creature is camouflaged with slime but also enjoys stinging helpless prey. And all of us, I imagine, or at least I hope, have been pondering the answer." At this point he looked up from his paper briefly, then lowered his head again. "You've probably guessed that Jillian didn't mean a creature from the animal kingdom. She meant a human creature. She meant one of us. Or she meant all of us."

Herb paused again. Anders raised his chin and tried to catch his eye, but failed.

"Well, I'm not going to speculate on exactly who she meant," Herb went on, "but I think we all should keep her riddle in mind in the future. We all need to be kinder to one another, that's what Jillian was trying to say, and when ever I think of Jillian, kindness is the word that comes immediately to mind, and I've heard a lot of you use that word here this evening. I'm sorry Jillian's friend Lazlo Heinz isn't here to speak to us, he's still over in Ireland with Jillian's family, but he wanted me to tell you students in particular that Jillian always spoke about how wonderful and talented you were. She used to tell him how she was the luckiest and proudest teacher in the world. And I guess that's all I have to say." And Herb, muffling a sob, left the lectern, his eyes downcast, and walked back to his seat while some of the students started to sniffle.

"Anders!" Emily poked him.

He looked down at his fist. He'd torn the sachet open and was scattering dried petals all over his legs. He brushed them off. He was covered with sweat but nothing had happened. Why couldn't Herb Dorsey have said what he really meant? What was all this stuff about kindness?

The soloist rose and sang "The Bard of Armagh" as everyone filed out, groping for tissues. The students hugged each other and the faculty hurried by, heads lowered. Just as he stepped out on the sidewalk, Anders spotted the young woman in a gray silk dress who had told the story about the tattoo. He had a strong urge to ask her why Jillian had picked a starfish—did a starfish have anything to do with the riddle she'd posed—but the gray silk dress was joined by a blue silk dress, and the two started across the grass together. There was no way Anders could have followed without looking conspicuous.

~ Some nights Anders woke up covered with sweat that felt like slime. Other nights his skin seemed to prickle as if it were covered with stinging cells. He knew it was all psychosomatic, but that knowledge didn't help banish the obsession, and he lay awake for hours thinking about the riddle or wondering about Jillian's starfish tattoo while listening to Emily's gentle snores. His tailbone hurt him when he sat at the computer to work on his assigned portion of the department's self-study report that he had to finish by August. He had a stiff neck, and a burning sensation in his side. But when he went to his doctor for his annual checkup and prostate test, he mentioned none of these symptoms, and other than slightly elevated cholesterol, he was perfectly normal.

All right, he told himself, if the answer to Jillian's riddle, what creature is covered with slime like a clown fish but also stings its prey like a sea anemone, really is Anders Peterson, so what? What did it matter if a dead woman thought he wasn't a nice person? Nobody else at the party had pinned the answer to the riddle on him, as far as he could tell. Some may have provided their own name as the answer, or simply thought Jillian meant some slime ball politician or high level administrator. He was crazy to let this thing bother him so much.

He wrote a check for the scholarship fund in Jillian's name. He wrote checks for the heart fund, the cancer fund, the arthritis fund, the Alzheimer's fund, Easter Seals, the local animal shelter and the ASPCA. Emily was gone most of the day, involved in an institute for special education, but she noticed his moodiness at dinner.

"You need to get out more," she said, stabbing at her grilled lamb chop.

"I'll do the grocery shopping tomorrow," he said.

"Good. And would you drop those bags of old clothes into the Goodwill box?"

"Sure," he said. He looked at her smooth, plump face, almost unlined though she was in her late forties, and wondered if she ever felt guilty about anything. Even though her two grown up children from her first marriage still called with all kinds of problems, she never looked ruffled or upset. He wondered if she'd given any thought to Jillian's riddle.

"I was wondering," he said, "you remember the party—where Jillian had the heart attack—did you—"

"Did I what?" She looked at him blankly.

He couldn't ask her about the riddle. What if she told him that he, Anders, was the answer. Did he really want her to admit that she was married to a slimy creature who preyed on the weak. "Did you happen to see her tattoo," he blurted out instead.

"See her tattoo? Whose tattoo?"

"Jillian's tattoo. On her shoulder. Remember that student at the service talked about her getting the tattoo of a starfish."

"Yes. What about it?"

"I was just wondering if you'd seen it."

Emily shook her head. "I didn't get that close to her. Why? You're not thinking about getting a tattoo, are you?" She laughed.

He laughed, too, and changed the subject.

The next day at the grocery store Anders was pushing his cart down the cereal aisle when he spotted a tall woman in a pink sundress with a canvas shoulder bag who looked familiar. As he got closer he realized that it was Mrs. Herb Dorsey, and he scrambled through his brain trying to remember her first name. She had the dazed, hypnotized stare of a shopper and began to maneuver her cart right past him. The cart was filled with packages of diapers and toilet paper.

"Hello there," he said. "How are you?"

The woman stopped and smiled, but it was clear that she had no idea who he was. "I'm Anders Peterson," he said. "One of your husband's colleagues. We've met a couple of times at department functions."

He saw that the name did ring a bell. Her eyes hardened, and she nodded. She was going to go past him, but he shifted his cart to the left, blocking her path. She was trapped by the oatmeal.

"How's Herb?"

"He's fine."

"When are you leaving town?"

She smiled stiffly. "At the end of the summer."

"Need any help moving."

"We don't need any help moving." She didn't add "from you" but the words hung there as she backed up her cart.

"Tell Herb I said hello."

She'd already turned her cart back up the aisle. She looked over her shoulder, smiled politely, and started to wheel away.

Anders took a deep breath. If he'd had any doubt about the way Herb Dorsey had answered Jillian's riddle, his wife had just put it to rest. She despised him. He was the slime covered stinging creature who had preyed on her husband.

But suddenly she stopped her cart. She took a couple of steps back down the aisle and looked at him with determined cheerfulness. "Oh, by the way, we're having a little cook out Saturday night," she said. "Why don't you and your wife stop by? Herb's brother in Seattle sent him some fresh salmon steaks. It'll be fun."

Anders swallowed. "Well, maybe," he said. "I'll talk to Emily."

"Just give us a call. Bye." She smiled and walked back to her cart.

Anders' face felt like it was steaming. He remembered Herb's talk about kindness at the memorial service, and clenched the bar of his cart so hard that his fingers ached.

After he'd loaded his groceries into the SUV, he took the two shopping bags of old clothes from Emily's annual spring closet cleaning and headed around to the back of the store. A truck was pulled up at the loading dock, and a man in a green uniform was unloading cases of soft drinks. As he walked around the truck to the large Goodwill bin and opened one of the doors, he heard a plane coming over, flying low. The roar seemed even louder than usual, and he glanced up to see a jet with an unfamiliar logo. He was just hefting his first bag into the bin when a sudden warm shower sprayed across his face and shoulders. He smelled something foul, and to his amazement realized that he was covered with a slimy liquid.

"What the hell!" the delivery man cried out.

"I'm all wet," Anders called, swiping at his face with a shirt he pulled out of the other bag. He laughed.

"What the hell's going on? What is this stinking stuff."

The plane was dipping down in the direction of the airport. "Something came out of the sky." Anders handed the man one of Emily's old skirts from his bag, and watched him towel off.

The delivery man wiped his wet head. "This is crazy. We better call the police. I'll go get one of the guys inside. What if this stuff is poisonous? Jesus Christ. Just fell out of the fucking sky. One minute you're doing your job, next you get splashed from a clear blue sky."

"It wasn't meant for you," Anders said.

Anders waited while the delivery man went for help. He looked up at the cloudless sky and raised his dripping arms. He was covered from head to feet with stinking slime. Now he knew for sure what he was. The riddle had been answered; he didn't have to torment himself any longer. He was as bad as he'd feared. Later, when the police told him that a charter jet with engine trouble had dumped its fuel after takeoff so that it could land again safely, he drank a Coke while they consulted with the Pollution Control Agency. Jet fuel wasn't as toxic as gasoline. He and the delivery man were just advised to shower and wash their clothes by hand, and some protective barriers were set up in the parking lot. Anders washed his hands with the grocery store hose, carefully spread old clothes on the driver's seat, and drove home feeling more cheerful than he had in years.

Michael Stephens

COINCIDENCES

"That was back in the old days," my friend said, "when I used to believe in coincidences." Now he no longer believed in them. It was the one thing in life that he had become profoundly skeptical of. Coincidences: just the word suggests a flabby connectedness, ruled by chance, that certainly his own life and maybe my own life too belies. There really was nothing in his life to suggest that certain events were fortuitous. Nothing in this life seemed merely accidental. My friend no longer saw these connections and said, "My God, but wasn't that a fluke!" Or: "How often would you see that happen?" He was talking about dumb luck, and how such a concept had been banished from his everyday life, but also from the precincts of his life's greater design, its universal pattern.

The moment my friend said this, I understood exactly what he meant; in fact, this friend had a knack for such revelations, seemingly ordinary, until their resonance kicked in, and I saw just how profound his remarks had been.

This telephone conversation I was having with him reminded me of another I had had with him months earlier. That one centered around a mutual acquaintance of ours who found himself on the deep end of reality. Paranoia began to rule our buddy's life. Not just mind-numbing paranoia I'm talking about Big Voices, Combustion, Violent Dreams (waking and sleeping), real post-traumatic-stress kind of shit, with the human vehicle kicked into full register after-burner hallucinatory them against us me against you kind of stiff-armed paranoia. Our acquaintance had picked up some drugs, thinking that might quiet the voices, but the drugs only intensified the bad vibes. Our buddy was left filibustering the traffic on Second Avenue in midtown Manhattan, only this was not your average homeless crazy. This was an educated but also dangerous man, one who had been trained in all the combat skills and martial arts, a real-life commando, a former Force Recon marine, double dipping his life away with drugs and paranoia, commando knives in his pockets, bandoliers slung across his chest and inside his fatigue jacket, with several pistols salted away inside his pants in those ancillary pockets on the legs that military clothing had. Our mutual friend—to borrow a phrase from Dickens—had become dangerous to himself and everyone, including his new wife, around him. But he was a good man, like I said, our buddy, and so my friend (the one I had been discussing coincidence with) said, "We need to say a prayer for X," and I agreed, we did need to say a prayer.

I intended, not when I hung up the telephone, but later that night to say a prayer for the salvation and recovery of my buddy's life, probably at the end of the day, just before I went to sleep and reviewed the events of the past twenty-four hours. But my friend who was concerned with coincidence and its lack thereof in his life saw the prayer's necessity being more immediate.

"Dear Lord," he said into the receiver at his end, "may You in Your mercy watch over our poor fucking friend X, watch him and guide him and be good to this crazy son-of-a-bitch, show your kindness and eternal love for our fucking buddy, and make him well again, for he is one sick and paranoid motherfucker, lurching about these streets, and he needs your fucking guidance, so provide him with a way back to the values of his crazy fucking life, make him safe from his own fucking deranged emotions, and help him to believe that his fucked-up feelings are not correct ones, goddamnit, but only drugged up ones which have fooled him into believing that You are not present in his fucking life, extend Your divine hand to our friend and touch him, this fucking buckeroo, as You so often do, at the point of his fucking need, A-fucking-men."

"Amen," I said, even though I had no intention of wanting to be a part of this prayer, which, after all, made me uncomfortable. Still, the prayer reflected two deep aspects of my friend—his deep spirituality and his equally deep streetness. Because I knew this man well, I also knew that nothing in his prayer was contradictory, however it may appear to a stranger on the surface; that this was a deeply, even a profoundly spiritual man, who after all had his unique method of prayer, almost like drama itself, full of tensions, a combination of the sacred and the profane, the way the early Greeks first envisioned prayer and spirituality in their rituals to Dionysis, the dithyramb appropriate to the spiritual and the mundane, in fact, really a collision of those two worlds.

It was not until later, reflecting upon this spontaneous prayer, that I saw how lovely it really was. At first I only felt embarrassed that my friend would speak like this on the telephone, because neither of us were churchgoing or God-fearing people, though both of us had come the long way around to spirituality, in through the back door in the House of the Lord as it were and ever shall be. He was a drug addict; I was an alcoholic. Neither of us had had our drug of choice in many years. That's what made my friend's prayer so special finally; this was not about a religious hierarchy but rather the spiritual ministrations offered to a desperate acquaintance. When I thought about the prayer later I realized that our mutual friend would not be away for long because that very prayer which had been uttered on the telephone would bring him back to life. That prayer, I thought, was the grace that had been missing in X's life. And it was; and it did work; and he did come back to the world. Our buddy eventually got free of the drugs, the paranoia deflated, and he got help.

So when my friend mentioned his nonbelief in coincidences I had to shake my head in agreement, knowing that I didn't believe in coincidences either. Too many things in our lives particularly had occurred to belie such a notion. There was nothing random about such gifts. Without God's help, I would have been a dead man six years ago; I would have bought the farm or wound up permanently crazy on some back ward, or I would have murdered someone and found myself locked up in jail for ever and a day. But I need to think back to those days six years ago to understand just how the patterns work, how there really are no coincidences.

I had collapsed on Broadway on a hot, humid late June afternoon in Morningside Heights, and eventually I would be taken, not right away, but some time later, by two undercover detectives to Saint Luke's Hospital Emergency Room. It was one hundred degrees outside with one hundred percent humidity, and people were dropping like insects. All the Emergency Medical Service ambulances were in use, and even overuse, which is why I got taken to the emergency room by two undercover cops, the closest support in the area. When I collapsed, I couldn't get up right away. Then I did. A construction worker came over and asked if I was all right. I'm all right, I said, and went on, but I was not all right. I had this tremendous pressure in my head and a terrible pain on the side of it; my legs were weak and wobbly, and my balance was not right. I decided to go back home. But I didn't make it home. Instead I stepped into a neighborhood saloon and told the bartender I was not feeling well; he took one look at me and told me to put my head down in a back booth and then he came back with a large glass of brandy, but I didn't need booze. The headache became worse and worse, so I asked him to call the EMS and to call my wife and tell her what had happened and to meet me at Saint Luke's emergency room, which is what she did. By the time I got to the hospital I couldn't walk or talk, so by then they had no idea what the matter was. I was put into some kind of intensive care unit, given an i.v., and left to languish with the other fallen patients, one man with a heart attack from ditch-digging, the other a heart attack from being out of shape, overweight, and old. Eventually that day ended and I got to go home, diagnosed, not with a stroke, which is what they thought at first because I couldn't talk or move my limbs, but rather with severe dehydration and acute migraine. But that was not the end of it. I should have known right then and there that something was the matter, but I did not. I continued to drink, take valium and phenobarbs, smoke cigarettes and consume gallons of coffee, not eating right, working around the clock to complete a book that already was overdue.

Nothing worked the old way anymore, though. My drinking, which was formidable, suddenly became erratic; one night I could drink like there was no tomorrow, consuming alcohol from early in the afternoon until late at night. Other days I'd be drunk on my ear after one gulp. Still, I had no awareness then that drinking might be the problem; I thought that I had some kind of physical malady that was affecting my ability to drink. I thought that maybe I was over-stressed from working too hard on the book.

Two weeks of pure hell were passed, drinking, writing, taking pills, smoking, becoming garrulous and quarrelsome at the drop of a fork, really beginning to go off the deep end. I had lost my bearings; I was adrift in the sea of my alcoholism, and it had been drifting all my life, since I was a kid in my early teens, and I had been a daily drinker since I was fifteen. Now I was forty-two-years old, a writer, an occasional teacher, a sometimes journalist. When I was a boy, my brothers and I used to joke about one of our alcoholic aunts and her alcoholic boyfriend, and how pathetically drunk the two of them used to get, so stoned out that they couldn't even open their own cans of beer, so they used to give us nickels for opening their beers, which we sipped from, then handed to them, watching their hands shake, their faces contort as the cold liquid oozed down their parched throats, and once their nerves got steadier, one of them lit another strong, unfiltered cigarette, coughed, and went back to the alcoholic haze. I swore that I would be many things, but I would not become as pathetic as that red-headed, Irish aunt and her hopeless boyfriend, both of them reeling and incoherent at our dining room table on Long Island, or royally ensconced in some nook in a saloon in East New York underneath the elevated train line on Broadway or out in the sailor bars at Coney Island or red-faced drunk in my grandmother's house on Macdougal Street, reeling and rocking, shouting and cursing, threatening and cajoling, trying to stand and too drunk to get up. I vowed never to become like Aunt Katherine and her boyfriend Gene. But there I was sixteen or seventeen days after I had collapsed on Broadway and wound up in the local emergency room, my hands shook, I couldn't focus my concentration, and I was too weak to open—yes, just like Gene and Katherine—a can of beer.

"Open this for me," I said to my daughter.

She was twelve years old at the time, and she looked at me with compassion, but also this note of sadness, maybe even the way I once looked at my aunt and her boyfriend.

"Dad," said my daughter, "you shouldn't drink this." Then she paused and said: "You're an alcoholic."

And I was, and had known it for a long time, but I never thought that my own daughter thought that I was one, too. To her, I had been her father, a knight of the round kitchen table, the man who read her fairy tales, nursery rhymes, and children's books when she was a child, and now the one who listened to her stories or plays which she wrote, who discussed reading assignments and proofread her term papers, pointing out grammatical and spelling errors or suggested a better, more colloquial way of putting something in words.

She finally opened the can of beer that I couldn't open, and in many respects, I was more pathetic than my crazy red-headed aunt and her emaciated boyfriend from the Brooklyn ghetto where we all originated from. In those days, it took pressure on the church key to punch two triangular holes into the can—and the cans were a lot thicker and stronger than they are today—and all I had to do now was pull the tab on the lid, snap it back and guzzle.

That was no coincidence.

Doctors had told me to stop drinking; my wife had told me; a brother in recovery had tried to get me to stop; even the barflies in the local old-man's saloon told me that I drank too quickly and too much and I ought to lay off the sauce for awhile. But I told everyone that they did not understand, and I thought they did not, not understanding how thick the denial was. That's where grace enters into this. I was too thick with denial to allow reason to invade my life; I was too physically, mentally, and spiritually gone to understand how bad off I was. Instead, I was offered this gift, and that is where coincidence becomes a meaningless term. I needed to be provided with a daughter who loved me enough to warn me who I was and what I was doing, and that was all I needed to stop.

Again: no coincidences here.

So I stopped drinking. That can of beer that I could not open became the last drink of alcohol I have had from then until now, which is not to say that some day I might fall out of grace and pick up again. That is a distinct possibility that I am forever aware of. The thought is ever present that I am cured, or, worse, that I am not really an alcoholic, so why not have one more drink? That's the nature of the disease, that dis-ease, that uncomfortability. Two voices forever war inside of me: one of them wants my destruction, wants me insane, incarcerated or dead, while the other wants me whole and well. These are never coincidental voices; they are incredibly powerful voices, not miscellaneous ones, not random shouts in the head. Each works overtime. If I forget that I only have this grace for just today, I am lost, too. All I have is the present. The past no longer matters; certainly I can't afford to regret any of it. If I possess any kind of radiance, it comes with the simple fact that I am powerless; I have surrendered everything I lost, and now I can, being a special kind of loser, get on with my life.

But first I had to detox, and foolishly I did this myself, going to bed for a week, I mean, just giving up everything and going to bed, and not getting out of bed, not turning on a light or letting in any light through the closed blinds for a whole week. I peed in a pot next to the bed, and other than water and vitamins, I was too sick to take any food. At the end of this time I called and was admitted into Smithers, the alcohol treatment facility on the East Side of Manhattan, and there I went, still drying out, crazy as a loon, spastic, wired, hallucinating, for twenty-eight days.

That was no coincidence, especially how that name—Smithers—jumped into my consciousness from I don't-know-where. Smithers! It was as if the name had been placed into my brain by an angel. Certainly until that moment I had no memory of the name, not able to remember where all those big-time athletes went, nor remembering that Smithers out-patient at Roosevelt was where my friend Joel went when he got sober eighteen years earlier. It was no coincidence how I picked up the telephone book and that was the page I came to immediately, nor was it a coincidence that only the day before I had been approved for a cheaper medical insurance which had a one-shot coverage for alcohol and drug treatment. Nothing was coincidental from that point onward when my daughter suggested what I really was, telling me what I was—an alcoholic—instead of thinking all those years that it was family, bad upbringing, craziness, artistic temperament, ethnicity, or the peculiarities of my own education.

It was no coincidence which allowed me not to kill myself, though each day for six months I thought of doing just that, because I had become so depressed, so despairing of ever feeling good again, and, once again by the grace of God, I woke up on a New Year's Day, not hungover, but alive and alert and well, full of vitality and even joy, for the depression had been lifted at the moment when I went outside and walked down Broadway at seven in the morning, seeing all the drunks and drug addicts reeling home or shanghaied and marooned on the islands in the middle of Broadway, bereft of any clue of where they were, what they were doing, or even who they were this early in the morning. None of them looked happy; they were no longer new- year revelers, but rather the old year's desperados, the rejected and outcast, brain-fogged, body-clotted, spirit-empty, the walking zombied, the dead alive, and, then, there I was, alert and fresh, ready to go into the new year, a new man, full of a new life, thankful, grateful for the first time, blessed, touched by grace, not drunk, I was sober, and well, I was going down Broadway, glad to be alive. None of that was a coincidence.

For the greater part of coincidence is not its seeming pattern but its accidental nature. Coincidences occupy the same position simultaneously, have identical dimensions, happen at the same time during the same period; they correspond exactly, are identical. Okay. I can accept all of that; I can agree that so much of my present life has this *seeming* coincidentalness to it. Yet the key word is not the coincidence but the "seemingness" of it, because the world I now occupy, unlike the drunken world I left behind where there were no seams between the real and the imagined, the truth and my lies, so that everything seemed to be one thing or the other, and what did it matter anyhow? so that the world I now occupied had nothing to do with seemed but rather, as Hamlet said to his mother Gertrude, does not seem but is. Being was far more powerful than seeming; living one's life belied any notion of accidental forces converging to inspire that state of grace. Being is not an accident but the outcome of a gift, the occasion of a celebration of life. That is why I have become so skeptical of coincidence; it is too accidental and seeming, whereas the nature of my present world is the thing itself, a world of gratitude and grace, a world of connections, between myself and other things, but, more important, my connectedness to other people. This is our planet, I think, and there is nothing coincidental about that connection; it is as real as it will ever get.

In a world without coincidence, there is only the universal ring of gratitude. What holds this universe together is grace, a connective tissue as resilient as steel and as soft as the petals on roses. In a world of grace, there are no coincidences, only human connections. The coincidental always seems to be planned or arranged, so that I might agree with that part of it. Life now seemed to have a design. And if life had a design, it was not accidental. If this was not an accident, how could it be coincidental? I asked. Of course, there is plenty of evidence to contradict me. One can suggest convincingly that this universe—particularly this murderous century—only reinforces the possibility of the merely accidental in everything. Coincidence is not only alive and well; it is our guiding principle. Life, after all, is ridiculous; it is an absurd construct. True, I think, for Nietzsche said as much, and so did Sartre, and Camus confirmed it further.

Then I recall something that Camus wrote in an essay on Sartre that "the realization that life is absurd cannot be an end, but only a beginning." Likewise coincidences abound everywhere. Yet they are not the final act in a seemingly random universe. Once I despaired at the very act of breathing; I hated being alive, and could not wait to get to the end of my life, to be gone, to become nothing once again. Then all of that changed. How I changed I don't know, nor do I care to analyze why I changed at all. Instead, I acknowledge the difference that took place. Now when I wake in the morning, I'm suffused with gratitude. At what? you might ask. Of course, at being alive, the very thing that once troubled me so much that it made me want to die. I feel different today because I am different today. Once again I have been given twenty-four hours in which to rejoice at this act of being. This zany, optimistic attitude reminds me of another insight I once found in Camus. He wrote that "the world is beautiful, and outside it there is no salvation."

That is what a coincidence really is—a concept outside the beautiful world of being; it is an idea which lacks for its own salvation. Coincidences are anxiety-filled moments of false desire, a desperate attempt to impose our order upon the pattern of the universe. This brings me back to my friend's spontaneous prayer on the telephone, which in turn reminds me of yet another friend who once shouted at a crowded corner on Broadway in Manhattan, "I believe in God," he screamed into the beautiful sunshine of a spring afternoon, "and that's the fuckin' truth." There it is, I thought. It is finally the difference between a truth—a *fuckin'* truth, as my exuberant friend said—and a shallow observation of reality, a weak fact such as a coincidence. Coincidence is a kind of metaphysical journalism, whereas its opposite, the lack of coincidence, the physical world imbued with grace, is a philosophical moment of truth, an insight deeper than any fact could ever anchor itself to the known world. I can only be grateful to my friends for these insights.

Arturo Vivante

THE CRICKET

A cricket was chirping in the kitchen. Under the sink? Behind the stove? He could not tell. For a moment he even wondered if it weren't outside. No—the sound was too distinct for that. It was within. But where? The shrill, piercing note had a ubiquitous quality. It filled the room the way its companions outdoors filled the night. The only difference was that outside a choir was playing; this was a solo. And his only company. Playing for him. No—playing for itself, his presence absolutely irrelevant to it. It would chirp on if he left the kitchen and went upstairs to his bedroom. It wouldn't miss him. But he would miss it. Sometimes, for reasons unknown to him, it stopped, and the silence that followed soon became a tingling sound as the crickets outside took over. Or was it merely the tingling of the night, the night making "a weird sound of its own stillness"? Everything was so very still.

He had no radio, no television. To hear the news he sometimes went out to his car. He was alone in this house, one of several reserved for the faculty of the college where he had come to teach. He had been here three days. There were four other rooms, but so far no one else had shown up. Classes hadn't yet begun, that must be the reason. He was new and had come early, taking literally the college's recommendation to arrive right after Labor Day. The others, old hands, and most of them—from what he had heard—weekly commuters from New York, would wait. But any time now, someone would arrive, he was sure. Another day passed, however, and he was still alone. He and the cricket.

Outside, squirrels and chipmunks leapt from branch to branch, with a wavy motion and lightness that astounded him. At night, an owl hooted in the distance, more softly even than mourning doves cooed. Were he a bird, such a sound, he was certain, would be hard to resist. It was too entrancing, tempting, seducing; he would move and betray his presence, his whereabouts. Early in the morning, flickers would peck at the shingled walls of the house and wake him more effectively than an alarm clock. The sharp pecks struck more rapidly than the rapid spacer on his electric typewriter, or intermittently, like a loud, irregular escapement. On the lawn there were trees laden with ripe apples that no one picked and that fell "to bruise themselves an exit for themselves." The grounds of the college were extensive—the nearest house was at least a thousand feet away. Beyond the lawn, to the south, he walked into a field of corn much taller than he was. Soon he was quite hidden, felt himself disappearing from view, becoming invisible to any observer. Not that there were any observers—of his species. It was good to hide in freedom, as in a wood.

In the distance, almost on every side, were mountains, their outlines like great wings aslant, the open wings of a seagull. It was rather pitiful that he should make the comparison—he missed his village by the sea where his home and family were.

He returned inside to have a cup of coffee in the kitchen, and heard the cricket. How tirelessly it went on, and for what purpose? Was it simply *joie de vivre*, a song of summer, a song of summer dying? Or was it a love song, played to a mate who wasn't there, a lonely call that one might come and join it?

He sipped his coffee—instant, with a little milk—in the bare kitchen, so distant from the one at home, where there were two of his children's paintings, a Russian icon, a bronze relief of crabs over the stove, a copper pitcher from Arabia, many pots and pans on display; where his wife made Italian coffee, and where people kept dropping in—they lived right in the center of the village. Here, apart from the sink, the stove, the refrigerator, the table and two chairs, there was almost nothing, and no one. Yes, someone—he heard a door on the ground floor being opened and steps coming his way. A middle-aged, slender, mild-looking, bespectacled man, with reddish hair brushed down and curling at the lobes of his ears, appeared and stopped at the threshold as if surprised to see him.

"Hello," he said to the newcomer.

"Hello," the man replied. "I thought I was alone."

"I did too."

They laughed. "Thaddeus Dolmen," the man said.

"Emilio Buti."

They shook hands.

"That's an unusual name," Emilio said.

"Yes, people don't know what nationality. It presents certain advantages," Thaddeus said in a slight, not unpleasant foreign accent.

"I won't ask you any passport questions. When did you arrive? Oops, there's one!"

"What do you teach, may I ask?"

"A prose workshop, a course on late nineteenth-century and early twentieth-century novels, and some Italian. And you?"

"History of ideas, literary criticism and theory of language."

"That sounds very intellectual."

Thaddeus pursed his lips, exhaled and tilted his head as if to brush aside the remark. "I am a structuralist and a semioticist," he said. "What novels are you doing, may I ask?"

"Controversial ones—novels that were hard to publish; *Resurrection,* because of the Czar; *Tess of the D'Urbervilles* and *Women in Love,* because of the morals of the time; *The Portrait of the Artist as a Young Man* and *Remembrance of Things Past* because they were considered underplotted."

"Interesting," Thaddeus said, then began talking rapidly about other novels that he thought were ahead of their times—novels that for the most part Emilio didn't know; English, French, Scandinavian, German, Russian, and even Italian novels—and with such enthusiasm in three cases that Emilio thought he had better write down their titles and the names of their authors. He wondered if he had ever met anyone so erudite. Thaddeus came very close as he spoke, and more than once Emilio felt a droplet of saliva landing on his face. But never mind. It was worth it. He thanked him, which only encouraged Thaddeus to say more. With considerable zeal, he dictated two other titles and spelled out the authors' names for him. Next, he recommended a book on Dante that was unknown to Emilio. He felt so ignorant. I shouldn't be teaching, he thought. I ought to be painting houses, or gardening, though I am not very good at those things either. Oh God, what is it that I do well?

Thaddeus paused for breath, and, to his relief, Emilio heard the cricket chirp. Such a familiar, simple sound.

"A cricket," he said to Thaddeus.

"Ah," Thaddeus said, and went toward the sink. He tapped the sink. Immediately the cricket stopped chirping; then, after a moment, it began again. Once more Thaddeus tapped the sink. Again there was stillness. "He stops," Thaddeus said, "then resumes. Stops and resumes. It is funny."

"Yes. Well," Emilio said, smiling, "I guess I'd better go back up to my room and do some reading."

"Oh, there is another novel you must read. This one 1910."

Dutifully Emilio took pencil and paper again while the other dictated. "Well, thank you," he said. "You've given me quite a bit of homework. I really feel very well equipped now."

"Oh, you are welcome," Thaddeus said with a discounting gesture, as if he had offered him two peanuts, then looked down at the floor at a rather large bug, and, before Emilio could say stop, Thaddeus had crushed it under his shoe.

"No!" Emilio said.

Thaddeus stepped aside, uncovered a crumpled little heap from which two long legs stuck out, flattened.

"The cricket! You killed it."

Thaddeus looked at it and shrugged his shoulders, then rubbed his shoe on the floor. "And there's another book—" he went on.

But Emilio wasn't about to listen. "No," he said, softly, and left the kitchen. As he went into his room he still had in his hand the slip of paper he had written the names on. He looked at it the way one looks at a distasteful object and, tearing it to pieces, threw it into the wastepaper basket.

Eugene Wildman

THE LAST DAYS OF ATLANTIS

I

"You're thinking," Mimi says. "If you're not thinking you should be talking."

Mimi is opposed to thinking; she values spontaneity and possibility and pure expression of being. "Do whatever you do," she is always lecturing Todd, "only don't get lost in your head." What Mimi likes doing more than anything is talking.

Todd blinks and rubs his eyes, trying to clear the sleep away; he is not quite there yet. Images flicker and wink out: a cat in a doorway, an enormous Buddha, a girl with a serpentine smile. Like traces of an earlier existence. He wonders if he was dreaming about Da. Or was that Mimi smiling?

Lately she has been starting his day by calling in with her newest dreams. She has several of them each night, which she wakes up from and immediately writes down. She keeps a notebook by her bedside, a discipline begun more than twenty years ago, and now the many accumulated notebooks contain the record of an inner self over nearly half a lifetime. Mimi is so in touch with her internal process that she easily alters the content of bad dreams and produces recurrences with the outcome she likes.

Todd can never remember his dreams and he keeps hoping he will show up in hers. He would like to be the man of her dreams, but for now he is only their captive audience. For a moment more he holds himself back, and then his resistance falls away and he lets himself float on the sound of her voice.

~ Mimi is always lost in these nocturnal sagas, trying to find a way home; there is always something about water. In this installment she is at a strange hotel set at the shore of an unknown lake. The rooms are empty and she wanders the hallways searching for a purse filled with jewelry that somehow she has mislaid. Outside there is a flash of lightning; a door flies open and two of her sisters emerge from one of the rooms. They look cautiously about them, and then they notice her. There are six girls in the family in all, and an equal number of brothers, but only the three appear here. Her sister Margie is present, the one she is closest to in age, and also the one she likes best. Her younger sister Connie is there too, the *femme fatale*, who had an affair with her husband. Till Connie came along Mimi was the youngest. Everyone called her Mei-mei, which means younger sister. That is where she got her American name. The sisters walk outside to the lake, where a shadowy form rises from the water. The shape stands with arms outstretched, as if beckoning, and with that she wakes up.

~ She wants to know what Todd makes of it, but he is not sure what to say. There is the matter of rivalry among the sisters. Margie is happily married, to a man he suspects Mimi has a crush on. Connie, the other, stole her husband, though that was ten years ago. Todd is curious which of the three the shadow was reaching out to. But is this a can of worms he wishes to open up, first thing in the morning yet?

"Even in your sleep you play hard to get, what's the big megillah?" Todd says.

"How profound," Mimi says, but he can tell that she is pleased.

He wonders for the thousandth time what went wrong between them. How could everything have disappeared so suddenly? It is hard to take this reversal seriously, not to look for some meaning inside it, some clue that may lead to a way back. Mimi of course would find that absurd. She clings to the here and now. Even the suggestion of an underlying meaning is sufficient to produce an outburst from her. "Things are what they are," she would say. "If anything was there we would be in bed now." But he knows something about disappearances too.

~ These dark strangers have figured before, always in odd, aqueous settings. Streets and buildings dissolve around her, plunging her into murky depths where the stranger either rescues or pursues her. These scenarios mirror her life. In China the family moved from village to village, one step ahead of the Japanese army. Her father was a famous general, a leading light in Kuomintang circles, and they would have been killed or put in prison, dangled as bargaining chips. Afterward came Hong Kong and Taiwan, and a desperate stretch in the U.S. where she moved from state to state. The dreams reveal a rootless core, someone who is at home everywhere yet nowhere.

Occasionally a breath of humor shines through. Once the stranger turned out to be a brother who is gay and there was great merriment as well as mutual embarrassment. Another time, entering a theater, she spots the stranger again, watching from a storefront window that sports a sign saying PRAWN SHOP.

Mostly they are romantic intrigues, often with a certain scatological flair. In one she is at her mother's house when some prominent Japanese arrive. Desperate to relieve herself and unable to find anywhere else, she goes inside a priceless vase which the visitors apparently covet. Urns and baskets and steaming bowls appear with regularity. Women smoke cigars in her dreams, and men, sometimes women too, smear her with food and lick it off. Lately she has taken up cigar smoking herself. Waste matter often floats through the water, but somehow she emerges untainted and untouched.

II

Mimi sits across from him holding a cigar, turning it with her fingertips, looking at it musingly. They have come from *Wings of Desire*, a movie where angels see only in black and white, except for those moments when they feel human. Then the screen leaps into color. Now they have stopped for a nightcap. The place is crowded and the tables are jammed together and theirs is much too close to the bar. You almost have to shout to be heard.

"I don't love you," Mimi says.

"All right," Todd says, "it's enough."

"You don't turn me on," she says, puffing on the cigar again. She tilts her head back and blows a cloud of smoke.

"I got the message," he says.

"If I wanted it we would have had it before. I know how to get what I want." She gives the cigar another turn and puts it back in her mouth.

"You stuck a knife into my heart," he says.

"That's your story," she says.

"That's right, it's my story and I don't like it," he says.

"Then stop telling it," she says. "Take your knife out of your own heart and stop being such a victim."

They have known each other since he got back from Bangkok, on the trail of the Thompson mystery. Jim Thompson was a legend when he vanished, twenty-five years before. Seemingly gone up in smoke. The story was a sensation when it broke. Celebrity expat, millionaire silk merchant, and very possibly a spy. Todd was bursting with ideas—on a tear, on fire, feeling like a rocket blasting off. He was closing in, he could sense it. That was over two years ago, twenty-six months today. He is still on fire, but this is Mayday. Now the publisher is gone as well, the project is out in the cold. The mystery too has ground to a halt, is just a mass of notes; the rocket has crashed and burned.

Mimi had placed a personals ad describing herself as an artsy type, one time FOB, had it with cheating SOB's, seeking to meet a superior man, long fingers a plus. She has her own graphic design business, whence the artsy part. But why the contentiousness, was it real or put on? And what of the reference to the superior man? Ironical echo of the *I Ching*? It turned out she was frank to a fault, did not have a clue what irony meant. In the end the ad intrigued him and he responded. He sent her a tracing of his hands and they talked on the phone and arranged to meet at an espresso place they both liked. When he saw her walking through the door he felt an electric shock. Everything he wanted was coming toward him.

~ He regards her as retribution for Da, a balancing of accounts, divine justice. They are paired in his mind, merged almost, as if they themselves are lovers. Da is the woman he lived with in Bangkok. Her real name is Suchada—Da is a nickname—and there is a story that goes with it, about a virtuous girl, the primal Da, accused of being unfaithful by the king. She protests her innocence but to no avail and the furious ruler has her beheaded, whereupon her blood, transformed into a rainbow, shoots from her body up to the sky. The day he left Da was devastated, rushing from the terminal, sobbing bitterly, unable to hold herself back any longer. She writes him often and in his replies he tries vainly to soften the blow.

He had prayed at the Rama Shrine that he would meet someone, burned incense, placed a wreath of flowers, picturing the woman he had in mind. A few days later the picture came alive. They fell in love, but then all at once his feelings somehow were gone. It was as mysterious to him as it was to her. He could not recapture what he felt before. Now he is being repaid in kind.

Today another letter came. She has not written in awhile and feels awkward, but she thinks about him always, dreams of him. Things are very bad. She is thinking of returning to her village, entering a temple, living as a nun. Last month her brother died. A truck transporting a load of fish swerved into his car, killing him and her half-sister. It is the rainy season and the roads are dangerous. She is alone in the world and has no one to turn to. Can he send money? She knows she has asked too often already, this would be the last time.

How different these are from her first letters. Todd wonders if she is really writing them. He should compare the handwriting with the earlier ones. It would make a nice piece. Some enterprising friend acquires his address, and along with her scuzzy foreigner boyfriend concocts these heart-rending letters he gets. He could send back a letter mirroring hers, describing how dreadful things are for him. But he is afraid of what else he may bring down on himself.

III

He listens to the whoosh of a car in the distance, like the sound of a boat at the Floating Market. With his eyes closed Todd sees the river, winding like a serpent around the city. Whether held protectively or in a lethal embrace no one can ever truly know. The streets twine sinuously out from the bank, so many serpent heads on the Buddha's crown. On the far side a temple spire points an admonishing finger to the sky. When he opens his eyes it is all gone.

Sometimes he thinks his life is a dream and he tries to wake up but does not know how. He remembers the day he first arrived, stepping from the terminal at Don Muong airport, squinting in the light and looking up. A white balloon shimmered in the sky, like a sign from above, which in fact it was. It was a promotion for Kismet, a line of perfumes being introduced in the stores. The balloon was in the shape of an elephant and was 150 feet long. The newspapers called it "The Great Sky Elephant." The sky is about the only place they have not looked for the missing man whose life he had come in search of.

Maybe he will phone the bar today. It is mostly in the mornings that Todd thinks of calling. Perhaps because here the day is just starting, while there where she is already it is dark. The sudden, deep darkness of the tropics. At the Lucky Star the night is beginning and Da is putting on her face. It is tomorrow there. Out of reach in time and space she sits at her dresser playing with her hair, doing her nails, adding the final touches. Soon, with a last look around, she will put out the light and leave quickly, her face blank, revealing nothing.

The letters have begun to weigh on him. Last month was the downpayment on the house her aunt has put up for sale. Before that was the CAT scan, dizzy spells, something about a blood clot. Before that her best friend Tuk walked off with the money before that. Todd would like her to have security, a place to call her own. His friends laugh and tell him he is a fool, he is supporting a whole village, a province, and he replies so what, then so be it. Besides, he knows what he knows. Your tongue may lie but your eyes cannot, and Todd has looked into hers. He reaches over, punches the numbers, and one of the hostesses comes on the line. "Allo," she says and sets the phone down. He does not know the voice, though how would he, more than two years later. Bar girls come and go all the time. A year is a lifetime in the bars. He waits but no one comes back on the line. Above the din of voices in the background he can hear the tape deck booming out. Stevie Wonder, "I Just Called to Say I Love You," that at least has not changed. He tries to pick out bits of conversation, even a word here or there. But it is not possible, it is just din.

Twice it rained, unseasonable downpours, just after he got there. And then a month later again. They were sitting in his room sopping wet, Da laughing, shaking her head. "You always bring the rain," she said. He remembers her excitment when he bought her reading glasses. She kept refusing, insisting she could do without them, but in the end relenting and now she wore them everywhere, almost never taking them off. The room suddenly filled with magazines, Da jubilant, bursting out, "Before, my eyes are dark!" Then later, after they made love, "You give me my eyes, you cannot give your heart." Da and her way with words, he thinks, what does it matter if the stories are false.

IV

Todd sits on a packing crate in a storage area at the international terminal. A group of workers, Mexican mostly who speak no English, are sorting Christmas tree ornaments, taking them from cartons and placing them in others, writing what kind and how many there are in Magic Marker along the sides. Yesterday the trees were stacked neatly in rows. He is here with Mimi who is supervising the shift, a favor for Jeri, a close friend, a landscape architect who has the airport contract. There is nothing for Todd to do but watch.

Mimi is wound as tight as he has seen her. She comes over every now and then to ask the name of an ornament. When he is unable to say, she looks annoyed. "I'm not the Christian," he protests, whereupon Mimi glares; in fact she was converted when the family lived in Hong Kong. She asks him to roll up the sleeves of her sweater, her hands are dirty, she explains. The left one goes smoothly enough, but the right is harder because her blouse sleeve is bunched and she yanks her arm impatiently back.

Driving up they had their old familiar argument about why couldn't he accept the way things were. A Chinese torch song from the Thirties was on the tape deck. The singer had a velvety textured voice and the melody was hauntingly beautiful.

"I feel the way I feel," Todd said. "How about you doing some accepting?"

"That's all your conversation," Mimi said.

"All right, it's my conversation," he said. "So we're conversing, so what?"

"So get out of your head just for once."

"I don't think I'm in my head."

"*I don't think I'm in my head.* Listen to yourself. Think is all you do."

The song came to an end and she rummaged through her stack of tapes, popped in Debussy's *The Afternoon of a Fawn.*

"That's more like it," he was about to say, "an afternoon of fawnication." Then he figured let it go. "Is this the time or place?" was the best he was able to come up with instead. "Do we have to go into it here?"

"I love that. *Is this the time or place?* You're so lost in your head."

"For god's sake, that's not true."

"You live in your head, for god's sake."

"Is my erection in my head?"

She shot a grudging smile. "With you it probably is."

"Why don't we find out," he said.

But Mimi was not listening anymore and they drove the rest of the way in silence. Every few seconds she kept changing tapes. "Nobody knows me like you do," she said, as they were pulling into the parking garage. "Don't you know what that means?"

"No, I don't know what," he said.

"I've turned into such a bitch," she said.

~ The workers watch Todd watching them. He takes out his notebook and jots impressions. *The women wear sweaters and dark skirts. The men are dressed in boots and Levis and have tooled leather belts.* They glance over and murmur in Spanish and he senses disapproval, even scorn. Why is he not dressed for work? What is he writing down? What is it between the woman and him, why is she so angry?

He wonders what flights are leaving tonight. Why put up with any more? Another word and he is off for Aruba, wherever that is, and then he remembers, an island off Venezuela. There was a piece on TV recently, something about a revolution in paradise.

In a few minutes he will go upstairs and check the departure board. Maybe there will be one for Bangkok and he will go back and live happily ever after in a cozy cottage for two with Da. Not even bother saying goodbye, just fall off the earth like Jim Thompson.

Mimi's friend returns with Bill, her partner and longtime companion. They were off in another part of the airport when he and Mimi arrived. They are tall, with faded blond hair, and look almost exactly alike. They remind him of an aging Tristan and Isolde. She is the one with the intensity, though; next to her Bill is flat. She is the beauty, and Mimi adores her.

Jeri and Bill round up the men and lead them to one of the other terminals where there is heavier, more physical work to be done. The women remain sorting ornaments, counting little glass cherries and throwing them into cartons. Other cartons are filled already with glass oranges, glass snowballs covered with glitter, silverfoil fans and stuffed Santas. There is even a box of female Santas in cute red pantsuits topped with little yellow wigs.

Suddenly Mimi is poking him, shaking her head, wagging her finger. "You don't like sticking to facts," she says. "Things are what they are, why can't you get it?"

"At last I see the light," Todd says. "So tell me, is there anything that is not what it is?"

"Yes, you! Because you're hopeless. Don't you know what it's like just to *be?* Not in your head, for once in your life. Free of your tapes, your identity, your *shit.* Finally, *really,* who you are." She turns and stalks away.

"That's right," he shouts, "I don't get it, because unlike you I'm not out of my head." If Mimi has heard she does not let on and suddenly he is famished. It is late, they have not eaten since lunch, and he calls out that he is going for sandwiches but gets no answer in return. Forget it, he thinks, they are too entirely different. He is tired of endlessly quibbling and arguing, feeling like a spectator trapped in his life.

Can this be what it was like for Thompson? Todd is disappearing also, out in plain view. Fine, he thinks, he will face the facts. Mimi is right, it is simple. He will tell her finally that he has had it, put a stop to the mess with Da. He deserves to have something too. He will dedicate himself to the project and stay with it all the way; a calling reclaimed, purpose recovered. It has always been a race with time, and his constant fear is that the remains will turn up. Some tourist or developer will stumble on the skeleton and that will be that, the bitter end.

People take off all the time, maybe he should approach it that way. And then it suddenly occurs to him, how could he not have considered this before, what if it was a hoax? What if Thompson, having tired of it all, of his double life as businessman-spy, simply walked away? Took a new identity and began again. Another Mimi, free of his tapes. Though Todd personally still believes the Golden Triangle is the key. He is convinced that poppies were involved, a drug ring piggybacking shipments of silk. Possibly CIA-sponsored. When Thompson learned of it his fate was sealed. Only why did he never report what he knew? Or was that the fatal misstep, that he did?

There are too many possibilities, that was the catch from the start, and as Todd makes his way through the maze of corridors it strikes him that he may not find his way back. Could he wish for a better windup? It is like his vision of solving the mystery, cutting through the tangles of secrecy and lies. There is no way anyone can know the truth, even to conceive it is madness. He opens a door and climbs a flight of stairs, already picturing the headlines in the paper: HOPE FADES FOR MAN LOST IN AIRPORT.

~ In the departure lounge people mill about, expressions of shock and dismay on their faces. "I can't believe it," a woman says, her voice small and quavering. She is close to tears. A few feet away a crowd is clustered in front of a TV set.

"What's going on?" Todd asks.

"See for yourself," the woman answers, "the whole downtown is underwater."

On screen a crew of workmen is pouring sand and maneuvering pumping equipment into place. A tunnel wall has apparently been breached and the Chicago River is flooding the Loop. A city official is on the scene offering reassurances. "There is no need for alarm," he says, "the situation is under control." Cut to the anchorman who declares, "What the public will now demand to know is why there were no precautions in place. Was this an accident waiting to happen?"

The cafeteria is at the end of the terminal, so he nods to the woman and continues on his way. There is a long line and service is slow, and by the time he has gotten his sandwiches and come back the TV is off, the woman is gone and the waiting area is empty. A cleaning crew is buffing the floor.

He wonders if Mimi and her friends have heard. He cannot get the footage out of his mind, the water rushing up from the ground, like a scene from the Atlantean endtime, the workcrews trying frantically to contain it. When he gets back, before he can say a word, he sees that something has happened. The Mexican women are standing with their coats on, looking uncomfortable, waiting to leave. "We finished up early," Mimi says, her voice hoarse and hollow. Mimi and Jeri stare at each other, seem to sink into each other, then Jeri turns to Bill and slaps him. You can see the red spot on his cheek. Bill rubs it where he was struck, shaking his head and smiling sheepishly, then raising his hands as if in surrender. Todd keeps looking from one to the other, and suddenly it comes together. Boxes in boxes, he thinks to himself. Meet the dark stranger. Not so dark after all. The reason she ran her ad in the first place and then, like that, broke it off. The outside seems only an extension, almost as if the city itself has entered one of her dreams; the flood hardly more than a sign of whatever is raging within.

He notices the glass snowball in her hand, watches unable to say a word as she slowly begins to squeeze. She stares helpless at her own hand, mouth half-open, then seems to stagger, and a carton tips over. A pool of glitter spreads on the floor. Like powder, he thinks, from the wings of a butterfly. Luckily for Mimi the skin is not punctured, but she looks frightened all the same. He reaches over to look at her hand and this time she does not pull it away.

"It just broke," Mimi says.

"Just like that?" Todd says.

"Yes, like that," she says. Her lips press together, he can see the tension, and he knows enough not to push. Time later for things past and talk of new beginnings.

As they walk through the corridors to the parking lot he thinks again how different they are. She runs from meaning while he yearns for it; she savors dreams while his are unknown. When they get in the car he can feel her exhaustion. For all the problems she causes him she is so surprisingly, unexpectedly slight. Such tiny shoulders to rest his hopes on. He wonders what her dreams will be now.

"Do women always come to you?" Mimi says.

"I came to you," Todd says.

"I advertised for you," she says.

She reaches for a tape and puts it in the deck, the Chopin *Ocean* étude. They sit quietly as the music swells, and then as the car begins to move he notices glitter on his hands too.

Russell Working

INMATES

1

There was no announcement. The priest simply appeared one day, fleering out the windows and shambling about the old rectory, his new home, on the outskirts of Port George, a Northern California coastal town that has since become notorious for the bludgeoning death of an African-American prisoner who had thrown his feces at the guards. But in 1987 the town was still debating whether to endorse the construction of a supermaximum-level state prison out by the tidal mudflats, and the region was five years away from the boom that would draw Wal-Mart and Bi-Rite to town and fill Cafe 24 and Ideal Drugs with construction workers and architects and then wives of the guards and the battered, forgiving girlfriends of inmates, women who stuffed the mail bags with perfumed letters and aspired to pregnancy during conjugal visits. The mills were closing, the congregation was shrinking, and the assignment of this priest was taken in some quarters as an insult, an old gnome presiding over the death of a parish. Even Louise Shippen's Church/Scene profile of the new cleric in *The Daily Record-Searchlight* was lacking the breathless piety one usually found in her copy, whether the topic was lesbian Methodists or the Mennonites who sued to stop teachers from pledging allegiance. Ms. Shippen was interested in Eastern mysticism and seemed irritated by a priest who "lived for four years in Asia, but never found time to investigate its ancient spiritual heritage." "Plenty to keep me busy in the parish," he chimed.

For a year, since the retirement of Father Roy, St. Stephen's had prayed for a priest, and now in reply came this mild French Canadian Jesuit with a face that made babies cry. There was no way to be polite about it. One could not put a finger on anything specifically abnormal: it was the combination of features that added up to something monstrous: his lower eyelids drooped, revealing bloodshot white and only the slit of a pupil, and he grimaced grotesquely when smiling; his nose had been broken, like a boxer's, and his checks were as hollow as the punt of a champagne bottle. Father Jules was gaunt and bent, and despite his age, his gray hair had a henna tinge, as if he were dyeing it. It made you squirm to stare at him for the course of an hour-long mass, excluding the time his back was to the congregation (exposing a dented, bald pate) while he raised the host and knelt and raised it again, and then turned to reveal a visage such as one might have discovered in a Victorian ward for the criminally insane. But he seemed a good man, and in the end one can grow accustomed to anything. At least, everyone thought, we've got a priest again.

The congregation had trouble getting a fix on him. Some priests like to hector you on subjects they know nothing about, marriage for example, like some bachelor uncle who, angry at a young nephew's pleasure in the company of women, persists on warning his girlfriends about his intentions, but Father Jules was different; he seemed pained at having to offer the slightest reproof. This was good, perhaps, yet one sensed he repressed a great deal. It was January, and he slept in the rectory for a week before he mentioned to anyone that the heating was broken.

Father Jules rapidly settled in to his tasks. He baptized infants in their miniature wedding dresses, warbled mass in tones of utmost despair, limped around the yard planting garlic bulbs, thanked the ladies for the dinners they dropped off but was once seen to scrape an entire casserole into the garbage in back—he was that fussy about what he ate. He rambled in sermons quoting Sir Thomas More, Nelson Mandela, Randall Terry, Terry Anderson, Solzhenitsyn.

To everyone's surprise, the priest soon became friends with Tom Corcoran, algebra teacher, city councilman, and varsity basketball coach—and Corcoran, despite the Irish name, was not even a Catholic. They were the unlikeliest pair, the broken old priest and the youthful coach: divorced, affable, six-foot-six and a touch beefy, yet so handsome that he still, at thirty-nine, received love letters from girls who had hardly begun shaving the down from their legs. He was never quite able to denude the cleft in his chin of whiskers, so that it had a vaguely obscene quality, like the backside of a man in the shower. There was something Southern in his accent. You wanted him to like you. When he made his opinion known on the council, even those who had shown up to yell about, say, the proposed sewer bond issue, hastened to preface their criticism by lining up their views with his: "Well, I agree with what Tom said, but . . ."

The priest was a basketball fan, and he was seen at every Port George High School game. It was less widely known, however, that Lafon was a former high school basketball coach himself, not to mention a center (and fullback, during football season) for the Jesuit college he had attended decades ago in Montreal. Around town Corcoran said it was obvious that Lafon, who would have been tall had his spine not been so bent, had been injured on the field. The coach wasn't exactly sure how it had happened: a leap for a pass, a ferocious tackle, a late hit, a flying elbow in the days before helmets had face masks, a broken nose and crushed vertebra. In any case, Corcoran admired the priest's perseverance amid adversity. True, this virtue was also evident in the kid with cerebral palsy who lowed when he talked, puttered through the halls on what looked like a golf cart, and still managed to pull straight A's. But Corcoran found something tragic in an athlete struck in his prime by accident or illness—look at Lou Gehrig. Perseverance! For years he had been knocking this into the heads of the queers and wussies and women and geeks who tried out for his teams.

Corcoran had drafted the priest his first week in town for the pre-game locker room prayer (this honor was rotated among the clergy, and there had not been a Roman Catholic for some time), but their friendship began in earnest the night the coach dropped by with a housewarming gift, a bottle of Kentucky bourbon. The priest offered Corcoran a drink, and the coach said no, really, save it, you don't have to break it open tonight; but of course he did, especially when he learned that the coach had no one waiting at home. Lafon said this surprised him; despite the fulfillment he found in the service of God, his deepest burden was the loneliness, sitting alone in a restaurant with a plate of mussels and a glass of sauvignon blanc, while at the next table over sits a man with a wife of thirty years and five children and a grandchild or two, and they laugh and sample each other's dinners and engage in ordinary conversation about an idiotic employee or a kitchen that needs remodeling, interrupting themselves from time to time to admonish a child or admire a crayon camel scribbled on a placemat; at such times you see what you're missing. Plus you eat faster, Corcoran said. It's impossible to prolong your dinner for more than fifteen minutes when you're alone, and you feel ripped off if it's a nice restaurant and you've forked out twenty bucks, wine included. Precisely, the priest said. Which is why he was surprised a good-looking young fella like Corcoran was single. The coach found something sad in this man's acknowledgement of loneliness. He mentioned his divorce, changed the subject to basketball.

They spent the evening talking—or rather, Corcoran talked, for the most part, he later recalled with embarrassment (he had not realized how starved for conversation he was), while Father Jules listened. For some reason Corcoran went on about his son Cody. The boy was a natural athlete, but he had never shown any interest in basketball until this season, the year of his parents' divorce, when he tried out for and made varsity, as if to hurl in his father's face some message Corcoran had yet to decipher. Suddenly the coach was ashamed of the intimate turn of the conversation. Do people always spill their guts while chatting with priests? he wondered. The guys must get sick of it. So he switched to his personal theory of mental preparedness. When Father Jules did vouchsafe an opinion, Corcoran was surprised at a nagging sense of his own ignorance and even fraud, as in a dream where one must land a 747 or conduct brain surgery. The coach was used to being heeded and respected. People sought his opinion, particularly on matters relating to his areas of expertise: sports, mathematics, juvenile delinquency, the tourism sub-committee, and the water/sewer issue in the urban growth boundary. But although he had a master's in education and doctorate in kinesiology, he was unable to grasp Father Jules' theory of sports science, which was derived from a fusion of John Wooden and Thomas Aquinas' doctrine of the prime mover. His half-spectacles settled on his nose, the priest quoted Summa Theologica.

"Isn't that the entire science of the game: transforming the potency to act—and of course knowing when to strike?" Lafon said. "It's a beautiful thing to see a pass hurled into a crowd of defenders, and a center appears at that precise instant from nowhere and grabs the ball and flips it in—not dunks it: too crass; simply rolls it off the palm and the fingers, backwards."

"That's the part that's impossible to teach," Corcoran said. "Instinct."

"Don't get me wrong: I'm not saying your boys should read Thomas to bone up on strategy," the priest added, and Corcoran wondered if the priest was pulling his leg.

"We're only up to Augustine," he said, and Lafon laughed.

"Drills," he went on, more to himself than the coach. "I always loved watching the drills. Three boys weaving down the court, firing the ball back and forth, never dribbling, never traveling. Or when offense passes around the key, and the entire defense shifts with the ball, as if it were a field of gravity. That for me always had the satisfaction of mathematical equation."

"That's one thing basketball never reminds me of: math," the coach said. "And I teach it."

The priest was helpless at the little repairs that had to be done at the rectory, and Corcoran took on projects there, hanging a curtain, repairing a toilet that flushed on its own every few minutes as if a ghost were hitting the handle. When he learned that a moving van would be dropping off Lafon's books and other personal articles, Corcoran rounded up a work detail, which annoyed church members who would have been happy to help.

For starters he drafted his son. Cody was a sixteen-year-old with frizzy hair like a mushroom; despite a slight stammer, he was a show-off, a clown, popular with the girls because of his prowess in three sports. Admirers egged him on. Without an audience, Cody never would have stolen the hood ornaments from sixteen Mercedes at Jim's Classic Foreign Autos last year, or tried to pull down the Grants Pass caveman statue with Corcoran's own pickup after that school's homecoming game last November. Cody lived with his mother, and the boy's eyes still flashed with the anguish and affront that had come over him the day his parents sat him down and said they couldn't go on like this anymore. At practice Corcoran sometimes caught Cody staring at him; on weekends, when the boy stayed with his father, they saw little of each other, for Cody was always out with his friends. But with his son present, Corcoran could count on enough help to unload whatever a priest accumulates over a lifetime.

There was too much help, really. Corcoran and two kids cleared out the minivan (not a moving van, it turned out) while Cody and another boy screwed around. The priest wandered about in an abstracted state, opening boxes randomly, rediscovering lost books, thumbing through a history of the Lakers, which he tried to discuss with Corcoran just as the coach was hefting a box containing a multiple-volume history of the Latin mass. Having doffed his clerical garb for the day, Lafon cut a ridiculous figure, in sandals, dark socks, a Hawaiian shirt, a sweater he must have found at a St. Vincent De Paul, and pants as absurdly baggy as a skateboarders'.

When Corcoran tried to move a bookcase, the priest, suddenly efficient, lurched foreword to help. "That's OK, Father," Corcoran said. "We'll take care of it. Zawacki! Make yourself useful." Kyle Zawacki grabbed the other end of a bookcase, and they carried it toward the living room wall. The boy was the best player Corcoran had ever coached, but he had been arrested last summer for slamming his twenty-year-old girlfriend into the wall until she lost consciousness. The jury acquitted him, though. He had scored thirty-three points in the state quarterfinals that year. Suddenly Zawacki guffawed and dropped his end of the bookcase.

"Hey! You nearly threw my back out of joint," Corcoran said. "Pay attention."

"Sorry, coach."

But as soon as they lifted the bookcase Zawacki started snickering again.

"What's with you?" Corcoran said.

"Nothing. Cody is just being a dork."

"Cody, don't be a dork. And don't say 'dork' around a man of the cloth, Zawacki, you'll make his ears burn."

Corcoran turned to wink at the priest. What he saw was this: Lafon ambling across the room, reading, while Cody, bent double like a hunchback, gimped along behind in imitation of the priest. The boy ogled his friends with a bug-eyed, hunchbacked expression, and they snorted, wept, suffocated their laughter.

"Cody!" the coach said. Lafon glanced back and saw the boy. Agonizingly, the priest registered no anger. He ducked into the study with a pained expression. "You!" Corcoran said, grabbing Cody by the arm. "Outside!"

In the front yard the coach demanded, "What the hell were you doing?"

"What do you mean?"

"You know what. Give me forty burpies."

"Dad, I was only kidding."

"Fifty. One more word and you're grounded this weekend."

Cody dropped on the frosty lawn and launched into his burpies: down, two, three, one. Down, two, three, two. . . . He did not take his eyes off his father.

"I am so pissed I can hardly speak," said Corcoran. "What were you trying to prove, gimping around like that? How would you like it if I joked about—"

Cody's eyes widened in anticipation of a jab at one of his shortcomings (his stammer, his inability to master even the simplest mathematics equation), and Corcoran felt a pang and cut himself off. He had a sudden awareness of how much pain his divorce had inflicted, of his utter failure not only as a father but even at the modest goal he had declared when Cody was born—to always be his son's friend—and the thought was too much to consider right now. He broke a switch from a crab apple tree and whacked the trunk seven times. Down, two, three, thirty-one. Down, two, three, thirty-two. Suddenly he felt like a slave driver and threw the switch on the roof.

When Cody was finished, he blurted out, as if to justify himself, "You keep acting like Father Lafon's some big football hero. Well, he's not, he's just an ex-con. His back was broken in prison, that's why he's all hunched over."

"That's bullshit. Who told you that?"

"Zawacki's dad heard it from a priest who stayed at their motel."

"Zawacki's dad? Oh, right. Chip Zawacki was probably stoned at the time. If Father Jules was ever in prison, he was a chaplain. They wouldn't let him be a priest if he was an ex-con. It's like with teachers."

"I swear to God, that's what he said."

"So what was Father Jules supposedly in for?"

"Something about being a communist."

"Son, I've got news for you: communists are atheists."

"Thank you. Dad, I appreciate that information." Cody added, "Maybe it's a lie. Why don't you ask him?"

"You know, I'm really not interested in this discussion. What interests me is seeing you apologize for being such a jerk."

They returned to find the old man dusting a battered leatherbound Erasmus on his shirt. As Cody spoke his stammer became so pronounced he could barely get the words out: "Father Jules, I'm sorry. I didn't mean anything."

The priest licked his finger and scrubbed at a spot. His ears had turned scarlet, but otherwise he showed no embarrassment. "That's all right, my son." Then he smiled grotesquely. "You know, Cody, I wasn't always like this."

2

The next day it snowed, swirls of white that scumbled the redwoods across the valley, drifted in particulate eddies in the middle distance of the courtyard, and descended like wafers around Corcoran. The snow splotched his hair and dark woolen coat like spatters of plaster. For the first time he could remember in eight months, Corcoran was happy. Trotting up the stairs to the gym, with its brick-and-stucco facade and barrel roof jumbled with chimneys and air conditioners, he glanced at the humanities building, where a skeleton hung in a third story window of an art class. Lately the skeleton had seemed a grim reminder of mortality, but today someone had placed a red derby on its head, rendering the collection of bones no more fearsome than a Halloween costume.

Inside, somebody had cut the lights after seventh period P. E., and the coach groped through the lobby and stumbled around in the dark gym until he found the switch. The lights came buzzing on gradually, so that the room proceeded from night to day in a continuum of imperceptible degrees, as a full moon is given birth by a dark horizon. Corcoran swung his whistle by its string around his finger, and surveyed the old gym where he had spent every winter afternoon for nine years. The place was redolent of old wood and varnish and dusty heating vents and the acrid sweat of adolescence. Above the stage hung posters from rallies ("SASQUATCHES—JUST DO IT") and pennants from conference championships as ancient as 1922. Varsity now played in the new gym, and this building was relegated to P. E., practice, and J. V. games.

Corcoran wheeled out a cart full of leather basketballs and palmed one—rhino-skinned, hyperinflated, brown with sweat and dirt. It had a delicious fullness in his hands. Dribble: the ball springs from the floor. Corcoran hooked a shot from the top of the key. The ball swished through the net and bounded back to him. He fired from the corner, and the ball ricocheted violently inside the rim and went down for three. The players began drifting in after a three-mile run, varsity in red, J. V. in white with the word "DEFENSE" across the butt, and Corcoran returned his ball to the cage, for it was unseemly for a coach to be caught shooting a basket.

He blew his whistle and hollered, "All right, all right, gentlemen. Bleachers. Let's go. We ain't got all day."

The boys ran the bleachers while dribbling balls, up one row and down the next, making sure to hit every step from row A to ZZ. In a game the basketball bounces with a singular thud, but in practice, with twenty balls concurrently thumping, there is no individual drumbeat: the whole gym rumbles as if in an earthquake.

When the boys finished their laps, Corcoran had them run a great circle around the court. Each kid jump-shot, grabbed his rebound, dribbled pell-mell for the other basket, shot again. Corcoran and Tim Harris, the assistant coach, stood under each basket with their forearms wrapped in foam rubber pads. As each player drove in for the shot, a coach gave him a shove, to simulate the rough and tumble of a game.

Horton, Glazier, Zawacki, Pennington, Van Der Heuvel, Mann—the boys came at Corcoran, one flushed face after another, biting their lips when they set up to shoot. They had lost the intensity of the first days of the season, when they still believed Corcoran could harangue and exhort a championship out of them, and still feared his wrath should they fall short. Now they were 10-7, with three straight losses, and, surveying the schedule ahead, it was conceivable they would not win another game this season.

Corcoran bumped McDonough, who came down on the coach's foot. "Shit!" they both said. Corcoran thumped McDonough on the back of the head. "Sorry, coach," the boy said.

At the far end of the court Cody was showing off, feinting right and going left around Harris. He spun the ball behind his back and dunked it. Harris (idiot!) didn't rebuke Cody, and so the other boys followed suit, with smart-ass dribbling and Globetrotter lay-ups, and the drill fell apart.

"Gentleman, I want to see a base-line jumper," Corcoran shouted, but the kids at the other end of the court chose not to hear. And Corcoran had to concentrate on the boys coming at him:

De Boer, a debate team member whose dad sold Japanese cars. Marks, who covered junior high sports as a stringer for *The Record-Searchlight*. Adams, who already had a drunk driving record. Kremicki, who could swear in Spanish after a summer bossing a crew of Mexican tree planters.

Corcoran harassed and thumped each kid. They barely tried. At sixteen or seventeen boys should not be so resigned. At thirty-nine a coach should not let them get away with it.

Humphrey, Knox, Pedersen, Cox.

Dingell, Dowell, Drager, Knox.

Corcoran.

Who drove straight for his dad with a glower that recalled Zawacki the day he was arrested on the assault and battery charge. At the last minute Cody feinted right and whirled left. It was a fine move, and all Corcoran could do was foul the boy as he went up to shoot: he shoved him, hard. Cody managed to release the ball as he crashed to the floor. Corcoran heard the net swish behind him.

He blew his whistle and stopped the drill. "I want a base-line jumper. I don't want a Goddamned hook or a lay-up. Now, Cody, get off your ass and get moving."

For a moment Corcoran was afraid Cody, groaning on the floor and clutching his knee, was seriously hurt. But the boy stood and limped toward the door, holding the ball against his hip.

"Cody!" Corcoran said. He wanted to ask. Are you OK? but that couldn't be done, not in practice, not in the face of such defiance. So he said, "You walk out, you're out of here for good."

For a moment Corcoran thought Cody would throw the ball at him. Instead he drop-kicked it into the bleachers and limped out of the gym. At the door on his way out he slugged the wall. The kids watched Corcoran.

"All right, gentlemen, let's go," he shouted, and the rumble of dribbling resumed.

Corcoran noticed a dark figure hunched in the bleachers with his chin on his palm. "Excuse me!" he shouted. "Practice is closed." Then he realized it was Lafon, who compounded Corcoran's embarrassment by waving broadly as if from the far side of the fairgrounds. He hobbled down the bleachers.

"Oh, Father Jules, I'm sorry, I didn't recognize you. You don't have to go."

"Rules are rules."

Glazier came dribbling at the coach, and Corcoran tore his attention from the priest and bumped the boy.

It was dark when he left the gym, and Cody was nowhere to be seen. The snow had stopped, and in the courtyard the slush was trampled and muddy. The lights were still on in a third story window of the humanities building, where the skeleton dangled by its chain, like the remains of a traitor hung from the city gates. From his office he phoned Cody at his mother's. "He came home crying," Karen said. "I hope you're proud of yourself." She hung up.

That night Corcoran dropped by the rectory with another bottle of bourbon. He felt the need to justify his outburst with Cody, but when he pulled up, he suddenly grew angry—why the hell did he owe Lafon an explanation?—and he remained in his car, wringing the paper bag around the bottle neck. The rectory was dark except for the study, where the priest sat at a desk by a curtainless window. In this light his expression was distorted and the hollows in his cheeks exaggerated, like a face in a photograph of prisoners of war. The thought brought a stab of sadness.

Sighing, he got out, stuck the bottle in his coat pocket, and nudged the car door closed with his hip. At the sound, the priest looked up. The anonymity vanished; he had reassumed his own elegiac ugliness.

Lafon was not surprised to see Corcoran, but he blushed as he accepted the bourbon, as though embarrassed at the implication that he needed to be kept in booze.

And anyway, they skipped the bourbon and drank Rob Roys, a favorite of Lafon's, in his study, surrounded by old volumes in Latin, Hebrew, Koine, Attic, Chinese. For book ends the priest used small sculptures he had acquired in Asia: teak elephants and tigers, a miniature ivory Taj Mahal, a metal scribe with a wise and bemused countenance, and a porcelain Confucian Buddha such as one might see in a Vietnamese immigrant's doughnut shop, with a maple bar and a cup of coffee and a garland of flowers laid out in offering before it. The priest sat on a couch and tucked an orthopedic pillow in the small of his back.

Corcoran flipped a chair around backward and perched on it. Abstractedly he swirled the cherry in his martini glass; finally realizing he had not tasted his drink, Corcoran sniffed the liquor and threw down a gulp. His face contorted with the expression of a cat coughing up a hairball. "The hell's this, airplane fuel?" he asked. The priest assented, then inquired about the team. Corcoran understood this as an invitation to talk about Cody, and he produced from his wallet a sixth-grade school picture which he had carried for five years—the babyish face, the eagerness, the Disneyland t-shirt that was later torn up when Cody fell off a horse and landed in a blackberry bush.

"He's almost grown up," the priest said, and returned the photograph.

"I hate it when that happens. You know, he was such a sweet little guy; now all I see is this anger, this brooding. Jules, it's the most terrible thing to have your son turn on you. I deserve it. I was unfaithful; I'm sure you figured that out" (though from the look on his face, the priest had not), "and because Karen and I no longer loved each other, maybe I wanted her to find out. But Cody had no idea, he never saw the divorce coming. Whenever he looks at me, I see these accusing eyes."

He had never expressed such sentiments to anyone, and he blushed. Abruptly Corcoran said, "So how long were you there? At practice, I mean."

"Fifteen minutes. I don't know."

"Not your most Thomistic drill today."

"Room for improvement."

"I'm not usually like that—well, OK, I'm always like that, in terms of yelling when I get torqued; you know that from watching me at games. But I don't normally knock my kids around."

"That was quite a shove you gave him."

"I guess I was still teed off about the other day when he started following you around." The coach cut himself off. The priest was not fooled, and was possibly offended, by the implication that Corcoran pushed Cody in retaliation for the boy's mimicry. "Well, it wasn't that. It's just, I'm a jerk sometimes. I can't stand kids who defy me to my face, and my own son—. I used to think you can mold character, but now I believe my influence is negligible. Even with my boy. Especially. I wish he'd never tried out for the team."

"He knows you think that."

"You talked to him?"

"I found him in the hallway slugging the wall. (I've always wondered why jocks do that.) He said he wanted to play basketball because he was afraid you would forget him after the divorce."

"Then how come he's so damned defiant about it? He told you that?"

The priest nodded. For a moment the men drank in silence.

Finally the coach ventured, "Jules, I know this is stupid, but I thought you should know there's this rumor going round. Actually, it was Cody who heard it, so consider the source—but he said that you were in prison. I told him it was ridiculous, but he claims to have heard it in town."

The priest drained his glass, rose painfully, and retreated into the kitchen, and Corcoran was faced with the horrifying realization that in addition to being a lousy husband and a father, he had now behaved like the worst sort of small-town gossip and passed on hurtful nonsense under the guise of friendship. Lafon did not return. Apparently he was supposed to leave now. But just as Corcoran stood to go, the priest returned with a tray bearing bottles of scotch and dry vermouth, and a jar of maraschino cherries. He mixed them each a second Rob Roy and began talking about his coaching days, when he was a missionary in China. Corcoran had always imagined Lafon at a school in Pittsburgh or Buffalo, coaching a small but tough team of Irishmen and Italians and Croatians and perhaps even blacks in the days before schools were supposed to have been integrated; he was disappointed to learn it was a mission school in Harbin, four decades ago.

Chinese basketball players! It sounded like a joke. But Lafon insisted his teams were not bad, at least not under the circumstances; his best kid had been a center named Tseng.

~ *He was not a good player [Lafon said] in the way you think of it: a skilled athlete. He was just huge, for China, anyway: six-four: one of these giants who dominate the sport in their own country, but when they play in the West, they are merely average, and terribly clumsy, I might add, and everyone runs circles around them. Our game strategy was simple: you just lobbed the ball down court to Tseng, and he shot and bounced it off the backboard two or three times, always rebounding over the heads of the others, until the ball went in. But he made up for that in his determination in school; he was a great student, a wonderful boy. Parents were converts.*

This was 1950, not long after the Reds seized power, and I was keeping my head low: saying mass, teaching, coaching. They were already expelling foreign missionaries, but when the Korean War broke out, everything went to hell. The government's hostility increased, old friends didn't recognize you on the streets, and I now knew firsthand of doctors, priests, and teachers who had disappeared. The Russians were already pulling out—before the Japanese occupation, there had been a hundred thousand of them in town, and the city had a dozen onion-domed churches, some of them truly beautiful. Anyway, the people who would talk to me said I should leave while I could, but I loved China, and I somehow believed that love would spare me; the same hubris and naiveté was manifested by those Americans and Europeans who stayed on in Beirut until they became hostages—professor-converts to Islam, spouses of Muslims, reporters who thought the subtleties of journalistic objectivity would be appreciated by people who do not hesitate to blow up children; all believing themselves to be immune to the hatred of the West. But sometimes at night, I dreaded what might happen: I tossed and turned in bed as the wind blew down out of Siberia, and started awake whenever a branch rapped the windows or the dog barked.

The police came during a blizzard. They beat me and ransacked the school and tore apart the rectory walls with crowbars—looking for hidden radios or propaganda tracts—and after a cursory questioning I was jailed in a cell with eight other inmates, each more politically advanced than I, particularly the cell chief, who painstakingly explained, as if to an idiot, that it would be best if I searched my heart and immediately confessed everything.

~ "You were a prisoner in China?" Corcoran exclaimed, but the priest shook his head and raised his bony hands to deflect any admiration, and cried. "Wait, wait; hear me out."

~ The formal interrogation took place in a room that smelled like a slaughterhouse and had an asphalt floor with a drain in the center. I remember wondering, as I stood with my head bowed respectfully, about the drain, and only after I was beaten did I understand: as I was dragged away another prisoner came in and mopped my blood down the hole. At a table my inquisitor sat, a judge with the profound gaze of the ascetic, the insane. He was a former dock worker, and his teeth were broken and jagged like a shark's, the result of a beating by nationalist soldiers—so he told me bitterly, as if I had been party to this crime.

There was also a stenographer, a handful of guards, and a chalkboard, on which a guard would occasionally write things I said. I could not understand why certain phrases were chosen. It did not make any sense.

"Let me outline the facts of the case," the judge said. "We know you have had extensive spy contacts with the imperialists dating back to the war. We have evidence of perverse activities you have engaged in. We have proof your so-called basketball team was in fact an espionage organization for the purpose of sabotage, corrupting youth, and teaching counterrevolutionary values."

"This is absurd," I said. "I was arrested because I am a priest; I thought China still allowed freedom of religion. This is persecution."

"You're only partly right: yes, in China there is freedom of religion. Therefore, what is occurring tonight cannot be persecution. You must be guilty of something. Our conversations will guide us to the answer of this question: Guilty of what? So tell me."

When I would not cooperate, he ordered the guards to handcuff my hands in front of me and jam a pole through my elbows behind my back. They beat me unconscious, roused me with water, beat me again.

At some point I was dragged back to my cell. The other prisoners took shifts keeping me awake, pinching and slapping me whenever I dozed off, demanding to know what it was that I was withholding. I believe I did not sleep for two weeks, although my mind was too confused to make any sense of those weeks, I was hallucinating, I was having conversations with my boys and my older brother and the Blessed Virgin herself.

You must understand that at this time you become so confused and desperate for sleep, you rack your brains trying to understand what it is they are asking you, and how you can render it without compromising yourself or injuring others. All have sinned and fallen short of the glory of God. Is it so much to admit this? No. I have always believed I am a sinner—a traitor, if you will—before God and man.

And that is the first step. For man is a guilty creature, and in such conditions you draw up mental ledgers of deeds you at some level regret. And the very formation of such ledgers opens a crack through which they will eventually gain access to one's reservoirs of shame and guilt: guilt for your petty failures and great transgressions; for losing your temper with a student who subsequently never returned to school; for the fact that you, a servant of Christ, employed a servant of your own at the rate of a few cents a day (oh, they were good; they quoted Matthew 20:26–27 to me, and I began sobbing; I was a broken man by then). Guilt real and imagined.

The priest buried his face in his talons, and Corcoran thought he would cry; but he reemerged and said flatly: "It's not so hard to get to a man."

Suffice it to say I started by confessing to something that I thought would not implicate my boys: I said I forced them, against their will, to listen to the anti-communist radio broadcasts of a certain Dutch priest. This was unbelievably stupid of me. I didn't know that this now rendered them, too, in need of "thought reform." The judge—I always had the impression he was snapping at an insect with his broken teeth when he shouted at me—showed me a photograph of myself with Tseng and his parents.

"You know this boy?" he said.

I said, "I think he was in seminary with me." (My mind was going, you see.)

"He was one of your basketball players."

"Oh, yes. You're right, of course."

"Do you remember his name?"

"I don't know."

"This is Tseng. You remember him? He has been arrested."

Suddenly everything about the boy returned—his large hands, the lisping way he spoke Latin—and I cried. He continued, "We know he was working with you to supply information to the CIA."

I was confused. It did not make sense. "Tseng?" I said. "I'm sure you're wrong, I don't think he would do this."

"Don't lie to my face!" the judge exploded.

"I don't remember. For heaven's sake, I just don't remember."

"Then we will help you."

The judge ordered the guards to bind me. They laid me face-down with my mouth open on a concrete block and kicked the back of my head. That's how I lost my teeth. They nearly drowned me in a tub, revived me, drowned me again. I can't tell you how water terrifies me. They broke a collarbone, cracked my sternum and two ribs, stomped me until I passed out. A medical officer would give me injections so that I would be conscious to feel everything. They fractured my hip and my back, so I later learned from the X-rays they took in Hong Kong after I was released. Apparently I'm lucky I can walk. They beat my body into what you see now.

To make a long story short, I was "reformed." Everyone is, to one degree or another—even the heroes—though perhaps not as shamefully as I. One day I talked so rapidly, the stenographer had to slow me down.

They were particularly keen on radios, so I confessed to making secret transmissions for the Vatican.

I said my life's work had been spying for British intelligence.

I admitted to all kinds of perversion with nuns, with prostitutes, with children.

The judge asked me to write a letter to each of my players, confessing I had been a Western spy all along and the purpose of basketball had been to instill in them capitalistic values of competition. That letter still pains me. I knew it would be used in their interrogations, should they be arrested, or simply to discredit me in their eyes; but at the time I believed it was true.

From then on my treatment became milder, and they even had a doctor examine me with an intent of healing and not extending and intensifying the duration of my pain. The interrogations continued, but in the place of the brutish judge was a missionary-educated man, a former candidate for the priesthood, who assumed the air of a schoolmaster who has your interests at heart and has infinite patience for this lesson. I was put in a new cell full of reformed missionaries, and we engaged in discussions on the purification of one's mind from bourgeois sentiments. You need to understand, we weren't pretending. I passionately believed in the historical dialectic, and yet somehow, I never ceased believing in Christ. Consciously this made sense to me, as it somehow does to Liberation Theologians. But my unconscious mind rebelled against it; panic attacks awoke me at night, and I prayed to Mary and meditated on her purity in contrast to my sins, until I finally slept.

We counseled other prisoners to our level of understanding. And so one day I was sent to talk to a man in solitary. When they opened the cell door he lay in the fetal position on the floor, a small, naked man, like an overgrown Somali baby: all skin and bones, except for his bloated hands, which had been crushed.

His face, in profile, was puffy and unrecognizable. As I approached him I realized his shortness had been an optical illusion of the cell. He was remarkably tall. It was Tseng. They were starving him to death.

As I began talking, he regarded me with anguish, and only as I saw myself in his eyes did I realize how thoroughly I had fallen. I wanted to ask his forgiveness. But I didn't. I didn't. I felt myself stepping back from emotion, into a state of tranquility, and I lectured him on the sin of pride.

He cut me off: "I never believed that letter until I saw you; I thought it was a forgery."

"My son, you must understand the futility of one man standing against history."

"Father, go away," he said.

"I'll pray for you—pray for courage."

I meant it, but he said, "How dare you talk to me about prayer?"

I was too ashamed to reply.

"Get out of here, please, stop poisoning me—you don't know how hard it is already."

I returned to the hall and talked with the guard so that I would not think or feel that which was forbidden. He could see I was upset.

"Don't worry," he said by way of comforting me. "He'll die soon."

The most severe manifestations of brainwashing lasted only a year or so after I had gotten back to the West. But in a subtle way, I suppose it still is there now; the strongest sense of all is guilt that I wasn't able to resist, that I had betrayed God and my people and my boys. And the knowledge of how frail selfhood is.

3

That night was drummingly recalled, the next morning, in Corcoran's bursts of stuffy drymouthed self-castigation, damning himself for his initial awkward silence when the priest had finished, for his idiotic joke about how half his own team was probably going to end up in prison, for offering further details about his affair, not excluding the herpes (Christ! and to a priest!), for his inability to offer any assurance of pardon. Beyond that the night, considered now, from his bed the next morning, was a blank. Apparently he had drunk more after he got home—four beer cans were crushed beside his bed. When after vomiting he slumped to the kitchen and opened the refrigerator looking for mineral water, he discovered his wallet, his keys, and a great quantity of pennies and nickels and paper clips in the butter compartment. His inability to remember how or why these articles had ended up on a shelf by the orange juice made him rage at himself again. What if you'd killed somebody driving home in that condition?

Corcoran avoided Lafon for a week. At first this was intentional; he needed distance, and because he did not hear from Lafon he supposed the priest felt the same.

Eventually, however, he dropped by the rectory, after practice one Tuesday, then again on a Sunday afternoon. No one answered his knock. On the second occasion Corcoran slipped under the door a note on a subscription card that had slipped from a *Sports Illustrated* in his car:

Hey Lafon, we're losing without our good luck priest. What are you up to these days?

—TC

(The priest would understand the attempt at a joke: they had been losing even when he was attending the games.)

It was a time of solitude and estrangement, especially from his son. The first weekend Cody was sick and remained at his mother's, the next he said he was thinking about going skiing at Mount Bachelor with some friends. One day after school Corcoran spotted Cody crossing the courtyard, and he called him inside the old gym. The lights were again out, and as the coach groped around the walls ("You'd think I'd be able to find the damn switch after all these years"), he heard a sigh: Sheesh. Forget the lights, Corcoran thought, and in the shadowy foyer with the boy side-lighted through the window by an overcast day, he launched into the speech he had been mulling for the last two weeks. Corcoran had intended to apologize. But speeches never work, reconciliation is impossible, and the only direction we move is apart. Cody was sullen, and as they talked, the coach felt a pain in his stomach, a physical sense that discipline and authority, the only material he possessed for building a winning team out of small-town mediocrities, was slipping from his grasp. There are reasons for drills, he was saying, they draw a team together into something greater than the sum of its parts, something that functions with a mathematical precision—

"If you're trying to talk me into joining the team again, you're wasting your breath," Cody said.

"I'm trying to tell you you won't get anywhere in life if you act like a butthead."

Cody walked out. Now it was Corcoran who felt like slugging the wall.

~ But that Sunday morning he was sleeping in when the phone rang. He knocked the receiver from the bedside table, groped around groggily, said "What?" not hello.

"Dad?"

"Cody! Hey, you woke me up, dude. What's happening?"

"I'm at St. Stephens," he said, and before Corcoran could voice his amazement, the boy added, "Father Jules isn't here yet."

"Well, it's only, God, Cody, it's not even 8:30. Most churches start at 10 or 11, don't they?"

"The early mass starts at 8, and nobody's seen Father." Father. "I was afraid something happened to him."

When Corcoran arrived, a clutch of parishioners had gathered in front of church, watching a pair of old men knock at the rectory next door. Cody stood in a planter and peered in a window. Corcoran strode over in the sweats he had slept in and a Sasquatches warmup jacket. Catching a glimpse of his father, Cody rolled his eyes—whether at Corcoran's appearance or at the old men's incompetence, it was unclear; but Corcoran also detected in the boy's eyes a plea for help.

"Are you the locksmith?" one old man said. "Oh, coach, I should've known you. I doubt Father has gone far: the car's still here. This young fella here checked the garage."

Corcoran tried the front door knob. It turned, but the chain was latched. "Jules?" he called. He glanced at the others, who shrugged. He shouldered the door in.

On the floor of the study they found the priest. He had collapsed while praying, it appeared, for he lay on his side next to a kneeling rail, clutching a rosary, his knees pulled to his chest. "Oh, my God," Cody cried. The old men crossed themselves.

Corcoran felt Lafon's pulse at the throat. Then he gathered the bony priest in his arms and shoved through the crowd that had followed him into the manse. "We'll take him to Harbor View. Cody, get the keys out of my pocket. You're driving."

He lay Lafon on the back seat of the pickup, then Corcoran joined him in back and cradled the priest's head.

"And don't get us killed on the way," he said when the boy nearly backed into a log truck roaring down the highway.

Cody was florid, and he was jutting his jaw as Corcoran himself did when he was angry.

"You OK?" Corcoran said.

The boy nodded.

"How long you been going to church?"

"Couple of weeks." He ground the gears as he worked the shift. "It's something to do."

At the emergency room the nurses undressed the unconscious priest, and the coach was shocked at the scarred, emaciated body: rib cage, bony limbs, swollen belly. The nurses slipped on a hospital gown, carelessly exposing his shriveled genitals, missing a testicle. They took his pulse and blood pressure, attached an IV, slipped on an oxygen mask, hooked him up to a computer that monitored pulse and blood pressure.

The coach took Lafon's hand. Just then a doctor parted the curtain, nodded at the Corcorans, washed his hands as the nurse gave a report, and examined the patient. After a few minutes he turned to Corcoran.

"How long has he been like this?"

"I think he said since the 1950s. He was injured in a football game."

The doctor started to say something. Then he shook his head and went on with his examination—thumping the ribcage, listening with his stethoscope. "I find it hard to believe you didn't notice your father's condition. Does he live with you?"

"He's not my father."

"The nurses said—"

"He's a priest."

The doctor considered this.

"Somebody should have noticed. Do you people even look at this man when he, whatever you call it, does communion? I haven't seen anything like it since I worked at a refugee camp in Ethiopia." The doctor straightened himself and said, "Malnutrition. Your priest is starving to death."

There were complications—kidneys, heart, a case of bronchitis that was threatening to expand into pneumonia—and Lafon remained in the hospital, drifting in and out of consciousness, while Corcoran and Cody sat with him. The coach described the games the old man had missed. Cody found a Cosmopolitan in the lobby and thumbed through it. Corcoran nearly asked, "Can't you find something other than that garbage?" but he bit his tongue. As if reading his mind, Cody tossed the magazine in the trash.

Finally a nurse entered and announced that several parishioners had been waiting for some time, could the Corcorans please wrap up their visit. So the coach leaned close to the unshaven cheek and hairy ear and told Lafon they must leave. Did he want to pray or something before they went? The priest nodded, eyes closed. What now? Corcoran looked at Cody in desperation. The boy began reciting the Lord's Prayer.

The Corcorans had never been a religious family, but Cody kept the prayer plodding along, and the coach kept up most of the way, until the line about forgiving our debts. But then the priest's eyes opened, glassy and tormented, as if at the sight of a terrible chimera. Corcoran said, "Forgive us this day—" and then stumbled. He let Cody finish; he could not find his way to the end.

Contributors

CHIMAMANDA NGOZI ADICHIE was born in Nigeria. Her short fiction won the 2003 PEN/David Wong award, as well as an O. Henry Prize. Her first novel, *Purple Hibiscus,* was published in October 2003.

CHRIS AGEE'S first collection of poems, *In the New Hampshire Woods,* was among the finalists for the 1994 Kingsley Tufts Poetry Prize. His new collection, *First Light* was among the finalists for this year's National Poetry Series in the U.S. A selection of his poetry is included in the anthology *The Book of Irish American Poetry,* edited by Daniel Tobin. His collection of Balkan essays, *Journey to Bosnia* will be published next year.

SANDRA ALCOSSER'S *Except by Nature* received numerous awards, including the James Laughlin Award from the Academy of American Poets. James Tate selected *A Fish to Feed All Hunger* to be the Associated Writing Programs Award Series winner in Poetry. Alcosser co-directs the graduate writing program at San Diego State University and is currently the Richard Hugo Professor at the University of Montana.

DICK ALLEN is the author of seven collections of poetry, including *The Day Before: New Poems,* published by Sarabande Books and *Ode to the Cold War: Poems New and Selected.* He has received many awards for his poetry, including writing grants from the Ingram Merrill Foundation and the NEA. His poems have appeared recently in *Atlantic Monthly, Gettysburg Review, Boulevard,* and *Georgia Review.*

MICHAEL ANANIA'S recent poetry collections include *Heat Lines, Selected Poems,* and *In Natural Light.* He also is the author of a novel, *The Red Menace.*

JAN LEE ANDE'S books include *Instructions for Walking on Water* and *Reliquary.* Her poems appear in *New Letters, Image, Mississippi Review, Nimrod, Bellevue Literary Review,* and *Poetry International.* She teaches poetry, poetics, and history of religions at Union Institute & University.

ROBERT ARCHAMBEAU'S books include *Word Play Place: Essays on the Poetry of John Matthias, Vectors: New Poetics,* and *Home and Variations,* which was published by Salt. He teaches at Lake Forest College.

RENÉE ASHLEY has twice been awarded the Kenyon Review Award for Literary Excellence. Poems from her collection, *The Revisionist's Dream*, have appeared in *Threepenny Review*, *Poetry*, and *Georgia Review*, among others.

JENNIFER ATKINSON'S second book of poems, *The Drowned City*, won the 2000 Samuel French Morse Prize. She teaches creative writing and literature at George Mason University.

NED BALBO'S second collection, *Lives of the Sleepers*, received the 2004 Ernest Sandeen Poetry Prize. "Aristaeus Forgiven," a poem from that manuscript was awarded the 2003 Robert Frost Foundation Poetry Award. His first collection was *Galileo's Banquet*.

MARY JO BANG is the author of *Louise in Love* and *The Eye Like a Strange Balloon*. Her most recent collection of poems is entitled *Elegy*. She teaches at Washington University of St. Louis.

TINA BARR'S work has appeared in *Boudary 2*, *Chelsea*, *Crab Orchard Review*, and *The Southern Review*. A chapbook, *The Fugitive Eye*, was selected by Yusef Komunyakaa as the winner of the Painted Bride Quarterly contest and published in 1997. She directs the Creative Writing Program at Rhodes College in Memphis.

MIKE BARRETT, a poet, teaches in Missouri. He is the founder and Creative Director of Anvil/lyre Studio.

CHRISTIAN BARTER'S poems have appeared in *Georgia Review*, *Tar River Poetry*, *Louisville Review*, and others. He is a crew leader for Arcadia National Parks's trail crews.

WENDY BATTIN is a poet, teacher, and director of the Contemporary American Poetry Archive. She is the author of *Little Apocalypse* and *In the Solar Wind*, a selection of the National Poetry Series from Doubleday.

NICKY BEER is a creative writing PhD student at the University of Missouri at Columbia. Her poems, reviews, and nonfiction have appeared in *Cider Press Review*, *Clackamas*, *Columbia*, *Indiana Review*, *New Orleans Review*, *Nerve*, and others.

CAROLINE BERGVALL lives and works in England. She has had texts featured in a number of magazines in England and North America. Recent texts include *Fig* and *Goan Atom: Jets Poupee*. Work also includes collaborations on performances and text-based installations. She is Director of Performance Writing at the Dartington College of Arts in Devon, England.

RICHARD BLANCO is the author of a book of poems, *City of a Hundred Fires,* and poems of his have appeared in *The Nation, Michigan Quarterly, TriQuarerly, Indiana Review,* and *Americas Review.*

EAVAN BOLAND is director of the Writing Program at Stanford University. She has been writer in residence at Trinity College and University College Dublin. She has also been the Hurst Professor at Washington University and Regent's Lecturer at the University of California at Santa Barbara. She is on the board of the Irish Arts Council and a member of the Irish Academy of Letters. She has published ten volumes of poetry, including *In a Time of Violence* and *An Origin Like Water: Collected Poems 1967–1987.* Her most recent published book is *Domestic Violence.*

WILLIAM BRONK (1918–1999) was a poet and the author of more than 15 books of poems and essays and a winner of the American Book Award in 1982.

RICHARD BURNS has lived in Italy, Greece, the USA, and Yugoslavia. His perspectives as a poet combine English, French, Mediterranean, Jewish, Slavic, American, and Oriental influences. In the 1970s, he founded and ran the (now almost legendary) international Cambridge Poetry Festival. His work has been translated into eighteen languages.

JARDA CERVENKA has won many awards for his fiction, and has published two collections of short stories, the most recent being *Revenge of the Underwater Man.*

YANBING CHEN obtained his MFA in fiction writing at Notre Dame. In recent years he has become well known as a translator of Bei Dao and other contemporary Chinese poets.

SHARON CHMIELARZ has had poems in *Prairie Schooner, The Iowa Review* and *The Seneca Review.* One of her books is *The Other Mozart,* a verse biography about Nannerl Mozart.

KEVIN CLARK'S first full-length collection of poetry, *In the Evening of No Warning,* was published in 2002. His poems have appeared in numerous magazines and collections, including *Antioch Review, Georgia Review, College English,* and *Black Warrior Review.*

MICHAEL COLLINS is the acclaimed author of eight books, including novels and short stories which have been translated into seventeen languages. Collins holds an MA in Creative Writing from the University of Notre Dame and a doctorate in Creative Writing from the University of Illinois. He has taught at various colleges, including The Art Institute of Chicago and Western Washington University. While working for Microsoft Corporation, Collins penned his award-winning novel, *The Keepers of Truth.* His most recent novel is *The Death of a Writer.*

ROBERT CRAWFORD works as professor of Modern Scottish Literature at the University of St. Andrews. He won an Eric Gregory award in 1988 and was one of twenty poets selected for the Poetry Society's "New Generation Poets" promotion in 1994. He has twice won a Scottish Arts Council Book Award, and four of his collections have been Poetry Book Society Recommendations.

ROBERT CREELEY (1926–2005) was a poet and author of more than sixty books. He is usually associated with the Black Mountain poets. He served as the Samuel P. Capen Professor of Poetry and the Humanities at SUNY Buffalo, and lived in Waldoboro, Maine, Buffalo, New York, and Providence, Rhode Island, where he taught at Brown University. He was a recipient of the Lannan Foundation Lifetime Achievement Award.

TONY D'SOUZA earned his MFA from the University of Notre Dame. He has contributed fiction and essays to *The New Yorker, Playboy, Salon, Esquire, McSweeney's, Tin House,* the *O. Henry Prize Stories, Best American Fantasy,* and elsewhere. His first novel, *Whiteman,* received the Sue Kaufman Best First Fiction Award from the American Academy of Arts & Letters. His second novel, *The Konkans,* appeared in 2008.

SEAMUS DEANE'S poetry collections include *Gradual; Rumours; History Lessons;* and *Selected Poems.* His non-fiction includes *Celtic Revivals: Essasys in Modern Irish Literature 1880–1980; A Short History of Irish Literature; The French Englightenment,* and *Revolution in England 1798–1832.* He is General Editor of *The Field Day Anthology of Irish Writing.* His first novel, *Reading in the Dark,* appeared in 1996.

CORINNE DEMAS is the award-winning author of two story collections, two novels, a memoir, *Eleven Stories High: Growing Up in Stuyvesant Town, 1948–1968,* and numerous children's books. She is professor of English at Mount Holyoke College and a fiction editor of *The Massachusetts Review.*

DEBRA DI BLASI is the author of *The Jirí Chronicles & Other Fictions, Prayers of an Accidental Nature,* and *Drought & Say What You Like.* Awards include the Thorpe Menn Book Award, James C. McCormick Fellowship in Fiction from the Christopher Isherwood Foundation, Eyster Prize for Fiction, Web del Sol's Best Web Fiction, and a Cinovation Screenwriting Award. She is president of Jaded Ibis Productions, a transmedia corporation™.

RAY DIPALMA is a poet and visual artist who has published more than forty collections of poetry, graphic work, and translations with various presses in the US and Europe. He was educated at Duquesne University and the University of Iowa.

JAMES DOYLE'S book, *Einstein Considers a Sand Dune,* won the Steel Toe Books 2003 Contest. His most recent collection is *Bending Under the Yellow Police Tapes.* He has work in *Cimarron Review, Green Hills Literary Lantern,* and *Willow Springs.*

KEVIN DUCEY'S first book, *Rhinoceros,* is available from Copper Canyon. He lives in Madison, Wisconsin.

RICHARD ELMAN (1934–1997) was a novelist, poet and critic who taught for many years at the Bennington College Summer Writing Workshops in Vermont. He published over 25 books; his last was a memoir of sorts, *Namedropping* (1999).

JOHN ENGELS (1931–2007) authored eleven volumes of poetry and was a professor of English at St. Michael's College in Colchester, Vermont, for 45 years. A graduate of the Iowa Writer's Workshop, he received numerous awards and fellowships for his work, including the National Endowment for the Arts, the Guggenheim and Rockefeller foundations, the Bread Loaf Writers' Conference, the Fulbright Program, and others. Additionally, he was a finalist for the Pulitzer Prize for his book *Walking to Cootehill.* His collected poems, *Recounting the Seasons: Poems, 1958–2005* was published in 2005.

ED FALCO'S most recent books are *Sabbath Night in the Church of the Piranha: New and Selected Stories, Wolf Point,* and *In the Park of Culture. Acid,* his short story collection, won the 1995 Richard Sullivan Prize. He lives in Blacksburg, Virginia, where he teaches writing and literature in Virginia Tech's MFA program. He also edits *The New River,* an online journal of digital writing.

BETH ANN FENNELLY'S recent books are *Tender Hooks* and *Unmentionables.* Her first book, *Open House,* won the 2001 Kenyon Review Prize. She has received fellowships from the National Endowment for the Arts and the Breadloaf Writers' Conference, and she was Diane Middlebrook Fellow at the University of Wisconsin. Fennelly is an assistant professor of English at the University of Mississippi.

ANNIE FINCH is the author of four volumes of poetry and poetry in translation. Finch's recent works include *Calendars*; a reissue of her early long poem, *The Encyclopedia of Scotland*; and a book of essays on poetry, *The Body of Poetry: Essays on Women, Form, and the Poetic Self.* Since 2005 she has served as Director of the Stonecoast graduate creative writing program at the University of Southern Maine.

JAMES FINNEGAN works in the field of financial institution insurance. Infrequently, his poems have appeared in literary journals. In 2001 he founded the NewPoetry List: http://wiz.cath.vt.edu/mailman/listinfo/new-poetry.

ROY FISHER is a poet and jazz pianist. He was one of the first British writers to absorb the poetics of William Carlos Williams and the Black Mountain poets into the British poetic tradition. His books include *The Dow Low Drop* and *The Long and the Short of It.*

JOHN GALLAHER is the author of the books of poetry, *Gentlemen in Turbans, Ladies in Cauls,* and *The Little Book of Guesses,* winner of the Levis Poetry Prize, from Four Way Books. He is currently co-editor of *The Laurel Review* and GreenTower Press.

RICHARD GARCIA is the author of *Rancho Notorious.* His poems have recently appeared in *Sentence, Crazyhorse,* and *Ploughshares.* He is the recipient of a Pushcart Prize, and one of his poems is included in *The Best American Poetry 2005.*

AMINA GAUTIER is assistant professor of English at St. Joseph's University in Philadelphia. Her short stories have appeared in several literary publications, and she is a contributing editor of *Storyquarterly Magazine.*

ROBERT GIBB is the author of several books of poetry: *World Over Water, The Burning World, The Origins of Evening,* which was a National Poetry Series winner; *Late Snow*; *Momentary Days*; *The Winter House*; and *The Names of the Earth in Summer.* His awards include a National Endowment for the Arts grant, four Pennsylvania Council on the Arts grants, a Pushcart Prize, the Wildwood Poetry Prize, and the Devil's Millhopper Chapbook Prize.

REGINALD GIBBONS is professor of English and Classics at Northwestern University. His most recent publications are his eighth book of poems, *Creatures of a Day* and a volume of translations of Sophocles, *Selected Poems: Odes and Fragments.* He has also published a collection of very short fiction, *Five Pears or Peaches*; a novel *Sweetbitter*; and other works.

ALBERT GOLDBARTH'S books of poetry have twice received the National Book Critics Circle Award. His current collection is *The Kitchen Sink.*

BARRY GOLDENSOHN is professor emeritus of English at Skidmore College. His poetry collections include *The Marrano, East Long Pond, Uncarving the Block,* and *Dance Music.*

LORRIE GOLDENSOHN is a poet and critic whose book, *Elizabeth Bishop: The Biography of a Poetry,* was published in 1992 and nominated for a Pulitzer Prize.

JEFFREY GREENE is the author of *To the Left of the Worshiper* and *American Spirituals,* which won the 1998 Samuel French Morse Prize. He was also the winner of the Randall Jarrell Prize and the Discovery/The Nation Award. His work has appeared in *The New Yorker, The Nation,* and many other journals and anthologies. He lives in Paris.

DEBORA GREGER has published six books of poetry: *Movable Islands, And, The 1002nd Night, Off-Season at the Edge of the World, Desert Fathers, Uranium Daughters,* and *God.* She has won the Grolier Prize, a Discovery/The Nation Award, the Award in Literature from the American Academy and Institute of Arts and Letters, the Peter I. B. Lavan Younger Poets Award, and the Brandeis University Award in Poetry. She was a winner of the Amy Lowell Poetry Traveling Scholarship and has received grants from the Ingram Merrill Foundation, the National Endowment for the Arts, and the Guggenheim Foundation.

ROBERT HAHN is a widely-published poet, essayist, and translator. His books of poetry include *All Clear* and *No Messages.*

CORRINNE CLEGG HALES is the author of *Underground, Out of This Place,* and *January Fire,* winner of the Devil's Millhopper Chapbook Prize. Other awards include two National Endowment for the Arts Fellowship Grants and the *River Styx* International Poetry Prize. She writes about the American West.

MARK HALPERIN is professor emeritus of English at Central Washington University, and the author of several poetry collections, including *Time As Distance* and *Falling Through the Music.*

JERRY HARP is a visiting assistant professor of English at Lewis and Clark College, and is the author of *Creature* and *Urban Flowers, Concrete Plains,* among other poetry collections.

MARY KATHLEEN HAWLEY has had her poems published in journals including *The Bloomsbury Review, Another Chicago Magazine,* and *The Spoon River Poetry Review.* Her first collection of poetry is entitled *Double Tongues.*

JUSTIN HAYNES is a graduate of the MFA program at Notre Dame. He also received a fiction fellowship from the Fine Arts Work Center in Provincetown, as well as a Djerassi fiction fellowship at the University of Wisconsin at Madison.

SEAMUS HEANEY is the 1995 winner of the Nobel Prize in Literature.

BRIAN HENRY is associate professor of English and creative writing at the University of Richmond. He is the author of *American Incident, Astronaut, Graft,* and *Quarantine,* among others.

ROALD HOFFMANN is the 1981 Nobel Prize winner in Chemistry, shared with Kenischi Fukui. He is the Frank H. T. Rhodes Professor of Humane Letters at Cornell University.

JANET HOLMES is author of *F2f, Humanophone, The Green Tuxedo,* and *The Physicist at the Mall.* Her work has twice been included in the annual Best American Poetry anthologies, and she has received numerous prizes and honors for her writing, including grants from the Bush Foundation, the McKnight Foundation. the Minnesota State Arts Board, and The Loft. She is director of Ahsahta Press, an all-poetry publishing house at Boise State University, where she has taught in the MFA program since 1999.

ALISON JARVIS received the Lyric Poetry Award from the Poetry Society of America and the Guy Owen Prize from *Southern Poetry Review.* Her poems appeared, most recently, in *Chelsea, Cream City Review, Gulf Coast, Notre Dame Review, Seattle Review,* and *Southern Poetry Review.* A psychotherapist in private practice, she lives and works in Manhattan.

DEVIN JOHNSTON received his PhD in English from the University of Chicago. His research interests include contemporary and modern American literature and creative writing in poetry and fiction. He has written several works of poetry, and he is currently writing a book of essays on birds, pastoralism, and poverty in modern poetry. His two poetry collections are entitled *Aversions* and *Telepathy.*

PAUL KANE'S most recent collection of poems is *Drowned Lands.* A recipient of NEH and Guggenheim Foundation fellowships, he teaches at Vassar College.

ROBERT KELLY'S latest books are *Lapis* and *Shame/Scham.* Forthcoming are *The Language of Eden* and *May Day.* He teaches in the writing program at Bard College.

R.M. KINDER won the 2005 University of Michigan prize for a collection of short stories titled *A Near-Perfect Gift.* Another of her short story collections, *Sweet Angel Band,* was awarded the Willa Cather Award in 1991. Her prose has also appeared in *Other Voices, Short Stories,* and *The New York Times.*

JOHN KINSELLA is an Australian poet, novelist, critic, essayist and editor. His writing is strongly influenced by landscape and he espouses an 'international regionalism' in his approach to place. He has also frequently worked in collaboration with other writers, artists, and musicians. Important collections of his work include *Doppler Effect, Peripheral Light,* and *The New Arcadia.*

JOHN KOETHE is Distinguished Professor of Philosophy at the University of Wisconsin at Milwaukee and the first Poet Laureate of Milwaukee, where he lives. His collection *North Point North* was a finalist for the Los Angeles Times Book Prize, and his collection *Falling Water* won the Kingsley Tufts Award. In 2005 he was a Fellow of the American Academy in Berlin.

SANDRA KOHLER'S second collection of poems, *The Ceremonies of Longing,* won the 2002 AWP Award Series in Poetry. A previous collection, *The Country of Women* appeared in 1995. Her poems have appeared recently in *Colorado Review, Women's Review of Books, Diner,* and *Inkwell.*

SUSANNE KORT is a psychotherapist practicing in Jalisco, Mexico. Her poems have appeared in *Grand Street, Northwest Review, Indiana Review, The Journal, North American Review, Seattle Review, Antioch Review,* and others in the U.S., as well as journals in Ireland, Canada, and England.

MARILYN KRYSL has published seven books of poetry, three of stories, work in *The Atlantic, The Nation, The New Republic,* and other journals, in *Best American Short Stories 2000,* O. Henry Prize Stories, and the Pushcart Prize Anthology. She is former Director of the Creative Writing Program at the University of Colorado, Boulder, and a founding editor of the literary journal *Many Mountains Moving.* Her newest collection of stories is *Dinner With Osama.*

JOHN LATTA earned an MFA in Creative Writing at the University of Virginia and a PhD in English at the State University of New York, Albany. His first collection of poems, *Rubbing Torsos,* appeared in 1979. A recent collection, *Breeze,* won the 2003 Ernest Sandeen Prize in Poetry. He has received numerous awards, including two creative writing fellowships from the National Endowment for the Arts. His poems have appeared in dozens of magazines and other publications, including *Boston Review, New American Writing, Gettysburg Review, Jacket,* and *Chicago Review.*

DENISE LEVERTOV (1923–1997) published more than twenty volumes of poetry, including *Freeing the Dust,* which won the Lenore Marshall Poetry Prize. She was also the author of four books of prose, most recently *Tesserae,* and translator of three volumes of poetry. From 1982–1993, she taught at Stanford University.

MOIRA LINEHAN has had work accepted by *Image, New Orleans Review, Orion, Poetry East, Prairie Schooner,* and *Sou'wester.* Her poetry collection, *If No Moon,* appeared in 2007.

WILLIAM LOGAN is the author of seven books of poems: *Sad-faced Men, Difficulty, Sullen Weedy Lakes, Vain Empires, Night Battle, Macbeth in Venice,* and *The Whispering Gallery.* He is a regular critic of poetry for the *New York Times Book Review* and writes a biannual verse chronicle for the *New Criterion.*

GEORGE LOONEY's books include *Animals Housed in the Pleasure of Flesh, Attendant Ghosts,* and *Greatest Hits 1990–2000.* His poetry has earned him a National Endowment for the Arts Creative Writing Fellowship, and two grants from the Ohio Arts Council. In 2003, poems of his won The Larry Levis Editors Award for Poetry from *Missouri Review.* He is co-director of The Chautauqua Writers Festival, and serves as editor-in-chief of *Lake Effect* and translation editor of *Mid-American Review.* He is associate professor of English and creative writing at Penn State Erie, where he is program chair of a brand new B.F.A. in creative writing he designed.

SHERYL LUNA'S collection of poetry *Pity the Drowned Horses* won the first Andres Montoya Poetry Prize sponsored by the Institute of Latino Studies and the Creative Writing Program of the University of Notre Dame. She has received scholarships from the Provincetown Fine Arts Work Center and the Napa Valley Writer's Conference. She teaches at the University of Colorado at Boulder.

DEREK MAHON'S honors include the Irish American Foundation Award; a Lannan Foundation Award; a Guggenheim Fellowship; the Irish Times/Aer Lingus Poetry Prize, the American Ireland Fund Literary Award; the C. K. Scott Moncrieff Translation Prize for his translation of *The Selected Poems of Philippe Jaccottet;* the Eric Gregory Award; and the David Cohen Prize for Literature. He is a member of Aosdána and lives in Dublin.

GERARD MALANGA lives in Brooklyn, New York. He is a poet and photographer, and author of *Archiving Warhol: Illustrated History, Scopophilia: The Love of Looking,* and *Rosebud,* among other publications.

MICHAEL MARTONE is professor of English and Director of the Creative Writing Program at the University of Alabama where he has been teaching since 1996. He is the author of five books of short fiction including *Seeing*

Eye, Pensées, The Thoughts of Dan Quayle, Fort Wayne Is Seventh on Hitler's List, Safety Patrol, and *Alive and Dead in Indiana.* He has edited two collections of essays about the Midwest: *A Place of Sense: Essays in Search of the Midwest* and *Townships: Pieces of the Midwest.*

DAVID MATLIN is a novelist, poet, and essayist. His collections of poetry and prose include the books *China Beach, Dressed In Protective Fashion,* and *Fontana's Mirror.* He teaches at San Diego State University.

CRIS MAZZA is the author of over a dozen books of fiction, most recently *Waterboy.* She lives in Blacksberry Township, Illinois, and is director of the Program for Writers at the University of Illinois at Chicago.

JAMES McMICHAEL is professor of English at the University of California at Irvine. He is the author of several poetry collections, including *Capacity, The Lover's Familiar,* and *The World at Large.*

ROBERT McNAMARA is the author of *Second Messengers* (poems), and the translator of *Birajmohan and Other Poems,* by the contemporary Bengali poet Sarat Kumar Mukhopadhyay. He has published articles on Ezra Pound, T. S. Eliot, and Rabindranath Tagore, and has given papers on teaching writing in the disciplines.

CHRISTOPHER MERRILL has published four collections of poetry, including *Brilliant Water* and *Watch Fire,* for which he received the Peter I. B. Lavan Younger Poets Award from the Academy of American Poets; translations of Aleš Debeljak's *Anxious Moments* and *The City and the Child*; several edited volumes, among them, *The Forgotten Language: Contemporary Poets and Nature* and *From the Faraway Nearby: Georgia O'Keeffe as Icon*; and four books of nonfiction, *The Grass of Another Country: A Journey Through the World of Soccer, The Old Bridge: The Third Balkan War and the Age of the Refugee, Only the Nails Remain: Scenes from the Balkan Wars,* and *Things of the Hidden God: Journey to the Holy Mountain.* His work has been translated into twenty languages. He has held the William H. Jenks Chair in Contemporary Letters at the College of the Holy Cross, and now directs the International Writing Program at the University of Iowa.

PETER MICHELSON has published three volumes of poetry and two books of prose, and edited an edition of *The Extant Works of Max Michelson,* who was his grandfather and one of the original Imagist poets. He is professor emeritus at the University of Colorado.

CZESLAW MILOSZ (1911–2004) was the 1980 Nobel Prize winner in Literature.

SIMONE MUENCH is assistant professor of English at Lewis University. Her poems have been published in *Paris Review, Indiana Review, Poetry, Bellingham Review,* and *POOL.* She is a recipient of an Illinois Arts Council Fellowship, the 49th Parallel Award for Poetry, the Charles Goodnow Award, the AWP Intro Journals Project Award, and the Poetry Center's 9th Annual Juried Reading Award. Her book *The Air Lost in Breathing* received the Marianne Moore Prize for Poetry.

PAUL MULDOON'S main collections of poetry are *New Weather, Mules, Why Brownlee Left, Quoof, Meeting the British, Madoc: A Mystery, The Annals of Chile, Hay, Poems 1968–1998,* and *Moy Sand and Gravel,* for which he won the 2003 Pulitzer Prize. His tenth collection, *Horse Latitudes,* appeared in 2006.

JUDE NUTTER was born in North Yorkshire, England, and grew up in northern Germany. Her poems have appeared in numerous international journals and anthologies, and she is the recipient of several awards and grants. Jude Nutter's first collection, *Pictures of the Afterlife,* was published in 2002. *The Curator of Silence* won the Ernest Sandeen Prize from the University of Notre Dame and was awarded the 2007 Minnesota Book Award in Poetry. Her third collection, *I Wish I Had a Heart Like Yours, Walt Whitman* is forthcoming from the University of Notre Dame Press. In 2004 she spent two months in Antarctica with the National Science Foundation's Writers and Artists Program. She has been living and working in Minneapolis since 1998.

JERE ODELL'S poetry has appeared in *A.C.M., Mudfish, First Things, Alaska Quarterly Review,* and *The Possibility of Language.*

ANDREW OSBORN teaches literature and writing at Whitman College in Walla Walla, Washington. His poetry and articles about poetry have appeared in such publications as *American Letters & Commentary, Bat City Review, Contemporary Literature, Denver Quarterly,* and *The Wallace Stevens Journal.*

ERIC PANKEY is the author of five collections of poetry. His poems, essays, and reviews have appeared in *Antaeus, Antioch Review, Gettysburg Review, Grand Street, Iowa Review, Kenyon Review, New Republic, New Yorker, The Quarterly, Shenandoah,* and many other publications. Winner of the Walt Whitman Award from the Academy of American Poets, Pankey has received numerous grants supporting his work. He has taught creative writing at several colleges, including Washington University in St. Louis, the University of Iowa, and, currently, George Mason University. He lives in Fairfax, Virginia.

SUZANNE PAOLA'S book, *Glass*, came out in the Quarterly Review of Literature Poetry Award Series. Her poems have appeared in *Ploughshares, Willow Springs,* and *Southern Humanities Review.* She is also the author of the award-winning poetry collection *Bardo.* She is associate professor of English at Western Washington University.

ELISE PARTRIDGE is the author of *Fielder's Choice,* shortlisted for the Gerald Lampert Award for the best first book of poetry in Canada.

TOM PAULIN'S collections include *A State of Justice,* winner of a Somerset Maugham Award; *The Strange Museum,* which won the Geoffrey Faber Memorial Prize; *Liberty Tree,* and *Fivemiletown,* which explores Northern Irish Protestant culture and identities. Later collections include *Walking a Line* and *The Wind Dog,* which was shortlisted for the T. S. Eliot Prize. The *Invasion Handbook* is the first installment of an epic poem about the Second World War.

DEBORAH PEASE has published in numerous journals including *AGNI, Denver Quarterly,* and *The New Yorker.* She is a former publisher of the *Paris Review.*

JOHN PECK'S recent books are *Collected Shorter Poems 1966–1996,* and *Red Strawberry Leaf: Selected Poems 1994–2001.*

PAUL PETRIE has published work in many magazines, including *The Atlantic, Commonweal, The Formalist, The Harvard Magazine, The Hudson Review,* and *The New Yorker.* He has also published several poetry collections, including *The Runners, The Academy of Goodbye,* and *Rooms of Grace.*

DONALD PLATT is the author of two volumes of poetry, *Fresh Peaches, Fireworks, & Guns* and *Cloud Atlas.* His poems have appeared in many journals, including *The New Republic, The Nation, Paris Review, Poetry, Kenyon Review, Georgia Review, Ploughshares, TriQuarterly, Virginia Quarterly Review,* and *Southern Review,* as well as in *The Best American Poetry 2000* and in *The Pushcart Prize XXVII and XXIX.*

GÖRAN PRINTZ-PÅHLSON (1931–2006) was a world-renowned poet, critic, translator, and scholar.

JAMES S. PROFFITT is a freelance journalist in Cincinnati. His poems and fiction have appeared in *Rattapallax, Tampa Review, Rattle, West Wind Review,* and elsewhere.

KEVIN PRUFER is the author of three books of poetry and the editor of two anthologies. He also serves as Editor of *Pleiades: A Journal of New Writing,* an international magazine of poetry, fiction, essays, and reviews; Associate Editor of *American Book Review*; and Vice President/Secretary of the National Book Critics Circle. He is professor of English at the University of Central Missouri.

JAMES D. REDWOOD is a professor at Albany Law School. His fiction has appeared in the *Virginia Quarterly Review, Black Warrior Review,* and elsewhere.

PETER ROBINSON is professor of English and American Literature at the University of Reading. His recent books include *Selected Poetry and Prose of Vittorio Sereni, The Greener Meadow: Selected Poems of Luciano Erba, The Look of Goodbye,* and *Talk about Poetry: Conversations on the Art.*

PATTIANN ROGERS has published eleven books, most recently *Firekeeper, Expanded and Revised Edition, Generations,* and *Song of the World Becoming, New and Collected Poems, 1981–2001.*

IRA SADOFF is the author of seven collections of poetry, most recently *Barter* and *Grazing,* as well as a novel *Uncoupling* and *The Ira Sadoff Reader.* He teaches at Colby College.

JOHN PHILLIP SANTOS is the author of *Places Left Unfinished at the Time of Creation,* which was a National Book Award finalist in nonfiction. Santos also was an Emmy nominee in 1988 for "From the AIDS Experience: Part I, Our Spirits to Heal/Part II, Our Humanity to Heal," and in 1985 for "Exiles Who Never Leave Home."

HILLEL SCHWARTZ is a cultural historian, senior fellow at the Millennium Institute, and author of *Century's End: An Orientation Manual Toward the Year 2000.*

NEIL SHEPARD, a professor in the Writing and Literature program at Johnson State College in Johnson, Vermont, grew up in Leominster, Massachusetts. Shepard earned his MA in Creative Writing at Colorado State University and his PhD at Ohio University. His poetry collections include *I'm Here Because I Lost My Way* and *This Far from the Source.*

REGINALD SHEPHERD is the editor of *The Iowa Anthology of New American Poetries.* He is also the author of five books of poetry, *Fata Morgana, Otherhood,* a finalist for the 2004 Lenore Marshall Poetry Prize, *Wrong, Angel, Interrupted,* and *Some Are Drowning,* winner of the 1993 AWP Award in Poetry. Shepherd's work has appeared in four editions of *The Best American Poetry* and two Pushcart Prize anthologies, as well as in such journals as *American Poetry Review, Conjunctions, Kenyon Review, The*

Nation, The New York Times Book Review, Ploughshares, Poetry, and *Yale Review.*

FRANCES SHERWOOD has published five novels: *The Book of Splendor, Green, Vindication, Betrayal,* and *Night of Sorrows.* In addition, she has published numerous short stories, and has had work appear in *Best American Short Stories* and *The O. Henry Award* collections.

CHARLES SIMIC is a former Poet Laureate of the United States. He is the author of more than sixty books, and his work has won numerous prestigious awards, including the Pulitzer Prize for *The World Doesn't End.* In 1995 Simic was elected to the American Academy of Arts and Letters.

R.D. SKILLINGS is chairman of the writing committee of the Fine Arts Work Center in Provincetown, and is the author of *How Many Die* and *Where the Time Goes* among other books.

FLOYD SKLOOT is a nonfiction writer, poet, and novelist whose work has appeared in such distinguished magazines as *The New York Times Magazine, Atlantic Monthly, Harper's, Poetry, American Scholar, Georgia Review, Sewanee Review, Southern Review, Boulevard, Creative Nonfiction,* and *Shenandoah.* His works include *In the Shadow of Memory, Patient 002,* and *A World of Light.*

KEN SMITH (1938–2003) was a poet and the author of *The Poet Reclining: Selected Poems 1962–1980* and *Shed: Poems 1980–2001.*

MIKE SMITH holds degrees from the University of North Carolina at Greensboro, Hollins College, and Notre Dame. His poems have appeared in *Borderlands, DIAGRAM,* the *North American Review,* and the *Notre Dame Review.* Poems are forthcoming in *Main Street Rag* and *Zone 3.* His chapbook, *Anagrams of America,* is on-line at *Mudlark: Electronic Journal of Poetry and Poetics.* His first book of poems is titled *How to Make a Mummy.*

MAURA STANTON'S most recent books of stories are *Do Not Forsake Me, Oh My Darling,* and *Cities in the Sea.* Her stories have appeared in *Ploughshares, Water~Stone, TriQuarterly,* and many other magazines. She won the Nelson Algren Award from the *Chicago Tribune.* She teaches in the MFA Program at Indiana University.

LISA M. STEINMAN teaches at Reed College and co-edits the poetry magazine, *Hubbub.* She has received NEA and Rockefeller fellowships and has also published two books about poetry, *Made in America* and *Masters of Repetition.* Her poems have been published in *Massachusetts Review, Prairie Schooner, Women's Review of Books,* and elsewhere. Her poetry collections include *Lost Poems, Ordinary Songs, All That Comes to Light, A Book of Other Days,* and *Carslaw's Sequences.*

MICHAEL STEPHENS is the author of *Circle's End, The Brooklyn Book of the Dead,* and *Season at Coole,* among others.

STEPHANIE STRICKLAND is a print and new media poet. Her fourth book, *V: WaveSon.nets/Losing L'una,* has a Web component, http://vniverse.com. Other works include *True North, The Red Virgin: A Poem of Simone Weil,* and *Ballad of Sand and Harry Soot.* She has taught literary hypermedia as part of experimental poetry at Brown, Hollins, University of Montana-Missoula, Boise State, Sarah Lawrence, Georgia Tech, and Parsons.

MARCELA SULAK is assistant professor of Literature at American University. She is working on a book entitled *1920s New York as a Construction Site for Modernist "American" Poetry.* Her poetry chapbook, entitled *Of All the Things that Don't Exist, I Love You Best,* is forthcoming. Other poems have appeared in such journals as *Fence, Indiana Review, River Styx,* and *Quarterly West.*

BRIAN SWANN'S latest books are *Autumn Road,* winner of the Ohio State University Press/The Journal Award for 2005, and *Snow House,* winner of the 2005 Lena-Miles Wever Todd Poetry Prize.

BRIAN TEARE has published poetry in *Ploughshares, Boston Review, Provincetown Arts, Verse,* and *Seneca Review,* among other journals. His first book, *The Room Where I Was Born,* won the 2003 Brittingham Prize and the 2004 Triangle Award for Gay Poetry.

MARIA TERRONE'S second book of poetry, *A Secret Room in Fall,* won the 2005 McGovern Prize from Ashland Poetry Press. Her first book, *The Bodies We Were Loaned,* appeared in 2002. Her work has appeared in such magazines as *Poetry, Hudson Review, Crab Orchard Review,* and *Poetry International.* She is the recipient of the *Willow Review* Award for Poetry, the Elinor Benedict Poetry Prize for *Passages North,* and the Allen Tate Memorial Award for *Wind.*

DIANE THIEL is the author of six books of poetry, nonfiction and creative writing pedagogy: *Echolocations,* which received the Nicholas Roerich Prize from Story Line Press; *Writing Your Rhythm: Using Nature, Culture, Form and Myth; The White Horse: A Colombian Journey;* and *Resistance Fantasies.*

RYAN G. VAN CLEAVE is the Jenny McKean Moore Writer-in-Washington at George Washington University. He has taught creative writing and literature at Clemson University, Florida State University, the University of

Wisconsin at Madison, the University of Wisconsin at Green Bay, as well as at prisons, community centers, and urban at-risk youth centers.

ARTURO VIVANTE (1923–2008) is best known for his short stories, seventy of which appeared in *The New Yorker. Solitude and Other Stories* appeared in 2004; *Truelove Knot: A Novel of World War II* appeared in 2007.

ANTHONY WALTON has written for a variety of publications including *The New York Times* and *7 Days*. His book *Mississippi* appeared in 1997, and he co-edited *The Vintage Book of African American Poetry* with Michael S. Harper.

MARLYS WEST received her MFA from the James A. Michener Center for Writers at the University of Texas at Austin. The University of Akron Press published her book, *Notes for a Late-Blooming Martyr: Poems,* in 1999. She was a 2002–2003 Hodder Fellow at Princeton University,

EUGENE WILDMAN is a former editor of the *Chicago Review* and a winner of several Illinois Arts Council awards for fiction. His main interest is in the short story, though most of his early work was experimental. He was the editor/"composer" of the *Chicago Review Anthology of Concretism,* the first collection of visual poetry to appear in this country; that was followed by *Experiments in Prose,* an assemblage of nonlinear and mixed media texts.

ERIC G. WILSON is Z. Smith Reynolds Faculty Fellow and associate professor of English at Wake Forest University.

DAVID WOJAHN is the author of seven collections of poetry: *Interrogation Palace, Spirit Cabinet, The Falling Hour, Late Empire, Mystery Train, Glassworks,* and *Icehouse Lights.* He is also the author of *Strange Good Fortune,* a collection of essays on contemporary verse.

RUSSELL WORKING is a reporter and fiction writer whose short stories have appeared in publications ranging from *Atlantic Monthly* to *Zoetrope: All-Story.* He is the author of the collections *The Irish Martyr* and *Resurrectionists.*

BARON WORMSER has received the Frederick Bock Prize for Poetry and the Kathryn A. Morton Prize along with fellowships from Bread Loaf, the National Endowment for the Arts, and the John Simon Guggenheim Memorial Foundation. In 2000 he was writer in residence at the University of South Dakota. For eight years he led the Frost Place Seminar at the Frost Place in Franconia, New Hampshire.

CHARLES WRIGHT has published fourteen volumes of poetry as well as translations of Italian poets Eugenio Montale and Dino Campana. He has also produced two collections of nonfictional essays and interviews, *Halflife* and *Quarter Notes*. He has won numerous awards for his verse, including a PEN Translation Prize, an Ingram Merrill Fellowship, a Lenore Marshall Prize for *Chickamauga*, a Pulitzer Prize and National Book Critics Circle Award for *Black Zodiac*, and an Award of Merit Medal from the American Academy of Arts and Letters.

MARTHA ZWEIG'S poems have appeared widely in literary journals including: *Northwest Review, Manoa, Boston Review, The Journal, Ploughshares, Literary Imagination, Gettysburg Review, The Progressive, Field,* and *Beloit Poetry Journal.*

Acknowledgments

Over ten years a number of people have contributed to the success of the *Notre Dame Review.* One of the first was the *Review*'s first managing editor, Jere Odell, who, along with Valerie Sayers, is responsible for its interior design. The first Editorial Board consisted of four names, the current editors and Sonia Gernes and Henry Weinfield. There were eight editorial assistants at first, all students in the creative writing program: Yanbing Chen, Julia Cosmides, K. T. P. di Camillo, Stephen P. Hidalgo, Andrew Hughes, R. C. MacRorie, Leigh McEwan, and one PhD student, Jessica Maich. (The other Managing Editors, members of the Advisory Board and Editorial assistants will be listed below.) We would also like to thank the Deans who created a budget for the *NDR*: Harry Attridge, Mary Ellen Koepfle, and Mark Roche, all of the School of Arts & Letters. We would also like to thank Sam Hazo for all his support and all our other "Sustainers," especially our two Anonymous donors. The covers have been done with the assistance of the university's graphics division, particularly Patrick Ryan and Paul Wieber. We have had two primary printers: McNaughton & Gunn, Inc. and Premier/Batson. And a number of distributors: Bernard DeBoer, Inc., Anderson News, International Periodical Distributors, Ubiquity Distributors, Media Solutions, and Ingram Periodicals. And we need to thank all the writers who have sent us their manuscripts, even, or most particularly, those we have not published. Without the ambition of strangers no literary journal can flourish. We would like to thank Barbara Hanrahan, Rebecca DeBoer, Katie Lehman, and Margaret Gloster at the University of Notre Dame Press for their support. And here are the names, not yet listed, of the staffs of our first ten issues: Julia Cosmides, Kevin Corbett, Amy Wray, Kathleen J. Canavan, Marie Munro, Michael G. Richards, Justin Haynes, Kelly Kearney, Angela Hur, James Walton, Matthew Benedict, Gerald Bruns, Seamus Deane, Stephen Fredman, Kymberly Taylor Haywood, Orlando Menes, Mike Smith, Joe Francis Doerr, Kevin Hart, Danna Ephland, and Francisco Aragon. Thanks to all.

Permissions and Credits

All authors have provided permission to reproduce their work in this anthology. Specific mention is made of works published separately from the *Notre Dame Review.*

CHRIS AGEE. "Dark Hay" in *First Light* by Chris Agee. Dublin: Dedalus Press. Copyright © 2003 by Chris Agee. Reprinted by permission of the author.

SANDRA ALCOSSER. "The Blue Vein" was made into a *livre d'artistes* with Brighton Press, a limited edition of 35 copies. Copyright © 2004 by Sandra Alcosser. Reprinted by permission of the author.

MICHAEL ANANIA. "Turnings" in *Turnings* by Michael Anania. Firenze, Italy: Bisonte. Copyright © 2005 by Michael Anania. Reprinted by permission of the author.

ROBERT ARCHAMBEAU. "Victory Over the Sun" in *Home and Variations* by Robert Archambeau. Cambridge: Salt Publishing. Copyright © 2004 by Robert Archambeau. Reprinted by permission of the author.

RENÉE ASHLEY. "Some Other Woman Speaks to Elpenor after His Fall from Circe's Roof" in *The Revisionist's Dream* by Renée Ashley. New York: Avocet Press. Copyright © 2001 by Renée Ashley. Reprinted by permission of the author.

JENNIFER ATKINSON. "Conturbatio, Cogitatio, Interrogatio, Humilitatio, Meritatio: Ghazal on the Five Petals of the Salt Spray Rose" in *The Drowned City* by Jennifer Atkinson. Boston: Northeastern University Press. Copyright © 2000 by Jennifer Atkinson. Reprinted by permission of the author.

NED BALBO. "After Hitchcock" in *Lives of the Sleepers* by Ned Balbo. Notre Dame, IN: University of Notre Dame Press. Copyright © 2005 by Ned Balbo. Reprinted by permission of the author.

MARY JO BANG. "To Dance the Tarantella" in *The Downstream Extremity of the Isle of Swans.* Athens: University of Georgia Press. Copyright © 2007 by Mary Jo Bang. Reprinted by permission of the author.

TINA BARR. "The Purpose of Jewelry" in *The Gathering Eye* by Tina Barr. Dorset, VT: Tupelo Press. Copyright © 2003 by Tina Barr. Reprinted by permission of the author.

CHRISTIAN BARTER. "The Lost World of the Aegean" in *The Singers I Prefer* by Christian Barter. Fort Lee, NJ: CavanKerry Press. Copyright © 2005 by Christian Barter. Reprinted by permission of the author.

WENDY BATTIN. "And the Two Give Birth to the Myriad of Things" in *Little Apocalypse* by Wendy Battin. Ashland, OH: Ashland Poetry Press. Copyright © 1997 by Wendy Battin. Reprinted by permission of the author.

CAROLINE BERGVALL. "More Pets" in *Fig: Goan Atom 2* by Caroline Bergvall. Cambridge: Salt Publishing. Copyright © 2005 by Caroline Bergvall. Reprinted by permission of the author.

RICHARD BLANCO. "October Crosswords" appears as "Empty Crosswords" in *Directions to the Beach of the Dead* by Richard Blanco. Tucson: University of Arizona Press. Copyright © 2005 by Richard Blanco. Reprinted by permission of the author.

EAVAN BOLAND. "The Harbour" in *The Lost Land* by Eavan Boland. New York: W. W. Norton, Copyright © 1998 by Eavan Boland. "The Harbour" originally appeared in *The New Yorker.*

WILLIAM BRONK. "Subject Matter," "The Immortals," and "The Mute Deaf of the World" in *The Cage of Age* by William Bronk. Jersey City, NJ: Talisman House Publishers. Copyright © 1996 by William Bronk. Reprinted by permission of the Trustees of Columbia University.

RICHARD BURNS. #50 from *The Manager* by Richard Burns. London: Elliott & Thompson. Copyright © 2001 by Richard Burns. Reprinted by permission of the author.

ROBERT CRAWFORD. "Alford" in *Selected Poems* by Robert Crawford. London: Jonathan Cape, 2005. Reprinted by permission of the author.

ROBERT CREELEY. "Histoire de Florida" (excerpt) in *Life and Death* by Robert Creeley. Copyright © 1998 by Robert Creeley. Reprinted by permission of New Directions Publishing Corporation.

JOHN ENGELS. "The Orders" in *Recounting the Seasons: Poems, 1958–2005* by John Engels. Notre Dame, IN: University of Notre Dame Press. Copyright © 2005 by John Engels. Reprinted by permission of the author.

ED FALCO. "Essay on the Eve of War" and "The Body of a Woman" in *In the Park of Culture* by Ed Falco. Notre Dame, IN: University of Notre Dame

Press. Copyright © 2005 by Edward Falco. Reprinted by permission of the author.

ANNIE FINCH. "A Letter to Emily Dickinson" in *Calendars* by Annie Finch. Dorset, VT: Tupelo Press. Copyright © 2003 by Annie Finch. Reprinted by permission of the author.

ROY FISHER. "And on That Note: 6 Jazz Elegies" in *The Long and the Short of It: Poems 1955–2005* by Roy Fisher. Copyright © 2005 by Roy Fisher. Reprinted by permission of Bloodaxe Books.

RICHARD GARCIA. "The Peaceable Kingdom" in *The Persistence of Objects* by Richard Garcia. Rochester, NY: BOA Editions. Copyright © 2006 by Richard Garcia. Reprinted by permission of the author.

ROBERT HAHN. "Elegiac Quarrel: Conclusion" as "Epilogue and Unraveling: Pig-Headed Father, Churlish Son" in *No Messages* by Robert Hahn. Notre Dame, IN: University of Notre Dame Press. Copyright © 2001 by Robert Hahn. Reprinted by permission of the author.

CORRINNE CLEGG HALES. "Girl at a Barbed Wire Fence" in *Separate Escapes* by Corrinne Clegg Hales. Ashland, OH: Ashland Poetry Press. Copyright © 2002 by Corrinne Clegg Hales. Reprinted by permission of the author.

MARK HALPERIN. "The Elegant Ladies of Tallinn" in *Time as Distance* by Mark Halperin. Kalamazoo, MI: New Issues Press. Copyright © 2001 by Mark Halperin. Reprinted by permission of the author.

JERRY HARP. "A Man Who Was Afraid of Language" in *Creature* by Jerry Harp. Cambridge: Salt Publishing. Copyright © 2003 by Jerry Harp. Reprinted by permission of the author.

SEAMUS HEANEY. "The Watchman's War" in "Mycenae Lookout" from *The Spirit Level* by Seamus Heaney. Copyright © 1996 by Seamus Heaney. Reprinted by permission of Farrar, Straus and Giroux, LLC.

ROALD HOFFMANN. "Tsunami" in *Soliton* by Roald Hoffmann. Kirksville, MO: Truman State University Press. Copyright © 2002 by Roald Hoffmann. Reprinted by permission of the author.

JANET HOLMES. "The Yellow Period" in *The Green Tuxedo* by Janet Holmes. Notre Dame, IN: University of Notre Dame Press. Copyright © 1998 by Janet Holmes. Reprinted by permission of the author.

DEVIN JOHNSTON. "Los Angeles" in *Aversions* by Devin Johnston. Richmond, CA: Omnidawn Publishing. Copyright © 2004 by Devin Johnston. Reprinted by permission of the author.

PAUL KANE. "The Desert Father" in *Work Life: New Poems* by Paul Kane. New York: Turtle Point Press. Copyright © 2007 by Paul Kane. Reprinted by permission of the author.

JOHN KOETHE. "The Maquiladoras" in *Sally's Hair* by John Koethe. New York: HarperCollins. Copyright © 2006 by John Koethe. Reprinted by permission of the author.

JOHN LATTA. "The Limits of Language" in *Breeze* by John Latta. Notre Dame, IN: University of Notre Dame Press. Copyright © by John Latta. Reprinted by permission of the author.

DENISE LEVERTOV. "The Cult of Relics" from *Sands of the Well* by Denise Levertov. Copyright © 1996 by Denise Levertov. Reprinted by permission of New Directions Publishing Corporation.

WILLIAM LOGAN: "After the War" from *The Whispering Gallery* by William Logan. New York: Penguin. Copyright © 2005 by William Logan. Reprinted by permission of the author.

GEORGE LOONEY. "Faced with a Mosque in a Field of Wheat" in *The Precarious Rhetoric of Angels* by George Looney. Buffalo, NY: White Pine Press. Copyright © 2005 by George Looney. Reprinted by permission of the author.

SHERYL LUNA. "Sonata on Original Sin" in *Pity the Drowned Horses* by Sheryl Luna. Notre Dame, IN: University of Notre Dame Press. Copyright © 2005 by Sheryl Luna. Reprinted by permission of the author.

DEREK MAHON. "River Rhymes" in *The Hudson Letter* by Derek Mahon. County Meath, Ireland: Gallery Press. Copryight © 1995 by Derek Mahon. Reprinted by permission of the author.

CRIS MAZZA. "Breeding" in *Dog People: A Novel* by Cris Mazza. Minneapolis: Coffee House Press. Copyright © 1997 by Cris Mazza. Reprinted by permission of the author.

JAMES McMICHAEL. "From the Homeplace" in *Capacity* by James McMichael. Copyright © 2006 by James McMichael. Reprinted by permission of Farrar, Straus and Giroux, LLC.

CZESLAW MILOSZ. "Wanda" in *New Collected Poems, 1931–2001* by Czeslaw Milosz. Copyright © 1995 by Czeslaw Milosz. Reprinted by permission of HarperCollins.

SIMONE MUENCH. "The *Melos* of Medusa" in *Lampblack & Ash* by Simone Muench. Louisville: Sarabande Books. Copyright © 2005 by Simone Muench. Reprinted by permission of the author.

PAUL MULDOON. "Long Finish" in *Poems 1968–1998* by Paul Muldoon. Copyright © 2001 by Paul Muldoon. Reprinted by permission of Farrar, Straus and Giroux, LLC.

JUDE NUTTER. "Grave Robbing with Rilke" in *The Curator of Silence* by Jude Nutter. Notre Dame, IN: University of Notre Dame Press. Copyright © 2006 by Jude Nutter. Reprinted by permission of the author.

JERE ODELL. "Fruit Fly" in *The Possibility of Language: Seven New Poets,* ed. Jeffrey Roessner. San Jose: Writers Club Press, 2001.

ANDREW OSBORN. "Homing" in *Plato's Aviary* by Andrew Osborn. Ridgefield, CT: The Aldrich Museum of Contemporary Art. Copyright © 2003 by Andrew Osborn. Reprinted by permission of the author.

ERIC PANKEY. "Does Not Sunder" in *Reliquaries* by Eric Pankey. Keene, NY: Ausable Press. Copyright © 2005 by Eric Pankey. Reprinted by permission of the author.

SUZANNE PAOLA. "Tenure at Forty" in *Bardo* by Suzanne Paola. Madison: University of Wisconsin Press. Copyright © 1998 by Suzanne Paola. Reprinted by permission of the author.

ELISE PARTRIDGE. "Gnomic Verses from the Anglo-Saxon" in *Fielder's Choice* by Elise Partridge. Montreal: Véhicle Press. Copyright © 2002 by Elise Partridge. Reprinted by permission of the author.

JOHN PECK. "Violin" in *Red Strawberry Leaf: Selected Poems, 1994–2001* by John Peck. Chicago: University of Chicago Press. Copyright © 2005 by John Peck. Reprinted by permission of the author.

DONALD PLATT. "Late Elegy in Spring for Larry Levis with Caravaggio & Horses" in *Cloud Atlas* by Donald Platt. West Lafayette, IN: Purdue University Press. Copyright © 2002 by Donald Platt. Reprinted by permission of the author.

KEVIN PRUFER. "Trompe L'Oeil" in *The Finger Bone* by Kevin Prufer. Pittsburgh: Carnegie Mellon University Press. Copyright © 2002 by Kevin Prufer. Reprinted by permission of the author.

REGINALD SHEPHERD. "Polaroid" in *Otherhood: Poems* by Reginald Shepherd. Copyright © 2003 by Reginald Shepherd. Reprinted by permission of the University of Pittsburgh Press.

CHARLES SIMIC. "De Occulta Philosophia" in *The Voice at 3 a.m.: Selected Late and New Poems* by Charles Simic. Orlando, FL: Harcourt. Copyright © 2003 by Charles Simic. Reprinted by permission of the author.

FLOYD SKLOOT. "Near the End" in *The Evening Light* by Floyed Skloot. Ashland, OR: Story Line Press, Copyright © 2001 by Floyd Skloot. Reprinted by permission of the author.

KEN SMITH. "The Donegal Liar" *Shed: Poems 1980–2001* by Ken Smith. Copyright © 2002 by Ken Smith. Reprinted by permission of Bloodaxe Books.

LISA M. STEINMAN. "Potatoes, Cabbages, Leeks, Plague, War" in *Carslaw's Sequences* by Lisa M. Steinman. Tampa: University of Tampa Press. Copyright © 2003 by Lisa M. Steinman. Reprinted by permission of the author.

STEPHANIE STRICKLAND. "WaveSon.Nets 14–18" in *V: Wave.Son.Nets/ Losing L'Una* by Stephanie Strickland. New York: Penguin. Copyright © 2002 by Stephanie Strickland. Reprinted by permission of the author.

BRIAN SWANN. "Eschatology" in *Autumn Road* by Brian Swann. Columbus: Ohio State University Press. Copyright © 2005 by Brian Swann. Reprinted by permission of the author.

BRIAN TEARE. "Poem Between Line Breaks" in *The Room Where I Was Born* by Brian Teare. Madison: University of Wisconsin Press. Copyright © 2003 by Brian Teare. Reprinted by permission of the author.

MARIA TERRONE. "Rereading the History Book: Centuries XX and XXI" in *A Secret Room in Fall* by Maria Terrone. Ashland, OH: Ashland Poetry Press. Copyright © 2006 by Maria Terrone. Reprinted by permission of the author.

DIANE THIEL. "Changeling" in *Echolocations* by Diane Thiel. Ashland, OR: Story Line Press. Copyright © 2000 by Diane Thiel. Reprinted by permission of the author.

ARTURO VIVANTE. "The Cricket" in *Solitude and Other Stories* by Arturo Vivante. Notre Dame, IN: University of Notre Dame Press. Copyright © 2004 by Arturo Vivante. Reprinted by permission of the author.

EUGENE WILDMAN. "The Last Days of Atlantis" in *The World of Glass* by Eugene Wildman. Notre Dame, IN: University of Notre Dame Press. Copyright © 2003 by Eugene Wildman. Reprinted by permission of the author.

BARON WORMSER. "Bernard Baruch" in *Mulroney & Others* by Baron Wormser. Louisville: Sarabande Books. Copyright © 2000 by Baron Wormser. Reprinted by permission of the author.

CHARLES WRIGHT. "High Country Canticle," "Morning Occurrence at Xanadu," "Night Thoughts Under a China Moon," and "Waking Up After the Storm" in *Scar Tissue* by Charles Wright. Copyright © 2006 by Charles Wright. Reprinted by permission of Farrar, Straus and Giroux, LLC.

Issues and Authors

No. 1—Inaugural Edition (Winter 1995)

Michael Anania
William Bronk
Julia Budenz
Robert Olen Butler
Michael Collins
Christopher Jane Corkery
Richard Elman
Jaimy Gordon
Robert Hass
Mary Kathleen Hawley
Seamus Heaney
Marilyn Krysl
Denise Levertov
Derek Mahon
Peter Michelson
Czeslaw Milosz
Susan Neville
John Peck
Ernest Sandeen
Melita Schaum
Beryl Schlossman
Marci Sulak
Anthony Walton
David Wolinsky

No. 2—Dangerous Times (Summer 1996)

Renée Ashley
Wendy Battin
David Black
Corinne Demas Bliss
Fred Chappell
Stuart Dischell
Richard Elman
Edward Falco
David Katz
Jesse Lee Kercheval
Marilyn Krysl
Konstantinos Lardas
Gus Pelletier
Michael Perkins
Göran Printz-Påhlson
Barry Silesky
Stephanie Strickland
Kymberly Taylor
James Weil
Kathleene West

No. 3—Eros and the Skull (Winter 1997)

Michael Anania
Mike Barrett
William Bronk
Kathy Fagan
Ed Falco
Beth Ann Fennelly
Reginald Gibbons
Heather O'Shea Gordon
Jennifer Anna Gosetti
Corinne Hales
Phillip Holmes
Janet Holmes
Caherine L. Kasper
John Latta
Bret Lott
Cris Mazza
Steve Moriarty
Gordon T. Osing
Robert Pinsky
Ira Sadoff
Hillel Schwartz
Michael Stephens
Richard Tillinghast
Linda Vavra
John Witte
David Wojahn

No. 4—Public Life, Private Lives (Summer 1997)

Robert Archambeau
Susan Bergman
Eavan Boland
Robert Boyers
Richard Burns
Esther Cohen
Catherine Daly
Beth Ann Fennelly
Barry Goldensohn
Janet Holmes
David Hoppe
Colette Inez
Suzanne Paola
John Peck
Michael Schneider
Barry Silesky
R. D. Skillings
John Howland Spyker
Maura Stanton

No. 5—Age and Envy (Winter 1998)

Robert Archambeau
Mary Jo Bang
Libby Bernardin
Anne Bingham
Janet Bloch
William Bronk
Robert Creeley
Joe Francis Doer
Randall Dwenger
Stephen Gibson
Elizabeth Gold
Lorrie Goldensohn
Carl A. Gottesman
Rick Hards
Susan Howe
David Jones
William Logan
Michael Martone
John Montague
Steve Moriarty
Paul Muldoon
Jere Odell
Peter Robinson
Pattiann Rogers
Charles Simic
Keith Tuma
Arturo Vivante
Amy Wray

No. 6—Is It Art? Is It Politics? (Summer 1998)

Robert Archambeau
Willis Barnstone
Libby Bernardin
Mark Brazaitas
Joe Francis Doerr
Richard Elman
Martha Gies
Jerry Harp
Laurie Hogin
Roman Huk
Robert Lietz
William Logan
George Looney
Michael Martone
Christopher Merrill
Peter Michelson
Yasumasa Morimura
Jere Odell
Linda Scheller
R. D. Skillings
Ken Smith
Marcela Sulak
James L. Weil

No. 7—Work (Winter 1999)

Michael Anania
Roger Brown
Richard Burns
Page Dougherty Delano
Martha Gies
Martha Greenwald
Corinne Clegg Hales
Robert Hahn
Kymberly Taylor Haywood
Marilyn Krysl
Dorthea Lange
George Looney
Jessica Maich
Emer Martin
William McGee Jr.
Kathleen McGookey
G. F. Michelson
Suzanne Paola
Piotr Parlej
Ricardo Pau-Llosa
Jeff Roessner
Balthus Klossowski de Rola
Melita Schaum
Floyd Skloot
Pauline Stainer
M. G. Stephens
Virgil Suárez
Igor Webb
Scott C. Withiam

No. 8—Place/Displacement (Summer 1999)

Jan Lee Ande
Neil Azevedo
Sean Brendan-Brown
Stacy Cartledge
Yanbing Chen
Sharon Cournoyer
Robert Crawford
Kevin DiCamillo
John Engels
Ed Falco
Rob Faivre
Robert Hahn
Corrinne Clegg Hales
Samuel Hazo
George Held
Christie Hodgen
Teresa Iverson
Alison Jarvis
Harriet McBryde Johnson
David M. Katz
Linda A. Kinnahan
John Latta
Kelly Le Fave
Diane Mehta
Orlando Ricardo Menes
G. E. Murray
John Peck
Don Pollack
Kevin Prufer
Kelly Ritter
Peter Robinson
Jason Salavon
David Sanders
Melita Schaum
Tom Smith
David Starkey
Lee Upton
Eugene Wildman
Baron Wormser

No. 9—Soft Millenium (Winter 2000)

Robert Archambeau
Julianna Baggott
Laton Carter
Jarda Cervenka
Susanne Davis
Annie Finch
Norman Finkelstein
James Finnegan
Geoffrey Gardner
Robert E. Haywood
Kurt Heinzelman
Janet Holmes
Teresa Iverson
Anthony Libby
Robert McNamara
Gerard Malanga
Mary Ann Moran
Claes Oldenburg
John Peck
James S. Proffitt
Peter Robinson
CarolAnn Russell
Geoff Schmidt
Peter Dale Scott
Reginald Shepherd
Barry Silesky
D. James Smith
Corinna Vallianatos
Ryan G. Van Cleave
Gordon Weaver
David Wojahn
Martha Zweig

No. 10—Body + Soul (Summer 2000)

Alison Armstrong
Mike Barrett
Jill Peláez Baumgaertner
Ace Boggess
Peg Boyers
Jarda Cervenka
Nancy Donegan
Andrew Epstein
Reginald Gibbons
David Green
Robert Hahn
Glenna Holloway
Devin Johnston
Eduardo Kac
R. M. Kinder
Marilyn Krysl
Susan Grafeld Long
George Looney
Malinda Markham
Michael McCole
Michael B. McMahon
James McMichael
Christopher Merrill
Carolyn Moran
J. Morris
Simone Muench
Paul Muldoon
Jere Odell
Andrew Osborn
Michael Perkins
R. D. Skillings
Ken Smith
Laura-Gray Street
Virgil Suárez
Maria Terrone
Ryan G. Van Cleave
Martin Walls
Henry Weinfield
Terence Winch
Daniel Weissbort
Wayne Zade

No. 11—Musics (Winter 2001)

Jeff Allen
Michael Anania
Robert Archambeau
Renée Ashley
Jennifer Atkinson
Ned Balbo
Charles Bernstein
Julia Budenz
William Doreski
James Doyle
Roy Fisher
John Gery
Stuart Greenhouse
Corrinne Clegg Hales
Mark Halperin
Jeremy Hooker
Devin Johnston
Catherine Kasper
John Kinsella
Susanne Kort
John Latta
Jeffrey Levine
Norman Minnick
Michael Olin-Hitt
Paul Petrie
Kevin Prufer
Jennie Rathbun
Frances Richey
William Rushton
Michael Russell
E. M. Schorb
Jonathan Stolzenberg
Stephanie Strickland
Virgil Suárez
Peter Swanson
Diane Thiel
Anthony Walton

No. 12—Grief Mornings (Summer 2001)

Seth Abramson
Chris Agee
Sandra Alcosser
Ned Balbo
Tama Baldwin
Adam Berlin
John Breedlove
Frances Padorr Brent
Christopher Brisson
Thomas Butler
Richard Cecil
Christopher Chambers
Philip Dacey
Joe Francis Doerr
Alice Elman
Joan Frank
Martin Galvin
Barry Goldensohn
Feebe Greco
Jeffrey Greene
Brian Henry
Roald Hoffman
Janet Holmes
Karen I. Jaquish
Richard Kenefic
John Kinsella
Sandra Kohler
David Kroll
Lorene Lamothe
Richard Lyons
James Magorian
Linda Mannheim
Michelle Margolis
Diane Mehta
Jere Odell
Gary Pacernick
Donald Platt
Kevin Prufer
Christopher Ripple
Michael J. Rosen
Jane Satterfield
Jason Schossler
Scott M. Silsbe
R. D. Skillings
J. David Stevens
Stephanie Strickland
Virgil Suárez
Brian Teare
Susan Terris
Dennis Trudell
Igor Webb

No. 13—Green (Winter 2002)

Sandra Alcosser
Anonymous
James Bertolino
Mary Biddinger
Sarah Bowman
Matthew Brennan
Brad Buchanan
Richard Caddel
Patricia Corbus
Karen Craigo
Tony D'Souza
Seamus Deane
Joe Francis Doerr
Eric P. Elshtain
Beth Ann Fennelly
Matthew Fluharty
Alice B. Fogel
Reginald Gibbons
Able Meadlaw Greene
Randolph Healy
James Himelsbach
Devin Johnston
Robert Kendall
Moira Linehan
Emer Martin
Susan Harper Martin
Walt McDonald
Brenda Miller
Paul Muldoon
Lisa Norris
Tom Paulin
Ricardo Pau-Llosa
Allan Peterson
Frances Richey
Peter Riley
Peter Robinson
David Roderick
Donelle Ruwe
John Phillip Santos
Melita Schaum
Ken Smith
Lisa M. Steinman
Lars-Håkan Svensson
Diane Thiel
Daneen Wardrop
Andrew Zawacki

No. 14—Traveling (Summer 2002)

Kathleen Aponick
Walter Bargen
Tina Barr
Christian Barter
Robert Bense
Eileen Berry
Rebecca Black
Susan Briante
Nadia Herman Colburn
Tony D'Souza
James Doyle
Shannon Doyne
Rikki Ducornet
Beth Ann Fennelly
Charles Freeland
Kenneth Frost
John Gallaher
Geoffrey Gardner
John Gery
Mark W. Halperin
John Hennessy
Catherine Kasper
Philip Kobylarz
Dale M. Kushner
Stacey Levine
William Logan
David Matlin
Jill McDonough
Peter Michelson
Patrick Moran
Linda Lancione Moyer
G. E. Murray
Martin Ott
Robert Parham
Elise Partridge
John Peck
Kathryn Rantala
Peter Robinson
John J. Ronan
Michael Salcman
Neil Shepard
Richard Spilman
Donna Baier Stein
Lisa M. Steinman
Robert Stewart
Marcela Sulak
Arturo Vivante
Daniel Weissbort
Tony Whedon

No. 15—Histories (Winter 2003)

June Frankland Baker
Richard Blanco
Ben Brooks
Kurt Brown
Peter Carpenter
Basil Cleveland
Chad Davidson
Joanne Diaz
Debra Di Blasi
Ray DiPalma
Joe Francis Doerr
Amina Gautier
Barry Goldensohn
Robert Hahn
Jonathan Hartt
Brian Henry
Cynthia Hogue
Teresa Iverson
Jesse Lee Kercheval
John Kinsella
Marilyn Krysl
Jeffrey Levine
David Matlin
Robert McNamara
Wayne Miller
John Minczeski
Simone Muench
Barbara Nickel
Andrew Osborn
Eric Pankey
John Pursley III
Nicole Louise Reid
Beryl Schlossman
Vera Schwarcz
Sean Singer
R. D. Skillings
Brian Swann
Keith Tuma
Wallis Wilde-Menozzi
Rynn Williams
James Matthew Wilson

No. 16—Apprentice and Apostrophe (Summer 2003)

Jeffrey Bahr
Jarda Cervenka
Earl Coleman
Debra Di Blasi
James Doyle
Ed Falco
John Gery
Chris Glomski
D. R. Goodman
Lea Graham
Debora Greger
Kerry Hanlon
Henry Hart
Robert Hass
Sandra Kohler
Susanne Kort
John Latta
Moira Linehan
Sarah Livingston
Peter Marcus
Christopher Merrill
Czeslaw Milosz
Robert Murphy
Adela Najarro
Mary Elizabeth Parker
Erik Anderson Reece
Peter Robinson
John J. Ronan
Morgan Lucas Schuldt
Floyd Skloot
Sofia M. Starnes
Brian Teare
Maria Terrone
Susan Thomas
Eric Tretheway
Doug Trevor
Susan Varon
Rebecca Warner
Brian Weinberg
Henry Weinfield

No. 17—Sportin' Life (Winter 2004)

Forrest Aguirre
Francisco Alarcón
Michael Anania
Francisco Aragón
Sharon Chmielarz
David Citino
Matthew Cooperman
Silvia Curbelo
John Engels
Melissa Fraterrigo
Jean Gallagher
Tess Gallagher
Richard Garcia
Rigoberto González
Maurice Kilwein Guevara
Jerry Harp
Kevin Hart
Dennis Hinrichsen
Glenna Holloway
Dionisio Martínez
Valerie Martínez
Michael Martone
María Meléndez
Ricardo Pau-Llosa
Deborah Pease
John Peck
Donald Platt
Rebecca Reynolds
Peter Robinson
Emily Rosko
Melita Schaum
Floyd Skloot
Ken Smith
Mike Smith
Adam Sorkin
Virgil Suárez
Diane Thiel
Liliana Ursu
Robert Vasquez
Jeanne Murray Walker
Brian Weinberg
Marlys West
Wallis Wilde-Menozzi

No. 18—Near and Far (Summer 2004)

Chimamanda Ngozi Adichie
Dick Allen
Michael Anania
Jan Lee Ande
Ned Balbo
Christian Barter
Robert Bense
Charles Boer
Stacy Cartledge
Sean M. Conrey
Patricia Corbus
Glenn Deutsch
Kevin Ducey
Robert Estep
Carla Falb
Beth Ann Fennelly
Steve Gehrke
Robert Gibb
Debora Greger
Mark Halperin
Raza Ali Hasan
Justin Haynes
Samuel Hazo
Paul Kane
Robert Kelly
Gary J. Maggio
Nadine Meyer
Michael Northrop
Jude Nutter
John Peck
Mary Quade
Jay Rogoff
Neil Shepard
R. D. Skillings
Marcela Sulak
Brian Swann
Keith Taylor
Diane Thiel
Jennifer Tonge
Pete Upham
Martin Walls
Eric G. Wilson
Ruseell Working
Charles Wright

No. 19—&Now/And Then (Winter 2005)

Joe Amato
mIEKAL aND
Camille Bacos
Peter Baestrieri
Mary Jo Bang
Mike Barrett
Caroline Bergvall
Charles Bernstein
R. M. Berry
Jenny Boully
cris cheek
Lucy Corin
Lydia Davis
Tom Denlinger
Debra Di Blasi
Amy England
Brian Evenson
Kass Fleisher
William Gillespie
Alexandra Grant
Tim Guthrie
Scott Helmes
Mrylin Hermes
Michael Joyce
Eduardo Kac
Catherine Kasper
Cynthia Lawson
Paul Maliszewski
Mark Marino
Steve McCaffery
Nick Montfort
Noam Mor
Sheila E. Murphy
Lance Olsen
George Quasha
Scott Rettberg
Davis Schneiderman
Mike Smith
Stephanie Strickland
TNWK
David Ray Vance
*
Robert Archambeau
Jeffery Bahr
Simeon Berry
Regina Derieva
Ed Falco
Stephen Fredman
Debora Greger
Mark Halperin
Paul Kane
Kristen Kaschock
John Kinsella
John Koethe
Kathryn Kruger
Sheryl Luna
Michelle Margolis
Bill Meissner
Tom O'Connor
John Peck
Paulann Petersen
James D. Redwood
Claudio Rodriguez
Frances Sherwood
Brain Swann
Keith Taylor
Maria Terrone
Steve Timm
TNWK
James Walton
Daneen Wardrop
Martha Zweig

No. 20—Lunar Auguries (Summer 2005)

Pippa Coulter Abston
Gabriel Arquilevich
Craig Beaven
Nicky Beer
Richard Blanco
Anne Blonstein
David Citino
Kevin Clark
Michael Clark
Michael Coffey
Tony D'Souza
Joe Francis Doerr
James Doyle
Kevin Ducey
Robert Estep
Amina Gautier
Robert Gibb
Albert Goldbarth
Robert Hahn
Henry Hart
Robert Kendall
John Kinsella
Susanne Kort
William Logan
Gerard Malanga
David Matlin
Martin Nakell
James Nohrnberg
John Peck
Raymond Perreault
Elizabeth Rees
Michael G. Richards
Jeffrey Roessner
Frank Rogaczewksi
Thom Schramm
Neil Shepard
John Shreffler
Rita Signorelli-Pappas
R. D. Skillings
Frederick Smock
Michael Spence
Maura Stanton
Ryan G. Van Cleave
Chris Wallace-Crabbe
Marlys West
Ginny Wiehardt
James Matthew Wilson
Emily Young